Also by Len Deighton

NONFICTION

Fighter: The True Story of the Battle of Britain

Airshipwreck

*Blitzkrieg: From the Rise of Hitler
to the Fall of Dunkirk*

FICTION

The Ipcress File

Horse Under Water

Funeral in Berlin

Billion-Dollar Brain

An Expensive Place to Die

Only When I Larf

Bomber

Declarations of War

Close-Up

Spy Story

Yesterday's Spy

Catch a Falling Spy

SS-GB

XPD

Goodbye, Mickey Mouse

Berlin Game

Mexico Set

London Match

WINTER

a novel of a Berlin family

WINTER

a novel of a Berlin family

LEN DEIGHTON

ALFRED A. KNOPF NEW YORK 1987

THIS IS A BORZOI BOOK
PUBLISHED BY ALFRED A. KNOPF, INC.

Copyright © 1987 by B. V. Holland Corporation

All rights reserved under International and Pan-American
Copyright Conventions. Published in the United States by
Alfred A. Knopf, Inc., New York. Distributed by Random
House, Inc., New York. Published in Great Britain by
Century Hutchinson Ltd., London.

Library of Congress Cataloging-in-Publication Data

Deighton, Len, [*date*]
Winter: a novel.

I. Title.
PR6054.E37W56   1987   823′.914   87-45842
ISBN 0-394-55177-X

Manufactured in the United States of America

FIRST EDITION

*". . . readers should remember that the
opinions expressed by the characters
are not necessarily those of the author . . ."*

JAMES JONES

WINTER

a novel of a Berlin family

Prologue

Nuremberg 1945.

Winter entered the prison cell unprepared for the change that the short period of imprisonment had brought to his friend. The prisoner was fifty-two years old and looked at least sixty. His hair had been thinning for years, but suddenly he'd become a bald-headed old man. He was sitting on the iron frame bed, sallow and shrunken. His elbows were resting on his knees and one hand was propped under his unshaven chin. The prison authorities had taken from him his belt, his braces, and his necktie, and the expensive custom-made suit from Berlin's most famous tailor was now stained and baggy. And yet the dark-underlined eyes were the same, and the pointed cleft chin made him immediately recognizable as a celebrity of the Third Reich, one of Hitler's most reliable associates.

"You sent for me, Herr Reichsminister?"

The prisoner looked up. "The Reich is kaputt, Germany is kaputt, and I'm not a minister: I'm just a number." Winter could think of no way to respond to the bitter old man. He'd become used to seeing him sitting behind the magnificent hand-carved desk in the tapestry-hung room in the ministry, surrounded by aides, secretaries, and assistants. "Yes, I sent for you, Herr Doktor Winter. Sit down."

He sat down. So it was all to be formal.

"I sent for you, Winter, and I'll tell you why. They told me you were in prison in London awaiting interrogation. They said that any of us on trial here could choose any German national we wanted for

3

our defense counsel, and that if the one we chose was being held in prison they'd release him to do it. It seemed to me that a man in prison might know what it's like for me in here."

Winter wondered if he should offer the ex-Reichsminister a cigarette, but when—still undecided—he produced his precious cigarettes, the military policeman in the corridor shouted through the open door, "No smoking, buddy!"

The ex-Reichsminister gave no sign of having heard the prison guard's voice. He carried on with his explanation. "Two, you speak American . . . speak it fluently. Three, you're a damned good lawyer, as I know from working with you for many years. Four, and this is the most important, you are an Obersturmbannführer in the SS. . . ." He saw Winter's face change and said, "Is there something wrong, Winter?"

Winter leaned forward; it was a gesture of confidentiality and commitment. "At this very moment, just a few hundred yards from here, there are a hundred or more American lawyers drafting the prosecution's case for declaring the SS an illegal organization. Such a verdict would mean prison, and perhaps death sentences, for everyone who was ever a member."

"Very well," said the prisoner testily. He'd always hated what he called "unimportant pettifogging details." "But you're not going to suddenly claim you weren't a member of the SS, are you?"

For the first time since the message had come that the minister wanted him as junior defense counsel, Winter felt alarmed. He looked round the cell to see if there were microphones. There were bound to be. He remembered this building from the time when he'd been working with the Nuremberg Gestapo. Half the material used in the trial of the disgruntled brownshirts had come from shorthand clerks who had listened to the prisoners over hidden microphones. "I can't answer that," said Winter softly.

"Don't give me that yes-sir, no-sir, I-don't-know-sir. I don't want some woolly-minded, fainthearted, Jew-loving liberal trying to get my case thrown out of court on some obscure technicality. I sent for you because you got me into all this. I remembered your hard work for the party. I remembered the good times we had long before we dreamed of coming to power. I remembered the way your father lent me money back when no one else would even let me into their office. Pull yourself together, Winter. Either put your guts into the effort for my defense or get out of here!"

Prologue

Winter admired his old friend's courage. Appearances could be deceptive: he wasn't the broken-spirited shell that Winter had thought; he was still the same ruthless old bastard that he had worked for. He remembered that first political meeting in the Potsdamer Platz in the 1920s and the speech he'd given: "Beneath the ashes fires still rage." It had been a recurring theme in his speeches right up until 1945.

"We'll fight them," said Winter. "We'll grab those judges by the ankles and shake them until their loose change falls to the floor."

"That's right," he said. It was another one of his pet expressions. "That's right." He almost smiled.

"Time's up, buddy!"

Winter looked at his watch. There was another two minutes to go. The Americans were like that. They talked about justice and freedom, democracy and liberty, but they never gave an inch. There was no point in arguing: they were the victors. The whole damned Nuremberg trial was just a show trial, just an opportunity for the Americans and the British and the French and the Russians to make an elaborate pretense of legal rectitude before executing the vanquished. But it was better that the ex-Reichsminister didn't fully realize the inevitable verdict and sentence. Better to fight them all the way and go down fighting. At least that would keep his spirits alive. With this resolved, Winter felt better, too. It would be a chance to relive the old days, if only in memories.

When Winter got to the door, the man called out to him, "One last thing, Winter." Winter turned to face him. "I hear stories about some aggressive American colonel on the prosecution staff, a tall, thin one with a beautifully tailored uniform and manicured fingernails . . . a man who speaks perfect German with a Berlin accent. He seems to hate all Germans and makes no allowances for anything; he treats everyone to a tongue-lashing every time he sends for them. Now they tell me he's been sent from Washington just to frame the prosecution's case against me. . . ." He paused and stared. He was working himself up into the sort of rage that had sent fear into every corner of his ministry and far beyond. "Not for Göring, Speer, Hess, or any of the others, just for me. What do you know about that shit-face *Schweinehund?*"

"Yes, I know him. It's my brother."

———

Prologue

One of the American lawyers, Bill Callaghan—a white-haired Bostonian who specialized in maritime law—said, after reading through Winter's file, that the story of the brothers read like fiction. But that was only because Callaghan was unacquainted with any fiction except the evidence that his shipowning clients provided for him to argue in court.

Fiction had unity and style, fiction had a beginning and a proper end, fiction showed evidence of planning and research and usually attempted to impose an orderly pattern upon the chaos of reality.

But the lives of the Winter brothers were not orderly and had no discernible pattern. Their lives had been a response to parental expectations, historical circumstances, and fleeting opportunities. Ambitions remained unfulfilled and prejudices had been disproved. Diversions, digressions, and disappointments had punctuated their lives. In fact, their lives had been fashioned in the same way as had the lives of so many of those born at the beginning of the twentieth century.

Callaghan, in that swift and effortless way that trial lawyers can so often command, gave an instant verdict on the lives of the Winter brothers. "One of them is a success story," said Callaghan, "and the other is a goddamned horror story." Actually, neither was a story at all. Like most people, they had lived through a series of episodes, most of which were frustrating and unsatisfactory.

1899

"A whole new century."

Everyone saw the imperious man standing under the lamppost in Vienna's Ringstrasse, and yet no one looked directly at him. He was very slim, about thirty years old, pale-faced, with quick, angry eyes and a neatly trimmed black mustache. His eyes were shadowed by the brim of his shiny silk top hat, and the gaslight picked out the diamond pin in his cravat. He wore a long black chesterfield overcoat with a fur collar. It was an especially fine-looking coat, the sort of overcoat that came from the exclusive tailors of Berlin. "I can't wait a moment longer," he said. And his German was spoken with the accent of Berlin. No one—except perhaps some of the immigrants from the Sudetenland who now made up such a large proportion of the city's population—could have mistaken Harald Winter for a native of Vienna.

The crowd that had gathered around the amazing horseless carriage—a Benz Viktoria—now studied the chauffeur, who, having inspected its engine, stood up and wiped his hands. "It's the fuel," said the chauffeur, "dirt in the pipe."

"I'll walk to the club," said the man. "Stay here with the car. I'll send someone to help you." Without waiting for a reply, the man pushed his way past a couple of onlookers who were in his way and marched off along the boulevard, jabbing at the pavement with his cane and scowling with anger.

Vienna was cold on that final evening of the 1800s; the temperature sank steadily through the day, until by evening it went below

7

freezing point. Harald Winter felt cold but he also felt a fool. He was mortified when one of his automobiles broke down. He enjoyed being the center of attention when he was being driven past his friends and enemies in their carriages, or simply being pointed out as the owner of one of the first of the new, expensive mechanical vehicles. But when the thing gave trouble like this, he felt humiliated.

In Berlin it was different. In Berlin they knew about these things. In Berlin there was always someone available to attend to its fits and starts, its farts and coughs, its wheezes and relapses. He should never have brought the machine to Vienna. The Austrians knew nothing about such modern machinery. The only horseless carriage he'd seen here was electric-powered—and he hated electric vehicles. He should never have let his wife persuade him to come here for Christmas: he hated Vienna's rainy winters, hated the political strife that so often ended in riots, hated the food, and hated these lazy, good-for-nothing Viennese with their shrill accent, to say nothing of the wretched, ragged foreigners who were everywhere jabbering away in their incomprehensible languages. None of them could be bothered to learn a word of proper German.

He was chilled by the time he turned through big gates and into an entranceway. Like so many of the buildings in this preposterous town, the club looked like a palace, a heavy Baroque building writhing with nymphs and naiads, its portals supported by a quartet of herculean pillars. The doorman signaled to the door porters so that he was admitted immediately to the brightly lit lobby. It was normally crowded at this time of evening, but tonight it was strangely quiet.

"Good evening, Herr Baron."

Winter grunted. That was another thing he hated about Vienna: everyone had to have a title, and if, like Winter, a man had no title, the servants would invent one for him. While one servant took his cane and his silk hat, another slipped his overcoat from his shoulders.

Without hat and overcoat, it was revealed that Harald Winter had not yet changed for dinner. He wore a dark frock coat with light-gray trousers, a high stiff collar, and a slim bow-tie. His pale face was wide with a pointed chin, so that he looked rather satanic, an effect emphasized by his shiny black hair and center parting.

"Winter! What a coincidence! I'm just off to see your wife now."

"A whole new century."

The speaker was Professor Doktor Franz Schneider, fifty years old, the best, or at least the richest and most successful, gynecologist in Vienna. He was a small, white-faced man, plump in the way that babies are plump, his skin flawless and his eyes bright blue. Nervously he touched his white goatee beard before straightening his pince-nez. "You heard, of course. . . . Your wife: the first signs started an hour ago. I'm going to the hospital now. You'll come with me? My carriage is here, waiting." He spoke hurriedly, his voice pitched higher than normal. He was always a little nervous with Harald Winter; there was no sign now of the much-feared professor who met his students' questions with dry and savage wit.

Winter's eyes went briefly to the door from which Professor Schneider had come. The bar. Professor Schneider flushed. Damn this arrogant swine Winter, he thought. He could make a man feel guilty without even saying a word. What business of Winter's was it that he'd had a mere half-bottle of champagne with his cold pheasant supper? It was Winter's wife whose pangs of labor had come on New Year's Eve, and so spoiled his chance of getting to the ball at anything like a decent time.

"I have a meeting," said Winter.

"A meeting?" said Professor Schneider. Was it some sort of joke? On New Year's Eve, what man would be attending a meeting in a club emptied of almost everyone but servants? And how could a man concentrate his mind on business when his wife was about to give birth? He met Winter's eyes: there was no warmth there, no curiosity, no passion. Winter was said to be one of the shrewdest businessmen in Germany, but what use were his wealth and reputation when his soul was dead? "Then I shall go along. I will send a message. Will you be here?"

Winter nodded almost imperceptibly. Only when Professor Schneider had departed did Winter go up the wide staircase to the mezzanine floor. Another member was there. Winter brightened. At last, a face he knew and liked.

"Foxy! I heard you were in this dreadful town."

Erwin Fischer's red hair had long since gone gray—a great helmet of burnished steel—but his nickname remained. He was a short, slight, jovial man with dark eyes and sanguine complexion. His great-grandparents had been Jews from the Baltic city of Riga. His grandfather had changed the family name, and his father had converted to Roman Catholicism long before Erwin was born. Fischer

9

was heir to a steel fortune, but at seventy-five his father was fit and well and—now forty-eight years old—Fuchs Fischer had expectations that remained no more than expectations. Erwin was a widower. He wasn't kept short of money, but he was easily bored, and money did not always assuage his boredom. His life had lately become a long, tedious round of social duties, big parties, and introductions to "suitable marriage partners" who never proved quite suitable enough.

"You give Bubi Schneider a bad time, Harald. Is it wise? He has a lot of friends in this town."

"He's a sniveling little parasite. I can't think why my wife consulted such a man."

"He delivers the children of the most powerful men in the city. The wives confide in him, the children are taught to think of him as one of the family. Such a man wields influence."

Winter smiled. "Am I to beware of him?" he said icily.

"No, of course not. But he could cause you inconvenience. Is it worth it, when a smile and a handshake are all he really wants from you?"

"The wretch insisted that Veronica could not travel back to Berlin. My son will be born here. I don't want an Austrian son. You are a German, Foxy; you understand."

"So it's to be a son. You've already decided that, have you?"

Winter smiled. "Shall we crack a bottle of Burgundy?"

"You used to like Vienna, Harald. When you first bought the house here you were telling us all how much better it was than Berlin."

"That was a long time ago. I was a different man then."

"You'd discovered your wonderful wife in Berlin and Veronica here in Vienna. That's what you mean, isn't it?"

"Don't go too far, Foxy."

The older man ignored the caution. He was close enough to Winter to risk such comments, and go even further. "Surely you've taken into account the possibility that it was Veronica's idea to have the baby here."

"Veronica?"

"Consider the facts, Harald. Veronica met you here when she was a student at the university. This is where she first learned about love and life and all the things she'd dreamed about when she was a little girl in America. She adores Vienna. No matter that you see it as a second-rate capital for a fifth-rate empire; for Veronica it's still the home of Strauss waltzes and parties where she meets dukes, duchesses, and princes of royal blood. No matter what you say, Harald, Kaiser Wilhelm's Berlin cannot match Vienna in the party season. Would you really be surprised to find that she had contrived to have the second child here?"

"I hope you haven't . . ."

"No, I haven't spoken with her, of course I haven't. I'm simply telling you to ease the reins on Bubi Schneider until you're quite sure it's all his fault."

Winter stepped away and leaned over the gilt balcony. Resting his hand upon a cherub, he signaled to a club servant on the floor below. "Send a bottle of the best Burgundy up to us. And three glasses."

They went to a long, mirrored room, the chandeliers blazing from a thousand reflections. A fire was burning at the far end of the room. The open fireplace was a daring innovation for Vienna, a city warmed by stoves, but the committee had copied the room from a gentlemen's club in London.

Over the fireplace there was a huge painting of the monarch who combined the roles of emperor of Austria and king of Hungary and insisted upon being addressed as "His Apostolic Majesty, our most gracious Emperor and Lord, Franz Josef I." The room was otherwise empty. Winter chose a table near the fire and sat down. Fischer stood with his hands in his pockets and stared out the window. Winter followed his gaze. Across the dark street a wooden stand had been erected for a political meeting held that morning. Now no one was there except two uniformed policemen, who stood amongst the torn slogans and broken chairs as if such impedimenta did not exist for them.

"I've never understood women," said Winter finally.

"You've always understood women only too well," said Fischer, still looking out the window. "It's Americans you don't understand. It's because Veronica is an American that your marriage is sometimes difficult."

"You told me at the time, Foxy. I should have listened."

"No European man in his right senses marries an American girl. You've been lucky with Veronica: she doesn't fuss too much about your other women or try to stop you drinking or going to those parties at Madame Reiner's mansion. For an American woman she's very understanding." There was a note of humor in Fischer's voice, and now he turned his head to see how Winter was taking it. Noticing this, Winter permitted himself the ghost of a smile.

A waiter entered and took his time showing Winter the label and then pouring two glasses of wine with fastidious care.

Fischer sipped his wine, still looking down at the street. The plain speaking had divided the two men, so that now they were isolated in their thoughts. "The wine steward found you something good, Harald," said Fischer appreciatively, pursing his lips and then tasting a little more.

"I have my own bin," said Winter. "I no longer drink from the club's cellar."

"How sensible."

Winter made no reply. He drank the wine in silence. That was the difference between them. Fischer, the rich man's son, took everything for granted and left everything to chance. Harald Winter, self-made tycoon, trusted no one and left nothing to chance.

"I was here this morning," said Fischer. He motioned down towards the street where the political demonstration had been held. "Karl Lueger spoke. After he'd stepped down there was fighting. The police couldn't handle it; they brought in the cavalry to clear the street."

"Lueger is a rogue," said Winter quietly and without anger.

"He's the mayor."

"The Emperor should never have ratified the appointment."

"He blocked it over and over again. Finally he had to do as the voters wanted."

"Voters? Riffraff. Look at the slogans down there—'Save the small businessman'; 'Bring the family back into church'; 'Down with Jewish big business'—the Christian Socials just pander to the worst prejudice, fears, and bitter jealousy. 'Handsome Karl' is all things to all men. For those who want socialism he's a socialist; for churchgoers he's a man of piety; for anyone who wants to hang the Jews, or hound Hungarians back across the border, his party is the one to vote for. What a rascal."

"You're a man of the world; you must realize that hating foreigners is a part of the Austrian psyche. How many votes would you get for telling those people down there that the Jew is brainier than they are, or that these immigrant Czechs and Hungarians are more hard-working?"

"I don't like it, Foxy. Lueger is becoming as popular as the Emperor. Sometimes I have the feeling that Lueger could *become* the Emperor. Suppose all this hatred, all this *Judenhass,* was organized on a national scale. Suppose someone came along who had Lueger's cunning with the crowd, the Emperor's sway with the army, and a touch of Bismarck's instinct for *Geopolitik.* What then, Foxy? What would you say to that?"

"I'd say you need a holiday, Harald." He tried to make a joke of it, but Winter did not join in his forced laugh. "Who is the third glass for, Harald? Am I allowed to know that?" He knew it wasn't a woman: no women were ever permitted on the club premises.

"The mysterious Count Kupka sent a messenger to my home today."

"Kupka? Is he a personal friend?" There was a strained note in Fischer's normally very relaxed voice.

"Personal friend? Not at all. I have met him, of course, at parties and even at Madame Reiner's mansion, but I know nothing about him except that he is said to have the ear of the Emperor and to be some sort of consultant to the Foreign Ministry."

"You have a lot to learn about this city, Harald. Count Kupka is the head of the Emperor's secret police. He is responsible to the Foreign Ministry, and the minister answers only to His Majesty. Kupka's signature on a piece of paper is all that's needed to make a man disappear forever."

"You make him sound interesting, Foxy. He always seemed such a desiccated and boring little man."

Fischer looked at his friend. Harald Winter was clearly un-daunted by Kupka. It was Winter's bravery that Fischer had always found attractive. He admired Winter's audacious, if not to say reck-less, business ventures, and his brazen love affairs, and his indiffer-ence to the prospect of making enemies like Professor Schneider. Sometimes Fischer was tempted to think that Harald Winter's cour-age was the only attractive aspect of this ruthless, selfish man. "We've known each other a long time, Harald. If you're in trouble, perhaps I can help."

"Trouble? With Kupka? I can't think how I could be."

"It's New Year's Eve, Harald. At midnight a whole new century begins: the twentieth century. Everyone we know will be celebrating. There is a State Ball where half the crowned heads of Europe will be seen. Why would Count Kupka have to see you tonight of all nights?"

"It is something that perhaps you should stay and ask him yourself, Foxy. He is already twenty minutes late."

Fischer finished his glass of wine in one gulp. "I won't stay. The man gives me the shudders." He put the glass on the table alongside the polished one that was waiting for Count Kupka. "But let me remind you that tonight the streets will be empty except for some drunken revelers. For someone who was going to bundle a man into a carriage, or throw someone into the Danube, tonight would provide a fine opportunity."

Winter smiled broadly. "How disappointed you will be tomorrow, Foxy, when it is revealed that Count Kupka wanted no more than a chance to ride in my horseless carriage."

In fact, Kupka didn't want a ride in Winter's horseless carriage; or if he did, he made no mention of this desire. Nor was Count Kupka the desiccated and boring little man that Winter remembered. Kupka was a broad-shouldered man with large, awkward hands that did not seem to go with his pale, lined face and delicate eyebrows that had been plucked so that they didn't meet across the top of his thin, pointed nose. Kupka's head was large: like a balloon upon which a child had scrawled his simple, expressionless features. And, like paint upon a balloon, his hair—shiny with Macassar oil— was brushed flat against his head.

Kupka was still wearing his overcoat when he strode into the lounge. His silk hat was tilted slightly to the back of his head. He put his cane down and removed his gloves, holding his cigar between his teeth. Winter didn't move. Kupka tossed the gloves down. Winter continued to sip his Burgundy, watching Kupka with the amused and indulgent interest that he would give to an entertainer coming onto the stage of a variety theatre. Winter could recall only two other men who smoked large cigars while walking about in hat and overcoat, and both of those were menials in his country house. It amused him that Kupka should behave in such a way.

"I am greatly indebted to you, Winter. It is most kind of you to consent to seeing me at such short notice." Kupka flicked ash from his cigar. "Especially tonight of all nights."

"I knew it would be something that couldn't wait," said Winter with an edge in his voice that he did nothing to modify.

"Yes, yes, yes," said Kupka in a voice that suggested that his mind had already passed on to the next thought. "Was that Erwin Fischer I passed on the stairs?"

"He was taking a glass of Burgundy with me. Perhaps you'd do the same, Count Kupka?"

"There is nothing that would give me greater pleasure, Herr Winter. . . ." Before Winter could reach for the bottle and pour, Kupka held up his hand so that gold rings, some inset with diamonds, sparkled in the light of the chandeliers. "But, alas, I have an evening of work before me." Winter poured wine for himself and Kupka said, "And I will be as brief as I can."

"I would appreciate that," said Winter. "Won't you sit down?"

"Sometimes I need to stand. They say that, at the Opera, Mahler stands up to conduct his orchestra. Stands up! Most extraordinary, and yet I sympathize with the fellow. Sometimes I can think better on my feet. Yes . . . your wife. I saw Professor Doktor Schneider earlier this evening. Women are such frail creatures, aren't they? The problem concerning which I must consult you comes about only because of my dear wife's maternal affection for a distant cousin." Kupka paused a moment to study the burning end of his cigar. "He is rather a foolish young man. But no more foolish than I was when young, and no more foolish than you were, Winter."

"Was I foolish, Count Kupka?"

Kupka looked at him and raised his eyebrows to feign surprise. "More than most, Herr Winter. Have you already forgotten those hotheads you mixed with when you were a student? The Silver Eagle Society you called yourselves, as I remember. And you a student of law, too!"

Despite doing everything he could to remain composed, Winter was visibly shaken. When he spoke his voice croaked: "That was no more than a childish game." He drank some wine to clear his throat.

"For you perhaps, but not for everyone who joined it. Suppose I told you that the anarchist who killed our Empress last year could also be connected to an organization calling itself the Silver Eagle?" Kupka glanced up at the portrait of the Emperor and then warmed his hands at the fire.

"If you told me that, then I would know that you are playing a childish game."

"And if I persisted?" Kupka smiled. There was no perceptible cruelty in his face. He was enjoying this little exchange and seemed to expect Winter to enjoy it also. But for Winter the stakes were too high. No matter how unfounded such accusations might be, it would need only a few well-distributed rumors to damage Winter and his family forever.

"Then I would call you out," said Winter with all the self-assurance he could muster.

Kupka laughed. "A duel? Save that sort of nonsense for the Officer Corps. I am no more than an *Einjährig-Freiwilliger,* and one-year volunteers don't learn how to duel." Kupka sat down opposite Winter and carelessly tapped ash into the fireplace. "Now that I see the label on that bottle of wine, perhaps I could change my mind about a glass of it."

Winter poured a glass. The work of the picador was done, the temper and the weaknesses of the bull discovered: now Kupka the matador would enter the ring.

"About this lad," said Kupka after sipping the wine. "He borrowed money from your bank."

"Hardly my bank," said Winter. He'd come prepared. Kupka's message had mentioned this client of the bank.

"The one in which some unnamed discreet person holds eighteen thousand nominee shares. The one in which you have an office and a secretary. The one in which the manager refers all transactions above a prescribed amount to you for approval. My wife's distant cousin borrowed money from that bank."

"You want details?"

"I have all the necessary details, thank you. I simply want to give you the money."

"Buy the debt?" said Winter.

"Plus an appropriate fee to the bank."

"The name was Petzval; he said his family was from Budapest. The manager was doubtful, but he seemed a sensible lad."

"Petzval, yes. My wife worries about him."

"A distant cousin, you say?"

"My wife's family is a labyrinth of distant cousins and so on. A fine wine, Winter. I have not seen it on the wine list," said Kupka, and poured himself some more. "She worries about the debt."

"What does she think I will do to him?" Winter asked.

"Not you, my dear friend. My goodness, no. She worries that he will get behind in his payments to you and go to a moneylender. You know what that can lead to. I see so many lives ruined," said Kupka without any sign of being downcast. "He wants to write a book. His family have nothing. Believe me, Winter, it's a debt you will be better without."

"I will inquire into the facts," said Winter.

"The payment can be made in any way that you wish it—paper money, gold, a certified check—and anywhere—New York, London, Paris, or Berlin."

"Your concern about this young man touches me," said Winter.

"I am a sentimental fool, Winter, and now you have discovered the truth of it." Ash went down Kupka's overcoat, but he didn't notice.

A club servant entered the lounge looking for Winter. "There is a telephone call for you, Herr Baron."

"It will be the hospital," explained Winter.

"I have detained you far too long," said Kupka. He stood up to say goodbye. "Please give my compliments and sincere apologies to your beautiful wife." He didn't press for an answer; men such as Kupka know that their requests are never refused.

"*Auf Wiedersehen,* Count Kupka."

"*Auf Wiedersehen,* my dear Winter." He clicked his heels and bowed.

Winter followed the servant downstairs. The club had only recently been connected to the telephone. Even now it was not possible for a caller to speak to the staff at the entrance desk; the facility whereby wives could inquire about their husbands' presence in the club would not be a welcome innovation. The instrument was enshrined upon a large mahogany table in a room on the first floor. A servant was permanently assigned to answer it.

"Winter here." He wanted to show both the caller and the servant that telephones were not such rarities in Berlin.

"Winter? Professor Schneider speaking. A false alarm. These things happen. It could be two or three days."

"How is my wife?"

"Fit and well. I have given her a mild sedative, and she will be asleep by now. I suggest you get a good night's sleep and see her tomorrow morning."

"I think I will do that."

"Your baby will be born in 1900: a child of the new century."

"The new century will not begin until 1901. I would have thought an educated man like you would know that," said Winter, and replaced the earpiece on the hook. Already the bells were ringing. Every church in the city was showing the skills of its bellringers to welcome the new year. But in the kitchen a dog was whining loudly: the bells were hurting its ears. Dogs hate bells. So did Harald Winter.

"What good jokes you make, Liebchen. *"*

Martha Somló was beautiful. This petite, dark-haired, large-eyed daughter of a Jewish tailor was one of twelve children. The family had originally come from a small town in Rumania. Martha grew up in Hungary, but she arrived in Vienna alone, a sixteen-year-old orphan. She was working in a cigar shop when she first met Harald Winter. Within three weeks of that meeting he had installed her in an apartment near the Votivkirche. Now she was eighteen. She had a much grander place to live. She also had a lady's maid, a hairdresser who came in every day, an account with a court dressmaker, some fine jewelry, and a small dog. But Harald Winter's visits to Vienna were not frequent enough for her, and when he wasn't with her she was dispirited and lonely.

Harald Winter's mistress was no more than a small part of his curious and complex relationship with Vienna. He'd spent a lot of time in finding this wonderful apartment with its view of the Opera House and the Wiener Boulevard. From here she could watch "Sirk-Ecke," a sacred meeting place for Vienna's high society, who paraded up and down in their finest clothes every day except Sunday.

Once found, the apartment had been transformed into a show-place for Vienna's newly formed "Secession" art movement. A Klimt frieze went completely round the otherwise shiny black dining room, where the table and chairs were by Josef Hoffmann. The study, from writing desk to notepaper, was completely the work of Koloman Moser. Everywhere in the apartment there were examples of Art Nouveau. Martha Somló felt, with reason, that she was little more than a curator for an art museum. She hated everything about the apartment that Harold Winter had so painstakingly put together, but she was too astute to say so. Winter's American wife, Veronica, had made no secret of her dislike for modern art, and the end result of that was the apartment in Kärntnerstrasse and Martha. If Martha made her true feelings known, there was little chance that Winter would get rid of his treasures; he'd get rid of her. It would be easier, quicker, and cheaper.

"I love you, Harry," she said suddenly and without premeditation.

"What was that?" said Winter. He was in his red silk dressing gown, the one she'd chosen for him for his thirtieth birthday. That was six months ago: now they hardly ever went anywhere together. Since his wife had become pregnant with this second child, he'd become more distant, and she worried that he was trying to find some way to tell her he didn't want her anymore. "I think I must be getting deaf; my father went deaf when very young."

She went to him and threw her arms round his neck and kissed him. "Harry, you fool. You're not going deaf; you're the strongest, fittest man I ever met. I say I love you, Harry. Smile, Harry. Say you love me."

"Of course I love you, Martha." He kissed her.

"A proper kiss, Harry. A kiss like the one you gave me when you arrived this afternoon hungering for me."

"Dear Martha, you're a sweet girl."

"What's wrong, Harry? You're not yourself today. Is it something to do with the bank?"

He shook his head. Things were not too good at the bank, but he never discussed his business troubles with Martha and he never would. Women and business didn't mix. Winter wasn't entirely sure about women being admitted to universities. On that account he sometimes felt more at ease with women like Martha than with his own wife. Martha understood him so well.

"Do you know who Count Kupka is?"

"My God, Harry. You're not in trouble with the secret police? Oh, dear God, no."

"He wants a favor from me, that's all."

She sat down and pulled him so that he sat with her on the sofa. He told her something about the conversation he'd had with Kupka.

19

"And you found out what he wanted to know?" She stroked his face tenderly. Then she looked at the leather document-case that Winter had brought with him to the apartment. He rarely carried anything. Many times he'd told her that carrying cases, boxes, parcels, or packages was a task only for servants.

"It's not so easy," said Winter. She could see he wanted to talk about it. "My manager asked for collateral. This fellow owns land on the Obersalzberg. All the paperwork has been done to make the land the property of the bank if he defaults on the loan. I have now changed matters so that the loan has come from my personal account. Luckily the land deed is already made over to a nominee, so I get it in case of a default."

"Salzburg, Harry? Austria?"

"Not Salzburg; the Obersalzberg. It's a mountain a thousand meters high. It's not in Austria: it's just across the border, in Bavaria."

"In Germany?"

"And that's going to be another problem. I'm not sure it's possible to turn everything over to Kupka."

"He'll say you're not cooperating," she said. She had heard of Kupka. What Jew in the whole of the empire had not heard of him? She was sick with fear at the mention of his name.

"Kupka is a lawyer," said Winter confidently.

"That's like saying Attila the Hun was a cavalry officer," she said.

Winter laughed loudly and embraced her. "What good jokes you make, *Liebchen*. I'm tempted to tell Kupka that one."

"Don't, Harry."

"You mustn't be frightened, my darling. I am simply a means to an end in this matter."

"Just do what he says, Harry."

"But not yet, I think. Tonight I'm meeting this mysterious fellow Petzval at the Café Stoessl in Gumpendorfer Strasse. Damn him— I'll get from him everything that Kupka won't tell me."

"Remember he's a relative of Kupka's, and close to his wife."

"Rubbish," said Winter. "That was just a smokescreen to hide the true facts of the matter."

"Send someone," she suggested.

He smiled and went to the leather case he'd brought with him. From it he brought a small revolver and a soft leather holster with a strap that would fit under his coat.

"What good jokes you make, *Liebchen*."

"If Kupka has his men there, a pistol won't save you."

"Little worrier," he said affectionately and kissed her.

She held him very tight. How desperately she envied his wife; the children would always bind Harry to her in a way that nothing else could. If only Martha could give him a wonderful son.

1900

A plot of land on the Obersalzberg.

It was dark by the time that Winter pushed through the revolving door of the Café Stoessl in the Gumpendorfer Strasse and looked around. The café was long and gloomy, lit by gaslights that hissed and popped. There were tables with pink marble tops and bentwood chairs and plants everywhere. He recognized some of the customers but gave no sign of it. They were not people that Winter would acknowledge: the usual crowd of would-be intellectuals, has-been politicians, and self-styled writers.

Petzval was waiting. "A small Jew with a black beard," the bank manager had told Winter. Well, that was easy. He sat at the very end table facing towards the door. He was a white-faced man in his late twenties, with bushy black hair and a full beard so that his small eyes and pointed nose were all you noticed of his face.

Winter put his hat on a seat and then sat down opposite the man and ordered a coffee, and brandy to go with it. Then he apologized vaguely for being late.

"I said you'd go back on your word," said Petzval.

It wasn't a good beginning, and Winter was about to deny any such intention, but then he realized that such an opening would leave him little or no room for discussion. "Why did you think that?" asked Winter.

"Count Kupka, is it?" Petzval leaned forward and rested an elbow on the table.

A plot of land on the Obersalzberg.

Winter hesitated but, after looking at Petzval, decided to admit it. Kupka had claimed Petzval as a relative and had not asked Winter to keep his name out of it. "Yes, Count Kupka."

"He wants to buy my debt?"

"Something along those lines."

Petzval pushed his empty coffee cup aside so that he could lean both arms on the table. His face was close to Winter, closer than Winter welcomed, but he didn't shrink away. "Secret police," said Petzval. "His spies are everywhere."

"Are you related to Kupka?" said Winter.

"Related? To Kupka?" Petzval made a short throaty noise that might have been a laugh. "I'm a Jew, Herr Winter. Didn't you know that when you made the loan to me?"

"It would have made no difference one way or the other," said Winter. The coffee came, and Winter was glad of the chance to sit back away from the man's glaring eyes. This was a man at the end of his tether, a desperate man. He studied the angry Jew as he sipped his coffee. Petzval was a ridiculous fellow with his frayed shirt and gravy-spattered suit, but Winter found him rather frightening. How could that be, when everyone knew that Winter wasn't frightened of any living soul?

"I'm a good risk, am I?"

"The manager obviously thought so. What do you do, Herr Petzval?"

"For a living, you mean? I'm a scientist. Ever heard of Ernst Mach?"

He waited. It was not a rhetorical question; he wanted to know whether Winter was intelligent enough to understand.

"Of course: Professor Mach is a physicist at the university."

"Mach is the greatest scientific genius of modern times." He paused to let that judgment sink in before adding, "A couple of years ago he suffered a stroke, and I've been privileged to work for him while pursuing my own special subject."

"And what is your subject?" said Winter, realizing that this inquiry, or something like it, was expected of him.

"Airflow. Mach did the most important early work in Prague before I was born. He pioneered techniques of photographing bullets in flight. It was Mach who discovered that a bullet exceeding the speed of sound creates two shock waves: a headwave of compressed gas at the front and a tailwave created by a vacuum at the back. My work has merit, but it's only a continuation of what poor old Professor Mach has abandoned."

"Poor old Professor Mach?"

"He's too sick. He'll have to resign from the university; his right side is paralyzed. It's terrible to see him trying to carry on."

"And what will you do when he resigns?" He sipped some of the bitter black coffee flavored with fig in the Viennese style. Then he tasted the brandy: it was rough but he needed it.

Petzval stared at Winter pityingly. "You don't understand any of it, do you?"

"I'm not sure I do," admitted Winter. He dabbed brandy from his lips with the silk handkerchief he kept in his top pocket, and looked round. There was a noisy group playing cards in the corner, and two or three strange-looking fellows bent over their work. Perhaps they were poets or novelists, but perhaps they were Kupka's men keeping an eye on things.

"Don't you realize the difference between a high-velocity artillery piece and a low-muzzle-velocity gun?"

Winter almost laughed. He'd met evangelists in his time, but this man was the very limit. He talked about the airflow over missiles as other men spoke of the second coming of our Lord. "I don't think I do," admitted Winter good-naturedly.

"Well, Krupp know the difference," said Petzval. "They have offered me a job at nearly three times the salary that Mach gets from his professorship."

"Have they?" said Winter. He was impressed, and his voice revealed it.

Petzval smiled. "Now you're beginning to see what it's all about, are you? Krupp are determined to build the finest guns in the world. And they'll do it."

Winter nodded soberly and remembered how the Austrian army had been defeated not so long ago by Prussians using better guns. It was natural that the Austrians would want to know what the German armament companies were doing. "Count Kupka is interested in your job at Krupp? Is that it?"

"He wants me to report everything that's happening in their research department. By taking over the debt he can put pressure on me. That's why I want the bank to fulfill its obligations." Petzval kept his voice to a whisper, but his eyes and his flailing hands demonstrated his passion.

"It's not so easy as that."

"You have the land on the Obersalzberg. It's valuable."

"Even so, it might be better to do things the way Count Kupka wants them done."

"You, a German, tell me that?"

Warning bells rang in Winter's head. Was Petzval an agent provocateur, sent to test Winter's attitude towards Austria? It seemed possible. Wouldn't such military espionage against Krupp be arranged by Colonel Redl, the chief of Austria's army intelligence? Or was Count Kupka just trying to steal a march on his military rival? "It might be best for everyone," said Winter.

"Not best for me," said Petzval. "I'm not suited to spying. I leave that sort of dirty work to the people who like it. Can you imagine what it would be like to spend every minute of the day and night worrying that you'd be discovered?"

"You could make sure you're not discovered," said Winter.

"How could I?" said Petzval, dismissing the idea immediately. "They'd want me to photograph the prototypes and steal blueprints and sketch breech mechanisms and so on." He'd obviously thought about it a lot, or was this all part of Count Kupka's schooling?

"It would be for your country," said Winter, now convinced that it was an attempt to subvert him.

"Have you ever been in an armaments factory?" said Petzval. "Or, more to the point, have you ever gone out through the gate? At some of those places they search every third worker. Now and again they search everyone. Police raid the homes of employees. I'd be working in the research laboratory and I am a Jew. What chance would I have of remaining undetected?"

Winter glanced round the café. Despite their lowered voices, this fellow's emotional speeches would soon be attracting attention to them. "I'm sorry, Herr Petzval," Winter said, "but I can't help you further."

"You'll pass it to him?" Was it fear or contempt that Winter saw in those dark, deep-set eyes?

"You read the agreement and signed it. There was nothing to say it couldn't be passed on to a third party."

"A third party? The secret police?"

"Raise money from another source," said Winter. It seemed such a lot of fuss about nothing.

"I'm deeply in debt, Herr Winter. I beg you to take the land and let me have the money."

"I couldn't agree to that. Your prospects . . ."

"What prospects do I have if Kupka prevents me from leaving the country?"

"If Kupka prevents you from leaving Austria . . ." For a moment Winter was puzzled. Then he realized what the proposal really was. "Do you mean that you came here hoping that I would refuse to do as Kupka demands but not tell him so until you were across the border?"

"You're a German."

"So you keep reminding me," said Winter. He gulped the rest of his brandy. "But I have business interests here, and a house. How can you expect me to defy the authorities for a stranger?"

"For a client," said Petzval. "I'm not a stranger; I'm a client of the bank."

"But you ask too much," said Winter. He got up, reached for his hat, and tossed some coins onto the table. It was more than enough to pay for his coffee and the brandy, as well as any coffees and brandies that Petzval might have consumed while waiting for him. *"Auf Wiedersehen,* Herr Petzval." As Winter walked down the café, he heard some sort of commotion, but he didn't turn until he heard Petzval shouting.

Petzval was standing and shaking his fist. Then he grabbed the coins and with all his might threw them at Winter. At least two of the coins hit the glass of the revolving doors. Winter flinched. There was a demon in this fellow Petzval. Two waiters grabbed him, but still he struggled to free himself, so that a third waiter had to clamp his arms round Petzval's neck.

"Damn you, Winter! And damn your money! I curse you, do you hear me?"

Winter was trembling as he pushed his way through the revolving doors and out into the darkness of Gumpendorfer Strasse. Of course the fellow was quite mad, but his curses were still ringing in Winter's head as he climbed into his horseless carriage. He couldn't help thinking it was a bad omen: especially with his second child about to be born at almost any moment.

A plot of land on the Obersalzberg.

———

Winter woke up and wondered where he was for a moment before remembering that he was in his Vienna residence. It seemed so different without his wife. Usually a good night's sleep was all that Harald Winter needed to recuperate from the stresses and anxieties of his business. But next morning, sitting in his dressing room with a hot towel wrapped across his face, he had still not forgotten his encounter with the violent young man.

Winter removed the hot towel and tossed it onto the marble washstand. "Will there be a war, Hauser?" Winter asked while his valet poured hot water from the big floral-patterned jug and made a lather in the shaving cup.

The valet lathered Winter's chin. He was an intelligent young man from a village near Rostock. He treasured his job as Winter's valet; he was the only member of Winter's domestic household who unfailingly traveled with his master. "Between these Austrians and the Serbs, sir? Yes, people say it's sure to come." The razors, combs, and scissors were sterilized, polished bright, and laid out precisely on a starched white cloth. Everything was always arranged in this same pattern.

"Soon, Hauser?"

The valet stropped the razor. He was too bright to imagine that his master was consulting him about the likelihood of war. Such predictions were better left to the generals and the politicians, the sort of men whom Winter rubbed shoulders with every day. Hauser was being asked what people said in the streets. The sort of people who lived in the huge tenement blocks near the factories; workers who lived ten to a room, with all of them paying a quarter of their wages to the landlords. Men who worked twelve- and even fourteen-hour days, with only Sunday afternoons for themselves. What were these men saying? What were they saying in Berlin, in Vienna, Budapest, and London? Winter always wanted to know such things, and Hauser made it his job to have answers. "These Austrians like no one, sir. They are jealous of us Germans, hate the Czechs, and despise the Hungarians. But the Serbs are the ones they want to fight. Sooner or later everyone says they'll finish them off. And Serbia is not much; even the Austrians should be able to beat them." He spoke of them all with condescension, as a German has always spoken of the Balkan people and the Austrians, who seemed little different.

Winter smiled to himself. Hauser had all the pride—"arrogance" was perhaps the better word—of the Prussian. That's why he liked him. Hauser steadied his master's chin with finger and thumb as he drew the sharpened razor through the lather and left pink, shiny skin. As Hauser wiped the long razor on a cloth draped over his arm, Winter said, "The terrorists and the anarchists with their guns and bombs . . . murdering innocent people here in the streets. They are all from Serbia. Trained and encouraged by the Serbs. Wouldn't you be angry, Hauser?"

"But I wouldn't join the army and march off to war, Herr Winter." He lifted Winter's chin so that he could bring the razor up the throat. "There are lots of people I don't like, but I can see no point in marching off to fight a war about it."

"You're a sensible fellow, Hauser."

"Yes, Herr Winter," said Hauser, twisting Winter's head as he continued his task.

"We are fortunate to live in an age when wars are a thing of the past, Hauser. No need for you to have fears of riding off to war."

"I hope not," said Hauser, who had no fears about *riding* off to war: only gentlemen like Herr Winter went off to war on chargers; Hauser's class marched.

"Battles, yes," said Winter. "The Kaiser will have to teach the Chinese a lesson, the English send men into the Sudan or to fight the Boers—but these are just police actions, Hauser. For us Europeans, war is a thing of the past."

Hauser turned his master's head a little more and started to trim the sideburns. He cut the sideburns a fraction shorter each time. Side whiskers were fast going out of fashion and, like most domestic servants, Hauser was an unrepentant snob about fashions. He always left Winter's mustache to the end. Trimming the blunt-ended mustache was the most difficult part. He kept another razor solely for that job. "So the Austrians won't fight the Serbs?" said Hauser as if Winter's decision would be final.

"The Balkans are not Europe," said Winter, turning to face the wardrobe so that Hauser could trim the other sideburn. "Those fellows down in that part of the world are quite mad. They'll never stop fighting each other. But I'm talking about real Europeans, who have finally learned how to live together, and settle differences by negotiation: Germans, Austrians, Englishmen . . . even the French have at last reconciled themselves to the fact that Alsace and Lorraine are German. That's why I say you'll never ride off to war, Hauser."

"No, Herr Winter, I'm sure I won't."

There was a light tap at the door. Hauser lifted his razor away in case his master should make a sudden move. "Come in," said Winter.

It was one of the chambermaids; little more than fourteen years old, she had a Carinthian accent so strong that Winter had her repeat her message three times before he was sure he had it right. It was the senior manager from the Vienna branch of the bank. What could have got into the man, that he should come disturbing Winter at nine-thirty in the morning at his residence? And yet he was usually a sensible and restrained old man. "Very urgent," said the little chambermaid. Her face was bright red with excitement at such unusual goings-on. She'd seen the master being shaved; that would be something to brag about to the parlormaid. "Very, very urgent."

"That's quite enough, girl," said Hauser. "Your master understands."

"Show him up," said Winter.

Hauser coughed. Show him up to see Winter when he was not even shaved? And this was the tricky part: shaving round the master's mustache. Hauser didn't want to be doing that with an audience, and there was the chance that Winter would start talking; then anything could happen. Suppose his hand slipped and he made a cut? Then what would happen to his good job?

"I'm deeply sorry to disturb you, Herr Winter," said the senior manager as he was shown into the room. This time the butler was with the visitor, instead of that scatterbrained little chambermaid. Hauser noticed that the butler's fingers were marked with silver polish. That job should have been completed last night. These damned Austrians, thought Hauser, are all slackers. He wondered if Winter would notice.

"It's this business with Petzval," said the senior manager. He had big old-fashioned muttonchop whiskers in the style of the Emperor.

Winter nodded and tried not to show any particular concern.

29

"I wouldn't have disturbed you, but the messenger from Count Kupka said you should be told immediately. . . . I felt I should come myself."

"Yes, but what *is* it?" said Winter testily.

"He died by his own hand," said the senior manager. "The messenger emphasized that there is no question of foul play. He made that point most strongly."

"Suicide. Well, I'm damned," said Winter. "Did he leave a note?" He held his breath.

"A note, Herr Direktor?" said the old man anxiously, wondering if Winter was referring to a promissory note or some other such valuable or negotiable certificate. And then, understanding what Winter meant, he said brightly, "Oh, a suicide note. No, Herr Direktor, nothing of that sort."

Winter tried not to show his relief. "You did right," he said. He felt sick, and his face was flushed. He knew only too well what could happen when things like this went wrong.

"Thank you, Herr Direktor. Of course I went immediately to the records to make sure the bank's funds were not in jeopardy."

"And what is the position?" asked Winter, wiping the last traces of soap from his face while looking in the mirror. He was relieved to notice that he looked as cool and calm as he always contrived when with his employees.

"It is my understanding, Herr Winter, that, while the death of the debtor irrevocably puts the surety wholly into the possession of the nominated beneficiary, the bank's obligation ends on the death of the other party."

"And how much of the loan has been paid to Petzval so far?"

"He had a twenty-crown gold piece on signature, Herr Direktor. As is the usual custom at the bank."

"So this small tract of land on the Obersalzberg has cost us no more than twenty crowns?"

"The money was to be paid in ten installments. . . ."

"Never mind that," said Winter. "There was no message from Count Kupka?"

"He said I was to give you his congratulations, Herr Winter. I imagine that . . ."

"The baby," supplied Winter, although he knew that Count Kupka did not send congratulations about the birth of babies.

A plot of land on the Obersalzberg.

Count Kupka obviously knew everything that happened in Vienna. Sometimes perhaps he knew before it happened.

"My darling!" said Winter. "Forgive me for not being here earlier." He kissed her and glanced round the room. He hated hospitals, with their pungent smells of ether and disinfectant. Insisting that his wife go into a hospital instead of having the baby at home was another grudge he had against Professor Schneider. "It's been the most difficult of days for me," said Winter.

"Harry! You poor darling!" his wife cooed mockingly. She looked lovely when she laughed. Even in hospital, with her long fair hair on her shoulders instead of arranged high upon her head the way her personal maid did it, she was the most beautiful woman he'd ever seen. Her determined jaw and high cheekbones and her tall elegance seemed so American to him that he never got used to the idea that this energetic creature was his wife.

Winter flushed. "I'm sorry, darling. I didn't mean that. Obviously you've had a terrible time, too."

She smiled at his discomfort. It was not easy to disconcert him. "I have *not* had a terrible time, Harry. I've had a son."

Winter glanced at the baby in the cot. "I wanted to be here sooner, but there was a complication at the bank this morning. The senior manager came to talk to me while I was shaving. At home, while I was shaving! One of our clients died. . . . It was suicide."

"Oh, how terrible, Harry. Is it someone I know?"

"A Jew named Petzval. To tell you the truth, I think the fellow was up to no good. The secret police have been interested in him for some time. He might have been a member of one of these terrorist groups."

"How do you come to have dealings with such people, darling?" She lolled her head back and was glazy-eyed. It was, of course, the aftereffects of the anesthetic. The nurse had said she was still weak.

"It was one of the junior managers who dealt with him. Some of them have no judgment at all."

"Suicide. Poor tormented soul," said Veronica.

Winter watched her cross herself and then glance at the carved crucifix above her bed. He hoped that she was not about to become a Roman Catholic or some sort of religious fanatic. Winter had quite

31

enough to contend with already without a wife going to Mass at the crack of dawn each day. He dismissed the idea. Veronica was not the type; if Veronica became a convert, she was more likely to be a convert to Freud and his absurd psychology. She'd already been to some of Freud's lectures and refused to laugh at Winter's jokes about the man's ideas. "It's a good thing you're not running the bank, my dearest Veronica. You'd be giving the cash away to any bare-assed beggar who arrived with a hard-luck story." He moved a basket of flowers from a chair—the room was filled with flowers—and noticed from the card that the employees of the Berlin bank had sent them. He sat down.

"I want to call him Paul," said his wife. "Do you hate the name Paul?"

"No, it's a fine name. But I thought you'd want to name him after your father."

"Peter and Paul, darling. Don't you see how lovely it will be to have two sons named Peter and Paul?"

"Have you been saving up this idea ever since our son Peter Harald was born, more than three years ago?"

She smiled and stretched her long legs down in the bedclothes. She'd chosen two names her American parents would find equally acceptable. She wondered if Harry realized that. He probably did; Harry Winter was very sharp when it came to people and their motives.

"All that time?" said Winter. He laughed. "What a mad Yankee wife I have."

"You are pleased, Harry? Say you're pleased."

"Of course I am."

"Then go and look at him, Harry. Pick him up and bring him to me."

Winter looked over his shoulder, hoping that the nun would return, but there was no sign of her. She was obviously giving them a chance for privacy. Awkwardly he picked up his newborn son. "Hello, Paul," he said. "I have a present for you, child of the new century." He was a pudgy little fellow with a screwed-up face that seemed to scowl. But the baby's eyes were Veronica's: smoky-gray eyes that never did reveal her innermost thoughts. Winter put the baby back into the cot.

"Do you really, Harry? How wonderful you are. What is it, darling? Let me see what it is."

A plot of land on the Obersalzberg.

"It's a plot of land," said Winter. "A small piece of hillside on the Obersalzberg."

"A plot of land? Where's Obersalzberg?"

"Bavaria, Germany, the very south. It's the sort of place where a man could build himself a comfortable shooting lodge. A place a man could go when he wants to get away from the world."

"A plot of land on the Obersalzberg. Harry! You still surprise me, after all this time we've been married." Through the haze of the ether that was still making her mind reel, she wondered if that represented some deep-felt desire of her husband. Did he yearn to go somewhere and get away from the world? He already had that beastly girl Martha to go to. What else did he want?

"What's wrong?" said Winter.

"Nothing, darling. But it's a strange present to give a newborn baby, isn't it?"

"It's good land: a fine place with a view of the mountains. A place for a man to think his own thoughts and be his own master." He looked at the baby. It was happier now and managed a smile.

1906

"The sort of thing they're told at school."

"You have two delightful little boys, Veronica," said her father. He watched through the window of the morning room as the solemn ten-year-old Peter pushed his radiantly joyful little blond brother across the lawn on a toy horse. The children were in the private gardens of a big house in London's Belgravia. It was a glorious summer's day, and London was at its shining best. An old gardener scythed the bright-green grass to make scallop patterns across the lawn. The scent of newly cut grass hung heavily in the still air and made little Pauli's eyes red and weepy. Cyrus sniffed contentedly. Their English friends urged them to come to London in "the season," but the Rensselaers preferred to cross the Atlantic at this time of year, when the seas were calmer. "No matter what I'm inclined to say about that rascally husband of yours, at least he's given you two fine boys."

"Now, now, Papa," said Veronica mildly, "let's not go through all that again." She was wearing a long "tea gown" of blue chiffon with net over darker-blue satin. Such afternoon gowns gave her a few hours' escape from the tight corsets that fashion forced her into for most of the day. It was a lovely, loose, flouncy creation that made her feel young and beautiful and able even to take on her parents. She pulled the trailing hem of it close and admired it.

"She's given Harry two fine boys," Mrs. Rensselaer scoffed. "Isn't it just like a man to put it the wrong way around? Who endured that dreadful hospital in Vienna, when there was a bed-

34

room and our own doctor waiting for her in New York City?" They were getting at her again, but she was used to it by now. She noticed how much stronger her mother's high-pitched Yankee twang sounded compared with her father's softly accented low voice. She noticed all the accents much more now that her life was spent amongst Germans. She wondered if her spoken English had now acquired some sort of German edge to it. Her parents had never mentioned it, and she knew better than to ask them.

"I couldn't have come home to have the baby, Mother. You know I couldn't." She suppressed a sigh. For six years they'd nursed this resentment, and still it persisted.

Her father watched the children cross the road hand in hand with their nanny and heard the front door as they came in time to have a wash before tea. He said, "I travel across the Atlantic regularly, Veronica, and your mother usually accompanies me. It's ridiculous for you to go on pretending that you can't come home for a visit when we come here to London every year without fail." He thrust his hands into his pockets. "By golly, when I first came to Europe, I sailed on a four-masted barque; now your mother and I sleep in staterooms with running water, and eat dinners that wouldn't disgrace the Ritz."

Cyrus G. Rensselaer was a distinguished-looking man in his mid-fifties. He had a shock of black hair combed straight back, pale-blue eyes, and a large mustache. He made no concessions to the warm weather: he wore a black barathea morning suit with a fancy brocaded waistcoat, and a loose tie with a silver pin through the knot. Yet there was a certain unconventional look to him—his hair was longer than was fashionable—so that sometimes, on the steamship coming over, fellow passengers thought he might be a famous musician or a successful painter. This always pleased Cyrus Rensselaer, because he often said that he would have become a painter had his father not thrashed him every time he wanted to stop studying engineering.

"I know, Father. You've told me all that in your letters. But Harry is a German; the boys are German. I think of Germany as my home now." The difficulty was that her parents spoke no foreign languages, and their one visit to Berlin for the wedding in 1892 seemed to have deterred both of them from ever going to the continent of Europe again.

"You were able to go to Vienna and have the baby, darling,"

35

explained her mother. "Papa feels that coming back to New York wouldn't have been all that much more of a strain."

"The baby was early, Mother. We were in Vienna and the doctor said I shouldn't travel." She looked at her parents; they were unconvinced. "Harry was furious about it. He'd made all the arrangements in Berlin. Poor little Paul—Harry used to call him 'the little Austrian dumpling' until I made him stop saying it."

Her father pulled a gold hunter from his waistcoat pocket and looked at it. "Didn't your Harry say he'd be back for tea?"

"He's lunching at the club."

"He likes clubs," said her father.

"It's some mining deal . . ." explained Veronica. "Someone has discovered a cure for malaria. They think it's something to do with mosquitoes. Harry says that if it works it will really open up the darkest part of Central Africa."

"It's not a woman, is it?" whispered her mother.

"No, it's not a woman, Mother."

"How can you be so sure?" her mother asked.

"I'm sure, Mother. Harry's not so smart about women as he is about money."

Mr. Rensselaer did not like hearing Harald Winter praised, and he certainly didn't like to hear him praised about his investing and banking skills, at which he considered himself pre-eminent. "I'm surprised your Harry isn't investing in flying machines," he said sardonically.

Veronica looked up at him sharply. "You underestimate Harry, Papa. You think he'll invest money into any crazy scheme put up to him. But Harry is clever with money; he would never put it into the hands of people like that."

"I'm darned if I ever know what to make of your Harry," said her father. "He spends money on such toys as this Daimler Mercedes and then takes you down to a cabin on the Obersalzberg and makes you manage with only a couple of local servants. I didn't pay for your education so that you could wash dishes and sweep the house."

"It's not a cabin, Papa, more like a hunting lodge. The land passed to Harry because of a bad debt. He gave it to Pauli as a christening present. Now he's built the house there. I love going there. It's the only time I have Harry all to myself. And we take two maids from the Berlin house, as well as the cook, Harry's valet, and the chauffeur."

"It sounds like a lot of work for you, darling," said her mother. "And walking for five miles! We could hardly believe it when we read your letter. We couldn't picture you walking so far. Don't you get lonely?"

Veronica smiled. "I have Harry and the children; how could I ever be lonely? And, anyway, we have plenty of neighbors."

"What sort of neighbors? Peasants? Woodcutters?"

"No, Papa. Some fine families have houses there. It's become very fashionable; musicians and writers . . . some of them live there all year round."

"It sounds like an odd kind of christening present. Harry should have sold it and put the money into some investments for your Pauli."

"I want Pauli to have it, Papa. Last year the woodcarver in the village carved a big sign—"Haus Pauli"—that will be fixed over the gate. It's the most beautiful place in the whole world: meadows, pine trees, and mountains. Behind us there is the Hohe Göll and the Kehlstein mountain. From the window of the breakfast room we can see for miles, right across Berchtesgaden or into Austria."

"It's southernmost Bavaria. I looked on the atlas. That's too far for us to travel," said Rensselaer in a voice that precluded any further discussion.

The Scots nanny brought the boys in promptly at four. Their hands and faces were polished bright pink, and a brown circle of iodine had been painted on Pauli's newly grazed arm. It was always blond Pauli who fell: he was the unlucky one. Or was he careless or clumsy? Either way, he was always cheery and smiling. Peter was quite different; he was dark, sober, and composed, a thoughtful little boy who'd never been babyish like his young brother. They kissed their mother and Granny and Grandpa dutifully and then, in response to the bellpull, the maids brought tea, with the best china teacups and silver pots. And there was Cook's homemade strawberry jam, which went onto the freshly cooked scones together with a spoonful of pale-yellow Cornish cream.

Tea was poured, plates distributed, cakes cut, and sugar spooned out. Throughout the hubbub of the afternoon tea, Rensselaer remained standing by the window; his teacup and saucer and a plate with scones and cream were on the table untouched. He had started his engineering career out west, working in places where a man soon learned how to handle hard liquor, his two fists, and

37

sometimes a gun. The way in which he'd gained admittance to New York's toughest business circles, and then to its snobby society families, was as much due to Rensselaer's clumsy honesty, disarming directness, and awkward charm as to his luck and mining skills. But he'd never acquired the social grace that his wife expected of him, and this sort of fancy English tea was a ceremony he didn't enjoy.

"Are you keeping up the Latin?" Rensselaer asked Peter. He was a thin, wiry child, dressed, like his little brother, in cotton knickerbocker trousers with a sailor-suit top. He had the same dark hair that his grandfather had, and the same pale-blue eyes. There was no other noticeable resemblance, but it was enough to make them recognizably kin.

"Yes, sir." Peter was a graceful little boy, slim and upright, standing face to face with his grandpa and answering in clear and excellent English.

"Good boy. You must keep up the Latin and the mathematics. Your mother always got top grades in mathematics when she was at school in Springtown. Did she tell you that?"

"No, sir. She didn't tell me that." There was an awkward relationship between Veronica's parents and her sons. The Rensselaers were unbending, not understanding that children were no longer treated in the formal and distant way that they had treated their daughter.

"And what are you going to be when you grow up, young Peter?" Rensselaer asked him. How he wished the children hadn't had these very short Prussian haircuts. He was used to children having longer hair. These "bullet heads" were unbecoming for his grandchildren, and he resented Veronica's allowing it.

"I'm going to fly in the airship with Count Zeppelin," said Peter.

His little brother looked at him with respect bordering on awe, but Mr. Rensselaer laughed. "Airship! That's rich!" he said and laughed again.

Pauli laughed, too, but Peter went red. To help cover his embarrassment, Mary Rensselaer said, "Would you like to come and see us in America, Peter? We'd love to have you visit with us."

"Next year I go to my new school," said Peter.

"You're boarding them, Veronica?" she asked her daughter.

"No, Mother. It's a day school. Harry doesn't like boarding schools except well-supervised military schools. He says there are always bullies. Harry says it makes the English the way they are."

"No harm those Germans of yours becoming more like the English," said Mr. Rensselaer. "A little bullying at boarding school might have done that bellicose little Kaiser Wilhelm a power of good." He marked this observation with a sound that might have been a chuckle or a snort, then wiped his nose on a very big red cotton handkerchief.

Veronica glanced nervously at the boys, then said, "Harry says the Kaiser has done wonders for Germany. He's brought us closer to Austria, and that's a good thing."

"It's a good thing for Harry, because of his business interests in Austria, but the Dual Alliance, as they call it, has frightened Russia and France into closer ties, and whatever France does, Britain does, too. The Kaiser's heading himself into a lot of trouble, Veronica. I want you to remember that when you are reading your newspapers."

"Harry says all that war talk is just nonsense the newspaper writers invent to sell the papers."

Mr. Rensselaer leaned down to talk to Peter. "You remember that your mother is an American, young man. And that makes you half American, too. Never mind about flying in airships with Count Zeppelin; you come to New York City and you'll see things that will make your eyes pop. America is the only country for a young man like you: farmlands that stretch to the horizon and beyond, and railroads crisscrossing the whole continent. You come to America and discover what it's like to breathe the air of free men." He reached out to put his hand on the child's shoulder.

Peter pushed his grandfather's hand away and turned on him. "I don't want to go with you. I hate you. You're a bad man to say nasty things about His Majesty. He's my Emperor. Germany has to be strong, to fight the French and the English and the Russians. Then the world will respect the Kaiser. I'll never go to America—never, never."

The smile froze on Pauli's face. For a moment the four grownups were too embarrassed to react. They watched this ten-year-old's outburst without knowing what to do about it. Cyrus Rensselaer felt a sudden sense of isolation. He'd spent a lot of time looking forward to this meeting with his daughter and his grandsons. They were his only heirs. But instead of the two amiable, tousled, freckle-faced kids he was expecting to see, he was suddenly faced with two militant Teutons. Rensselaer was shocked and speechless. No one moved until six-year-old Paul—sensing that something awful had happened—let out a howl and began to cry more loudly than he'd ever cried before. Then the nanny grabbed the hand of little Paul and tried to grasp Peter's hand, too, but he ran from the room and slammed the door behind him with all his might.

Veronica said, "Take them both up to their room, Nanny. You can tell Peter that his father will hear about this when he gets home."

"Yes, madam," said the nurse. "I really don't know . . . It's not like Peter. . . ."

"That will be all, Nanny," said Grandpa Rensselaer. When the children and nanny had gone, he went to the sidetable and poured himself a whiskey. He downed it in one gulp.

"It's the journey . . . and the excitement," said Veronica when her father turned back to face her. "Peter is usually the quiet one. Peter is polite and thoughtful. It's Pauli who gets overexcited." She spoiled the little one, and she knew it. Did this sudden outburst mean that Peter felt neglected and was demonstrating his discontent?

"It's that husband of yours," said Rensselaer. "You can see what sort of ideas he puts into the children's heads . . . Count Zeppelin . . . airships, and all this nonsense about Kaiser Wilhelm, 'my Emperor.' It's time I had a word with your Harald."

"Please don't, Father. It's none of Harald's doing. He spends little enough time with the children." She smoothed her satin dress nervously.

"Someone's been filling the boy's head with mischievous twaddle," said Rensselaer.

"It's the school, Father. It's the sort of thing they're told at school."

Cyrus Rensselaer's influence and popularity were evident that evening. His twenty-two dinner guests provided a cross section of Britain at the height of its power. On Mary Rensselaer's right sat an Indian prince, a delicate old man with an Eton accent so pronounced that sometimes even the other English guests had trouble understanding him. Facing her there was a weatherbeaten infantry colonel who'd soldiered through the empire. In the Transvaal he'd won his Queen's newly founded Victoria Cross, and in Afghanistan he'd left an arm.

Dominating the table with his anecdotes there was a plain-speaking Yorkshireman, sole owner of a steelworks from which had come enough metal to build a complete Royal Naval Battle Squadron. And listening with delight there was a Peer of the Realm: a handsome, bearded youth who'd inherited half a million acres of northern England. He was rich on coal from a couple of mines he'd never seen, and on rents from a dozen villages that he couldn't, when asked, name.

The women were as formidable as the men, and just as surprising. The Indian princess could speak a dozen languages, and her German was faultless. The wife of the steelmaster had been painted by Degas, and the bank official's wife had been a lady-in-waiting to the late Queen. A buxom woman with a glittering diamond collar had run a hospital in the Sudan before marrying a man who owned several thousand miles of Latin American railways.

The dining room was designed to complement such eminent company: fine paintings, carpets, linen, crystal, and silver. And the food and wines were memorable.

Harald Winter was overwhelmed. Even his Berlin-tailored evening dress felt wrong, especially when he found all the other men wearing white waistcoats instead of the black ones that were still fashionable in Berlin. In Berlin he was treated as a wealthy and influential—not to say powerful—man. But he felt different in the presence of these people. They were relaxed and courteous, but Winter was not such a fool that he didn't see their arrogant self-confidence. Though they complimented him on his excellent English, he knew the way they ridiculed any sort of foreign accent. Their exaggerated politeness and modest disclaimers were the veneer that overlaid their rough contempt for foreigners such as Winter, and for his banking house, of which they all told him they'd never heard.

"I'm completely out of touch nowadays," one of the guests—a financial expert—told him apologetically. "The only bankers I remember are the really big ones. . . . Getting old, you see." He tapped his head and turned away to speak with someone else. Winter felt humiliated.

Rensselaer was just as bad. He'd spent most of the meal talking to the Indian princess. Winter wondered if his father-in-law guessed that he urgently wanted to put a financial proposition to him. He'd been trying to have a private word with his host since arriving back from a disappointing business lunch. Was he avoiding him? Surely not. Rensselaer was as keen on a profitable deal as any other man in the financial world. It was just as well they were houseguests. Perhaps he could have a word with Rensselaer after these dinner guests had gone.

"You look pensive, darling," Veronica told her husband when the men joined the ladies in the drawing room. "Is everything all right?"

"Everything is fine," said Winter. It was no good telling his wife how much he disliked these people. Veronica and her family were the same as the rest of them, so he simply told her she was looking wonderful in her long pale-green silk dress. She'd never perceive the way in which these rich and powerful guests of her father's despised the little German banker and the nation from which he came.

"I'm not a pork butcher," he peevishly responded when the woman with the diamond collar asked him what he did for a living in Berlin. It was a silly remark and simply revealed his nervous exasperation.

"My grandfather was a butcher in Leeds," she cheerfully told him. "Even now I can remember the wonderful roast beef we always had at his house."

Winter was embarrassed at her response. He desperately tried to make amends for his gratuitous rudeness. "I have a bank," he said and, in keeping with this English obsession for modesty, added, "a very small bank." She laughed. No matter what one did, somehow the English always knew how to make a foreigner feel a fool.

The two boys, in the nursery bedroom at the very top of the house, heard the clatter of carriages and the sounds of the guests leaving soon after midnight. Peter, lost in a dream about airships, went back to sleep almost immediately, but little Pauli was still worried about his brother's outburst that afternoon. Paul had none of the cleverness that distinguished his elder brother but, perhaps in compensation for this, the little blond child had an instinct about what went on in other people's minds. He knew that his grandfather was deeply hurt by what his brother had said. Peter was like that:

he had the capacity for cruelty that comes so easily to the self-righteous.

Now Pauli stayed awake worrying about what would happen to Peter. Perhaps he'd be sent away. He'd heard of children's being sent away. They were sent away to jobs, and to schools, and sometimes sent away to the army or the navy. Pauli had no idea of what happened to those who were "sent away," but now it was dark, and the flickering nightlight made strange shadows on the ceiling and on the wall, and all sorts of frightening ideas about being sent away occurred to him.

He called to his brother, but Pauli's voice was faint and Peter's sleep was not interrupted. Pauli got out of bed and decided to wake up Nanny; she'd be angry, of course, but he knew she'd pick him up and cuddle him and put him back to bed with reassuring words that sometimes little boys like Pauli want to hear in the middle of the dark night.

Pauli was halfway down the top flight of the back stairs by the time he fully realized that he wasn't in his home in Berlin. He walked up and down the line of closed bedroom doors trying to decide which one to try. It was then that he heard voices from somewhere below. He continued down the servant's stairs until he got to the ground floor. The voices were coming from a room at the back of the house. It was Grandpa's study—a small back room where Cyrus Rensselaer went to smoke. Here he kept a comfortable old leather chair, a desk where he could write, and a locked cabinet that contained his very finest French brandy and his favorite sourmash bourbon, which he brought with him because the London wine merchants had never heard of it.

From his position on the landing, Pauli could squeeze into a space where empty steamer trunks were stored, and from there he could look through an open fanlight and see into the room.

Grandpa was sitting in the big leather chair, alongside the coal fire that was now only red embers and gray ash. Pauli's father was perched on the edge of the writing desk. His father looked uncomfortable. Both men had cut-glass tumblers in their hands. Grandpa was smoking a big cigar and Daddy was lighting one, too. Pauli could smell the smoke as it curled up into his hiding place. Grandpa took the cigar from his mouth and said, "Never mind all the stories about a cure for malaria, Harry. If you are trying to raise capital for your bank, it means your bank is in trouble."

43

"It's not in trouble," said Winter. He tugged at the hem of his black waistcoat and silently cursed his Berlin tailor for not knowing that in England it was passé.

"When people start saying a bank is in trouble: it's in trouble."

Harald Winter said, "It's a chance to expand."

Rensselaer interrupted him. "Never mind the bullshit, Harry; save that for the suckers. My friends in the City tell me you're not sound."

Winter stiffened. "Of course it's sound. Half the money still remains in German government bonds."

"Damnit, Harry, don't be so naïve. It's not sound because your aluminum factory may not be a success. Suppose the aluminum market doesn't come up to your expectations? How are you going to pay back the money? Your investors think all their money is in government bonds. It's bordering on the dishonest, Harry."

Winter sipped his drink. "The electrolytic process has changed aluminum production. The metal is light and very strong; they're experimenting with all kinds of mixtures, and these alloys will revolutionize building and automobiles, and they'll find other industrial uses for it."

"Sure, sure, sure," said Rensselaer. "I've heard all these snake-oil stories. . . . There's always a claim where some guy will strike gold or oil . . . and it's always next week. I grew up on all that stuff."

"I'm not talking about something that might never happen," said Winter. "I'm talking about using aluminum alloys."

"Aluminum: okay. I made a few inquiries. In 1855 it cost a thousand Reichsmarks per kilo; in 1880, twenty Reichsmarks; now I can buy it for two Reichsmarks a kilo. What price will it be by the time your factory comes into full-scale production?"

"I'm not selling aluminum, Mr. Rensselaer." He always addressed his father-in-law as "Mr. Rensselaer," always expecting him to suggest he called him "Cyrus" or "Cy" as his friends did; but Cyrus Rensselaer never did suggest it, even though he called his son-in-law "Harry." It was another example of the way Harald Winter was deliberately humbled. Or that was how it seemed to him. "I'll be selling manufactured components that bolt together to make the rigid framework for airships."

"Then why the aluminum factory? Buy your materials on the open market."

"I have to have an assured supply. Otherwise I could sign a

contract and then be held to ransom by the aluminum manufacturers."

"It's my daughter I'm thinking of, Harry. You haven't told her that you are going to put every penny you can raise into producing metal components for flying machines. I sounded her out this afternoon: she thinks you're cautious with money. She trusts you to look after the family."

Winter drew on his cigar. "These zeppelins are going to change the world, Mr. Rensselaer. A year ago I would have shared your skepticism. But I've seen Zeppelin's first airship flying—as big as a city block and as smooth as silk."

"And as dangerous as hell. Don't you know those ships are full of hydrogen, Harry? Have you ever seen hydrogen burn?"

"I know all the problems and the dangers," said Winter, "but, just as you have your contacts here in London, I have friends in the Berlin War Office. At present the General Staff is showing strong opposition to all forms of airship; the soldiers don't like new ideas. But the Kaiser has personally ordered the setting up of a Motorluftschiff-Studien-Gesellschaft: a technical society for the study of airships. It's still very secret, but it's just a matter of time until the army orders some big rigids from Count Zeppelin."

"That's all moonshine, Harry. I hear that Zeppelin's second ship, which flew in January, turned out to be a big flop. They say its first flight is going to be its one and only flight."

"But Count Zeppelin is already building LZ 3, and it will fly about twelve weeks from now. Make no mistake: he'll go on building them."

"Maybe that just shows he doesn't know when he's licked. And who can say how the airships will shape up when the army tests them?"

"Do you realize how much aluminum goes into one of those airships? They weigh almost three tons. Thousands of girders and formers go into each ring. I've done some sums. Using Count Zeppelin's first airship as a yardstick, I'd need only six-point-seven-three percent of an airship's aluminum requirement to break even and pay back the interest."

Even Rensselaer was visibly impressed. "But we're talking about every red cent you possess, Harry. Why not a smaller investment?"

"I could have a smaller investment; I could do without the aluminum factory and be at the mercy of my suppliers. I could have half an interest and have only nonvoting shares, but that would mean someone else was making the decisions about who, what, why, and where we sell. That's not my way, Mr. Rensselaer: and it's not your way, either."

Rensselaer scratched his chin. "I've spent half my working life trying to talk people out of these kinds of blue-sky investments. But I can see I'd be wasting my time trying to talk you out of it." Rensselaer got up from his chair for enough time to flick ash into the fire. "J. P. Morgan bought up steel companies to make U.S. Steel, and he's made himself one of the most powerful men in the U.S., maybe one of the most powerful men in the whole damned world. It looks easy, but don't think that you can corner the market in aluminum and become the J. P. Morgan of Germany. The European market just doesn't work that way."

"I know that, Mr. Rensselaer."

"Do you?" He slumped back into his chair. "That's good, because I meet a whole lot of people who try to get me involved in financing crackpot schemes like that."

"It's just bridging."

"It's *not* bridging, Harry!" Suddenly Rensselaer's voice was louder. Then, as if determined to control his temper, he lowered it again to say, "We're talking about guarantees that will go on until 1916. Ten years! A hell of a lot of things could happen between now and then."

"I have most of it, Mr. Rensselaer."

"You need nearly a million pounds sterling, Harry, and that's a hell of a lot of dough when you've got no collateral that I'd want to try and realize on."

Winter knew that his father-in-law had decided to let him have the money. He smiled. "It's a great opportunity, Mr. Rensselaer. You'll never regret it."

"I'm regretting it already," said Rensselaer. "I've always tried to stay clear of government agencies in all shapes and forms. Especially I've avoided armies and navies. Now I'm going to find myself with a million pounds sterling invested in the army of the Kaiser: a man I wouldn't trust to look after my horses. What's worse, I'm going to have the security of my investment depending upon his bellicose ambitions."

Rensselaer knew his words would offend his son-in-law, but he was angry and frustrated at the trap he found himself in. When

Winter wisely made no reply, Rensselaer said, "It's for Veronica's sake—you know that, of course—and I'll want proper safeguards built into the paperwork. I'll want your life insured with a U.S. company for the full amount of the loan."

"It's the Kaiser's life you should insure," said Winter. "My death would make no difference to the investment."

"Here's to the Kaiser's health," said Rensselaer sardonically. He raised his glass and drank the rest of his whiskey.

Winter smiled and decided not to drink to the Kaiser's health. In the circumstances it would seem like lese majesty.

Little Pauli crawled out of his hiding place and went slowly upstairs, trying to figure out what the two grownups had been talking about. By the time he found his bedroom again, only one part of the scene he'd witnessed was clear to him. He shook Peter awake and said, "I saw Daddy and Grandpa. They were smoking cigars and talking. Daddy made Grandpa drink to the health of His Majesty the Emperor. He made him do it, Peter."

Peter came awake slowly, and when he heard Pauli's story he was skeptical. Little Pauli hero-worshipped his father in a way that Peter would never do. "Go to sleep, Pauli; you've been dreaming again." He turned over and snuggled deep into the soft down pillow.

"I haven't been dreaming," said Pauli. He wanted Peter to believe him; he wanted his big brother to treat him as an equal. "I saw them." But by the time morning came, he was no longer quite certain.

1908

"Conqueror of the air— hurrah!"

In Friedrichshafen it was cold, damned cold. There was very little wind—the zeppelins could not take off in a wind—but November is not a time of year when anyone goes to the shores of the grim, gray Bodensee unless he has business there. Across the calm water of the lake, the Swiss side was clearly visible and the Alps were shining in the watery winter sunlight.

Harald Winter had persuaded his wife to stay in the car. It was Winter's pride and joy. A huge seven-and-a-half-horsepower Italian car, just like the one that won the Peking-to-Paris Road Race with twenty days' lead! And yet, with its four-speed gearbox, so reliable and easy to use that Winter sometimes took the wheel himself. He'd had it parked down by the waterfront under the trees near the Schlosskirche, so that Veronica would have a good view of the airship and the shed that floated on the lake. She was well wrapped up, and under her feet was a copper foot-warmer that could be refilled with boiling water. And if she got too cold, the chauffeur would drive her back to the Kurgarten Hotel in Friedrichshafen, where the zeppelin people had provided for the Winter family a comfortable suite of rooms.

But Harald Winter was at the lakeside, nearer to the activity. He was excited; he would not have missed this occasion for all the world. Together with his two boys—Peter twelve and Pauli eight— he'd been given a place from which he could see everything. He would have been flying in the zeppelin but for the stringent terms of the life insurance that his father-in-law had made a condition of the loan.

They'd seen the floating shed being revolved to eliminate any chance of a crosswind's damaging the airship as it came from out of its tight-fitting hangar. Now they watched as the white motorboat took its distinguished guests out to LZ 3; the new modifications made her the finest of the airships. The crowd cheered spontaneously. After the tragic destruction of LZ 4 last year—in a gesture that no foreigner would ever understand—the spontaneous generosity of the whole nation brought Count Zeppelin six million marks in donations. Much of the money had been sent within hours of the disaster. So these cheers were not just for the airship. There was something exhilarating in the atmosphere here today. The zeppelin was fast becoming a symbol of a new, exciting Germany, whose scientific inventions, paintings, music, and, more important, growing naval strength had made a real nation from a collection of small states. And not just a nation, but an international power of the first rank.

"That's the Kaiser," whispered Winter to his sons. "He's wearing that long cloak or you'd see all his medals. Next to him is Prince Fürstenberg and then Admiral Müller and General von Plessen. The thin one is the Crown Prince."

"Why isn't Count Zeppelin with them?" Peter asked. The boys were wearing gray flannel suits, specially tailored for the occasion, and large cloth caps that their mother thought were "too grown-up-looking" for them.

"He is," said Winter. He was wearing a tight-fitting chesterfield and top hat, a formal outfit suited to someone who would be presented to the Kaiser. "He's facing His Majesty, but he's not wearing his old white cap today; he's dressed up for the occasion."

They watched the airship come out on the surface of the lake, and then there was an interminable delay while the royal party inspected the airship, and another while it was given the final adjustments for the flight. After the Prince and Princess of Fürstenberg were safely aboard, the ballast was offloaded piece by piece, until the moment came when the great silver machine shuddered and floated free.

The roar of the engines echoed across the cold, still water of the

49

Bodensee, and then the nose tilted up and the airship climbed slowly into the gray sky and, rolling slightly as it went, headed down the lake. The airship's silver fabric was shining in the pale sunlight as it came steadily back to where the shore was black with onlookers. There were more loud, uncoordinated cheers as it passed over the boat from which the Kaiser and his entourage watched.

But it was after the landing of LZ 3 that the boys were proudest of their father. For Harald Winter was invited to take his two sons out to the floating shed to watch Kaiser Wilhelm making his speech.

Every available inch of space was used. Illustrious generals, spiked helmets on their heads and chests crammed with medals, and admirals with high, stiff collars and arms garlanded with gold, were all crowded shoulder to shoulder. Standing behind von Zeppelin— the seventy-one-year-old ex–cavalry officer whose single-minded endeavor was today celebrated—they saw Dr. Hugo Eckener, whose conversion to the zeppelin cause had made him even more zealous than his master. Next came Dürr, the engineer, Winter with the two children, and then senior design staff and an official from the engine factory.

"In my name," began the Kaiser suddenly, his voice unexpectedly shrill, "and in the name of our entire German people, I heartily congratulate Your Excellency on this magnificent work which you have so wonderfully displayed before me today. Our Fatherland can be proud to possess such a son—the greatest German of the twentieth century—who through his invention has brought us to a new point in the development of the human race." At this, one or two of the generals and admirals nodded. One of the design staff edged aside to give little Pauli a better view.

The Kaiser looked round his audience, drew himself up into an even more erect posture, and continued: "It is not too much to say that we have today lived through one of the greatest moments in the evolution of human culture. I thank God, with all Germans, that He has considered our people worthy to name you as one of us. Might it be permitted to us all, as it has been to you, to be able to say with pride, in the evening of our life, that we had been successful in serving our dear Fatherland so fruitfully. As a token of my admiring recognition, which certainly all your guests gathered here share with the entire German people, I bestow upon you herewith my high Order of the Black Eagle."

"Conqueror of the air—hurrah!"

Count Zeppelin stepped one pace forward. Over his head the Kaiser put the sash, and then embraced him three times and called, 'His Excellency Count Zeppelin, the conqueror of the air—hurrah!"

From the crowd in the distance, cheers could be heard. For Winter and his two sons it was a day they would never forget.

It was already getting dark by the time Winter and the boys got back to the hotel in Friedrichshafen. Nanny was sent to have dinner alone in the restaurant so that the boys could have theirs served in the sitting room of their suite. Harald Winter was excited by the events of the day, and at times like this he liked to have a few extra moments with his sons.

A solicitous waiter in a white jacket brought the meal and served it to the children course by course. There was turtle soup and breaded schnitzels with rösti potatoes, which the Swiss, across the lake, did so perfectly. When no one was looking, Peter took forkfuls of Pauli's cabbage—Pauli hated cabbage—so that he wouldn't get into trouble for leaving it on his plate. And after that the waiter flamed crêpes for them. It was the first time that their father had permitted them to have a dish containing alcohol and, despite the strong flavor, the boys devoured their pancakes with great joy, slowing their eating to prolong this happy day forever.

After Nanny had taken the boys off to bed, Harald had a chance to express his happiness to his wife. They were in the bedroom; Veronica's maid had gone. Harry was fully dressed in his evening clothes and his wife was making a final selection of jewelry. She had already put three different diamond brooches on her low-cut ball gown and rejected each. She was wearing a wonderful new Poiret dress from Paris, a simple tubular design with a high waist. She knew the new Paris look would create a sensation at the ball tonight. But on such a neoclassical design the jewelry would be all-important. She didn't want to get it wrong. "What do you think, Harry?" She turned away from the mirror enough for him to see her hold the diamond-studded gold rose against her.

"You're very beautiful, my darling," he told her.

"I'm thirty-four, Harry, and I feel every year of it. My shoes hurt already, and the evening has not even started."

"Change them," said Harry.

"The pink silk shoes would look absurd," she said.

He smiled. That was the way women were: the pink shoes looked absurd, the white ones hurt; there was really no answer. Perhaps women liked always to have some problem or other: perhaps it was the way they accounted for their disappointments. "Did you see His Majesty?"

"I got so cold, Harry. I just waited until the airship lifted away. Then I came back for a hot bath."

"The boys saw him. He looked magnificent. He's a great man."

"I'll just have to slip them off at dinner."

"The LZ 3 is to be delivered to the army right away. And as soon as the LZ 5 is completed—and has done a twenty-four-hour endurance flight—they want that, too."

"I know. You told me. It's wonderful."

"You realize what it means, don't you?"

"No," she said vaguely. She'd heard it all before. She wasn't listening to him; she was looking at her shoes.

"It means we'll be rich, darling."

"We're already rich, Harry."

"I mean really rich: tens of millions . . . perhaps a hundred million before I'm finished." He sat down, reaching behind him to flip his coat tails high in the air like a blackbird alighting. You could tell a lot about a man by the way he sat down, she decided. Her father always lifted his coat tails aside carefully, making sure they'd not be creased.

"We're happy, Harry. That's the important thing."

"Dollars, I'm talking about, not Reichsmarks."

"What does it matter, Harry? We're happy, aren't we?" She looked up at him. Somewhere deep inside her there arose a desperate hope that he would embrace her and tell her that he would give up his other women. But she knew he would not do that. He needed the women, the way he needed the money. He had to be reassured, just as little Pauli needed so much reassurance all the time.

"It doesn't matter to you," he said, and she was surprised at the bitterness in his voice. He was like that; his mood could change suddenly for no accountable reason. "You were born into wealth. You have your own bank account and your father's allowance every year. But now I'll have as much money as he's got. I won't have to kowtow to him all the time."

"I haven't noticed you displaying servile deference to Papa," she said. She gave him all her attention.

He ignored her remark. "The army will buy more and more airships, and the navy will buy them, too. I had a word with the admiral today. They're already planning where the bases should be. Nordholz in Schleswig-Holstein will be the biggest one; then others nearby. Revolving sheds built on turntables—the North Sea is too rough for floating the hangars."

"Schleswig-Holstein? Why would they want them so far north? The weather there is not suited to airships. You said they'd need calm weather today."

"Use your brains, Veronica. Germany has the only practical flying machine in the world. The experimental little contraptions that the Wright brothers have made can scarcely lift the weight of a man. What use would those things be for bombing?"

"Bombing? Bombing England?"

"This has been Count Zeppelin's idea right from the start. I thought everyone knew that. He conceived these huge rigid airships as a war-winning weapon."

"How ghastly!"

"It's how progress comes. Leonardo da Vinci developed his great ideas only to help his masters fight wars."

"But bombing England, Harry? For God's sake. What are you saying?"

"Don't get excited, Veronica. I wish I hadn't started talking about it."

"War? War with England? But, Harry, it is no time at all since the King of England went to Berlin. The children saw them both going through Pariser Platz in the state coach. The Kaiser is King Edward's nephew. It's unthinkable. It's madness!" This came in a gabble. It was as if she thought that she had only her husband to persuade and everything would be all right.

It was not an appropriate time to remind her that Kaiser Wilhelm made no secret of his hatred for his uncle the English King. Only the previous year, Winter had been one of three hundred dinner guests to whom the Kaiser had confided that King Edward was "a Satan." But his wife needed assurance, so he went to her and put his arms tightly round her. By God, she was beautiful. Even at thirty-four she outshone some of the younger ones he bedded. He

53

hated to see her distressed. "There will be no war, my darling. I guarantee that. England will see sense. When the time comes, England will see sense. The English are a nation of compromisers."

"I pray to God you're right."

"They say the mustard manufacturers get rich from the dabs of mustard people leave on their plates. And we'll get rich in the same way, darling. From selling the soldiers weapons they'll never use."

1910

The end of Valhalla.

Both boys liked to visit Omi. Harald Winter's widowed mother, Effi, lived in a comfortable little house on the coast, near Travemünde. They went each summer, with Nanny, Mama, and Mama's personal maid. From Berlin they always got a sleeping compartment in the train that left from Lehrter Bahnhof late at night and arrived at Lübeck next morning. They alighted from the train and watched the porters pile the luggage onto carts. The children were taken to see the locomotive, a huge hissing brute that smelled of steam and oil and of the burned specks of coal that floated in the sunlit air. Omi always met them at the station in Lübeck. But this time she wasn't there—only the taxi. It was a big one—a Benz sixty-horsepower Phaeton, more like a delivery van than a car—and it could seat sixteen people if they all crammed together. The driver was a white-haired old fellow named Hugo who would laboriously clamber up onto the roof. There, on its huge rack, he'd strap a dozen suitcases, Mama's ten hat boxes, a traveling rug inside which were rolled a selection of umbrellas and walking sticks, and four black tin trunks so heavy that he'd almost overbalance with the weight of them.

The house itself was a gloomy old place with lace curtains through which the northern sunlight struggled to make pale-gray shadows on the carpet. Even in the dusty conservatory that ran the length of the house, the warmth of the summer sun was hardly enough to stir the wasps from their winter torpor.

Omi always wore black, the same sort of clothes she'd worn back in 1891, when Grandfather died. She spent most of the day in the room on the first floor: she read, she sewed, and for a lot of the time she just remembered. The room was furnished with her treasures and mementos. There were two large jade dragons and a whole elephant tusk engraved with hunting scenes. There was a big photo of her with Opa on their wedding day, and portraits of other members of the family, and there were stuffed birds in glass cases and green plants that never bore flowers. She called the little room her "salon" and she received her visitors there—although visitors were few—and looked out the window across the Lübecker Bight to the coast and the water that became the Baltic Sea.

Peter and Paul wouldn't have looked forward so much to their visits had it not been for the *Valhalla*. The *Valhalla* was a small sailing boat that had once belonged to Opa. In his will Opa had bequeathed the little boat to a neighbor. But whenever the two Winter boys arrived, the *Valhalla* was theirs. The neighbor didn't know his sailing boat was called the *Valhalla*. On its bow was painted the same name that had been there when Winter bought it from a boatbuilder in Travemünde: *Domino*. But for the boys it was always called *Valhalla:* the hall in which slain warriors were received by Odin.

The *Valhalla* gave the boys a unique chance to be away from any kind of supervision. They took little advantage of this cherished freedom except to laze and, more important, to talk and argue in that spirited and curiously intimate way that children only do when no adults are within earshot.

"You'll change your mind again before you are fourteen," Peter told his ten-year-old brother with all the mature authority of a fourteen-year-old. "I wouldn't go to cadet school; I'd hate it. I'm going to be an explorer." He trailed his hand in the water. The wind had been swinging round for the last hour or more, so that Peter had had to adjust the sail constantly. Now the boat was moving fast through the choppy water of the bight. The sun was a white disc seen fitfully behind hazy clouds. There was little heat in the sun. Visitors did not come to this northern coastline to bask in the sunshine; it was a brisk climate, for active holidaymakers.

The boys were dressed in yellow oilskins and floppy hats, just like the real sailors who sailed the big ships out of Kiel, along the coast from here. The younger boy, Paul, was crouched in the stern, hugging his knees. His hair was long and had become even more blond as he got older. People had said that his hair would darken, but adults had been wrong about that, as about most other vital things he'd wanted to know. He said, "You're good at mathematics. You'd have to be good at mathematics for exploring, wouldn't you?"

"Yes," said Peter, who'd recently come top in mathematics.

"I'm no good at anything except sports: hockey, I'm good at hockey. Papa says the cadet school will be best for me. I'll never be any good at mathematics."

"No, you won't," said Peter.

Paul looked at his elder brother. It was a simple statement of fact: Paul was no good at mathematics and never would be. Adults all said that he was young and that soon he'd understand such scholastic subjects. The adults perhaps believed it, but it wasn't true, and Paul preferred to hear his brother's more brutal answer. "And then after cadet school I'll be a soldier and wear a uniform like Georg." Georg was a young soldier who was walking out with one of the housemaids in Berlin.

"Not like Georg," said Peter. "You'll be an officer and ride a horse and parade down Unter den Linden and salute the Kaiser on his birthday."

"Will I?" said Pauli. It didn't sound at all bad.

"And go off and fight the Russians," said Peter.

"I wouldn't like that so much," said Paul. "It would mean leaving Mama and Papa." He loved his parents as only a ten-year-old can. His father was the person he envied, respected, and admired more than anyone in the whole world; and Mama was the one he ran to when Papa scolded him.

"There's more wind now," said Peter. The sail was drumming and there were white crests on the waves. "Take the helm while I fix the sail."

Big storm clouds moved across the hazy sun. It went dark quite suddenly, so that the sky was almost black, with only a shining golden rim on the most distant of the clouds, and a bright shimmer of water along the horizon. "Is it a storm?" said Paul. Two years ago they'd sailed through one of the sudden summer squalls for which this coast was noted. But that was in a bigger boat and with a skillful yachtsman, Dr. Schapiro, in charge.

"It's nothing," said Peter. But as he said it, bigger waves struck the hull with enough force to make loud thumping noises and toss the small boat from side to side.

57

"Pull the rudder round," said Peter.

The little blond boy responded manfully, heaving on the tiller to bring the boat head on to the waves. "But we're heading in the wrong direction now. We're heading out to sea," said Paul. The waves were getting bigger and bigger, and when he looked back towards Omi's house the coast was so far away that it was lost in the haze of rain. Paul was frightened. He watched his brother struggling with the sail. "Do you want me to help?"

"Stay at the tiller," called Peter loudly. He'd heard the note of fear in his young brother's voice. He let go a rope for long enough to wave to encourage him. It was then that one of those freak waves that the sea keeps for such moments of carelessness hit the boat. The deck was slippery and Peter's wet shoes provided no grip upon the varnished woodwork. There was a yell and then Pauli saw the sea swaddle his brother into a dirty-green blanket of water and bundle him away into the fast-moving currents.

Peter had never been a strong swimmer and, hit by half a ton of icy-cold sea water, the breath knocked out of his lungs, he opened his mouth. Instead of the air he needed, he swallowed cold salty water, and felt his stomach retch at the taste of it. Sucked down into the cold water, he somersaulted through a dim green world until he no longer knew which way was up.

"Peter! Peter!" There was nothing but milky-looking waves and mist, and the boat raced on before the gusting wind. Pauli jumped to his feet to pull the sail down, and before he could move aside the tiller was torn from his hands strongly enough to whack him across the leg, so that he cried out with the pain of it. He couldn't reef in the sail, he knew he couldn't: it was something his brother always attended to. "Peter! Please, God, help Peter."

Some distance away from the boat, Peter came to the surface, spluttering and desperately flailing his arms so that he got no support from the water. Still encumbered in his yellow oilskin jacket, he slid down again into the hateful green, chilly realm from which he'd just fought his way. He closed his mouth only just in time to avoid a second lungful of sea water, and let the water close over him, twisting his arms in a futile attempt to claw his way back to the surface. The green water darkened and went black.

When Peter saw daylight again, the waves were still high enough to smash across his head. Like leaden pillows, they beat him sense- less and scattered a million gray spumy feathers across the heaving

The end of *Valhalla.*

sea. He could see no farther than the next wave and hear nothing but the roar of the wind and the crash of water. It seemed like hours since he'd been washed overboard, and—although it was no more than three minutes—he was physically unable to save himself. His small body had already lost heat, till his feet were numb and his fingers stiffening. Besides the temperature drop, his body was bruised and battered by the waves, and his stomach was retching and revolting at the intake of cold salty water.

There was no sign of the *Valhalla,* but even had it been close there would have been little chance of Peter's catching sight of it through the gray-green waves and the white, rainy mist that swirled above them.

No one ever discovered why little Pauli jumped off the stern of the *Valhalla* and into the raging water that frightened him so much. Many years later explanations were offered: his wife said it was a desperate wish to destroy himself; a prison psychologist interpreted it as some sort of baptismal desire; and Peter—who heard Pauli talk about it in his sleep—said it was straightforward heroism and in keeping with Pauli's desire to be a soldier. Pauli himself said it was fear that drove him from the safety of the boat into the water: he felt safer with his brother in the sea than alone on the boat. But that was typical of Pauli, who tried to make a joke out of everything.

Little Pauli was a strong swimmer and, unlike his brother, he was able to divest himself of the oilskin and prepare himself for both the coldness and the strength of the currents into which he plunged. But, also like his brother, he was soon disoriented, and couldn't see past the big waves that washed over him constantly. He swam—or, rather, flailed the heaving ocean top—hoping he was heading back towards the coast. Above him the clouds raced overhead at a speed that made him dizzy.

The squall kept moving. It passed over them as quickly as it had come, moving out towards Bornholm and Sweden's southern coast. The racing clouds parted enough to let sunlight flicker across the waves, and then Pauli caught sight of the yellow bundle that was Peter.

Had Peter been completely conscious, it's unlikely that the smaller child would have been able to support his brother. All drowning animals panic; they fight and thrash and often kill anything that comes to save them. But Peter was long past that stage. He'd given up trying to survive, and now the cold water had produced in him that drowsiness that is the merciful prelude to exposure and death.

Peter's yellow oilskin had kept him afloat. Air was trapped in the back of it, and this had pulled him to the surface when all his will to float had gone. They floated together, Pauli's arm hooked round his brother's neck, the pose of an attacker rather than a savior, and the other arm trying to move them along. The coast was a long way away. Pauli glimpsed it now and again between the waves. There was no chance of swimming that far, even without a comatose brother to support.

They were floating there for a long time before anything came into sight. It was a boy at the oars of a brightly painted rowboat, trying to get to the *Valhalla*, who saw first a yellow floppy hat in the water, and then the children, too. The oarsman was little more than a child himself, but he pulled the two children out of the water and into his boat with the easy skill that had come from doing the same thing with his big black mongrel dog, which now sat in the front of the boat, watching the rescue.

The youth who'd rescued them was a typical village child: hair cut close to the scalp to avoid lice and nits; teeth uneven, broken, and missing; strong arms and heavy shoulders, his skin darkened by the outdoors. Only his height and broad chest distinguished him from the other village youths, that and the ability to read well. To what extent it was his height, and to what extent his literacy, that gave him his air of superiority was debated. But there was a strength within him that was apparent to all, a drive that the priest—in a moment of weakness—had once described as "demoniacal."

The seventeen-year-old Fritz Esser looked at the two half-drowned children huddled together in the bottom of his boat and—despite the pitiful retching of Peter and the shivers that convulsed Pauli's whole body—decided they were not close to death. He rowed out to where the poor old *Valhalla* had settled low into the water, its torn sail trailing overboard and its rudder carried away. "It will not last long," he said, "it's holed." Pauli managed to peer over the edge of the rowboat to see what was left of their lovely *Valhalla*, but Peter was past caring. Esser, aided by the black mongrel, which ran up and down the boat and barked, tried to get the *Valhalla* in tow, but his line was not long enough, and finally he decided to get the two survivors back to dry land.

The end of *Valhalla.*

He put them in an old boat shed on the beach. It was a dark, smelly place; the only daylight came through the chinks in its ill-fitting boards. Inside there was space enough for three rowboats, but it was evident that only one boat was ever stored here, for most of the interior was littered with rubbish. There were furry pieces of animal hide stretched on racks to dry. There was flotsam, too: a life preserver lettered "Germania—Kiel," torn pieces of sails and old sacks, broken oars and broken crates and barrels of various sizes arranged like seats around a small pot-bellied iron stove.

Esser wrapped sacking round the boys and poked inside the stove until the sparks began to fly, then tossed some small pieces of driftwood into it and slammed it shut with a loud clang. The necessity of closing the stove became apparent as smoke from the damp wood issued out of the broken chimney. It was only after the fire was going that the boy spoke to them. "You're the Berlin kids, aren't you? You're from the big house where old Schuster does the garden. Old Frau Winter. Are you her grandchildren?" He didn't wait to hear their reply; he seldom asked real questions, they found out soon enough. "You come here with your mother, and the flunkie, and your father comes sometimes, always in some big new automobile."

Peter and Pauli were huddled together under some sacking that smelled of salt and decaying fish. As the stove flickered into life, and the air warmed, the hut became more and more foul. But the children didn't notice the odor of old fish or the stink of the tanned hides. They clung together, cold, wet, and exhausted; Pauli was looking at the flames in the tiny grate, but Peter's eyes were tightly closed as he listened to Fritz Esser's hard and roughly accented voice.

"I hate the rich," Esser said. "But soon we'll break the bonds of slavery."

"How will you do that?" asked Pauli, who, typically, was recovering quickly from his ordeal. It sounded interesting, like something from his *101 Magic Tricks a Bright Boy Can Do.*

Esser racked his brains to remember what the speaker from the German Social Democratic Party had actually said. "Capitalism will perish just as the dinosaurs perished, collapsing under the weight of its own contradictions. Then the working masses will usher in the golden age of socialism."

61

Half drowned he might be, but Pauli could perceive the majesty of that pronouncement. "Is that how the dinosaurs perished?" he asked.

"You can scoff," said Esser. "We're used to the sneers of the ruling classes. But when blood is flowing in the gutters, the laughing will stop."

Pauli had not intended to scoff but decided against saying so while the role of scoffer commanded such a measure of Esser's respect.

"We have a million members," Esser continued. He spat at the stove and the spittle exploded in steam. "We're the largest political party in the world. Soon they'll start to arm the workers and we'll fight to get a proper Marxist government."

"Where did you find out all this?" Pauli asked. It sounded frightening, but the strange boy was not unfriendly: just superior. His chin was dimpled and his brown eyes deep and intense.

"I go to meetings with my father. He's been a member of the SPD for nearly ten years. Last year Karl Liebknecht came here to give a speech. Liebknecht understands that blood must flow. My father says Liebknecht is a dangerous man, but my uncle says Liebknecht will lead the workers to victory."

"Did your father tell you about the dinosaurs and the blood in the streets and all that?" asked Pauli.

"No. He's soft," said Esser. He stoked the fire to make it flare. "My father still believes in historical evolution. He believes that soon we'll have enough deputies in the Reichstag to challenge the Kaiser's power. If Germany had a proper parliamentary democracy, we'd already be running the country."

Pauli looked at his savior with new respect. It would be just as well to remain friends with a boy who was so near to running the country. Peter had opened his eyes. He had not so far joined the conversation, but it was Peter who, having studied Fritz Esser, now identified him. "You're the son of the pig man, aren't you?"

"Yes, what of it?" said Fritz Esser defensively.

"Nothing," said Peter. "I just recognized you, that's all." Peter coughed and was almost sick. The salt water was still nauseating him, and his skin was green and clammy to the touch, as Pauli found when he hugged his brother protectively.

For Pauli and Peter—and for many other local children—the pig man was a figure of rumor and awful speculation. A small thickset figure with muscular limbs and scarred hands, he was not unlike some of the more fearful illustrations in their books of so-called fairy stories. The "pig man" wore long sharp knives on his belt and went from village to village slaughtering pigs for owners too squeamish, or too inexperienced with a knife, to kill their pigs for themselves. He was to be seen sometimes down by the pond engaged on the lengthy and laborious task of washing the entrails and salting them for sausage making. So this was the son of the pig man. This was a boy who called the pig man "soft."

In an unexpected spontaneous gesture of appreciation, Pauli said goodbye to Fritz Esser with a hug. Forever after, Pauli regarded Fritz Esser as the one who'd saved his life. But Peter's goodbye was more restrained, his thanks less effusive. For Peter had already decided that little Pauli was his one and only savior. These varying attitudes that the two boys had to the traumatic events of that terrible day were to affect their entire lives. And the life of Fritz Esser, too.

It was the pig man himself who took the boys home. Still wrapped in the fusty, stinking old sacks that gave so little protection from the remorseless Baltic wind, they rode on the back of his homemade cart drawn by his weary horse. It was more than seven kilometers along the coast road, which was in fact only a deeply rutted cart track. The smell of rancid fish and pork turned their stomachs and they were jolted over every rut, bump, and pothole all the way. When they got to Omi's, the pig man and his son were given a bright new twenty-mark gold coin and sent away with muted thanks.

It was only after the Essers had gone that the two children were scolded. Who would pay for the boat? How did they come to fall overboard? Didn't they see that a storm was coming up? How could they not come directly home after being rescued? All three women asked them more or less the same questions; only the manner of asking was different. First came the regimental coldness of Omi's interrogation, then the operatic hysteria of Mama's, and finally that of their Scots nanny, who, after their hot bath with carbolic soap, put them under the cold shower and toweled them until their skin was pink and sore.

The children took their chastisings meekly. They knew that such anger was just one of many curious ways in which grownups manifested their love. And they'd long ago learned how to wear a look of contrition while thinking of other things.

Now that they no longer had the *Valhalla,* the children spent their days on the beach. They walked back along the coast road to Fritz Esser's boathouse. Very early each morning, Esser went out in his boat to fish. He caught little: he had neither tempting bait, good nets, nor the skills and patience of the successful fisherman.

The boys always arrived in time to welcome him back. But Fritz never showed any disappointment when his long hours of work had provided nothing in return. He was always able to manage the crooked smile that revealed a wide mouth crowded with teeth. Every day, of course, the children hoped to see him towing the *Valhalla* back to them. And each day their hopes diminished, until finally they went to see Fritz just for something to do.

Despite the disparity in age, Fritz Esser enjoyed the company of the two children. He let them help him with painting and repairing the boats he was paid to look after. He showed them how to sew up torn sails and caulk the seams of boats that belonged to holidaymakers who'd left them too long out of the water. And all the time he lectured them with the political ideas that came from the booklets he read and the conversations he liked to listen to in the bar of the Golden Pheasant on the Travemünde road, and to the words of his hero Karl Liebknecht.

At the back of the Golden Pheasant there was a big room that was used for weddings and christenings and meetings of the SPD. That was where, last year, Fritz had listened enraptured to the fiery little Karl Liebknecht. In his pince-nez, neatly shaped black mustache, well-brushed black suit, and high, stiff collar, this thirty-nine-year-old member of the Prussian diet looked more like a clerk than a revolutionary, but from his very first words his speech revealed his passions. He denounced the international armaments industry, "the clique who mint gold from discord." He denounced the Kaiser and Bendlerstrasse, where the generals "at this very moment are planning the next war." He denounced the Russian Tsar and all the "parasites" that made up Europe's royal families. He denounced the capitalists who owned the factories and the police who were their lackeys. He denounced the rich for exploiting their riches and the poor for enduring their poverty.

A big crowd filled the Golden Pheasant that Friday evening.

Most of them had come because he was the son of the great Wilhelm Liebknecht (close friend of Karl Marx and a leader of the short-lived revolutionary republic of Baden), not because they wanted to hear this arrogant and unattractive man, whose only notable achievement so far was to have served an eighteen-month prison sentence for treason.

Karl Liebknecht had none of the qualities that a successful orator must have. His clothes made him look more like one of the cold-eyed bureaucrats they all feared and detested than like a man who would lead them to the golden land they were looking for. His educated *Hochdeutsch* and his manner—urban if not urbane—set him apart from this audience of fishermen and agricultural workers. Liebknecht's message didn't appeal to men who were looking for immediate improvement in their working conditions rather than an ultimate world revolution.

Only the very young have time enough for the sort of promises that Karl Liebknecht gave his audience that night. And only a few local youngsters like Fritz Esser were moved by this strange man.

Although the Winter boys had only a hazy idea of what it was all about, something of the excitement that Fritz Esser showed was communicated to them. And Fritz liked striding up and down declaiming the principles of Marxism to this enraptured audience of two. Pauli loved the sounds of Esser's words, though the fiery rhetoric of hatred held no meaning for him. Peter sensed the underlying belligerence, but Fritz Esser's flashes of easy humor and his simple charm won him over. And when Esser told them that as fellow conspirators they mustn't repeat a word of what he said to the policeman, to their family, to any of their household, or even to anyone else in the village in case Fritz was sent to prison, the two boys were totally devoted to him. What a wonderful thing it was to share a secret with a boy who was almost a man. And what a secret it was!

During the final week of their summer vacation, Uncle Glenn arrived. Veronica's younger brother, Glenn Rensselaer, had a habit of turning up unexpectedly all over the world. The first Veronica heard about his visit to Europe was a telegram from the post office of a liner due to arrive at Hamburg next day: "Arriving Thursday with friend. Love, Glenn." There was a flurry of domestic preparations and, for Veronica, speculation, too. Who was the friend, and was this just Glenn's jocular way of announcing that he had come to Europe on his honeymoon?

The speculation ended when Glenn arrived Friday noon, together with an Englishman named Alan Piper. They'd met on the ship coming over from New York: "The *Kaiserin Auguste Victoria:* twenty-five thousand tons. The biggest liner in the world, and she's German." It was typical of Glenn that he delighted in the achievements of the Old World almost as much as those of his own countrymen. Glenn had insisted that, since Piper had a month or two to spare before reporting back to the Colonial Office in London, he should accompany him on his tour of Germany, beginning at the house in Travemünde.

Alan "Boy" Piper spent much of his time apologizing for all the extra work and trouble he was causing to the household. He apologized to Veronica so many times that Glenn finally said, "Don't be so goddamned British. They have slaves to do all the work in this country. And Veronica loves a chance to speak a civilized language."

He was right about his sister. Her mother-in-law had not been well for a few days and was allowed only bread and beef broth, having it served in her upstairs room. So Veronica played hostess to the unexpected houseguests, and there was no need to speak anything but English.

Veronica adored her young brother but she was also enchanted by the shy Englishman. He was a little older than Veronica, an unconventionally handsome man with short brown—almost ginger-ish—hair, a lean bony face, and curiously youthful features that had long ago earned him his nickname Boy. He insisted that his life had been uneventful compared with her brother's. From Merton College, Oxford, he'd gone to South Africa, and stayed there working as a colonial government official, although, as Glenn pointed out, he'd been there right through some of the bloodiest encounters of the Boer War.

"He's a soldier of fortune, like me," said Glenn Rensselaer.

"Nothing so exciting as that, I'm afraid," said Piper modestly. "My father was a government official in Africa, and so far I have simply followed in his footsteps." He smiled. He had the face of a youngster—fresh and optimistic, and unwrinkled despite the African sun.

"So what are you doing in Germany, Mr. Piper?" said Veronica. She took care to address him as "Mr. Piper," and yet there was a mocking note in her voice that some might have said was flirtatious. "Is it another excursion among the natives?"

"Indeed not, Mrs. Winter. I'm on leave. This visit to Germany, as delightful as it is already proving to be, was quite unplanned. When I returned to London to start this year's leave of absence, I was very disappointed to learn that I would not be returning to Africa. The two Boer Republics we fought, and the Cape and Natal, become what is to be called the Union of South Africa. I would like to have been there to see it."

"South Africa's loss is our gain," said Glenn.

"I will drink to that," said Veronica.

The Englishman picked up his glass, looked at her and saw those wonderful smoky-gray eyes, and, after a fleeting moment, smiled.

Veronica looked down as she drank her wine, and yet she could feel the Englishman's eyes upon her and, despite herself, she shivered.

"My life has not been nearly so colorful as your brother's, Mrs. Winter. I believe him to be one of the most extraordinary men I've ever met."

"Really?" She was pleased to look at her brother and smile. "What have you been up to, Glenn?"

Piper answered for him. "He's been everywhere and done everything. He's even panned for gold on the Klondike."

"And a lot of good it did me: I finally sold out my claims for three hundred dollars and some supplies."

"He's worked for Henry Ford and turned down a job with the U.S. Army team that surveyed the Panama Canal. He's broken horses, repaired automobiles, and even flown an aeroplane."

"An airplane?" said Veronica; even she could still be surprised by Glenn's doings.

"Just the once," said Glenn. He bent forward and forked some more cold pork, without waiting for the table maid to offer it, trying to cover his embarrassment at Piper's laudatory remarks. Having swallowed it, he took a sip of wine and wiped his lips. "There was a guy on the ship coming over, a rancher. I'd worked for him a couple of times. He spent half the voyage filling Boy's head with tales about me. You know how Texans like to spin a yarn to a Limey."

"And why exactly are you in Germany, Glenn?" she asked her brother.

"Dad told me that your husband knows Count Zeppelin. I was hoping he'd arrange an introduction for me."

"Count Zeppelin? Is he so famous that they've heard of him back home?"

"They've sure heard of his airships," said Glenn. "Last September there was some kind of air show in Berlin. . . ."

"Yes," said Veronica. "Berliner Flugwoche at Johannisthal. There was a prize of one hundred fifty thousand marks. Harald took the boys. They were there when an airplane flew from Tempelhof to Johannisthal: ten kilometers!"

"Orville Wright was in Berlin at that time. And down in Frankfurt they had an airship meet: the Internationale Luftschiffahrt Ausstellung." He pronounced the German words with difficulty. "And suddenly a lot of people are taking a new interest in airships: especially big rigid airships. I want to see one of them, fly in one, and find out what they're like to handle."

"But surely you heard—the latest one, *Deutschland,* only lasted a couple of weeks. It's a complete wreck. There were amazing pictures in the newspapers."

"Oh, sure. LZ 7: I know about that. But he still has the LZ 6 flying, and a trip in that will suit me fine."

Veronica turned to the Englishman. "And you, Mr. Piper, do you share this obsession with flying machines that seems to be sweeping the world?"

"Up to a point, Mrs. Winter."

"He's just being polite," said her brother. "I talked him into coming with me to see the zeps, because he can speak the lingo. I can't speak German, and I don't suppose Count von Zeppelin is going to be able to speak English."

"You'd better learn not to call him Count von Zeppelin: von Zeppelin or Count Zeppelin, but not both together."

"Is that so?" said Glenn thoughtfully. "I know these Europeans get darn mad if you get their titles wrong. There was an Italian countess I once met in Mexico City. She wanted me to . . ." He stopped, having suddenly decided not to go into detail.

Veronica laughed. She realized that the account of Glenn's colorful experiences with horses, motorcars, and canals had been carefully edited in order not to offend her.

"And so you speak German, Mr. Piper?" she asked as the servants cleared the plates.

"For my work I had to learn some Cape Dutch, Mrs. Winter. It seemed foolish not to persevere with my German."

"He reads the kind of intellectual stuff you like, Veronica. I offered him my brand-new copy of *Lord Jim* when he was sitting alongside me on the promenade deck. And darn me if he didn't wave it away. He said he doesn't read Conrad because he doesn't stretch the mind. I felt like punching him in the ear. That's how we first got talking."

Piper—even after his three months' stay in America—had still not got used to this direct style of speaking. "I didn't exactly say that, Glenn. . . ."

"He's reading *Das Stunden-Buch* in German!" added Glenn Rensselaer. "It took me half an hour to learn how to pronounce the title." Veronica noticed the mutual regard of the two men; somehow friendships between women didn't flourish so easily and quickly.

"I'm afraid that Rilke is too much for me," Piper admitted. "All that symbolic imagery requires a better knowledge of Germany and Germans."

"Oh, but it's a wonderful book," said Veronica. "Don't give up."

"I've tried so hard. The chapter I'm reading now: I've reread it, dictionary in hand, at least four times."

"Perhaps if we read a few pages together . . ." Veronica stopped and hurriedly poured cream over the sliced peach. She hadn't meant to say that. . . . She made her racing mind stop. She'd never looked at, not even thought of, another man in all the years she'd been married. When she first discovered that Harry had installed that very young girl Martha in an apartment in Vienna, she'd gone to pray in the Votivkirche, and so steal a glimpse at the street where his mistress was living. Yet, even in that hour of anguish, she had never thought of betraying him. But then she'd never met a man who might be able to tempt her to betrayal. Now, suddenly, she realized that.

"That would be most civil of you, Mrs. Winter," said the Englishman. "Sometimes it's just a matter of understanding the heart of the author. Just a few pages properly understood might open a new world to me."

"I'm not a scholar," said Veronica. "I'm a thirty-five-year-old *Hausfrau.*" It was her clumsy attempt to change direction.

"I can't let that go unchallenged," said Piper. "I cannot think of anyone in the world more likely to change my life."

69

On the day that Father arrived, it rained without stopping. Not just the cold, thin drizzle through which the boys would walk, bathe in the ocean, or, in the happier days of the *Valhalla,* sail. It fell in great vertical sheets of water from slow-moving gray clouds that came from the North Sea to rain upon the bight.

While everyone prepared for Harald Winter's arrival, the boys wandered through the house, getting in everyone's way and feeling low. On previous days, Uncle Glenn or his English friend Mr. Piper had kept them entertained with stories, tricks, and card games. Pauli particularly liked Mr. Piper's magic and even learned to do some of the conjuring tricks himself. But today the two houseguests had gone to look at the wonderful old city of Lübeck and were not expected back until evening. By that time Father would have arrived.

Peter finally found something to do. Cook let him help prepare the vegetables. She needed the extra hand because the scullery maid was sick and the kitchen maid had been ordered away to ready the rooms on the second floor that Harald Winter and his wife used when both were there together.

After a brusque rejection by his grandmother, who wanted to sleep, Paul went in search of his mother. He found her in the turret room at the top of the house. It was a tiny circular room with a wonderful view of the countryside. This was where she liked to sleep when Father wasn't with them. She was looking through her clothes in the wardrobe, taking her dresses out one by one and examining them before putting them on the bed for her maid to take to the other bedroom.

Paul stared at his mother. She did not look well. Her face was white but her eyes were reddened as if she'd been crying. "What is it?" she said. She sounded angry.

"Nothing," said little Pauli. "Can I help you, Mama?"

"Not really, darling," she replied. Then, seeing Pauli's disappointment, she said, "You can take my jewelry case downstairs. It will save Hanna a journey."

Pauli always coveted his mother's jewelry case. It was made of beautiful blue leather and lined with soft blue velvet. Inside, it was fitted with little drawers and soft pockets and velvet fingers upon which Mama's rings were fitted. Pauli couldn't resist playing with all the fittings of the box. It was such fun to pull out each drawer and see the sparkling diamond brooches or strings of pearls lying within. He looked at Mama, but she was completely occupied with her dresses—choosing one for Papa's return, Pauli decided. He continued to play with the jewel box. Suppose it was a pirate ship and each drawer concealed a cannon, and as some unsuspecting boat came along . . . Oh dear: the contents of a drawer fell onto the carpet. How clumsy he was. He felt sure he would be scolded, but today it seemed as if nothing could divert her attention from her dresses.

Pauli picked up the tiny gold earrings, the large gold earrings, the pearl earrings, the diamond earrings that Mama wore only with her long dresses and pendant earrings. Two of each. He counted them again and then saw a silver earring on the carpet. Then there must be another . . . rolled under the bed, no doubt. He went flat on the floor to find it. Yes, there it was. And . . . there was something else there, too. He pulled it out. A wristwatch. A large gold wristwatch with a second hand.

"What are you doing, Pauli?"

"I found a watch, Mama."

"What do you mean, Pauli?"

"I found it under the bed, Mama." He showed her the wristwatch proudly. It was a fine Swiss model with a leather strap and roman numerals like the church clock.

"Oh my God!" said his mother.

"It belongs to Mr. Piper, Mama. I noticed him wearing it." He looked at his mother. He'd never seen her so horror-struck.

"Yes," she said. "I borrowed it from him. Mine stopped last night at dinner."

"Shall I give it to him?" said Pauli.

"No, give it to me, Pauli. I'll tell the chambermaid to put it in his room."

"I know which is his room, Mama."

"Give it to me, Pauli. He might be angry if he hears I've dropped it on the floor."

"I won't tell him, Mama."

"That's best, Pauli." His mother clutched the watch very tight and closed her eyes, the way children do when making a wish.

Three days after Papa arrived, everyone went to Kiel and stayed in a hotel. It was a momentous trip. Mama wore her new ankle-length motoring coat and gauntlet gloves. Papa drove the car. Its technology was no longer new, but he loved the big yellow Itala and clung to it, even though some people thought he should drive a German car. It was the first time he'd taken the wheel for such a long journey, but he knew that Glenn Rensselaer was able to make running repairs and the chauffeur was ordered to stay near the telephone at Omi's house just in case something went very badly wrong. Glenn sat beside Harald Winter, the Englishman and Mama at the back, the two children in the folding seats. There were no servants with them. The servants had gone by train. As Harald Winter said, "It will be an adventure."

It was not just an excursion. Harald Winter didn't make excursions: he had an appointment in the Imperial Dockyard. The next day, while a sea mist cloaked the waterfront and muffled the sounds of the dockyards, he met with a young Korvettenkapitän and two civilian officials of the purchasing board of the Imperial German Navy. Harald Winter had not been forthcoming about the subject of his discussion. It concerned the prospect of a naval airship program, and that was categorized as secret. The department was already named—it was to be the Imperial Naval Airship Division—but so far it consisted of little beyond a name on the door of one small room on the wrong side of the office block. Last year the appearance of the German army's airship Z II at the ILA show in Frankfurt am Main had made the future seem rosy. But this year everything had gone wrong. The destruction of that same airship—one of the army's two zeppelins—in a storm near Weilburg an der Lahn in April was followed by the loss of Count Zeppelin's newly built *Deutschland* in June. To make matters worse, a competitor of Zeppelin had built a semirigid airship that not only beat Zeppelin's endurance record by over an hour but arrived at the autumn army maneuvers complete with its own mobile canvas shed. Now all the admirals and bureaucrats who'd delayed the decisions about purchasing zeppelins were congratulating themselves upon their farsightedness.

But while Harald Winter was sitting across the table from the earnest young naval officer and two blank-faced officials, his wife, children, and guests were on the waterfront admiring the assembled might of the new German navy.

The end of *Valhalla.*

"Look at them," said Glenn Rensselaer, indicating a dozen great gray phantoms just visible through the mist. "German shipyards have never been so busy. The one anchored on the right is a dreadnought." He used his field glasses but failed to read any name on the warship.

"Three dreadnoughts last year, and four built the year before that," said Piper. Today the Englishman was looking like a typical holidaymaker, in his striped blazer and straw hat. "That makes the German navy exactly equal to the strength of the Royal Navy." He took the glasses Glenn Rensselaer handed him but didn't use them to look at the ships.

"No," said Glenn. "You British have eight dreadnoughts and at least three more on the slipways." He wore a cream pin-striped flannel suit with his straw boater at an angle on his head. The incoming sea-mist had made it too cold for such summer attire on this promenade. He had a long yellow scarf and now he wound it twice round his neck. Veronica noticed and wished she'd chosen something warmer. The cotton dress with its *broderie anglaise* trimmings was made specially for this holiday, but the dressmaker had not calculated on the spell of cold weather.

The Englishman nodded. "Perhaps you're right."

"And what exactly is a dreadnought?" said Veronica.

"Oh, Mama!" said young Peter, looking back from where he was climbing on the railing to get a better view. "Everyone knows what a dreadnought is." Little Pauli climbed up beside his brother.

"It's a new type of battleship," said the ever-attentive Piper.

"They all look the same to me," said Veronica.

"Maybe they do," said Rensselaer, "but when the British built HMS *Dreadnought* in 1906 it made every other capital ship obsolete. Steam-turbine engines, bigger guns, and all to a common caliber: faster and more deadly than anything previously built. Now the strength of any navy is measured by the number of dreadnoughts they have. It took that Kaiser of yours a couple of years to get started, but now he'll bust a gut rather than let the Royal Navy outgun him."

"Get down, Peter," Veronica called to her son. "You'll make your trousers dirty, and we haven't brought any more with us." The Englishman smiled at her. "It's so difficult without the servants," said Veronica.

Glenn Rensselaer took back his field glasses again and studied

73

the big dreadnought. "Do you think they brought her through the canal, or is she too big?" Now that the Nord-Ostsee-Kanal directly connected Germany's North Sea Fleet with the Baltic Fleet, it had vastly increased Germany's naval potential. Still using the field glasses, Glenn Rensselaer eventually answered his own question: "Too big, I think. That's probably why they are working so hard to make it wider and deeper." Even without the glasses one could see the sailors moving about the deck in their white summer uniforms. From the size of the sailors it was easy to judge the dimensions of the huge battleship. "She's big," said Glenn Rensselaer, "very big."

Veronica, hampered by the fashionable hobble skirt, had walked on, and now Piper followed her. The crisp cotton dress with its high, tight lace collar and the lovely new hat with silk bow and artificial flowers made her look wonderful, and she knew it. The others were out of earshot by the time he caught up with her. It was the first chance for Veronica to speak privately with the Englishman since her husband had arrived, but she said only, "I wish my brother wouldn't speak so disrespectfully of His Majesty. It has such a bad effect on the children."

"I know, Mrs. Winter, but your brother means no harm, I'm sure of that." He smiled at her and she smiled back.

She felt very happy. It really didn't matter what was said. She loved the Englishman and he loved her. There was no need to say it. There was no need to say anything at all, really.

They'd hoped that the mist would lift, but it was one of those days when the Kiel Bight remains shrouded in fog until nightfall. When they got back to the hotel, Harry had still not returned from his meeting. Alan Piper ordered tea. Glenn chaffed him about this curious English ritual, but they all sat together in the glass-sided lounge, exchanging small talk, until the Englishman took the restless boys outside to the promenade for another look at the warships.

Left without them in the lounge, Veronica turned to her brother and said, "There won't be a war, will there, Glenn?"

He looked at her and took his time before replying. "Dad is convinced that there will be. The folks would like you to come back home; I guess they tell you that in their letters."

"Yes, they do." She poured more tea for herself. She didn't want it, but she was nervous.

The end of *Valhalla.*

"This year you didn't get to see them in London." He sat back in the armchair and crossed his legs. Big bony skull, wide cheekbones, and easy smile—sometimes he looked so like Father, and so like little Paul. She'd not noticed before how much of a Rensselaer her son looked.

"It would be so easy for them to come here." She didn't want to talk about her parents. It would make her feel guilty, and she didn't want to feel guilty.

"Dad's not too fond of the Germans; you know that. And since the sudden death of the King of England, the Kaiser is determined to prove himself the master of Europe. Dad says he's dangerous, and I agree."

"It's just not fair," said Veronica. "Everyone blames the Kaiser, but all he wants to do is make Germany as strong as the other powers. What's so bad about that?"

"It's the way he goes about it: he struts and rants and always wears that damned army outfit with the spiked helmet. That military posturing doesn't go down well in Paris and London and New York. They like statesmen to wear dark suits and carnations and make speeches about peace and prosperity."

"Harry says that European armies are only suited for colonial wars."

"Suited, maybe. But they are fast becoming *equipped* for something far more destructive. What about these airships that can float right over big towns and toss explosives down on the city hall? Look out the window and see the guns on that dreadnought: one of those ships could shell a coastal city and remain out of sight while doing it. And what about these huge conscript armies that Prussia has had for over a hundred years? You don't need conscript armies for colonial scraps. Right? Back home I've been down through the South. . . . I walked through the ruined streets of Richmond, Virginia, and it's enough to make you weep. The same goes for cities in the Carolinas and Georgia. What is it—forty-five years back? And they still haven't rebuilt everything that the fighting destroyed. And the bitterness remains. . . . It's terrible, and that's the kind of war that these damned Europeans are going to have, unless I miss my guess."

"You frighten me with such talk, Glenn."

"I promised Dad that I would have a serious word with you. Don't you ever miss your friends and your folks and your fam-

75

ily? How can you be happy with all these foreigners all the time?"

"I don't want to say anything hurtful, Glenn, but these 'foreigners' are my friends and my family now." Glenn would never understand how much Berlin meant to her. She loved the city: the opera, the ballet, the orchestras, the social life, and the intellectual climate. She loved the crazy, uncomplaining, shameless Berliners, with their irrepressible sense of humor. She loved the friends she'd made, and her husband, and her incomparable sons. How could Glenn expect her to abandon everything that made life worth living and start all over again in a cultural wasteland like New York City?

"Do you mind if I smoke my pipe? I can't think properly without a taste of Virginia." From the pocket of his double-breasted flannel jacket he took a tobacco pouch, safety matches, and a curly meerschaum pipe.

"I don't mind, but maybe it's not permitted here. There's a smoking room at the back of the restaurant."

"Baloney! People smoke everywhere nowadays. People smoke on the street in New York, even women."

"That sounds horrible."

He lit the pipe, which was already charged with tobacco. "It was the flies that got me started," he said between puffs at the pipe. "I was working on a ranch in Texas, and the smoke was the only way you could keep them out of your eyes and mouth. I saw guys go crazy."

"I'd love to see New York again," she admitted with what was almost reluctance. "Just for a visit."

"You'd never recognize New York City these days, sis. I know your husband is reckoned a big shot in that automobile of his. But I stood in Herald Square and saw it jammed so tight with automobiles that none of them could get going." He laughed and puffed his pipe. He'd affected a pipe when he first came to see her in Germany, the year after Peter was born; Glenn was seventeen then. He'd tried to look grown-up but he'd choked on the tobacco smoke, and she'd brought him fruit when he went to bed feeling sick. She felt a sudden pang of regret that she'd left her family so young. They'd grown up without her, and she'd grown up without them.

"And Dad and Mama like it in New York?" she asked.

"They don't spend much time downtown anymore. But, sure, Dad likes it. While your Harry was betting on airships, Dad was betting on the automobile. He invested in steel, oil, and rubber and is getting richer by the minute." He puffed on his pipe again. "You didn't mind my bringing Boy with me?"

"Of course not, but if I'd known earlier, I could have had things better prepared. Those little rooms you have . . ."

"The rooms are fine, sis, and I'm sorry we just descended on you. I didn't realize how sick your mother-in-law is. It must make a lot of work for you."

"It's good to see you, Glenn. Really good."

"Boy is stuck on you; you know that, don't you?" he blurted out. She had the feeling that he'd been trying to find a way of saying it ever since they'd first begun to talk.

"Yes, I know he is."

"You get to know what a man's like when you drink with him. And I've knocked around a bit, sis. I've met a lot of people since I last saw you. He's a regular guy."

She said nothing for a long time. He was her brother, and she felt she should respond. "He wants me to go away with him."

"Boy does?" He was discomposed. He thought she'd just be flattered, and laugh. He wished he'd not mentioned it.

"I don't know what to do, Glenn. The children would never understand. Peter would feel I'd betrayed them, and Pauli just dotes on his father."

"Buck up, sis. It's nothing to cry about."

Glenn could not advise her; she'd known that before confiding in him. Glenn was her younger brother: their relationship precluded any chance that he could talk to her about such things and keep a sense of proportion. "Please don't say anything to anyone, Glenn. I'm still trying to make up my mind. Boy wants me to bring the children, too."

Glenn Rensselaer shook his head in amazement. "You're a dark horse."

"I love him, Glenn. I don't know how it happened in such a short time. I thought it was something that only happened in books and plays. But I love Harry, too." She turned her head away as the tears welled up in her eyes.

"Divorced women are not received in our sort of society." He had to warn her. Glenn was a good man. He'd only wanted to make her happy, and now he found himself involved in her moral dilemma, the sort of thing he couldn't handle.

"I couldn't go without the children, Glenn. . . ."

"It's a big step." That bastard Harry, despite his philandering, would probably deny her a divorce: he detested the Englishman, Glenn could see that. So his sister would be living in sin in a society where such sinners were punished here on earth. The idea of that happening to his sister pained him. And yet Harry was a swine. . . .

"I couldn't take Harry's sons from him and give them to another man. That would be a sin, wouldn't it?" She wiped her tears away.

"We only have one life. I'm not a priest."

"Hush! They're coming in," said Veronica, catching sight of Piper and the two children coming up the path. As the doorman swung open the doors, the sound of a ship's band playing on the sea front came to their ears. They were playing Sousa; such bold Yankee music sounded strange in these German surroundings.

Harald Winter's final meeting with the representatives of the Imperial German Navy's purchasing board had not left him in the best of moods. The meeting had ended with a gesture that Winter regarded as provocative. One of the civilians produced photographs of the army's latest airship, the *Parseval III,* flying over Leipzig. Manufactured by Zeppelin's brilliant rival, August von Parseval, it was a most efficient flying machine. It was big: its envelope contained five thousand cubic meters of gas. It had two hundred-horse-power engines and carried eight passengers. And yet the whole contraption could be deflated and taken away by horse-drawn wagon. This miracle was achieved by having no rigid metal frame-work. But the prospect of airships without a rigid metal framework had little or no attraction for Harald Winter. He left the meeting in a rage.

He snapped at the hotel staff and at his personal servants. When he was unlocking his decanters for a drink before dressing for dinner, he even found fault with the children.

"They are getting out of control," he said.

"How can you say that, Harry? Everyone remarks on how well behaved they are."

"They're allowed to roam all through the hotel. And Pauli even pesters me when I'm working."

"And you snap at him. I wish you'd be more patient with little Pauli. He adores you so much, and yet you always reject him. Why?"

"Pauli must grow up. He's like a little puppy that comes licking your hand all the time. He wants constant attention."

"He wants affection." Harald Winter had never shown much affection to her or to the boys. He'd always said that earning money should be sufficient evidence of a man's love for his family.

"Then let him go to Nanny. What do I pay her for?"

"Harry, how can you be so blind? Little Pauli loves you more than anyone in the whole world. You are his life. You hurt him deeply when you send him away with angry words." She didn't want to pursue the subject. She tried to decide whether she could endure her corset as tight as this for the entire evening. Some women were abandoning corsets altogether—it was the new fashion—but Veronica still kept to the old styles.

Harald Winter poured brandy for himself and added a generous amount of Apollinaris soda water. He drank some and then turned his attention to the faults of their guests.

"They act like a couple of spies," he complained. "Do you think no one notices them out on the promenade using their field glasses and making sketches of the warships?"

"Spies?" said Veronica. "You're speaking of our guests; and one of them is my kith and kin."

Harald Winter realized that he'd gone too far. He retracted a little. "I didn't mean your brother, I meant the *Engländer.*"

"No one was making sketches, Harry, and the field glasses belonged to Glenn."

"Piper is obviously a spy," said Winter. He had never really liked the English, and this fellow Piper, with his absurdly exaggerated good manners and the attention he gave to Veronica, was a prime example of the effete English upper class.

"You sound like a character in those silly books the children read. If the ships are secret, why are they anchored here for everyone to see? And if you are convinced that Mr. Piper is a spy, why bring him here?"

"It's better that he be someplace where the authorities can keep an eye on him," said Winter.

"You didn't repeat these suspicions to the people at Fleet Headquarters?"

"I felt it was my duty." He put his glass down with more force than was necessary.

79

"Harry, how could you! Mr. Piper is our guest. To report him as a spy is . . ."

"Ungentlemanly?" asked Harry sarcastically. Nervously he smoothed his already well-brushed hair. A German wife would know better than to argue about such things.

"No gentleman would do it, Harry," she told him. "No English gentleman would do it, and neither would a member of the Prussian Officer Corps. The officers to whom you reported your suspicions of Mr. Piper will not see it as something to your credit, Harry." It was the first time she'd confronted him with such direct imputations. Harry's already pale face became white with anger.

"Damnit, Veronica. The fellow is sent to South Africa without any army rank. He learns to speak Afrikaans and wanders around anywhere that trouble arises. Then the fighting ends and, when you'd think Piper's expertise is most needed, the British give him a year's leave and he decides to go and look at zeppelins. But before that he turns up in Kiel, studying the most modern units of the Kaiser's battle fleet through powerful field glasses."

"Must you Germans always be so suspicious?" she said bitterly. "It was you who suggested bringing him to Kiel. You knew the Fleet would be here for the summer exercises—you told me that yourself. Then you report him for spying. Have you taken leave of your senses, Harry? Or are you just trying to find some perverse way to show these naval people how patriotic you can be?"

Her accusation hit him and took effect. His voice was icy cold, like his eyes. "If that's the way you feel about us Germans, perhaps you'd be happier among your own people."

"Perhaps I would, Harry. Perhaps I would." She rang the bell for her bath to be run. She would be pleased to get back to her mother-in-law's house. She didn't like hotels.

Those final summer days at Travemünde marked a change in the children's lives. They became both closer together and further apart. They were closer because both children knew that Pauli's desperate leap overboard had saved his brother's life. Both carried that certain knowledge with them always, and although it was seldom, if ever, referred to even obliquely, it influenced both of their lives.

The end of *Valhalla.*

They became further apart, too, for that summer marked the time when their carefree childhood really ended and they both, in different ways, faced the prospect of becoming men. Pauli, genial and anxious to please, did not relish the prospect of going to cadet school and becoming a member of the Prussian Officer Corps, and yet he accepted it, as he accepted everything his parents proposed, as the best possible course for someone of his rather limited abilities.

Peter's ambition to be an explorer was, like so many of Peter's ambitions, a way of describing his desire for freedom and independence. Peter was strong and respected strength, and his narrow escape from drowning made him see that strength came not only from intellect or muscles: strength could come from being in the right place at the right time. Sometimes strength could come from loving someone enough to jump into the sea. Peter had always considered his little brother weak, but now he wasn't so sure.

The last two days at the house near Travemünde were filled with promises and farewells: false promises but sincere farewells. Glenn and his English friend were the first to go. When would the boys come and see Glenn in New York? Soon, very soon.

Then Peter and Paul went off to find Fritz Esser. He was in his boat shed, chopping wood and bundling it for kindling. He said he was sorry that the *Valhalla* had never been found again. Perhaps it would turn up. Wrecks along this coast reappeared as flotsam on the beaches after the autumn storms. "See you next year," the boys told him.

"I won't be here next year. My papers will come for the army, but I won't go. I'll be on the run."

"Where will you hide?" asked Pauli. They had both come to admire the surprising Fritz Esser, but little Pauli hero-worshipped him.

"People will shelter me," said Esser confidently. "Liebknecht says the Party will help."

In the corner of the old hut Peter spied splinters of beautifully finished white hull, just like that of the *Valhalla,* but he didn't inspect them closely. Sometimes it is better not to know.

Along the beach they saw the pig man. He grinned and waved a knife at them: they waved back to him and fled.

The boys said goodbye to Omi, too. They heard their father

whisper to Mama that by next year Omi might no longer be here. They kissed Omi goodbye and promised to see her next year.

Veronica went up to the little turret room and spent a few minutes alone there. She would never see the Englishman again: she knew that now. She could never go away without the children, and yet she could not bring herself to take them away from her husband.

1914

War with Russia.

Despite all his previous misgivings, Paul was not unhappy at his military school. In fact, he rather enjoyed it. He enjoyed the unvarying routine, and he appreciated the way everyone accepted his scholastic limitations. It was all very strange, of course. Most of the other boys had come from *Kadettenvoranstalten*—the military preparatory schools—and they were used to the army routines and the shouting and marching and the uniforms that had to be so clean and perfect. Cleanliness had never been one of Paul's priorities, but luckily a boy named Alex Horner, who'd come from the military prep school at Potsdam, helped the fourteen-year-old through those difficult early days of April when they first arrived.

Nothing at Gross-Lichterfelde was quite as he'd imagined it. He'd expected to be trained as a soldier, but his daily routine was not so different from that of any other German high school except that the teachers wore uniforms and he was expected to march and drill each afternoon. He'd hoped to be taught to shoot, but so far he'd not even seen a gun.

His father had told him that the Emperor had to approve each and every entrant to this, the Prussian army's only cadet school, and that only the sons of aristocrats, army officers, and heroic lower ranks could be admitted. The truth was somewhat different: most of the cadets were, like Paul, the sons of successful businessmen or of doctors, lawyers, bureaucrats, and even wealthy farmers. Only a few of the boys had aristocratic families, and most of these were the second or third sons of landowners whose estates would go to their elder brothers.

Alex Horner was typical of these disappointed younger sons. His father owned four big farms in East Prussia and had served only a couple of years in the army. Alex owed his place at Lichterfelde to the efforts of an uncle who was a colonel in the War Office.

It was Alex who always pulled Paul out of bed when reveille was sounded at six o'clock and got him off to the washroom before the cadet NCO came round to check the beds. A quick wash and then buttons. It was Alex who showed him how to use a button stick so that no metal polish marked his dark-blue tunic: a sleepy boy at the other end of the room who once tried polishing his buttons last thing at night instead of before breakfast discovered how quickly brass dulled, and served a day under arrest. Thanks to Alex, Paul was usually one of the first outside ready to be marched off to the standard Lichterfelde breakfast of soup and bread and butter. But the most important reason that Pauli had for liking Alex Horner was that Alex had seen Pauli crying his heart out on the night he first arrived, and Alex had never told a living soul.

Marching back from breakfast along the edge of the parade ground that morning in July, Paul remembered April 1, the day he'd arrived. That was over three months ago; it seemed like years. His father had insisted that Mama shouldn't come, and Paul appreciated his father's wisdom. He was quite conspicuous enough in the big yellow Italian motorcar with Hauser at the wheel. The Winters had lost two chauffeurs, who went to drive Berlin motor buses, so Hauser, the valet, had now learned to drive the car, and he'd promised to teach the boys, too, as soon as they were tall enough to reach the foot pedals.

Paul could look back now and smile, but that very first day at the Königlich Preussische Corps des Cadets at Lichterfelde—or what he'd now learned to call Zentralanstalt—had come as a shock. Although the band was playing, it didn't offset the fuss the parents were making. The poor boys, with their tearful mothers and odd-looking fathers, knew they would be teased mercilessly about every aspect of their parents, and everything they did and said within the hearing of their fellow recruits.

Now it was summer, almost eight o'clock, and the sun was very low and blood-red in an orange sky. Soon it would be hot, but the morning was cool, and a march to breakfast and back again was almost a pleasure. Crunch, crunch, crunch. Paul had learned to take pride in the precision of their marching. For the boys with years of cadet training already behind them it was all easy, but Paul had had to learn, and he'd learned well enough to be commended—and allowed to shout orders to the cadets on one momentous occasion. Halt! There was much stamping of boots while the cadet NCOs saluted the lieutenants, and the lieutenants saluted the Studiendirektor. Then, file by file, all two hundred cadets marched into the chapel for morning service.

"Something has happened," whispered Alex. The chapel was gloomy; the only light came through the small stained-glass windows.

"War?" said Paul. The darkness and the low, vibrant chords of the organ provided a chance for furtive conversations. There was a clatter of hobnailed boots when one of the seniors stumbled as the back row was filled. Then the doors were closed with a resonant thump.

The boy next to him was a senior—one of the *Obertertia,* the boys permitted to go to rifle shooting in the afternoons. "The Serbs have replied to the Austrian ultimatum."

"Everyone knows that," whispered a boy behind them, "but will the wretched Austrians fight?"

"Quiet!" called a cadet NCO. "Horner and Winter, report to me after Latin class."

Paul stiffened and looked down at his hymnbook. It was always like that: the junior year got punished and the senior boys escaped. Was it because their sins were overlooked, or had they become more skilled at talking without moving their lips? Alex kicked Paul in the ankle; Paul glanced at him and grinned. He hoped it would mean nothing worse than being put on half lunch ration—the other boys always helped out, and the last time he'd eaten even better on punishment than he normally did—but if he got a three-hour arrest this afternoon he'd be late home, and then he'd have Father to answer to. Paul hated to be in disfavor with his father. His brother, Peter, had always been able to shrug off those fierce paternal admonitions, but Paul wanted his father to admire him. He wanted that more than anything in the whole world. And it was Friday: this weekend he'd arranged for Alex Horner to come home with him, and a detention now would mess everything up.

"Hymn number 103," said the chaplain mournfully, but no more mournfully than usual.

Paul and Alex escaped with no more than a fierce reprimand. Luckily their persecutor wasn't one of their own NCOs but a senior boy who didn't want to miss his riding lesson. Normally at 4:30 p.m.—after doing two hours of prep—there was drill on the barracks square, but at noon this day the boys were told that they were free until dinner, and that those with weekend passes could go home. It was another sign that something strange was in the air.

And as Alex and Paul went to their train at the Lichterfelde railway station, they noticed that civilians deferred to them in a way that was unusual. "After you young officers," said a well-dressed businessman at the door of the first-class compartment. There was an element of mockery in this politeness, and yet it was not entirely mockery. The ticket inspector touched his hat in salute to them. He'd never done that before.

The boys did not read. They sat erect, conscious of their uniforms, styled like those of the post-1843 Prussian army, rather than the new field-gray ones. Military cap, white gloves, blue tunic, poppy-red cuffs and collar with the double gold braid that marked Lichterfelde cadets, and on the black leather belt a real bayonet.

In the other corner of the compartment, the man who'd ushered them inside sat reading a copy of the daily paper. The big black headline in Gothic type said "Russia mobilizes."

From the Potsdamer railway station they walked through the center of Berlin: past the big expensive shops of Leipziger Strasse, and then along Friedrichstrasse. Everywhere they saw groups of people standing around as if waiting for something to happen. There were more women on the streets nowadays—shopping, strolling, exercising dogs; the shorter skirts enabled women to be out and about in a way they never had before. The narrow Friedrichstrasse was always busy, of course; here were offices, shops, cafés, and clubs, so that it never stopped, night or day. But today it seemed different, and even the wide Unter den Linden was filled with aimless people. At the intersection of the two streets—one of the most popular spots in all Berlin—was the boys' destination: the Victoria Café and the best ice cream in town.

They got a table outside on the sidewalk and watched the traffic and the restless crowds. A No. 4 motor bus went past; on its open top deck were half a dozen soldiers. They were flushed of face and singing boisterously. The bus was heading towards the Friedrich-strasse railway station, where there were always military policemen. Alex predicted that they would be in cells within half an hour, and there was little chance that he would be wrong.

Everything was bright green, the lime trees were in full leaf, and the birds were not frightened of the noise, not even of the big new motor buses. Only when the band marched past did the birds fly away. Alex said the band was that of the 3. Garde-Regiment zu Fuss marching back to its barracks at Skalitzer Strasse. They wore white parade trousers and blue tunics and gleaming helmets, and the music sounded fine. Behind them was a company of infantry in field gray. They looked tired and dusty, as if they'd been on a long route march, but when they got to the corner of Friedrichstrasse there were some cheers from civilians standing there, and the soldiers seemed to stiffen up and smile.

The waiter brought the boys the big platter of ice cream they'd so looked forward to on this hot day, and they started eating greed-ily. At the next table two men were arguing about whether Russia had really mobilized or whether it was just another rumor or an-other way of selling newspapers. New editions of the daily papers were appearing on the streets every hour, and the vendors came calling the new headlines with a desperate urgency.

"Will they send us to the front?" Paul asked his friend between mouthfuls of ice cream. Alex's time at the military prep school and the skills he'd already shown made him an authority on all things military, and Paul always deferred to him.

"Not right away," said Alex, finishing the last of his chocolate ice cream and starting on the raspberry one. "But they'll need officers once the war starts. Perhaps they'll graduate us quickly."

"No one could be commissioned before they were seventeen at least, could they, Alex?"

"I'm not sure," said Alex. "But if we fight the Russians they'll need everyone they can get. The Russians have a very big army. My father will have to go: he has a reserve commission in the cavalry. He wants me to go into the cavalry, but I'm going to fly in the army airships."

"My father has a factory that builds airship parts," said Paul. He wiped a dribble of ice cream from his chin. "My brother likes airships, but I wouldn't much like to fly. I prefer horses." In fact, Pauli found the prospect of flying in an airship quite terrifying, but that wasn't something he'd confide to anyone: not even Alex.

After finishing their ice cream they walked up Unter den Linden, just to see what was happening. From the Victoria Café they went past the cathedral, over the "museum island," and then returned to the enormous block of the Royal Palace. The sentries had been doubled outside the palace, and a crowd was staring up at the empty stone balcony, hoping the Kaiser would appear, but the Kaiser was at sea with his Fleet. Some of the crowd began to sing "Deutschland über alles," until a dozen policemen appeared and, after a lot of shouted orders and pushing, moved them along.

When the boys eventually got back to the Winter house, it was four o'clock. Hauser opened the door. Hauser was growing a beard; progress was slow, and each weekend Paul noted its development. "The master is in the study with Herr Fischer," said Hauser, "and your mama has a headache and is sleeping. Your father said you are to see Nanny right away."

Paul took his friend up to the top floor. It was a big house, as Alex, on his first visit here, noticed. It had the smell of newness. There had been many such fine new homes built in Ku-damm over the last twenty years or so. There was wood paneling, rich carpets, and wonderful furniture. And although Alexander's own home in far off Königsberg had fine furniture and just as many servants, if not more, the Winter house was in such faultless condition that he was frightened of leaving a footprint on the perfectly brushed carpet or a fingermark on the polished handrails. But Alexander was enough of a snob to know that these big houses near the Ku-damm were the mansions of the nouveaux riches. The established tycoons had villas in Grunewald, and the aristocracy their palaces on the Tiergarten.

Paul found his nanny in her room, packing her case. "I'm off, back to Scotland, young Paul," she said. She looked at him as if expecting a reaction but, not knowing what he was supposed to say, Pauli stared back at her without expression. "Be good to your mother, Pauli," she said. Her eyes were red. She leaned over and gave him a peck on his forehead. Then she reached for the cup of tea she always liked to drink at four o'clock in the afternoon. She put condensed milk in it. Afterwards, for all his life, Paul never smelled condensed milk without remembering her. "It will seem strange after nearly sixteen years with you all." She gulped some tea and said, "Your father thinks it's best, and he knows." Her voice was rough. She was on the verge of tears, but Paul didn't realize that. He watched her folding her aprons and packing them carefully into the big scarred suitcase. He'd never seen inside the case before: outside it was stained and scuffed and covered with torn hotel labels, but inside its leather was like new. Dutifully the boys stayed with her, watching her pack, until Paul glanced at Alex and made a face. Then, unable to think of anything more appropriate, he said, "Goodbye, Nanny," and with no more than a perfunctory kiss on her cheek he took Alex off to his "playroom," which had been called the nursery when Nanny first arrived so long ago, before Paul was born.

While the two boys were setting out the train set, downstairs in his study Winter was drinking brandy with his guest, Erwin "Fuchs" Fischer. The lunch had been a protracted one, as lunches tended to be when Winter wanted to discuss business, for Winter was not a man who rushed his hurdles.

"The loss of both naval airships last year—how did the Count take that?" asked Fischer. Asking how von Zeppelin had reacted to the crashes was just a roundabout way of asking how Winter had reacted.

Winter smiled. He was a dapper man and his hair, now parted on the left side of his head and allowed to grow longer, had grayed at his temples. But he was handsome—undeniably so—even if he was somewhat demonlike with his pointed chin and dark, quick eyes. And always he was optimistic. It seemed as if nothing could get him down. "Zeppelins have flown thousands and thousands of kilometers since 1900. Those sailors in L 1 were the very first deaths in any Zeppelin airship. And that was due to a squall; there was no structural failure."

"You always were a good salesman, Harry." Fischer grinned. He had now inherited the big complex of metal companies that his father had built up in over thirty years of trading. Harry Winter was trying to persuade him that a big cash investment in his aluminum business would be to their mutual benefit, but Fischer wasn't so sure. He didn't know much about the light-alloys business, and he was frightened of bringing ruin to his father's work. The added responsibilities had aged him suddenly. The great helmet of hair had now thinned so that his pink scalp was visible, and his eyes were dark and deep-set.

Winter said, "A light cruiser—the *Köln*—radioed a storm warning, but . . . Well, we don't know what happened after that."

"Except that L 1 crashed into the sea and fourteen sailors died." Fischer scratched his nose. He didn't want to do business with Harald Winter. He enjoyed his friendship, but he didn't trust his judgment. Winter was too impulsive.

"Airships are safe, Foxy. But freak weather conditions are something no one can provide against."

Fischer sipped his brandy. The food and drink were always first-class at Winter's place, he had to admit that. And he lived in grand style. Fischer looked round at the magnificent inlaid desk, the leather-bound editions of Goethe, Schiller, and Shakespeare that he actually read, and the exquisite Oriental carpets that he wasn't afraid to walk upon. Winter was not known for giving big parties or having a box at the opera, but in his own quiet way he lived very, very well. "Then, just five weeks later, the navy lost the L 2. It burned and fell from the sky. How does the Count explain that one, Harry?"

"They took her up to 'pressure height' too fast, and hydrogen was valved from the gas cells."

"I read all that, Harry. But, damnit, why did the hydrogen ignite?"

"The navy fitted big windscreens to the gondolas to provide a bit of protection from the air stream. The leaking gas went along the underside of the envelope—combining with enough air to make a very explosive mixture. From the keel those damned windscreens took it down to the gondola and the red-hot parts of the engines."

Fischer stroked his lips nervously. "The navy say that von Zeppelin approved their modifications," he persisted. If Harald Winter wanted him to invest in his aluminum company, Fischer might let him have some small token payment for the sake of their friendship, but it would be no more than the company could afford to write off. And even for that Fischer was determined to drive a hard bargain.

"No," said Winter. "He simply sent his congratulations on the way the finished airship looked."

"Having a stand-up row with Grossadmiral von Tirpitz at the funeral didn't improve matters for him."

"Count Zeppelin's an old man," said Winter.

"We're all getting older, Harry, even you. What were you last birthday, forty-four?"

"Yes," said Harry.

"And I'm sixty-two. We've known each other a long time, Harry. I should be getting ready for retirement, not learning how to run this damned company of mine."

Pleased with the opening thus provided, Winter said, "It makes sense: an investment with me would make good sense, Foxy."

"Aluminum? My instinct is to diversify out of metals."

"Exactly what I'm offering. The five million Reichsmarks you invest will be for an aero-engine company and an air-frame assembly plant."

"You said it was for aluminum."

"No, no, no. That's just the collateral I'm offering to you. The extra money is for airplane manufacture."

"Haven't you got enough troubles in aviation, Harry? Two naval rigids crashed. Who's going to buy your aluminum now?"

"The navy are committed to the airship program. They have built airship bases along the northern coast and are building more. The money is allotted and the personnel are being trained. They can't stop now. They'll buy more and more. And so will the army."

"I suppose you are right. And now it's to be airplanes, too?"

"Airplanes will be needed to protect the airships and to attack enemy airships, too."

"So the war is certain, is it, Harry? Not just newspaper talk?" To some extent this was provocation, but it was also a question. Harry Winter mixed with the military people; he'd know what the current thinking was. "Is war a part of the company's prospectus?"

"You sell the navy a battle cruiser and they use it for twenty-five years. Sell the army artillery pieces and they last ten or fifteen years." He sipped his drink. "But aircraft are fragile."

"And are expendable in war in a way that battleships are not expendable?"

"War or no war, airships and airplanes get damaged easily. Men have to be trained to fly, so there are many crashes. Everyone knows that, including the men who fly them. A constant supply of new machines is going to be required by the military."

"You're a cold-blooded devil, Harry."

"I don't make the decisions, Foxy, I simply react to events."

"I can't give you an exact answer, Harry. My son Richard will have to agree. But we'll participate."

Harald Winter relaxed. He'd got what he wanted. He knew Foxy would try to whittle the five million down to one million or less. But what Foxy didn't realize was that Harry only wanted his name. He had several investors who'd readily put their money in when they heard that Fischer was convinced. "Is Richard a director now?"

"I'm not going to keep my son out of the business the way my father excluded me right up to the day he died. He's thirty-three years old. Richard is a junior partner and gets a chance to decide on everything important. What about your two boys?"

"Little Paul seems happy enough at Lichterfelde. He's a genial chap, always laughing. The army will be good for him; he has no head for business."

"And Peter?"

"He'll go to university next year, and then he'll get a position with me. I'm arranging for him to be excused his military service and simply be replacement reserve. There are plenty of men for the army: the population has grown by leaps and bounds. And my factories are now vital to the army and navy. If he works hard, I'll make Peter a junior partner."

"Lucky boy. Is that what he wants to do?"

"You know what young people are like, Foxy. He has this mad idea of becoming a musician. He doesn't understand what a musician's life is like."

"Is he talented?"

"They tell me so, but talent is no guarantee that a man will earn a living. On the contrary, the more talent a man has the less likely he is to do well."

"Surely not?"

"The scientists in my factory, the engineers who design the engines and the structures: what talents they have, and yet they will never get more than a simple living wage. Most of them could make far more money in the sales department, but they are too interested in their work to change. Talent is an impediment to them. Look at all the penniless artists desperate to sell their work, and the musicians who beg in the street."

"And so you've forbidden Peter to study music?" asked Fischer provocatively.

Winter knew that Fischer was baiting him in his usual amiable way, but he responded vibrantly. "If he wants to study music, that's entirely up to him. But he can't expect to enjoy himself playing music while others work to supply him with money."

"You'd cut him off without a penny?" said Fischer with a smile. "That's hard on the boy, Harry."

"If he wants to inherit the business, he must work. I have no patience with people like Frau Wisliceny, who gives the boy these crazy notions."

"Frau Wisliceny—Professor Wisliceny's wife? But her 'salon' is the most famous in Berlin. The world's finest musicians take tea there."

"Yes, Frau *Professor* Doktor Wisliceny, I should have said. . . . And so do all sorts of other riffraff: psychologists, painters, novelists, poets, and even socialists."

Fischer decided not to reveal the fact that he had tea there regularly, too, and spent happy hours talking to the "riffraff." "But if Frau Wisliceny thinks your son Peter has talent . . . What does he play?"

"Piano. I won't have one in the house, so he goes there to practice. My wife encourages him, I'm afraid. At first they thought that they'd force me to buy one for him, but I wouldn't yield. Professor Wisliceny must be a strange fellow to put up with it. How did he make his money?"

Fischer smiled. "Ah, that rather goes against your theory. The professor is a very clever chemist . . . synthetic dyestuffs."

"He made money from that?"

"These aniline dyes save all the time, trouble, and expense of getting dyes from plants, minerals, or animals. He makes a lot of money selling his expertise. You should bear him in mind, Harry, when you are making Peter toe the line."

Winter was not amused. "I'm not talking about scientists. I don't want a musician in the family."

"Too bohemian?"

"I'm not fond of the Wislicenys. People like that should not encourage the troublemakers."

"They are good people, Harry." He wanted to calm Winter's anger. "And the three Wisliceny girls are the prettiest in all Berlin. The youngest one, Lisl, would be a match for your youngest boy." Fischer couldn't resist teasing Harry Winter. "She's a gifted little girl: plays the piano at the *conservatoire.*"

"A little more brandy?" said Harry Winter.

The question was never answered, for at that moment they heard one of the maids screaming. She screamed twice and then came racing—falling almost—down the front stairs, the ones the servants were not permitted to use. "She's dead. The mistress is dead!"

Harry Winter rushed to the door and stepped out of his study fast enough to catch the hysterical girl in his arms. "Stop it!" he shouted so fiercely that for a moment she was silent. "Sit down and stop that stupid noise."

"She's dead," said the girl, more quietly this time but with great insistence. She was shaking uncontrollably.

Winter ran up the stairs two at a time. He was no longer as fit as he'd once been, and the exertion left him breathless as he raced into his wife's room.

Veronica, fully dressed in a long green tea gown but with her golden hair disarranged, was sprawled across the bed. Winter rolled her over and then gently lifted an eyelid to see her eye.

"My God!" said Fischer, who'd followed him into the room. "It smells like a hospital in here. What's wrong?"

"She's all right." Winter looked at his friend and hesitated before saying more. "It's chloroform. My wife takes it in order to sleep."

"Shall I send for a doctor?"

"No, I know what to do." Winter went to the door and said to the chambermaid, "Send Frau Winter's personal maid to help her to bed. And tell Hauser that Frau Winter is unwell. He's to keep the children and the servants from disturbing her."

Fischer looked round the room. This was Veronica's sanctum: floral wallpaper and bows and canopied bed. Harry's bedroom— more severely ordered with mahogany and brass—was next door.

"It's happened before?" said Fischer as Winter closed the door on the maid and turned back to him.

"Yes," said Winter. He went to the bed and looked at his wife. Why had she done this to him? Winter was too self-centered to see Veronica's actions as anything but inconveniences.

Fischer looked at him with sympathy. So this was why Veronica was not much seen lately in Berlin society. Chloroform wasn't taken to combat insomnia; it was a drug taken for excitement by foolish young people or by people who could no longer face the bleak reality of their world. Veronica was American, of course; all this talk of war must have put a strain on her. "How long has this been going on, Harry?"

There was no point in telling lies. "We went to Travemünde in the summer of 1910. Her brother, Glenn, was with us. It started about that time." He picked up the empty bottle and the gauze pad, sniffed at it, and grimaced. "I'm damned if I know where she gets the stuff."

"It's easy enough to get, if you want it badly enough," said Fischer, who knew about such things. "Any pharmacist stocks it, and hospitals use it by the bucketful." He looked at Harry, who was now sitting on the bed embracing his unconscious wife. "Is everything all right between you?" Fischer was one of the few men who could be so candid with him.

"I love her. I love her very much." Winter fingered the things on his wife's bedside table: a Bible, a German-English dictionary, and some opened letters. Winter put the letters into his pocket. He wanted to see who was writing to his wife. Like most womanizers, he was eternally suspicious.

"With respect, Harry, that's not what I asked."

"There are no other men. Of that I'm sure."

"So what now?" Fischer was embarrassed to find himself suddenly at the center of this domestic tragedy. But Harald Winter and his wife were old friends.

"I'll have to send for the Wisliceny woman. She's become Veronica's closest friend. She looked after her when this happened before." He looked up at Fischer. "It's not life and death, Foxy. She'll come out of it."

"Perhaps she will, but it's damned serious. You must talk to your wife, Harry. You must find out what's troubling her. Maybe she should see one of these psychologist fellows."

"Certainly not!" said Winter. "I won't have some damned witch doctor asking her questions that don't concern him. She must pull herself together." Winter hated to think of some such fellow— Austrian Jews, most of them were—prizing from his wife things that were family matters. Or business secrets.

"It's not so easy, Harry. Veronica is sick."

Winter still felt affronted by his wife's behavior. How could she make this scene while Fischer was their guest? "She has servants, money, children, a husband. What more can she want?"

Love, thought Fischer, but he didn't say it. Was Harry still making those frequent trips to Vienna to see his Hungarian mistress? And how much did this distress Veronica? From what he knew of American women, they did not readily adapt to such situations. But Fischer did not say any of this, either; he just nodded sympathetically.

Winter looked at his pocket watch. "It's so late! What times she chooses for these antics. Little Paul has brought a friend home from his military school, and my elder son, Peter, will be arriving soon."

But, however much Winter tried to put on a bold face, it was obvious to Fischer that Veronica's overdosing had shaken him. Winter had even forgotten about his investment program and Fischer's contribution to it. You're a damned hard man, thought Fischer, but he didn't say it.

At that time, Peter was at Frau Wisliceny's house off Kant Strasse. He'd spent two happy hours practicing the piano under the critical but encouraging supervision of Frau Wisliceny. But now he was drinking coffee in the drawing room, accompanied by the eldest of the three Wisliceny daughters. Her name was Inge. She was tall, with a full mouth that smiled easily, and dark hair that fell in ringlets around her pale oval face.

"You will have to tell them, Peter," she said. "Your parents will be even more angry if you delay telling them."

"My father has made up his mind that I go to university this year."

"To study what?"

"Law and mathematics."

"Surely he'll be proud that you've joined the navy?"

"It will spoil his plans: that's what he will be concerned with. I think he's already decided the exact date on which I will become a junior partner. He has my life all planned. You don't understand how trapped I feel. Your mother is so understanding."

"But joining the navy is such a drastic way to escape him."

"There will be a war," said Peter.

War with Russia.

"There may not be a war. My father says the General Staff encourage these stories when they want more money."

"It's too late now," said Peter. He grinned. He captivated her with his wavy hair and his smiles; he was so handsome, and in a naval officer's uniform he would look wonderful. She was very young— only three and a half months younger than Peter—but already she had set her heart upon capturing him. He didn't know that, of course: she let him think that it was no more than a pleasant and casual friendship. And yet, when he was not with her, she ached for him, and when he was expected, she spent hours in front of the mirror getting ready for him. Her youngest sister, Lisl, was the only one who suspected her secret. Sometimes she teased her about this serious-minded pianist and made Inge blush.

"Are you accepted?"

"Yes. I am accepted for officer training and then for the Imperial Naval Airship Division."

"That's dangerous," said Inge, not without a note of pride. She was a catlike creature. She shook her head enough to make her lovely hair shine, and when she looked at him, those wonderful deep-green eyes were for him alone.

"It's what I want to do. I wouldn't like it on ships. I nearly drowned once, and I've never really liked the water since."

Inge smiled. She never got used to the way in which he confided such secrets to her. What other eighteen-year-old boy would have admitted to being frightened of the sea? "I wouldn't tell the navy that, Peter," she said. "I don't think they would relish appointing a naval lieutenant who didn't like the water."

Peter laughed.

Frau Professor Wisliceny, a large, imposing woman, sailed majestically into the room. "Your mama is not well," she announced without preamble. She went to the mirror and glanced at her reflection before turning back to Peter. "You'd better come with me, Peter."

1916

"What kind of dopes are they to keep coming that way?"

The elderly American and his son were sitting in the library of the Travellers Club in London, drinking whiskey. They had the whole room to themselves. The club was quiet, as it always was at this time of the evening. Those members who had dined in were taking coffee downstairs, and the few theatregoers who dropped in for a nightcap had not arrived. Nowadays the risk of zeppelin raids persuaded most people to go home early. London—despite the presence of hordes of noisy, free-spending young officers—was not the town it had been before the war.

"It sounds damned dangerous," said Cyrus G. Rensselaer. He was sixty-five years old but he looked younger. His hair was a little thinner and gray at the sides, but the pale-blue eyes were clear and his waistline was trim. He felt as fit as ever. It was only looking at his thirty-six-year-old son that made him feel his age.

Glenn Rensselaer looked tired. "Sometimes it is dangerous," he agreed. "Most of them are only kids straight from school." For a year he'd been working as a civilian flying instructor for the Royal Flying Corps, and lately he had been training pilots for night flying. It was a new skill, and the casualty rate was alarming. "But the zeps come at night, so that's when the British have to fly."

"Haven't they got anti-aircraft guns?"

"Not enough of them, and the Huns seem to know where the guns are. But the zeps are slow, and planes can chase them. They are damned big, and sometimes you can spot them better from up there." He looked at his father and saw that, behind the sprightliness, the old man was aging. "When did you get back from Switzerland, Dad?"

"Yesterday afternoon. The train from Paris was packed with British officers, wounded mostly. Poor devils. Not many of them will fight again. I went to bed right away and slept the clock around."

"You're in a hotel?"

"The Savoy. It wasn't worth opening the house for just a few nights. To tell you the truth, I'm thinking of selling it. If the war hadn't brought property prices so low, I would have let it go last year, when you said you didn't want to use it."

"The war must end soon, Dad. You'll need a place in London." He wasn't sure whether his father would still be young enough for the rigors of transatlantic crossing by the time these remorseless Europeans had fought themselves to a standstill, but he felt it was his duty always to encourage his hopes and plans. Cy Rensselaer's wife, Mary, had died unexpectedly the previous year, and he didn't want his father to go into what people called a decline.

But Glenn needn't have worried about that. "Well, as a matter of fact, I was going to have a word with you about family matters, son."

"Sure, Dad. What is it?"

"Would you think I'm crazy if I told you I'm going to get hitched again?"

"Hitched?" For a moment he didn't understand. "Hitched" was not the sort of word that his father used. That he used it now was a measure of Cy Rensselaer's embarrassment. "Married, you mean?"

"Yes. Remarried. Is it too soon? I know you loved Mom."

"Whatever is best for you, Dad. You know that."

"Do you remember Dot Turner? Bob Turner's widow."

"Turner Loans, Savings and Realty?"

"She's got three boys. A nice woman. I met her at a dinner party last Christmas, and we get along just fine. Do I sound like an old fool, Glenn?"

"No, Dad, of course not."

"I get lonely sometimes. I miss your mother. She did everything for me. . . . It's just the companionship."

"I know, Dad. I know."

"She wouldn't take the place of your mother. No one could do that. . . ."

"It's a great idea, Dad," said Glenn, still trying to get used to the prospect of having a new mother.

"She's too old to have a family or anything. It's just companionship. She's got all the money she needs, and her boys wouldn't take the Rensselaer name. It wouldn't make a jot of difference to you or Veronica."

"Sure, Dad, sure." He looked at his father and smiled. The old man leaned out and touched his son's arm. He was happier now he'd got it off his chest.

"And if you want the house here in London, I'll turn it over to you."

"I live on the airfield. It's comfortable enough out there. The Royal Flying Corps have even given me a servant—'batmen,' they call them. And I enjoy being with the youngsters. They are full of life and they talk nothing but flying. But tell me about Switzerland."

"I wanted to take the train and go right through to Berlin, and see dear Veronica," said the old man, "but the ambassador was so strongly against it."

"You must be careful, Dad. A lot of people would misunderstand a trip to meet a German partner."

"What do you mean, Glenn?"

"Harald Winter is your partner, and he's making airplanes and airships for the Germans. The British are in the middle of a desperate war. Your trip to meet Winter could be construed as a betrayal by your British friends."

"I wish to God I'd never loaned the money to him."

"But it's been a good investment for you?"

His father's voice was hoarse and hesitant. "He's doing okay. He got into aviation at the very beginning, and he's been very shrewd. He builds only under license from other manufacturers, so he doesn't have all the worries about designing new ships and selling new ideas to the military."

"And Winter had no difficulties about meeting you in Switzerland? The British say that Germany is virtually under martial law."

"The Zeppelin company is in Friedrichshafen on the Bodensee. From there he had only a short trip on the ferryboat to Romanshorn. And Winter has become an important factor to the wartime economy; he's a big shot now."

"I can imagine how he struts around."

"You never liked him, did you?" said the old man. "I was always against him, too, but this time . . ." He shrugged. "He looks really worn out. I might have passed him on the street without recognizing him. And he's really concerned about Veronica. I never realized how much she meant to him."

"Is he still running around with other women?"

"How can I know that?" said his father.

"I wish she'd come home."

"We all wish she'd come home, Glenn. But it's her life. We can't live her life for her. And now that she's ill, I have to say that Harald has done everything for her. She's seen specialists in Berlin and Vienna, and she has a nurse night and day."

"I've never understood exactly what's wrong with her."

"No one seems to know. The war came as a shock to her, and now that Peter is serving with the Airship Division, she's obviously worried about him. But it's more complicated than that. Harald says she seems to have lost the will to live. It happens to some women, of course. Their children grow up and they find themselves beyond the age of childbearing. Somehow they feel useless."

"Especially if their husband spends all his spare time with his mistresses."

"We can't be sure about that, Glenn."

"Men like him don't change."

"We all change, Glenn. Some more than others, but we all change. Women have to feel needed, but maybe men have to feel needed, too. Maybe that's why we all have this compulsion to go on working even when we have enough money to live in style."

"Poor Veronica."

"It's pointless for her to worry about Peter. But that boy has a mind of his own. I remember how he went for me because I let slip a few home truths about Kaiser Bill. Even though he was just a child, he let fly at me. I was mad at him at the time, but when I thought about it I had to admire the little demon. It takes guts to challenge your grandfather in such circumstances. He's a plucky kid. No surprise to me that he upped and joined the navy airships."

"The boy has a better chance than he'd have with an infantry regiment on the Western Front. Did you see the casualties the British suffered on the Somme in July? Column after column after column of names in the newspapers. Neither side can keep on like this. Two years ago, right here on the streets of London, I saw crowds cheering the prospect of fighting the Germans, but there are not many cheers left anywhere now. Even the fliers I teach make grim jokes about how long they expect to last."

"Winter gave me photos of his two boys. I should have brought them. Peter is big. In his naval officer's uniform he is a handsome young man. He's tall and dark, with eyes just like Veronica. Peter is the solemn one—dedicated and scholarly. He's a German through and through, but he's like the best sort of Germans I knew before the war: solid, honest, and reliable. Harry is so proud of them."

"I saw Peter in Berlin the summer the war started. Veronica took me to see a friend of hers, Frau Wisliceny. Did you ever meet the Wislicenys?"

"I met the professor here in London one time."

"Frau Wisliceny got Peter to study music. He played the piano for us. It sounded kind of good to me, but I don't understand any of that classical music. It seemed to me that Peter was more interested in the three daughters. The youngest one—Lisl, I think her name was—was obviously crazy about him. Yeah, he's a nice kid."

"Mathematics and music. Harry said that Peter was interested in nothing else."

"Fathers don't always know what sons are interested in," said Glenn.

"I wish like hell you'd get interested in some lovely daughters," said his father.

"I'm interested in all kinds of daughters, Dad. But I don't want to marry any of them right now."

"Those two boys of Harry Winter's are the only grandchildren I've got, Glenn. You tell me that maybe I shouldn't cozy up to him on account of the war, and maybe you're right. But I'm getting old, Glenn, and there's no sign of you providing me with heirs. Those two boys are all I've got."

"I didn't realize how much that kind of thing meant to you, Dad."

"At one time it didn't mean a thing. But you get to being sixty-five and you look at the work you've done and you look at the money you've stacked away, and you start wondering what it's all for."

"I just don't know enough about business. . . ."

"It wasn't intended as any kind of reproach, my boy. You've lived your own kind of life, and I respect it. You seldom ask me for anything. . . . To tell you the truth, I wish you asked for more, and asked more often. A man wants to feel his son needs him now and again. . . ."

"I always . . ."

"Let me finish. I'm just trying to explain to you why I didn't go over there and sell out my holding in Winter's factories and tell him to go to hell."

"I didn't criticize you."

"I know you didn't, but over the recent months you've made it clear that you would have handled Harry differently. I wanted you to understand why I go along with the bastard."

"I understand, Dad." Glenn wondered whether marrying Dot Turner was his father's excuse for taking over the Turner kids. This sudden interest in young people was something to do with growing old.

For a few moments Cyrus was silent. When he spoke again it was in a quieter voice. "The younger boy, Pauli, is an unmistakable Rensselaer, with that big Rensselaer jawline and wide, flat head. He's never done well at school—he just scrapes by each term, Harald tells me—but he's such a character. A regular Yankee Doodle; I've always said he was a real little Yankee. And what a charmer. Always laughing, takes nothing seriously, not the Kaiser, not military school, not the war, not Harry. He adores Veronica, of course, and she dotes on little Pauli. He's coming up to his final year at military school. Soon he'll be at the front. Harry worries about both boys. He hated it when Peter went into the Airship Division, but Pauli has always been the baby of the family. You should hear Harry's stories about little Pauli. He adores him. The thought of him leading a platoon of infantry in a bayonet charge is not easy to face. And, like you say, everyone knows what kind of casualties there are among young infantry lieutenants. The thought of it—plus his worries about Veronica—is wearing Harry down."

At that moment a servant entered the library. After unhurriedly adjusting the edges of the curtains, he said to the older man, "The secretary's compliments, Mr. Rensselaer, and I am to inform you that there is an air-raid warning."

"Thank you," said Rensselaer calmly. He drank a little whiskey before asking his son, "What exactly does that mean, Glenn? Aren't you supposed to be the expert on zeppelin raids?"

"The German zeppelins take off from their bases after lunch. One, two, anything up to a dozen airships fly out over the North Sea and then they hover there, just over the horizon, where the British can't see them, and well out of range of any airplane. They sit out there for hour after hour, waiting for the light to fade. When it gets dark, they sail in and bomb their chosen targets."

"Sounds kind of spooky."

"Maybe. Hurry and wait: that's the way the military always do things. But the Royal Navy have learned to take advantage of that ritual. They have listening posts along the eastern coast, and they pick up the radio messages that the zeppelins send to each other while they are waiting out there. Sometimes they are even able to discover what the target is going to be."

"And tonight London is the target."

"Nowadays London is always a target, and usually the main one."

"And what are we supposed to do now?"

"There are probably shelters down in the cellar. Some clubs even have sleeping arrangements. But I usually go up to the roof and watch the fireworks."

"Then what are we waiting for?"

"The nights are beginning to get chilly now, Dad. I think we'll need our overcoats, and maybe a bottle of Scotch."

Sitting on the chimney parapet that night in 1916, with his son beside him and a bottle of whisky to hand, was something Cyrus Rensselaer remembered vividly for the rest of his days. The strange life the old man had led, the traveling and the hard work, had prevented him from seeing his son grow up in the way that other, luckier men did, watching their sons and helping them as they faltered into adulthood. But to some extent this night compensated for that lost relationship. Tonight the two men drew together, not as proud father and dutiful son, but as two friends with common interests and values who enjoyed each other's company.

Glenn, too, remembered this night for as long as he lived, not just for the events they witnessed but because it was the high point of his relationship with his father.

"My boys will be excited," said Glenn.

"Will they be in the air?"

"Not yet. They'll probably be sitting on their butts waiting for a sighting."

"Then?"

"Then they have to take off in the dark and climb like hell. The zeps can get damned high nowadays. An airplane pilot has to be darned nifty to get in among them before they bomb and climb away. But they'll try. They'll chase after those zeps until their gas tanks run dry. Then comes the bit they all dread, landing in the dark—it's a bitch. We've lost too many good boys in accidents; sometimes I wonder if it's worth it."

"What do you mean by that?" said the elder man, although he could not repress a shudder. If landing in the dark was the most dangerous part of the mission, what were the chances that Glenn would survive the job of teaching these boys how to do it?

"Maybe we should let them come in and bomb. Now that Londoners have learned how to darken the town, central London has become more difficult to find on a dark night, and that's the only kind of night the zeps come. And even when they bomb, they seldom hit anything of military value or kill more than half a dozen people."

"Sounds mighty callous, Glenn."

"The British lost fifty thousand infantry before lunch on the Somme a few weeks back."

The old man sighed. "Well, maybe you are right. But it would rile me to think of those Germans cruising overhead unchallenged."

"It's politics, Dad. The politicians wouldn't dare leave London undefended, even if it was the right thing to do. The voters would never stand for it. My boys wouldn't stand for it, either. . . ." He drank. "Especially now that we have rich civilians offering rewards for anyone who downs a zep."

"I was reading about that."

"Three thousand five hundred pounds sterling for any pilot who gets himself an airship, and any time at all someone is likely to chip in another bagful of gold. That's enough to set one of my boys up for life."

"Are you still flying with your buddy Piper, the Englishman you met on the boat?"

"The one that went for Veronica."

"Veronica?"

It was the whisky, of course. Glenn could have bitten his tongue off. "It's a long time ago."

"Veronica. My Veronica?"

"You remember how I went to stay at old Frau Winter's house that summer when they were all on vacation there. It was long before the war . . . 1910, I think. I was starting that tour around Germany that I did with 'Boy' Piper. I'd just met him, and we spent a week with the Winters."

"Never mind the goddamned filibuster," said his father. "What happened?"

"Hell, nothing *happened,* Dad. But Boy wanted Veronica to marry him. He was crazy about her. He still is. He never got married, and once, when he left his wallet and stuff in my locker—Royal Flying Corps pilots are not allowed to carry personal effects when they're in the air—a photo of Veronica fell out. He made some silly joke about it being a photo of his sister, but I recognized Veronica all right. Then, after that, he always carried it with him, like a lucky piece."

"Jesus! How did Harry react to all this?"

"I told you, Dad, there was nothing to react to. Boy just fell head over heels in love with Veronica. I think she went for him, too, but she figured she had to stay with Harald because of the boys."

"You mean you even discussed this with Veronica?" His father was incredulous. "She knew Piper was in love with her? It sounds like a damned funny business."

"We were in a hotel in Kiel. Veronica told me that Boy had asked her to go away with him. She had to tell someone, and she couldn't tell Harald. She was in love with Boy, there was no doubt about that. I could see it in her face."

"And what did you say?"

"I wish I'd told her to go with Boy. He's a great guy; she would have been happy with him. And Harald is a louse."

"Well, I'm glad you told me about this," said Cyrus bitterly. "I'm relieved that your mother never found out."

"No one will find out. I never even discussed it with Boy."

"And is your friend Piper still working with you?"

"The lucky dog got command of a squadron on the Western Front. Can you imagine that? He's over forty years old. And he didn't even learn to fly until the war began. How the devil he fixed it, I'll never know. Not fighters, of course, but even so . . ."

"What's that across there?"

"Searchlights. That will be a zeppelin; they always come in that way, from the northeast. Some of them mistake the river Lea for the Thames and drop their bombs there, which can be bad luck if you live out that way."

"More searchlights."

"I think they've got him. See the little sparks—bluish-white flickers. That's the anti-aircraft shells exploding. Maybe you can hear them."

"Well below him."

"We haven't got enough long-range high-velocity guns."

Glenn's father noticed that "we" hadn't got the guns. Although Rensselaer senior was an unreserved Anglophile, he was, above all, an American, and determined to stay out of this European quarrel. He was tempted to lecture his son on the subject, but he wisely decided that this was not the time or place. "There must be a dozen searchlights there."

"The defenses concentrate there because that's the way the Germans come."

"What kind of dopes are they, to keep coming that way?"

"No, they are smart to come that way. The Thames estuary is wide. The zeps come over the water and they can get very close to London before making a landfall."

"More searchlights." There were much louder explosions from the other direction, somewhere south of the river—Southwark, probably—but the bombs were small ones and the sound was muffled. In the street below, a policeman cycled past, blowing blasts on a whistle.

"There's another zep there . . . maybe three or four. The searchlights are trying to find them all. They come in like that sometimes—three or four together—one zep is detected but the others slip past."

"They're coming this way."

"It's central London they are looking for. Look at the gunfire now."

"The searchlights have got him!" Despite the elder man's determination to stay neutral, the atavistic excitement of the hunt now brought him to his feet. Glenn steadied his father on the slippery moss that grew in the guttering. Now the silver fabric of the airship was gleaming as the stiletto-thin beams stabbed into it. There were half a dozen lights and, at the point of the pyramid, the fishlike airship. "He's hit!" For a moment the airship disappeared behind a cloud of white smoke. As it cleared, the fish was tilted at a crazy upward angle. "He's hit!"

"No. That's not smoke. He's dropping water ballast . . ."

Boom, boom, boom. Like distant thunder came the sound of high explosive, much lower and more vibratory than the crack of the guns. The building shook.

". . . and his bomb load, too. Now he's lightened, he'll climb for dear life."

"What's that?" Colored flares lit the sky bright red.

"They're Very pistol lights. One of my boys telling the guns to stop firing while the airplanes try. Look at that zep go!" Without bombs and water ballast, the zeppelin rose at an astonishing speed, so that the searchlights slid away and the airship disappeared into the dark night.

"Has he escaped?"

"Maybe. Somewhere up there two of them are playing a game of hide and seek. There's a little scattered cloud to the north. If I was the zep captain, I'd be making for it."

"And if you were the airplane pilot, you'd be heading that way, too."

They continued to stare towards the northeast. "It's damned cold tonight," said Rensselaer senior. He shuddered.

Suddenly there was a red glow in the sky. Small at first; then, like a Chinese paper lantern, the great airship became a short red tube that lengthened as the flaming hydrogen burst from one gas cell to the next, until the whole shape of the airship was depicted in dull red. Then at one place the flames ate through the fabric and were revealed as bright orange. Only then, as the aluminum melted, did the zeppelin cease its graceful forward motion. Halted, it became a cloud of burning gas around a tangle of almost white-hot metal, and then, slowly but with gathering speed, the great airship fell from the sky.

"Oh my God!" cried Rensselaer senior. No hatred now for friend or foe. He turned away and covered his face with his hands. "It's horrible, horrible!" Glenn Rensselaer put his arms round his father's shoulders and embraced him in the way that his father had so often comforted him as a child.

"You're a good, reliable officer."

On the wall of the office there was a calendar advertising "the margarine that Germans enjoy." It was there because some thoughtful printer had provided for each day a small diagram of the phases of the moon. The week before and the week after the new moon were marked in red ink. For the zeppelin service, knowing which nights were to be dark and moonless was a matter of life and death.

Lieutenant Peter Winter sat at the desk under the calendar. He wore the dark-blue uniform of the Imperial Navy, complete with stiff wing collar that dug into his neck as he bent over his work. From this window, on those very rare moments when he looked up from his task, he could see the hard morning sunlight shining on the zeppelin sheds, the hydrogen plant, and the flat landscape of the sort that he'd known as a child at Travemünde, not so far away.

"Can I get the twelve-noon train, Peter?" Hans-Jürgen, a fellow Berliner, was today taking the dispatch case to the ministry. If he caught the early train, he'd have a chance to see his girl.

"Fifteen minutes, no more," promised Peter without looking up from his labor. When he'd volunteered for the Navy Airship Division, he'd never guessed how much of his time he'd spend at a desk, filling out forms and signing long reports about things he only half understood. Compared with this drudgery, working for his father would have been stimulating. On the other hand, working for his father would not have provided him with the naval officer's uniform, of which he was secretly so proud, or the bombing trips over England, which he found both daunting and stimulating. Stimulating because he was at the period of physical and mental development when humans suddenly discover who and what they are. And Peter had discovered that he was courageous. The flights did not frighten him in the way that some of his comrades were frightened.

He signed the form and slapped it into the box while grabbing the next pile of paperwork. It seemed absurd that each zeppelin commander had to file seven copies of each flight log. Then came the route charts and endless lists showing the precise time that ballast was jettisoned and the exact amount of it. The weather forecast was compared with the actual weather conditions; the name, rank, number, and age of each crew member had to be entered each time, and their behavior throughout the mission noted. The times of takeoff, changes of course, bombing, and landing were all here. Attached, on separate sheets submitted by the navigating officers, there were observations of enemy targets, and descriptions of any shipping seen en route. These had all been signed and then verified and countersigned by the commanders. All of it would soon be filed away and forgotten in some dusty Berlin office. Sometimes he felt like screaming and shoveling the whole pile of it into the wastepaper basket. But he plodded steadily on—with glances at the clock so as to have it all ready in time for his friend to catch the Berlin train.

There was no opportunity for Peter Winter to get to Berlin and see his girl, Lisl, the youngest of the Wisliceny girls—for tonight, according to the the margarine calendar, was to be dark. And Peter was due to take off at 1:30 P.M. There would be no time for lunch.

And yet he must get to Berlin soon. Inge Wisliceny seemed to have some idea that *she* was his girl. He liked Inge, but only as a friend. It was her sister Lisl that he was seriously attracted to, and this would have to be explained to Inge. Inge would be hurt; he knew that. Losing Peter to her young sister would be especially wounding, for Inge was rather haughty about her sisters. He didn't look forward to it, but it would have to be done.

Inge was too serious, too conventional, and too intense. In some ways she was too much like Peter, though he'd never admit that. Lisl was young—childlike sometimes—irreverent, impudent, and quite outrageous. But Lisl made him laugh. Lisl was someone he wanted to be with on his precious brief trips to Berlin.

The paperwork was only just completed in time for Peter to change into his heavy leather flying clothes, which came complete with long underwear. When he arrived at the airship, hot and sweaty, the engines were already being run up. Within the confines of the iron shed the noise was deafening. Their shed companion, an old zeppelin that dated from the first weeks of the war—her crew called her "the Dragon"—was already out on the field.

"Achtung! Stand clear of propellers!" the duty officer in charge of the ground crew shouted. The engineers let in the clutches and engaged the gears. One by one the big Maybach engines took the

weight of the four-bladed wooden props, and the engines modulated to a lower note. A cloud of dust was kicked up from the floor of the shed.

Peter swung aboard and almost collided with men loading the bombs: four thousand pounds of high explosive and incendiaries. As he stepped aboard, the airship swayed, and one of the handling party unhooked a sack of ballast from the side of the zeppelin. Its weight approximated that of Peter, so that the airship continued in its state of equilibrium within the shed.

He climbed into the control gondola, a tiny glass-sided "room" two yards wide and three yards long. The others were already in position, and there was little space to spare. Above the roar of the engines came the constant jingle of the engine-room telegraph and the buzz of the telephones. The noise lessened as the engineers throttled back, until the engines were just ticking over. Then they were switched off and it became unnaturally quiet.

The captain—a thirty-three-year-old Kapitänleutnant—nodded in response to Peter's salute, but the rudder man and the man at the elevator did not look up. Hildmann, the observation officer—a veteran with goatee beard—immediately said, "Winter, go and take another look at the windsock. This damned wind is changing all the time. . . . No, it's all right. Carl is doing it." And then, to the captain, he said, "All clear for leaving the shed." The observation officer then climbed down from the gondola in order to supervise the tricky task of walking the airship out of the shed.

There was the sound of whistles, and the command "Airship march!" as the ground handling party tugged at the ropes and heaved at the handles on the fore and aft gondolas to run the airship out through the narrow shed door. Peter leaned out of the gondola and watched anxiously. The previous month, in just such a situation, the airship had brushed the doorway and suffered enough damage to be kept grounded. For that mistake their leave had been canceled, and leave these days was precious to everyone. When the stern came out of the shed, there was a murmur of relief.

"Slip astern!" The rearmost ropes were cast off, and she began to swing round so rapidly that the men of the handling party had to run to keep up with her. Then, with all the ground crew tugging at her, the airship stopped. Hildmann climbed back aboard and, with a quick look round, the captain gave the order to restart engines. In response to the ringing of the telegraphs, one after another the warmed engines roared into life. "Up!" The handling party let go of the leading gondola and she reared up at an angle.

"Stern engines full speed ahead!"

Now the handling party holding the handles along the rear gondola could not have held on to it without being pulled aloft. Suddenly the ship was airborne, and every man aboard felt the deck swing free underfoot, and the airship wallowed in the warm afternoon air. It would be many hours before they'd feel solid ground again.

The engineer officer saluted the captain before climbing the ladder from the control room up to the keel. His fur-lined boots disappeared through the dark rectangle in the ceiling. He was off to his position at the rear-engine gondola. He would spend the rest of the flight with his engines. The other men moved to take advantage of the extra space.

Now that the airship was well clear of the roofs of the sheds, the motors were revved up to full speed. There was no real hurry to reach the rendezvous spot in the cold air of the North Sea, but when so many zeppelins were flying together, it always became something of a race.

There were twenty-three in the crew. They knew one another very well by now. Apart from two of the engine mechanics and the sailmaker—whose job it was to repair leaks in the gas bags or outer envelope—they'd all trained and served together for some ten months. They'd flown out of Leipzig learning their airmanship on the old passenger zeppelins, including the famous *Viktoria-Luise.* They were happy days. But that was a long time ago. Now the war seemed to be a grim contest of endurance.

Oberleutnant Hildmann, the observation officer—who was also second in command—was a martinet who'd served many years with the Baltic Fleet. It was he who had assigned Peter to navigation. Actually this was the steersman's job, but Peter's effortless mental arithmetic gave him a great advantage when it came to working out endless triangles of velocity. It was a skill worth having when Headquarters radioed so many different wind speeds, and in the black night they tried to estimate their position over the darkened enemy landscape.

Peter had been given a sheltered corner of the chilly, windswept control gondola in which to spread his navigation charts. Now he scribbled the airship's course and her estimated speed on a piece of paper, and tried to catch glimpses of the North German coast. Upon the map he would then draw a triangle, and from this get an idea of what winds the night would bring.

There was cumulus cloud to the north, and a scattering of cirrus. The forecast said that there would be scattered clouds over eastern England by evening. That was good news: cloud provided a place to hide.

When they reached Norderney—a small island in the North Sea used as a navigation pinpoint—Peter spotted several other zeppelins. The sun shone brightly on their silver fabric. One of them, well to the rear, was easily recognized as the Dragon: her engines were worn out with so many war flights over these waters, so that her mechanics had to nurse the noisy machinery all the way. Nearer was the L 23, with another naval airship moving through the mist beyond. It was a big raid today. Rumors said that there were a dozen naval airships engaged, and three or four army airships, too. Perhaps this would be the raid that would convince the British to seek peace terms. The newspapers all said that the British were reeling under the air raids on London, and the foolhardy British offensive along the river Somme in July had been a bloodletting for them.

For Peter, London was just a dim memory. It seemed a long time ago since he had last visited his grandparents in the big house there. He remembered his grandfather and the big English fruitcakes that were served at four o'clock each day. He remembered the busy streets in the City, where Grandfather had an office, and the quiet gardens and the street musicians to whom Grandfather always gave money. Especially vividly he recalled the piper, a Highlander in kilt and full Scots costume. He seemed too haughty to ask for money, but he stooped to pick up the coins thrown from the nursery window. The piper always came by about teatime, and the little German band came soon after. The bandleader was a big fellow with a red face and furious arm movements. He was astonished when Pauli responded to their music with rough and rude Berlin slang.

Peter's memories of London had no meaning for him now. His boyhood desire to become an explorer was almost forgotten. The war had changed him. He'd lost too many comrades to relish these bombing missions. He was proud of his active, dangerous role, but when victory came he'd be content to spend the rest of his life in Berlin.

The whistle on the speaking tube sounded. Peter took the whistle from the tube, which he then put to his ear: "Hello?" It was the lookout reporting the sighting of a ship: a German destroyer heading for Bremen. Peter noted it in the log and went back to his charts. They were at the rendezvous. Now commenced the worst part of the mission. Here at the rendezvous there would be hours of waiting, the engines ticking over just enough to hold position in the air. A skeleton crew on duty and anything up to a dozen men in hammocks slung along the gangways. No one would sleep; no one ever slept. You just stretched out and wondered what the night would bring. You remembered the stories about the airships that had broken up in mid-air or burst into flames. You wondered if the British had improved upon their anti-aircraft gunfire or perfected the incendiary bullets that the fighter planes fired.

The whitecapped sea would soon darken. But the days were long up here in the sky. Although the sun sank lower and lower, the waiting airships remained bathed in its light, glowing with that golden luminosity that is so like flame.

"Winter. Leave whatever you're doing and go to the number-two gun position: the telephone is not working."

The observation officer was not a bad fellow, but he, too, succumbed to the nervousness of these waiting periods. Peter knew that there was nothing wrong with the telephone. The gunners were down inside the hull, out of the cold airstream, trying to keep warm. Once you got cold there was no way to get warm again: there was no such thing as a warm place on a naval airship. And who could blame the gun crew? There was no chance of enemy aircraft out here, so far from the English coast.

"*Ja,* Herr Oberleutnant. Right away." Peter saluted him. Saluting was not insisted on in such circumstances, but Hildmann, like most regular officers of the old navy, didn't like the "sloppy informality" of the Airship Division.

Peter climbed the short ladder that connected the control gondola to the keel. To get to the upper gun position took Peter right through the airship's hull. As he walked along the narrow gangway, he looked down through the gaps in the flapping outer cover and could see the ocean, almost three thousand feet below. The water was gray and spumy, speckled with the last low rays of sunlight coming through the broken cloud. Peter didn't look down except when he had to. The ocean was a threatening sight. He had never enjoyed sailing since that day when he'd nearly drowned, and the prospect of serving on a surface vessel filled him with horror.

Some light was reflected from below, but the inside of the airship was dark. Above him the huge gas cells moved constantly. All around him there were noises: it was like being in the bowels of some huge monster. Besides the rustling of the gas cells there was the creaking of the aluminum framework along which he walked and the musical cries of thousands of steel bracing wires.

It was a fearsomely long vertical ladder that took him up between the gas cells to the very top of the envelope. Finally he emerged into the daylight on the top of the zeppelin. Suddenly it was very sunny, but the air was bitterly cold and he had to hold tight to the safety rail. It was a curious place up here on the upper side of the hull. The silver fabric sloped away to each side, and the great length of the airship was emphasized. What an amazing achievement it was for man to build a flying machine as big as a cathedral.

Peter stood there staring for a moment or two. To the portside he could see two other zeppelins. They were higher, by several hundred feet. Ahead was a flicker of light reflected off another airship's fabric. That would be the old Dragon fighting to gain height. She'd caught up with the armada. It was good to see her so close; Peter had friends aboard her. They were not alone here in the upper air.

It was late afternoon. Still the airships glowed with sunlight. Soon, as the sun sank lower, the airships would darken, one by one, darken like lights being extinguished. Then, when even the highest one went dark, they would move off towards England. Peter shivered; it was cold up here, very cold.

"Hennig!" called Peter loudly. He knew where the fellow would be hiding: all the gunners took shelter, but Hennig was the laziest.

"What's wrong, Herr Leutnant?" He emerged blinking into the light and behind him came the loader, a diminutive youth named Stein, who followed the gunner everywhere. Stein was a Bolshevik agitator, though so far he'd been too sly to be caught spreading sedition amongst the seamen. Still, his cunning hadn't saved him from several nasty beatings from fellow sailors who opposed his political views. Hennig was not thought to be a Bolshevik, but the two men were individualistic to the point of eccentricity, and neither would be welcomed into other gun teams. So they had formed an alliance, a pact of mutual assistance. Erich Hennig pushed his assistant gently aside. It was a gesture that said that, if there was any blame to be taken, he would take it. "What's wrong, Leutnant?" he said again. Hennig was a slim, pale youth of about Peter's age. His dark eyes were heavy-lidded, his lips thin and bloodless.

"You should be at the gun, Hennig."

"*Ja,* Herr Leutnant." Hennig smiled. It was a provocative and superior smile, the smile a man gave to show himself and others that he was not subject to authority. It was a smile for Peter Winter alone: the two men knew each other well. Winter had known Hennig since long before both men volunteered for the navy. Erich Hennig lived in Wedding; his father was a skilled cooper who worked in the docks mending damaged barrels. The apartment in which he grew up, with half a dozen brothers and sisters, was cramped and gloomy. At school Hennig proved below average at lessons, but he earned money by playing the piano in *Bierwirtschaften*—stand-up bars—and seedy clubs. It was a club owner who brought Erich Hennig's talent to the attention of the amazing Frau Wisliceny. And through her efforts Hennig spent three years studying composition and theory at the *conservatoire.* By the time war broke out, Erich Hennig was being spoken of as a talent to watch. In April 1914 he'd given a series of recitals—mostly Chopin and Brahms—at a small concert hall near the Eden Hotel. There was even a paragraph about it in the newspaper: "promising," said the music critic.

Peter had met Hennig frequently at Frau Wisliceny's house. Once they'd even played duets, but no friendship ever developed between them. Hennig was fiercely competitive. He saw the privileged Peter Winter as a spoiled dilettante who lacked the passionate love for music that Hennig knew. He'd actually heard Peter Winter discussing with the Wisliceny daughters whether he should pursue a career in music, study higher mathematics, or just prepare himself for a job alongside his father. This enraged Hennig. For Hennig it was a betrayal of talent. How could any talented musician—and even Erich Hennig admitted to himself, if not to others, that Peter Winter was no less talented than himself—speak of any other career?

"When the telephone rings, you make sure you answer it," said Peter.

"I do, Herr Leutnant." He continued leaning against the gun.

"You should be standing to attention, Hennig."

"I'm manning the gun, Herr Leutnant."

The wretch always had an answer ready. And Peter well knew

that any complaint about Hennig would not be welcome. Hennig played piano in the officers' mess. He could be an engaging young man when he tried, and he had a lot of supporters amongst the senior ranks. When the beer and wine were flowing and the old songs were sung until the small hours of the morning, Hennig became a sort of unofficial member of the officers' club. It would be a foolish young officer who punished him for what might sound like no reason but jealousy. For Peter would never be able to play the sort of music that got a party going. In this respect he admired Hennig's talent and envied those years that Hennig had spent strumming untuned pianos for drunken clubgoers. Hennig always found under his fingertips the right melodies for the right moments. And he remembered them. He knew the tune the Kapitänleutnant had danced to the night he met his wife. He knew those bits of Strauss that the observation officer could hum. He knew when the captain might be induced to sing his inimitable tuneless version of "I'm Going to Maxim's" and changed key to help him; and he knew the hymn tunes for which there were words that could be sung only after the captain departed.

Peter Winter's musical talent was the talent of the mathematician, and, as was the case with most mathematicians, Bach was his first musical choice. Peter's love for Bach was a reflection of his upbringing, his social class, and the time and place in which he lived. There was a measured orderliness and formality to Bach's music: a promise of permanence that most Europeans took for granted. Playing Bach, Peter displayed a skill and devotion that Hennig could never equal. But Hennig never played Bach. And Peter never played the piano in the officers' mess, where Bach was not revered.

Peter went to the telephone, swung the handle round until the control gondola answered. "Upper gun position. Testing," said Peter.

"Your voice is loud and clear, Herr Leutnant," said the petty-officer signalman.

Peter replaced the earpiece. "Carry on, Hennig," he said.

"I will, Herr Leutnant," said Hennig. And as Peter started on the long and treacherous vertical ladder, he heard the loader titter. He decided it was better not to hear it.

As he picked his way back down the ladder to the keel, he thought about his exchange with Hennig. He knew he'd come out of it badly. He always came out of such exchanges badly. He didn't have the right temperament to deal with the Hennigs of this world. He had tried, God knows he'd tried. Early in their first training flights, on one of the old Hansa passenger zeppelins, he'd talked to Hennig and suggested he apply for officer training. Hennig had taken it as some subtle sort of insult and had rejected the idea with contempt.

But in the forefront of Peter's mind was the fact that Hennig had lately become more than friendly with Lisl Wisliceny, whom Peter considered his girl. Particularly hurtful was the latest letter from Lisl. Until now she'd been pressing Peter to become engaged to her. Peter, reluctant to face the sort of scene that his father would make in such circumstances, had found excuses. But in her latest letter Lisl had written that she now agreed with Peter, that they were both too young to think of marriage, and that she should see more people while Peter was away. And by "people" she meant Erich Hennig. That much Peter was certain about. Only after Peter had taken Lisl to the opera did young Hennig suddenly begin to show his interest in this, the youngest of the Wisliceny daughters. And Hennig got far more opportunities to go to Berlin than Peter got. For the other ranks there were two weekend passes a month if they were not listed on the combat-ready sheet or assigned to guard duties. But officers were in short supply at the airship base. And, as any young officer knows, that meant that the junior commissioned ranks worked hard enough to prevent this shortage of officers, bringing extra work to those with three or more gold rings on their sleeve.

Damn Hennig! Well, Peter would show him. Little did Hennig realize it, but his insolence, and his pursuit of Peter's girl, would be just what was needed to make Peter into the international-class pianist that Frau Wisliceny said he could become. From now on he would practice three hours a day. It would mean getting up at four in the morning, but that would not be difficult for him. There was a piano in the storage shed. Though it was old and out of tune, that would be no great difficulty. Peter could tune a piano, and there was a carpenter on the Dragon who would help him get it into proper working order, a decent old petty officer named Becker. He'd worked as an apprentice in a piano factory and knew everything about them.

For the next half-hour Peter was kept busy with his charts. Having missed his lunch, he became hungry enough to dip into his ration bag. The food supplied for these trips was not very appetizing. There were hardboiled eggs and cold potatoes, some very hard pieces of sausage, and a thick slice of black rye bread. There was also a bar of chocolate, but for the time being he saved the chocolate. If they went high, where even the black bread turned to slabs of ice that had to be shattered with a hammer, the chocolate was the only substance that didn't freeze solid. He took a hardboiled egg and nibbled at it. If he could get down to the rear-engine car, there might be a chance of some hot pea soup or coffee. The engineering officer let the mechanics warm it on the engine exhaust pipes. In some of the zeppelins there was constant hot coffee from an electric hot plate in the control gondola, but on this airship the captain wouldn't allow such devices to be used because of the fire risk.

When his calculations were complete, Peter turned to watch the men in the control gondola. At the front was a seaman at the helm. He steered while another crewman beside him, at the same sort of wheel, adjusted the elevators to keep the airship level. This was said to be the most difficult job in the control room, although Peter had never tried his hand at it. A good elevator man was able to anticipate each lurch and wallow and turn the wheel to meet each gust of wind. The control gondola was like a little greenhouse into which machinery had been packed. The largest box, a sort of cupboard, was the radio, for keeping in touch with base and with the other airships. There was the master compass with an arc to measure the angle to the horizon, a variometer for measuring descent or climb, an electric thermometer to measure the temperature of the gas in the envelope, and there were the vitally important ballast controls. At the front, where the captain stood alongside the helmsman, was the bomb-release switchboard and a battery of lamps for signaling and for landing.

Tonight's plan was simple: the main body of airships would attack London, approaching from over the Norfolk coast while two army airships were sent north to fool the defenses by making a feint attack along the river Humber. The plan itself was good enough, although its lack of originality meant that the British would not be fooled.

And the attack started too early. Even the captain, a man whose formal naval training prevented him from criticizing the High Command or his senior colleagues, said it was a bit early when the first of the airships moved forward from the place at which they'd hovered for three hours. The whole idea of waiting was so that the sky would be totally dark when the airships crossed the English coast-line. But it wasn't dark. Even the English countryside, some six thousand feet below them, was not quite darkened. Peter had no trouble following the map. He could see the rivers, and many of the villages were brightly lit. And that meant that the British could see them. The alarms would go off, London would be made dim, and civilians would go to the bomb shelters. Worse, the pilots would stand by their planes and the gunners would load the guns; their reception would be a hot one.

All the time he watched the horizon; there was always some sort of glow from London, no matter how stringently the inhabitants doused their lights. Then he spotted it, and as they came nearer to London Peter could see the looping shape of the river Thames. There was no way that could be hidden. Suddenly the guns started. Flickers of light at first as the gunners tried to get the range, but then the flashes came closer. Staring down, Peter spotted the Houses of Parliament on the riverbank. And then the shape of London—well known to him more because of his study of target maps than because of any memories that the sight evoked—was recognizable.

"Prepare for action! Open bomb doors!" He noted the exact time: 2304 hours. At first he was going to advise dropping bombs on the Houses of Parliament, but the briefing clearly said railway stations. There were two right below: Waterloo and Charing Cross. Peter signaled and the captain ordered the first lot of bombs released. There was a series of flashes as they hit, and though Peter could imagine the terror and destruction they had brought, he had no deep feeling of remorse or regret. The British had had every chance to stay out of the war, but they had decided to interfere, and now they must face the consequences.

Crash! The second lot of bombs were striking somewhere south of the river. It was mostly just workers' housing on that side of the water. The captain should have awaited Peter's signal, but everyone got excited. There were more explosions, though without any corresponding lights on the ground. He suddenly realized that it was the sound of the British anti-aircraft guns. They were very close, and for the first time on such a war flight Peter felt a little afraid.

At least there were no searchlights here in the very heart of town. The British had concentrated their searchlights to the northeast and along the approaches. They could be seen there now, steadily moving in search of the zeppelins that were behind them. Wait: they were clustering together. They'd caught someone. Two more anti-aircraft shells exploded, very close. In the gondola Pete heard the captain order the firing of a red Very pistol light. It was a trick—pretending to be a British fighter plane ordering the guns silent—but the "color of the night" was changed sometimes hour by hour, and the gunners were not often tricked. The light went arcing out into the darkness, a red firework sinking slowly.

"Drop water ballast forward!" murmured the captain, and immediately the orders were given. Peter hung on tight, knowing the the airship would tilt upwards to an alarming angle as she began to rise. There was the whoosh of water rushing through the traps. There she went! The gunfire explosions dropped away below them like the repeated sparking of a cigarette lighter that would not ignite. They continued to rise. Here in the upper air it was dark and cold.

By now a dozen searchlights had fastened on the airship behind them, to the north. "The Dragon!" said a whispered voice in the gondola. How could it be the Dragon? She'd been ahead of them. Of course, she was always very slow. Those old engines of hers were the subject of endless grim jokes. They'd been promised new engines again and again, but all the new engines were needed for new airships.

The telephone rang and was answered by Hildmann. "Number-two gun position report enemy aircraft," he said.

"Switch off engines!"

The silence came as a sudden shock after so many hours with the throbbing sound of the engines. Everyone throughout the airship remained as quiet as possible and listened.

It was Peter, staring down to the townscape below, who spotted him, a large biplane climbing in a wide circle, trying to get into position for an attack. The fighters liked to rake the airships from stern to nose, using the new explosive and incendiary bullets. "Fighter!" He pointed.

The captain bit his lip and turned his head to see the instruments. The airship was still at the slightly nose-up angle that provided extra dynamic lift.

Suddenly all was gray: the sky, the ground, and all the windows. The zeppelin had passed up into a patch of cloud. Now, with all speed, the airship was "weighed off." The upward movement ended and the airship stopped, engines off and completely silent, shrouded in the gray wet cloud. The mist around them brightened as the searchlight beams raked the cloud's underside and made the water vapor glow.

They could hear the airplane now. It had followed them into the cloud and passed near on the starboard side, its engine faltering as the dampness of the cloud affected the carburetor. It circled once, as if the fighter pilot knew where they were hiding, and then, after another, wider circle, the sound of the plane's engine grew fainter.

"Restart engines!" The clutches were engaged till the props were just turning, treading the air so that the airship scarcely moved. They waited five minutes or more before dropping more water ballast and recommencing their upward movement. Suddenly they were out of the cloud and the stars were overhead. They were very high now and could see a long way. Over northern London clusters of searchlights were still moving slowly across the sky, searching for the airships heading back that way.

Peter provided a course to steer, and slowly—the engines weakened on this thinner air—they headed for home. Everyone was watching the horizon, where the English defenses were concentrated. Every few minutes there was a flicker of gunfire, like fireflies on a summer's evening. That was the gauntlet that they must also run.

"Look there!"

One by one the searchlights swung over to one point in the sky, forming a pyramid with a silvery shape at its tip. Then the silvery shape went red. At first the red glow was scarcely brighter than the searchlight beams below it. Then it went to a much lighter red, as a cigar tip brightens at a sudden intake of breath.

"My God!" Even the captain was moved to cry out aloud. Everyone stared. Flight discipline, rank, was for a moment forgotten. All stared at the terrible sight. None of them had seen such a thing before, except in their nightmares. The stricken airship flared white like a torch, so bright that it blinded them, and they were unable properly to see the dull-red sun into which it changed before dropping earthwards. Then the fiery tangle vanished into a cloud, and the cloud turned pink and boiled like a great furnace.

It was in the silence that followed that the telephone rang. The observation officer—Hildmann—answered tersely. He looked round the control gondola and stared at Peter. If there was a job, then Peter was the one likely to be spared from duties here in the car. The course home was set, and the charts were already folded away, the pencils in their leather case in the rack over the plotting table.

So it was Peter who was sent to speak with the sailmaker. The gas bags were holed; the captain must know how badly. Was it the small punctures that the scout's machine guns made, or the far more serious jagged tears from shell fragments? Were the leaks low down, or were they in the upper sections of the bags, where a leak meant the loss of all the gas it held? Peter looked around to find an extra scarf and the sheepskin gloves that he'd removed to use the pencils. It would be cold back there inside the envelope, even colder than it was here in the drafty control gondola. He'd found only one glove by the time Hildmann shouted to him again. No matter: he'd keep his hand in his pocket.

He went up the ladder again. It was dark and dangerous picking his way along the keel between the lines of gas bags. It was like walking down the aisle of some echoing cathedral, except that huge silky balloons floated inside and filled the whole nave, from floor to vaulting.

Some of the giant bags were hanging soft and empty. It was here that the sailmaker was already at work, patching the leaks. He called down from the darkness: "Herr Leutnant." The sailmaker was clinging to the girders high above him. Peter climbed with difficulty. The lack of oxygen made him feel dizzy.

It was while Peter was inspecting the damaged gas bags that the anti-aircraft battery scored its hit. There was a loud bang that echoed in the framework. The airship careened, remained for a moment on its side, so that everything tilted and the half-emptied bags enveloped the two men. Peter fought the silky fabric aside as the airship rolled slowly back and then steadied again. "What the devil was that?" said the sailmaker. Peter didn't reply, but he knew they were hit, and hit badly. It was a miracle that there was no fire. "Stay here," said Peter. "I'll find out what's happened."

When he got back to the control gondola, it was in ruins. The rear portion of the car was gone completely, and a large section of the thin metal floor was missing, so that, still standing on the short communication ladder to the keel, Peter could see the landscape

123

thousands of feet below them. The helmsman and rudder man were nowhere to be seen: the explosion had blown them out into the thin air.

There was broken window celluloid everywhere, and the aluminum girders were bent into curious shapes, like the tendrils of some exotic vine. The body of the captain—hatless to reveal an almost bald head—was sprawled on the floor in the corner, his head slumped on his chest. The observation officer had survived, of course: Hildmann was a tough old bird, the sort of man who always survived. He had somehow scrambled across the two remaining girders and got to the front of the car. He was manning the elevator wheel. When he saw Peter coming down through the hatch, he pointed to the wheel that controlled the rudders and then went back to his task.

"How bad?" Hildmann asked him after Peter had swung himself across the gaping hole to take his place at the wheel and steer for home.

"The gas bags? Two of them are bad, and some of the holes are high. But the sailmaker is a good man, and his assistant is at work, too."

The observation officer grunted. "We can let it go lower, much lower." His voice was strained as he gasped for breath. Hildmann was no longer young. At this height the lack of oxygen caused dizziness and headaches, and every little exertion seemed exhausting. Peter's clamber down into the car had made his ears ring, and his pulse was beating at almost twice its normal rate. In the engine cars, and up on the gun positions, men would be suffering nausea and vomiting. It was worth going high to avoid the defenses, but today they hadn't avoided them. "A lucky shot," said Hildmann, as if reading Peter's mind.

"There will be more guns along the coast," warned Peter.

"We must risk that. The gas will be escaping fast at this height; soon we'll lose altitude whether we want to or not. And the engines will give us more power lower down."

Peter didn't answer. Hildmann was deluding himself. The pressure inside the bags would make little difference. Whatever they decided, the airship was continuing to sink, due to the lost hydrogen from the punctured gas cells. Peter was having difficulty at the helm of the great ship. He had never touched the wheel before; the seamen given this job were carefully chosen and specially trained.

Holding the brute, as it willfully tried to fly its own course through the open sky, was a far harder task than he ever would have believed. He had new respect for the men he'd watched doing it so calmly and effortlessly. And as the thought came to him, he realized that now he would never be able to tell them so: both men had long since hit the ground at terminal velocity, which meant enough force to indent themselves deep into the earth.

"Is he patching the holes?" said Hildmann.

"The sailmaker and his assistant," affirmed Peter. "They can't work miracles, though."

In other circumstances Hildmann might have considered Peter's reply insubordinate, but now he seemed not to notice the apparent disrespect.

"We're sinking still," said Hildmann, at last facing the reality of their danger. "They'd better work fast." The airship dropped lower and lower until the altimeter—an unreliable device worked by barometric pressure—warned them they were as low as they dared go in darkness. Then it became a battle to stay in the air. In other parts of the airship, crewmen, on their own initiative, began to throw overboard everything that could be spared. Desperately men dumped the reserve fuel, ammunition boxes, then ammunition; finally, as they crossed the coast near Yarmouth, the guns went, too.

"Can you work the radio?" asked Hildmann.

"I can try, Herr Oberleutnant." The radio looked to be in bad shape, the glass dials shattered and a fresh bright-silver gash across its metal case. There was little or no chance that it would still be working. The clock over it had stopped, a mute record of the exact moment the shell burst struck.

"We'll probably come down in the sea. We need to know the position of the nearest ship."

And find it, thought Peter. He had only the haziest idea of their present position, and finding such a dot in the North Sea would need a navigational skill far beyond his own crude vectors and sums. But for a moment he was spared such tests; there was no question of his leaving the helm until a relief could be summoned, and the telephone link was severed.

"Better not look down," said Hildmann in a voice that was almost avuncular.

Had the old man just discovered that? thought Peter. The void beyond the gap in the car's floor was the most terrifying sight he'd ever seen. After that first shock he'd kept his eyes away from the jagged hole. "*Jawohl,* Herr Oberleutnant!"

"You're a good, reliable officer, Winter."

"Thank you, Herr Oberleutnant," said Peter, but he wished the observation officer hadn't said it. It was too much like an epitaph. He had the feeling that Hildmann had said it only because their chances of survival were so slim. It would be just like him to be writing their final report in his head before going to meet his Maker.

"Request the Oberleutnant's permission to change course five degrees southwards."

"Why?" asked Hildmann.

"The compass must be wrong. Dawn is coming up."

The observation officer stared at where the horizon would be if the night had not been so very dark. Then he saw what Peter had been looking at for five minutes: a dull-red cotton thread on the silky blackness of the night. Hildmann looked at his watch to see whether the sun was on schedule. "Yes, change course," he said, having decided that it was.

The dawn came quickly, changing the sky to orange and then a sulfurous yellow before lighting the gray sea beneath them. Cross-lit, the choppy water was not a reassuring sight.

"Is that the coast ahead?"

"Yes, Herr Oberleutnant."

"Won't need the radio now."

"No, Herr Oberleutnant."

"Just as well. I don't think it's working."

"I don't think it is, Herr Oberleutnant."

"Do you think we'll be able to get it down in the right place?"

"I think we can, Herr Oberleutnant." Hildmann would have been outraged by any other response, but he smiled grimly and nodded. Peter wondered how old he was; rumors said he was a grandfather.

"We lost the Dragon."

"Yes, Herr Oberleutnant." Trees appeared behind the desolate sandy coastline. They were very low. He stared down into the darkness.

"Good men on the Dragon."

"Yes, Herr Oberleutnant."

"Oh my God!"

Everything happened so suddenly that there was no time to avert the crash. The elevator cables had been in shreds for hours. Hildmann didn't realize that the movements of his wheel depended upon a single steel thread until the final thread snapped and the elevators slammed over to put the airship into a violent nose-down attitude. It all happened in only a few seconds.

First there was the sudden snapping of the control cables: bangs like explosions came as the released steel cables thrashed about, ripping through the gas bags and tearing into the soft aluminum. The lurch started Hildmann's wheel spinning and sent Hildmann staggering across the car so that he stumbled and was thrown half out of the hole in the floor. Then came the big crash of the airship striking the tree tops.

Branches came into the car from every side, and a snowstorm of leaves and wood and sawdust filled the control room, until the weakened gondola was torn into pieces by the black trees. There was a scream as Hildmann disappeared into the darkness below, and then the airship met a tree that would not yield, and, with a crash and the shriek of tortured metal, the vast framework collapsed upon him and Peter lost consciousness.

"My poor Harry."

In Vienna that same September morning it was bright and clear. The low-pressure region that had provided the zeppelins with cloud cover over England had broken. Southern Germany and Austria had blue skies and cold winds.

Martha Somló—or Frau Winter, as she had engraved on her visiting cards—was awake. She'd been an early riser ever since she was a child, when she'd got up at five every morning to prepare the work in her father's back-room tailor shop.

Harald Winter was sound asleep. He snorted and turned over. "Wake up! Harry." She had a tray with coffee and warm fresh bread.

He grunted.

"Wake up! You were snoring."

He rubbed his face to bring himself awake. "Snoring?"

"Yes. Loud enough to wake the street." She smiled sweetly and forgivingly.

He looked at her suspiciously. Veronica had never mentioned his snoring, nor had any of the other women he enjoyed on a more-or-less regular basis. "It's an ugly habit, snoring," he said.

He opened his eyes to see her better. She was wearing the magnificent silk dressing gown he'd bought for her on one of his trips to Switzerland. It was black and gold, with huge Chinese tigers leaping across it. He'd thought at the time how like Martha the snarling tigers looked. "It doesn't matter, darling. You can't help it," she said.

The truth was that Harald Winter did not snore, but teasing him was one of the few retaliations she got for being neglected.

She set the tray down on the bed and slid back under the bed-clothes. This was her very favorite time: just her and Harry at break-fast. He gave her a quick hug and kiss before taking a kaiser roll and waiting for her to pour his coffee and add exactly the amount of cream and sugar he liked. From the street below came the sound of horses' hoofs and wheels upon the cobbles and the jingle of harness. It was a large contingent of field artillery moving off to the war. The noise continued for a long time, but neither Harry nor Martha went to the window to look. Soldiers had become too common a sight in the streets of Vienna for breakfast to be interrupted.

Prompted by the sounds of the horse artillery, Martha said, "The war's going badly for us, isn't it, Harry?" She removed the tray to the side table and came back to bed.

"It goes up and down: wars are always like that."

"And you don't care, as long as you sell your airships and planes, and make lots of money."

"My God, but you are a little firebrand, aren't you?"

He grabbed her wrist and clutched it tight. It hurt, but she wouldn't give him the satisfaction of complaining. In fact, his physi-cal strength attracted her even when it was directed against her. In the same way, her strong-willed antagonism fascinated him. She was the only woman who openly defied him.

"I heard there were wooden airships now," she said spitefully, "and smaller, collapsible ones better than Count Zeppelin makes."

He smiled. "I have persuaded the navy that airships made of wood and glue are not suitable for use over the sea in bad weather."

"You think only of money!" she said.

He released her arm and said softly, "How can you say that, you little bitch, when I have two sons fighting for us?"

"I'm sorry, Harry. I didn't mean it."

He gently pulled the silk negligee from her shoulders so that he could look at her pale body. "You are exquisite, darling Martha. All is forgiven in your embrace." It was the frivolous, supercilious manner he adopted for their bouts of lovemaking. It was a way of avoiding any serious discussion.

But as he reached for her there was a knock at the bedroom door. Martha twisted away from his hand and, pulling her dressing gown tight, went to the door.

It was her maidservant. He couldn't hear what was said. Despite reassurances from his physician, he was convinced that he was growing deaf.

"What is it?" he said as she returned to the bed. "Come back to bed, my little tiger." But she remained where she was, a petite, pale figure, her face forlorn, with jet-black hair tumbling over her eyes till she pushed it back with her small, perfect hands.

"The zeppelins over England last night . . . five didn't return. Your son Peter . . ." She couldn't go on. Tears filled her eyes.

"My Peter . . . What?" He got out of bed, and went to her and held her. She was sobbing. "My poor Harry," she said.

It was almost noon next day when Peter started to regain his senses. Even before he tried to open his eyes, he smelled the ether in his nostrils. The hospital room was filled with yellow light: the sun coming through a lowered blind. When he moved his feet—an exploratory movement to discover if he was all in one piece—he felt the stiffly starched sheets against his toes. It was only then that he realized he was not alone in the hospital room. Two men in white coats were standing near the window, looking down at a clipboard.

". . . the only one to escape from the forward gondola," said one voice.

"And completely unharmed, you say?"

"Just scratches, bruises, and the finger."

"Did he lose the finger?"

"No, he had the luck of the devil. I just removed the tip of it."

"And it was the left hand, too; well, I can't imagine that that will make a scrap of difference to any young chap."

"Unless he was a pianist . . ."

"And the pianist—Hennig, isn't it?—was the one with the broken ankle. God moves in strange ways; I've always said that."

"It's a curious war, isn't it? The zeppelin staff plan to bomb

Saint-Omer's town hall when all the top Allied military commanders are there together with the King of England and the Belgian King. And the Kaiser forbids it."

"You disagree?"

"After a night spent looking at the cruelly mutilated bodies of so many very young men, I simply say it's a curious war."

Peter heard one of them hang the clipboard back on its hook before they went out of his room, but he kept his eyes closed and pretended to be asleep.

In England the next day, visitors went to the wreckage of the zeppelin that had been shot down near London. Frederick William Wile—onetime Berlin correspondent of *The Daily Mail*—wrote: ". . . even those who felt most bitterly about the brutality of raids upon unarmed civilian populations could not refrain from pity at the sight."

Wile continued: "It is one of the traditions of the Hohenzollerns that the King of Prussia must ride across the battlefields on which his soldiers have fallen and look his dead men in the face. Trench warfare and a decent regard for his own skin have prevented William II from carrying out this ghoulish rite in his war. But I wish some cruel Fate might have taken the Kaiser by his trembling hand yesterday morning and led him to that rain-soaked meadow in Hertfordshire, and bade him look as I looked at the charred remains of human wreckage which a few hours before was the crew of an Imperial German airship. I wish Count Zeppelin, the creator of the particular brand of Kultur which sent the baby-killers to their doom, might have been in the Supreme War Lord's entourage. I wondered, standing there by the side of that miserable heap of exposed skulls, stumps of arms and legs, shattered bones and scorched flesh, whether the Kaiser would have revoked the vow he spoke at Donau-Eschingen in the Black Forest eight years ago when he christened the inventor of airship frightfulness, 'the greatest German of the twentieth century.' "

1917

Not so loud, voices carry in the night.

Paul Winter had been called "little Pauli" for so much of his life that, now seventeen years old, he still thought of himself in that way. He had the cherubic face that made some lucky men youthful and attractive all their lives. Some of the others called him "Lucky." So what rotten luck that a member of the Prussian Officer Corps on active service on the Western Front should be attached to this wretched Royal Bavarian infantry regiment. What was "little Pauli" doing sitting in this deep dugout on the Western Front, listening to the muffled thumps of enemy shells exploding? The morning bombardment had started with the adjoining sector, but now they were landing closer and closer. He tried to push the fears out of his mind and concentrate upon writing a letter to his parents. The dugout was dark; he had only the light of one flickering candle. He used a penknife to sharpen the stub of his indelible pencil, and he gave a deep sigh.

But this introspection didn't mean that he felt in any way sorry for himself. The last remnants of self-pity had been eliminated during his years at the cadet school. Pauli accepted life day by day as it came but that didn't mean that he never asked himself why his life had for so long consisted of spartan food, strict discipline, and so little rest. A regime to which had lately been added gluey mud, mortal danger, and long periods of boredom. Pauli was at heart an easygoing, pleasure-loving fellow who wanted only to live and let live.

My dearest parents,
Thank you for the parcel. It arrived safely. It was so kind of Cook to knit the socks for me, but they are very big—two sizes too big. No matter, one of the other men will benefit. I shared the tin of meat with only my friend Alex but we had a little party to eat all the other food. You must not worry about me. I am many miles away from where the real fighting is taking place. Most of the time I am in Headquarters and cannot even hear the artillery fire

He stopped writing. Perhaps that was going too far. Even back in Brussels they could hear the artillery fire, and his parents might well know that. He added:

except when the wind blows from the west. Peter is coming to see me today. I will have lunch with him at Headquarters.

He wondered what to say next. Several times reduced almost to despair by the cold, filth, mud, and cruel loss of friends, he'd attempted to write a letter that truthfully described what it was like here. But each time he'd abandoned the effort and scribbled the same sort of reassuring banalities that everyone else sent home to keep the family ignorant and happy. So he wrote:

The weather here is good for this time of year and the war is going well for us. I must end this letter now. It is very early in the morning and I have a lot to do.
I will write again—a longer letter—after Peter's visit,
Your loving son,

Carefully he signed it and read it again before he put it into an envelope. He was always promising "a longer letter" but he never wrote longer letters, just short thank-you notes. Though he wrote wonderful letters in his mind, he never got them on paper. He felt constantly guilty about neglecting his parents. He knew how much they liked to hear from him and how much they worried all the time. Did all sons feel such guilt about their relationship with their parents? Most specifically, did his brother, Peter, feel guilty about his relationship with them? He knew the answer to that even before asking the question. Peter didn't neglect them. He wrote a long informative letter to them every week. Pauli had seen the letters piled up high on his father's desk. They read them again and again. And yet he knew that they didn't worry about Peter as they did about him, especially since Peter was taken off flying duties after the crash. Since Christmas 1916 Peter had been assigned to liaison duties in Brussels, and his life was no more dangerous than it would be at home in Berlin. Here on the front line, life was more hazardous; the regiment had lost fourteen officers in five weeks; five dead and nine wounded. From his pocket he took the postcard that Peter had sent arranging their meeting. For the thousandth time he made sure he had the date, time, and place right. He put the postcard away again with other cards from Peter that made a bundle so thick he couldn't button his breast pocket over them. Ever since cadet school, Peter had sent postcards regularly: every two weeks, never more than three. Sometimes it was no more than a sentence—a joke, a greeting, a memory from the past, one of their nanny's oft-repeated Scottish aphorisms. How did Peter know how important the cards were to him? Pauli never told him and never even responded to them. Peter, Peter, Peter. How he missed him.

"Runner!" The command was that of a Prussian officer. Pauli was always a little surprised to hear the voice coming from himself.

"Herr Leutnant?" The man almost fell down the steps and into the dugout. He was typical of the farm boys who made up most of the regiment. The rest of them were older men with families or physical disabilities that had kept them out of the war until last year, when the casualties meant that more and more men were needed. They were only half trained. The regiment should not be holding a section of the line: it should be at a training camp, where these fellows could learn to march and shoot. On the ranges, half of them couldn't even hit the target, let alone score. The machine-gun teams were pitifully slow at stripping the guns or even at clearing them when they jammed. If the British infantry decided to attack on this sector, they would be able to walk through. Or at least that's the way it appeared to those who hadn't seen the state of the British soldiers facing them. But Pauli had spoken with enough British prisoners to know that the winter of endless rain, and the waterlogged trenches, had brought enemy morale down to a point where some Tommies were thankful for the prospect of a dry POW camp away from the fighting.

The theory held by the generals at Imperial Army HQ was that a few experienced NCOs and some trained Prussian officers for each company would work a miraculous transformation in this fighting force, but of course it wouldn't. The "trained Prussian officers" were no better than boys from cadet schools, some with less training than Pauli. And as for the experienced NCOs, they were too damned experienced. They were disillusioned veterans, many of them only recently discharged from hospital, men who had hoped to spend the rest of the war in safe jobs with training units. Now they were back in the front line, but instead of being with their comrades, they were wet-nursing this raggle-taggle bunch of stupid peasants, some of them not even Bavarians, kids with incomprehensible Austrian accents or unpronounceable Hungarian names. No wonder there were mutterings of discontent, Marxist leaflets, and, every now and again, a wound that looked suspiciously like something that might have been self-inflicted.

He put the letter into an oilskin pouch to protect it from the mud, the rain, and the runner's filthy hands. "Take this letter to Regimental Headquarters and tell the clerk to put it with the officers' mail so that it goes off this morning. Do you understand?" There was a crash that made the candle flicker, and some dried pieces of mud fell from the lintels overhead. "That's not very close: the other side of the railway lines . . . even farther, perhaps." It was an automatic reaction, done always to reassure whoever was nearby. Pauli buttoned his precious stub of indelible pencil into his jacket.

"Yes, Herr Leutnant." The boy didn't believe it, of course; the runners got about and knew what was happening. The British artillery were softening up the communications trenches so that no reserves would get here when they attacked. Rumors said that it would come in two or three days' time. Lots of British patrolling lately—that was usually a sign of an impending attack. Pauli knew all about it because he was the only officer in the regiment who spoke fluent English. He was called upon to interrogate the prisoners or sort through the personal effects of the British dead before the things were sent back to the intelligence officers. Two days, three at the most. A sergeant from the South Wales Borderers had virtually admitted it to him.

The soldier took the oilskin packet and stumbled over his rifle butt, striking his helmet against the low doorway as he hurried up the steps and out along the trench. Pauli watched him without comment: Pauli, too, was inherently clumsy. He, too, stumbled up the steps more times than not. Why were some people like that, no matter how hard they tried? Pauli would have loved to be adroit and elegant, but he couldn't even dance without stepping upon his partner's feet.

As the antigas flap on the door swung back, a heavy smell of fresh cordite and the stink of the latrine buckets came into the dugout. Oh well, it was a change from the steady smell of unwashed bodies and putrefaction that was the normal atmosphere down here.

"What's the time?" From one of the wooden bunks built into the far wall a figure swung his legs to the floor and then slowly emerged from the blanket that cocooned him. Alex Horner—Pauli's close friend at the cadet school—had found himself attached to the same regiment. Both boys had hoped to be assigned to one of the better Prussian units—cavalry, guards, or dragoons—instead of this collection of conscripts. But they were together, and that was the one consolation in the whole miserable, tormented existence they led.

"Next time I'm in Wertheims department store, I'll get you a watch with an illuminated face," said Pauli sarcastically.

"Well, that might be a long time," said Alex. He rubbed his chin to decide whether he needed a shave badly enough for the company commander to admonish him. He decided to risk it: seventeen-year-old chins did not show much stubble per day. Leutnant Alex Horner was already acquiring the look of the Prussian officer. A duel at cadet school had left him with a saber cut along his jaw, and the lice-infested conditions here on the front line required him to have his head almost shaved. But he was not yet the austere, unbending Prussian figure: he smiled too much, for one thing, and his nose was pert and upturned, the sort of nose more often to be seen on farmers' daughters than on Prussian officers.

"It's three-thirty-two," said Pauli.

"What a terrible time to be awake."

"Stand-to in fifteen minutes." At dawn the front-line trenches had to be manned, because it was the best time for the British to attack. But, since the trenches were full of infantry, it was also a good time for the British to strafe them with a barrage of mortar shells.

Alex Horner groped on the floor to find his cigarettes. Together with the matches, he found them in his steel helmet. Unlike most of the soldiers, Alex Horner couldn't sleep with his helmet on his head. When he'd got his cigarette lit, he tied up the laces of his boots and buttoned up his woolen cardigan, his jacket, and the overcoat in which he'd been sleeping. He moved slowly, as a man does when drunk. Stress, lack of rest, and the stodgy food so lacking in protein made them all a bit robotic.

"If only the army had not disbanded their airships . . ." said Alex. He put some eau de cologne on a dirty handkerchief and wiped his face with it.

"Well, they have," said Pauli, who'd heard Alex's sad story a hundred or more times.

"My application was completed and approved. The physical exam would have been no more than a formality. I'm a hundred percent fit; you know that, Pauli."

"I know," said Pauli. He couldn't be too rude to his friend; they both needed someone to complain to. In the absence of any other sympathetic friends, they told each other the same stories over and over again.

"I'd be flying by now."

"Perhaps you could transfer to the Naval Airship Division."

"They'd never allow that; you know they wouldn't."

"I'll talk to my brother when I see him. Perhaps he could arrange something for you."

"I even bought those books on engine repair and maintenance."

"Airships are dangerous. My brother, Peter, was shot down."

"You talk to him. Perhaps if I was prepared to go in as a midship-man . . ." They both knew that there was no possible chance that he'd be permitted to transfer to the navy, but by common consent they talked of it often.

"Have you got your pistol belt and the flashlight? It's time to go, Alex."

"It's the monotony that gets me down. We'll stand to and freeze for an hour; then we'll spend ages while the captain inspects every rifle barrel."

"Not this morning; this is Easter Saturday. Wake up, Alex! We're assigned to check the sentries and then be at the old supply line when the wiring party returns."

Alex nodded, but he didn't abandon his moaning. "Then, when the breakfast is coming, the British will mortar the communication trenches and those fools will drop our breakfast into the mud, the way they did three times last week. On Monday I only got a bread roll and half a cup of coffee."

Not so loud, voices carry in the night.

"Don't you ever think of anything else but food and drink, Alex?"

"What else is there?" It was Alex's "morning moan." Pauli had got used to his friend's bad moods, which came immediately after waking. In another hour he'd be his normal cheery self again. Until then he needed to moan. "I suppose the planes will come over any time now."

"It's too early. The attacks last week were planes coming back from patrol. The English patrol planes go out at dawn and come back about half an hour later. Perhaps the English pilots will stay in bed for Easter."

"Where are our planes?"

"The British believe they must enter our airspace every morning. They say it keeps up their fighting spirit. They send the infantry patrols over to our trenches for the same reason. They are frightened that their soldiers will lose their appetite for the war unless they are sent often to fight us."

"Is that what you find out when you speak with the prisoners?"

"They make no secret of it."

"Is Leutnant Brand on duty this morning?" Alex asked, making the inquiry sound as casual as possible, and yet the imminent encounter with the dreaded Leutnant Brand was uppermost in the thoughts of both young men.

"Yes, he's duty officer."

"Jesus Christ!" Alex rubbed his beard again and regretted not shaving, for Leutnant Heinrich Brand was a tyrant, a cruel man who lost no opportunity to make the lives of his junior officers a misery. Brand was thirty-two years old, the son of a baker in a village near the Austrian border. He'd entered the Bavarian cavalry as a boy and risen to the rank of Feldwebel by 1914. It was a rank beyond which he would never have been promoted except for the coming of the war. By the end of December 1914 he was a senior NCO in the regimental training camp. But it was on the Eastern Front, in the fighting of early 1915, that he saved the life of his commanding officer. Attacking Cossacks cut his cavalry regiment to pieces as they retreated through woodland that became marsh and then an open piece of ground that gave the Russian cavalry a chance to demonstrate their superior skill and reckless courage. Brand got the Iron Cross and a commission for that day's hard fighting. But the same

137

officers who applauded Brand's bravery did not want to share their mess with this coarse-accented villager, and Brand soon found himself amongst strangers. And this time he was not even in the cavalry.

It was dark and cold, and there was rain in the air. The wind was singing in the massed barbed wire that filled no-man's-land. As Pauli and Alex plodded their way along the duckboards, which made a slatted floor for the deep trench, both were thinking of Brand. The Leutnant saved his particular hatred for these two products of the Prussian army's most exclusive officer-cadet school. Brand envied them. He would have given almost anything to have the panache, the style, and the background—to say nothing of the proper Berlin accent—of the two youngsters.

"I hate him," said Alex Horner as they negotiated the zigzag trenchline, the skirts of their greatcoats heavy with accumulated mud. The sky was clear, with a thousand stars and a moon that was almost full and very yellow. The night was bitterly cold. Underfoot the duckboards had frozen hard into the mud, so that they didn't sink under the boys' weight the way they usually did in the daytime.

"Not so loud," said Pauli. "Voices carry in the middle of the night like this. Last night I could hear the stretcherbearers taking the casualties back to the medical post near Regimental HQ, and that's a long way away, isn't it?"

"What about that Englishman in no-man's-land last week? Did you hear him sobbing?"

"I heard him cursing," said Pauli. They were both speaking in whispers now as they plodded along the trench.

"That was later," said Alex. "That was at the end. Imagine being out there with a leg shot off. Do you ever think about that, Pauli?"

"No, I never think about it," said Pauli. In fact, like all the rest of them, he found that such ideas haunted his thoughts and gave him nightmares. The shouting and weeping of the mortally wounded Englishman had affected all who heard him. Even Leutnant Brand was heard to curse the dying man.

They reached the first sentry. He was standing on the fire step looking over the parapet. Even the farm boys could look heroic in such a pose, cloaked in a muddy blanket and as still as a statue. "Any sign of the wiring party?" Pauli asked.

"No, Herr Leutnant," the sentry answered without turning his head. Sentries soon learned how dangerous it was to make any sort of movement that might be seen by the British snipers. Twice in the

Not so loud, voices carry in the night.

last week snipers had killed sentries. Both times the casualties had been men wearing glasses. It was assumed that the moonlight—or in one case a flare—had glinted on the glass. One of the officers had suggested that men with eyeglasses be excused sentry duty, but in a second-rate unit like this, with so many men from lower medical categories, it would have been an unfair burden on the rest of them.

"No movement anywhere, Herr Leutnant," said the sentry.

It was the same at the next sentry, and the next. But this didn't mean that there was no one out there in the twisted, tangled chaos of no-man's-land. The British patrols could move silently and swiftly. They used trench knives and clubs. More than once in the last month a British raiding party had come right over into the German front-line trenches and got out again before the alarm could be sounded. They were trying to get an officer prisoner—that was usually the reason for such raids: an officer prisoner and secret papers that might help their intelligence find the place where the German armies joined, for such a place was an ideal one to attack when the big offensive came.

"Leutnant Brand should never have sent out a wiring party on a night like this," said Pauli. "It's too light."

"The wire was broken."

"The wire is always broken. It's murder to send men out to mend it on a night like this."

They turned the corner and started down the "old supply line." These trenches, captured from the British, were poorly made by German standards. The British infantry always improvised them, with only shallow dugout shelters roofed with corrugated iron sheets and none of the deep dugouts that were standard design when the German engineers constructed their front-line positions. No one liked this section of the front line. Apart from the inferior workmanship, the trench system was all the wrong way round: the old fire steps faced east and there were "saps," bombing sections and machine-gun positions, all on the wrong side, so that they were vulnerable to enemy gunfire. Worst of all was the smell. This section of the line was littered with ancient corpses that were integrated into the earthworks.

The much-feared Leutnant Brand was standing on the fire step in order to look across the endless shiny mud of no-man's-land. He wasn't using a periscope or the pierced steel that offered some protection. He liked to show how fearless he was: he liked to be thought of as brave to the point of madness. "Crazy Heini," the men called him, and he was proud of that nickname—although he would have severely punished anyone heard using it.

He got down from the fire step. "Horner! Winter! You're both late. You'll go on report." They weren't late, of course—they were three minutes early—but there would be nothing gained from arguing with him. The major would, in any case, believe what Brand told him, or at least the major would pretend to believe it. The major was worn out; he did whatever was easiest, and arguing with Brand was heavy going. Brand knew the regulations word for word—he'd learned them when he was a junior NCO—and now the major had long since learned that he was no match for Brand's sort of "lawyer's talk."

"Young officers should be setting an example to the men," said Brand. He always said that, but each time he said it as if it was a new, fresh, and original observation that should be carefully noted. "Horner! You haven't shaved. You people think that you are a law unto yourselves. You think a Bavarian regiment isn't good enough for you Prussians. Well, I'll have to persuade you it is. And if punishment is the only way, then punishment it shall be!" Brand did everything he could to speak like a gentleman, but when he got excited his Bavarian accent thickened.

Pauli looked at him. When he'd first heard about this Bavarian sergeant major who'd become an officer on the battlefield, he'd expected to see some red-faced, beer-bellied old fellow with a big nose and a huge mustache. But Brand was younger than the other company commanders, slim-hipped, and rather handsome. His nose was thin and bony and his forehead high, with trimmed eyebrows and quick, crazy eyes. His eyes moved all the time, as if he was constantly expecting to be assaulted. When he took off his helmet, as he did when looking through the trench periscope, one could see that his hair was not cropped close to the skull in the way that he insisted all the others under his command had their hair cut. Brand's hair was of medium length and wavy. Somehow, even here in the front-line trenches, he always managed to find ways of keeping clean. He wore a long waterproof coat that he'd got from a British-officer prisoner—"trenchcoats," the British called them—and under it his uniform, complete with Iron Cross medal on his pocket, was relatively clean and dry. In his hand Brand carried a riding crop with which he liked to point at people or things, prod soldiers who needed prodding, or simply slap his thigh reflectively. He slapped his thigh with it now.

"You're both going to work hard today, my friends. Winter will go back to the village and bring a burial party up to number-three post. It's time we got rid of those bodies: it stinks down there." Slap, slap, went the riding crop against the skirt of the trenchcoat. He turned to Alex and nodded. "Horner! The major wants someone to supervise the detail rebuilding the long dugout. It should have been finished two days ago. Hurry them up. I'll be along later to see what's happening."

Pauli said, "I'm going back to Divisional Headquarters today, Herr Leutnant. My brother is coming. The major gave permission."

"You'll do as you're told, Winter. I want those bodies buried *tout de suite.*" Leutnant Brand liked to use French phrases; the officers in his cavalry regiment had all done so.

"My brother is coming from Brussels. The major asked the colonel: it's all official."

"The war is official, too," said Brand. He was enjoying himself now. He looked at both of them and gave a grim smile, as if inviting them to join in the fun. Then he slapped the skirt of his trenchcoat with the riding crop. "Family reunions take place with the commanding officer's permission, but even then they are subject to the needs of the military situation. I don't know if your brother is a slack, good-for-nothing nincompoop like you, Winter. He probably is. But unless he is a complete idiot he'll know that the army comes first. Right, Winter? Understand now, Winter?"

Leutnant Brand was unusually agitated that morning, and the reason for this became clear when the Vizefeldwebel came to report that the wiring party had still not returned. Brand went back to surveying no-man's-land, but this time he used the trench periscope. The sky had gone blood-red, and it was getting lighter every minute. If the wiring party—twelve men—were still alive somewhere out in the mud, their chances of surviving through the day were slight. The British would shoot up anything unusual out there; it was the standard practice for both sides. Anything that might be some new sort of weaponry was to be feared, ever since the tanks had appeared last year. And today the weather forecast said the wind was from the west, a light breeze, which would exactly suit the British if they decided on another gas attack. What would happen to the wiring party then? They had gone out wearing the bare

141

minimum of equipment—some without helmets, even—and it was doubtful there would be one gas mask amongst the lot of them.

"You two, get going!" said Brand as he remembered that they were still waiting his orders. "And don't let me see you slacking off. Remember what I said: you are going to set an example to the men."

The Vizefeldwebel watched the exchange with a blank face, but Brand was not willing to let the old man stay out of it. As he watched the two officers hurrying back along the trench, he smiled to show that he was really a good fellow, an ex-Feldwebel who knew that young officers were lazy rogues. But the old man didn't respond to the smile.

Once Pauli and Alex got back to where the communication trenches started, Pauli said, "I so wanted to see my brother. I miss him. It's nearly a year, and he's come all the way from Brussels."

"Just go," advised Alex. He knew what the meeting meant to his friend: Pauli had been talking of little else for the last two weeks. "The burial party don't need you to watch them work. They won't slack on that detail: you can be sure of it. They'll work to get that stinking job done as quickly as possible."

"They'll need an officer to collect the identity discs from the bodies," said Pauli doubtfully.

"Rubbish!" said Alex. "The NCO will do that. It's Winkel, a good fellow."

"Brand will find out."

"How will he find out? Will you tell him? Will I tell him? Winkel won't make trouble."

"He'll go and check on the burial."

"Not Brand. He won't go near number three until they are all buried. Brand doesn't like that sort of job. That's why he always gives them to us to do: it's the worst thing he can think of to do to us."

"I promised Peter. . . ."

"Go! Go! I told you, go."

"I'll go as far as the village and talk to the NCO in charge of the burial party."

"I told you, Winkel is in charge. What are you going to say to him? That you're frightened of Brand but you are going to disobey him anyway?"

"I suppose you're right."

Not so loud, voices carry in the night.

"Tell no one. Get the ration truck from the village and go to HQ. Is that where you're meeting your brother?"

"Yes."

"Well, get going. It's a long walk. I'll cover for you. I'll have plenty of opportunities to get away from the party rebuilding the long dugout. It will take them ages yet. You know the way it's flooding. Only an idiot like Brand would make them persevere with that job." He slapped his friend on the arm.

"Thanks," said Pauli. His fears and doubts began to fade as he hurried back along the trench towards Divisional HQ. He decided to consult his brother about dealing with Leutnant Brand. Peter would know how to handle him; Peter knew everything. The more he thought about it, the happier he was. The prospect of seeing his brother again filled him with joy.

It was a long way to HQ. To start with, it was just over half a kilometer along communication trenches before the road was reached, but in the drizzling April rain it seemed much farther. At places the trench walls had collapsed, and there was a constant movement of men coming the other way. Pauli had to ease his way past ration details and had to wait while reinforcements came through, so it was nearly an hour before the trenches gave way to a sunken road. The road—little more than a track in places—was unseen by even the best positioned of the British artillery observers, and safe from everything except the odd salvo of twenty-five-pounder fire that greeted any dust that was raised at the crossroads. And in this weather there was no dust.

At the crossroads were three military policemen. Two of them were squatting in a dugout shelter roofed with galvanized iron. All three were young, not much older than Pauli. Chains at their collars supported the small metal gorgets that were the badge of their trade and caused their fellow soldiers to call such unpopular men "chained dogs." But theirs was an unenviable job. They were there not only to check the papers of any soldiers leaving the front-line area but also to keep the traffic moving through this place in which the British artillerymen were so interested. Such a task would produce more regular casualties than even the front-line infantry suffered. Pauli felt somewhat better to find that there were more dangerous jobs than his own.

Pauli asked one of the policemen the way. He knew the way, but he still felt nervous about deliberately disobeying Brand's order, and talking to the military policeman was somehow reassuring. The policeman—a well-fed fellow with a pale, pocked face and a straggling mustache—welcomed a chance to talk. He was not insubordinate, nor was he properly deferential to the difference in rank. Pauli had found this same "man-to-man" attitude amongst some of the men in his regiment, often the older men with families. It was usually the mark of a man who has resigned himself to the inevitability of death.

"The general found a conspicuous landmark for himself," said the military policeman. There was a note of derision in his remark. Conspicuous landmarks were not eagerly sought after in this war-torn terrain. "A château with two pointed towers . . . I was on duty there until last month. You'll see the ruins of a church as you get into the village. Then there's the officers' brothel—you'll see the signs—and then look for the sentries on the right. But it's a long way yet." He didn't ask to see Pauli's papers. Pauli wondered if an officer could be shot for such disobedience. With Brand quoting the appropriate rules and regulations, it seemed highly likely. He wished he hadn't come, but it was too late now.

"You'll get a ride on the ration wagon," said the policeman. "It will be coming back this way. Wait in the shelter, if you want to."

"I'll keep going," said Pauli. The other two policemen might not be so negligent about his written orders, or, rather, his lack of any.

"I'm not even German," said the policeman. "I was born in Vienna." It was hardly necessary to say it: the man spoke with a strong nasal, Viennese accent.

"So was I," said Pauli.

"Really? I wish we were there now, don't you?"

It was at this point that Pauli felt the policeman's familiarity had become insubordinate, but even now he didn't want to upset the fellow. "Soon we will be," said Pauli.

"Yes, Herr Leutnant," said the policeman. Sensing the young officer's resentment, he saluted. The rain made his helmet shiny and ran down his face like tears. Of course the man didn't believe that Pauli had been born in Vienna. Pauli had never had a Viennese accent—although he could mimic one with commendable accuracy. He'd grown up to know the voices of Berlin, and his voice, although not his manner, was that of the Officer Corps.

Not so loud, voices carry in the night.

By the time he started walking again, it was raining heavily. He passed the bloated, rotting corpses of two huge horses. Alongside, a broken wheel stood like a grave marker. The stench was overpowering. Pauli buttoned his overcoat tight against his neck and took off his steel helmet to wipe the sweat from his head and face. To some extent he was sweating with the exertion of his walk, but he felt hot with fear, too.

Only a few hundred yards past the crossroads, he got a ride on the ration wagon that was going back to the depot empty. He sat up beside the driver—a taciturn man, thank goodness—and watched the rain-washed Zeeland horses plod along the ridged track. Their pace was little faster than he'd made on foot, but up here on the driver's platform was better than picking his way between the submerged potholes and deep mud patches. The landscape was dull, misty, and monochrome. There was little movement except for military traffic on the road and a few peasants who, despite everything, clung desperately to their patches of soil.

It was nearly 9:00 a.m. by the time he reached Divisional HQ, situated—as the policeman had promised—in a grand house. There was a large paddock and a dozen magnificent cavalry horses grazing there. They looked at Pauli as he walked past, then went back to their fodder. Clerks were bivouacked in the orchard, and there was a soup kitchen sited in what must once have been an herb garden. Pauli didn't want to go the officers' canteen in case he saw someone from his regiment, so he asked the Feldwebel for something to eat and got a metal cup of hot dried-pea soup with two miserable bits of sausage floating in it. Both soup and sausage were bland and almost tasteless, but it warmed him.

In the grand, marble-paved entrance hall an NCO wearing the smart uniform of a Bavarian rifle regiment was seated at a table. Around him was a constant traffic of messengers, while noisy young staff officers were grouped at the foot of the great staircase. Their voices were not of the sort that Pauli had heard on the parade ground at Lichterfelde; they were the shrill, excited voices of wealthy young aristocrats. The NCO stared at Pauli. Men straight from the battlefield were seldom seen this far behind the lines, and the NCO clerk—who'd not been to the trenches—had never before seen an officer so dirty.

After his inquiries Pauli went up the magnificent staircase and found Peter in an upstairs room talking to an elegant-looking captain. The captain was about forty years old and wore the badges of a heavy cavalry regiment. His striped armband marked him as a staff officer from Corps HQ. Peter and the captain were laughing together as Pauli went into the office and saluted.

Peter! This was the moment he'd risked so much for. This was the meeting he'd waited for so impatiently. Peter! He wanted to throw his arms around his beloved brother and hug him, but that wasn't something he could do in the presence of a stranger. So he stood anxiously smiling at Peter.

"So this is the brother?" said the captain, and both men laughed again. Pauli envied the way his elder brother could make friends so easily. Peter was able to bridge the gap that rank and age created. Peter could even laugh and joke with his father, whereas Pauli was always treated like a baby, both by family and by strangers. Whenever Pauli got away with some misdeed or other, it was always by means of his charm, but Peter talked to other men as an equal, and that was what Pauli so admired. This relaxed and sophisticated elder brother of his would never have endured the bullying of Leutnant Brand; he would have found some way of dealing with him. But God only knows how.

Peter stood up and clasped Pauli's offered hand. "Pauli," he said, "Pauli."

Without taking his eyes from his brother for more than a moment, Pauli sat down on a hard wooden chair. It always seemed strange to sit on a proper chair after a long spell in the trenches.

"I'll leave you together," said the staff officer. "There's not much doing over the Easter weekend. Most of the staff are probably in Brussels on leave."

The friendly staff officer gave Peter and Pauli the use of the little office room and even sent a soldier to serve them coffee and schnapps.

"You're in a terrible state," said Peter when they were alone together. He was staring at his younger brother's dark-ringed eyes and shaved head and at his rain-drenched greatcoat and mud-caked boots. As Pauli loosened his collar, he caught sight of a dirty undervest, too. "Haven't you had time to change into a clean uniform?" It was the voice of the grown-up brother admonishing the baby about his gravy-stained bib, but Pauli didn't allow the condescension to spoil things.

For a moment Pauli didn't reply. He knew, of course, that the civilians didn't realize that the front line was no more than a filthy ditch from which the sound of bronchial coughing could be heard across no-man's-land, and where pneumonia was as deadly as enemy bullets and shells. But that his brother should think it was someplace where clean uniforms and pressed linen were available shocked him. "There was no time," said Pauli. He wished he could take Peter to the trenches and show him what it was like. He'd never understand otherwise. No one could visualize it. It was useless to explain.

"It's an officer's first task to set an example," said Peter primly. "Surely they taught you that at cadet school." Oh, God, how like Leutnant Brand he sounded, thought Pauli. But Peter smiled suddenly and the mood changed. "You've grown so big, Pauli. So big across the shoulders . . ." Was that Peter's polite way of saying that Pauli had not grown much taller? Pauli had always wanted to be as tall as his brother, ever since he could remember, but now he knew he would never be tall, slim, and elegant: he'd always be short, thickset, broad, and clumsy.

"You're promoted," said Pauli. Perhaps his elder brother's shiny new gold ring on that so very clean, neatly pressed naval uniform had gone to his head.

"Oberleutnants are little more than office boys in Brussels, where I work," said Peter. But, in a gesture that belied his modesty, he brushed his sleeve self-consciously as he spoke.

"You're looking well, Peter." He made no mention of his elder brother's mutilated hand and tried not to look at it. Peter's injury frightened him in some way that the firing line did not. Peter was family: an injury to him injured Pauli.

"There's no reason why I shouldn't be back on flying duties. As an Oberleutnant with my experience, I'd probably get command of one of the new high-altitude zeppelins. I even tried for the High Seas Fleet. But the damned medical board won't clear me. Sometimes I wonder whether Father hasn't found some way of keeping me from active duty."

"There's no doubt he'd try if he got the chance," said Pauli. They both knew that their father would have done anything to keep Pauli from the Western Front, and for Pauli his efforts had obviously failed.

"Now that the army have stopped using airships, Father probably has less influence with them. But the navy still listen to him."

"When did you last see him?" asked Pauli. He scratched himself. Fleas were a fact of life in the trenches—and lice, too—but Pauli noticed his brother's look of horror as he realized he was lousy.

"Christmas. I got seven days' leave. Everyone hoped that you'd come home, too."

"Training. I got a twenty-four-hour pass for Christmas. No one was permitted to leave the barracks. Even the colonel stayed."

"The infantry are winning the war," said Peter.

"We're not winning the war," said Pauli. "We're being shot at, and we're shooting back. We are not winning the war. We *will* win it, of course—no one doubts that—but for the time being it's a sort of stalemate. Neither side advances more than a few meters, and the English leave battalions of dead on the barbed wire."

"At least the Russians are kaputt," said Peter.

"We don't get much news where we are."

"It started in March; there were food riots in Petrograd, and when the troops were called out they shot their officers and joined the mob."

"My God!"

"You didn't hear?"

"Only that the Tsar abdicated and a provisional government was formed. The troops joined in? It's true?"

"Including the Imperial Guard. Some say it started in the Imperial Guard, but even in Brussels it's difficult to get reliable news. Each newspaper story contradicts the one before. A fellow I know on the Supreme Command at Spa told me the little I know."

"What will happen now?"

"The Russians can't go on fighting much longer. In Berlin there are rumors that the Kaiser has arranged for Marxist revolutionaries to be given safe passage across Germany to return home to Russia."

"The Kaiser would allow such a thing? Never!"

"The revolutionaries have always been opposed to the war—the world brotherhood of man, and so on. So, if they took power in Petrograd, they would immediately order a cease-fire. If we have no enemy to fight in the East, all our divisions would be turned to face the French and the British. The war could end within the month."

"It sounds too good to be true."

Peter nodded his agreement and said, "What will you do when it ends, Pauli? Will you stay in the army?"

"What else am I fit for? I have no head for banking or business, and even if I did have, I'm not sure that I'd get along well enough with Father to be working alongside him every day. What about you?"

"No more piano playing." He held up his gloved hand. "I'll go to college. If Father wants me to study law, I'll do it. Then, if I don't get along with him, I can go into a law practice somewhere."

"Tell me about dear Mama. . . . It's such a long time."

"She still has the awful American accent, but her German is much better now. She found people would be rude to her, thinking she was British. It made her improve her German in a way that nothing else ever did."

"Rude to Mama? Who would be rude to her?"

"People standing in the food lines."

"Mama standing in the food lines?"

"Mother has changed, Pauli. Just as the Jews have become so determined to prove their patriotism, so Mama and other foreign-born Germans feel that they must outdo everyone else in the struggle to win the war. She helps the wounded soldiers to write letters home, she rolls bandages, and even makes speeches at War Loans rallies."

"But she was so sick."

"Then the war has cured her sickness. When you go back to Berlin, you will not recognize her, Pauli."

"And what of Father?"

"Work, work, work. Did you hear that Hauser joined the army?"

"Old Hauser? Father's valet? But he must be at least forty years old."

"Thirty-eight years old. I'm surprised they took him, but he shaved off that awful beard and gave a false age to the recruiting officer. He's now a driving instructor at a transport school in Frankfurt. And from what I hear from Father, he's lording it with stories about how he used to drive Papa's old Itala."

"How does Father manage without him?"

"It's amazing. Father drives himself almost everywhere."

"And women?"

His brother hesitated. It was a taboo subject, or had been until now. "He goes to Vienna a great deal," said Peter finally.

"I thought that was finished."

"So did poor Mama, I think."

"I wish Father could see how ridiculous it makes him look," said

Pauli. He loved his father and respected him to the point of reverence, but now he'd reached the age at which he judged him, too.

"Does it make him look ridiculous? Most of his friends seem to admire and envy him. We are the only ones who think him ridiculous, and that's just because we feel sorry for Mama."

"Perhaps she would have been happier with the Englishman."

"Which Englishman?"

"Surely you guessed that the Englishman, Piper, wanted her to go away with him."

"Mama?"

"Mama had a love affair with the Englishman. At Travemünde, when we lost the *Valhalla*."

"Are you crazy, Pauli?"

"It took me a long time to understand what had happened between them. But now I look back at it, I can see how desperately unhappy she was for years afterwards."

"The Englishman? The spy?"

"He was no spy. That was just Papa's way of attacking him."

"Are you saying that Mama had a love affair with the Englishman and that Papa knew about it?"

"I found his wristwatch under Mama's bed. . . ." There, he'd said it. A thousand times it had been on the tip of Pauli's tongue to reveal the secret, but now he'd said it. And now he regretted it.

Peter closed his eyes. "It's incredible," he said at last.

"Incredible or not, it's true. I think Mama was afraid I would blurt out something that would betray her secret."

"But you never did?"

"I didn't understand the significance of finding the watch there until years later. But then, when Mama took the chloroform in the summer of 1914, and Frau Wisliceny came round to look after her . . . That night, when I went in to kiss Papa good night, I noticed that he was piecing together torn fragments of a letter. It must have been a letter to Mama from the Englishman."

"I wish you hadn't told me," said Peter. "I feel besmirched by it."

"Don't be absurd," said Pauli. "Does Mama have no right to be with someone who loves her?"

"She has Father."

"And Father has half a dozen other women. He has no real, deep love for Mama. Sometimes I think he might have married her only for the Rensselaer money."

Peter was affronted. He could hardly believe that Pauli had changed so much. Pauli had always been in awe of Father. "If you were not my brother I'd call you out for saying that."

"A duel?" Pauli laughed. "You think I'd care about losing my life in a duel? Where I am, I see men maimed and dying every day. I stood next to a sentry last week while a shell splinter trepanned him. His brains spattered into my face. You complain about my dirty uniform. Do you know what the stains on my jacket are? Blood; the blood of boys who forget to lower their head at the right time, or make too much noise mending the wire at night. Would you like to know about the stains on my trousers, Peter? Feces! I shit myself with fear every time I hear the whistle of a mortar bomb or shell, or hear at night the movement of a few rats, which might in reality be a British raiding party coming to bury a trench knife in my throat. It's quick and quiet, the throat, you see. You learn how to cut a man's throat while holding a hand very tightly over his mouth so that he doesn't scream."

"You did this, Pauli?" His elder brother's eyes were wide and his face had gone pale. "Killed with a knife?"

"Half a dozen times. I have a superior officer—a contemptible cad—who thinks young Lichterfelde graduates like me should be exposed to maximum danger. He tells us that. He also told me that I mustn't come here today. I suppose that shocks you, too. I came here today—in this dirty uniform of which you so disapprove—having defied the lawful orders of a superior officer. And I shall do it again whenever it suits me."

"You are insane, Pauli."

"No, *I'm* not insane, but sometimes I think His Majesty must be insane to continue with this mad war."

"Pauli, you must see a doctor. You *are* insane." Peter looked round fearfully, astounded to hear such treasonable talk from his young brother.

"Perhaps you're right. Then come to the front line with me, Peter, and perhaps you'll become insane, too. But I promise that you'll lose all fears of death, disgrace, or anything else that fate has waiting for us." Pauli reached forward to take the glass of schnapps that the captain had sent to them, and he downed it in one swallow.

When Peter spoke again, his voice was soft and low, his tone more conciliatory. "Whatever may be the truth of it, Pauli, I beg you, for your own sake and for that of the family, to leave such thoughts unspoken. It can be very dangerous. People might even think you are mixed up with these crackpot radical groups who are so outspoken against the war."

"After this war I want things to be different, very different, but I'm not a Spartacist, if that's what you mean."

"I know you're not. That man Liebknecht is a traitor and a swine. It's a good thing he's gone to prison. But now the Tsar's been deposed, everyone who says anything against the war is lumped together with the revolutionaries. In the North Sea Fleet we have already had some serious insubordination, bordering on mutiny. The admiral jumped on it vigorously, I'm glad to say. I was sent to Wilhelmshaven with the legal team. Do you know who I saw there? Fritz Esser."

"Fritz? That rogue?" Pauli laughed. "Was he the ringleader? With all his hero-worshipping talk about his precious Karl Liebknecht, I wonder how the navy ever accepted him."

"If he was the ringleader he was too cunning to be caught. He's found himself some soft job in the supply branch and is already a petty officer."

"A petty officer. I thought he was illiterate."

"Esser? Of course not, Pauli. Can't you remember all those books and pamphlets he'd read about the coming revolution?"

"Yes, you're right."

"You thought the world of him."

"We both did," said Pauli, "but we laughed at him, too."

"I'm not laughing now, Pauli. Esser and his ilk are dangerous men. Make no mistake, Germany has many such uneducated, treacherous fools, who will sell out their country if they get the chance."

"Sell out their country? To what?"

"I don't know . . . they don't know, either . . . some fantasy about a world revolution and the brotherhood of mankind. They want power, Pauli. I saw these people at close hand when we were preparing the court-martial evidence in Wilhelmshaven. Many of them were simple men—stokers, mostly—but among them were some trained agitators, well equipped to argue their crackpot political theory with lawyers, or anyone else."

Not so loud, voices carry in the night.

"It's all finished now?"

Peter glanced round nervously. "No, it's not finished, I'm afraid. We put a few troublemakers behind bars, but there are too many Essers at large. Back home, civilians are working regular twelve-hour days and food is very short, thanks to the British naval blockade. So many tired and hungry workers provide opportunities for rabble-rousers. Unless conditions improve soon, I'm afraid we'll see more and more trouble from servicemen and civilians."

"I've never heard anything of this before, Peter."

"I didn't intend to talk about it."

"We don't hear anything at the front."

"This revolution in Russia will give Liebknecht and the Rosa Luxemburg woman encouragement to renew their efforts. The radicals will bide their time, and when they make their bid for power they'll be ready to spill blood. Not only their own blood, either!"

The two of them sat for several minutes, looking at each other and drinking the delicious coffee that was available to these lucky men who fought their war behind desks. Then there were loud voices in the corridor, the sort of anxious exchanges seldom heard in these quiet corridors. Suddenly the door opened and the staff captain came in, looking agitated. With no more than a nod to the two officers, he grabbed papers from a tray on his desk and retrieved others from the top of a cabinet. "The Americans have declared war," he said over his shoulder as he sorted through his papers.

"Are you sure?" asked Peter. It was impossible to take in. America was thousands of miles away, and their army was negligible. Even if their army was enlarged, the U boats would make sure the Americans never got to Europe. And yet . . .

"The American Congress ratified it yesterday. What a thing to happen at Eastertime!" He threw papers into a file. "Do you realize what it means?"

"Will they send armies to Europe?" said Pauli. Already they were stretched to the limit to hold the front.

The captain said, "We must disengage from the Russians and crush the French with one quick, massive offensive before the Americans arrive." It sounded like something he'd been told.

"Is such a thing possible?" said Peter.

"We will discover in good time," said the captain. He dropped a handful of papers against the desktop to get them straightened. "If we haven't won the war by Christmas, it will be the end of the

Fatherland. The end of everything we're fighting for.'' Peter looked at the staff officer and was disturbed by his demeanor. Perhaps the Americans would make a difference. There were so many of them, and their resources were limitless.

As the captain went out through the door, Pauli could see, at the top of the grand staircase, the general who commanded the division and two aides. They were magnificently attired: swords, *Pickel-hauben,* gleaming boots, and chestfuls of orders and decorations. He got only the briefest glimpse of the three men, but all his life Pauli remembered the scene in every small detail, even the way in which the general was holding his Turkish cigarette in a jade holder.

The two brothers had not resumed their conversation when they heard the distant explosion of an enemy shell. The rumble of gunfire had been a background to their talk, but this one was nearer, about three miles away. They went to the window in time to see the plume of brown smoke that marked its fall. By that time another shellburst shook the glass. The second round landed only slightly closer.

Peter said, "It's the first time I've been on the receiving end of it."

"A heavy-caliber gun," said Pauli. "Somewhere up there a couple of men in an observation plane are trying to locate us. I don't know why they find it so difficult: a big mansion like this with two big spires."

"It's not so easy when you are up there," said Peter. "In this sort of poor light, through the overcast, it all looks gray. In evening or morning sunlight the shadows make it easier."

"Then why do they always come over in such bad weather?" said Pauli.

Peter gave a grim smile. It seemed so safe and simple to those who stayed on the ground. "The poor devils want to disappear into the clouds if our fighters get near them or the anti-aircraft fire does." As he said it, small black puffs of flak appeared in the sky to the south, but they could see no sign of the artillery-spotting plane.

"The fliers won't hang around long," said Pauli. "And these long-range guns can fire only a few rounds at a time. Then the barrels are worn out. War is a damned expensive business, as the taxpayers are discovering."

"When we win, the French will pay reparations, as they did last time."

Not so loud, voices carry in the night.

"Ah! When we win," said Pauli.

They stood in silence, looking at the shattered landscape. The grounds of the château had been beautifully cultivated for a couple of hundred years, but now the whole place had been ravaged by the soldiers. The orchard was no more than tree stumps, the lawn a camp, and everywhere a quagmire. Farther away, the woodland had been scavenged for firewood through three winters of war; and the country roads, built for carts and carriages, were churned by endless divisional horse-drawn traffic and the occasional staff car and truck.

"Was it terrible?" asked Pauli, still staring out the window. "The zeppelin flights, the raids over England, and the crash: was it terrible?"

"The raids were all right. I didn't realize what danger we were in until, on the final one, I saw an airship burn in the sky." Peter's voice was different now: the voice Pauli remembered from when they'd exchanged confidences in the darkness of the nursery. "I was so frightened, Pauli, that my hands were shaking. She was gone. . . . The whole airship was gone in a few seconds. So many friends . . ."

"And you crashed."

"That wasn't so bad, but they operated on my hand three times and I was convinced that I would relive my fears . . . scream or reveal my cowardice under the anesthetic."

"And did you?"

"God knows."

"Papa told me that most of your crew were killed."

"We were hit over the English coast—gunfire—the control gondola was damaged and we lost some of the officers. We limped back across the North Sea, sinking lower all the time. I thought we'd get home in one piece, but it was not to be. Most of the casualties came when we hit the trees. The observation officer, an elderly chap named Hildmann—the staff captain just now put me in mind of him—was killed. While he was alive I didn't ever give Hildmann a thought, but after he was dead I realized how much I owed to him. He'd looked after me right through all the training flights and on our first war missions over England. After a man is dead you can't say thank you."

"And Hennig was with you?"

"He survived, the insolent little swine."

"And he's married Lisl Wisliceny, I hear."

"Yes, a flashy ceremony—Frau Wisliceny arranged it all, of course—and a big reception in the Adlon afterwards."

"Mama wrote me a letter."

"Mama had to go: Frau Wisliceny is her best friend. She's a fine woman. Yes, Mama went, but Papa was in Friedrichshafen with the airship people." Peter said it with satisfaction. He was pleased that his father had found a reason to stay away from the wedding of the hateful Hennig.

"Did you want to marry her?"

"Lisl? Yes, once I did. Or at least I thought I did. But then, as I realized the way in which she was playing a game with me and Hennig—playing us off one against the other—I didn't love her anymore."

"They're all pretty girls, the Wislicenys."

"I was close to Inge once. . . ." He turned suddenly. "By God! I've just thought of something. If America has declared war, Mama is an enemy alien. They might make us resign our commissions, Pauli."

"You're a selfish pig, Peter. Instead of worrying about your commission you should be worrying about poor Mama. She must be feeling terrible about it. Let's pray she'll not be sent to an intern-ment camp like the English civilians have been."

"Yes, of course, you're right. I should have been thinking of her. But it will affect us, too, Pauli. It could make things very difficult for both of us."

A light tap came and the office door opened immediately. A man stepped inside, a formidable figure, a captain, fortyish, with hard gray eyes and a mouth like a rat trap. He nodded to Peter and without any preliminaries asked Pauli for his papers. Pauli knew it was the end for him as soon as he saw the metal gorget at his neck. A Feldgendarmerie officer complete with Bavarian-style shako, and sword hung with ornamental knot. "You are absent without leave, Leutnant Winter. You have absented yourself from your post while on active service. From the front line . . . It's a death-penalty offense. I suppose you know that?" A slight Bavarian accent: it wasn't the voice or the manner of a career soldier, but there was that touch of informality that professional policemen use to make apprehended men amenable. Pauli guessed that he'd once been a senior police officer in Munich or some such town.

Not so loud, voices carry in the night.

Pauli didn't reply. He knew what was expected of a Prussian officer. He stood rigidly at attention, as he'd stood for so many hours on the parade ground at Lichterfelde. He'd known, deep down, that it was going to happen, and now it had happened. His guts were churning, but in some ways it was a relief. Now all he had to do was face his punishment. He'd always been better able to face the consequences than to worry about them.

He had plenty of time to think about what he'd done. He was held for two nights in the cells at Divisional HQ before facing his court-martial. But for his colonel, Pauli would probably have faced a firing squad. It was the colonel—prematurely aged from sending so many youngsters into battle—who gave such a glowing account of Pauli's bravery and devotion to duty. It was the colonel who put such emphasis on Pauli's extreme youth, and it was the colonel who arranged that Leutnant Brand not appear in person.

But Brand's written deposition was carefully worded. He must have spent many hours upon the document, and he covered every eventuality, even to the extent of finding the military policeman with whom Pauli had spoken at the crossroads. The verdict was inescapable.

The sentence came like a slap in the face, but Pauli didn't flinch. Six months with a Punishment Battalion. Everyone knew that a spell with a Punishment Battalion was intended as a deferred death sentence. Such units were used only where the fighting was most bitter and the personnel were considered expendable. But the one consolation was that his Field Post Office address didn't reveal what had happened, so his parents believed he was simply transferred to another regular infantry regiment.

And thus it was that Pauli endured the worst of the fighting of that year, so that afterwards some men did not believe that he could be a veteran of so many infamous fields of battle. But he did not survive the year unharmed. Though his skin was intact, his soul was hardened—"as hard as Krupp steel," he sometimes claimed after a few drinks. He had learned to suffer without complaint, to hurt without whimpering, and to kill without emotion.

And yet, paradoxically, there were aspects of him that stayed unchanged. Outwardly he remained genial, careless, clumsy Pauli. He was too anxious to please ever to become really sophisticated. And now more than ever he relished the simple pleasures of life.

Unlike his brother, Peter—who was austere, cultivated, and brimful of ambition—Pauli served his sentence and went back to active duty asking no more than to sit down now and again to a big bowl of beef stew, smoke twenty cigarettes a day, and have an extra half-hour in bed on Sunday morning.

1918

"The war is won, isn't it?"

Leutnant Pauli Winter had never been in no-man's-land like this before. He'd never known it in the full foggy raw light of morning. Like all the other front-line infantry, he'd come here only at night, on patrols to mend the great jungle of rusty barbed wire, which was constantly damaged by shell and mortar fire, or to raid the enemy trenches. Always under cover of darkness.

Until now his world had consisted only of narrow trenches and dark dugouts. The sky, seasonally gray, azure, or black with rain clouds, had been only a narrow slot framed by the muddy edges of the trench parapet. No one in his right mind raised his head above the parapet to stare across at where the unseen English inhabited their own subterranean dominion.

It was impossible to remember all the stories he'd heard about no-man's-land. There were stories about fierce animals that were said to live out here, skulking in their warrens and emerging by night to feast on the dead and dying. And certainly some of the noises they'd all heard encouraged the belief. Other soldiers' stories said there were men living out here in this great churned-up rubbish tip. Deserters of all nationalities were said to have formed a community, a bandit gang, who lived deep in the ground, stole money, watches, and personal possessions from the bodies that littered the ground, and fed upon stores plundered from both sides of the line. It was all nonsense, of course, but hugging the ground out here, the barrage whistling overhead, the earth stinking of cordite, feces, and decomposing flesh, made such yarns seem only too likely.

But today was March 21, 1918, the start of the great attack that was going to break the British-held front line and end the war with a victory for the Kaiser. Pauli and two of his company—his runner and his youthful sergeant major—were crouched in a shell crater about a hundred meters in front of the German lines. The rest of his company were similarly hidden nearby, and so were other "storm companies" crouching unseen in no-man's-land all along the front line.

The three men had their hands clamped over the sides of their heads to protect their eardrums against the deafening roar of the German guns. The preparatory bombardment had been going on for nearly five hours. Now it was nine-forty, and the guns would stop, and in the pearly light Pauli would lead his men into the attack.

"Nothing could have lived through that," shouted Feldwebel Lothar Koch as the artillery fire lessened. Koch was young—he'd given a false age to get into the army—a pimply fellow with a square protruding jaw that moved as he chewed on a plug of tobacco. Partly due to the immense pride his promotion had given him, he was still optimistic about the outcome of the war. Deep down in his heart, young Koch entertained the hope of being commissioned, or at least becoming a noncommissioned deputy officer by the time he took part in the promised victory parade through conquered Paris. He looked at the other two men with his mournful eyes. They both stared back at him blankly. "Nothing could have lived through that," repeated Koch.

Pauli touched the silk stockings under his collar: black, a pair of them knotted to form a long scarf that wound around his neck five times. It prevented the collar of his uniform from chafing his neck, and also reminded him of a glorious few hours in Brussels with a girl he'd met in church! He looked at his pocket watch—wrist-watches did not survive in these conditions—and up at the heavy fog. Thank God for it. He dragged himself to his feet. His uniform was caked with mud; his canvas bag of stick grenades felt heavier than ever. "Bugler!" he shouted, and from a muddy hillock nearby the bugler slowly pushed up through a chrysalis of heavy mud. "Sound the advance."

On every side German "storm troops" emerged from the incredible collection of broken debris that littered the ground. They met

with the clattering sound of a British Lewis gun and some intermittent rifle fire from Tommies who had not been rendered useless by
the artillery's systematic destruction of the British front-line trenches. But the fog was too thick for the British to see what was
happening, and the fire that greeted their advance was aimed into
the white mist, so that only a few unlucky Germans screamed and
fell. Pauli heard calls for stretcherbearers and a bugle sounding the
advance.

"Is the company advancing?" Pauli asked the young Feldwebel.
There was mud in his mouth, and he spat it out and wiped his face
with a dirty lace handkerchief. Her handkerchief! Her name was
Monike. She spoke the Belgian sort of *Plattdeutsch* that he could
understand. A tall, slim, shy creature with wonderful green-gray
eyes, heart-shaped face, and all the mysterious promises of a first
love. She'd taken him home and given him chicken soup that her
mother had left on the stove for her. Thick chicken soup with beans
and carrots. He loved Monike. He thought of her every day. And
wrote her long letters, every one of which he carefully tore up.

"Yes, Herr Leutnant. The company is advancing." Koch could
see through the fog no better than his company commander, but
they both knew that the men would do as they were ordered. They
were Germans, and their readiness to obey instructions was a measure of their civilization, and their tragedy.

Pauli kept running over the uneven ground. With the swirling
white fog wrapped round him, he stumbled into potholes and
tripped over the roots of trees, sandbags, corpses, balks of ancient
timbers, and large sheets of corrugated iron that, together with
untold other stuff, littered this old battlefield. The intelligence reports said no-man's-land was two hundred meters wide at this place,
but now it seemed much wider.

Sergeant Major Koch, a thin, wiry figure, was just a few paces
ahead of him: hurrying as best he could, ungainly and uncertain
about the going. His machine gun was slung over his shoulder, and
in his hands he held a huge set of heavy-duty wire cutters. Bullets
zinged past, but the German bombardment was now no more than
a few desultory bangs and crashes far in the enemy's rear areas. How
soon before the British artillery and mortars began to lob their
explosives into no-man's-land? Surely they must have guessed that
the five-hour bombardment was a prelude to an infantry assault.
Or were the British pulling their howitzers and field artillery back

into safer, rear areas? Such defeatism was too much to hope for. Or was it?

Now Koch had started cutting through the wire. The artillery had done their job well: endless fields of wire—so carefully tended by the night patrols from both sides—were now a shambles. Koch found the weakest parts of this metallic thicket and cut a path just wide enough for the infantry to follow through. The wire sprang back with a loud noise like a peal of bells. At night such carelessness would have brought a burst of fire and almost certain death, but now speed was all that mattered. The stolid Koch, crouched low, went chopping his way through the undergrowth of rusty tendrils.

Behind Pauli the bugler was sounding "close up!"—the prearranged call to indicate the way through the defenses.

"Koch! Get back, damn you."

Once through the last of the wire, Pauli pushed ahead of his sergeant major. In the storm companies it was a matter of pride that the company commander led his men into battle. More bullets came now: closer, for they no longer zinged but cracked like a ringmaster's whip. Chest-high. Alongside him, two men bowed low to die, heads down, snorting and gurgling briefly as the blood flooded into their lungs. He ran on, stumbled, and touched the silk stockings—or, rather, made a gesture in the direction of his throat—Monike had said that she would be his good luck. It was a childish thing to say, for she was a child, and he believed it, because, for all his brutal experiences, he, too, was little more than a child. She hadn't given him the stockings, of course. She was not that sort of girl. He'd taken them from the laundry basket in her bedroom.

More firing of rifles and machine guns. Over to the left—and very close—there came the sound of a heavy Vickers gun, stertorous, like a wheezing generator. But it was too late now to worry about bullets. Pauli found himself on the brink—the parapet—of the foremost enemy trenchline. He jumped. It was almost three meters deep. Burdened as he was with bombs and machine pistol, his weight took him right through the damp duckboards that formed the floor of the trench. The rotten wood snapped with a loud noise, and Pauli went deep into mud, so that he had to bend and extricate his boots from the broken slats. Thank God this section of the trench was unmanned.

He ran along the trench, splashing his way through the stagnant, watery mud. God! Did the British stand in this shit night and day?

He came to a surprised-looking British soldier. Pauli pulled the trigger of his pistol and the youngster was punched backwards by the force of the bullets. He sank down without any change in the expression upon his pinched, pale face.

Pauli ran on, along the communications trench and then to a junction with the support trench. Here the conditions were even worse: he was ankle-deep in stinking mud. The trenches were unmanned here. Had the British gone over the top to face the attackers, or fled? A sign marked the rear trench "Pall Mall," and there were other painted wooden signs pointing the way to Company HQ and a field dressing post.

The trench lines zigzagged to minimize the effects of blast. At the next turn, half a dozen khaki-clad soldiers were bunched in the corner at the entrance to a dugout. They were wide-eyed with fear. Two of them were sitting on the fire step, hugging themselves. Their uniforms were blackened with rain, and the heavy wet cloth hung on them like a dead weight. Pauli swung aside. From behind him Koch fired a burst from his MP-18, and the brown-coated soldiers stiffened and grew taller before toppling full-length like lead toys.

As they ran forward again, a British officer put his head out of his dugout immediately ahead of them and shouted loudly. He was a middle-aged fellow with a neat mustache. He looked not unlike Pauli's father.

Pauli stopped, undecided what to do, but Koch hit the officer with the butt of his gun and then threw two stick grenades down through the dark entrance and raced on. There was a tremendous bang and muffled screaming. Pauli looked back. He saw the British officer as the blast caught him. The wretched man was blown to pieces in a pink cloud of blood. The mangled body, its khaki sleeve and insignia intact, hit the sides of the trench. Round the upper part of the arm was a mud-stained white armband with a red cross on it. The dugout was of course a temporary casualty station. Too late now.

Ahead of them the sound of firing and, emerging from the white fog, more men. *"Wer da?"* He climbed up one of the trench ladders and ran along the edge of the parapet.

"Don't shoot! Don't shoot!" They were Germans from the next company. *"Wer da?"* More challenges as gray-uniformed men appeared like wraiths in the dispersing fog. Pauli recognized the faces of some of them. The bugler sounded the close-up signal again. Pauli saw their officer, a captain named Graf, a thin, irritable man with a red nose, his heavy steel helmet grotesquely large for his small ferret face.

"Keep going, Winter. We've got them on the run."

"*Ja*, Herr Hauptmann." He turned and shouted to the rest of his men to hurry. The Punishment Battalion had changed Pauli. At one time he would have been terrified by a man like Hauptmann Graf. Now it took a great deal more to frighten him.

There was a loud roar behind him, and the narrow trench was suddenly lit by a brilliant orange glow. Pauli turned to see the great balloons of ignited fuel ripping a hole through the white fog. The flame throwers were systematically burning out the dugouts all along the support trench. Poor devils—even a bayonet in the guts is better than that.

They hurried on; the earth was firmer behind the support trenches and the fog much thinned. Crossing the sunken road that the British had used for their supplies and reinforcements, the Germans chased across the open ground. No one was firing at them now. To the left was a forest of tree stumps, the trunks short, broken, and bared white like pencil stubs. To the front of them the ruins of a village, with only waist-high walls remaining. The church had been devoured by the war: its relics and valuables stolen, its doors and pews chopped into firewood, the roof collapsed, its lead improvised into drains for waterlogged trenchlines, and its tower reduced to rubble by artillery fire to deprive the British of an observation post.

Behind the village were twenty or thirty brown-clad soldiers, British service troops without rifles, an officer wearing the badges of the Royal Engineers, and two men carrying wooden crates. At the first sign of the Germans, they raised their hands in the air. The Germans, in too much of a hurry even to rob them, pointed back the way they'd come. Reluctantly the British shambled off to the east, walking slowly, in the hope that a counterattack would free them before they got to the German rear.

In the ruined village was a mobile bath unit. It had been abandoned hastily by men who'd left behind parts of their uniforms, towels, webbing, and even a rack of Lee-Enfield rifles. But even the sight of clean hot water and the wonderful fragrance of disinfectant and soap did not halt the advancing Germans.

They pressed on. Pauli was fit and strong, but the pace was wearing. He sniffed the air. Was it gas? And if so what type? Not mustard gas anyway. That was the one most to be feared, but the plan of attack said that the artillery would only put mustard into British rear areas, into which the Germans would not advance. So it couldn't be mustard. Could it? He stopped and bent down to prod loose a clod of earth and sniff at it. Foolhardy, but it was what was expected of men in the storm companies. He started running again and swung his gas mask round to the front of his belt as he ran. Soon they slowed: the pace was too demanding even for young, fit bodies, and there was no sign of the enemy.

Walking now. The girl came back to his mind. The house was empty, she said, her parents visiting her grandmother. They'd kissed and ended up in bed. First time for Pauli and first time for the girl. What a fiasco. All his sexual fantasies shattered by two minutes in bed. The girl had cried. I'm still a virgin, she'd said. Then, her mood changing, she'd laughed. Well, it wasn't funny for him. He'd fled from the house with only the stockings around which to weave stories for his fellow soldiers. But by the time he'd got back to his company, he had no wish to mention her to anyone. There was no one to whom he could confide his story. He was in love; he wanted her too much to talk about her. What a fool he'd been. If only he'd let the relationship develop at its own pace. Then perhaps he wouldn't have got the letter telling him that she never wanted to see him again. He blamed himself unceasingly: a girl you meet in church doesn't expect to be treated like a whore.

Twice they were halted by pockets of determined resistance: fierce Scots veterans whose rapid, accurate rifle fire caused severe casualties among the by-now careless Germans. Soon the regiment's trench-mortar units arrived, and after a relentless pounding the Scotsmen came out, calling, "Kamerad!"

By this time it was late afternoon, and already the wintry daylight was beginning to go. They moved on again. They were all more cautious now, and tired. On the left, the bugler for the next company was sounding rally. Pauli stopped and his bugler did the same. Time for re-forming, and a moment for the fleet of foot to recover their breath and the slower men to catch up.

A runner from Battalion Headquarters told him to consolidate his position and take possession of a British twelve-inch howitzer battery several hundred meters to the west. They found it without trouble. Hauptmann Graf was already there. His men were energetically plundering the enemy stores.

The captured battery was a revelation to the German storm troops. The Germans were trying on the superb sheepskin coats that the British supplied to their sentries, and there were many who wanted one of the fine leather jerkins. More than one fellow was striding around in British officers' hand-sewn leather boots. In the officers' mess were all manner of forgotten luxuries, including Stilton cheese, smoked salmon, and a dozen unopened cases of Scotch whisky.

Pauli looked around with interest and apprehension. These were specially selected and well-trained soldiers. Given the order, they'd abandon their booty and continue the advance. But what of the ordinary German conscripts behind them? What would they be doing tonight?

Pauli decided that such conundrums were best left to the generals. He went to report to Captain Graf. "It's disgraceful," said Graf. He took off his heavy helmet. He was a jug-eared little man, gnomelike: a homosexual, it was whispered. But, homosexual or not, Graf was a fearless soldier, respected by every man in the regiment. "Shells were ready and fused. I blame the officers. No attempt to disable the guns: dial sights in position, breech blocks in full working order. It's disgraceful."

"Yes," said Pauli, amused that Graf should be so indignant about the enemy's lack of soldierly dedication.

"Cowards."

"We must have come five kilometers," said Pauli. "There's never been a breakthrough like this before."

Captain Graf grunted. He was smoking and holding in his hand a gold-colored tin of fifty English cigarettes. "Try one," he said and offered the open tin.

Pauli lit one up and, after breathing out the smoke, said, "If the advance has been the same all along the battlefront, we must have captured a huge piece of ground."

"Like them?" said Graf. "English cigarettes: damned good."

"Yes," said Pauli. He'd never smoked anything so delicious. He studied the pale tobacco appreciatively and decided that if he ever became rich enough he'd smoke such cigarettes all the time. In the sandbagged shelter behind Graf, one of the men had found a gramophone and was winding it up. "Do you think we'll go all the way to the coast, Herr Hauptmann?"

"The coast?"

"The war is won, isn't it?"

"Look at those stores, Winter," said Captain Graf, turning to look at the German soldiers gobbling the captured food. "Last week I severely punished four of my men who'd ground up horse fodder to make flour. They said they were hungry. They were, of course. We are all hungry. We ration out the shells to our artillery. We don't have enough rubber to make more gas masks." He blew smoke. "Have you seen what's in that mess hut, Winter? Food for the rank and file. Tinned beef, plum jam, good white bread, that yellow English cheese. Did you see how much of it there is? They told us the English were starving, didn't they?" He sniffed. "No, the war is lost, Winter. The courage of our young men and our meager supplies of shells and bullets can't prevail against this sort of plenty."

"The war is lost?" said Pauli. Captain Graf was a tough regular officer from a good regiment, not the sort of fellow who was easily discouraged.

"The war is lost," said Graf. "No matter how much ground we occupy, we cannot win." The gramophone started playing "Poor Butterfly." For a moment the two officers listened to it. "Get your casualty returns sorted out. The infantry will be close behind us. They'll pull the storm companies back later tonight, or before first light in the morning."

Pauli looked to where Koch and other men of his company were sitting on the ground, too exhausted even to join in the plundering. How could the war be lost? It wasn't fair; it just wasn't fair.

"The damned war's not *over."*

"I wish to God that you'd stop saying the war's over," Peter told his father. He was propped up on an armchair in the drawing room of his parents' house in Berlin. His dark-blue naval officer's tunic was resewn where it had been ripped, and the gold was missing from one sleeve of it. His left leg was in splints and his face badly bruised. "The damned war's *not* over and perhaps never will be."

"They signed the armistice nearly two months ago," said his father gently. His son was in pain and frustrated by his immobility.

167

"The British navy is still blockading us. Our people are starving. The warships of the High Seas Fleet have red flags flying from their mastheads. There are bands of armed ruffians in the streets shooting at each other. That traitor Liebknecht has been carried shoulder-high through the streets by soldiers wearing the Iron Cross—and has made a speech from the balcony of the Royal Palace. The army has disintegrated. The Kaiser has run away to Holland. How can we negotiate a peace treaty? We have nothing to bargain with." It was a cry of pain. The defeat seemed to have affected Peter more deeply than any of the rest of the Winter family. Attacked in the street by a group of Spartacists, he'd been knocked to his knees by clubs and rifle butts. There is little doubt that this drunken, vicious little mob would have killed him, but for another mob that came along and started a brawl, during which Peter escaped. Since then he'd been confined to the house and had done nothing but stare out the window and brood on the consequences of the chaos in the streets below.

Pauli Winter got up from the armchair. He was wearing the better of his two army uniforms. It was far from the elegant costumes in which Prussia had sent officers to war. Its motley stains had not been removed by scrubbing and cleaning, and its shape had not been improved by regular baking in the delousing ovens. The fine leather boots he'd gone to war wearing were long since lost, and he wore simple boots and gray puttees like the ones worn by the storm troops. "I must get back to Battalion Headquarters," said Pauli. "I'll see you tomorrow, Peter." He was in fact on a twenty-four-hour pass, but Pauli found that a couple of hours in the gloomy house near Ku-damm was all he could endure. He'd bought a few cheap presents from a department store in Leipziger Strasse, and now he placed them carefully under the Christmas tree in the corner. One of the servants had found a few logs, and today, with Christmas so near, a fire was burning in the stove. On the sideboard he noticed that all the family photos were arrayed, their silver frames gleaming. There they were in 1913, the happiest of happy families: two smiling children and Mama and Papa standing proudly behind them. How long ago it seemed. The family had changed dramatically since then. Now—with riots in the streets and Bolsheviks occupying Winter's factories—even a log on the fire was a treat to be relished. Harald Winter was stunned by the sudden change in his fortunes, and Peter had become a crusty invalid. Now it was Mama who held them all together, ventured onto the streets, coaxed food from the shop-keepers, and persuaded the servants to keep working.

"Battalion Headquarters! With that ridiculous little Captain Graf in command," said Peter scornfully. "You still go on pretending, do you? Your Freikorps battalions are just a lot of uniformed gangsters, and Graf is no more than a brigand."

"That's not true," said Pauli. It was because they were so close that Peter knew where to put the knife. "The Freikorps is a fine organization, and the army fully approves. There are thousands of us: disciplined and armed. And not just in Berlin—they are being formed all over Germany. Every one of our soldiers is a volunteer signed on month by month. In the East they will be defending our borders now that the army are withdrawing. The Poles, and the rest of them, would have been looting Berlin by now if it wasn't for the Freikorps units out there."

"Then why don't you march eastwards?" said Peter.

"Because, like you, we are temporarily immobilized. When the transport and our orders arrive, perhaps we'll go." Pauli's tone was mild, not just because he remembered the good times they'd shared, but because he was frightened that Peter might thoughtlessly blurt out something about the court-martial and Pauli's assignment to a Punishment Battalion. He'd do almost anything to prevent his parents from finding out about that.

"An under-strength battalion commanded by a captain?" said Peter sarcastically. "Four machine guns, an antique tank, and two armored cars? What sort of battalion is that?"

"The next time the Reds try to take over Berlin, you'll see," said Pauli. He put on his field-gray overcoat and steel helmet and tightened the strap under his chin before reaching for his belt and pistol.

"What's that crooked cross sign you've painted on your helmet?" his father asked.

"It's called a swastika. Many of the Freikorps units wear it to distinguish us from the regular army."

"Be very careful, Pauli. Remember what happened to your brother."

Pauli did remember. Peter had been beaten up just because of the "imperial insignia" on his officer's uniform. Many army and navy officers had been similarly beaten—and several murdered—by jeering and catcalling thugs who were determined to blame the officer class for the war and its outcome.

"I wear a private's greatcoat and no badges," said Pauli.

"But you have an officer's sidearm," said his father.

"And I'll use it, too," said Pauli. "I'd be grateful for a chance to pick off a few of the bastards who tried to kill Peter."

"Don't say goodbye to your mother: she'll only worry until you telephone."

"I'll telephone if I can, but the telephone lines are sometimes cut."

"Take care of yourself, Pauli," said his father. "Those mutinous swine are holding the Chancellor to ransom. . . . My God, who could have guessed it would come to this? The Chancellor held prisoner by Marxist hooligans." They embraced, and as he grasped him in his arms Pauli was struck by the slight, frail frame of his father. Although not yet fifty years old, Winter had grown old and tired and apprehensive. Perhaps it was only temporary, but it was a sad transformation in a man the boys remembered as always dynamic and rather frightening.

Harald Winter regarded his son with equal sorrow. The war had made Pauli into a ruffian. He was brusque and dismissive of all the values that Harald Winter revered. This new Pauli who'd come back from the war was someone his father found difficult to cope with. As much as he'd disliked the dependence that Pauli had demonstrated as a child, he preferred that to the new rough-spoken man he'd become. In other words, like many fathers, Harald Winter hated to see that his son had grown up.

Pauli took the S-Bahn to Alexanderplatz. The trains were running normally, but as Pauli walked towards the palace he kept a wary eye open for marauding bands of troublemakers. He saw a small procession of factory workers—women, too—going over the *Schlossbrücke.* They were not armed, but they carried red banners and chanted slogans, so he remained in the shadows until they passed. It was as well to be cautious. Schinkel's beautiful little guardroom—designed like a Greek temple—was brightly lit and he could see soldiers inside, some of them huddled in blankets on the stone floor. Were they loyal soldiers assigned to duty by the High Command, or Bolshevik renegades? There was no way to know. He hurried past.

The Royal Palace, or what was usually called just the Schloss, was lit only by light from the cathedral across the road, but against the darkening sky he could see the red blanket that mutinous sailors had hoisted up. The palace had had no official residents ever since the Kaiser abdicated and ran away to Holland. It was at present the home of about three thousand bellicose revolutionary sailors of the self-styled "People's Naval Division," who were now holding the head of government for ransom.

Pauli kept walking along Unter den Linden. The streetcleaners were not in evidence, and in places Pauli had to clamber over piles of snow. Only the streetcar tracks had been systematically cleared of it. Despite the occasional sounds of rifle fire—and sometimes even the explosion of a grenade—the shops were open, and some taxicabs, buses, and streetcars were still running. But the shortage of fuel meant that there were more horses: ancient *Droschken* with half-starved animals plodded through the snow. There were a few shoppers hurrying home past street peddlers selling crudely made paper Christmas decorations and hot chestnuts.

Pauli crossed the road to avoid the crowd milling around the gates of the Russian Embassy. Since April 1918 the Imperial Russian Embassy had been called the Soviet Embassy. At the 1918 party conference, Lenin had told the delegates that ". . . we shall go under without the German revolution." And in response the new staff, of no fewer than three hundred people, had been frantically circulating Bolshevik agitators, ready cash, and crateloads of revolutionary literature throughout Germany. The new ambassador—a wealthy Jewish philanthropist from the Crimea—had had hoisted across the embassy's façade a huge red banner that urged, "Workers of all countries, unite!" Soon afterwards he'd been deported back to Russia, but the banner remained.

Guarding the Interior Ministry were three men with rifles slung over their shoulders. Round the corner was a truck with more armed men; their shabby, makeshift uniforms and red armbands identified them as members of an irregular band recruited by the new police chief—Emil Eichhorn—a radical of the extreme left. On the corner of Wilhelmstrasse were some women, one of them weeping uncontrollably. They were on their way back from Dorotheen Strasse, where the army's casualty lists were still being displayed, with new names every day. The fighting had ended, but corpses were still being identified. Pauli walked past them and crossed back across the road to the Adlon Hotel.

He checked his helmet, overcoat, and pistol belt at the cloakroom. The elderly attendant showed no surprise. He placed the gun and helmet on a shelf with silk hats and gave Pauli a small yellow ticket. Pauli went into the bar. There was a crowd in here, but the heating was not working, and some customers had their overcoats on. He had arranged to meet Alex Horner here and, true to form, Alex was sitting near the door with a bottle of wine in an ice bucket at his elbow. An extra glass was in place. From the dining room next door came the high-spirited music of a gypsy band.

"How goes the army command?" said Pauli. He sat down and waited for the waiter to pour his wine.

"Excellent!" said Alex. "And how are things at home?" Alex was not in uniform. He was wearing a smart new gray flannel suit, white shirt, and dark tie, but no one in the bar—or in Berlin, for that matter—could possibly have mistaken him for anything but a Prussian of the Officer Corps.

"Peter is still moaning. Papa won't leave the house and says it's on account of the influenza epidemic. Mama has become something of a tyrant, but she still manages to serve meat, even for lunch: sauerbraten today. I had two helpings."

"Your mother is a woman of infinite resource," said Alex.

Alex had secured an excellent job—or, rather, his influential relative in the War Department had secured it for him. After the failure of the big German offensive of 1918, he was sent to Supreme Headquarters in Spa, Belgium, and appointed an aide to the military governor of Berlin.

The present military governor was a rather disreputable civilian, but that didn't prevent Alex from lording it over his old friend, for there was a great difference between duties on behalf of the headquarters of the Imperial German Army and being with the Freikorps, an *ad hoc* assembly of enthusiastic volunteers consisting almost entirely of men the army had no place for.

Alex liked to give his friend insightful anecdotes about life among the generals. For a few minutes Alex entertained him with stories about the new commander of the German Army. "General Groener is a good sort," said Alex. "He's highly intelligent and not at all stuffy."

"He's a Schwab," said Pauli before sipping some wine. "Get rid of all these damned Prussians, I say." It was a Riesling from Alsace, just cold enough, and it tasted delicious. Goodness knows when he'd taste its like again: under the terms of the armistice, Alsace was now a part of France once more.

Alex grinned. Although Pauli was born in Vienna to an American mother, his upbringing was hardly less Prussian than his friend's, but there was a running joke that Alex was a Prussian of the most inflexible old-fashioned kind and Pauli was the oppressed Southerner. The friendship between the two boys was based on a long time together and mutual respect. And yet, right from the time they'd first met at Lichterfelde, Pauli was the admirer and Alex, by common consent, was granted an edge of seniority. The admiration that Pauli had always shown for his elder brother, Peter, was reflected in his respect for Alex. And, typically, Alex responded to this faith that Pauli showed by revealing to him his most treasured secret. Alex said, "Although the Chancellor is being held prisoner in his office, there's a secret telephone line from the Chancellery to the army. Chancellor Ebert has asked the army for help."

"Good God!" said Pauli. Everyone believed that the mutinying sailors had cut all the lines from the Chancellery and that Ebert—the new socialist head of government—was being held incommunicado.

"That's just between the two of us," said Alex. "It's a closely guarded secret, not to be passed on even to your father."

"Just as you say, Alex. But it changes things, doesn't it?"

"Yes, and the army will do what has to be done," said Alex enigmatically. "Those mutinous pigs will find out what it means tomorrow."

"Christmas Eve?" said Pauli. "Why?"

"Are you in a hurry?" said Alex languidly.

"I've got all the time you need," said Pauli, sipping some more wine and leaning forward to hear what Alex had to tell.

"It all began on November 9," said Alex.

"Everything did," said Pauli.

That much was true: everything began on November 9, 1918. The army's commanders—too arrogant to face the consequences of their own defeat—had sent some unfortunate civilians through the wire of no-man's-land to seek an armistice from the Allies, as the Turks and Austrians had already done. During that Saturday, the Imperial German Army ceased to exist as a unified fighting force. Red flags were flying all over the land as soldiers' committees took control. Alex Horner, on one of his regular visits to Supreme

Headquarters from Berlin, was shown the reports. It was amazing: the army's command structure collapsed like a deck of cards. "Riots in Magdeburg"; then, early in the afternoon, "7th Army Corps Reserve District rioting threatened." Halle and Leipzig were declared "Red" by 5:00 p.m., and soon afterwards Düsseldorf, Halstein, Osnabrück, and Lauenburg went, too. So did Magdeburg, Stuttgart, Oldenburg, Brunswick, and Cologne. By this time the soldiers at Supreme HQ had stopped saluting the officers, and some of the offices were deserted. At 1900 hours, news came that the general officer commanding 18th Army Corps Reserve at Frankfurt was "deposed." It was all over. By early evening Kaiser Wilhelm, Emperor of Germany and "All-highest Warlord," was sitting in the dining car of his private train, waiting for it to leave the siding and start the journey that would take him to exile in Holland.

In Berlin the socialist Cabinet, which had been created without any legal transfer of power, could not contain the disorder. They ordered the army to rip up sections of railway line and so interrupt the trainloads of mutinous soldiers and sailors that were arriving in the capital in ever-increasing numbers. When Alex arrived at the Lehrter station, in a train that had taken two and a half days to reach Berlin from Belgium, he was startled to see that army machine-gun teams commanded a field of fire along every platform and the main concourse. Troops were occupying the gas and electricity works, the government buildings on Wilhelmstrasse were all guarded, and there were even armed soldiers outside some of the town's finest restaurants.

By the time that Leutnant Horner reported to Berlin's military governor, that governor was a socialist civilian named Otto Wels. The Imperial Army's Berlin garrison having deserted—and having no more than a handful of civil policemen at his disposal—Wels had put together a force of ex-soldiers and armed civilians. Most of the rifles had been bought from the deserters who, standing alongside the flower girls, were doing a brisk trade at the Potsdamer Platz at two marks per gun. Even the "army's" trucks had been purchased in this way from the deserters. Wels had given his scratch force the grandiose title of Republikanische Soldaten—the Republican Soldiers' Army—but they were a motley collection difficult to distinguish from the extreme left Sicherheitswehr that the Police President employed, or from any of the other armed mobs who patrolled the city looking for victims and plunder. Moreover, Wels's army was infiltrated by many Spartacists and the extreme-left "Independents."

It needed only one visit to the military governor's office to convince Alex Horner that his officer's uniform was not suitable attire. He bought a suit in a tailor's shop in Friedrichstrasse—the first ready-made suit he'd ever worn—and went back to work feeling less uneasy. But he did notice the way that the carefully positioned beggars watched him as he arrived. There were few beggars to be seen on the streets in these early days of the revolution. Most of the uniformed ex-servicemen who stood outside the department stores and food shops hoping for money still had enough dignity to be offering a tray of bootlaces, matches, or candles. Yet these fellows made no pretense of being pedlars, and Alex was convinced that they were spies. Police spies, Bolsheviks, Spartacists, and foreigners, too: the city was alive with spies of all shapes and sizes, and of every political color. Berlin had always been a city of spies and informers, and it probably always would be.

Berlin's most serious problem was created by the naval mutineers who'd arrived from the Northern naval bases and settled themselves into the Imperial Palace. The fiasco of this People's Naval Division turned sour when the sailors became more menacing and demanded their "Christmas bonus." The sailors had been under the influence of Karl Liebknecht ever since occupying the Imperial Palace. And it was Liebknecht's declared intent to bring down the moderate socialist government of Friedrich Ebert—a forty-seven-year-old ex–saddle maker—by anarchy and confusion. Having the sailors demand ever more money was very much to Liebknecht's taste. If Ebert was frightened by the extortion and paid out the money, the government would demonstrate their weakness. If they moved against the sailors, it would be a sign that they were the sort of treacherous, reactionary, anti–working-class government that Liebknecht said they were. Either way it would make things easier for Liebknecht to seize power and set up his Leninist regime.

It was December 20 when the sailors announced that they'd spent the first 125,000 marks the government had paid them for "guarding" the Imperial Palace. Now they wanted more money.

Alex Horner was in the anteroom of the Chancellor's private office when Otto Wels came out with Ebert. It was the first time Alex had seen the Chancellor at such close quarters. He was an imposing figure, broad and muscular, with jet-black hair and a large mustache and small beard. The government had agreed to pay more money, but first the palace must be evacuated and the People's Naval Division reduced to six hundred men. The money would be paid only after the keys of the emptied palace had been given to Otto Wels.

On the morning of the day on which Alex and Pauli met, Alex had hurried down to the lobby of the Chancellery in response to a phone call from one of the secretaries. A delegation of sailors were being taken to one of the drawing rooms that were situated to the side of the fine Empire vestibule. One sailor was carrying a leather case that he said held the keys of the Imperial Palace. They wanted their money.

"Herr Horner is one of the military governor's assistants," said the secretary who was dealing with the sailors. He was a sniffy little man with the curt and superior manner that distinguishes career bureaucrats.

The spokesman for the sailors, a tall petty officer with crooked teeth, asked for Alex Horner's identity papers. Luckily Wels had arranged such formalities as soon as the young officer got back to the revolution-stricken city. Taken to a Reichstag office by an attendant wearing the livery of the old regime, he'd been given a pass by a woman clerk wearing a red armband. It was an inexpertly printed card on stiff red paper. It said that Horner was "authorized to maintain order and security in the streets of the city." Accompanying it was an identity card issued by the "Workers' and Soldiers' Council" saying he was "trustworthy and free to pass." Neither document mentioned his military rank, and if the woman issuing the papers to him knew him to be an army officer she gave no sign of it. From the way she handled the office files, it looked as if she was occupying the same desk as she had before the revolution. Most of the workers were doing the same thing that they'd done during the Kaiserzeit without the red bands and banners. For the Berliner, life was simply a matter of exchanging time for money and money for food. Even during the shooting, the buses ran on time and the water and electricity supply continued normally.

Having scrutinized Horner's papers, the petty officer showed him *his* card in return. "Petty Officer Esser." How curious that so many of these revolutionary servicemen clung so tightly to the badges and titles and privileges of the old regime.

Esser politely but firmly explained to Horner and the secretary that the political committee of the People's Naval Division had decided that they'd not deal with Otto Wels, who, although a social-ist, was "a class enemy."

"Then give the keys to Herr Barth," suggested Alex. He was grateful that the secretary had not revealed the fact that he was an army officer.

"Herr Barth is in a meeting and cannot be disturbed." The secretary expected them to hand the keys to him and depart with-out further delay. Despite wearing a small red ribbon in his buttonhole—a sartorial accessory that had been adopted by many middle-class office workers during the previous few days—the man did not hide his impatience and his distaste for the unwashed revolutionaries.

"Then get him out of the meeting," suggested Alex.

The secretary shook his head to show that there could be no question of interrupting the commissioner. Emil Barth was amongst the most radical of the commissioners, but these wretched socialists had quickly adapted to the bureaucracy of Wilhelmstrasse: meet-ings, meetings, meetings. And the bureaucrats had easily adapted to their new masters.

"That would be impossible," said the secretary. He was an el-derly man with rimless spectacles, bushy eyebrows, and a celluloid collar that was going yellow at the edges, like the documents that were to be seen on every side.

"Try," suggested Alex, and the sailors vociferously agreed.

Now there were more arguments and some telephone calls. Ev-eryone who might have placated the sailors had gone to lunch, and the revolutionaries were becoming angrier every minute.

Before the problem was resolved, a messenger came rushing into the lobby with an urgent request for Alex Horner. He must go immediately to the office of Herr Otto Wels. Wels had been kid-napped.

It was not difficult to discover what had happened. Wels's staff were standing in the corridor talking in loud voices. Some of the women were sobbing. They told how another group of sailors had entered the building by a side door, found their way upstairs, and demanded the Christmas-bonus money from Wels. Wels was heard to say they'd get no money until he had the key.

Which of the sailors was the first to strike Wels makes no differ-ence, for soon he was beaten and frog-marched back to the Imperial Palace, which the sailors obviously had no intention of leaving.

According to a message that Alex received later that day from a paid informer, Wels was beaten with rifle butts and thrown into a rat-infested cellar.

That afternoon a large party of the sailors went back to the Chancellery. They were in a bitter frame of mind. They pushed their way into the lobby, posted armed guards at every exit, and took control of the Chancellery telephone exchange. No one—not even the Chancellor—would be permitted to enter or leave the building. They had Wels as a hostage and they wanted their money.

Pauli had listened to Alex Horner's long story with intermittent attention. He'd studied the other people in the bar, with particular interest in the younger women. He'd had so little free time since the war began—so little time amongst civilians—that he'd still not got accustomed to the shorter skirts and the display of female ankles. Women had worn full-length skirts since ancient Greece; surely there was something apocalyptic about the new fashion. If not apocalyptic, certainly provocative, especially when some of the younger ones wore these flesh-colored stockings!

Between them they'd finished one bottle of wine and were nearly at the bottom of a second one. Now Pauli realized that Alex had reached a stage in his story when some contribution from Pauli was expected. "What did you mean about the sailors' finding out something tomorrow?"

Alex glanced back over his shoulder to be sure he wasn't overheard. Next door the gypsy band was playing sad Hungarian ballads. "The Chancellor used the secret telephone link to summon help from the army. Groener is sending troops. We'll crush those Red swine once and for all."

"Sending them here? To the Imperial Palace?"

"The government is a prisoner, Pauli. They are being held hostage by those people. Groener has ordered several squadrons of the Imperial Horse Guards from the Potsdam barracks to march. They'll be here by midnight."

"Will the troops fire on the sailors?"

"The Imperial Horse Guards have remained loyal to their officers. There are a few other reliable men coming. Artillery, too. They'll blast their way into the palace."

"The sailors won't stand much chance against artillery."

"The damned war's *not* over."

"They've brought it on themselves. I've no sympathy for those gangsters."

"That fellow Esser you mentioned. I know him."

"The petty officer?" Alex's blasé mask dropped and he registered surprise. "How the devil did you come to know a fellow like that? From the Punishment Battalion?"

Pauli laughed. "No, the real rogues don't end up in the Punishment Battalions, Alex. The real ones end up as generals. We both know that."

Such remarks made Alex nervous. He looked round again to make sure they weren't overheard; even so he disassociated himself from such sentiments. "I'm not sure about that, Pauli," he mumbled.

"I'd like to try and get Esser out of there," said Pauli.

"Get him out?"

"He's a good sort."

"There are no 'good sorts' there, Pauli. They are all scum."

"I can't leave him to be killed," said Pauli. "He was my friend. He's the son of a villager from where my grandparents lived."

"It's too dangerous," said Alex.

"Don't be a fool," said Pauli. "No one's going to harm me simply for going along to the palace to have a word with Esser."

"You're in uniform."

"A private's uniform."

"These people are mutineers, Pauli. One look at you and they'll know you're a member of the Officer Corps. And the Freikorps is the avowed enemy of the revolution."

"I'll have to go. Was it midnight you said the soldiers will arrive?"

"On your honor, you mustn't warn them," said Alex.

Pauli smiled. "You must be joking, Alex. No secrets remain secret in this town for more than half an hour."

"Then I shall come with you. Perhaps I can persuade them to release Wels."

"That would be a feather in your cap, Alex."

Alex nodded seriously and swigged the last of his Riesling. "The more I come to think of it, the more amusing it sounds. Let's go, Pauli."

It was only a short walk down Unter den Linden from the Hotel Adlon to the Imperial Palace. As they came out of the hotel, the street was illuminated by the lights of the British Embassy. The Armistice Commission were said to be using it, but there was no sign of British soldiers there. From the far side of the Pariser Platz, close to the Brandenburg Gate, they heard a brass band playing energetically: a Christmas carol. It sounded like a military band, but there was no way to be sure. Beyond the gate, the Tiergarten was being used as a military camp, but no one knew the allegiance of the soldiers. Probably the men were just remaining close to the army soup kitchens that had been set up there. Half a meter of snow had fallen upon Berlin, and the sounds of the city were muffled under the white blanket, so that even the music of the band was distant and muted. They plodded on, icy impacted snow under their feet.

"You've changed, Pauli. You've changed a lot."

"We've grown older," said Pauli, dismissing the idea. His father was always talking about the way Pauli had changed. Hadn't Peter changed? Hadn't Mama changed? And hadn't Harald Winter changed most of all?

"It's more complicated than that," persisted Alex. "Was it the Punishment Battalion?" They'd been together many times since Pauli had served his sentence, but until now the Punishment Battalion had been a taboo subject.

"Changed in what way?"

"You're tougher, more determined. In the old days you wouldn't have come looking for trouble. You'd have let a fellow such as Esser fend for himself."

"The Punishment Battalion was nothing. It was a relief to get away from that pig Brand. Sometimes I pitied you for still having to endure the brute."

"But they sent you into all the hardest fighting."

"It wasn't so bad. It made a man of me. I learned how to survive—survive when all the odds were against survival, survive when all around me were dying."

"And after that you went to serve in a *Sturmbataillon*. Tell me about that. Was it like the Punishment Battalion?"

"It was like nothing you've ever seen. With more such units we would have won, Alex."

"It wasn't the lack of storm battalions, Pauli. It was these damned civilians who stabbed us in the back. As an officer I remain loyal to the government, but it's hard to forget that these politicians we take orders from are the cowards and socialists who railed against the army all through the war. . . ." He stopped; even now his officer training inhibited him against such outbursts. "But tell me about the storm battalion."

"No rifles: carbines, and lightweight machine pistols, and small flame throwers. Everything was designed for lightness and fast movement. Even the other ranks got pistols. Special uniforms, leather pads on elbows and knees. No cartridge pouches—we stuffed rounds into our pockets. Round our necks we carried bags of grenades. We were unstoppable . . . and ruthless."

"They took you as a Stosstruppführer."

"They didn't care that I'd been in a Punishment Battalion, if that's what you mean. Yes, they made me a Stosstruppführer. There were plenty of vacancies: officers always had to lead their men into the attack. Only young, unmarried men were accepted, and the physical was the strictest I've ever had."

"I envy you the experience, Pauli. The storm battalions have become a legend. But you were lucky to survive."

"You mustn't believe *all* the stories you hear, Alex. Storm troops were kept in the rear until they were needed for some special task; even then they took us most of the way by truck. And we had lots of leave, and the food was always the very best available."

"You sound nostalgic, Pauli."

"Let me explain something to you, Alex. You grew up wanting to be an army officer. But I never wanted to go to cadet school. It was my father's idea. I loved my father—I still do—but my father has no respect for me; he thinks I'm brainless, and he doesn't care about anything except brains, especially the sort of brains that know how to make money. My elder brother doesn't give a damn about Father, but he's the one my father loves. I realized that I didn't have the brains that my brother, Peter, has, so I went to the cadet school the way Papa wanted. Now soldiering is the only trade I know."

"Well, now the workers' and soldiers' committees are taking over all your father's factories, it's ended up making little difference to you."

"Papa will find a way; he always does."

"But you seemed happy enough at Lichterfelde."

"Yes, I came to like it. I've always been adaptable: younger brothers have to adapt to what everyone else wants. And I liked the respect that an officer's uniform got for me. Do you remember, Alex? Members of the Officer Corps were gods. I loved all that, Alex, the bowing and scraping that I got from civilians. I loved being saluted, and the way that people stood aside to let me pass in the street and let me be served first in shops."

"I suppose we all did. And yet here we are: me skulking in civilian clothes and you masquerading as a private soldier." Pauli looked at his friend. Alex was wearing a gray bowler hat and an old-fashioned Inverness—a loose-fitting gray overcoat with attached shoulder cape. It wasn't a particularly odd costume amid the curiously garbed people to be seen on the city's streets, but it was hardly appropriate for a Prussian officer.

Pauli nodded. "And I even loved the Kaiser. I loved the idea that someone knew what was best for Germany and what was best for the army and the Officer Corps and what was best for me. And when the war went on and all sorts of riffraff like Brand managed to get commissions, I still didn't care, because those people weren't real officers: the Prussian Officer Corps was still a small elite that outsiders couldn't enter." They walked in silence for a few moments while Pauli collected and ordered his thoughts. "And then came the Sturmbataillon. It was a world I'd never known. It let me be myself. I wish you'd been with me, Alex."

"You said that in one of your letters."

"We spoke using *'du,'* officers and men alike. I called my men by their first names, and often we'd be sitting around talking together with no rank deferentials. Arguing politics, or talking about what kind of Germany we'd have after the war."

"And did any of you guess it would be like this?" Alex whipped his walking stick through the heaped snow.

Pauli snorted. "Who could have guessed it would end like this? No one! Who would have guessed that the Kaiser would run away so that Fritz Esser and his friend Liebknecht would be sitting in the Imperial Palace? Who'd guess that a collection of half-baked intellectuals and socialist draft dodgers would be running Germany as a ramshackle republic, and that the Imperial Horse Guards would be answering their call for help?"

"I thought you were about to tell me that your time with the common man had provided you with a new understanding of the socialists, Pauli."

"Socialists are dreamers. The time for dreaming is long past.

Our Fatherland is dying, and no one goes to help." He kicked the top from a mountain of snow, so that it shattered into a white cloud.

When they got to Friedrichstrasse they had to wait for the traffic before they could cross the road. It was astounding how life went on, seemingly unaffected by the fact that the city was in the throes of revolution. Even while shooting could be heard, the Christmas shoppers crowded the pavements and the motor buses kept going. There was the smoky smell of roasted chestnuts and the sound of American jazz music from one of the nearby clubs. A shop assistant and a chauffeur were loading dozens of colored parcels into a large car while a fur-coated matron counted them. It was hard to believe that the dull thuds heard earlier that day had been mortar shells exploding, and that right now artillery was on its way to assault the Imperial Palace.

"Civilians have their own affairs to attend to," commented Alex as they crossed the road, dodging a taxicab.

"Making money, do you mean?" said Pauli scornfully.

"You can't live without it."

"There are other, more important things than money, Alex. That's what I learned with the storm troops, and that's what many of our Freikorps volunteers believe."

"Are they men from your old storm troops?"

"In my battalion a dozen or so are old comrades. That's what made me join. If recruiting continues as at present, I'll have my own company next month."

Alex Horner chuckled. "And all this time I've been thinking that you'd become old and cynical, Pauli. While really you are the same fervent optimist and dreamer that I've always known."

"You can mock me, but . . ."

"I'm not mocking you, Pauli. We all feel the same way. Everyone I know and respect feels more or less the way that you do. They all feel frustrated watching this damned government being treated with contempt by every rascal at home, and spat upon by Paris, London, and Washington."

"But you remain aloof? Or are you just fatalistic?"

"If the mob wants to be ruled by the Spartacists, then so be it. I'm a professional soldier; I'll obey lawful commands from the army, just as the Russian army do under Lenin."

Pauli shook his head. "You are too naïve, Alex. Do you really think that Lenin represents the Russian worker? Lenin's party is a tiny, noisy, violent group that seized power and then slaughtered all the opposition. Now, here in Germany, Ebert's socialists are in the majority but the Spartacists are already trying some of Lenin's tricks to get power in Germany. And then heaven help Liebknecht's opponents. They'll be put against the wall and shot without trial."

Behind them they heard the sound of marching men coming down Unter den Linden from the direction of the Tiergarten. In the darkness the soldiers' hobnailed boots were striking sparks from the paving. They were Uhlan Guards. The two young officers watched approvingly as the soldiers wheeled into the entrance to the university. There were few such trained and disciplined units left in the whole of Germany.

As the two men got closer to the Imperial Palace, Unter den Linden became more crowded. There were the usual streetcorner groups of men in makeshift uniforms. Most of them had their rifles slung over the shoulder muzzle-down in what had become the style of all the revolutionaries. But these armed men were outnumbered by sightseers who'd arrived in response to the rumors that were now being spread across the city. They wanted to see how the army was going to tackle the bellicose sailors. Or, as another rumor had it, they wanted to watch the army's monarchists staging a counterrevolution.

When Alex and Pauli reached the main entrance of the palace, three sentries were there, pale-faced youngsters with soft sailor hats and bandoliers crossing their chests. They were warming their hands at a bonfire on the pavement. In the fire could be seen bits of antique furniture, its polish and gilt bubbling and blistering in the flames. They asked the guards for Esser. It took a long time to find him. Alex and Pauli stood by the fire and tried to see into the courtyard. Even from their limited view of the interior it was clear that the sailors were excited and frightened by the prospect of a pitched battle with the army units that were marching from Potsdam.

After about fifteen minutes an armed sailor took them inside and upstairs. Esser, typically, had bivouacked in the Empress's private apartments, and that is where they were taken. Although the whole place had been ransacked, many of the personal possessions of the royal occupants were in evidence. Lace jackets and long ball dresses were still hanging in the Empress's dressing rooms. Her writing desk had been broken into, and sheets of stationery and envelopes were scattered round, presumably by those people who'd been hawking examples of the royal correspondence round the streets. On the floor were powder boxes, some hairbrushes, combs, and silver frames from which photos had been wrenched.

And yet the overall impression of this sanctum was of charmless vulgarity, an ostentatious collection of frivolous knickknacks that might be expected in the house of some nouveau-riche tradesman.

"The chairman of the sailors' and workers' emergency committee will come in five minutes," announced a bearded sailor.

"Is that Fritz Esser?" Pauli asked.

"Yes, Comrade Esser," said the sailor. "You are not permitted to touch anything or to leave the room on pain of death; do you understand?"

"Yes, we understand," said Leutnant Horner. He had by now grown used to the extravagant rhetoric of the revolution.

For "Chairman" Fritz Esser of the People's Naval Division it had been an eventful day, even when compared with the other crowded days of the past few weeks. But, as had happened so often since those early days of November 1918, he'd been outguessed and outmaneuvered and eventually shouted down.

The trouble was that Esser never properly evaluated his opposition. It had been like that right from the time the naval mutinies began. Fritz Esser was usually the first to spot an opportunity, but he lacked the skill and cynicism to follow through his advantage.

For instance, the Spartacists and the left-wing radicals of the Independents had always expected that the revolution, about which they'd talked for years, would begin amongst the tired, frightened, and exhausted front-line soldiers, rather than amongst sailors or civilians. It was Fritz Esser who'd persisted with his secret meetings and inflammatory leaflets directed at the crews of the battleships and battle cruisers of the High Seas Fleet, which had spent almost the entire war anchored in the Northern ports.

It was Esser—in a secret report to one of Liebknecht's acolytes—who'd told them that fighting men would be the last ones to mutiny. That was evident here in the seaports, where there was little interest in Karl Marx amongst the U-boat crews or the men who'd chosen dangerous duty with the torpedo boats and destroyers that regularly sailed out to fight the enemy. The men who came to his meetings were the crews of the big ships: conscripts from the cities, bored, discontented men who chafed at the restrictions of military life and had nothing to do but parade, chip rust, and paint their towering steel prisons. These men, who had never heard a shot fired in anger, were the ones who listened to Esser's dreams of tomorrow.

Even the previous summer, after Esser had encouraged men of the battleship *Prinzregent Luitpold* to walk ashore at Wilhelmshaven in defiance of orders—a crime for which two of Esser's fellow believers faced an army firing squad—the Spartacists did not believe that the High Seas Fleet was a fertile ground in which their agitators could scatter the seeds of revolution. Esser's reports were ignored. In September a Spartacist leader told Esser that the Naval High Command's reforms—"food committees," elected by the sailors, were henceforward to distribute the rations—had removed the promise of further revolt.

It was only when, posted to Kiel, Esser had got the real mutinies going there that the Spartacist leadership started to take notice. But even then they were lukewarm and pointed out that the mutiny was only a reaction to being ordered to sea for a final suicide battle with the British navy. The Spartacists' political committee in Berlin seemed offended by the fact that the sailors lacked political motivation. They insisted that this mutiny would never become the workers' revolution they wanted.

Esser and his friends ignored the dicta from Berlin. It was one of Esser's young disciples whose speeches prompted the stokers on the battleship *Helgoland* to draw their slicers through the coals, bring them out on the floor plates, and damp the fires with the hoses. Without heat enough to make steam, Admiral von Hipper's order to put to sea could not be obeyed.

And when the U-135 threatened to torpedo the *Thüringen* unless its mutineers surrendered, it was one of Esser's converts who persuaded the *Helgoland*'s gunners to level their sights at the submarine. That Esser wasn't present for this fiasco, which ended with the mutineers in prison, did not change his proud claim to have started the revolution. For within a few days not only Kiel but dozens of other towns and cities as well were under the control of workers' and sailors' councils. The army did nothing to put down the revolt: it was too widespread.

And so, when Esser got to Berlin with the vanguard of the mutinying sailors who now called themselves Volksmarine, or People's Naval Division, he expected to be greeted with praise and thanks by the Spartacist hierarchy. But Esser was brushed aside as the politicians took control of the revolution in which they had shown so little belief. Esser became no more than a minor party functionary, a chairman for a committee that until today was asked to do nothing more important than arrange duty rosters for the cleaning of the billets and settle disputes between the numerous drunks, thieves, and petty criminals who soon attached themselves to the sailors.

The important decisions about Spartacist policy—or lack of any—were being made by the same people who'd given Liebknecht and Rosa Luxemburg such bad advice in the past. Self-serving men with hard eyes, dark suits, and sharp city accents dismissed Esser and his like as country bumpkins without the sort of political sophistication that was needed to steer the forthcoming revolution, which would sweep the temporary socialist government from power and replace it with uncompromising authoritarian rule.

And yet the men and women who could hear only Esser's country accent would have done well to study his conclusions, for Esser was shrewd and perceptive. Esser's report on the irregular army formations—Freiwillige Landesjägerkorps or Freikorps—now springing up all over Germany was something the Spartacist leaders would have done well to read. Esser had become an expert on discontent, and he was able to distinguish the discontent of the sailors he'd helped to bring to a state of mutiny and the sort of discontent that was furnishing the Freikorps with more men than they could properly clothe and arm.

Few sailors of the Naval Division had seen any action in the war. Typically they were unmarried ex–factory workers with no fixed addresses. Some of them went on regular forays of looting and housebreaking and even demanding money from well-dressed people in the streets, always disguising their crimes with neat political labels. The sailors remained in the Imperial Palace because they were being provided with payments by the government—who were frightened of them—and because it was warmer and more comfortable than the street to which they would otherwise be relegated. As long as Liebknecht and Luxemburg encouraged them, they would cheer the Spartacists' speeches.

The men of the Freikorps were a totally different proposition, as Esser pointed out. The Freikorps recruits came largely from front-line soldiers. For these men the world was divided into "the front" and "the rear." The rear were the civilians who'd made so much money in the war factories and the bosses who owned them. The rear were the bankers and the financiers, the pacifists who'd made speeches against the war, and the "November criminals" who'd signed the armistice. Although officers were excluded from the People's Naval Division, the Freikorps soldiers readily included their battle-hardened officers as part of their exclusive fraternity.

Perhaps it was while compiling his neglected report that Fritz Esser began to discover something about himself. Esser had never been in battle. His naval service had been spent in the comparative comfort and the indisputable safety of Imperial Naval barracks. And although he'd never admitted it, Esser felt uneasy about his passive role in this great "war to end wars," for Esser—despite his revolutionary declarations—had the inborn respect for the warrior that so burdens the German soul.

Endless bickering, inarticulate committees meeting long into the night without reaching any conclusions, had wearied and disillusioned him. And on this Monday evening, the 23rd day of December, 1918, Esser had reached the end of his patience. The prospect of the Imperial Palace's coming under attack by loyal units of the army frightened him, and he made no secret of his fear. Even the light artillery that informers said were being readied at Potsdam would be enough to blow the main doors in, and the effect of shrapnel fire in these confined spaces would not bear thinking about.

And yet trying to get this simple fact understood by his committee had proved far beyond his power. Not that any of the committee members offered a sensible alternative to his suggestion that they open talks with Ebert and release their hostages—Otto Wels in particular—as a gesture of good faith. He was shouted down by cries of "Traitor!" and "No surrender!" rather than defeated in rational discussion. Finally Esser exploded with rage. He yelled obscenities at these pompous pen-pushers—*Bonzen,* he called them—and stormed out of the meeting. It was then that the messenger came to say that two army plenipotentiaries were waiting for him downstairs. This was the beginning of the end. He felt frightened. Now what was he supposed to do? Temporize, yes, but how?

"I am Esser, committee chairman. What is it?" Esser fixed them with his dark, piercing eyes. Pauli immediately recognized his friend, who'd grown into a barrel-chested giant, pea jacket open, red neckerchief at his throat, and sailor cap on the back of his close-cropped head.

"Fritz! Remember me, Pauli Winter? Travemünde."

Esser didn't recognize Pauli. His eyes went to Alex Horner. He recognized Horner from the meeting in the Chancellery; he was some sort of military aide to Otto Wels. It was to be expected that the army would send him to parley about the release of Berlin's military governor. Esser had opposed the idea of holding the socialist politician here as hostage: it was nothing better than kidnapping and extortion. Such tactics would not endear the People's Naval Division to the working class. Esser knew the working class: they were moralists.

"Come away from the palace, Fritz. I want to talk to you."

Esser went to the window. It was dark outside, but he could see the crowds. He thought he could see the lights from the cathedral shining on steel helmets. But steel helmets didn't mean that the army had arrived; half the population of Berlin seemed to be wearing steel helmets and carrying guns. He turned back to look at the two men. The fellow from Wels's office was unmistakably a Prussian officer, despite the bowler hat, walking stick, and long overcoat. The other was dressed in a battered army greatcoat and a steel helmet with a swastika painted on the front. They shouldn't have let him in here with that pistol strapped to his belt, but it was too late now.

"Fritz!" said Pauli once more.

He recognized him now. The kid from the big house at Travemünde: Paul Winter. Perhaps it was going to be all right. He grabbed the young man's outstretched hand. "What the devil are you doing here? Did the army send you?"

"The army? No."

"Good God, Pauli, the guards only brought you in here because they thought you were sent by the army to negotiate with us."

"Come and have a beer, Fritz."

Esser turned to Alex Horner. "You haven't come here to ask for the release of Otto Wels?"

Alex was on the point of saying, To the devil with Wels. Instead he told Esser, "Herr Winter is my friend."

"Then let's go and drink beer!" said Fritz Esser loudly. He smiled to show his crooked teeth. "I'll buy you more beer than you can drink, young Winter."

"That might be a lot of beer, Fritz."

"It's not a trick?" said Esser, his face suddenly darkening.

"You have my word," said Alex Horner formally. He clicked his heels.

"My friend is a Prussian stuffed shirt," Pauli told Esser, "but under that shirt there is a goodhearted fellow."

"I'll trust you," said Esser. It seemed a long time since he'd trusted anyone very much, but now he wanted to shed the worries of the day and forget, forget, forget. Let those know-it-alls of the committee continue their arguments without him. "Where shall we drink?" Just to be on the safe side, he strapped a belt and pistol around his waist. He ran his hand back over his bristly hair and felt his scalp damp with sweat, then plonked his cap back on his head.

Pauli had his answer ready: "There's a *Kneipe* behind the Spittelmarkt: Guggenheimer's place. Know it?"

The choice of venue reassured Fritz Esser. Guggenheimer was a Jew with half a dozen children, all of whom attended the university, with varying degrees of success. His bar was a student hangout with cheap food and strong beer. All sorts of odd people went there. It was the sort of place that a sailor, a Freikorps man, and a smartly dressed civilian might be able to drink together without getting unwelcome attention.

Alex stole a glance at his friend. Had it all been planned by Pauli? He could be devious and cunning: it was a part of his nature that few people knew. And yet Pauli was sincere, too; that was what so beguiled Esser.

"The pay is not important," said Pauli Winter after several tankards of Guggenheimer's best dark beer had been consumed. "It's the comradeship: men you can trust with your life. Good fellows, every one of them. But the money is good, too. Every volunteer has a daily basic pay of forty marks, and now the government are adding another five. Then there's the food: two hundred grams of meat and seventy-five grams of butter and a quarter-liter of wine. Plenty of beer and cigarettes, too." He held up his beer. "In our canteen this would cost us almost nothing. But a lot of the men join because Freikorps service counts towards their pension. Take you, Fritz," he added, as if taking an example entirely at random. "You'd be taken into the Freikorps at your present naval rank and pay—in fact, you'd become my sergeant major, because I'm getting my own company next month—and your Freikorps service counts towards your pension. Plus the regular family allowance will immediately start again for your parents. How are they, by the way?"

"My father is not well," said Fritz Esser absent-mindedly.

"I'm sorry to hear that," said Pauli. It was a part of Pauli's charm that he could express his genuine sorrow that the "pig man" was unwell, then immediately continue his description of life in the Freikorps, without seeming uncaring. "People who can handle the administration side are difficult to find. The storm battalions were not noted for their paperwork. But now we can only get pay, allowances, food, and all the other supplies we need if the office work is properly done. These socialists are all bureaucrats, you see; we have to play their game."

"Why do we have to play their game?" Esser inquired. "I don't trust this government."

Alex nodded agreement and leaned forward to hear Pauli's reply.

"For the time being," said Pauli. "When the right time comes, Germany will have proper leadership."

"An emperor?" asked Alex Horner.

"Perhaps," said Pauli. "But somehow I think we've seen the end of the House of Hohenzollern. His Highness lacked the qualities of a true Prussian soldier-king, and no one who's seen the Crown Prince at close quarters would hope he'd be any better."

"Heartily agreed," said Alex Horner, and belched. Esser took off his old patched jacket and hung it over the back of his chair. His bare arms were covered with tattoos: serpents, girls' names, and expressions of fidelity in elaborate scrollwork.

"Get more beer," said Pauli.

"It's my turn," said Fritz Esser. He was the oldest of the three men and determined to pay his way. He got up and walked to the counter with only the slightest unsteadiness.

With Esser out of earshot, Alex Horner whispered, "You'll never recruit this wretch to your damned Freikorps Graf." Alex didn't like Captain Graf, the diminutive homosexual who ran his private army like some medieval warlord, but he was cautious about voicing such thoughts to Pauli, who'd become something of an apologist for this strange man.

"There's not one there who could take on the job of a sergeant major," said Pauli.

"Not one where?"

"In the company that I'll take over next month. Good soldiers, good fighters, good comrades, but no skewer upon which I can fix them."

"You'll never do it, Pauli. The fellow's a Spartacist."

"He'll see reason," said Pauli complacently. "Fritz is a sensible fellow."

"You mad fool. Did you have this in mind right from the start?"

Before Pauli answered, Esser was back with three foaming steins of beer. He slammed them on the table. "Drink, drink, drink," he urged. He looked round to see who was seated nearby. "And then there are a couple of things you must tell me about this Freikorps business."

Fortified with several liters of Guggenheimer's beer, the trio went down Leipziger Strasse, visiting various bars, until they turned north along Friedrichstrasse, where the nightlife was even more raucous: male and female prostitutes mingling with beggars, drunks, and pickpockets, and from every side the frantic sounds of recently arrived American jazz.

Fritz Esser never went back to the Imperial Palace. When, early on that Christmas Eve morning, the army's artillery opened fire on the palace, Esser didn't even hear the gunfire, for he was in an upstairs room over a club behind the Schiffbauerdamm Theatre, asleep in the arms of a half-undressed nightclub hostess.

As 1918 tottered to a close, Fritz Esser was enrolled in the Freikorps. On the other side of the city, Liebknecht joined his Spartakusbund to the Independent Socialists and the Revolutionary Shop Stewards, called his new political entity the Communist Party of Germany, and began arming his supporters.

Everywhere in Berlin the madness continued: lines of hungry people formed outside bakers' shops, and butchers', too, and stared into expensive restaurants, where war profiteers and their gloriously attired women gobbled champagne and caviar. On the Western Front the Allies had stopped fighting but their naval blockade continued, and thousands of Germans died of malnutrition. Throughout Europe the influenza virus decimated the tired and hungry population; it brought death to seventeen hundred Berliners in a single day.

"The damned war's *not* over."

Whatever reservations Fritz Esser had had about serving under the command of his young friend soon evaporated as Pauli Winter led his company across the rooftops of Wilhelmstrasse despite Spartacist snipers across the street. Soon Pauli had repaid any debt he owed Esser for hauling him from the sea so long ago. More than once Pauli saved his sergeant major from death or injury. Once his strong arms saved Esser from sliding off the rain-swept slates into the street below. Esser had followed Graf and the others along the ridge of a saddleback roof. It required balance, daring, and speed, and Fritz Esser, burdened with rifle, bandoliers, and a heavy bag of grenades, had none of these in adequate amounts. He slipped on the icy ridge tiles, and his rifle went across the slates and down into the street far below. As Esser started his fall, Pauli grabbed him by the greatcoat collar and held him spread-eagled across the steep roof, while men on the roof on the far side of Wilhelmstrasse fired at him. Only with great difficulty was the unfortunately heavyweight Esser dragged to safety. Pauli laughed about it. Under fire the clumsy Pauli became another man: not just commander of "Winter Company," he was also the most audacious and skilled fighting man in that very formidable unit, Freikorps Graf.

Once, during the heavy fighting in the center of the city, the two men met briefly with Leutnant Alex Horner. It was during the violent fighting of January 11, 1919, when Freikorps units battled their way into the Police Headquarters on Alexanderplatz, where Spartacist resistance was fierce. It was something of a massacre. The defenders' morale was weakening as they realized that Liebknecht's communists were not going to win power by force. Pauli and Esser were amongst the first inside the Police Headquarters courtyard. Esser lobbed a stick grenade through a downstairs window, and both men scrambled into the smoke-filled wreckage; the others followed without hesitation. Now the defenders fell back, room by room, floor by floor, but the merciless Freikorpskämpfer slaughtered everyone they found.

Alex Horner protested at the slaughter. He took his formal objections to Captain Graf. But the Freikorps men were in no mood to listen to technicalities from the regular army. They left no one alive.

The regular army, too, had men who gave no quarter. A few days later an informer reported the presence of Rosa Luxemburg and Karl Liebknecht in a middle-class apartment in Wilmersdorf. The captive pair were taken to the Eden Hotel, near the Memorial Church, which the Horse Guards were using as their headquarters. After a brutal interrogation they were murdered, and with their deaths "Spartacus week" ended.

During this respite the Freikorps reformed and refitted, and Leutnant Pauli Winter lost his sergeant major. Fritz Esser had, in his brief service with his company, shown only moderate aptitude for infantry tactics, and unless Pauli was at his side he didn't have the combat experience or the reckless bravery that most of the others showed. But there had been time to recognize the administrative skills he'd learned during his naval service. Fritz Esser was promoted to be an assistant to the battalion adjutant. Then, just two weeks later, after the adjutant was hospitalized, Esser was made battalion adjutant.

Whatever extravagant claims are made for the democratic style of the Freikorps units, there was strong opposition to making Esser an officer. So he became adjutant with that strange compromise rank that the German army invented for such social dilemmas. He was made a Feldwebel-Leutnant, so that he could do an officer's job with officer's badges and shoulder straps and officer's pay without being the social equal of his peers. It was an arrangement that made all concerned very satisfied.

The man that Fritz Esser now worked alongside was Captain Georg Graf, and he was not an easy man to get along with. Despite first appearances, the little Munich-born career officer with big ears, red nose, and unconcealed homosexual preferences wasn't a figure of fun to anyone who'd fought alongside him, anywhere from Verdun to Alexanderplatz. He was mercurial, violent, and unforgiving.

Fritz Esser and Captain Graf—both men difficult and argumentative by nature—worked amicably together. Pauli Winter teased Esser that Graf had fallen in love with him, because that idea made the unmistakably heterosexual Esser nervous. Esser stoically replied that he admired Graf for his physical bravery under fire and appreciated the very real concern he showed for the men under his command. But, whatever the exact nature of the relationship, the mutual regard Esser and Graf showed for each other was genuine and lasting. And that was just as well, for Feldwebel-Leutnant Esser became Graf's *de facto* second in command. When Graf was not available, Esser was always consulted. "What would Captain Graf probably want . . . ?" The question was always phrased in such a way that Esser gave an opinion rather than an order, but his underlying authority was undisputed, and Graf supported his adjutant's decisions, whatever his true feelings may have been about some of them.

Feldwebel-Leutnant Esser's assignment to Headquarters did not mean there was any change in the relationship between him and Pauli Winter. They were very close. Esser was grateful to Pauli for bringing him into the battalion, and though Esser could never replace his brother, Peter, in the role of mentor and protector, or Alex Horner as conscience and example, Fritz Esser was the most priceless of companions. Fritz could be outrageously funny, and he had a sharp eye for the sort of cant and humbug that the new socialist government plentifully supplied every day. Fritz was not a committed socialist; nor was he a communist or a Marxist. And whatever was the political creed that bound the Freikorps men together, Fritz Esser had no heartfelt devotion to that, either. Fritz Esser was an anarchist by both conviction and nature, and Pauli found his anarchistic attitude towards life not only amusing but illuminating and instructive, too.

When Freikorps Graf moved out of Berlin, first to Halle and then to Munich, Esser's role as quartermaster, mother superior, slavemaster, and general factotum earned the respect of the entire battalion. En route there was always a hot evening meal ready, a dry place to sleep, and some sort of breakfast, too. Every soldier in the battalion had well-repaired boots and fifty rounds of ammunition in a bandolier in case there was trouble with the local populations, who sometimes preferred their communist committees to the freebooting warriors. And if on occasion they had to march too far, then that was because not even the amazing Fritz could keep all the ancient trucks in good enough repair to transport a battalion of men. Besides, soldiers marched—everyone knew that. Freikorpstruppen liked to march and shoot and sleep rough; that was why they were in the Freikorps. People who didn't like such hardships and the comradeship that went with them remained civilians, and all good Freikorpskämpfer despised civilians of every political creed.

1922

"Berlin is so far away, Harry, and I miss you so much."

The Austrian countryside was bleak and cold, and by five o'clock in the afternoon the darkening sky was streaked with the red light of the setting sun. Martha Somló and Harald Winter had skated round and round long after all the other skaters—villagers mostly; the Viennese did not come this far to find ice—had gone.

She loved the hiss of the blades cutting into the ice, and the way her face tingled in the cold wind. She loved the harmony with which they moved together, and she enjoyed Harry's arm firmly around her waist as they raced across the ice at reckless speed.

The dinner they were served in the private rooms upstairs at the White Horse was simple country food, but there was nothing better than a veal stew on a cold winter evening. They had their warm apple strudel, and tiny glasses of powerful Schwarzbeer schnapps from the nearby farm, while sitting in front of a roaring log fire. The logs were trimmings from the orchard, the smoke smelled of the fruit, and the sap still inside the wood made the fire crack and bang and throw sparks.

"Must you go back tomorrow?" she asked. They had been in bed. Now she was sitting on the floor by his feet, naked except for an ornate gypsy-style shawl that she'd wrapped herself into. He'd made her scrub off all the powder, cream, and lipstick. He cared nothing about the new fashions: in Harald Winter's world only whores and chorus girls painted their faces.

"I shouldn't have stayed so long," said Harald Winter.

"Berlin is so far away, Harry, and I miss you so much."

"Why are you selling the bank?" Every time she passed the bank in Ringstrasse she felt proud of knowing Harry.

"Only my share of the bank." He stared into the fire as if hoping to see a bright future there.

"Why?"

"It will make no difference to us, little one. I will still come to Vienna." He touched her hair gently, and she closed her eyes as he stroked her head.

"But not so often."

"I am not rich anymore," said Winter. He was rich, of course, very rich by the standards that most people employ to measure wealth. But he could not provide Martha with the luxuries—the carriage and servants—that she'd once enjoyed, and he felt humiliated by his economies.

"It doesn't matter," she said. She turned to look at him by the light of the flames. He looked tired and ill, but she knew now that Harald Winter's business failures affected him in the way that other men are affected by infirmities or disease. "I'll always be here waiting."

"I'm setting up a trust fund for you in Switzerland," he said. "It will be enough to live comfortably whatever happens."

"You are a wonderful man, Harry. What would I do without you?"

"Many people say things will get even worse. Some of the banks might crash. It's better to sell."

"Berlin is so far away, Harry, and I miss you so much." He leaned forward and bent over to kiss her. If only it could be like this forever, he thought. But, just as quickly, the thought was gone. Harald Winter would find life like this unendurable after a week or so, and he was sensible enough to know that.

1924

"Who are those dreadful men?"

The birthday party that Harald and Veronica Winter put on for their younger son, Pauli's twenty-fourth birthday, was the first real birthday party he'd had since he was a child. Although unsaid, it was his parents' celebration of Pauli Winter's first term at university, his return to civilian life. The lovely old house was ablaze with lights and noisy with the excited chatter of more than fifty guests and a ten-piece dance band. In a grim sort of joke that was typically *berlinerisch,* the invitations were overprinted upon billion-mark banknotes. Back before the war, an unskilled worker in one of Harald Winter's factories earned twenty-five marks a week, but the staggering inflation of the previous year had seen the value of Germany's paper money plunge to a point where one U.S. dollar bought over two and a half billion marks. Foreigners came across the border from Holland and Czechoslovakia and bought land and mansions with handfuls of hard currency. Then finally the madness ended. The Reichsbank issued its new Rentenmarks, one of which was worth one billion in the old currency. As if in celebration, Aschinger, the famous restaurant near the Friedrichstrasse railway station, offered one main dish, a glass of beer, a dessert, and as many rolls as you cared to eat for just one new mark. Inflation had stopped.

As the smoke cleared, it was apparent that the middle classes had suffered most: in the final few terrible weeks most people's life savings totaled not enough to buy a postage stamp. But some Germans had not suffered. Harald Winter had almost doubled his fortune. Like many industrialists, he was allowed to borrow from the Reichsbank, which, in the manner of most government departments, reacted very slowly to the events of the day. Thus, even when the Reichsbank was charging its top rate of interest, Harald Winter could continue borrowing and repaying at rates far, far below that of inflation. And by 1924 the five-million-Reichsmark debt due to his father-in-law was nothing like enough to buy a meal at Aschinger. It could be renegotiated to almost anything Harald Winter decided.

But not everyone present at Pauli's birthday party this evening had been as fortunate and as astute as Winter. Many of them had had at least a part of their money in government securities, and now they were talking about the law of December 8, 1923. The socialist government had decided that their own debts were to be advantageously revalued—for instance, the reparations due to France—but the millions of holders of now worthless government securities would not be compensated.

"By God!" said Frau Wisliceny, who'd come with her daughters and, to Peter Winter's indignation, brought her son-in-law Erich Hennig. "I'm beginning to believe that ruffian Hitler is right about the rogues who govern us." Frau Wisliceny had not mellowed with age—a big, handsome, matronly woman in an elaborate but decidedly unfashionable Paris gown that she'd had since before the war. Frau Wisliceny eschewed the new fashions for the sake of which women sacrificed their long hair and exposed their legs. Her voice was firm and decisive, and she prided herself that she was as well informed as anyone in Berlin and happy to argue about art, music, or politics with any man present.

"Surely you would not wish to be ruled by such a rascal?" said Richard Fischer. Foxy Fischer's son, now forty-three years old and running the family's steel empire, had left his aging father in order to flirt with Inge until Frau Wisliceny moved into the group. Not that Frau Wisliceny would oppose a marriage between the two of them or object to Richard's flirting. Richard Fischer was the most eligible of bachelors, and her eldest daughter was getting to an age when to be unmarried was noticeable. But Inge had not given up hope of marrying Peter Winter, and as long as he remained single she had eyes for no one else.

"You'd better lower your voice," Erich Hennig advised.

"That little Captain Graf over there is one of Hitler's most notorious strongarm men, and the big brute with him is his so-called adjutant."

"I'm not frightened to speak my mind," said Fischer. He, too, was a big fellow, and his full beard, along with the confident manner that his riches provided, made him a formidable adversary in any sort of conflict.

"Hitler will go to prison anyway," said Frau Wisliceny, in an attempt to avoid any friction that might arise between her son-in-law and Fischer. "Even the Bavarians won't let him get away with an armed putsch against their legally elected government."

"I'm not sure he will," said Peter Winter. He was tall and slim, with a pale complexion that had come from long hours studying his law books. In his well-fitting evening suit he was as handsome as any man in the room. He'd let his dark hair grow unfashionably long, so that it touched the top of his ears. Inge eyed him adoringly. Peter was not the sort of man every girl would want: some said he was an unbending snob, too old-fashioned for the fast-moving permissiveness of Berlin in the twenties. But Inge had decided that there could be no other man for her, and now that her sister Lisl was married . . . "My class in law school went to Munich last week. We spent some time with the prosecution people, and they let us see the evidence."

"But there is nothing to prove," said Lisl. "Hitler's guilty. It was an attempt to seize power by armed force. It's simply a matter of sentencing him."

Peter looked at her before replying. Marriage to the awful Hennig obviously agreed with her. She looked well and happy and was even more self-confident than he remembered. Most of her friends had predicted that she'd be crushed by the opinionated, dogmatic, domineering Hennig, but the opposite had happened: it was Lisl who made all the decisions, and when it came to political opinions Hennig deferred to his beautiful young wife.

Peter said, "You only need half an hour in Munich to realize that this is no criminal trial, it's more like an election. What jury will send a war hero such as General Ludendorff to prison?"

Lisl replied, "We're not talking about Ludendorff, who everyone knows is only half dotty. We're talking about Hitler, a madman."

"I don't know how carefully you follow Hitler's speeches," Peter told her with the dispassionate moderation that he'd learned from his law professor. "But I read through some of his speeches. Hitler is being described as 'the new Messiah' and he cultivates this. He condemns moral decay, corruption, and vice and is able to rally round him people with very differing views: that is his skill."

"I've heard all that tosh," said Fischer. "But if you listen to Hitler, you'd think that all the vice and corruption in the world are here in Berlin." He stroked his beard and looked to Inge for approval. She smiled at him but then turned back to look at Peter.

"He does," agreed Peter mildly. "But that appeals to the Bavarians. They like to see Berlin as the base of centralism, the home of the Prussian military—which they fear and despise—and Protestant Berliners as the greatest obstacle to their aim of restoring a Bavarian kingdom, complete with Catholic monarchy. Hitler skillfully panders to all these feelings."

Fischer said, "And those Bavarians. Those damned southerners see Berlin as a place controlled by Jewish capitalists. It suits their anti-Semitic nature."

The band started playing a Lehár waltz. "It's a crime not to be dancing," said Frau Wisliceny. "Inge, is this dance booked?"

"No, Mama."

Frau Wisliceny looked pointedly at Richard Fischer, who immediately asked Inge to dance.

Peter would have asked her sister Lisl to dance, if only as a way to annoy Hennig, but Hennig was too quick for him and whirled his wife away onto the dance floor with no more than a curt nod to them.

Someone invited Frau Wisliceny to dance and, left alone, Peter Winter turned to watch two soldiers who were standing near the bar. One of them was Fritz Esser, of course. There was no way of avoiding recognition of the debt he owed him, but he didn't have to approve of the fellow's activities or of the horrid little homosexual who'd come here with him. And Peter thought it appalling that the two men should have arrived in their comic-opera uniforms. Captain Graf was wearing the modified uniform of an army captain. Esser wore a new sort of uniform: brown shirt, breeches, boots, and Sam Browne–style leather belt and shoulder strap. Both men were members of the uniformed "army" that the notorious Captain Ernst Röhm commanded—under ever-changing titles—as a military arm for Hitler's National Socialist Party. "Storm troopers," they called themselves.

Peter Winter hated the Nazis almost as much as he hated the communists. He distrusted their cavalier use of words such as "freedom," "honor," "bread," and "security." He believed that only stupid people could define the failings and opportunities of this complex world by means of trite catchall mottos.

Deep down he had always hoped that by some miracle he'd wake up and find himself back in a well-ordered world run from the Imperial Palace by that autocrat Kaiser Wilhelm, who cared nothing for what the Reichstag decreed. But, gradually and grudgingly, he'd come to believe that the new postwar constitution provided a truly democratic framework by means of which Germany would again become the greatest nation in the world.

Despite his distaste for socialism, Peter Winter was that evening one of the very few people in the Winter house—or, indeed, in the whole city—who supported Ebert, the socialist president. Germany must be run by the law; that was why he was studying to be a lawyer. The organized violence of communists and Nazis was a threat to the law, to the stability of German middle-class society, and therefore to everything that Peter held dear.

So Peter Winter found it difficult to conceal his hostility as he walked over to where Captain Graf was talking to Fritz Esser. He hated these men not only for what they were but because of their continuing association with Pauli. He had a sense of foreboding that made him want to protect his younger brother from these unpleasant rascals. At least he'd been able to persuade Pauli to leave Graf's wretched Freikorps. Had he remained in Munich with them much longer, there was little doubt that Pauli would have become a Nazi storm trooper and been here tonight in one of these ridiculous uniforms.

"Not dancing, gentlemen?" said Peter provocatively. He signaled to the waiter for more champagne for his guests. They knew who he was, of course: Graf had met him before, and Esser had known him from the time he'd pulled him out of the sea off Travemünde.

"We are talking business," said Graf. He had a notebook in his hand, and he was wearing steel-rimmed spectacles to read from it.

"Come along! This is a celebration. Drink! Dance! Have fun!"

Neither of the two men could decide how to respond to Peter's friendly words, but both knew they were being mocked. As he turned his head, Graf's spectacle lenses flashed with the reflections of the grand chandeliers, and his fierce eyes showed anger.

When the servant had poured wine for both men, Esser lifted his glass in salute. *"Prosit!"* he said and grinned broadly. Peter bowed and took his leave of them.

"The place is full of Jews," Graf told Esser once Peter Winter had gone. "And the Winter family have grown rich and fat feasting on the corpses of our comrades."

"Our time will come," said Esser. He put a thumb into his belt and stood surveying the dancers like a lion tamer.

Captain Graf was looking at the far end of the room, where four young girls in scanty sequined two-piece outfits had suddenly started their dance. Captain Graf didn't share Esser's appreciation for half-naked girls, and he turned away with a scowl on his face. "Jewish, capitalist filth!" said Graf.

Esser grunted and continued to watch the floor show. The girls were Pauli Winter's idea; they'd been specially brought over to the house from a *Revue-Bar.* Esser recognized the dancers, and the girls knew him. His face was known at every drinking place in Berlin, from the Kempi on Leipziger Strasse to the sleazy little bars on Invalidenstrasse where pimps plied their trade. Esser, unlike Graf, liked girls. He drank his champagne. He had long ago learned that everything of which Captain Graf disapproved was "Jewish, capitalist filth," and until now he had never dared to contradict his boss. But the past year had seen a change in Esser's loyalties. He'd been close enough to the Nazi Party leadership to know that Graf's hero—and immediate commander—Röhm was not blindly loyal to Hitler. Soon there must come a confrontation between Röhm's uniformed SA—Sturmabteilung—and the gray-faced civilians of the Nazi Party leadership, and Esser had decided that, whether Hitler got a prison sentence or not, his future was with "Der Chef." "They are damned good dancers," said Esser defiantly and applauded the *Revue-Bar* girls. Captain Graf snorted angrily, stuffed his notebook back in his breast pocket, and strutted off towards the upstairs smoking room and bar.

Pauli Winter saw Graf's tiff with Esser from the dance floor. Pauli was transformed. No longer in the haircut that he'd had since entering cadet school, which had made his skull into a furry pink billiard ball, his blond hair was long enough to fall forward across his eyes.

His new evening suit—from his father's tailor—fitted close upon his stocky, muscular figure, and many female eyes watched him with interest as he waltzed with one of the Guggenheimer daughters. His student life had revealed a new aspect of Pauli, for he was a sociable young man who enjoyed parties, girls, drinks, and dancing more than lectures and books. On this account his first exam results had been so poor that he'd not yet told his father about them. Sometimes he wondered why he'd let his parents persuade him to go to university, but they had been determined to get him out of the Freikorps. They were hypocrites. They applauded the way the Freikorps fought the communists but deplored Graf and the men who did the fighting.

It was not easy to adapt to the schoolroom again after the violent rough-and-tumble of the Freikorps. But Peter was at the law school, too, and Peter sorted out all the problems in that rather imperious way that he did everything. But even Peter couldn't help Pauli get better marks. Corporation law was not something that interested Pauli very much but, as usual, Pauli wanted to please his parents. He wanted to please everyone: he knew it was a foolish weakness, but he too often agreed to whatever was required of him rather than be subjected to long arguments.

When the dance ended, Pauli applauded the band and thanked Hetti Guggenheimer. She was a pretty girl—dark hair and large brown eyes with lashes that she too readily fluttered at young men. Hetti Guggenheimer was one of Pauli's fellow first-year students. She was studying medicine and always got top marks. Hetti's next dance was booked with someone else, but she went through the motions of referring to her card before excusing herself to Pauli. Pauli didn't mind too much. There were lots of pretty girls here, and he was popular with the girls. Although he'd never grown as tall as his brother, Pauli had the American good looks of the Rensselaer family. His cheekbones set high in a bony skull, large intense eyes, and wide smile had made him look like the sort of actor that Hollywood casts as a cowboy. And, like the archetypal cowboy, he was soft-spoken, easy-tempered, and uncomplaining. Now, taking his leave of Hetti, he went back to where he'd left his beer and looked round the room. He saw Esser and Graf having what was obviously some sort of argument and watched Graf go strutting upstairs angrily. Pauli smoothed his disarrayed hair, tucked in his rumpled shirt, and went over to Esser. "Is everything all right, Fritz?"

"Everything is just fine."

"I saw Captain Graf come past me. He looked angry."

"You know what he's like, Pauli. His anger passes."

"You usually get along so well with him."

Esser drank champagne and Pauli realized that he was thinking about his reply. Finally he said, "Things have changed since the old days, Pauli. After you left us to go to school, the battalion became different." It was nearly a year since Pauli had left them to start the cramming course he'd taken before the entrance exam. Ten months of living with his parents. It seemed much longer. Much, much longer.

"Different how?"

"Too many youngsters. Spiteful kids who never went to the war and want to show how tough they are. And I miss Berlin."

"And Graf?"

"He's become too pally with Röhm, and I don't get along with Röhm. He's too damned ambitious to be a soldier. He plays politics." Esser looked round to be sure he wasn't overheard. "I went to the Führer and told him what was happening."

"The Führer? Hitler?"

"I told him that Röhm is looking for an opportunity to take over. With the Führer in prison, Röhm could take control of everything."

"Perhaps Röhm will be sentenced to a long prison term, too."

"It's possible. But Röhm has remarkable friends and supporters: in the army, in the Bavarian government, and in the judiciary, too. They all know that sooner or later the Nazis will come to power."

"So you believe the Nazis will get into power," said Pauli. The idea of that small, cranky organization's forming a government seemed unlikely.

"Good men will be needed then, Pauli. Reliable men like you. When you've finished at law school, there will be a good job waiting for you."

"With the Nazis?"

"All the top men are lawyers. I'm even thinking of studying law myself."

Pauli slapped him on the shoulder. "You could do it, Fritz. I would help you."

He laughed self-consciously. "I'd need coaching. I left school when I was fourteen."

"We'll talk about all that next week, when we have lunch. So you are a Nazi?"

"Yes, I am a secret member. That cunning bastard Röhm tries to keep us brownshirts separated from the Party. Röhm still has dreams of ditching Hitler and restoring the monarchy, but the Führer knows what he's doing."

"I hope you know what *you're* doing, Fritz," said Pauli. He was flattered that Esser had taken him into his confidence, for these were days when any small disloyalty was enough to get a man murdered.

"I have a nose for what's what. I'm not really a soldier; I'm a political person. I always have been," said Esser.

"What will happen next? Your Hitler is certain to get a long prison sentence, isn't he?"

"We'll bide our time," said Esser. "Adolf Hitler is the man Germany needs; we must wait for him, however long."

"For God's sake, be careful, Fritz. You said Röhm is a ruthless bastard. If he finds out that you're betraying him . . ."

"I know how to handle him. He's a homosexual, like Graf. There are too many homosexuals around Röhm; that's one of the things I don't like about the situation in Munich. I treat them all like spoiled brats. One day the Führer will deal with them. Until then those pansies need me. Röhm is hiding guns for the army—secret dumps all over the country. More than twenty thousand rifles, machine guns . . . even artillery." He grinned. "Without my office files they'd never know where anything is to be found."

"Alex Horner is here tonight. You should talk to him. One day he'll end up as chief of the General Staff. There might be a time when an influential friend in the Reichswehr would be useful to you." Pauli wanted his friends to be friends with one another. It was something of an obsession with him.

Fritz Esser downed his drink. "Thanks, Pauli. But don't worry about me. I know what I'm doing. Sometime we'll go out and get drunk and I'll tell you some stories about the Munich putsch that will make your hair curl. It nearly came off! I marched alongside the Führer. I was in Odeonsplatz when the police opened fire. The Führer was no more than thirty paces from me. He was still wearing his evening suit, with a trenchcoat over it. The man next to him was shot dead; he pulled the Führer down with him. Captain Göring was wounded. Only Ludendorff ignored the gunfire and marched on through the police cordon. It was a wonderful experience, Pauli."

"It was a fiasco," said Pauli, not unkindly.

"One day you'll regret you were not with us. We made history."

"Have another drink, Fritz. And then let's see if we can find Alex. I want to get the two of you together."

At that moment Pauli's old friend Leutnant Alex Horner was smoking a cigar in Harald Winter's study and being quizzed by Winter and old Foxy Fischer. The study had never been refurnished since the Winters first moved in. The walls were lined with more or less the same books, and the floor covered with the same richly colored Oriental carpet. The same inlaid mahogany desk occupied one corner, and the only light came from the green-shaded desk lamp. Everything was clean and well cared for, but the footstools, like the polished leather wing armchairs, were scuffed and scarred by carelessly held cigars and the marks from drink glasses. The study, more than any other room in the house, had escaped unchanged over these eventful years, and Harald liked it all just the way it was; even the engraved portrait of Kaiser Wilhelm remained on the wall.

This evening the air here was blue with cigar smoke from the three men. The deferential attention the young man was receiving was flattering for him, but he was not surprised by it. For Leutnant Horner had recently been able to see for himself what was Germany's most closely guarded secret: the newly established German military installations in Soviet Russia. Now the two men wanted a first-hand account of this astounding political development.

"Did you visit all the factories?" asked Fischer. He was seventy-two years old, totally bald and frail, but he would not give up cigars and brandy.

"I really don't know, but I went to some of the most important ones." Alex's face had become hard and set into the inscrutable expression that the German army expected of its elite Prussian Officer Corps. His nose was wider, and the dueling scar that had been on his cheek so long had become more livid with age.

"The Junkers airplane factories, near Moscow and Kharkov," supplied Harald Winter, to show he was already well informed. He looked especially sleek. He'd spent the earlier part of the evening dancing. Harry enjoyed dancing, and tonight he'd made sure of partnering most of the attractive young women here. At fifty-four he was still a better dancer than any of the younger men, and he was only too pleased to demonstrate it.

Alex Horner nodded. "There were twenty-three of us. We traveled separately. I didn't, for instance, visit the poison-gas factory—it's in a remote part of Samara Oblast—or any of the plants where artillery shells are manufactured. Ordnance specialists were sent there, and aviators reported on the flying schools. My assignment was to visit the tank training schools that we run in cooperation with the Red Army."

Fischer crushed his cigar into the ashtray with unnecessary force. "I don't like it, I'll tell you. The idea of showing Bolshevik murderers how to use tanks and planes is madness. Those swine will attack us the first chance they get."

"Your fears are unfounded, Foxy," said Harald Winter, and smiled at the strongly expressed views. "The Versailles Diktat forbids us to have planes and tanks. The Soviets have not signed the Versailles Treaty, and their cooperation is exactly what we need. The Russians want our expertise, and we have to have secret testing grounds." The neatness of the deception pleased him.

"You are being carried away by the prospects," Fischer told Winter. "I, too, want to get my factories fully working again, but I can't keep a tank production line secret."

Winter hesitated and a nerve in his cheek twitched. Then he admitted, "I have already supplied the army with modern planes. All-metal airframes. Aluminum alloys, *monocoque* construction, far advanced over the flimsy old wooden contraptions that were used in the war. I'd desperately like to hear how they are faring in field conditions in Russia. The army won't let me send my technical experts there." He looked at Horner, half hoping that he would offer to arrange for this, but Horner looked away.

"Perhaps I'm getting too old," said Fischer. "My son Richard thinks as you do: he's obsessed with the designing of all these wretched tanks, to the point of neglecting our other clients. I tell him these Bolsheviks are treacherous and he laughs at me."

"We have a mutual enemy," said Horner. He blew a smoke ring and admired it. The drink and the conspiratory atmosphere had gone to his head.

"Us and the Russians? The Poles, you mean?" said Fischer. "I have never believed that Poland was a serious threat to us."

There was a light tap at the door, and when Winter called "Come in" his wife entered. Time had been kind to Veronica Winter. She had lost little of the beauty that had turned men's heads when

Winter had first met her. She was thinner now than she'd been then, and her face, throat, and arms, revealed by the striped brown-and-yellow silk-voile evening dress she wore, were paler. But the serenity that made her desirable, and the smile that was so often on her lips, had gone. Veronica was perturbed.

"Harald!" she said, having indicated that the other two men should not stand up for her. "Who are those dreadful men?"

"Dreadful men?" said Winter. "Which men?" He flicked ash from his cigar. It was a sign of his irritation at being interrupted.

In an attempt to calm her, Fischer chuckled and said, "There are so many dreadful men in your house tonight, Veronica, that even your husband can't keep track of them."

"How can you say such a thing, Herr Fischer?" she replied, feigning offense. To her husband she said, "Two men in some sort of uniform."

Harald Winter said, "One of them is a fellow who calls himself 'Captain' Graf, one of the ruffians who took his private army down to Munich to fight the communists."

"Pauli's commander?" said Veronica.

"Yes, until our Pauli had enough sense to stay here and go to school."

"And the other?" said Veronica.

"Is there another?" said Harald. He looked at Fischer, who shrugged, and then to Alex Horner.

Horner answered her. "His name is Fritz Esser. He's a friend of Pauli, Frau Winter. An old friend."

"The name is familiar," she said doubtfully.

Alex added, "Back before the war he lived at Travemünde. Pauli recruited him into his Freikorps and he stayed with them."

"The Essers," said Harald Winter. "Yes, I remember the family. They lived in the village, near Mother. It's the little fellow who saved the children from drowning. Why do you want to know, darling?"

"People are asking me who they are, Harald. They hardly look like friends of ours. And now this Captain Graf person has gone up to the servants' rooms."

Winter got to his feet. "Whatever for?" he asked, but he guessed the answer before it came. There were two youngsters working in the house, and Captain Graf's homosexual activities had been given considerable publicity. Some said that threats of police prosecution on this account were the reason he'd taken his battalion from Berlin.

Veronica blushed. "I'd rather not say, Harald."

"I'll have the blackguard thrown out!"

Now the other two men were standing. Fischer put a hand out to touch Winter's arm. "Let someone else go, Harry. Graf is a dangerous fellow."

"Please allow me to attend to it," said Alex Horner with studied casualness. "Graf is, I regret to say, a member of the Officer Corps. His behavior directly concerns me."

Harald Winter didn't answer, nor did his wife. It was Fischer who replied to Horner's offer. "Yes, Leutnant Horner. That would be the best way."

There was a certain grim inevitability to the unfortunate business at Pauli's birthday party. Inviting Captain Graf to such a party was undoubtedly a mistake, but no one had expected him to accept the invitation. It was only because Esser was coming that Captain Graf came, too.

Once inside the house, Captain Graf drank his first glass of champagne far too quickly. It was French champagne. Where Harald Winter had got it no one knew, but once Graf had downed one he had another and then another. Then Esser found the cognac. Captain Graf's storm company had captured a French distillery during the 1918 offensives, and the bouquet brought happy memories of those exciting days so long ago. And Graf was a man as easily affected by memories as by alcohol. By the time he spotted the young under-footman and followed him upstairs, he was tight enough to miss his footing on the steps more than once.

Captain Graf afterwards maintained that he'd only been looking for a bedroom in which he could rest for an hour, but when Hauser—Harald Winter's longtime valet and general factotum—stopped Graf from entering a servant's room on the second floor, Captain Graf stabbed Hauser in the chest with a folding knife.

Hauser—in his mid-forties and gassed in the war—shouted and collapsed, bleeding profusely. One of the chambermaids heard the scuffle and found Hauser unconscious in a pool of blood. She screamed after Captain Graf, who was by then running down the back staircase with the bloody knife still in his hand.

It was Leutnant Alex Horner who intercepted Graf. He knew

the house from his many visits there, and guessed Graf's route of escape.

"Captain Graf? I believe—" Graf lunged at Horner with the knife, and Horner avoided the blade so narrowly that its tip slashed the front of his dinner jacket.

But Alex Horner was not the dressmaker's dummy that Graf mistook him for. His years at the front with Pauli and the vicious trench raids that Leutnant Brand had repeatedly assigned him to had produced reactions that were as instinctive as they were effective.

Horner swung aside and, as Graf completed his unsuccessful knife thrust, aimed a powerful blow at the captain's head. It sent him reeling, but Graf was a fighter, too. He recovered his balance and lunged again, so that Alex had to retreat up the narrow servants' corridor to avoid the slashes aimed at him. Graf grinned, but it was a drunken grin, and it encouraged Alex to take a chance. He kicked hard and high, knocking the knife aside. Horner grabbed the knife, and now it was Graf's turn to flee.

Graf found his way down the servants' stairs, through the pantry, and to the tradesmen's entrance at the rear, and slammed the heavy door behind him. The wooden frame had swollen with the damp of winter, and by the time Alex had wrenched it open, run through the yard, and reached the street, there was no sign of Graf except some footprints in the newly fallen snow.

Alex Horner stopped and caught his breath. He knew enough about fighting to know when to stop. He looked up the moonlit street; there were coaches waiting to collect guests, their coachmen huddled against the cold night, faces lit by glowing cigarettes, the breath of the horses making clouds of white vapor. It was very cold, as only Berlin can be, with a few snowflakes drifting in the wind and a film of ice on everything. The city was silent, and yet it was not the empty stillness of the countryside: it was the brooding quiet of a crowded, sleeping city. From somewhere nearby came the sound of a powerful motorcar engine starting, and the squeal of tires. That would be Graf; the fellow was often to be seen in his big motorcar.

Alex reached into his pocket for a cigarette and stood there on the street smoking as he thought about what had happened. Thank God, Graf had had plenty to drink—he'd have been a formidable adversary sober. Better to forget the whole business, he decided. Graf and his ilk had friends in high places and in the Bendlerblock the army bureaucrats were now referring to Röhm's storm troops as the "Black Reichswehr," treating them as a secret army reserve. Testifying against Graf might well mar his career prospects. Any last delusion that the army kept out of politics had long since gone. Getting promoted in this curious postwar army was like walking through a minefield.

By the time Alex Horner had finished his cigarette and returned to the party, it was almost as if nothing untoward had occurred. Hauser was in bed and being attended by a doctor, the bloodstains had been scrubbed from the carpet, the band was playing, and the guests were dancing as if nothing had happened. In fact, many of the guests were not aware of the murderous scuffle on the back stairs.

Peter Winter was dancing with a glorious girl in a decorative evening dress of a quality that was seldom seen in Germany in these austere times. The girl had brazenly approached Peter and asked him to dance. "I hear you're a good dancer, Herr Winter. How would you like to prove it to me?"

Her German was not good. The grammar was adequate, but the accent was outlandish. Not the hard consonantal growl of the Hungarian or the Czech, this was a strange, flat drawling accent of a sort he couldn't for a moment distinguish.

"Are you Austrian?" Peter asked.

She laughed in a way that was almost unladylike. "You flatterer! I heard you were a ladies' man, Peter Winter, and now I declare it's true. You know my German is not good enough for me to be Austrian. Is that what you say to any girl you encounter with a weird accent you don't recognize?"

Peter blushed. It was exactly what he said to any girl whose accent he couldn't place. "Of course not," he muttered.

"I'm from California, U.S.A.," she said. "We're almost family. Your mother was at school with my aunt."

"That's not family," said Peter.

She laughed. "You Germans all have such a wonderful sense of humor." But Peter was not amused to be the butt of her joke. "Well," she said, stretching her long, pale arms towards him, "aren't you going to ask me to dance?"

Peter clicked his heels and bowed formally. She laughed again.

Peter felt confused, almost panic-stricken, and this was a strange, new experience for him. He wanted to flee but he couldn't. He was afraid of this girl, afraid that she would think him a fool. He wanted her to like him and respect him, and that, of course, is how love first strikes the unwary.

"Yes, you dance quite well," she said as they stepped out onto the dance floor to the smooth romantic chords of "Poor Butterfly." Her name was Lottie Danziger and her father owned two hotels, three movie theatres, and some orange groves in California. She wore the most attention-getting evening dress of anyone there. It had a tubelike shape that deprived her of breasts and bottom. It was short and sleeveless, and its bodice was embroidered with bugle beads and imitation baroque pearls in the sort of Egyptian motif that had been all the rage since Howard Carter's amazing discoveries in Egypt's Valley of the Kings. The trouble was that the beadwork was so heavy that it made Lottie want to sit down, and so fragile that she was frightened of doing so.

Lottie was like no other woman that Peter Winter had ever met. She was not like the German girls he'd known, or even like any of the Rensselaer family. She was beautiful, with pale skin and naturally wavy jet-black hair, cut very short in a style that was new to Berlin, not like the short hairstyles that were necessary to get the close-fitting cloche hats on, but bobbed almost like a man's. She had dark, wicked eyes and a mouth that was perhaps a little too big, and very white, even teeth that flashed when she smiled. And she smiled a lot. Not the polite, tight-lipped smiles that well-bred German girls were taught, but big open-mouthed laughs that were infectious: Peter found himself laughing, too. But above all Lottie was intense; she was a fountain of energy, so that everything she did, from dancing to telling jokes about the young men she'd encountered on the ocean liner, was uniquely wonderful, and Peter was beguiled by every movement she made.

"I have a cousin Rachael who is my chaperone, darling. We couldn't possibly go without her." It was her crazy transatlantic style to call Peter "darling" right from the first moment, but her flippant use of the word made it no less tantalizing. Every suggestion he made for seeing her again was met with some wretched rule about her chaperone. She was playing with him: they both knew that she could meet with him alone if she really wanted to, and it was this that put an extra edge on their exchanges. She was so desirable that his need for her pushed all other thoughts and aspirations out of his head.

"But you don't look like a Rensselaer," she said, having for a moment silenced his attempts to arrange another meeting. She swung her head back to see him better and cocked it on one side, so that her dark, wavy hair shone in the lights. "No, you don't look like a Rensselaer at all."

She was teasing him, of course, but he readily joined her game. "And what do the Rensselaers look like?"

"Gorgeous. You have only to look at your mother to know that. The Rensselaers are the most beautiful family in the whole of New York. Why, when your uncle Glenn came back from the war he must have been getting on for forty years old, and yet there wasn't a girl in the city who didn't dream of capturing him. The groans and gnashing of teeth when he married were to be heard from Hoboken to Hollywood. Your uncle Glenn came here just after the war, didn't he?"

"He was an Air Corps major attached to the Armistice Commission. He wanted Mother to go back to New York, but Father was against it."

"Why?"

"He said it would look bad. All through the war he'd been saying that Mother was at heart a German. That was how he prevented her from being interned. How would it look, he said, if when the Allies won she went running back to America?"

"Her parents are too old to travel, and they'd give anything to see her again."

"Papa was adamant."

"Do all German families obey Father so readily?"

"I don't know," said Peter.

"In America your father would find life more difficult. You should have heard what my father said when I first told them I was coming to Europe."

"What did he say?"

"He cut me off without a penny, darling," she said with a laugh. "But eventually he came around." She hummed the melody: " 'Poor Butterfly,' it's such a beautiful tune, isn't it? I never hear it but I think of the war: all those poor butterflies that never came back."

"Yes," he said without being sure that he understood. Until now he'd not liked Americans, not the Rensselaers, not President Wilson, not any of them. They were not easy to understand. But this one—with her hair bobbed almost like a man's, and the fringe that came down to her eyebrows—was captivating. As he swung her past a huge arrangement of fresh-cut flowers, she extended her hand so that the fingertips brushed the blooms. It was a schoolgirl's gesture—she had to show the world how happy she was. Perhaps all Americans were like that: they were not good at secrecy, they had to demonstrate their emotions.

They danced on until they passed Inge Wisliceny dancing with Richard Fischer. Inge looked especially beautiful tonight. Long dresses and deep necklines were becoming on her. Lottie let go of Peter's hand to wave to her. Inge smiled sadly as they whirled past and disappeared. "And where is your uncle Glenn now?" she asked.

"Heaven knows. Somewhere in Europe. Every few weeks we get a postcard from him. He visits now and again and he's always sending gifts of food. He thinks we're starving."

"Many Germans are starving," Lottie reminded him. "But Glenn was always generous. He was my very favorite man. I was eighteen when he got married. I cried to think I'd lost him. I went to the East Coast just to be a bridesmaid. Handsome, clever, and brave."

"And rich, too," said Peter sardonically. He was getting rather fed up with this eulogy to Glenn Rensselaer.

"Not your uncle Glenn. He cares nothing for money, but his father is rich, of course."

"My grandfather, you mean; yes, he got rich from the war," said Peter. "They say that one out of every ten trucks the American army used came from a Rensselaer factory."

"You're not going to be one of those boring people who want to blame the war on war profiteers."

"So many people died," said Peter. "It's obscene to think that the fighting made anyone rich."

"So what would you prefer?" she said. "That the government own everything, make everything, and decide how much money each and every citizen deserves?"

"It might be better."

"You'd better stay away from politics, Peter Winter. No one will believe that you could be so *dumm* as to want to deliver yourself to the politicians."

"Yes. Long, long ago my brother, Pauli, told me more or less the same thing."

There was something touching about Peter Winter when he admitted to his shortcomings. "You're adorable," she said and brushed her lips across his cheek. He caught a whiff of her perfume. "Why are you staring at me?" he asked.

"I know you so well from your photographs. Your grandfather has pictures of you everywhere in his house in New York. And in the room where I practiced piano there is a photo of you at the keyboard. You must have been about ten or twelve. They told me you practiced three hours every day. Is it true?"

"I've given up the piano. I haven't touched a piano for years."

"But why?"

"My hand was injured."

"Where? Show me." She pulled his hand round into view. "That? Why, that's nothing. How can that make any difference to a real musician?"

"I can't play Bach with a fingertip missing." For the first time she heard real anger in his voice, and she was sorry for him.

"Don't be so arrogant. Perhaps it will prevent your becoming a professional pianist, but how can you not play? You must love music. Or don't you?"

"I love music."

"Of course you do. Now, tomorrow you will visit me and I will play some records for you. Do you like jazz music?"

"It's all right."

"If you think it's only all right, then you haven't heard any. Tomorrow you'll hear some of the best jazz music on records. I brought them from New York with me. You'll come? I'm staying with the Wislicenys."

"I know. Yes, I'd be honored." Listening to jazz music was a small price to pay for being alone in her room with this wonderful girl.

"The really great jazz is not on records. You should hear it in Harlem. Although you have to go to the black people's brothels in Memphis or New Orleans to hear the real thing."

Peter Winter turned his head away so that she didn't see his embarrassment. Even in this degenerate, wide-open city of Berlin one didn't expect well-brought-up young ladies to know what a brothel was, let alone to mention it in conversation with a man.

"Are you looking for someone?" she asked.

"My brother." It was not true, but it would do.

"Your father sent for him. I was there. Is something wrong?"

"Pauli invited some strange people."

"Sure, but it's his show."

"His birthday? Yes, but sometimes one's friends do not mix well with family."

"Will he get told off?"

"He'll get round it. Pauli can charm his way out of anything," said Peter.

"Do I hear a note of envy?"

"No." Peter smiled. How could he ever envy Pauli, except sometimes for the way that his parents indulged him? "He's always getting into the sort of scrapes that test his charm to the very limit. Goodness knows how he'll ever pass his law finals."

"I can't imagine your brother, Pauli, as a lawyer."

"And what about me?"

"Easily . . . a trial lawyer, perhaps. You have the style for that."

"And Pauli doesn't?"

She was cautious. Peter's readiness to defend his brother against any sort of criticism was something of which the Wisliceny girls had already told her. "Is there any need for him to do anything? Isn't it enough that he'll inherit half the Winter fortune and keep this fine old house going while you run the business?"

Peter smiled grimly. "Father would have something to say about that. Father is a man of the Kaiserzeit. . . . So, I suppose, am I."

"Yes, you are."

"And you don't object to us formal, humorless Teutons?"

"Object? Goodness, what could I object to? I'm not going to marry and settle down here. I'm just a tourist."

He hastily thought of something to say. "Pauli's not a fool. He's clever, and as brave as a lion."

"Poor butterfly . . ." she sang softly as they danced. She knew the words, and her soft, low, murmuring voice was bewitching.

"Keep your money. . . ."

Pauli loved and feared his father, but now the time had come for him to speak up for himself or be crushed by his father's personality.

He looked at the picture of the Kaiser that hung on the wall, and then he caught his breath and turned on his father. "You pretend it's a party for me, but who are invited to your grand house? Your rich friends and the people you want to impress, that's who. Do you know what I think about your friends and your party? . . ." He stopped. His mother's face had turned pale, and there was a look of such anguish there that he could not bear to hurt her more. Through the door he could hear the band playing "Poor Butterfly." It took him back to the first day of the 1918 offensive—the captured British battery, the tinny gramophone.

"Go on," said Harald Winter calmly. Deeply hurt by his son's outburst, he couldn't repress a secret feeling of satisfaction that Veronica was present to see his predictions come true. For Harald more than once had said that Pauli was an ungrateful wretch. It was his terrible experiences in the war, of course. Harald Winter had always been quick to explain the faults of those around him. Pauli had been through all sorts of hell, and that had affected him. Otherwise the boy would have been pleased to have such a lavish celebration held in his honor. As for Pauli's complaint that most of the people there were friends of his parents rather than his own friends, he should have the sense to understand that this was his chance to get reacquainted with people who matter. And, anyway, a formal dinner of this scale was not something that his Freikorps rowdies, or his noisy, loose-living student friends, would appreciate. Judging by what Winter heard at his club, the whole party would have become an orgy inside ten minutes.

Harald Winter told his son, "Captain Graf was invited at your insistence, as I understand it. How do you explain his disgraceful criminal conduct?"

"I fought alongside Graf, and many others like him. They fought the communists, and are still fighting them, to keep Germany safe for you and others like you. Who are you to sit in judgment on him? What did you do in the war except make money?"

"I haven't noticed that you decline the chance to spend a portion of it. You have a generous allowance, a motorcycle . . . your college fees, books, you run up bills at my tailor." Harald stopped, choked with indignation and anger.

"Keep your money. . . ."

"No, Pauli, no. Say nothing that you'll regret tomorrow," his mother pleaded.

"What loyalty do you show to your friends?" persisted Pauli. "Tonight you've invited all your aristocratic Russian refugee friends: princes, dukes, and duchesses, and even that old fool who claims to be a nephew of the Tsar. Do they know that aircraft built in your factories are helping to train the Red Army that kicked them off their grand estates?"

"The army don't ask my advice about where to use their aircraft," said Harald Winter calmly.

"I can't continue living in this house," said Pauli. "I should never have moved back here. It's stifling, constricting, like a prison, like a museum." To his mother he said softly, "It's better that I go, Mama: We live in such different worlds. You hate my friends and I have grown to hate your values."

"Decency and respect? What values are you talking about?" said Harald Winter. "Poor Hauser was stabbed by that madman Graf. Your friend Esser has drunk so much that he vomited on the morning-room carpet and knocked over a caseful of chinaware. How dare you tell me that you hate my friends and my values?"

Pauli shrugged. It was always like this when he was dragged into a row; he found himself arguing to support issues in which he didn't believe. He loved Hauser and despised Graf, but that didn't change the fact that his father's world was an ancient, alien place from which he must escape. "I'm sorry, Papa. Forgive me, but it's better that I leave. I will go to Hamburg or Munich or somewhere I can start again. I would never have got through my finals anyway. I am too stupid to study the law. But Peter will fulfill your hopes and expectations."

"Pauli . . ." said his mother.

"Let him go," said Harald Winter. "He'll be back when the money runs out. I've heard it all before. Let him discover what it's like to be a penniless beggar in these terrible times. He'll be back knocking at the door before the month is out."

Veronica said nothing. She did not believe that Pauli would come back begging for his father's help. And, in fact, neither did his father.

In the event, Pauli did move his effects from the house, but he didn't go to Hamburg or Munich. He moved into a room in the nearby district of Wedding in a boardinghouse run by a war widow, an intimate friend of Fritz Esser. Pauli declined to take any more payments from his father, but he did not give up his law studies.

It was Peter who spent hours pleading his brother's case. It was Peter who reminded his father of the terrible time Pauli had had in the war, and Peter who conspired with his mother so that the approaches were made when Harald was in a good mood.

Although Pauli took no more money from his father, his brother, Peter, transferred money to his bank account each month. Pauli's parents accepted this covert financial arrangement, and honor was satisfied. Pauli was happy to feel that he wasn't accepting money from his father, while his father was happy to know that in fact he was. And, as Harald Winter remarked to his wife, he didn't want Pauli to be driven to such a state of penury that he sold that house on the Obersalzberg.

Most important, Pauli got permission from the university to switch, starting the following term, from corporation law to criminal law. It was a study that Pauli found immediately interesting and relevant. To everyone's surprise, not least to Pauli's, he caught up quickly with his fellow students and came fifth from the top in his exams.

Coaching Fritz Esser in this subject was less successful, although with a great deal of effort Fritz got through his interim exams before abandoning his studies. One day, he promised, he'd go back and get his law degree. But meanwhile he'd become a full-time paid official of the Nazi Party and wholly occupied with politics.

Soon after Pauli left home, his uncle Glenn Rensselaer found his shabby lodging. Glenn was working for some American office-machinery company that had its main agency in Leipzig. He came often to Berlin and always brought Pauli presents. Pauli liked Glenn; he liked the way he came up to the top-floor garret room and did not stare around at the cracked linoleum, the newspaper pasted on the broken windowpanes to provide a modicum of privacy, the chamberpot under the bed, or the unshaded light bulb. Glenn seemed perfectly at home in the rat-infested tenement. The occasion of his arrival was usually marked by Glenn's presenting the landlady and certain other tenants with bottles of schnapps. Glenn said he got them cheap, but Pauli knew he paid full price at the shop round the corner. Glenn was like that.

When Pauli passed his final exams, it was Glenn who persuaded Harald to attend the ceremony, and Glenn who arranged dinner for twenty-four people at Medvedj, a smart restaurant on Bayreuther Strasse, and footed the bill for blini and caviar, borscht and kulibiaki, a gypsy trio, and all the trimmings in this fashionable restaurant where Berlin's Russian exiles liked to go when they could afford it. And when Glenn asked so casually what Pauli would do next, and Pauli gave a long, involved explanation about a company that had offered to provide him with an office and secretarial help on condition that he do some legal work for them, Glenn's congratulations sounded warm and sincere. But Glenn Rensselaer was no fool, and he guessed just as quickly as did Peter and Harald Winter that the "company" that was to play fairy godmother was the Nazi Party, and that Pauli was going to be defending some of the worst thugs involved in the streetfighting, assaults, and murders that had become a regular part of the German political scene.

When, the following October, Peter talked about becoming engaged to Lottie Danziger, Glenn Rensselaer gave Lottie a jade brooch bearing Peter's initials on the gold setting and gave Peter a watch engraved with the date of their intended engagement party. "Now," Glenn Rensselaer told them both, "you'll have to go ahead." And they did. It was another big party, this time at the Wisliceny house. Lottie's parents did not come. They had long before decided that Lottie was going to marry the eldest son of a West Coast oil tycoon, and they were angry to think of Lottie's marrying Peter Winter, a German. "Not so angry as I am," said Harald Winter to his wife the night he first heard the news: and many, many times afterwards. "I don't know what appalls me more," he said, "the thought of him married to an American or to a Jew."

His wife did not take this insult personally. During the war she had grown used to hearing her countrymen denigrated and insulted. Calmly she said, "How can you say that, when the Fischers are such close friends?"

"The Fischers are different."

"And Peter and Lottie plan to live in Germany. Think of her poor parents—six thousand miles away—they are losing her forever." It was an expression of Veronica's guilt. Now, as her father grew old, she thought about him more and more.

Harald Winter grunted. He felt not at all grateful to fate or to the girl. *Of course* they would remain in Germany. Peter hadn't taken complete leave of his senses, thank God.

1925

"You don't have to be a mathematician . . ."

"Explain?" said Glenn Rensselaer. "I can't explain it any better than I have there in the written report." The bald-headed young American behind the desk looked at him blankly. Glenn Rensselaer went on: "I guess you mean describe it in terms of its U.S. equivalents. Well, I can't do that, either. These Freikorps groups are just bands of armed men in makeshift uniforms. Usually their commanders are captains or majors, sometimes a colonel, and, rarely, a sergeant. They take their orders from whoever pays them, and sometimes they don't even obey their paymasters. Some of the officers behave like gangsters; some of the rankers are professional criminals. But some of these men are patriots and idealists. It's impossible to generalize about the Freikorps except to say—thank God—there is nothing in the U.S. that I can compare them to."

The man behind the desk still said nothing. Glenn Rensselaer looked round the gloomy little upstairs room on Washington's K Street. Ancient floral wallpaper, an old desk, some dented filing cabinets, a worn carpet, and in the corner a large brass spittoon, brightly polished. So this was the U.S. State Department's idea of a suitable office for its "research and intelligence subsection." Was it secrecy, parsimony, or neglect?

"On the other hand," said Glenn Rensselaer, more to break the silence than because he felt the man behind the desk was interested, "for a lot of people Germany right now is where everything is happening. The movies, legitimate theatre, the opera, popular music, light opera, orchestral music, science—from atomic physics to psychology—architecture, industrial design, painting . . . every damn thing." He stubbed out his cigarette and added, "Is all this boring you? I have the feeling that there are other things you'd rather be doing."

"Not at all," said the bald young official. "I find everything you tell me fascinating. But I'm likely to be the only person in the whole State Department who will read your report all through."

"Is that so?"

"The U.S. has lost interest in Europe, except to count how many battleships the British are building under the terms of the new treaty."

"You're talking in riddles."

"Forgive me: I don't mean to. What I should have said is that right now no one wants to talk about anything but Japanese naval strength. You must be familiar with the terms of the 1922 conference—a ratio of five British capital ships and three Japanese capital ships for five of ours. You don't have to be a mathematician to see that under the terms of that treaty the combined naval strength of the Japs and the Brits would gun us off both oceans."

"You don't have to be a mathematician," agreed Glenn Rensselaer. "You just have to be nuts."

Again came the inscrutable look. No reply. Perhaps Glenn should not have come here wearing this old jacket and flannels with his brightly patterned bow tie and knitted pullover. The man behind the desk was in a tight-fitting suit with a stiff collar. Glenn had forgotten what it was like in Washington, D.C.

Glenn persisted. "You're not seriously suggesting that we're likely to get into a fight against the British, are you?"

"It's our job to take into account even the most unlikely eventuality, Mr. Rensselaer."

"You guys are out of your minds. If we tangled with the Japs, the British would be alongside us." He got to his feet and the man got up, too.

"I'm sure you're right, Mr. Rensselaer," said the man in a voice that betrayed nothing of his thoughts. "Anyway, it was good of you to come. We don't get much first-hand news these days."

Glenn Rensselaer was glad to get back to his parents' house in New York. It was home to him, for his travels abroad made it convenient and convivial for his wife to share his father's large mansion. She got along well with Cy Rensselaer's second wife, Dot, and now that Dot's three sons had grown up and left home, she was company for the older woman.

When he returned from his trip to Washington, his father asked him about it, but Glenn was unforthcoming. Had he explained his reception at the bureaucrats' "secret" office, his father would probably have taken exception to the description. The Republican Party firmly controlled House and Senate. Calvin Coolidge was in the White House. The old man preferred to believe that the men in Washington knew what they were doing. It was a point of view difficult to sustain after a trip to the capital, which was perhaps why his father never went there.

So Glenn talked to his father about Germany. "Since the war you see on the streets this large rootless proletariat," Glenn told his father. "Mostly from the East: Poles, Czechs, Russians, Hungarians, Rumanians, gypsies, dispossessed smallholders and peasants, factory workers, and God knows who. In order to blame these badly dressed, incoherent outsiders for every misfortune from petty crime to factory closures and job losses, a name was required. So the Germans have decided to call them 'Jews.' "

"Don't make jokes about Jews, son. I can't abide it, never could."

"I'm not joking. Anti-Semitism is everywhere; you smell it in the air."

"That's not just in Europe, Glenn."

"No, but in France and England and here in the U.S., anti-Semitism is a form of envy. It's mostly directed at the rich, clever, and successful. The anti-Semite depicts the Jew as a man with a diamond tie pin, in a big automobile, smoking a cigar, and coming to collect the profits from his factory. In Germany they have that anti-Semitic envy, too. And it's especially strong there because the Jew plays a vital part in the cultural life of Germany. The movies, the theatre, publishing, and the art world are conspicuously dominated by Jews. But there's this other sort of anti-Semitism, too."

"Does it really matter?"

His father felt uncomfortable, but Glenn continued: "It's a downward-looking anti-Semitism. I'm talking about the fear of any strange-looking, penniless itinerant. Now, add that to the envy and you've got an explosive mixture. That's why Germany is unique. This double anti-Semitism comes from Germany's geographical position; that's why it's different from anything you find in other countries. And let me tell you that there are a hell of a lot of German politicians who know exactly how to stir up that mixture."

"Is it the Nazis you're talking about? Only last week there were pictures in one of the weeklies."

"There are others, but the Nazis are the most dedicated and the most dangerous. This fellow Hitler has renewed strength since being in prison. Politically it's the best thing that could have happened to him. He's a sort of romantic, and he understands that blend of sentimentality and cruelty that is uniquely German. He knows how to appeal to a lot of different Bavarian malcontents. Want to restore the monarchy? Hitler's your man. Feel the nice Bavarian Catholics are ill-treated by nasty Prussian Protestants? Hitler. Want to hear that the bureaucrats in Berlin are the cause of Bavaria's troubles? Want to hear that the General Staff—Protestant every one—lost the war? Lost your job? A Jew took it from you. Your factory went out of business? A Jewish boss did it and made a profit on the deal. Socialists organizing a strike you don't like? Communists fighting in the street? Everyone knows Moscow is run by Jews. You don't agree? Then either you are being duped or you are a Jew and a part of the conspiracy."

"That might sound good to voters in Bavaria, but it won't get mister Hitler very far if he wants to get into the national government. The way I hear it, Hitler is virtually unknown outside of Bavaria, and my guess is he'll stay that way."

"You don't know this guy. Don't imagine he has any kind of written manifesto that you can challenge him on. He's all things to all men. He trades on emotions, not facts. When he goes for the Reichstag he'll have a fresh set of answers ready. This guy is dynamite. We had an office in Munich. I've heard him speaking at his meetings. He holds people spellbound. He's full of spite, brimful of hatred and contempt. There is nothing constructive in what he says: just threats of what he'll do to the sort of people he blames for all the troubles."

"All politicians are negative," said his father. "A promise to punish the fortunate and soak the rich is always good for a few votes."

"But in Germany too many people are ready to believe in the quick and easy solution."

"It will all pass," said his father. There was a note of weariness detectable in his voice. His father was still so energetic that it was difficult to believe he was seventy-four years old, except when now and again the mask slipped. "It's the legacy of the war—defeat, disappointment, hunger. It will pass."

"I wish I could believe you, Dad. But the fact is that this poison is more prevalent among students than among any other sector of the population. Students—university students for the most part, fellows who were too young to go to the war—are more bitter about the defeat than the soldiers who were in the fighting. Veterans know in their hearts that the Germans were licked on the battlefield; the kids who weren't there like to believe all that "stab-in-the-back" stuff. And the kids are the ones who get violent. They are full of energy and full of hate. They are looking for a cause, and Hitler will provide it for them."

"For God's sake, don't tell the Danzigers any of this, Glenn. Lottie's father is worried sick at the idea of her remaining in Berlin. He always calls me up when he comes into town, and we usually lunch at the club. Some idiot friend of his sent him clippings from German newspapers. He had his office translate the stuff. I don't know what it said, but he's darned worried. So don't tell him, huh?"

"The club? Is Mr. Danziger now a member of the club?"

His father looked flustered. "Well, no. They still have that stupid rule about members . . . but taking a Jew in as a guest is okay."

Glenn could think of nothing to say. They sat in silence for a few moments. Outside there was the continual sound of motorcars; it was hard to believe that when he was a child the house had been so quiet.

"He's letting some little film company build movie lots and stages on his orange groves."

"Danziger?" said Glenn.

"Just a handful of cash and twenty-five percent of the movie company."

"Is it a good deal?"

"He's gone soft in the head, if you ask me. Twenty-five percent of nothing is nothing. Just like ninety-nine percent of nothing is nothing. And what's a movie company got in assets except its real estate?"

"Did you tell Danziger that?"

"Contracts, he says. Contracts with actors. Can you imagine how that would show on the auditors' books?"

"Movies are doing okay, aren't they?"

"Do you know how long it will take him to get real quality fruit growing there again?"

"Danziger can afford a few mistakes," said Glenn Rensselaer.

"I'm not sure he can," said his father. "The Danzigers are not rich."

Glenn smiled.

"I'm serious."

"I know you are, Dad, but I remember you telling me that his assets would total some five million dollars. How can you say he's not rich?"

The old man did not reply for a moment. He didn't think it was funny. But Glenn Rensselaer had noticed that this obsession with money, the raw measure of power that money represented, was one of the few ways in which his father's old age showed. "To tell you frankly, I wasn't happy to think of his eldest daughter marrying into the family. Lottie is a nice enough girl, of course, but not right for little Peter."

"Your 'little Peter' is now a qualified lawyer and a junior partner in Winter's holding company."

His father seemed not to have heard. "I couldn't say that to Danziger, of course."

"No, of course," said Glenn. In fact, old Cyrus Rensselaer's opinion of Lottie Danziger's suitability had not been sought by Harald Winter, by Veronica Winter, or by Peter Winter. And the old man had been hurt by that.

"I miss her," said his father suddenly.

"Veronica? But that's half a lifetime ago."

"I should never have agreed to her going to Europe. I had a strange premonition about it."

"Really?"

"But she was determined to go, and I wanted her to be happy."

There was a passion in the old man that he'd not heard before. The loss of his beloved daughter was an agony that had tormented him all this time.

"But that was more than thirty years ago, Dad."

"Wait till your children leave home; you'll find out what it's like."

"And me? Did you miss me?"

"Sure I did. But I worried about Veronica. She was such a sweet child. So helpless, so trusting . . . I hate that bastard. You know that, don't you?"

"Harry?"

"I'll pay him back." For the first time his father smiled. It was the crafty smile that only the old know. "He'll suffer as I've suffered. Then he'll know what he did to me."

"You mustn't blame Harry. He was an attractive man: powerful and ruthless in a way that Veronica found attractive . . ." Glenn stopped.

"Attractive in me? Is that what you were going to say?"

Reluctantly Glenn admitted it. "Yes, Harry is ruthless in that same way."

"And you didn't admire it?"

"It's not my style, Dad. And that was just as well—we would have fought."

"You're right, Glenn. You never fought me. You've been a good son. Did I never tell you that?"

"It's good to hear, Dad."

"Loyal. And I love loyalty. Just as I repay treachery. Want to know what I've done about Harry?"

"I'm not sure I do."

"I've fixed it so that Peter is offered the job of a lifetime. And Harald adores Peter, the eldest."

"A job?"

"A bank in Los Angeles. I recently bought a stake in it. They'll offer Peter Winter a vice-presidency. He'll come and live in America."

"A bank in Los Angeles?"

"I fixed jobs for two of Dot's boys in the bank there, and they are doing fine." Glenn nodded. He'd heard that the old man had gone to a lot of trouble for his stepsons. They, in return, had taken the name Rensselaer. "And Peter will do fine, too."

"I'd forget about it, Dad. You don't want to come between father and son."

"What about father and daughter?" the old man said shrilly. "That's what he did, that Harald Winter, the swine."

"That was natural. He fell in love. He didn't do it to give you a bad time, Dad."

"He fell in love with the Rensselaer money, that's what he fell in love with; everyone knows that."

"He was doing all right without it."

"He was on the verge of bankruptcy. I bailed that tinhorn out, not once but twice, and then he had the nerve to pay me back in confetti."

"Let him be, Dad. Veronica loves you; she'll visit you. Be patient."

"It's too late now. He'll find out what it's like. He'll find out and I'll have the laugh on him."

"Take it easy, Dad."

"He'll find out what it's like to lose your favorite child."

Glenn Rensselaer nodded but didn't answer. He'd always known that he wasn't his father's favorite, but hearing him say it hurt, hurt like hell.

"It's nothing to cry about."

Veronica Winter knew before her husband, and it was Lottie Winter who told her. The two women had become very close since Lottie's marriage to Peter. At first it had been no more than the comfort of an American voice, but over the months the relationship had become more like that of mother and daughter. Harald Winter didn't like it, of course—he'd never liked Lottie enough to welcome her as a daughter-in-law—but he was shrewd enough to know, right from the start, that he could do nothing to influence the relationship. So Veronica and her daughter-in-law had tea together regularly. It was an event to which both women always looked forward with great pleasure.

It was two weeks before Christmas when Lottie brought the exciting news about the job. An Italian-born vice-president of the bank had made a special journey from Milan, Italy, where he was consolidating a big loan and visiting some members of his family, just to put the matter to Peter in person.

"But it will be wonderful, Lottie. You'll be with your family again."

"Yes, it will be."

"Why so down-in-the-mouth?" said Veronica. She'd never seen her daughter-in-law like this before.

"I feel so at home here now. It has been so marvelous putting the home together for Peter that I can't face the thought of losing it all and starting again."

"But think of the sunshine and your family."

"I know, I keep telling myself that. But here I'm a person, a someone. At home my folks treat me like a child."

"Not now you're married, they won't, Lottie darling. Your mother will be transported to have you there with her."

"She's not my real mother. My real mother died in a railroad accident in Chicago when I was five."

"I'm sorry, Lottie; I forgot that."

"And my stepmother won't be so crazy about having to share Dad."

"I'm sure you're wrong," said Veronica.

"No, I know her too well. She loves me and I love her, but every letter she writes says how pleased she is that I'm settling down here."

"What about your father?"

"I'd like to go and see Dad, but a visit would be enough. A visit over January, February, and March, when the weather is so terrible here."

"And what about Peter?"

"I don't want to influence him one way or the other. It's his life: his career. And all the more difficult when a family business is involved."

"His father wouldn't disinherit him, Lottie."

"Now, don't get me wrong, Mrs. Winter. Money doesn't enter into it, but I reckon that a wife, if she's smart, doesn't give her husband advice about his career. Because if things go wrong she is likely to get all the blame. Men are like that; at least I figure they are."

"I'm afraid men are like that, Lottie."

The maid came in. Veronica had recently changed all the servants' uniforms so that they were no longer in ankle-length skirts. This parlormaid had a fashionably short black dress with a superb lace apron and cap. Lottie decided that her servants should be similarly modernized.

It was the complete silver tea service. Even though the two women knew that neither of their husbands would join them, plates, teacups, and cutlery were set for four, as always. As well as the traditional German plum tart there were brownies. Ever since the first tea they'd had together, Veronica always tried to arrange to have some American cookies or pastries prepared for Lottie. It had become a treat that they both looked forward to, a calculated touch of nostalgia.

When the parlormaid had poured tea, offered the neatly cut thin bread and butter, and departed with a curtsy, Veronica turned to her guest and said, "What is it, Lottie? I feel there's something else bothering you. Is there something wrong between you and Peter? Would it help you to talk about it?"

"Oh, Mrs. Winter!"

"I do wish you'd call me Veronica."

"Oh, Veronica," she said. Tears welled up in her eyes. "You've been so wonderful."

"Lottie, darling, what is it?"

"I'm pregnant."

"Are you certain?"

"I'm certain."

"Have you told Peter?"

"You're the first person I've told."

"It's nothing to cry about, Lottie darling. It's something to celebrate." Lottie continued to cry; the tears rolled down her face, and she didn't even try to dab them away. Veronica searched for something else to say: "And Peter will be overjoyed. He certainly won't take the job in California at a time like this. It would be too much for you . . . unless they'll wait a year."

"They won't wait," said Lottie, drying her eyes with a tiny lace handkerchief. "The position has to be filled by the end of January; they specially stipulated that."

"Peter wouldn't go there alone. He wouldn't leave you. I know he wouldn't, and I'd forbid it anyway."

Lottie sobbed more until she was gasping for breath. Veronica put her arms round the young woman to comfort her. "Lottie darling, you must pull yourself together. Sit back. Blow your nose, and have some tea."

"He'll turn down the job," said Lottie after she'd had a few moments to recover. "Peter will turn down the job, on account of the baby. Then he'll blame me forever afterwards."

"You silly child. Of course he won't. He'll be the happiest man in the world."

"Do you really think so?"

"Of course he will. And he'll be a marvelous father. You must tell him your news as soon as he arrives—I'll leave you together for a few moments—and we must get a cable off to your father and to my father, too. Everyone is going to be so excited at the news."

1927

"All they ask in return."

It was late May, a time when all Berlin is filled with the smell of linden flowers. The sun came spasmodically from behind ragged gray clouds, but it was not warm. Pauli sat outside to drink his tea and spend a few minutes watching the world pass by.

Pauli's face was known in all the most fashionable cafés of Berlin: the Monopol, the Josty, the Schiller, the Café des Westens. But the one he liked best was opposite the Memorial Church: the Romanische Café. Some said this was the most famous café in the whole of Germany; others said it was the most famous in the whole world. Yet there was always room to sit down, for it could hold over a thousand people. It was open day and night and always busy: a place where intellectuals came to discuss philosophy, couples came to talk about love, others came to argue about politics, write letters or memoirs, review new plays or write poems. There were famous faces to be seen here. Up in the balcony, where the chessplayers liked to sit, one could often see Emanuel Lasker, who'd been world champion for thirty-three years.

Some of the clients were outrageous; at least they would have been had there been anyone left in Berlin who could feel outrage at the sight of shaved skulls, dyed hair, or flamboyant costumes. Outside in the street it was easier to be outraged by the sight of crippled ex-servicemen begging in their ragged uniforms, the painted faces of the homosexuals, or the pinched white faces of the child prostitutes.

Inside the café there were always pedlars going from table to table: shoelaces, matches, *Literarische Welt, Die Rote Fahne,* a copy of the *Times* from London four days old. An angry-looking young man offered crayon drawings. The drawings, too, were angry: jagged and spiky deformed servicemen, lewd matrons in suspender belts and black stockings, and bemedaled officers with porcine faces and no trousers. He stopped to show the drawings to two well-dressed Swedish tourists. They went through his wares solemnly and thoroughly but they did not buy. Tourists rarely did. Perhaps they didn't want to take such things through the customs inspections. The young man offered the drawings at a cheaper price. The Swedish man shook his head; the woman laughed; the drawings were gathered up. Some said the young man merely sold the drawings; others said he was the artist. But no one knew the truth about it, just as no one knew the truth about anything in Berlin. It was better not to know.

There were newspapers hanging on sticks near the door. Pauli didn't take the National Socialist paper—from its pristine condition he guessed that no one else had read it, either. He selected the *Berliner Zeitung am Mittag,* an undemanding tabloid, and sat down. His usual waitress brought a glass of lemon tea and a schnapps. He always came here for tea after the lunch of sandwiches that he ate at his desk. He usually sat here for thirty minutes before returning to his office. It was the only way he got a break from work. All day long at his office people put their heads round the door: "I don't want to interrupt you, Pauli, but . . ."

And the office had not got any better since the Nazis' new Gauleiter, Josef Goebbels, had taken over Berlin. He was too damned enthusiastic, and the rank and file didn't like the levy of three marks a month that he demanded from them. There were fewer than a thousand Nazi Party members in Berlin; it wasn't the way to get recruits, and Goebbels's Rhineland accent—which sounds funny to the ears of Berliners—hadn't helped him. Strasser, the Regional Chief, opposed almost everything Goebbels suggested, and SA Leader Kurt Daluege—with his army of brownshirts—wouldn't cooperate with either of them. With three bosses trying to run the Berlin office, very little got completed, but there was no way that any of them would listen to Pauli Winter's suggestions. Especially when—as Goebbels reminded him—he'd not even bothered to join the party.

"All they ask in return."

At one time Pauli had allocated half a day to his private clients and the morning to work for the party, but it was now over a month since he'd done any private work at all. Many clients didn't like the proximity to the Party office or the way that uniformed SA men came banging in and out of his office without so much as a by-your-leave. And those who didn't care about his political affiliations grew tired of being so obviously a low priority on Pauli's work roster. It wasn't that Pauli was lazy: twice last month he'd actually fallen asleep in court, but he took on too much. Nor did his long hours of work bring much financial reward. The Nazi Party retainer didn't go far, and on individual payments they always argued about his bills.

"You're Herr Paul Winter, aren't you?" He looked up to see a woman of about sixty, perhaps older. She was wearing a good but ancient coat with an astrakhan collar. Her huge black hat, with a mauve veil wrapped round it, was secured by means of large ornamental hairpins. It was all out of style by many years: the sort of outfit his grandmother had worn at Travemünde before the war.

"Yes," he said. Awkwardly he put his newspaper down and got to his feet.

"You don't know who I am, do you?"

He knew exactly who she was, and at one time he would have said so, but now he'd become more wary. "I don't think I do."

"I am Frau Guggenheimer."

"Won't you sit down?"

"I mustn't keep you," she said, but she put down her parcel, a large brown paper one tied neatly with lots of string, and sat down on the chair he pulled out for her. She was the wife of Guggenheimer, the owner of a bar that students frequented. Hetti Guggenheimer, a girlfriend of long ago, was Frau Guggenheimer's daughter.

He waited for her to tell him what she wanted, but now that she'd summoned up the courage to approach him she seemed tongue-tied. He said, "How is your husband?"

She welcomed the chance to speak on the subject. "The student trade is not enough; it never was. And that side of town is not so lively now that the Royal Palace is empty. Even Friedrichstrasse is not what it used to be. The center of town has shifted. All the life is over here in Ku-damm nowadays."

"That's true. I'm sorry."

"And the Nazis don't want to give us any trade, of course, with us being Jewish."

"Perhaps he should sell up. Retire."

"He's got no money, Herr Winter. We lost all our savings in the big inflation. We don't even own the bar. We live well enough, I suppose, but we live from hand to mouth."

"Is there something you want, Frau Guggenheimer?"

"Nazis used to come into the bar and fight. Terrible fighting. They'd come in on those evenings when we were crowded and shout horrible things about Karl Marx or Lenin. There was always someone there who'd fight them. Some of these young fellows like to fight no matter how badly hurt they get. They'd smash the furniture and hit out with a chair leg or with a broken bottle. . . ."

"You say they used to do that? They stopped?"

"Now my husband pays them money every week, a contribution to Nazi Party funds. But we can't afford it, Herr Winter. They ask too much, and business is not good at this time of year."

"I know such things happen."

"You're with the Nazis, Herr Winter. Couldn't you say something to one of the top men there? We really can't afford it, and my husband worries. He's awake at nights thinking about what to do. We're getting into debt, and we've never been in debt before, ever."

"It's not really anything to do with me, Frau Guggenheimer. I'm just a lawyer they pay to advise them."

"Frau Weiss, who has the flower stall, said you helped her when those young communist boys were grabbing money from her cashbox."

"I wish she hadn't told you," said Pauli earnestly.

"She said you sent some of your Nazis to beat them up."

"That wasn't anything that I did, I assure you."

"And she's never had any more trouble from that day to this."

"Does your husband know you came to see me?"

"Of course not."

"Then please don't say anything to him. In fact, don't say anything to anyone. Will you promise me that?"

"I'll do anything, Herr Winter."

"I can't promise. I'll try."

She got up. "I remember you when you first came back from the war, and that was a long time ago, wasn't it?"

"A very long time ago."

"My Hetti went to your birthday party a few years back. She said it was wonderful."

"How is Hetti?" he asked politely.

"She's well."

"Good."

"It can't go on like this, can it, Herr Winter—all this fighting and hurting people and the prices of everything?"

"No, it can't go on, Frau Guggenheimer; something will happen."

He finished his tea and his schnapps and went back to the office. It was crowded, as usual. Unemployed party members sat in the anteroom reading, smoking, and telling the same stories over and over again. He went up to the Regional Chief's office. Strasser was out, but Fritz Esser was there. "Ah! Good. Fritz. Just the man I was looking for. Where are those two gorillas who were arrested at the Pharus Hall battle?"

Fritz Esser looked up from the plate of sliced sausage and rye bread that he had every day. "They're waiting downstairs," he said through a mouthful of food.

"Send them up now, Fritz."

The Pharus Hall was a large squalid room in Müllerstrasse in Berlin-Wedding. It was rented for meetings. There was no district of Berlin more solidly communist than Wedding, and no meeting place more regularly used by the communists than the Pharus Hall. That's why the new Gauleiter had chosen it for a well-publicized speech. The communists were of course waiting there for the Nazis to arrive, and the ensuing fighting was prolonged and bloody. Josef Goebbels had announced his intention of getting more publicity for his tiny Berlin Nazi Party, and he'd succeeded. Only the presence of a large contingent of Berlin police had restored order and prevented a massacre. Now it had become fashionable to call it the "battle of Pharus Hall," and these two roughnecks—arrested for kicking a policeman until he was unconscious—were still waiting to have their cases heard in court.

Although very different, they were both typical of the men who'd joined the SA. One was in his late thirties, an ex-serviceman with a gray, lined face, dark, deep-set eyes, and a gray mustache. His brown uniform shirt was clean and pressed with a neat darn on the collar. His army record was exemplary. Wounded twice and severely gassed during three years of front-line infantry service on the Western Front. Nearly a year in military hospitals. It was all in his file. Pauli would need such details for the courts if he was to keep the fellow out of prison. Usually the courts were more sympathetic to the right-wing political factions than to the communists, but when a policeman was the victim such fine distinctions counted for nothing.

The other one was scarcely a man: a pale, spotty-faced nineteen-year-old, nearly twenty, a huge hulk of a body but without the foundation of strength that proper nutrition provides. He'd left school when fourteen years old and had never had a proper job. His hair was dirty and his face not properly washed. His uniform was stained and rumpled. He was probably sleeping on the floor somewhere, or even in the street. His face too easily relaxed into the insolent smile that is the mask worn by the insecure and uneducated. Pauli noted it: one leering smile like that and the case would be lost immediately.

"Now, I don't know who's been going to Guggenheimer's bar and squeezing money from them. And if I ask around I don't suppose I'll get anyone to tell me." The two men exchanged brief grins. "But you're going to go to the Guggenheimers and tell them it's all been a mistake. You are going to tell them they are not to pay any brownshirt, or party member, anymore. And you're going to make sure that whoever has been engaging in this bit of private capitalism crosses the Guggenheimers off his list. Got it?"

"It's official policy now that all Jewish . . ."

"Shut up and listen to me. I don't want to know any of the details. The only thing that interests us in this room is what happens to you two when you go to court. Right?"

"Yes, Herr Doktor. Right," said the older man.

"And if the Guggenheimers are pestered anymore, you two are going to suddenly find yourself without adequate legal defense."

"That sounds like a threat," said the younger one.

"Oh, does it?" said Pauli. "Good, because that's exactly what it was."

The man with the gray mustache was subtler. He said, "It might be a bit difficult explaining why these bloody Jews are not to make a contribution to our funds."

Pauli stood up, leaned across his desk, and poked the man in the chest. "Well, my friend, you tell anyone who asks you that 'difficult' question that it was because I said so. You pass the word around!"

"Yes, Herr Doktor." He was an ex–army man: he liked taking orders. These SA men were all like that; that's why they liked dressing up in their brown shirts and peaked caps and big boots. They wanted someone to take over their lives and give them orders.

"Now get out. I'll get an adjournment for a few weeks. Come back on the first day of next month."

"Heil Hitler!" said both men in unison.

"That's right," said Pauli. "Heil Hitler."

"Your brother's a decent sort of fellow," said Fritz Esser to Pauli, having obviously come to this conclusion only recently. He tapped his cigar to put ash into an ashtray, but it went onto the tablecloth. Fritz was drunk.

"He's a stuffy sort of man, but he never lets anyone down," said Pauli. He was self-conscious about his affection for his brother. He didn't want people to think he depended on Peter in any way.

The room—lit only by the greenish light of two hissing and popping gas jets—was paneled in a dark wood, its botanical origin obscured by half a century of tobacco smoke and old varnish. On the wall were framed photos of a cycling club posing in groups with their machines after the races at Friedenauer Volkspark each year. The two men were sitting at a long dining table; the dinner was finished and all the guests had departed. The table was littered with ashtrays, plates, glasses, and bottles, and wine was spilled on the cream-colored linen cloth.

"What made the bloody fool marry a Jew?"

"They're very happy together," said Pauli.

"Oh, sure. She's beautiful and clever and witty and rich, but she's a Jew. Jews should marry Jews."

Pauli looked at him. "You sound like one of Goebbels's speechwriters. You don't believe all that stuff, do you?"

Fritz took him by the sleeve. "You saved me, Pauli. I don't mean saved my life during that damned streetfighting in 1919, although I'll be eternally grateful for that, too. But if you hadn't come to the Imperial Palace and saved me that night, I would have ended up selling matches in the gutter where I often see some of those stupid bastards from the People's Naval Division. But after you I owe everything to the party. They have given me everything. I had no education, no money, no influential friends or family, no nothing. But the party took me and gave me everything I've got. And all they ask in return is that I hate Jews. Is that something I have to question?" He let go of Pauli's sleeve and drank some schnapps.

"I didn't marry her; my brother did."

"So you saved his life?" said Esser. He spilled some drink down his shirt, drank the rest, and poured more. "I didn't know that on that day I fished you out of the sea. So you'd jumped in to help him?"

"I don't know what happened," said Pauli. He was embarrassed, just as he'd been embarrassed earlier in the evening when Peter had raised a glass and proposed the health of the brother who'd saved his life at the risk of his own. "Neither does he. We were only children, weren't we? But he insists that it all happened his way, so I go along with it."

Fritz half closed his eyes against the curling cigar smoke and smiled. He was a tough customer and something of a loner. Even for tonight's celebration he brought no partner. Despite his sly little sexy jokes and stories, he was seldom seen with women. Fritz said that was because all his lovers were married to other men, but sometimes Pauli wondered if that was true. The dinner had been held to celebrate Fritz Esser's departure to Munich. No one knew exactly what his new job was to be, but there was no doubt that it was a promotion. By now it seemed that Esser, like Captain Graf and certain other rising stars, was marked for a good job in the Nazi Party organization.

Pauli had organized the farewell party. It took place in a private dining room in Leipziger Strasse. The food and drink were all supplied by the Guggenheimers, not so far away. It amused Pauli to think that all these ardent Nazis had been eating Frau Guggenheimer's delicious food. Some of the dishes were traditional Jewish ones, but the people present couldn't distinguish between traditional German and Jewish dishes. Not many Germans could.

Pauli knew that having the Guggenheimers do the catering would be enough to persuade Peter and his Jewish wife, Lottie, to attend, and that was his chief motive in arranging it. Dr. Josef Goebbels had remarked on the food and stayed long enough to deliver a short speech of congratulation from which all trace of his

Rhineland accent had been eliminated. It was this polished performance—and the fact that he was the only one of the top Nazis
with a quick-witted sense of humor—that earned him a round of
applause from all present. Fritz said afterwards to Pauli that a man
who could change his hometown accent could change anything or
anybody.

Now it was two o'clock in the morning and all the guests had
departed. Only Pauli and Fritz remained, and they were both very
drunk. Fritz reached for a bottle of good apple brandy from the
crate that was far from empty. He cracked the wax from the top,
used the corkscrew to open it, and poured more for both of them.

All the male guests, including Pauli, had managed to find evening dress. Some—such as Peter Winter and Dr. Goebbels—even
had fine suits, cut to the latest fashion, with padded shoulders and
wide trousers. Only Fritz came in a lounge suit, soft shirt, and
colored tie. Was it indifference, or a studied declaration of his
egalitarian views? Pauli could not decide. "I wouldn't have Goebbels's job, not for anything," said Fritz Esser. "He's been sent here
on a make-or-break assignment."

"It looks like that," agreed Pauli. He offered a cigarette and Fritz
took one.

"Thanks. Yes, Strasser is getting too big for his boots—all that
stuff about government ownership of everything, and alliances with
the Russian proletariat—and he's not doing so well: in Berlin the
membership of the party is disappointing. On the other hand,
'Dummi-dummi' Daluege is doing well: the SA is growing by leaps
and bounds. No one knows the exact figures, but my guess is that
the SA outnumber the party memberships. If that can happen in
Berlin, it can happen everywhere. If it happens all over Germany,
Hitler will be displaced by Röhm, and the brownshirts will take
control."

"And the tail will wag the dog," said Pauli. Fritz had long ago
thrown his lot in with Hitler and the party. If Röhm and the brownshirts gained the ascendancy, all Fritz's calculations would come to
nothing. "But that won't happen," said Pauli.

"Why won't it?" Fritz wanted to be reassured.

"The party won't come to power by means of a putsch. Even
Hitler must realize that by now."

"So how?"

"He'll have to win votes, and that means the party will always keep control. It also means that the party will soon have to move everything to Berlin."

"You think so?"

"Suppose his putsch in Munich had worked. Do you imagine that he would have been allowed to form a Nazi power base in Bavaria by means of an armed overthrow? Of course he wouldn't—the government here in Berlin would have told the army to move against him, and they would have done so. He wouldn't have lasted a month."

Fritz got to his feet unsteadily and turned the gas taps. The mantle glowed greenish white. It was as if he thought the extra light would illuminate his thoughts. "But if the Berlin government had done nothing?"

"The army would have moved against him anyway. And if no one had acted, the French would have used Hitler's putsch as an excuse to occupy the whole of Bavaria, like they occupied the Rhineland."

"You're probably right," said Fritz with a sigh. In some ways he preferred the idea of an armed overthrow. It was simpler and quicker and easier than persuading the voters, and it was much more in line with his own sort of thinking. "I suppose he's sent Goebbels here because Berlin is so important."

"What's he got in store for you, Fritz?"

"One day I'll get a top job, Pauli, and you'll be with me."

"You should try to get the party to put you up as a candidate for the Reichstag."

"I'd like that. Think what my father would say." He thought about it and nodded. "The Führer rewards the faithful, and I've made myself important to him."

"Don't stay away from Berlin too long, Fritz. Munich will become a backwater."

"We've known each other a long time. Right?" His words were slurred but he was sincere enough. "You're my best friend, do you know that?" He put an arm round Pauli's shoulder.

"Sure, sure," said Pauli, although the idea was a complete surprise to him. Fritz Esser had so many friends, and the higher he rose in the party organization, the more friends he made.

"Bastards, most of them," said Fritz, as if reading his friend's mind. "You're the only one who's never asked me for a favor. Do you know that?"

"No."

Fritz looked at him. Pauli never tried to outshine him, never tried to take him over or push him aside. Pauli was the only man he knew who got genuine pleasure from his friends' advancement. "And you need a few friends, you old bastard." He clapped Pauli on the back so that he almost choked on his drink. "Only the other day I was asked why you had intervened to stop the Guggenheimers' paying their money."

"Oh, yes."

"And the party needs funds. Badly needs funds."

"So what did you say?"

A cough and a laugh. "What did I say? I said that you were protecting an informant."

" 'Protecting an informant.' I'm glad you told me what I was doing."

"I learned that one from you, you cunning little swine. I learned everything I know from you."

Pauli smiled. Fritz said, "What else do you know that I don't know?" He poured more apple brandy.

"Get close to Captain Göring," said Pauli. "If Hitler comes to power it will be through Göring's efforts. Göring is acceptable to the middle class. For all sorts of reasons, Göring will be the center of power. Hitler needs Göring. All the others will be satellites."

"You know who was chasing the Guggenheimer business, don't you?"

"No," said Pauli, although he had a sinking feeling in the pit of his stomach simply because he did guess who it was.

"Your friend Brand. He's just become a Sturmbannführer, under Viktor Lutze, in Elberfeld. He's going places, your old comrade Brand."

"I heard he was in the Ruhr SA."

"And he hates you, Pauli. He really hates you. What did you do to him?"

"Nothing," said Pauli. "He's just overendowed with hatred."

"Watch out for him, Pauli. If anything ever happens I'll do what I can. You know that, don't you?"

"Sure, Fritz. Thanks."

"He's out to get you." Fritz swigged the last of his apple brandy and then threw the empty glass at the wall. It was a thick, crudely made glass of the sort specially made for the hotel trade, but so violent was Fritz that it smashed into tiny fragments.

When Fritz tried to get up, he staggered and knocked his chair over. Pauli laughed. Fritz was very drunk, or he wouldn't have been saying these things.

"You're not frightened, are you?" said Fritz in his usual brutally direct way.

"Frightened of what?" said Pauli. He helped Fritz keep his balance, although he was equally drunk.

"That's right," said Fritz. But they both knew that Pauli was frightened. He'd miss having Fritz in the Berlin party office to protect him against the enmities and jealousy, petty spites and chronic vendettas that had become the way the Nazi Party worked. The top leadership believed that the law of the jungle provided the party with natural strength.

How would Pauli survive? Without Fritz he'd have no one to protect his back.

1929

"There is nothing safer than a zeppelin."

There wasn't very much upholstery remaining; that's why the sound of the piano echoed from the dirt-encrusted gilded angels in the domed ceiling, and down through the derelict space at the back of the dress circle where once had stood a beautiful oak counter and an elaborate mirrored bar.

Once it had been a big theatre. Now it wasn't really a theatre at all in the sense that that word is used in London, Paris, or New York. It had suffered at the hands of rioters and thieves. Back in 1920 a Freikorps had used it as their barracks, and after that the Reichswehr had stored here ammunition that the generals had wanted to hide from the Allied Armistice Commission. One of the most talented and avant-garde of the new producer-directors had leased it for a year and, when the rent was due, ripped out and sold off fixtures, fittings, and floor covering to get out of debt. So now it was a cold, drafty, uncomfortable shell. And it smelled of the cats that ran wild in the cellars. But even now, in the winter of 1929, the coldest winter in memory, people would still pay to come here if the show was good enough.

It was almost midnight; the run-through and some last-moment auditions had finished. Almost everyone had gone home. The stage and auditorium were totally dark except for one dim electric bulb hanging very low on one side of the stage to illuminate the piano. The theatre was empty but for the piano player and the woman leaning over him to see the scrawled script and manuscript notes from which he was playing.

"I adore it," said Lottie, starting to hum, following the melody her husband was playing on the piano.

"Yes, it's a wonderful melody." Peter was dressed in a dark-gray lounge suit with a bowler hat perched on the back of his head. It was not the way he'd ordinarily have worn his hat, but Peter had seen one of the Americans like that, and he now sometimes imitated it.

"And there are words, aren't there?" She was wearing a gigantic golden-colored fur coat. It was too cold here to take it off.

"You know Brecht: the words always come first, then Kurt writes the music." Peter sang; his voice was tuneful but soft and unsure: "Oh, the shark has lovely teeth, dear, and they cut you like a knife. . . ."

"Oh, stop. Why does he always write such stupid lyrics?"

"He's a poet."

"You all kowtow to him too much."

"I don't think so. You should see him directing actors, Lottie. Silly little girls become like stars when he talks to them."

"I love to watch you playing piano; you are so happy."

"It was your idea, Lottie. I'd given up all ideas of ever playing again. But now I sometimes think I'd like to leave Father and go into show business." He inserted silly, skillful cadenzas into the music.

"I hope you're not serious, Peter darling. These people are paupers. And you've got a wife and daughter to look after."

"I know, Lottie. I wasn't serious. If I worked in the theatre full-time, maybe I wouldn't find it so interesting and exciting. But it's a privilege to work with the great names: Piscator, Brecht, Kurt, and all the rest of them: Reinhardt, Jannings, Peter Lorre. . . ." He changed to play a few bars from "Moon of Alabama" and made it into something foolishly grand. Then he stopped suddenly. "I could never have taken that job in California and left all this behind; you know that, don't you?"

"I know it now, but at the time I didn't know working with Brecht mattered so much to you. You're getting quite famous."

"No, I'm not getting famous, except as the piano player with a half-finger missing." He rearranged the pages in front of him, took off his glasses, looked up at her, and smiled. She hadn't yet got used to seeing him in his horn-rimmed reading glasses. Peter hadn't got used to them, either, and now he briefly rubbed the little red marks they'd left on each side of his nose. "They use me because I'm cheap: in fact, free."

"That's not true, darling. The way you sight-read from all those scribbled notes and make a piano sound like a full band is a miracle."

"It's good enough for auditions and first rehearsals, and that's the exciting bit. Once the show is put on, I'm less interested in it."

"But how do you remain so good-tempered about all this communist propaganda? I remember a time when you would have walked out on songs like the ones in *Mahagonny*. They're not only communist but anti-American, too."

"Does that annoy you?" He was genuinely concerned, and she was touched by it.

"Yes," she said, "sometimes it does. Brecht is a pig, and his ignorance about America is phenomenal. Why does he always write about things he doesn't know about?"

"He's not a politician, darling. He's a poet. I don't think much about the content of the songs, and I don't think the audiences do, either. People come to be entertained. They come to escape the misery for a couple of hours of fantasy. Brecht makes 'Amerika' a place for his fantasies."

"You're too nice, Peter." She pulled the collar of the fur coat closer about her neck.

"Being married suits me. This damned piano is already going out of tune again. Look at that. . . ." He tapped a dead note.

"I love you."

He looked up, pursed his lips to show her he loved her, too, and continued playing.

She went to get his coat, gloves, and cane from the chair where he'd carefully set them. She knew he'd sit here playing the piano for another hour or so if she didn't drag him away.

Peter Winter could easily have been playing his own piano in his own comfortable home—Lottie had bought him a fine Bechstein grand for his thirty-third birthday—but he seemed to get some special sort of pleasure from playing this neglected old instrument, just because it was on the stage in this famous old theatre. Peter would have denied it strenuously had she said so, but he was unmistakably "stage struck." She'd seen it happen before. Her stepmother had wasted years dancing, desperate to get into show business. The house in California was still filled with photos of her in her stage costume. Lottie had always suspected that it was her stepmother who'd bullied her father into letting the movie people build hideous studios on their beautiful orange groves.

She put Peter's hat level on his head and draped his overcoat across his shoulders. "Come along, darling, or I'll start to think you don't like to be at home."

He kissed her. "It's a wonderful home, and there is nowhere else I'd rather be than at home with you and little Helena. And soon your parents will be here to see what a wonderful wife and mother you are."

"I wish they weren't coming on that wretched airship. I have nightmares about it."

"Don't be silly, darling. There is nothing safer than a zeppelin. They've been flying for twenty-nine years off and on, and not one passenger has ever been hurt. You can't say that about trains, cars, or ocean liners."

"What about all the people killed in the war? What about you and your injured hand?"

He frowned. "That was different. They weren't passengers: they were soldiers and sailors, and there were guns firing at them. No one is going to be firing at the *Graf Zeppelin.*"

"Suppose they're ill? Mother can't even handle a sea voyage comfortably."

"This flight around the world will make the Zeppelin company front-page news everywhere. Already the flight to Palestine was in the English and American newspapers; think what they'll say about its going completely round the world, stopping only at Tokyo, Los Angeles, and Lakehurst, New Jersey."

"They're not young anymore, Peter."

"They'll go from Los Angeles to Friedrichshafen in one week, having had a weekend in New York. It's a miracle, Lottie. There will only be about twenty passengers; my father had the devil of a job getting two tickets for them. Most of them are reserved for important government officials or journalists."

"I don't want to sound ungrateful, darling. It was a wonderful idea, and Daddy is terribly pleased about it. He says it's made him the most celebrated man in California."

"Invest this five dollars with me."

The *Graf Zeppelin* gleamed in the sunshine. This astounding flying machine was almost one year old. The airship first took to the air in September 1928, and since then it had attracted the attention of the whole world. But none of its previous flights had been more dramatic than this one. This was the final leg of a journey that had taken the great airship fully round the world. It had sailed almost silently across a thousand miles of Russia's wastelands, the angry Pacific Ocean, the pale American prairies, and the gray Atlantic waters. In the crowded streets of New York and Tokyo, just as in the quiet tundra and swampland, people had craned their necks and cheered the big silver fish as it floated along at a steady eighty-five miles per hour, awesome and unstoppable. Now, before dark, the airship would be back home again.

The breakfast things had been cleared away, and there was nothing to do but look down at the German countryside and work up an appetite for the lunch. The chef had been chosen from among all the Hamburg-Amerika Line's cooks, and the wines were suited to the excellent food that came from the small but well-equipped electric kitchen.

The *Graf Zeppelin* cruised at fifteen hundred feet, its shadow darting across forest and farmland. It was late summer; the sky was blue and the air was clear, so that below them the trees, farm buildings, and animals looked like toys.

"I just don't want the flight to end," said Mrs. Danziger as their airship crossed Germany, heading towards the Bodensee and the Zeppelin company's base at Friedrichshafen.

Her husband chuckled. "Didn't I tell you so?" Mr. Simon Danziger was a white-haired, rotund, somewhat cherubic little man in a pale-peach-colored suit that was unmistakably Californian.

"If anyone had told me it would be so smooth . . ." The sentence tailed away, as many of her sentences and ideas did. "And the engines, so quiet."

As the shiny silver airship had neared its destination, she had begun to worry about her hair. Back home she went to the hairdresser three times a week. She hated the idea of greeting her daughter and her son-in-law—and perhaps other members of the

family—with her hair not properly permed by someone she could
rely on.

She looked round the cabin. This room was no larger than the
big reception room at their home—or what they preferred to call
"the ranch house"—in Ventura County. But it had accommodated
twenty passengers for the whole flight. Here they'd been served
their three meals a day, and this had been the only place to sit apart
from the very cramped two-berth cabins. Of course she'd taken the
tour of the airship from stem to stern—all of them had done that,
just to vary the monotony of staring down at the green-gray ocean
for hour after hour. But one tour of the zeppelin was enough for
her. After that she'd spent most of the time sitting here in the large
cabin, talking to the other passengers or to the airship's officers.

It had been a wonderful surprise to find that one of the passengers who joined the airship at Lakehurst, New Jersey, was the son
of an old friend as well as being the uncle of Lottie's husband: Major
Glenn Rensselaer. He didn't normally use the army rank, but it
proved useful when pulling strings to get a ticket for this record-
breaking flight. As he'd explained modestly, and without describing
the dangers and skills of his work with the British fliers, most of his
wartime service had been spent as a civilian. But in the final few
months of 1918 he'd been officially gazetted to the U.S. Army so
that his knowledge of the German aviation industry could be available to the Armistice Commission. Nowadays he remained on the
Reserve.

Glenn Rensselaer was a brawny man who, despite his approaching fiftieth birthday, was as childishly excited by the flight as anyone
aboard. He still had lots of hair, and the blue "Rensselaer eyes"
were large and sincere. In many ways he was like his father, Cyrus,
except that no one would mistake Glenn for a successful painter, as
people had his father when he was fifty. Glenn had the leathery look
of the outdoors. And, quite apart from not looking like an artist,
Glenn didn't even look successful: his clothes were neither of top
quality nor well fitting. He wore a dark-gray-striped suit that yielded
nothing to the well-established fashion of boxy shoulders and "Ox-
ford-bag" trousers. It was the sort of outfit that could be bought in
a department store, such as Wertheims in Berlin, which is where
he'd bought it.

Glenn Rensselaer was a sociable man, and he'd conversed at
length with every passenger on the airship by the last day of the

flight. Most of the people aboard had some special interest in aviation, whether as serving officers, government employees, or journalists, and Glenn was interested to hear their opinions of the zeppelin. The Danzigers were almost the only people aboard who were not professionally interested in the workings of the airship, and with them Glenn's conversation was about the family into which their daughter Lottie had married, and about the granddaughter they were so anxious to see. Glenn Rensselaer's son, Cyrus, was eight years old, a beautiful, happy child, and the table was littered with snapshots.

But Glenn spent a great deal of time twiddling his thumbs, drinking strong coffee, and fidgeting with tableware. Like many of the other passengers, he found the total ban against smoking irksome. But with a few million cubic meters of highly flammable hydrogen close above their heads, he had no quarrel with this regulation.

"My husband, Simon, feels it the way you do," explained Mrs. Danziger. "He smokes cigars. Ever since we first met he's been in the habit of lighting up one of his big Havanas after lunch, and again after dinner. I never remember him skipping one except when he's been sick—not until now, that is."

"Nita," Mr. Danziger told his wife, "you'll have to have all our mail ready within the hour, or else it won't be accepted by the airship post office."

"Isn't it wonderful?" his wife said to Glenn Rensselaer. "When Simon heard that you could mail letters aboard, he had his office address envelopes for all our friends and Simon's business associates. Over one hundred letters."

"Two for each," said Mr. Danziger proudly. "One letter mailed on each sector. Mail sent on the Los Angeles-to-Lakehurst sector got different postmarks from the mail posted on the transatlantic leg. I'd say a lot of those folks will treasure a souvenir like that. Who knows, in time maybe it will become valuable."

"Simon collects German stamps," said Mrs. Danziger. "The mail sent on those first trips of the airship last year is already valuable."

"Not really valuable," protested Simon Danziger.

"Doubled in price," insisted his wife. "I'd like to see the rest of our investments do as well."

"Well, you'd be surprised to know, honey, that we have quite a few investments that look like they'll do much better than that before this year is through. The New York stock market is running wild lately."

"Simon takes care of that kind of thing," said Mrs. Danziger vaguely. "I've got no head for figures." She laughed. "Never did have."

Glenn Rensselaer said, "Some folks are getting a little worried about the market. Many stock prices are rocketing way past what they are worth in earnings: that's a dangerous sign."

"I don't get you," said Danziger.

Glenn hesitated. Talking about money was not something he enjoyed. He said, "I use a rough rule of thumb that a stock should be valued at about ten times its earnings. Now I'm watching folks pay fifty times the annual earnings! Radio Corporation of America went from eighty-five to four hundred twenty points—and RCA never paid a dividend at all!"

Danziger smiled. "Isn't it enough that the share prices keep going up?"

"Not if the stock is not really worth the price."

"Stocks are worth whatever they will fetch," said Mr. Danziger authoritatively. "The government stick to a cheap money policy because it's good for business. Well, darn it, it *is* good for business, and people are buying stocks as fast as they can. That's the American way; that's what I believe in."

"I don't have much in the way of savings," said Glenn Rensselaer, "but a couple of months back my father told me to put everything into government bonds, and I did just that."

"Your father is an old friend of mine, as you know. I never go to New York without we have lunch together. And Nita will tell you how much I admire his savvy as a businessman," said Danziger. "But businessmen get cautious. I'd say your father has become too cautious, Glenn. You take my advice, my friend. Take what money you've got and make a little cash while the chance is there. Anytime at all, the government will decide to let interest rates go up, but meanwhile Wall Street is the place to put your money, not government bonds."

"I'm sure you're right," said Glenn and smiled. He was obviously unconvinced.

Glenn's manner provoked Danziger to elaborate. He asked Glenn for a five-dollar bill and put it on the table to smooth it with the side of his hand. "Now, I want you to invest this five dollars with me—I did the same thing with my nephew last Christmas; it's an object lesson—and in six months I'll return it to you plus what it's made on the market."

"That's mighty nice of you, but . . . ."

Simon Danziger was enjoying himself. He chuckled to admit that it was a somewhat childish game. "Write your name right there on the bill, and some address where I can reach you in six months, and date it. . . . You'll see your profit and it will surprise you."

"Well, okay, Mr. Danziger." Glenn recognized in Simon Danziger the zeal of the newly converted.

Mrs. Danziger was more perceptive: she saw Glenn's embarrassment. "I'll get our mail together," she said, "and leave you men to talk business." She stood up. "Do you have any mail for the postal clerk, Mr. Rensselaer?"

"No, I don't have any mail. I'm not much good at writing letters, I'm afraid. I never got the hang of it."

"You know the Winter family well, Mr. Rensselaer," said Simon Danziger once the two men were left alone. "I must admit that I find the prospect of meeting them for the first time very daunting. Have you got any tips for me?" He tried to make it sound like a joke, but there was no mistaking the serious tone in his voice.

"I'm sure you'll like your son-in-law, Mr. Danziger. Peter Winter is a very sincere young man."

"And from the photos we've seen, a handsome man, too." He carefully placed Glenn's five-dollar bill in his pocket.

"Yes, that's true. And his mother is a truly wonderful woman."

"No doubt about that," said Danziger, "every letter my daughter writes is singing your sister's praises. I'd say that without your sister Lottie would have found it much more difficult to settle down over there in Berlin."

Glenn was cautious: it was a two-edged compliment. "I guess your wife would have preferred her to come home."

"Sure. We both would. But a wife has to arrange her life around her husband's business affairs. Nita knows that: everyone knows it. No, Nita appreciates the way your sister went out of her way to be so nice to our Lottie. It was a comfort to us both."

"The Winters are a swell family. Of course, Harald—Peter's father—is well known throughout Germany."

"A self-made man, so I hear. Started out with just a handful of cash and parlayed it into a fortune."

253

"Some of the stories are exaggerated," said Glenn. "Harald Winter wasn't a pauper when he started out . . ."

". . . and he's not sitting on a fortune now," Danziger finished the sentence. "Is that what you were going to say?"

"German industry has gone through tough times," said Glenn, choosing his words carefully. "Winter's corporations made a mint of money in the war, but when Germany lost, a lot of debts went unpaid. There were two factories in Alsace, so when Alsace became a part of France, those assets were lost. After the war, strikes, riots, and revolution turned Germany upside down, and he's only lately got himself back on his feet."

"The way I heard it, Harald Winter made a killing in the great inflation of 1923."

"That's correct, but in 1924, after the new money was introduced, the government demanded repayments from businesses that had profited too well on government loans. Harald Winter had to pay out on some of those old deals."

"You don't say? We've never heard anything about that."

"Now, don't get me wrong, Mr. Danziger. Harald Winter is a very rich and successful businessman, but he has his ups and downs. Lately he's been facing a lot of criticism from his codirectors. He could be ousted. I'm telling you all this so you realize that he needs his son Peter to handle some of the problems he's up against."

"That's real nice of you, Mr. Rensselaer. Maybe you know that a few years back Peter was offered a vice-presidency with a Los Angeles bank. My wife and I were mighty disappointed that they didn't come and live in California."

"I'm sure you were."

"But now for the first time I see the refusal in another light. The boy was being loyal to his father, and I respect him all the more for that."

"That's right."

"But my daughter wrote and told me that you'd advised him against taking that job."

Glenn was flustered. He fingered one of the snapshots of his eight-year-old son and laid it upon another, like a man playing patience. He hadn't reckoned that Peter would tell his wife, and that she would tell her parents. "Well . . . they were expecting the baby."

"As I understand it, you had confidential information about that bank, and you made a special trip to tell Peter that a job with them could prove disappointing."

Glenn bit his lip. This was a new aspect of Simon Danziger: he could be tough. "That's correct. My advice was to stay with his father."

"And he took your advice, but the bank is flourishing, the way I hear it."

"You are right. I was being overcautious, I guess."

"Just like with your treasury bonds?" Danziger turned his head to watch the countryside unrolling beneath them. It was rich, fertile land, green and lush in a way the California landscape never was. Yet this German earth was regimented in small rectangular parcels that varied little in size or shape.

"Just like that," said Glenn.

"I guess caution runs in the Rensselaer blood," said Danziger.

Glenn smiled and said nothing. He just couldn't decide how much of it was hostility. Maybe none. Maybe Danziger should just be taken at face value, like a T-bill.

"You can't just make them disappear."

Mr. Simon Danziger was variously described as a man of infinite sense and good judgment and as a cunning, parasitic loafer. This disagreement came from the way that Simon Danziger lived solely on profits and interest from his investments. At one time he'd tried to take personal control of the companies in which he invested, but found it both confusing and dull. From time to time he'd even bought small businesses, including three hotels, so that he could occupy himself with the decisions of management. Although this was more interesting for him, he'd seldom been able to contribute any ideas that bore fruit in prestige or profits. Now he let other people earn the money and didn't interfere with them.

Yet time never passed slowly for Simon Danziger: he was seldom if ever bored. He enjoyed long country walks; carefully planned dinner parties and the conversation around his table; arranging, and rearranging, "writing up," and adding to the collection of German stamps he'd inherited from his father; tending his small but elaborate garden; writing long letters (many of them to fellow stamp-collectors); and, above all else, reading.

Danziger was a voracious and omnivorous reader. A bookstore owner in Santa Barbara had come to know the Danzigers so well that he chose books and shipped them a dozen or more at a time. Seldom did his selection earn a complaint. Most of the books were, in the broadest sense, either art, biographical, or historical, books that helped the Danzigers "stay in touch with culture" from their home on the far side of the world.

So the Danzigers didn't come to Europe unprepared. A visit with them to the Greek and Egyptian collections of the New Museum left Peter Winter exhausted: his in-laws moved from room to room at a snail's pace and discussed each exhibit in wearying detail.

"I told you not to go!" Lottie reminded her husband with a laugh as he sank down in an armchair and sighed deeply. They were waiting in the sitting room of her parents' large, luxurious suite on the fourth floor of the Adlon Hotel. "My father has a pathological craving for culture; it's a disease endemic to certain regions of California."

"They never get tired."

"Do you know how long it takes on the train from Los Angeles to Chicago? And even then you are only in Chicago. My parents are starved for culture: starved!" Lottie was standing at the window watching the traffic in Pariser Platz. It had been raining, and the fallen leaves stuck flat and shiny on the road, like newly minted gold coins. She loved this view; it summed up Berlin for her. Across the Platz was the Brandenburg Gate and the long, long avenue that went right through the Tiergarten. "I wish we lived on this side of town; don't you, darling?"

"Only the other day you were telling your mother that all the smartest restaurants and chic shops were in Ku-damm."

"I didn't say they weren't, Peter. But this old part of town is the real Berlin. Unter den Linden, the palace, the Reichstag—these are the places that make the city unique."

Peter rubbed his face. "How I'll stay awake through the concert, I don't know."

"It's Bruckner, darling—sudden, loud, and discordant. Bruckner wrote music for people who might be tempted by sleep."

"I wish you'd seen your father when he first caught sight of the Queen Nefertiti bust. I was watching him. His eyes popped wide open. He shouted out loud. 'Golly!' he said, just like that: 'Golly!' "

"I felt like saying 'golly' myself when I first saw it."

"And he knows everything there is to know about Greek vases. Far more than I care to hear about, in fact."

She laughed. "Poor darling."

"Furthermore, your father actually corrected me on something I said about the Royal House of Hohenzollern. He knows more about even German history than I do."

"Well, you don't know much about German history. . . . I don't know why you are so astonished. I told you what my crazy parents were like long before they came."

"Yes, you did, Lottie darling. I just didn't believe you. And, Lottie, you must remind me to speak with the dining-room manager downstairs before we sit down. I'm the host tonight. It would be an absolute disaster if the cost of the dinner tonight went on your father's bill. If Uncle Glenn gets back from Hamburg in time there will be eighteen of us, quite a crowd. It's sure to go on very late, and I must be in the office tomorrow—I've missed so many days since your parents arrived, and tomorrow there's an important board meeting." He stopped. It was better not to tell her of the acrimonious disputes in the board room as an energetic group of directors fought to take control of the holding company. It wasn't the money. Papa had enough shares to give him a comfortable income, but the blow to Harald Winter's pride would be terrible to see. Peter prayed it wouldn't happen.

Lottie murmured assent, still looking out the window. "I hope Mother will be ready in time. I have to take a bath and change and I have someone coming in to fix my hair." Coming across Pariser Platz she saw a group of SA men, in their brownshirt uniforms and high boots, marching behind a swastika flag. She turned away from the window and looked at her watch. "Your brother won't come in his uniform, will he?"

"Uniform? Pauli? He's put on too much weight to fit into that these days."

"You said he'd become a brownshirt."

"No, darling. I said he'd joined the Nazi Party."

"Isn't that the same thing?"

"No, the SA, with their brownshirt uniforms, are quite separate. They're a rabble that that dreadful Captain Röhm recruited from Freikorps riffraff and chronic unemployed. They are closely allied to Hitler's Nazi Party, but there's a lot of friction between them."

"It's a fine distinction, isn't it?"

257

"No. The Nazi Party is a political party, like the socialists, the communists, the Center Party, and so on. They don't wear uniforms, perhaps just a small circular swastika badge in the buttonhole."

"I wish your brother wasn't a member."

Peter shrugged. "You know Pauli by now, Lottie. He's not exactly a zealot, is he? Pauli has even less interest in politics than I do. He joined the party because nowadays he gets almost his entire income from them. He thought it would look bad if he continued to say he didn't want to join. As a lawyer, you see, he has to be told many party secrets."

"I wish your brother had some other kind of work. He is a nice boy: I like him."

"I know. I told my father that we should have him in the family business, but things are difficult right now, and this job with the Nazis has been the making of him. When he got out of law school I wasn't even sure he'd be able to scratch a living. But now he's becoming quite influential in Berlin politics."

"Pauli is?"

"Oh, I don't mean he'll ever be a politician, but he has the ear of the Berlin party chiefs. Anyone who wants a favor from Goebbels or Strasser or from SA Leader Daluege goes to Pauli Winter. He's becoming a go-between for the Nazis and many of the top people."

"It's the anti-Jewish propaganda that is so wicked."

"I don't give that any attention."

"You won't forget that your daughter, Helena, is half Jewish, will you, Peter?"

"It's just their strategy. Pauli knows these people, and he says that it's only for vote-catching. Everyone knows that the anti-Jewish nonsense will all be dropped if they get any nearer to a majority in the Reichstag. In the coming year they'll begin to eliminate it from the program."

"What program? They haven't got a program, except hating the Jews."

"Nothing is going to happen to the Jews, Lottie. Don't get upset on that account. Look around you: the German economy would collapse without the Jews."

"But do the Nazis know that?"

Peter looked at his wife with concern. He hadn't realized how much the Nazi propaganda affected her. It was, of course, the presence in Berlin of her parents. Suddenly she was having to explain to them things she'd previously avoided thinking about. "Well, anyway," said Peter in an effort to relax her and end these childish fears. "How can they get rid of the Jews? They're Germans; they live here, don't they? You can't just make them disappear."

"Colonel Horner commanding."

The harvest had been gathered and it was the time of year when, since history began, the warrior had earned his pay. The water in the broad river flowed sluggishly through the rolling landscape, sweeping round the meadow that rose gently towards the tree-clad slopes where the gleaming birches had already shed their leaves. A whistle blew three times, and before the last blast ended three soldiers ran forward, disappearing from the drifting smoke, and then reappearing as an unexpected gust of wind clawed the smoke aside to reveal a platoon of engineers at the waterside. From them came the noise of a generator as the soldiers inflated supports of a pontoon bridge to improvise a raft.

A large gray-painted saloon car, its engine warmed and ready, started at the first swing of a starting handle and, still wielding the handle, a helmeted officer clamped a boot onto the running board of the accelerating motor, heaved himself into the passenger seat, and slammed the door.

The car slid on the wet grass before its heavy-duty tires took a grip. By the time the car reached the water's edge, the combat engineers had ramps in position. The car rolled onto the raft, the weight of it making water wash right over the inflated rubber supports. At the stern of the raft an engineer manipulated an outboard motor.

By the time the car was on the raft and secured, another gray-painted car was coming across the meadow. And then a third. They'd been concealed behind the cottages near the broken, half-submerged timber jetty where once there had been a ferryboat.

The men in the command post watched every move. "The first tank is ready to go," said the young Leutnant. His name was Rudolf von Kleindorf, and he was the baby-faced second son of an aristocratic World War I general. Von Kleindorf had not graduated from cadet school in time to serve on active duty, and now he showed an exaggerated respect for men like Horner, who'd fought in the war.

"Not enough smoke," said Oberleutnant Alex Horner, who was, for the purpose of this exercise, a colonel commanding a battalion of tanks. "Where are the smoke troops?"

"That's all the smoke we have," said von Kleindorf, his "chief of staff."

"Damn!" said Horner. "Set fire to one of those dirty little timber huts. Get fuel from the transport people—plenty of oil. Make black smoke. If the enemy see those rafts they'll guess that this is the *Schwerpunkt* and that our efforts upstream are a feint."

"There are people living in those huts," protested the "chief of staff."

"It can't be helped: we need the smoke."

Von Kleindorf energetically turned the handle of the field telephone and spoke into it, ordering the houses fired. But the officer at the other end said it was impossible. All of his motor transport was being used as "tanks." He could send men on bicycles, but it would take time to fill containers with fuel, and they would be difficult to carry by bike.

Alex Horner cursed again when he heard the reply.

"They are Arbeitskommandos," said von Kleindorf to explain the shortcomings of the transport unit. The AK were a secret reserve army formed from the remnants of the Freikorps. Formerly disguised as labor associations and sports societies, they were now dressed in army-style uniforms and under the command of Leutnant Colonel von Bock, chief of staff of the 3rd Reichswehr Division. Officially the AK were civilian laborers assigned to help the hundred-thousand-man army that the peace treaty permitted, but when there were no prying eyes around they became soldiers.

"Get the tanks going," said Horner. The smoke was thinning still more by now, and through his binoculars he could see the defenders on the other bank. If he could see them from the command post on the hillside, it was a reasonable guess that they could see the rafts. Out of sight, upstream, they'd soon be dragging into position the six wheelbarrows that were their assigned high-velocity antitank guns.

"Damn! Damn! Damn!" said Horner, who was not given to such displays of emotion.

Within three hours the battle was decided: the river crossing had been repulsed, the defenders had won.

"Colonel Horner commanding."

"It was a good idea," said von Kleindorf in an effort to comfort his commander. "No one ever thought of making the pontoon-bridge components into rafts before. If the transport company had fired the houses . . ."

Alex Horner's face gave no sign of any emotion whatsoever. "Who is the commander of the AK down there?"

Von Kleindorf consulted his notebook. "Brand. He's described here as a Sturmbannführer. A Sturmbann is a brownshirt battalion. The equivalent rank is major," he added, to warn Horner that the AK officer outranked him.

Horner said nothing.

Brand. It was a common enough name, but the officer who eventually appeared was the same tormentor Alex Horner had known so long ago and never forgotten.

"You sent for me, Oberleutnant?" Sturmbannführer Heinrich Brand asked formally. He had not changed much, the same "Crazy Heini," with his plucked eyebrows and the beady, quick-moving little eyes placed too close on each side of his thin nose. Impeccably turned out: Iron Cross first class on his pocket and swagger stick in his hand. The only false notes were the nicotine-stained fingers and, more noticeably, the gray mustache, its lower part dyed yellow by the cigarettes he constantly smoked.

"Where was the staff transport, Brand?" asked von Kleindorf. Brand stared at his questioner. Brand was in his mid-forties and a senior SA man, but these two kids—junior officers, neither of them even thirty—treated him like dirt. He recognized Horner, of course, and he knew that Horner recognized him. It was typical of these arrogant Prussian swine that Horner, the so-called commander, should remain aloof and silent, in the manner of some senior general out of the history books.

"Not available, Leutnant," said Brand. He didn't smile, but he let them see that he did not intend to apologize. "Leutnant": that was the brownshirt style. Not "Herr Leutnant"—that damned nonsense was finished.

"The commander's written orders were that one motor vehicle was to be kept for the transport staff."

"It was in use."

"For what purpose?"

"I was visiting the bridging unit."

"Why?"

"To inspect them. Most of them are my men."

"Are your AK men all brownshirts, Brand?"

"Yes, Leutnant, and all from Bavaria." It wasn't exactly true—nearly half of them were from the Ruhr—but he knew that the reply would get up the nose of these two Prussians. Brand saw no reason to stand rigidly to attention. As the AK commander, he should be treated with respect. He slapped his leg with the swagger stick. "The SA now outnumber the army," he told them gratuitously.

Von Kleindorf said nothing. Horner's face was set like granite.

"When we come to power," Brand told them, "the Sturmabteilung will become the nation's only bearer of arms. We will be a new sort of army."

"Will it deliberately disobey orders, as you did today?" von Kleindorf asked, and immediately wished he hadn't as he saw the satisfaction in Brand's face.

Brand gave no reply, and with ill-concealed anger von Kleindorf dismissed him. Brand saluted with a studied care that was insolent. He had no regrets. He didn't mind if his deliberate flouting of orders had caused the failure of the river crossing. The sun was sinking fast for Prussian stereotypes like Horner and von Kleindorf. A National Socialist order was about to dawn. Brand had the warm glow of the believer, and such men suffer no self-doubts.

It took until nightfall for the battlefield to be restored to the villagers who lived upon it. Not knowing how narrowly their homes had escaped extinction by fire, the residents of the cottages near the disused ferry gave the tired soldiers bits of hard home-made sausage and old dark bread.

Oberleutnant Alex Horner went to report to the "divisional commander"—Captain Niemann, a severe-looking man who'd ended the war as a hussar colonel and had taken the demotion to stay in the peacetime army. Then they began the night march back to barracks. It was a long journey. The men soon settled into that march time that trained infantry can sustain for hour after hour. The crunch of jackboot on loose-surface country road produced a rhythm that lulled the mind, and dulled the aches and pains that more casual walking brings.

The rearmost infantryman carried the oil lantern that regulations prescribed as a necessary precaution against traffic accidents, but the moon provided light enough for Oberleutnant Horner and von Kleindorf to see the whole column as they trudged on through villages where barking dogs greeted them as strangers. Horner and von Kleindorf were mounted on chargers—fine, big beasts that snorted and sneezed and danced and did not know that their role in war was to be confined to the symbolic and ornamental.

"Did you know that *Kerl?*" von Kleindorf asked, dropping, for the first time since the exercise had begun, the role of chief of staff.

"I was with him in the war," replied Alex Horner.

"He was in your regiment? An officer?" said von Kleindorf incredulously. Brand's surly manner and coarse accent were an unlikely asset for the mess of a smart regiment.

"No, I was in his," said Horner.

"Oh, the Bavarian Reserves you told me about."

"That's it," said Horner.

"Poor you," said von Kleindorf. "You don't think those SA ruffians could really become a part of the army, do you?"

"Not while I'm in it," said Horner. All the time he was thinking of the days to come: inquests, post-mortems, reports, and conferences. Alex Horner's failed river crossing was unlikely to come out well.

"What battalion is this?" It was the voice of Captain Niemann, out of the darkness. He was moving up to the front of his "division."

"First Heavy Panzer Battalion," said Horner, keeping to the terminology of the exercise. "Colonel Horner commanding." It was absurd, of course. He looked at his marching column: in manpower it was scarcely a company. With an army of only a hundred thousand men it would be difficult—after finding the support and lines of communication troops—to put together a couple of decent infantry divisions, let alone the panzer units, motorized infantry, and so on that this exercise envisaged. But if Captain Niemann was determined to hold on to his phantom division until the last moment, who could really blame him?

"Good night, Herr General," said Horner.

"Your financial adviser resigns."

Veronica had kept the Winters' house true to the splendid *fin de siècle* style. Over the years there had been new furniture, furnishings, and carpets, but the style was unchanged. Now, as the 1930s approached, she was conscious of the way that the gloomy drawing room, of which she'd always been so proud, was to her brother's American eyes like a museum.

The windows were heavily draped in yellow silk with chocolate-brown tassels, so that only limited daylight could fall upon the Oriental carpets. There was scarcely a glimpse of the patterned wallpaper, for the pictures, paintings, and carefully posed sepia family-portrait photographs were crowded together with ornamental plates and fans. Small pieces of chinaware, ivory, and silver bric-à-brac crowded the huge mirrored mantel-shelf, and were carefully arranged on side tables and in glass-fronted cabinets, so that Glenn Rensselaer was in constant fear of knocking something over.

"Harald should retire," Veronica told her brother.

"He's only fifty-nine; he's not sick, is he?"

"He's tired and he's bored and he's apprehensive."

"About the business?"

"About the world, about Germany, about the things that are happening here. Go ahead and smoke, Glenn. I can see you're dying to."

"I'm not sure I understand you, sis," said Glenn Rensselaer. "Yes, I would love to smoke, if you're sure you don't mind." He reached into the pocket of the suit he'd bought specially for this trip. He wanted to look smart for his sister, and on the shopwindow dummy this Glenurquhart check looked very presentable. But now, on him, it was already baggy and rumpled. He was getting out his pipe and tobacco pouch when there was a tap at the door. A chambermaid, complete with starched cap and apron, came in to attend to the stove. She fed coal into it and deftly swept the coal dust into a pan that she took away with her.

Only when the servant was gone did Veronica answer. "Unemployment is on the rise again."

"Everyone says Germany is booming."

"The boom has ended. Harald is predicting three million unemployed this coming winter, and he's usually right about such things. He thinks more unemployment will immensely strengthen the communists and the Nazis."

"Probably."

"And the Nazis are asking Harald for money. He's resisted so far, but most of the other big companies are making contributions to them."

"Why?"

"Don't be so naïve, Glenn. Because they don't want the communists to come to power and seize the factories. But for Harald there is a further complication: he has to consider Peter and Lottie."

"Well, he won't be helping Lottie and little Helena by financing the Nazis and bringing them into power, will he?"

"The Nazis will list Harald's companies among those with 'Jewish management' unless he donates a substantial sum to them. That could mean boycotts and demonstrations . . . strikes, too, perhaps."

"Does Peter know?"

"Peter is urging Harald to resist, but most of the other directors insist upon paying. It could probably be arranged that the payments be tax-deductible, so it wouldn't cost the company anything."

"Poor Harald."

"Until now he's resisted the Nazis, but they are becoming much more powerful every week. A severe winter and more unemployment might change everything for the worse."

"Has Harald spoken to Pauli about this?"

"For heaven's sake, Glenn. You must promise—Harald would die rather than ask Pauli for any sort of favor. The argument they had that night at Pauli's birthday party has never really healed."

"I'm sure Pauli bears his father no ill will," Glenn told her. "The other night, at the party for the Danzigers, they seemed to be on good terms."

"Pauli forgets the hurtful things he says, but his father doesn't."

Glenn puffed away at his pipe. "Back home they think that at long last Germans have come to see the advantages of parliamentary democracy."

"That will take a long time. The single voice of a strong emperor has always been to the German taste. Germans find the argument and conflict of our sort of politics confusing and disturbing. They don't like debate: they want decisions."

"You should know them by now, sis. You've lived here a long time."

"Too long, perhaps," she said.

"Is that so?"

"I've been thinking about going home, Glenn."

"The folks would be bowled over. Dad's seventy-eight this year; I think he's given up all hope of seeing you again."

"Tell me about Dad."

"Dot looks after him."

"What is she like?"

"I don't know. Sometimes I think she's a schemer. She had her three sons take the family name, and Dad put a lot of money into that bank to get partnerships for them. Her eldest son's little boy stays with us, and Dad seems more interested in him than in my little boy." He looked up and smiled at her. It was not like Glenn to express any kind of grievance. "Yes, you should go home."

"Perhaps I was wrong to wait so long, but at previous times I could see no way. . . ."

"A visit, you mean?"

"I don't know, Glenn. I love Harald and the two boys. And Lottie has become like a daughter to me. I would miss them all so much. And yet . . ."

"What is it, sis?"

"I don't want to die here, Glenn."

"Die? What are you talking about? You are only"—his brow furrowed as he quickly added five years to his own age to calculate— "fifty-four. You have half a lifetime in front of you."

"I know. I have no fears of death, or any premonition. It's just that I'd like to live out my old age in America. Does that sound crazy?"

"No, sis. Of course I understand. I know many people who feel exactly that way after living overseas. Have you spoken to Harald about this?"

"He'd be so terribly hurt, Glenn."

"But you are unhappy."

"Yes, I am."

"Would Harald go, too?"

"Not for a prolonged stay. In America he'd be like a fish out of water. His English is not very good, and he remains the most German German I've ever met."

It was not the first time that Veronica had discussed with Glenn the idea of returning to America. Each time she did so it was from some new aspect, and each time Glenn started off believing her. But, as in previous discussions of this kind, Glenn ended in doubt. Eventually he decided that she would never go back. She lacked the desire, the energy, that would be needed to sever herself, however briefly, from her life here in Berlin.

But Glenn saw how much his sister needed this curious fantasy about going home, and he was prepared to indulge her, despite the way her conversation went round and round, the deceptions and the self-deceptions and the devious ways she invented to temporize. He resolved that next time they spoke he'd confront her with the contradictions.

But the next conversation that Glenn Rensselaer had with his sister was under very different circumstances. It took place on the following Friday. Rensselaer had arrived at the emergency department of the Charité Hospital in response to a telephone call from the manager of the Adlon Hotel. A policeman had come to the hotel to bring news that one of their guests—Herr Simon Danziger—had been injured in a traffic accident.

It was said by people who know about such matters that Potsdamer Platz had become the busiest traffic intersection in the whole of Europe. Cars, delivery vans, and heavy trucks entered the Platz from a dozen different directions. Navigating across this mad whirlpool of motors and horse-drawn carts came the clanking streetcars, and everywhere deft cyclists and even more nimble pedestrians dashed through the torrent of traffic.

It was here—at the intersection with the recently named Friedrich Ebert Strasse—that, at eleven-fifty that Friday morning, Herr Simon Danziger was struck by a horse-drawn dray laden with twenty-six barrels of dark beer from the Neukölln brewery.

He was still conscious, and in great pain, while they rushed him to the Charité Hospital in the taxi from which he'd just alighted. He was prepared hurriedly and taken to an operating theatre on the top floor for major surgery.

The complex that is the Charité sprawls across Berlin's Mitte. These forbidding old buildings make up a gray stone fortress wedged between the slow-moving oily water of the river Spree and the canal. There was no waiting room, and Glenn Rensselaer spent the first half-hour standing awkwardly amongst the outpatients in a cold and drafty upstairs corridor. From here he enjoyed the view of a cobbled courtyard where two mechanics delved into the entrails of a Magirus ambulance.

Glenn Rensselaer felt conspicuous in his long fur-lined overcoat, homburg, gray gloves, and silver-topped cane. The poorly dressed people on the benches were hunched against the cold and stiff with their aches and pains. They looked at him with detached curiosity, as they looked at the senior medical staff who strode through, or at the sheet-covered trolleys that came clanking past them, dragged by men in soiled white coats and glistening rubber aprons. Only two green-uniformed policemen seemed relaxed and at ease. They stood by the door, smoking cigarettes that they concealed inside half-clenched fists, and blew smoke at the ceiling.

The next person to arrive was his sister, Veronica. She wore a magnificent sable coat that was adorned, as was her hat, with flecks of newly fallen snow. She was escorted by a fluttering little hospital official. He wore a frock coat, carried wads of official-looking papers, called her Frau Doktor Winter, and bowed his head continually to expose a balding patch on the top of his skull.

Veronica called to her brother and he joined them, to be shown into a warm office where there was the privacy and comfort that the fluttery man felt should be provided for the highly esteemed Frau Doktor.

"Are you family?" the fluttery man inquired.

"No, not family," said Glenn.

"No, of course not, of course not!" said the man, and was especially flustered at the idea of it.

Veronica was seated in the soft visitors' chair, and Glenn in the swivel chair behind the desk, when he returned to bring them the duty surgeon's prognosis. After a long description of Danziger's mortal injuries—a litany that Glenn couldn't understand and to which Veronica closed her ears—he said that there was no chance that Herr Simon Danziger could survive. He would expire, the man predicted—looking down mournfully at the papers in his hand—within the hour.

"Poor devil!" said Glenn Rensselaer when the man had departed.

"He was so full of life," said his sister.

"I was thinking of the driver of the beer dray."

"Yes, for him, too," said Veronica doubtfully.

There was a long silence. "Danziger went bust," said Rensselaer. "The first telegrams went out last Saturday night, calling in the margins. Danziger had sunk every last red cent into stocks on the New York exchange. We talked about it on the airship coming over."

"The 'crash'—I saw it in the papers, but I don't really understand . . ."

"Suckers kept buying: up and up and up and up it went. It had to go bang, and it crashed last weekend."

"And they didn't know it was about to happen?"

"Everyone on the exchange knew, unless they were plumb stupid. But the market makes money on every deal. The brokers will come out of this disaster richer than ever."

Veronica said, "You're saying Mr. Danziger deliberately stepped in front of . . . No, Glenn, no. That's too awful."

"I sure won't say it to Lottie or to Mrs. Danziger, but I'd bet a million bucks against an old shirt-stud that that's the truth of it."

"He was bankrupt?"

"Just about, I'd say. He told me that he'd scraped together every last asset he could find to play the market. Dad sent me a long telegram when the market closed on Monday. Told me what was happening behind the scenes. The time difference meant that I had the telegram soon after midnight."

"Did you tell Mr. Danziger?"

"I telephoned him at the Adlon and read Dad's telegram to him, leaving out the names of Wall Street tycoons who'd died by their own hand since the news broke. It was about one o'clock in the morning, Tuesday. I must have woken him up. He just grunted a thanks. I guess he'd already heard from his own broker. It was too late to do anything by then. That was the last time I spoke with him. I said to call me if I could help, but he never did."

"It's ghastly," said Veronica. "How will Mrs. Danziger manage?"

"I don't know. All she has is some shares in a movie studio, and that's not an asset easy to dispose of," said Glenn. He was thinking of his nephew Peter. If there was no prospect of an inheritance for Lottie, Peter was going to be tied to his father, and the safe, well-paid job there.

"I wonder if she'll have enough money to settle her bill at the Adlon. I'd better offer her those two rooms on the third floor. Will she want the funeral here in Berlin, do you think?"

"I don't think she has a lot of choice."

Mrs. Danziger would have preferred to take her husband's body back to America, and Lottie wanted her father buried with appropriate ceremony in the old Jewish cemetery in Grosse Hamburger Strasse, behind the Rote Rathaus, where the great Moses Mendelssohn was interred, but both ideas proved impracticable. Instead the funeral was held at the big Jewish cemetery at Weissensee.

Some people said that Pauli cared too much for his job with the Nazis to be seen at a Jewish funeral, but they were wrong. Pauli attended the funeral, dressed soberly in the dark suit he wore when attending the criminal courts. What's more, Pauli took a few moments at the funeral to do his father a favor. He told his father, in strictest confidence, that the Nazis would be more than satisfied with a quarter of the amount of money they were demanding from Winter Metal Alloys.

Mrs. Danziger was pleased to accept Veronica's offer of accommodation, and Glenn Rensselaer settled her bill at the Adlon. She stayed until after Christmas, not wishing to face the California party season alone.

It was a few days before Christmas when Mrs. Danziger had a letter from the insurance company that covered her husband's life policy. It said that they would pay. Glenn Rensselaer breathed a sigh and flushed down the toilet the five-dollar bill that Mr. Danziger had sent him just before he died. Had the assessors seen the cryptic note that accompanied it—"Dear Glenn, Your financial adviser resigns as of today. Please give my apologies to all concerned with the results. I did the best I could—Simon Danziger"—they might not have been so willing to categorize his death as accidental.

By the time Mrs. Danziger took the train to Bremerhaven to catch the S.S. *Albert Ballin* for New York, some of Harald Winter's pessimistic forecasts were coming true. And the effects of the New York crash came rippling into the European countries, so that their already unstable economies were buffeted by the storms.

In the month of January 1930 alone, the number of unemployed Germans rose from one and a half million to almost two and a half. In Berlin the factories were laying off workers at such a rate that in many parts of the city the streets were crowded with unemployed. They stood and stared vacantly about them, not knowing how to cope with their misery. Farms within walking distance of the city, as so many farms still were, had armed men guarding their crops.

The coalition government declared that there was not enough money to pay the normal unemployment benefit without incurring a deficit equivalent to about a hundred million dollars. This financial and political crisis came soon after the tenth anniversary of Germany's changeover to parliamentary democratic government. It wasn't easy to argue with those who said that the communists or the Nazis would do better.

Almost three years earlier, in 1927, the hundredth anniversary of the death of Ludwig van Beethoven, Artur Schnabel had created a sensation in Berlin by playing the complete Beethoven piano sonatas. It took seven Sunday-afternoon concerts, and Schnabel performed them in the Volksbühne, a theatre club created by means of trade-union financing and more usually associated with the radical left.

Schnabel's great success had an effect upon the Berlin musical establishment. It changed Erich Hennig's life. In February 1930, largely as a result of the continuous prompting of his wife, Lisl, Erich Hennig played Mozart piano sonatas before an invited audience.

In some ways it was a mistake. Erich Hennig did not have the subtle and disciplined lyricism that Mozart requires. Hennig was at his best supplying the more robust demands of Beethoven's piano concertos. But Hennig's two concerts were by no means a failure. His mother-in-law sent the invitations, and Frau Wisliceny was still a name to be reckoned with in the bitter and Byzantine power struggle that had always characterized Berlin's cultural life.

Those who might have dared to condemn Hennig's interpretation of Mozart were not present at the performances, and any comment they made was condemned as sour grapes. Hennig's Mozart was competent and charming and provided a turning point in Hennig's career. Until now he'd worked for a music publisher, but now he was signed by an agent. With three pupils, and the promise of more performance jobs, Hennig left his dull office job and became a professional musician.

And as his career changed, so did his political allegiances. Until this time he'd been a left-wing radical, regularly to be seen at Communist Party meetings. But beginning with his Mozart recitals, Hennig's political activities were less in evidence. The hammer-and-sickle badge was not displayed in the lapel of the black suit he wore when at the keyboard, and the bright-red tie was replaced by a quieter, patterned one chosen by his mother-in-law.

Other, more far-reaching changes dated from Hennig's Mozart recitals in February 1930. It was Pauli's presence at the recital hall off Ku-damm that caused Frau Wisliceny to invite him regularly to her house. Not always to her "salon," for Pauli Winter was not, and would never claim to be, an intellectual. "Mozart is about as far as I go," he told Frau Wisliceny, and anyone else who tried to discuss music with him.

He was welcome in many places nowadays, for Pauli Winter was not the little Pauli who had marched off to war. For one thing, he went everywhere nowadays in a smart black Horch convertible. On weekdays, on official business, the car was driven by a stern-faced young man wearing shiny high boots, breeches, and a brown shirt with swastika armband.

Pauli Winter enjoyed going to Frau Wisliceny's gatherings. She chose her guests carefully, so they were always people who reacted favorably to Pauli's jokes and chatter. Usually, after tea, Frau Wisliceny would persuade him to do some conjuring tricks. He'd feign reluctance, but she knew he enjoyed doing the tricks, because he always managed to have some new ones prepared. And his tricks were never silent. Four kings inserted into a deck became "four Turkish-carpet merchants arriving at their warehouse." There was always a funny story, and the end of the trick brought not only a gasp of surprise but also a hoot of laughter.

Pauli had the enviable ability to walk into a room filled with strangers confident that he'd make new friends: and he almost invariably did. Pauli could peel layers from a stranger and release some surprising prisoner trapped inside a reputation. No one but Pauli could have persuaded the pompous Erich Hennig to play a silly song like "Yes, We Have No Bananas!" and have got a revered actor like Emil Jannings to sing the nonsensical words.

Pauli's enemies said that he always wanted easy praise and appreciation. His father, on more than one occasion, warned him with that classic aphorism "Applause is the spur of noble minds, and the aim of weak ones," but Pauli was undaunted. Pauli was Pauli, and his nature was not so easily changed.

As with most successful entertainers, his disarming casualness concealed the great care with which he watched his audience. He knew which people present gave themselves to his jokes, tricks, and stories and which were determined to remain unimpressed. So he knew that Inge enjoyed them more than most.

And Frau Wisliceny appreciated the sight of Inge laughing. If only Lottie had not had her wedding reception at the Wisliceny house. She was their guest and there was no avoiding it, but the preparations for the wedding had turned the knife that was in Inge's heart. Her mother had wept for her, and began to doubt if Inge would ever be happy again. It was weeks before she would even leave the house, and her mother suffered with her. It was an agony greatly worsened by the unwillingness of either woman to admit that it existed. Sometimes Frau Wisliceny wondered if Peter Winter ever realized the consuming adoration that Inge had for him. Perhaps he did, for he seemed to contrive that he and Inge didn't meet at dinners or parties or any other gatherings.

So Frau Wisliceny was pleased to see that Pauli enjoyed entertaining Inge and some of his tricks seemed to be prepared for her alone. And when Inge went several times a week to the Romanische Café to join Pauli in his frugal lunch, or even when the lunches became less frugal and of longer duration, no one gave it any serious attention. Frau Wisliceny was relieved to see that Inge was once again taking an interest in the outside world. She guessed—rightly—that many of those early conversations were devoted exclusively to discussions about Peter.

It helped, of course. Pauli was a good listener, and it was far easier to explain her love of Peter to him, for he loved his brother, too. Neither of them considered any possible romantic developments of their meetings, even when the talk of Peter had dwindled to almost nothing. They enjoyed each other's company, and everyone knew that Pauli had lots of girlfriends: noisy, pretty, gregarious girls, none of them like the serious, beautiful, and intellectual Inge. She wasn't Pauli Winter's sort of girl. And yet Pauli was not blind to Inge's beauty. Her green, luminous eyes that could look so deep and so lonely, her long neck, long slim arms, and pale unblemished skin like porcelain made her someone he was proud to be seen with. And Inge discovered in Pauli someone she'd never known about, a man who was able to make her forget for a moment the ache she felt for Peter.

It was Pauli's blonde waitress at the Romanische Café who changed everything. She regularly exchanged vulgar jokes with all her male customers. One day she greeted Inge and Pauli with a typical Berlin joke that speculated on what they would be doing that afternoon following their lunch of a dozen oysters each and a bottle of Sekt.

Pauli was embarrassed, but to his surprise Inge responded by telling her in Berlin argot just how much she was looking forward to just such an outcome. A new relationship began immediately. The following day they went to Friedländer Brothers, next door to the Hotel Bristol, and chose a ring. And then to the "tea dance" at the roof garden of the Eden Hotel. Pauli could dance well when he wanted to, and now he wanted to. Within two weeks Inge and Pauli were officially engaged, and their marriage followed in May.

There was no opposition from the families. Any reservations that the Wislicenys might have entertained about Pauli's philistine tastes or political affiliations were entirely removed by Inge's obvious happiness. And all the Winter family agreed that Inge Wisliceny was a catch beyond any that Pauli could rightfully have expected.

Peter's wife, Lottie, was determined to remain Inge's friend, and despite the reservations that Inge at first showed, it was Lottie, far more than Frau Wisliceny, who helped Inge plan the wedding.

It was a spectacular event. Pauli's friend Alex Horner pulled strings at Bendlerstrasse and arranged for Paul Winter to be registered as an Oberleutnant of the Reserve so that he could have a military guard of honor at the ceremony. Each young officer was matched with a beautifully dressed bridesmaid, in the traditional German style. The couple came down the steps of the church under a canopy of drawn swords. This was Lottie's idea: since, as she pointed out, such a ceremony demanded that Pauli wear an army uniform, he could not possibly get married wearing the brown shirt and swastika of the SA, in which he'd recently been given honorary rank. Not even Dr. Goebbels, the Berlin party leader, would insist that anything could be more glorious for a German than to be married in army officer's uniform. And Pauli, with his wonderful blond hair, was the archetypal "Aryan" that Nazi mythology so admired.

Lottie and Inge had worked hard at the guest list to see that the reception was not only for the family but also a reunion of Pauli's old friends. There were men who'd been cadets at Lichterfelde with him and half a dozen men of his 1918 storm company, as well as close friends like Fritz Esser.

The presents were in keeping with the grandeur of the ceremony and reception. Richard Fischer gave the couple a twenty-place antique Meissen dinner service that had been in his family for several generations. Inge had refused Richard's marriage proposal, and now she wondered if this was his way of telling her that he'd never marry anyone else.

Harald and Veronica Winter gave them a large Mercedes tourer, as well as having the house on the Obersalzberg extensively extended and redecorated in preparation for their honeymoon there. Until this time it had been little more than a hunting lodge, with heavy rustic furniture and cheap printed fabrics. But now it became a country house, with a large dining room, a huge sitting room, and no fewer than five small but comfortable bedrooms. And, wonder upon wonder, Veronica, using the check sent by her father, had insisted upon an example of transatlantic profligacy: each bedroom had its own bathroom! This extraordinary extravagance had made the house one of the wonders of the Obersalzberg. Pauli took great pleasure in showing his house to his bride, and, to his great delight and Veronica's relief, she fell in love with it. She cherished it, and its proximity to the holiday home that Adolf Hitler used, and made Pauli promise to take her there regularly in winter, and in summer, too.

1930

A family Christmas.

The sound of a motorcycle engine carries for miles amongst the high mountains of the Obersalzberg. Lottie Winter heard it first—her hearing was almost superhuman—and when she went to the window and moved aside the curtain, she saw the motorcyclist's headlight miles down below them, on the Berchtesgaden road. Inge, Pauli, and Peter watched her cupping her hands round her face to see into the darkness.

"Are you expecting a visitor?" Lottie asked without turning away from the window.

The question remained unanswered for a moment; then Inge replied. "It could be going to the pension, the Türken Hotel, or to one of the farms."

"It's coming here," said Lottie. She shuddered. She had a premonition that it was a messenger bringing bad news.

"I can't think who it could be," said Inge. She, too, was now convinced that the motorcycle was coming to them. She switched out the light and pulled back the red silk curtain. Now through the windows they could see the mountain peaks, the snow lit by the waning moon. In the air there were snowflakes. For most of the year it was like this: the wind blew the snow off the mountains, so that the air was never completely free of whirling crystals.

It was Christmas 1930 when Pauli and Inge brought Lottie and Peter to the Obersalzberg, and this time their most famous neighbor was in residence nearby. Since 1923 Adolf Hitler had been a regular visitor to this small mountainside community in the shadow of the Hohe Göll near Berchtesgaden. He'd fled here after the putsch; upon his release from Landsberg Prison, he'd come here to finish writing *Mein Kampf.* Now he'd decided to have a residence permanently available here, and had rented a modest chalet from his half-sister.

Suddenly Adolf Hitler had become an important political leader. At the elections in September, Hitler won six and a half million votes. It increased the Nazi Party's twelve seats in the Reichstag to a staggering 107 seats. After the Social Democrats, the Nazis were the most powerful political force in Germany. Since the election, small groups of visitors—having made a special journey here—would sometimes linger at the curve in the road below the Türken Hotel, hoping to catch a glimpse of this fellow who called himself the Führer.

The world press took notice. In Britain, *The Times, The Sunday Express,* and *The Daily Mail* immediately published interviews with him. Hitler declared himself a bulwark against Bolshevism and warned the British that they would be militarily endangered by the Soviet Union if Germany fell to the communists.

Since his unsuccessful Munich putsch, Hitler always recognized how much he would need the support of the German army if he was ever to come to power. So, within a few days of the September election, Hitler promised that under a Nazi regime the army would become more powerful and more important and better equipped than ever before. As always, there was something in his promises for everyone except the Jews and the communists.

Pauli and Inge's mountainside house was higher than the Führer's Berghof and Inge usually saw him when he took his regular stroll in the deep, crunchy snow each afternoon before tea. Once, feeling rather foolish, she waved to him, but if he saw her he gave no sign of it.

It was Saturday. Peter and Lottie Winter had arrived the previous day. Knowing that Lottie followed the fashions so closely, Inge was wearing the new line: a bias-cut gray chiffon dress that fitted close at bust and hips. By now Inge's terrible longing for Peter's love had settled down and become no more than a dull ache. It was an ache she could live with, and she'd been determined to make both Peter and Lottie feel at home. That night, after a big dinner of roast kid, potato dumplings, and apple pancakes, the cook and maid had departed, and the four of them were sitting drinking coffee and brandy round the log fire, listening to Peter's stories about Bertolt Brecht, the playwright who'd become one of Berlin's most colorful anarchistic characters. In October, Brecht had brought a legal action against the Nero film company, which was making a movie of his *Threepenny Opera*. The legal proceedings had soon become as entertaining, and far more star-studded, than anything Brecht had ever staged. Actors, actresses, writers, poets, and more humdrum types of publicity-seekers made sure they were seen there, and the newspapers followed every move.

"Brecht is a monster," said Peter, who'd directed Brecht through this courtroom drama. "An amusing, talented monster, but a monster just the same. When I told him that he couldn't win and advised him to take the twenty-five thousand marks they offered as a settlement, he called me a capitalist lackey, jumped to his feet, and went striding out of court."

"But why couldn't he win?" Pauli asked as one lawyer to another.

"The film company brought witnesses to tell the court that Brecht had done almost no work on the film script; and Brecht provided me with nothing I could use to refute it."

"Bad luck," said Pauli. He knew the problem well: there had been some weeks when all the clients the Nazi Party provided for him were so guilty that nothing could save them. And some clients simply wouldn't help themselves.

"Oh, Brecht did all right," said Peter. "I persuaded the film company to give him sixteen thousand marks for agreeing not to go to the appeals court. I knew they wanted to get the matter conclusively settled quickly, so they could start filming."

"Isn't he a clever man?" said Lottie, who, sitting alongside her husband on the sofa, now hugged him. Inge smiled.

"I've learned quite a lot about the world of films and theatre in the last few years," said Peter.

"But not earned much money doing it," said Pauli.

"Tell him he should charge them proper fees," Lottie told Pauli.

"It's more fun than the work I do for Papa," said Peter. "And when *Mahagonny* opened in Leipzig, they gave me the best seats in the house."

"I wish we hadn't gone," said Lottie. "It was terrible. There were hundreds of storm troopers outside, waving protest banners and swastika flags. We pushed through them, but there were more demonstrators inside. There were fistfights in the auditorium, and some people were hurt. The police came: lots and lots of them. It was awful."

"You shouldn't have gone," said Pauli. "Brecht is a communist. He wants that sort of trouble: it gets him the publicity he likes."

"He's a genius," said Peter.

"Maybe he is a genius," said Pauli. "But why doesn't he use his genius to say something good about his own country? If Brecht had his way, he'd hand Germany over to his friends in Moscow."

"He's trying to stir up our thoughts," said Peter. "He likes to be provocative."

"Let him go and be provocative in Russia and see what happens to him," said Pauli. "Stalin is murdering his opponents by the hundred thousands. Why doesn't your friend Brecht write a play about that?"

"Sometimes Brecht goes too far," agreed Lottie.

"Perhaps he does," said Peter.

It was at this point that Lottie had heard the sound of the motorcycle and gone to the window. Their visitor was Fritz Esser, arriving unexpectedly, as he always did. Like many of the Nazi Party leaders, he'd leased a country house here in Bavaria, but in order to indulge his lifelong passion for sailing, he'd chosen the Ammersee, southwest of Munich. It took him over an hour on his BMW motorcycle to get to them. And, despite his ankle-length brown leather overcoat and fur-trimmed leather helmet, he would need some time by the fire and several drinks to thaw out properly.

Esser was a bearlike man: big, omnivorous, shaggy-coated, and sharp-clawed. Also like a bear, he could be elegant, cuddly, fast-moving, and vicious. He looked at them: the two brothers in dinner suits, and their wives in expensive new-fashion dresses. If Esser needed a reminder that his friends were from another world—a remote world with its own language, customs, and costumes—this moment provided that reminder.

Pauli introduced Fritz Esser to his sister-in-law. They shook hands warily. "A member of the Reichstag," repeated Pauli. "It's wonderful, Fritz." He poured coffee for Fritz and set the rum bottle out with the cream and sugar. Fritz preferred rum to brandy.

"Not even the Führer thought it was possible," said Esser proudly. "I wish my father had lived to see it."

"He would have been proud of you," said Peter dutifully, but he couldn't really imagine the "pig man"—a lifelong socialist—being proud of his Nazi son, even if that son was now a member of the Reichstag.

"Everyone was surprised." He looked up from his drink and met Pauli's eyes. They both knew that Pauli had suggested Fritz stand for election, and Pauli had done endless behind-the-scenes work to persuade the Nazis to back him. "No matter what they said afterwards, everyone was bowled over. Before the election they were hoping for thirty seats . . . fifty at the very most."

"And that's all you would have got under the American or British system of first-past-the-post," said Lottie. "It was proportional representation that inflated your gains."

"We're not in America," said Pauli sharply, as if to guard Fritz against his sister-in-law's tongue.

But Deputy Fritz Esser was far too happy to take offense at such remarks. "They never thought I'd do it," he said. "They say Göring helped the Chief assign the seats. They gave me my seat in Schleswig-Holstein, not because I'm from that part of the world, but because they hadn't the faintest hope that anyone could win it for us. Schleswig-Holstein! Good God, what could have been more hopeless for the party than that? They've voted liberal ever since anyone can remember up there. Everyone was astonished when the results came in."

He looked round at the others and smiled. Despite his old clothes, and his heavy body and darkly menacing eyes, Fritz had an energy and a willpower that made him attractive to men and to women. Anyone who'd heard his speeches glimpsed the captivating quality that was apparent to his friends. And yet Fritz never had any lasting relationships with women, as far as could be seen. Often he arrived with some glamorous young girl on his arm, but none lasted. Sometimes Pauli wondered if there was something wrong with Fritz, some flaw in his personality that Fritz could not come to terms with.

"Why did it happen?" asked Peter.

"No one knows: all the center parties suffered. Votes went to the communists and to us. The unemployed must have been a prime cause, but the Chief says that most of the first-time voters preferred us, and there were a lot of first-time voters in this election."

"Will Hitler work within the parliamentary system?" asked Lottie.

"Maybe," said Esser. He poured a generous amount of rum into his coffee and added sugar and cream, too.

"The system you've vowed to destroy," persisted Lottie.

"We'll make Germany great again," said Esser. He didn't want to get into an argument with this Jewish American intellectual: she was everything he despised. He was only being polite to her because Pauli was his closest friend, adviser, and confidant.

"Then why those disgraceful demonstrations in the Reichstag?" said Lottie.

"Now, that was Pauli's idea," said Esser. He looked at Pauli and grinned.

Pauli flushed. "It wasn't my idea, Fritz," he said awkwardly.

"You're too modest," said Esser. He enjoyed teasing Pauli. "On the night the election results came over the radio, I said to Pauli how angry the Führer was that Prussia had banned the wearing of our uniforms. He would have liked to see our deputies taking their seats in proper uniform. The Führer had said as much to me. He thought it was impossible to get round it, but young Pauli here found a way. He always finds a way. Pauli is the smartest fellow we have in the party."

"What was Pauli's idea?" said Peter.

"Taking our uniforms in with us and changing in the wash-rooms."

"Would someone explain it to me?" asked Lottie.

Quietly Peter said, "Once inside the building, the delegates enjoy parliamentary immunity. No one could stop them from wearing their Nazi uniforms, whatever the law says about it."

"It was a real pantomime," said Esser proudly. "We shouted and sang the old songs and told them what we thought of them. They tried to get the proceedings going, but there were too many of us, and the sight of our brown shirts drove them to a frenzy." He laughed.

"It sounds stupid," said Lottie angrily.

Esser laughed again at her anger, and Pauli laughed, too. They were like naughty schoolboys. She found it impossible to argue with them. "It's not funny," she said, but the more angry she became the more they laughed.

When they were quiet again and Pauli had replenished everyone's drinks, Pauli said, "Have you come to see the Führer, Fritz?"

"Tomorrow you will be introduced to him," Fritz Esser announced proudly. There was no need to say whom he was talking about: when Fritz spoke of his "Chief"—the Führer—there was a special note of respect in his voice. "Pauli and Inge, too. He has asked me to arrange it. He wants to meet all his neighbors, and of course he knows about Pauli's work in the Berlin Gauleiter's office." He finished his second coffee with rum; this time it was almost entirely rum.

"Does he?" said Inge. She had never had any interest in politics, but now that she was married to Pauli she supported the Nazis, for whom he worked. And, like any loyal and devoted wife, she wanted her husband's virtues to be properly rewarded.

"We all know what a damned difficult year it's been," said Fritz, rubbing his hands together before warming them again at the fire.

Inge didn't know. Pauli seldom discussed his work with her. Every night he came home looking as if he didn't have a care in the world.

"First, just after your wedding, when the Führer had his big row with Strasser. We were worried, I can tell you!"

"What was that about?" asked Inge. She looked at Fritz with great interest. Inge was a wonderful hostess: she drew people out.

Fritz knew she was pumping him, but he didn't mind. Inge was pretty and the wife of one of his best friends. And the rum was taking effect. "I was there, in the Hotel Sanssouci, when it happened. They nearly came to blows. Strasser wants a program of nationalization of industry and a whole lot of things that the communists want. The Chief called Strasser a commie and said he wouldn't nationalize Krupps, because government clerks would bring it to bankruptcy within a few weeks. It was quite a shouting match. Then a couple of days later the Berlin SA went on strike for more wages. . . ." He shrugged.

"What will happen about the SA? I'm so glad Pauli didn't wear a brownshirt uniform when we got married. There is always so much trouble with them." She looked at Pauli, who smiled but didn't comment.

"The trouble's not over yet. The Führer has asked Ernst Röhm to take command of the SA again."

"I thought he went to South America."

A family Christmas.

"Yes, we all thought we'd got rid of the fat swine, but now he's coming back."

"Pauli hates him."

"We all hate him; he's a cunning, deceitful pansy. And now he'll make sure all his homosexual friends are promoted back into the SA top ranks. He'll make life difficult for his enemies, and I'm one of his enemies."

"Why does the Führer want to use a man like that?"

"Since the election, people are joining the party and the brown-shirts in such numbers that we can hardly cope. With the party that's no real problem: we write their names and addresses in a book and they start paying us their contributions. But the SA has to be uni-formed, trained, and organized. Röhm knows all about that, so Röhm is the quickest solution to an urgent problem."

"Is Röhm coming here?"

"I hope to God he's not. I've got to have a few minutes with the Führer tomorrow. I was wondering . . ."

"A bed for the night? Of course, Fritz. I'll have your bags sent up to the corner room, the room with the balcony; you like that one, I know."

"Thanks, Inge. Not much baggage on a motorcycle: just the shoulder bag I left in the hall." He finished his third cup of coffee and rum and searched the pockets of his battered tartan, zip-fronted jacket to get cigarettes and matches. Pauli—always a good host—offered cigars from an inlaid humidor, but Fritz preferred the cheap, evil-smelling cigarettes he always smoked.

"When will we meet him?" Inge asked.

"Tomorrow, for tea. He's installed his half-sister over there as his housekeeper. She used to work as a pastry cook, and she makes the finest cream cakes I've ever seen; the Chief is very fond of cream cakes."

"Yes, we heard his widowed sister was living there. Angela, is it? Isn't there a brother, too?"

Fritz got up from the fender seat, where he'd been warming himself, and gave a little laugh—a snigger almost. "The Führer's half-brother, Alois, is a rather a touchy subject, Inge. He's been in and out of prison a number of times—some petty theft and then bigamy—and the last we heard of him, he's run off to live in England."

"The Führer's brother lives in England! That's extraordinary."

Fritz looked Inge straight in the eyes. "Yes, well, it's not something that has been given wide publicity, and I'd be obliged if you'd keep it to yourself."

She touched his arm in a gesture of reassurance. "Of course, Fritz."

"I've become very close to the Chief over the last few years, Inge. I've been loyal to him, and he's a man who respects loyalty. The Chief has a lot of good people round him: now more of them than ever, of course. But when the Führer has a problem, I'm proud to say he often turns to Fritz Esser. And Fritz never lets him down."

"And what does Fritz Esser do?" said Inge. "He goes to Pauli Winter."

"Exactly," said Esser.

Pauli smiled contentedly. Although he knew it to be a childish thought, he allowed himself to contemplate how perfect it would be if they all shared a house like this: together always. To be with Inge and Fritz and Peter and Lottie all the time was Pauli's idea of heaven.

Later that night, the two women were tidying the room. They had no living-in staff, and the two young village women who cooked and cleaned for them would not arrive until seven-thirty next morning. It being Sunday, they would come after Mass.

"You're not really going, are you, Inge?"

Inge was plumping up the cushions. She stopped and said, "To see the Führer?"

"The man is a monster."

"So is Brecht. Even Peter said so."

"That's different. Brecht doesn't rail against the Jews and threaten his opponents."

"But he does, Lottie. Brecht passionately hates everything that I love. He despises the soldiers who fought in the war for us. He says horrible things about officers, and Pauli and Peter were both officers. He hates the Homeland. He hates the church. He hates us!"

"I shouldn't have come," said Lottie. It was no good. Inge was one of the most intelligent German women she'd ever met, but . . .

"Don't be silly, Lottie darling."

"I'm not being silly!" said Lottie, a new, quiet anger in her voice.

Inge looked at her, not knowing how to deal with her. She'd never seen her sister-in-law on the verge of tears before. She'd never guessed that there were such strong emotions within her.

"Did you read the speeches Hitler just made at Offenburg and at the University of Erlangen?" Lottie asked her. "Everyone strives for expansion, he told them, and every people strives for world dominion. World dominion! He's a madman, I tell you."

"You mustn't take it all so seriously, Lottie," said Inge, much relieved to find that it was nothing more serious than Hitler's rhetoric that had upset her. "It's the sort of thing Germans want to hear. I am a German, and I understand these things. Please don't worry yourself."

"Perhaps we should go back to Berlin."

"Please don't go," said Inge. "It's so nice to see Peter and Pauli together. And it's Christmas."

"What is Christmas to me?" said Lottie. "I'm a Jew. Or have you forgotten that?"

"This obsessional hatred for the Führer."

Inge's mother-in-law, Veronica Winter, had met Adolf Hitler almost two years before. It was also at his house here on the Obersalzberg, and under similar circumstances. Veronica thought him "a horrible man." He fawned and smiled and behaved like the men she'd met at the salons in Vienna, hand-kissing men who hung around on the fringes of the art world being nice to rich old ladies.

But Inge and Pauli met a far more confident Hitler. Although the election success had not brought power, it had brought him the promise of power. There was not much hand-kissing now. They met a middle-aged man with unmistakable energy and determination. Not in any way like a peasant, he was obviously urban and quick-witted and might have been mistaken for a semiskilled foreman in one of Harald Winter's heavy-engineering factories. His carefully parted hair was almost unnaturally black, and his eyes were alert, but the color of his skin was gray and unhealthy. He wore a dark double-breasted suit with a Nazi Party badge in the wide lapel, and he made anxious little movements all the time: hand upon hip, then in pocket, raised fist, pointing finger, and hands clasped together.

Despite the violent and flamboyant speeches he'd made in the period leading up to the election, and his more recent ones at Offenburg and Erlangen, Hitler was today displaying the face of the respectable statesman.

For working-class audiences and students, Hitler concentrated on what they wanted to hear. He promised that everyone must be compelled to work, and that all income from investment would be abolished. Workers would nevermore be subjected to the "slavery" of interest repayments. All corporations would be nationalized, and department stores would be turned over to individual traders. Land would be redistributed to the peasants.

But today, for his prosperous neighbors, he talked of the injustice of the Versailles Treaty, the cooperation between workers and management that would bring a more prosperous Germany. He talked of his love for the mountains, his impoverished youth, and his ambition to see Germany and Austria united.

Hearing that Pauli Winter had been born in Vienna started the Nazi leader on a long, rambling account of his difficult days there. Only one light illuminated the darkness: the inspiring career of Karl Lueger, a man Adolf Hitler greatly admired. Once he had completed this short eulogy, uniformed aides made a passage for him, and the Führer moved away without waiting for any reaction.

Inge was thrilled. Years fell away, till her face shone with the excitement of a young girl. Nervously she ran her hand up the side of her face and back through her short-trimmed hair, holding her hand to her head as if trying to awaken herself from a dream.

There were many people in the chintzy little house with its fretwood and dried flowers and gingham. Too many for the cramped rooms, even when chairs and tables had been moved to make more space. In the corner was a piano—a present from his neighbors the Bechstein family—and Hitler sometimes played it. Besides aides, cronies, secretaries, bodyguards, and hangers-on, there was a crush of invited guests. Six of them were newly elected deputies, and Fritz Esser was amongst these. Inge was interested to catch a glimpse of Hitler's half-sister, Frau Angela Raubal. She was a cheerful, matronly woman who, Inge guessed from her appearance, had not given up hope of remarriage. Her daughter Geli was there, too, and had Inge been even better at guessing, she would have looked more closely at this plump twenty-two-year-old blonde who passed round the cream cakes. Before another year had gone,

Geli Raubal would be found shot dead in Hitler's Munich apartment, with Hitler's personal 6.35mm Walther pistol at her side, and be the center of speculation about "Uncle Alf's" love affairs.

But for Pauli, Hitler's half-sister and niece, and all the other local residents and high-ranking Nazis, were of only passing interest compared with the presence amongst the Führer's guests of Heinrich Brand. Pauli was horrified. He'd heard Esser's stories and other reports in the party papers of Brand's distinguished career as a brownshirt officer. And Alex Horner had told him of his encounter during the military exercises. But to see Brand face to face again was another matter.

An SA Obersturmbannführer now—a lieutenant colonel—and smartly turned out in beautifully cut riding breeches, and a well-fitting brown shirt on the pocket of which was an Iron Cross first class, exactly like the one the Führer wore. Had Pauli been prepared for this confrontation, it might have been endurable, but the sudden sight of his old tormentor made his stomach turn.

Pauli and Brand shook hands. Only a flicker of a smile from Brand revealed the hatred that he wanted made obvious to the younger man. Obersturmbannführer Brand, explained Fritz Esser, was setting up the headquarters for the return of the newly appointed brownshirt leader Ernst Röhm.

"Crazy Heini" was forty-five years old and, like his Führer, had grown less and less crazy with every step up the ladder of fortune. Brand had aged in the way that most people aged. His hair was gray and so was his mustache, but his eyes were the same as they always had been in so many of Pauli's worst nightmares. It wasn't just that they were set rather close to his thin, bony nose; the eyes were hard and glasslike, almost alive but not quite, moving always, and blinking like the eyes of a very expensive doll.

Pauli made polite comments about the important new post and how much he looked forward to meeting him again in Berlin. Brand touched his mustache and stared at Pauli, responding to his politeness with no more than a grunt. Pauli became nervous; he desperately wanted a cigarette, but they'd all been warned that the Führer didn't permit smoking.

Fritz Esser was suddenly at his elbow, persuading Pauli to repeat a joke that ended in a long speech in Austrian dialect, which Pauli could imitate so perfectly. He was halfway through before he remembered Hitler's strongly accented speech. He looked across the uncomfortably crowded room. It was damned hot in here, what with the wood stove and all these people. Hitler was at the window, surrounded by nodding, smiling sycophants. He was out of earshot, but Pauli had the feeling that this unfortunate joke would be repeated to the Führer. And Hitler's contempt for lawyers was well known.

When they got back home, it was dark. It got dark early in the mountains; that was the worst part of being there in the winter. Inge went upstairs to change into a dinner dress. Pauli poured himself a big glass of cognac and drank it too quickly. The shock of seeing Brand again had upset him. He decided that he wanted to talk about it to someone, and the depth of his fear was not something he wanted to reveal to Fritz Esser. Esser respected Pauli, and Pauli was determined to keep it that way. Pauli looked down at his hands. They were shaking so much that he'd already spilled some of his drink in pouring it out. Perhaps he should go and see one of these damned psychologists that were so fashionable nowadays.

But first he would speak about it with his brother. Peter understood him better than anyone. Peter wouldn't laugh at his fears. Peter would reassure him and give him advice, sensible advice, not the sanctimonious sermons that Papa delivered whether asked or not. It must have been fate that brought Peter here at this time of need. He went up to the big guest bedroom, the one with the balcony that provided a view of the legendary Untersberg. When there was no response to his knock, he tried the door. It opened, but Peter wasn't in, and neither was Lottie. And there was no sign of any of their clothes or personal possessions. On the dressing table there was an envelope. He opened it.

It was a polite note, thanking Pauli and Inge for their hospitality and the extra work the visit had made for them. There was an appropriate gratuity for the servants. But they'd had to return to Berlin suddenly. Peter was sure that Pauli would understand.

Pauli read the note again, and then a third time. He could hear Inge's bathwater running: it was no use going to her. He loved her dearly, but Inge wouldn't understand: he needed Peter. Pauli wanted to shout aloud, or at least to sob. But Pauli's days of crying had ended back when he used to cry himself to sleep in the cadet-school barracks at Lichterfelde.

He went downstairs and had another drink. It always took Inge a long time to bathe, change, and rearrange her hair. She liked to have some time to herself. When she came downstairs again, the fire was almost dead and Pauli was asleep on the sofa. She shook him, but the cognac decanter was empty and he was very drunk.

"Are you hungry, Pauli? There is ham and chicken." She touched his arm to wake him. "You haven't changed. . . . Pauli!" She switched the table lamp on. "Pauli!"

"Peter's gone home," he mumbled.

"Yes, I know."

"I love Peter," said Pauli drunkenly.

"Yes, you love your father and you love Peter. But can't you see that that's just your way of saying how much you depend on them?"

"I do depend on them."

"Then stop it! Pull yourself together, Pauli. Be a man. Start living your own life and making up your own mind about everything. I hate to see you abasing yourself to Peter. You're as good as he is; better, in fact."

"Why did he go?" asked Pauli.

"They were angry about our visit to the Führer," said Inge. "I heard him on the telephone ordering a car. It was Lottie, of course. She has this obsessional hatred for the Führer."

"You should have told me," said Pauli. "I wouldn't have gone if I'd known it would make that much difference."

"Yes, yes, yes," said Inge. "You would have refused to go, and what would have happened to us then?" She knelt on the carpet beside him and, holding him very tight, she kissed him. She loved this clumsy, silly Pauli, who never sent her flowers, never remembered her birthday, took her love for granted, as he expected her to do with his love. She loved him so much because he needed her to care for him. Germany had millions of unemployed, and many of them were lawyers. She wished Pauli would realize how lucky he was to have his fat salary and good job with the Nazis. It was all right for Lottie to air her opinions about what should be done, but her husband, Peter, had the security of the Winters' family business. Sometimes Inge resented the way that Pauli had been treated by his family. "Pauli, darling. I love you, I love you."

1932

"Was that more shouting in the street?"

In Berlin-Schöneberg, the evening of Sunday, April 10, 1932, was miserable. The sky had been overcast all day, it had got dark early, and the unrelenting rain was enough to persuade many people not to vote in the second presidential election. The whole city was plastered with election posters. Under the light of the streetlamps were regiments of Hitlers and rows of swastikas, shiny now in the persistent downpour. There weren't many people about, except for small squads of uniformed SA men, whose studded jackboots could be heard on the street, and sometimes their strident voices, too, as they sang their songs and looked for Jews to beat up or communists to battle with.

In fashionable Haberlandstrasse, a few houses from the apartment where Albert Einstein—the world's most famous scientist—had lived, the Isaac Volkmanns were preparing for a dinner party. The host was Isaac Volkmann, a prematurely balding thirty-six-year-old who would have been strikingly handsome but for the nose broken in a boxing match at school. Even so, his damaged nose, and a scar on his cheek, gave him the look of a slightly overweight pugilist, which some people, including his wife, thought attractive. But Volkmann was not a professional fighter; he was a fashionable dentist, whose clients included many of Berlin's most famous film and theatre stars. His particular skills included the fitting of beautifully made crowns and the general ability, by means of all sorts of magic tricks, to make a mouthful of crooked, yellow, neglected teeth into something even, white, and beautiful.

Frau Volkmann—a petite young woman with carefully plucked eyebrows and a sensuous mouth that too often pouted—was twelve years younger than her husband and still found the role of hostess somewhat stressful. For that reason the Volkmanns would often take their guests to a restaurant. Lately they had been favoring the newly furbished Restaurant Traube on Leipziger Strasse, with its tropical gardens and the tables arranged round a lily pond. Or the Café Berlin next door, where the orchestra was directed by Emil Schugalté, who before the revolution had been one of the most brilliant violin students of the *conservatoire* in St. Petersburg.

But tonight the Volkmanns were entertaining at home, in their apartment, where Isaac's superb collection of prints and paintings was on every wall. Feininger, Nolde, Grosz, and all sorts of bizarre examples of Dadaism. That magnificent collection was, it was whispered, the reason so many of Berlin's artists had notably fine teeth.

But Isaac Volkmann hadn't invited his guests to see his art collection. He was engaging in a tricky exercise in social engineering: trying to re-establish the former close relationship between the Winter brothers. The men had not taken a meal together since Peter's visit to the Obersalzberg at Christmas 1930. If it didn't work, if his two friends resented this contrived meeting—he'd not warned either of them—and there was some awful row, better, then, that it should take place at his home than in a restaurant for all the world to see.

This explanation did nothing to allay the fears of his wife, Lily. Since she was already worried about the cooking, the table arrangement, and the fact that by six o'clock that evening the fish for the second course had still not arrived, the last thing she wanted to contemplate was the chance of her guests quarreling.

"Oh, Lily. I forgot to mention that I invited that young English patient, too."

"Oh, Izzy. How could you!" She stamped her foot angrily.

"He's a nice young man. I thought Lottie might enjoy speaking her own language for a change."

"The table has been arranged for hours."

"Just one more diner, Lily, my sweetheart."

"An extra man. It's worse than asking two people. I can't possibly fit him in, Izzy."

"Nonsense, darling. Just move the flowers."

"Izzy, I spent all the morning doing those flowers."

"They'll look just as good on the side table there."

"I haven't got enough food."

"You have far too much. You always order far too much food: enough for double the numbers we invite. Sometimes I think that it must be that you had an impoverished childhood."

"Izzy. How could you do this to me? Do you hate me so much?"

"My darling, how could you say such a thing?"

"You'd better tell me about him, so that I don't say the wrong thing."

"He came to the surgery a week ago. In pain. A hairline crack in an upper front tooth. I saw immediately that it was a root canal."

"Izzy, I haven't got time for one of your lectures on modern dentistry."

"An Englishman. Twenty-three years old. Born to poor parents . . ."

"Did you ask him?"

"His teeth are in terrible condition. Poor parents, there is no doubt. He works for Dornier. A clever young man, very quick and amusing. He came today for a final checkup. I had a cancellation, so I was able to chat with him. On an impulse I invited him. Be nice to him, Lily."

"Am I ever anything but nice? I am too nice, that's my trouble. And what happens? I end up married to an inconsiderate brute who wants to make my hair turn gray. Why didn't you phone and tell me there was an extra man? I could have invited Lisl Hennig. Her husband is giving a recital in Breslau and won't be back until the weekend."

"Ah, the door. Someone must be very early."

"Izzy, it's not funny to try to make me more nervous than I already am. It's the fish."

"I know," said Isaac. "You have hours yet."

"I haven't even chosen what to wear."

"You look lovely just as you are, my darling." He put his arms round her.

"Izzy. Stop it. One of the servants might come in."

"Was that more shouting in the street?"

Dr. Isaac Volkmann's "experiment" seemed to work well. Volkmann was not a man who attempted such things without being confident of the outcome. He was about the same age as Pauli and had been with him in the storm battalion during the closing weeks of the war. He'd met him again after the war, and Pauli had been one of his very first patients; Peter Winter came to him soon after. Peter's contacts with the theatre world had brought Isaac some of his first celebrated patients. Isaac Volkmann felt obliged to both men, and the trouble he'd taken for tonight's reconciliation was a measure of his feeling about them both.

The brothers, and their respective wives, Lottie and Inge, talked and laughed together as if there had never been a difference of opinion about the visit to Adolf Hitler's private residence. Peter's wife, Lottie, just over the hurdle of her thirtieth birthday, had dispensed with the fringe she'd had for so long and let her lustrous black, wavy hair grow long enough to cover her ears. She wore a mustard-yellow silk-georgette dress with metallic-gold embroidery, a daring sort of color that only the exuberant Lottie could carry off with such style. And, never outdone, Inge, who had kept her hair short and boyish ever since bobbed hair had become fashionable, wore a conservative sleeveless black dress and a double rope of real pearls. Peter was slimmer, and his gaunt appearance suited him. His features had become more pointed with age—a hatchet face—unmistakably German. He looked, Inge noticed, more handsome than ever. The two brothers were in dinner jackets, like their host, but the Englishman, full of apologies, had arrived in a lounge suit, the most formal clothes he possessed.

Over the fresh asparagus the conversation was mostly about the new film about Frederick the Great. Otto Gebühr, who'd played Frederick the Great in the UFA comedy film *Das Flötenkonzert von Sanssouci,* was to repeat this role in the more serious film *Der Choral von Leuthen.* As Peter Winter said, the actor might not have been an exact likeness of that eighteenth-century monarch, but he was exactly what every German wanted to believe Frederick was like. Pauli, typically provocative, said that Richard Tauber, the singer from the Metropole Theatre, would be much better in the role of Frederick the Great. It was Lottie, of course, who said sarcastically that she could think of someone who could play the role of Frederick the Great better than either. The laughter was restrained. There was no

293

need for her to say whom she had in mind. This was election day, and even when Hitler's name was kept out of the conversation, he was not far from everyone's thoughts.

"He won't win," said Pauli. "That's obvious even to the Führer himself. But he'll show the world that a great many Germans want him as their leader." He passed the melted butter to Lottie without taking any. He was getting fat, and tonight he'd had trouble getting into his evening-dress trousers.

"What are you betting?" said Peter. "A third of the votes?" Peter could take melted butter, and all the other good things of life, and still remain slim. Why do some people get fat so easily? Peter looked lanky, long-haired, and "artistic": floppy bow tie and mustard-colored silk handkerchief in his top pocket. The handkerchief exactly matched his wife's dress. It really was too much. Peter tried to look like the theatrical crowd with which he spent so much time. His American grandfather was just the same: he loved to be mistaken for a painter.

"Yes, and anything up to fifty percent for Hindenburg. The rest for the communist," said Pauli in a voice that he kept flat and unemotional.

"It makes me shudder," said Volkmann. "The thought of your Nazis getting into power . . ."

"You've nothing to fear, Isaac," said Pauli.

"Are you crazy, Pauli?" said Isaac Volkmann. "Outside the department stores I see your brownshirts carrying signs saying, 'Don't buy from Jews.' How long before I have a brownshirt on my doorstep saying, 'Don't have your teeth fixed by a Jew'?"

"They're just signs," said Pauli. He was embarrassed.

"They're not just signs, Pauli. While I was passing Wertheims last week, I saw a couple of customers getting punched by brownshirt bully-boys just because they insisted on going in." Volkmann's face had gone red: it always did when he became excited.

"Then they should have gone to the police," said Pauli. "We don't claim to be above the law."

"When will you open your eyes, Pauli?" said Isaac. He had stopped, knife and fork in mid-air, eyes wide and fixed on Pauli, his old army comrade. He wanted to make him understand the validity of his fears. "Two policemen stood there and watched it happen. They did nothing. Germans can't rely on their police anymore. It's tragic."

No one said anything. Volkmann became calmer and ate some asparagus. "What do you think of all this, Mr. Samson?" Volkmann asked his English guest. Brian Samson was a handsome young man with light-brown wavy hair and the sort of straggling, lopsided mustache that young men are sometimes tempted to grow. He would have been very handsome except for the ruddy complexion that so often afflicts the British. He wore a gray worsted suit of English styling. The suit was of good enough quality, thought Volkmann, but how he would have liked to tell the young man that a celluloid collar—even a brand-new white one—spoiled everything. However, Volkmann knew enough about the world to know that Samson's plain blue silk tie explained a great deal about this young man. He'd met enough Englishmen who mattered to know that the men who made the decisions in England wore ties with stripes or patterns: "old school ties," the English called them. And Samson's hands were a worker's hands: scarred and callused, with oil and dirt that seemed to be under the skin, so that no amount of scrubbing would make them like the hands of a gentleman.

"I don't know what to think, Herr Doktor. . . ."

"Isaac. Call me Isaac, as my friends do."

"I'm an engineer. Designing, costing, and testing prototypes is about as much as my brain can deal with. I like things I can measure on a micrometer and calculate on a slide rule. I just haven't got the time, let alone the inclination, for politics."

There was confusion as three or four of the guests started to reply together and then stopped; everyone laughed.

"We all have a solution, you see," said Isaac, speaking to Samson, "but we all have a different one. That's what's troubling us in Germany."

"I've never been very religious," said Samson. "My mother was a Roman Catholic and my father a Church of England Protestant, so they compromised by bringing me up as an agnostic. . . ." He laughed briefly, as if perhaps he resented what his parents had done. "So I can't follow Hitler's religious persecution of the Jews. I don't see what the Nazis can hope to gain from it."

"It's not *religious* persecution," said Lottie, "it's racial."

"You'll have to explain the difference," said Samson.

"We've had persecution of the Jews in Europe for centuries," said Lottie. "But in the old days, if a Jew converted to the Christian faith, the persecution ended. Hitler offers no such respite. Hitler

295

hates the Jews because they are of Jewish race, not because of some subtle distinctions in their beliefs about God."

She stopped, but it was obvious that Lottie had more to say. Lottie glanced at Peter. She was always worried about embarrassing him. It was difficult to know when he was upset, and she still felt guilty about getting him to leave the house on the Obersalzberg so precipitately that Christmas. Peter smiled at her. He knew she was using the presence of the English guest as an excuse to air her fear and anger, but it was better that she did so.

"You can't leave it like that," said Samson. "Explain, please." Samson was an experienced and trained observer, so he noticed the way Lottie kept her husband always in view. There was nothing obvious about it, but Samson decided he'd never seen a woman so desperately in love, and he felt an irrational pang of jealousy for Peter Winter. He wondered if Winter realized how lucky he was.

Lottie said, "Hitler's Nazism, like Mussolini's Fascism, is a society at war. Its members are asked to make sacrifices and obey orders and put up with all kinds of indignities and deprivations because the society is at war." She looked quickly round the table to see how the others were taking it. Everyone except Inge was looking at her; Inge was concentrating on her plate. "Nietzsche worshipped the warrior. He said that the only role for man was fighting, and the only role for women giving birth to warriors. In order to swallow that sort of garbage, you have to persuade yourself that you are at war, threatened by a cunning and merciless enemy. Hitler has provided that enemy. Hitler's Germany, if it ever came, would be permanently at war with the Jew."

"I hope you're wrong, Mrs. Winter," said Samson.

Pauli laughed. He could not take that sort of intellectualization seriously. He said, "I wish you wouldn't all read between the lines. You don't pick your way through every line of the Communist Party manifesto. You don't take seriously every promise and threat in the speeches of the Social Democrats. It's only Hitler that you treat like a bogeyman. But Hitler is just as cunning a politician as the others. He knows how to handle a crowd and tell them the things they want to hear. Once in power he'll do what all politicians do once they've achieved their ambition: he'll drop all these nonsensical points. He'd make a good chancellor, the only man strong enough to stand up for Germany against the rest of the world."

Lottie said, "I don't know why you need someone to stand up

for Germany. The world's treating Germany generously, if you ask me."

"Come down from the mountain, Lottie," said Isaac Volkmann good-humoredly. "Look at the Versailles Treaty and you'll see how 'generously' the world is treating us." He glanced at the others for support. Even Samson nodded.

Lottie said, "Have you forgotten the terms Germany inflicted on France after winning the Franco-Prussian War?"

"Even worse, yes, but that was a long time ago," said Lily Volkmann, whose schooldays were nearer than those of most of the others present.

Lottie smiled. It was just what she expected them to say. "Then look at the terms Germany forced on the Russians when they stopped fighting in 1917. Look at the enormous areas of Russia the army occupied. Compared with that treaty, the terms the Allies drew up were lenient."

"That's all history now," said Dr. Volkmann dismissively. "It's not relevant."

"Yes, it is," said Lottie emphatically. "German schools are the root of all the problems. German schoolteachers have always taught that Germans were racially superior and destined to rule Europe. No sooner was the war over than the Weimar government encouraged schools to say that Britain, France, and Russia had forced Germany to go to war. Kaiser Wilhelm II appears in the classrooms as an apostle of world peace. From that kind of baloney it's a short step to anti-Semitism."

"You exaggerate, Lottie," said Inge gently.

Lottie smiled bitterly at her. "You know I don't," she said.

Frau Volkmann pressed a hidden buzzer to signal that the servants should come in and clear the dishes and serve the next course.

As a relief from the emotive political arguments, Isaac Volkmann asked leading questions of his English guest. Brian Samson told them of his childhood, which he'd spent as the only child of two domestic servants in a baronial estate in England's Midlands. When his father's employer bought a Rolls-Royce motorcar, Samson's father had been sent to the factory in Derby for a course in driving and maintenance. At that time such an instructional course for the customer's servant was included in the purchase price of the car. The young boy was thrilled at his father's good fortune and took a passionate interest in the wonderful car, so that by the time he left school, at fourteen, he was skilled enough to get a job in the local garage. Since then he'd studied at night school and got an intermediate engineering exam. But the chance of a job in the design department of the Dornier diesel-engine factory on the Bodensee persuaded him to defer taking his final exams for a year or two. Now he spoke excellent German (and had picked up adequate French on side trips to France) and was wondering whether to go back to England at all.

"If you get tired of your present job, Samson, come and see me," said Peter Winter. "We need skilled men in a factory my father's company is building in Bremen. You'd have good prospects."

"What sort of work would that be, Herr Winter?"

Winter continued removing the bone from his grilled sole. Then, encouraged by Samson's earlier remark that he was not interested in politics: "Aircraft engines. Very high-power, water-cooled, in-line designs . . . fuel injection, but petrol, not diesel."

Samson was immediately interested. "For fighter planes for the air force?"

Without looking up from his fish, Peter said, "There is no air force; the Versailles Treaty forbids it. Our engines go for export to Sweden and other countries."

"I have no objection to helping Germany build aircraft engines for export or for any other purpose, Herr Winter. The engines you describe are exactly what I have been working on. I'd be grateful for any introduction you can arrange."

Peter Winter passed a business card to Samson. "Come and see me. Phone me next week, and my secretary will make an appointment for us. Lunch, if you're free."

"That would be very convenient," said Samson. He had no illusions about the lunch, or the job he was being offered. The Winter companies had only recently gone into aircraft-engine design. An ex-employee of Dornier could provide them with all sorts of information, including what their rival was up to. Peter Winter would sound him out over lunch. That was how these things worked: it was like espionage.

"Good," said Peter.

Until now there had been nothing to indicate it was election day. But now from the street outside came the sounds of marching men, and then some shouting. Bayerische Platz, around the corner, was a favorite assembly place for the Nazi parades and rallies.

"Would I know his name?"

"Can the results be known already?" said Lily Volkmann. She asked her husband: he always seemed to know everything.

"Far too early," said Dr. Volkmann.

There were more shouts. No one got up from the table. Peter Winter said, "Tomorrow I will join the Social Democrats."

Pauli said, "We've had the Social Democrats since the war ended, and what has that got us but millions of unemployed, and streets not safe to walk down?"

"Was that more shouting in the street?" said Lily Volkmann nervously.

"It was more like screaming," said Brian Samson.

Dr. Volkmann poured more wine. No one spoke, and no one got up to look out the window.

"Would I know his name?"

For Pauli the dinner party with his brother was nothing short of rejuvenating. And the next day Peter phoned him and invited him to lunch at the luxurious wine restaurant that Lutter and Wegener (whose restaurant in the Gendarmenmarkt had been famous since the eighteenth century) had now opened in the West End of the city.

Their lunch was modest enough, and they drank no more than a bottle of Rhine wine and some French brandy, but Pauli was grateful for a chance to talk at length with his brother. He told him about his troubles at work. He'd been moved away from Party Headquarters to a dark little office near the Tempelhof S-Bahn station. It was a long way from his home in Pankow, and now that he no longer had a car and driver, he spent hours every day on the train. He had no secretary, either. These things were all said to be part of an attempt to cut back the expenses, but Pauli had seen the order that specifically named Paul Winter as one of the staff who didn't need either a secretary or an assistant. There had been many complaints. Most of Pauli's co-workers said the economies were Dr. Josef Goebbels's idea, but Pauli didn't believe it. It was Brand, of course, trying to force him out, or perhaps hoping that Pauli would complain or do something silly to get even with him.

"Then, for God's sake, leave them, Pauli," his brother urged. "We can always find a job for you somewhere in the firm."

"Another lawyer! You've got them coming out of your ears already. I've heard you say so."

"We'll get rid of someone." Peter had always been ruthless about such things. He didn't see it as a moral question; it was just a matter of administration.

"I wouldn't feel right about that, Peter. Thanks all the same."

"Then what will you do?"

Pauli toyed with his wine glass before answering. "I've been thinking about all the people I've got to know at the top of the tree."

"Yes, go and see the Führer."

"No, I couldn't. . . ."

"It was a joke, Pauli."

"Yes, of course."

"But how long will it all last, Pauli? These scandals will bring Hitler down. You must have seen those letters from Röhm that the *Münchner Post* published in March. Are you going to tell me that they were forgeries?"

"No, Röhm is an unrepentant homosexual. He makes no great secret of it."

"And now *Vorwärts* has a story about a murder plot against Röhm. It sounds like a madhouse. It sounds as if the SA is run by murderers, lunatics, and homosexuals. You don't belong among such people."

"You mustn't believe everything you read in the papers, Peter."

"What are you going to do?"

"Well, I know one old soldier in Munich who is said to wield influence with Röhm and some other top SA people. I know him well. I'm taking the train tomorrow."

"Would I know his name?"

"No," said Pauli and felt guilty, for Peter would have known his name only too well.

"Him and many more like him."

Pauli Winter had regained contact with Captain Graf when a letter arrived at Berlin Party HQ enclosing a list of books and asking to have them sent to his address in Munich. The clerk who authorized payment for such things queried the order, because the books were so different from the usual official demands by party and SA units. Captain Graf wanted old textbooks issued by the Kaiser's army. His list included such manuals as *Forage and Shelter for Cavalry Horses and Transport Animals Under Active Service Conditions, The Construction and Maintenance of Field Latrines, Parade Orders for Infantry Officers,* and *Divisional Operation: Test Papers for Staff Officers Under Training.*

News about the curious Captain Graf—his old army comrade and Freikorps commander—was always of interest to Pauli Winter. And he couldn't help noticing that the clerk's query was answered by an official letter from the SA chief of staff's office. It said that Captain Graf was engaged on work of great importance and was to be provided with any books and any other materials that he wanted. Even more remarkably, the letter was signed not only by Röhm's secretary: the chief of staff had scrawled his own signature on it, too.

Pauli had noted the address and, telling Inge only that he had to go to Munich "on business," he caught the sleeper that arrived in Munich's Hauptbahnhof at eight in the morning.

Pauli was not usually a worrier, but the pressure that he'd been under for the last few months had caused him to add about six kilos to his weight. Pauli was one of those people who nibbled between meals, and ate more and more when under stress. It was this extra weight that made Pauli wear his *Tracht:* his green loden breeches and decorated jacket had always been too large for him.

Tracht was exactly right for his visit to Bavaria. A man dressed in such local costume was sure of a welcome anywhere in the South. It was the right dress for any activity, from work to wedding. And Pauli—born in Vienna—had an incontestable right to wear it.

When he came out of the Munich railway station, it was a bright, clear morning, with the chilly wind from the Alps that made the Bavarian capital's weather so unpredictable. Pauli would normally have reported to the Brown House—the former Barlow Palace now used as Party HQ—but news of that would have got back to Brand. Pauli didn't want that; this was to be a purely private visit; not even Inge knew where he was going. He took a taxicab to Captain Graf's address. It was in the district of Giesing, one of the former villages that make up the town. At the end of the street were a small bridge and a stream and a couple of old farmhouses, enshadowed now by the big blocks of nineteenth-century apartment buildings. Pauli opened the street door of one such grimy tenement and entered a dark lobby, its walls covered with scratched green tiles. He squeezed past a dozen or more bicycles, which seemed inextricably locked together, and opened doors that gave onto a dimly lit staircase.

He found Graf's name on one of the two dozen postboxes and then climbed the stairs. He was out of breath when he got to the top—badly out of condition, not as in his army days, when he could run five kilometers before breakfast and enjoy every minute of it. He rang the doorbell and waited. On the other side of the door were voices. There was a long delay. Pauli looked out the dirty window. From here he could see down into the yard: a row of overfilled rubbish bins and a restless dog.

"Yes?" A beautiful young blond man had opened the door in response to the bell. "Your name?" The boy was wearing leder-hosen and a Bavarian-style shirt. The SA uniform was now banned.

"Winter. Oberleutnant Winter. I phoned." Too late, he realized that it might have been more appropriate to use his honorary SA rank, but he was still enough of a snob to prefer his army title. And so, judging by the label on the bell, was Hauptmann Graf.

"The captain is expecting you. Third door on the right. Go in."

Pauli had always remembered Captain Graf as a man of action, a man he'd marched with and fought alongside, a tough, ruthless, and cruel commander who ruled by fear and fought mercilessly. Pauli didn't expect to see him in this setting.

The large room was lined with books: hundreds, perhaps thousands of them, filling crudely made shelves and piled high on the floor. Graf himself was sitting at an old-fashioned carved desk, with more volumes spread round him. Some of the books were open for reference, and others had pages marked with slips of paper. Before him there was an open loose-leaf book in which he was writing in longhand. From the next room came the sound of a typewriter.

Graf looked at Winter sternly before greeting him. The *Tracht* that Pauli had chosen to wear was significant. *Tracht* was worn these days by men and women who believed that South Germany had its own destiny. The costume had become a symbol of patriotism and of traditional country life and of the Nazis who stressed these values so diligently.

"Winter! Sit down. Move those books from the chair! It's good to see you again. Coffee or schnapps? Or both?" Graf was the same ferret-faced little fellow, but his weathered face was wrinkled now and his body was bent. He took off his gold-rimmed spectacles and put them on the desk. He was wearing shiny brown leather high boots and a tight-fitting tunic. After a lifetime of uniforms he felt uncomfortable in anything else.

"Both," said Pauli.

"Hansl!" Graf yelled. "Coffee and my bottle." He watched Pauli moving the heavy books in order to sit down. "You're as fat as a pig, Winter. Exercise. You need exercise. Too soft. Everyone's too damned soft these days."

"You're right, Herr Hauptmann."

"Thirty minutes every morning. See that muscle?" He slapped his own arm and then looked at Pauli again. "My God, man, you are flabby. It's a disgrace."

"Yes, Herr Hauptmann. I want your advice. I know you're a busy man."

"Do you? 'Busy man.' What else do you know?"

"The Chief of Staff has given instructions that you are to be sent anything you ask for."

"Yes, I know. I got him on the phone. I won't have some little shit of a clerk questioning my instructions. Did you kick his ass?"

"He doesn't work for me," said Pauli. "I'm in the legal department."

"Ha!" said Graf. "Yes, I phoned the boss direct; I've known Röhm since he was a child. I could tell you some stories—I won't, but I could. I sentenced him to ten days in the cells. He was a cadet in those days. This is going back a long time, of course."

The coffee and schnapps arrived on a teak tray complete with a linen traycloth and polished silver spoons and cream jug. The young man who brought it looked apprehensive and kept his eyes down. "Sugar, cream . . . Schnapps cold? Yes," said Graf as he checked the tray in military style. "Get out." The boy departed without having spoken.

Pauli was nervous. It was now or never. "Do you know an officer named Heinrich Brand? An Obersturmbannführer."

"Know him? Of course I know him. Insolent bastard! I know all about him. Started off a ranker in a cavalry regiment. . . . Then some damned fool made him an officer. He's an upstart. Blood will out, Winter. I've always said that."

"I remember."

"Brand. An ambitious little peasant. Of course I know him."

"He's making life difficult for me, Captain Graf."

"A peasant! Who made him an officer? Answer me that."

"He's an Obersturmbannführer now."

"Rank counts for nothing. It's a matter of influence."

"Brand is close to the chief of staff."

Graf became agitated. "Is he? Who told you that? Do you know what I'm doing here, Winter? Let me show you." Graf went across to a cupboard and took a rolled sheet of paper from it. He waved the roll at Pauli. "As soon as we gain power, the SA will be merged into the army. Every one of our men will become a soldier. The chief of staff has appointed me to draw up the plans for that great day." He unrolled the large sheet of paper. He spread it on the desk and weighted the corners with books so they could see it. It was a complicated diagram showing the units of the German army, down to company level, and their present regional disposition, *Wehrkreis* by *Wehrkreis*.

Upon the drawing, in colored inks, were the names and numbers of SA units: SA *Standarten* had always been numbered to correspond with the old Imperial Army regiments. Now Graf's diagram showed how every army regiment would have a large brownshirt component to guarantee its loyalty to the Nazi regime.

Graf snapped his glasses on over his large ears and proudly stabbed a finger at his diagram. "The Reichsheer will be expanded so that each regiment will have one ordinary battalion—*allgemeines Bataillon*—and one brownshirt battalion." He moved his finger across the paper. "The staff arrangements are somewhat more complex. Eventually brownshirt officers will be represented in all arms, but for the time being the technical branches—engineers, artillery, and panzer—will have to remain the monopoly of the Reichsheer's trained officers."

"Has the Führer agreed to all this? I thought he had promised the generals that they would be the 'sole bearer of arms.' "

"The Führer? Come alive, boy. Wake up! The SA is more than four times the size of the Reichswehr, nearly half a million men. We don't have to bow and scrape to the soldiers, or to the Führer, either. We are the new army of National Socialism. When the little Austrian gets into power, it will be because we've put him there."

Pauli suppressed a shudder. He'd heard such ideas before, and even though Ernst Röhm was a fearless leader and a capable staff officer, the idea of that plump homosexual with his scarred face and coarse manners taking over the German army was unthinkable. "Does Röhm say this?" Pauli asked.

"You're not some damned spy, are you, Winter?"

"No, of course not, Captain Graf. But this is all a big surprise for me."

"And it will be a big surprise for some of those other fellows in Berlin, too, eh?" He winked.

"And Brand?"

He looked at Pauli for a moment before deciding he could confide in him. "Brand will be taken care of. Don't worry about our friend Brand. His name is on the list."

"The list?"

"The list of enemies, boy. You don't make an omelet without cracking eggs. Ever heard that expression? Yes, Brand is one of them. The chief of staff keeps Brand there in order to keep an eye on him. We know Brand reports to his damned Führer everything he sees and hears." Graf was still studying his diagram with great pride and interest.

"Killed? He'll be killed?"

Graf looked up. "There's no other way. It's been decided at top level. Him and many more like him."

"When?"

"When?"

"When will this happen??" said Pauli.

"When we assume power," said Graf, releasing his diagram from the weights and rolling it up again.

"This year?"

Graf shrugged. "I'm not a politician. You'd better ask your friend Esser. He's one of the high-ups nowadays."

"Do you see Fritz?" Pauli asked. It was a question that really meant, Does Fritz Esser know about Röhm's plans to take over the army no matter what anyone else says or does?

"Esser? Haven't seen him for years." Graf scratched his head pensively. "He owes me a favor or two. I hope he'll remember that."

"Fritz never forgets a friend."

"I'm not a friend," said Graf with pedantic precision. "But he owes me favors."

"Brand is making my life unbearable," said Pauli.

"I could talk to Röhm, but he hates complaints of that sort."

"No, don't say anything to anyone. I wanted your advice."

"Stick it out. That's my advice. Brand and all his cronies will be gone out of your life forever within a month of our achieving power. Stick it out, boy."

"Yes," said Pauli, and resolved to do so. He respected Graf's advice. Pauli needed someone to turn to: at cadet school, when Peter couldn't help, he'd turned to Alex Horner. In party matters he used to go to Fritz Esser. In this case, when Esser was in no position to help, he went to Graf. He admired men who were confident and decisive. He wished he were such a person, but it was such a strain being decisive, and decisive men made too many enemies. Pauli preferred to go along with the tide. Life was too short to be taken seriously. What was that joke he'd heard from his soldiers during the terrible fighting of 1918? "If you take life seriously you won't get out of it alive." He knew why rankers refused promotion. It was easier to be a private soldier, to take each day as it came, to comply with orders, and not to have all the problems that came with decisionmaking. Yes, damnit, he'd stick it out.

"Drink your coffee, Winter."

"I can see you're busy, Captain Graf."

"Never too busy to chat with an old comrade. Drink your coffee."

"After that I must go and leave you to your work."

The two men sat in awkward silence for a few minutes; then Captain Graf said, "That fellow who got hurt that night . . . ?"

"Hauser. My father's valet."

"Is he well?"

"Very well. He still works for my father."

"I'd had too much to drink, Winter."

"It's all forgotten, Captain Graf."

"Thanks to you, it all blew over, I think," said Graf.

"It's all forgotten," said Pauli again, embarrassed at the mention of the stabbing at his party so long ago. He finished his coffee, swigged back his schnapps, and got up to go.

When Pauli got to the door Graf said, "I never forget a favor, Winter. You leave Brand to me. I'll speak to the chief of staff."

"Thank you, Captain Graf," said Pauli.

It was still early, and Munich was one of Europe's most beautiful medieval towns. Pauli strolled back across the river and into the

center of the city. There was a Nazi demonstration assembling behind Marienplatz—big banners, slogans, and dozens of swastika
flags. On one side of the open square the brownshirts, complete
with brass band, were getting into their formations, and behind
them were dozens of men and women in the elaborate lacy national
costumes of Upper Bavaria. It was usual for the Nazis to combine
their new authoritarian urban creed with sentimental evidence of
their love of things natural, traditional, and rural.

Pauli turned aside lest he meet someone he knew. He walked
down as far as the *Viktualienmarkt:* he liked to smell the fresh fruit
and vegetables, and there were open-air eating places selling beer
and an array of fine sausages. It was almost lunchtime, and there was
enough sun to warm the air. He sat down at an iron table and
ordered *Maibock*—the dark Munich beer that is brewed in May—and
Munich-style white sausages with rye bread.

He was eating contentedly, and idly watching the girls strolling
in the market place, when a voice behind him said, "In Munich you
skin the weisswurst before you eat him, Winter, old comrade."

"Koch!" said Pauli. It was Lothar Koch, his Feldwebel from the
storm company, now dressed in an expensive black leather overcoat
and a Tirolean hat, complete with leather band and badger brush.
He was no longer that pimply youth; he'd become a mournful-
looking man in his early thirties with a large bulbous nose, bushy
black eyebrows, and dark rings under his eyes.

The two men shook hands, and Koch's face lit up with a smile
to reveal a gold molar amongst his sound, white, even teeth. "What
are you doing in Munich? I thought you lived in Berlin."

"A business trip. I'm catching the afternoon train back. And
you?"

"I've lived here for over five years now. I work for the party,"
he said, avoiding the word "Nazi," as so many did at that time. He
sat down uninvited. Koch was not a stickler for etiquette.

"So do I," said Pauli, relieved at not having to surmount a hurdle
that sometimes made social difficulties.

"I know. I've heard about you. I am with the 'Sicherheitsdienst
Reichsführer–SS.' " He smiled as if this was an inappropriate job for
him. The SD was the official name for the Nazi Party's private
security service.

"What do you do, Lothar?" The waitress came and Pauli ordered beer and weisswurst for his friend.

"I work for a young fencing champion named Reinhard Hey-drich. Know him? Too young for the war . . . One of these young lunatics who think they missed something good. You must know the type—Germany's full of them."

"And now?" Pauli asked. The white sausages arrived, complete with beer, bread, and the special sweet, dark mustard that goes with them.

"My boss is on the staff of Reichsführer Himmler. We have a little office at Türkenstrasse 23, here in Munich. Officially, since the government banned Nazi organizations, we are called the Presse und Informationsdienst."

"And unofficially? I mean, what do you do, Lothar?"

"My remarkable 'Reini' persuaded the Reichsführer that the whole damned organization is riddled with police and communist spies. We track down antiparty elements within the party. We report on the communists and we keep a file index on everyone we can think of." He laughed and stabbed a sausage to lift it from its dish of hot water. Once it was on his plate, he skinned it expertly and started to eat. Lothar had always been a hearty trencherman: it was strange that he didn't get fat. Maybe he worried a lot, thought Pauli, but he didn't look like a worrier. A sad fellow, perhaps; but not a worrier.

"Are there so many spies within the party?" asked Pauli.

"If Reini Heydrich wants them, I will provide them," said Koch.

"Be serious, Lothar."

"I am serious. My God, Pauli. This fellow Heydrich has only just joined the party—in no time at all he's on the Reichsführer's staff. From then on I can hardly keep up with his promotions. Last night there was a teleprinter message to say that as of July 19 he'll be formally appointed head of the SD, with the rank of Standarten-führer to take effect ten days later. Can you imagine what he's earning? And now, to cap it all, he's on a trip round all the SD offices in Germany."

"How many offices do you have in Germany?"

"Only a handful of informers here and there." He stuffed a piece of bread into his mouth and carried on talking. "That's just Reini's excuse for a jaunt: having his women, his luxury hotels, and his fancy restaurant bills paid for by the party." He ate sausage.

"Can he get away with that?"

Lothar had another mouthful of sausage but still he smiled.

"Who's going to stop him. Are you? Is some little party official in the cashier's office going to object? No. We know how things are done in the party, don't we, Pauli? Anyone who gets in the way of this cunning steamroller will find himself on a card-index file and then in hot—very hot—water."

"What sort of hot water?"

"I don't mean a scented bath. Reini knows how to deal with opposition, whatever else he doesn't know." There were no table napkins. Koch reached into his pocket and wiped the mustard from his lips with his handkerchief.

"Sounds awful," said Pauli.

"It's all a big joke," said Lothar. "The biggest bloody joke I know since that bastard Woermann got his ass shot off in no-man's-land, remember?"

"Yes." Pauli remembered. He'd remembered that along with a thousand other nightmares, but had never been able to find amusement in the memory.

From Marienplatz came the sound of the brownshirt brass band. It started with a rousing old Bavarian march from the days of the monarchy. That would bring the crowds: young and old. Only later would they play the solemn Nazi songs, and finally the sentimental ones, to create a serious mood for the speeches. Then, at the very end, would come the merry, catchy tunes for the collection boxes. It was all worked out in great detail.

"Damn it, Pauli, loosen up, man. If the law of averages was straight, we wouldn't even be here. We'd be manure under a piece of French farmland. If these stupid bastards want to spy on each other, that's all right by me. And the pay is good."

"Is it?" said Pauli.

"Ah!" He laughed again and waved a finger under Pauli's nose. "It's well over twice what I'd be getting if I'd stayed in Munich Police Headquarters, and I was a senior inspector." So he was a policeman. That explained the way he bolted his food: cops took their refreshment on the move; that went with the job. "You're a lawyer, aren't you?"

"Yes," said Pauli.

"My Reini is looking for a lawyer. He said so only last week. And eventually we'll have a proper Berlin office. If you played your cards right, you'd have a senior position there."

"I'm not sure I'd fit in."

"Don't be a damned fool. No one would fit in better. You've had police court experience, you're not one of these desk lawyers, you're wise to the ways of the real world."

Pauli nodded and wondered how Lothar Koch knew so much about him.

As if sensing this, Koch said, "I've seen you in court more than once when I've been sent to Berlin on prosecutions. You're sharp, Pauli. I've seen you in action, and you're damned quick."

"What would I be doing?"

"I tell you what you'd be doing: almost nothing. My Reini is nervous about falling foul of one of these liberal lawyers who enjoy making trouble for everyone these days. He likes everything legal, my Reini does. At present we take our proposals round to the lawyers at the Brown House. Well, that's bad security, isn't it? We need our own lawyer to run through our plans and okay them. You'd be our tame lawyer."

"It sounds good."

"It's as easy as skinning weisswurst, old comrade. Can I put your name up to my Reini when he gets back, exhausted, from his womanizing Olympics?"

"Yes, thanks, Lothar."

"You'll feel more at home with us, Pauli. More laughs and more freedom. You were never meant to be working with all those brown-shirted riffraff or those stiff-necked freaks from the party."

They sat and drank another beer and talked of old times. They talked of the trenches in 1918, and the friends they had lost there.

"I'll have to go now or I'll miss my train back," said Pauli, looking at his pocket watch.

"I'll walk over to the cab rank with you," said Lothar Koch.

They walked across the marketplace. When they said goodbye, Lothar Koch said, "You'll not regret joining us, my old friend. You're our sort." The band music from Marienplatz ended suddenly. There was only a brief pause before the first speech began. They were using amplifiers and loudspeakers, so that from this distance the voice was distorted into an incomprehensible shudder of sound from which only the odd word could be recognized.

"Lothar," said Pauli, on nothing more than an inspired guess, "did you know I was coming to Munich? Did you follow me today? Did you follow me from the railway station to see where I went, and

"Him and many more like him."

then follow me all the way to the *Viktualienmarkt* before talking with me?"

Lothar laughed, and this time Pauli could see two gold teeth. "There you are, Pauli, my old comrade—I said you would be at home with us!"

1933

"We think something is definitely brewing over there."

"Sometimes I think I've wasted my life," said Alan Piper. Though he was sixty years old, he had the same pink baby face and innocent eyes that at Oxford had earned him the nickname Boy. He was dressed in a suit of green Harris tweed, the shapeless sort of outfit such Englishmen wore on their country estates rather than here in government offices in London S.W.1. Piper offered his young visitor a cigar. He said it again—"wasted my life." There was a slight drawl in his voice, the warning that Englishmen like Piper used when they didn't want to be taken too literally.

Brian Samson took the cigar gratefully. He knew that few field agents ever met the European Controller, let alone got invited up to his top-floor ofice to enjoy a chat and a cigar. It was a pleasant room, but dark and shadowy, and furnished in a style that suggested the consulting room of an Edwardian physician. "Wasted, sir?" Piper tossed the matches and cutter to him. He cut the end from the cigar and put it in his mouth.

"Because the politicians take no notice of what we tell them, Samson. They think I sit up here inventing it all."

Samson laughed nervously. My God, this was as near as the senior staff of M.I.6 could get to mutiny. "I'm sure they don't," said Samson awkwardly.

"No, they believe it, all right, Samson." It was a firmer sort of voice now. "That's why they ignore it. Right, Glenn?" He looked at a man seated in the corner smoking a curly pipe.

"We think something is definitely brewing over there."

"Sure thing," said the man. He smiled. So "Mr. Rensselaer" was an American, thought Samson; he'd not noticed the accent when they were so briefly introduced. He could see it now: a middle-aged cowhand with weathered face and slow smile. He was younger than Piper: wide face, big-boned, with a lot of black hair, which was beginning to gray at the temples.

"And now Hitler's made it: Chancellor Hitler," said Piper. "It was inevitable, I suppose."

Samson got the cigar lighted and said, "Yes. He'll rule Germany forever. They'll never get rid of him. But it was inevitable," said Samson. "He knows how to appeal to middle-class Germans: the farmers, the schoolteachers, the doctors, and so on. The communists couldn't reach such voters as those."

"Then maybe you'll explain it," said Glenn Rensselaer gloomily. "Because it sure beats me."

Samson turned to see the American better and said, "The violence in the streets. Mobs—communists, Nazis, and troublemakers—roamed through the cities looking for a fight. No one was safe. For the middle classes—and lots of other people, too—nothing mattered except feeling it was safe to walk along the streets, and it seemed like only a Nazi government could bring back law and order."

"And he has brought back law and order?" Piper asked.

"Yes and no. In Berlin thousands of party members were appointed police auxiliaries. Certainly the communists have been suppressed. But most of the current lawlessness is due to his millions of brownshirts. They've set up improvised prisons in empty factories, warehouses, and cellars. They've locked up anyone they don't like. Many have been tortured to death. They are a law unto themselves, and they listen only to their chief of staff, Röhm."

"So how will Hitler deal with that?"

"You want my opinion or the facts?" said Samson.

"I have the facts in your report," said Piper. "I sent for you to get your more personal impressions."

Samson puffed at his cigar. "Since getting into power he's been as active as a wagonload of monkeys. The emergency decrees enabled Hitler to ban public meetings and newspapers, tap phones, intercept mail, search homes, and so on. But a reliable source told me that he is slowly taking control of the political police in every state in Germany and putting them under one man. This would be a big step towards total control. I mean *total* control."

"My knowledge of the German constitution is rusty," said Piper. "But I would have thought that was illegal."

"It is illegal," said Samson. "That's why it's all being done in secret. Even Interior Minister Frick seems not to be aware of what's happening."

"Who *is* aware?"

"Himmler. He'll end up as chief of the Political Police for the whole of Germany."

Samson glanced out of the window. Across the road was a beautiful Georgian house, and behind it the tops of the trees of Green Park. It was winter now—almost Christmas—and the trees were bare. There would be parties, paper hats, Christmas crackers, turkey, and pudding flared with rum. A sudden homesickness hit him. He'd love to live in England again. He'd had enough of boarding-houses and cheap hotels and interminable foreign voices.

Glenn Rensselaer said, "Perhaps Himmler is doing it in his own behalf."

"I don't think so, Mr. Rensselaer," said the young man. "In each state the Gauleiter will have to approve such a change to the state's police force. The Gauleiters are old Nazis, very touchy, very jealous of their powers. Only Hitler could persuade the Gauleiters to agree to such a change."

"Yes, and eventually Göring will also have to approve, if Himmler is to take over the Prussian Political Police," said Rensselaer reflectively. "Yes, Hitler would have to be a party to it."

"Make no mistake, sir, Röhm could win. The next heads to roll could be Hitler's, Goebbels's, Göring's, and Himmler's. Röhm is energetic and he has millions of men who'd back him against Hitler."

"Tell us about getting the job with Winter's organization," Piper asked the young man. He'd heard all he wanted to hear about Röhm's ambitions.

"It was luck, really. A dentist, a decent old cove, invited me to dinner, and Peter Winter was one of the guests. His brother, a Nazi Party lawyer, was there, too. Pauli, they call him. He let slip a couple of remarks that confirmed my other source. Peter Winter asked about my work. I just floated my job at Dornier past him, and he jumped at it. It was easy."

"We think something is definitely brewing over there."

"What do you think of Peter Winter?" said Glenn Rensselaer.

Samson thought for a moment before replying. "Very German. He even looks German. Authoritarian, very proper . . . and fair, I suppose. Not the sort who'd cheat anyone . . ."

Boy Piper nodded. Samson's description of Peter could pass as a description of Samson himself. It was always like that: men had a sharp eye for their own attributes when looking at others. But Glenn wanted to hear more. "Go on," said Rensselaer.

Samson said, "Sophisticated. Single-minded, perhaps narrow-minded in some ways. Speaks wonderful English: his wife is American, of course."

"Artistic?"

Brian Samson hesitated. He was no judge of art. "Playing the piano and so on? Yes, I heard that he's mad about the theatre, and plays jazz on the piano. But, after that one evening, I only met him in connection with work."

"And his wife?" Glenn Rensselaer had taken over the questioning.

"The American? Well, she's . . ."

"Jewish. Yes, she is."

"She told good jokes that night. A very clever woman. Attractive, too. And she seems to know a lot of history: I wouldn't like to get into a political argument with her. Outspoken about the Nazis—too outspoken, I'd say. Her husband gets embarrassed at some of the things she says." Samson looked at the two men, wondering what he was expected to say. He couldn't understand why the questioning had become so personal.

Piper decided to elucidate. "Life will get difficult for them under the Nazis, won't it, Samson?"

"Unendurable, sir."

"We were wondering whether to make an approach to Peter Winter. He could be useful to us. He knows a lot of things we'd like to find out more about."

"Offer him a job in England?" said Samson.

"Or America. He has relatives in America."

"Oh, yes, someone told me that his mother is American."

Piper did not deny or confirm this suggestion. He said, "Do you think the time is ripe? You worked for him; what do you think?"

Samson smoked his cigar for a moment. "He's very loyal to his father, sir. He might feel he was letting his father down. But the regime might start to put pressure on his wife. She loves him—that's obvious—but how much does he love his wife?"

"I see," said Piper. Samson noticed that the American was biting his lip.

Samson said, "But there's a close relationship between the brothers, too, unusually close. The older man treats his younger brother with exaggerated consideration. Anything you plan would have to take the younger brother into account."

"That's very useful, Samson. Well, thank you." The meeting was at an end. Samson wondered what he was expected to do with this magnificent cigar. He placed it carefully in the big cut-glass ashtray before he got up and shook hands with both men. "Ever meet the parents, Samson?" said Piper as Samson was about to leave the room. He couldn't resist asking.

"Only once, sir. They came to the Bremen factory. Old Mr. Harald was presenting certificates to young workers finishing their apprenticeship."

"What do you think of them? Did you see the American mother?"

"A nice old couple, sir." Samson looked from one man to the other. Piper looked a little flustered, and the American was wearing his slow smile.

"Thank you, Samson. Drop in on Tuesday morning. I'd like to see you again before you go back." Samson eyed the cigar but decided not to pick it up and continue smoking it.

When Samson had left the room, Glenn Rensselaer grinned broadly and said, "A nice old couple. It serves you right, Boy. For that young man we are both old fossils."

Piper ignored the remark. "What do you think?"

"He's a good kid."

"A lad like that should have gone to university. He left school at fourteen and educated himself in public libraries and night schools. It's a crying shame. With a decent education he might have ended up doing my job. As it is, unless something unexpected happens, he'll be lucky to end up downstairs in Registry."

"He'll be lucky to even survive," said Glenn Rensselaer. "The Nazis will tighten everything up. It will get more and more dangerous for him. You notice what he was saying about the Political Police? That was a cry from the heart, Boy."

"I know, but I can't pull him out yet awhile. He's one of the best men we have. He's a very experienced engineer, you see. He can get a job where others can't."

"It was good of you to let me sit in."

"I know you are going to Berlin next week. I particularly wanted you to hear that business about the Political Police all coming under one control."

"It's not really my department, Boy."

"I think it is, Glenn, because if my other sources have got it right, your nephew Paul Winter is one of the SS lawyers working on that development."

"Is he?"

"So if you learn anything that we could use . . ."

"Sure, Boy, sure." Wasn't that just like the British? They never gave anything away without strings being attached. Glenn sometimes regretted starting these unofficial exchanges of information. If the State Department got to hear, they'd roast him.

"We think something is definitely brewing over there, something big. We know for certain that Röhm now has a million paid, active brownshirts, with no fewer than three and a half million men on reserve. That is to say, five times as many men as the German army. We want to know everything there is to know about this new SS formation under Himmler. Whose side will he be on when the crisis comes?"

"Okay, okay, okay. If I find out what's cooking, I'll be sure to let you know."

"I would appreciate it, old chap."

"It's good to be back in Berlin, sis."

Glenn looked round the redecorated and refurnished drawing room of the Winter house in Berlin. All the old furniture had gone; everything was new. He sighed. Despite his enthusiasm for progress, there were some things he preferred unchanged.

It was Christmas. The mountain of presents he'd brought from all the family obscured the Christmas tree in the corner. From outside in the street came the sound of a band playing carols and the rattle of collection boxes.

"You're looking younger and more beautiful than ever, sis," he said.

"When are you going to bring your wife and little Cyrus to see us here in Berlin, Glenn? Your photos just make me long to see them and hug them."

"We had this crazy idea of coming over on the *Graf Zeppelin* when it returned from the Century Exposition in Chicago, but there was a waiting list for tickets about four miles long. The girl in the shipping office put our names down anyway, but I knew there was no chance."

"You should have written, Glenn. Harald still has dealings with the Zeppelin company. He might have been able to arrange it."

"I would have done that, but when I heard he'd been sick I thought it better not to bother him. We'll do it another time. Did you hear they're planning a new airship that will run scheduled transatlantic flights? Think of that, sis. We'll see each other a lot."

"That would be wonderful, Glenn. Tell me more about Dad."

"I've told you all there is to tell. They took him into the hospital that one night and gave him every sort of test. The doctor said he's as strong as a horse. He could easily live another ten years: the doctor said that. Of course, he's had to take things easy—no smoking and no booze—but otherwise he's just fine, sis."

"And he must adore having grandsons to spoil."

"Sure, and Cyrus was twelve this year. Dad took him out to lunch on his birthday—'little Cy,' we call him. Dad says that spoiling grandchildren is the only revenge a parent has."

"Little Cy. I'm so glad you named him after Dad. It was sweet of you."

"Yeah, Dad was pleased," said Glenn.

"And Dot's grandson Bret must be seven, the same age as Peter's Helena."

"It would be swell to get the whole family together."

"I can't imagine Harry crossing the Atlantic, even on an airship."

"Tell me about Harry. What's been wrong?"

"It all started with the Fischers. Last year, after the second presidential election, and Hitler's big share of the vote, Richard Fischer decided they should sell up."

"And leave Germany?"

"Yes, and go to Paris."

"But their home . . . and everything . . ."

"Yes, Foxy couldn't bear the thought of it. He's eighty-two, nearly as old as Dad. He was determined to stay put."

"It's good to be back in Berlin, sis."

"But why go?"

"The regime," said Veronica. Lately it had become a way of explaining every horrible thing that happened.

"But the Fischers are Roman Catholics. They were Catholics even before old Foxy was born."

"But the Nazis don't think like that. If your ancestors were Jews, you are a Jew."

"What happened?"

"They didn't go. Richard was arrested in August. Fuchs almost died of worry, and Harry went rushing around to everyone he knows."

"What was Fischer charged with?"

"No one could find out. They say he was interrogated for four days."

"But he got out?"

"He signed all his Fischer holdings over to the Nazis."

"That must have been worth millions."

"The Nazis seized Wertheims department store, too. Jewish property is being appropriated everywhere."

"But Richard is safe?"

"I don't know. He was arrested again in September. They say he'll be charged with changing Reichsmarks into Swiss francs. It may be all trumped up. They do that sometimes: just invent some offense and let you try to prove you are innocent."

"So what's happening now?"

"Poor Fuchs is with relatives in the country, and Richard has disappeared. The police won't say if they're holding him or not. He might have gone abroad. He has cousins in England."

"Couldn't Pauli find out anything?"

"No. Göring runs the police here in Prussia. Himmler—who Pauli works for—is in charge of Bavaria. Peter went along to Police Headquarters in Alexanderplatz and said he wanted to act as a lawyer for Richard Fischer and demanded to see him, but he got nowhere. I was worried that Peter might get into trouble, too."

"Thank God Lottie has kept her U.S. passport. What about little Helena? Has she got a German passport?"

"She's only seven years old, Glenn, so we don't have to worry about her for a little while."

"These people are maniacs," said Glenn.

"A lot of people support the Nazis," said Veronica. "At least they tell me they do." She became flustered in the face of such unbridled criticism of the new regime. The Nazis were not like other political parties who'd come to power. The Nazis were vindictive, spiteful, and very, very violent. Even in Berlin, these most outspoken of all Germans had quickly learned to curb their tongues. Nowadays only visitors like Glenn, and a few foolhardy opponents of the Nazis, voiced their innermost thoughts.

"I can understand why Harry got sick."

"He was so frustrated, Glenn. Before, he's always been able to go to the right people, or get lawyers, or find out the facts. But the Nazis thrive on secrecy. He became ill, and the doctor told him that if he didn't have a complete rest he wouldn't be responsible for his health."

"But now he's back at work?"

"Hauser drives him to the office at about ten-thirty. He has a look around, and then he comes home about three. But it's making too much work for Peter."

"But the companies are all run by directors. Isn't it time Peter took a holiday? You told me he hasn't been away for years."

"Poor Peter. He so hates working for the company. In the old days Harry had complete control, but now the directors have their own ideas about everything. Even though Peter tries to make sure that Harry's wishes are approved, sometimes Harry and Peter disagree. Peter is so much happier playing the piano. But in September Goebbels's Propaganda Ministry set up a 'Chamber of Culture,' with departments to control the theatre, the radio, the press, films, and so on. Peter, being married to a Jew and associated with Brecht—and the other Marxists, who have run away to America—will probably find it difficult to continue his work in show business." Veronica sighed. "Young Hennig has been doing so well with his piano recitals, and many people thought Peter much more talented. I wish you'd speak with him, Glenn. See if you could persuade them both to take a vacation—just a vacation—back home. It would do wonders for him. Sometimes I think he's forgotten that he's half American."

"Married to Lottie, I'd say that would be difficult."

She smiled. "Yes, you're right. Darling Lottie."

"And Pauli? We haven't talked of Pauli."

"Pauli. What can I tell you about him? He's still the same: he'll never change. The baby of the family. Marriage has worked wonders for him. Thank goodness he has Inge to look after him."

"But he lives in Munich?"

"Next year they'll be back in Berlin. With the Nazis in power, all the Munich offices will be coming up to Berlin."

"But you said that Göring runs the police in Berlin."

"Yes, dear, but that's all changing. By next summer, Pauli's department will be coordinating Political Police offices all over Germany, and he'll be working in Berlin. They've even asked me to look out for an apartment for them. It will be so lovely having them back here."

"Next week I will be going to Friedrichshafen. The *Graf Zeppelin* is having a complete mechanical overhaul, from *Spitze* to stern. On the way to Bodensee, I had a mind to stop over."

"Yes, do go and see him. Pauli would love that, Glenn. He's very fond of you. He's a real Rensselaer, and I've often thought you understand him better than anyone."

"I like him, sis, I really like him." Glenn looked round the room. All the old Biedermeier furniture had gone, in favor of modern pieces. Modern woven fabrics on low angular chairs, chromium and mirror everywhere, and a white carpet that he was constantly frightened of spilling coffee or ash upon. He guessed it was Harry's idea. Harald Winter prided himself upon his taste in modern art. It made the room lighter, of course, but for him this wasn't Berlin, this was more like some flashy new "roadhouse" on the New Jersey turnpike.

"If only they could have a child. I pray for them. It would transform Inge, and wouldn't Pauli be the most wonderful father any child could ever wish for?"

Glenn nodded and got up from his chair. Yes, that was true enough. Pauli, with his tricks and his jokes and his infectious laughter, would make any child happy. Glenn wished he'd spent more time with his two nephews. Now it was too late. Now they were men with their own lives to lead: they could have little use for an uncle, no matter how well meaning he might be. Sometimes he'd thought of bringing his wife here for a holiday, but not now. He didn't like what was going on in Germany.

He looked out of the window to see the crowded street below. It was almost Christmas and, except for the paths swept along the pavements and the roadway, there was snow everywhere. The shoppers looked happy enough, warm, well dressed, and busy. In the shopwindow across the street was an elaborate nativity scene, complete with a model donkey that nodded. The only jarring note was a bored-looking brownshirt on the corner outside Schachtmeister's *Konditorei* holding a sign that said "The true German does not buy from a Jew."

But Berlin did not belong to Hitler. Berliners had seen too many fakes and charlatans to be fooled easily. And Hitler's promises about restoring agricultural land to the peasants cut no ice with those factory workers who had so recently escaped the worse slavery of unmechanized farm labor. Nor did the Nazi talk of nationalizing factories appeal to Berliners, who could see here in the city the dismal result of enterprises run by bureaucrats. And if Berlin was ready to succumb to the fanciful promises of politicians, it would be to those of the left, for Berlin was "Red Berlin" and always had been.

"It's good to be back in Berlin, sis," said Glenn.

1934

"Gesundheit!"

Pauli had this filthy influenza. Inge said it was his fault for not wrapping up well, but anyway he couldn't shake it off. He'd been running a temperature for two days and he should have been in bed, and would have been except that Lothar Koch had made such a fuss. In any case, the last place he should have been at 4:30 a.m. on Saturday, June 30, 1934, was standing in front of the passenger buildings on the silent, empty, and icy-cold Oberwiesenfeld, the airport for Munich.

The breath of the two men condensed on the night air. "He left Bonn at two a.m.," said Lothar Koch. Behind the airport buildings a line of big cars was parked. The drivers had been sleeping. But now they'd been wakened and were wiping condensation from the glasswork and running the engines to have them warm and ready.

Pauli wiped his nose and didn't answer. It was all right for Koch. He was used to outdoor duties, and he had woolen underwear to wrists and ankles and his new heavy black leather overcoat. Leather was the only thing that offered protection against this sort of cold wind, and Pauli decided to buy one from the same shop where Koch had got his. It had a removable woolen lining in a hideously vulgar plaid, not even a genuine tartan. Pauli's Scots nanny had taught him to despise such fakes, and he had decided against buying the coat. But this morning he wouldn't have cared what the lining was like. Anything would have been warmer than his thin raincoat.

"Are you sure the Führer himself is aboard?" said Pauli. He huddled in the shelter of a mobile generator, but it gave little protection against the piercing wind. "Why would he come so early? He's not due in Bad Wiessee until eleven a.m."

"Something very special is happening. The teleprinters have been going all night," said Koch. "I was in the Brown House last night soon after Sepp Dietrich arrived with two Berlin Criminal Police officers. He'd come directly from a meeting with the Führer. He told me that two companies of the Leibstandarte are coming from Berlin-Lichterfelde. Does that bring back some happy memories?"

Pauli nodded and wiped his nose again. Lichterfelde barracks. It was odd to think of the black-uniformed LAH, Leibstandarte Adolf Hitler—the Führer's SS bodyguard—occupying the old Prussian-army cadet school. Nineteen fourteen—that was a long time ago. He'd been just a child, and the world was foolish and innocent. If only he'd known what was waiting for him.

"Oh, yes," said Koch. "The Leibstandarte are on their way by train to Kaufering, near Landsberg am Lech. Sepp Dietrich is meeting them there with transport to take them to Bad Wiessee."

"I don't see any special significance in that," said Pauli. "The Leibstandarte companies have to provide security for the Führer's meeting with Röhm."

"Röhm *and* all SA Obergruppenführer, and Gruppenführer and inspectors. All the SA top brass will be there," said Koch. "My pal from the Kripo got a look at the Führer last night. He said he was in a really bad mood."

Pauli nodded and sneezed into his handkerchief.

Koch added, "But the most significant thing of all, my friend, happened last Monday. The German Officers' Association expelled Captain Ernst Röhm. Expelled him! Why is the army distancing itself from him? I think those bastards know something we don't know."

"But which we soon will know," said Pauli, and wiped his nose. In this cold wind his eyes were watering, too. He felt like death. Whatever was going to happen, he fervently hoped it would happen soon, so that he could go home and go to bed.

There was the sound of a door slamming and a flash of yellow light from the building behind them. A man in blue coveralls and a leather jacket came out of a door marked "Weather Bureau" and told them the plane would be landing in ten minutes. Soon afterwards all the runway lights came on, revealing a layer of mist through which the lights shone like dandelion puffballs. Then they switched on the big floodlights that illuminated the apron where the passengers disembarked.

Now a group of people came from the airport buildings and stood looking at the northwestern sky. They didn't speak to one another. They stood like statues, still and silent. Some of the reception committee were easily recognized. They were mostly men from the Munich offices: personalities who had several closely written index cards devoted to them in Lothar's constantly updated SD records. There were a couple of army officers, and high-ranking officers of the SA, the SS, and the Nazi Party. The only ones not in uniform were two airport officials, who kept looking at their watches.

Pauli was the first person who spotted it in the streaky purple sky. It was the big three-engined Junkers that Lufthansa had refurbished specially for Hitler. It landed smoothly and taxied to where the steps had been wheeled into position. Lothar Koch and Pauli Winter kept well aside from the reception committee. Their orders would come from the office of Reichsführer-SS Himmler: that's how important it was. Meanwhile, Koch was writing in his tiny black notebook the name of everyone present. Koch kept a note of everything; it had become almost an obsession with him.

The aircraft's door opened, and as the first passengers emerged the reception committee formed a line, fidgeting about, like recruits on a parade ground, to be sure they were properly in position. The third man—a leather-coated figure—coming down the steep metal steps paused to look round, like an actor making his first appearance on a new stage. It was the Führer—there was no mistaking him—and even from this distance it was clear that he was agitated. After him came Josef Goebbels, lame and cautious on the steps, then Otto Dietrich, Hitler's press chief, and then—a dispatch case clamped tight under his arm, and keeping apart from the others—came Viktor Lutze, the SA leader in Hanover.

The Junkers cut its engines one by one, and in the silence that followed, Pauli heard Hitler tell the Reichsheer officers, "This is the blackest day of my life. But I shall go to Bad Wiessee and pass severe judgment. Tell that to General Adam."

Koch eyed Pauli and smiled sardonically. Now, slowly, it was becoming clearer to them. They both knew that Lieutenant General Wilhelm Adam, commander of the Reichsheer's 7th Division in Munich, was one of their regular sources of information about SA activities. If Röhm and his men were to be the target of some punitive action, General Adam would be only too pleased to provide the army's help. No doubt that was where Dietrich, the LAH commander, would get his trucks.

A tall man in the long black overcoat and peaked cap of the Allgemeine SS detached himself from Hitler's party and came over to them. "Which of you is the lawyer?" he asked. He wore the headquarters cuffband, a badge that identified him as one of the adjutants that Himmler's offices teemed with nowadays.

"I am," said Pauli.

"You'd better start now," he said. "Röhm's Headquarters Guard might put up a roadblock. You'd better have your story ready."

"I have false papers," said Koch. Even Koch was deferential to this august personage from the Reichsführer's office.

"Don't park near the Pension Hanselbauer. We don't want them alarmed."

"It's all prepared," said Koch. "I have chosen a place already."

"Very efficient," said the tall man in a voice that might or might not have been sarcastic. "Are you men armed?"

"Yes," said Koch.

"And you, lawyer?" As he said it, the adjutant looked away to see where Hitler's entourage were going.

"I have a pistol," said Pauli.

"And do you know how to use it?" asked the man. He was too young to have been in the war. It was typical of such upstarts that he wore an army saber instead of the SS sword that regulations prescribed.

"Yes," said Pauli, "I know how." Pauli did not share Koch's awe. He added, "Is the Führer going to Bad Wiessee?"

The tall SS adjutant looked at him with contempt. "You'd better get started," he said and turned away to rejoin Hitler's party, who were now getting into the cars.

"Don't ask questions," said Koch after they were on the road south. It was getting lighter every minute, and the cloudy sky changed from red to pink and curdled, like a bowl of soured cream. "That's one of the basic rules."

"It's a damned stupid rule."

"Perhaps it is," said Koch judiciously, "but it's a rule nevertheless. If you wanted so badly to know where the Führer is going, you
should have asked me."

"Why? Do you know where they're all going?"

"They're off to the Ministry of the Interior in Munich. The
Führer will give Minister Wagner a good talking to. After that they'll
come out to Bad Wiessee."

"How do you know?"

"I asked one of the drivers. That schmuck you asked had no idea
where they were going. That's what made him upset when you
asked."

Pauli laughed despite his misery. He liked Koch. Koch had the
right pragmatic approach; that's why he'd falsified his age to get into
the army, and that's why he'd become a sergeant major at some
ridiculously young age.

"And forget about roadblocks," said Koch. "Röhm's Headquarters Guard are in Munich. Does that oaf think we haven't been
watching their movements all the time?"

Bad Wiessee was a small resort near the Austrian border where
the elderly came to retire and the infirm to enjoy the iodine baths.
When the two men arrived in their car, the streets were empty. In
the sanguine light of early morning, the still water of the lake reflected the surrounding mountains and the tall peak of the Wall-
berg, which was, for the few brief weeks of summer, devoid of snow.

They parked in the back alley of the little Goldenes Kreuz Gast-
hof. From there they could see the road while remaining virtually
out of sight. Bad Wiessee is only fifty-four kilometers from Munich,
but it is high in the mountains, and in the unheated car Pauli shivered with the cold.

Inge had provided them with some cold meat, bread rolls, and
a small flask of hot soup. The soup would make Pauli feel better:
Inge's home-made soup always did. There was not much of it, and
he shared it between the two metal picnic cups.

For a few minutes the two men sat there chewing in silence, but
they watched the road constantly.

"Here they come now," said Koch. It was 6:30 a.m. He opened
the car door to tip away his untouched cup of hot soup. Pauli could
cheerfully have killed him.

Pauli turned his head towards the road but saw nothing. "Where?"

"They won't have their lights on," said Koch. "There!"

He could see them now, three vehicles coming slowly down the final stretch of road.

"Where's Dietrich and his Leibstandarte?" said Koch anxiously. "Oh my God! Where is he? How the hell can we protect the Führer if he goes in there now?"

The three cars rolled on right to the front door of the Pension Hanselbauer. Someone there must have been expecting the visitors, for the door opened immediately. Men tumbled out of the cars. Besides the Führer and his associates, there were six broad-shouldered, reliable men from the Political Police department in Munich.

"Come along!" said Koch. "This is us."

Pauli swigged down the rest of his soup, even though it burned his throat, and clambered out of the car into the colder air that came off the lake. Koch in the lead and Pauli chasing after him, they ran across the yard and entered the hotel building along with Hitler and the rest of them.

The proprietors—a man and wife—were up and dressed. Perhaps they were preparing breakfast for the fully occupied hotel. The woman hurriedly took off her apron and started to welcome the Führer formally. She even held the guest book ready for signing. Someone elbowed her aside roughly, Lutze grabbed the visitors' book, and they raced up the stairs. By now everyone had pistols drawn, even Hitler.

There was a banging of doors: they were looking for Röhm. There were shouts and screams. "No, not there!" More shouts. "He's not there, either!" A thump was heard as something or someone was knocked to the floor. Many of the SA leaders were in bed with young men. Lutze shouted the number of Röhm's bedroom—he'd read it from the visitors' book he'd snatched from the old woman. Now Lutze's role was clear: Lutze was Judas.

Someone was knocking at Röhm's door and shouting that he had something urgent to discuss. There was a delay, and then the door opened very wide. Röhm was dressed in pajamas. He stood in the doorway, heavy with sleep and blinking in the light. Hitler called him a traitor and Röhm shouted "No." Hitler said, "Get dressed. You're under arrest." His voice cracked with emotion. Röhm was his oldest friend, an associate and a supporter right from the very beginning, and still almost the only man who used the familiar *du* to the Führer.

Röhm, his scarred face flushed with anger, stared at him until Hitler turned away and banged on the door opposite Röhm's. SA Obergruppenführer Edmund Heines opened the door; behind him a young nude man was sitting on the bed, wide-eyed, and searching amongst the rumpled sheets for something to wear. Lutze pushed past Heines into the room. He opened the chest of drawers and wardrobe, looking for weapons, but there were none. Whatever the SA leaders had been doing, there was no evidence of armed revolt.

In the absence of Hitler's comments, Goebbels—the Führer's mouthpiece—was shouting "Nauseating!" and "Revolting!" from the other end of the corridor. Pauli stood watching. Otto Dietrich, the press secretary, caught his eye and shrugged. The two men had something in common. Pauli Winter was going to be asked to justify this madness in legal terms, and the press secretary would have to make it into something the public might swallow. Hitler croaked, "Take him out and shoot him," but no one was sure who was meant to be shot.

Heines heard it, however. He turned to Lutze and said, "Lutze, I've done nothing. Can't you help me?" Lutze, still rummaging through the wardrobe, said, "I can do nothing. I can do nothing."

Koch pushed his way along the corridor. "Come, Pauli." He seemed to know where he was going. He kicked open the unlocked door of a room and went inside. Pauli followed, pistol ready. There was no SA man to be seen in this bedroom, only a boy in bed: skinny, very young, little more than a child. Koch pulled the sheets from his naked body and the boy flinched, shielding his face with his hands, as if expecting a blow. Koch turned away from the bed and pulled open the wardrobe. At first there seemed to be only clothes hanging there. Then Koch shouted, "Out! Out, you bastard!," and a small hunched figure stepped out from the hanging garments.

He was completely naked. A pale, wrinkled body contrasted oddly with hands and head darkened by sunlight. It was Graf. Without his spectacles, he had to screw up his eyes to see Koch and Pauli more clearly. "Winter," he said in a subdued voice. "I thought it might be you."

Pauli said nothing. For a moment the two men looked at each other. There would be no pleas from Graf. Even now, humiliated and vanquished, he wouldn't ask for help. "You'd better get dressed," said Pauli. He handed the old man his gold-rimmed spectacles.

Koch watched the exchange with interest. He'd known all along, of course. And Lothar Koch couldn't resist telling you he knew. In a policeman it was a failing—perhaps Koch's only failing as a policeman.

From outside in the corridor, someone said, "Lock them in the cellars. We'll take them to Stadelheim." It wasn't clear who said it. Hitler was overcome with emotion and seemed almost incapable of speech. Perhaps it was Goebbels.

Pauli Winter and Lothar Koch drove behind the truck that took the arrested men to Stadelheim Prison. They went the long way, right round the southern end of the lake, through Rottach-Egern and Tegernsee, having heard that the men of Röhm's HQ Guard were waiting on the direct route back, hoping to rescue their charges.

By the time they got to Munich, the city was awake and at work. Armed men were in evidence everywhere. Nazi Party HQ in Briennerstrasse was completely sealed off—not by brownshirts or SS men but by armed soldiers of the Reichsheer. There were soldiers at the railway station, too, and plainclothes policemen were meeting every train and arresting SA leaders as they arrived for the scheduled SA conference with Hitler at 11:00 a.m.

At the prison, Pauli recognized most of the brownshirt leaders detained. Some of the most famous names in Germany were that day written into the prison records, for the SA had found supporters in high places. Ritter von Krausser, Manfred von Killinger, Hans-Peter von Heydebreck, Hans Heyn, Georg von Detten, Hans Joachim von Falkenhausen . . . Rumors abounded throughout the city, everyone was confused, and fear could be seen in almost everyone's eyes.

At the SD office, Pauli Winter was given a list of names and addresses. He would serve the warrant—no more than a typed note—and Koch would make the arrest. There were no police cars to spare, so they had to take a taxicab. They had found and arrested six wanted men before they stopped for a quick lunch. They went to the big *Bierkeller* opposite the prison. It was crowded with policemen, most of them on the same task as Pauli and Koch. By this time

Stadelheim Prison in central Munich was full. Prisoners were being taken up the road to where the old Royal Bavarian Gunpowder Factory buildings were now being used as a camp for "enemies of the state." Dachau concentration camp, they called it. Koch cursed their luck long and heartily. Dachau was seventeen kilometers away; the extra journeying was going to make much more work.

Pauli sat back, exhausted. His influenza had weakened him so that every exertion was too much. He drank his "soup with egg yolk" in the hope that it would give him more strength. It wasn't like Inge's. Inge's home-made soup—like everything else she did—was perfect. He loved Inge, and needed her, especially when he wasn't well. He was lucky to have such a wonderful, beautiful wife. She grumbled sometimes, but Inge did everything just the way he liked it.

Koch, who seemed to enjoy the excitement that the day had brought, was at the next table swapping stories with plainclothes-men from the Political Police desk. Someone said that Viktor Lutze had been declared the new chief of staff of the SA, so things didn't look too rosy for Röhm. There was a story going round that the Stadelheim Prison authorities had put Röhm back into the same cell that he'd occupied when arrested for marching alongside Hitler after the attempted putsch in 1923. If true, it was a grim sort of joke, but it was the type of black humor that policemen enjoyed. Koch and his cronies howled with merriment at the idea of it.

An even better story was that the team sent to arrest Dr. Ludwig Schmitt, an ally of Hitler's old enemy Strasser, had come back with Dr. Wilhelm Eduard Schmid, the well-known music critic of the *Muenchener Neueste Nachrichten.* "And," said the policeman telling the story, "once inside Dachau the poor old bastard was executed, so it's too late to do anything about it now." The other men drank their beer and exchanged self-conscious smiles. No one knew if it was true; there were many such stories going the rounds. And it was not only in Munich. Summary executions—officially sanctioned mur-ders—were taking place everywhere. The news just in said that in Berlin Dr. Erich Klausener—a director of the Reich Transport Min-istry and onetime head of the Police Section of the Prussian Ministry of the Interior—had been shot dead in his office by a uniformed SS man.

Pauli closed his eyes listening to Koch and his pals and tried to clear his blocked sinus. He was suffering. Koch told him to eat up, but Pauli just couldn't bear to. Once they were in the car again, Koch looked down at the paper and said, "The next on the list is SA Obersturmbannführer Heinrich Brand!"

Pauli almost jumped out of his skin "What? Brand?"

"Just a joke, Pauli, old friend. No, your Brand is far too smart to get caught in the mangle. Brand is to be on Lutze's new staff, from what I hear."

Koch looked at his watery-eyed, red-nosed friend and smiled. Koch knew about Pauli's court-martial, and his time with the Punishment Battalion. Koch had a spy in the army records office who checked up on everyone Koch needed to know about, but he never revealed that knowledge to Pauli, and had arranged the SD personnel files so that Pauli Winter's army record was unblemished. Koch regarded such little favors as the sort of thing any comrade would expect of another.

They arrested four more SA leaders that afternoon. The elderly brownshirts went meekly and with only mild complaints. It was the journey to Dachau that was so tiring. By 6:00 p.m. the two men reported back to the SD office in Zuccalistrasse 4. Pauli sank down behind his desk while Koch found for him the bottle of schnapps they kept in the filing cabinet. "What a day!" said Pauli, but just as he was signing out, a clerk told him that a lawyer was required at Stadelheim Prison. He was to report to SS-Gruppenführer Sepp Dietrich.

He found the well-known Leibstandarte commander in the courtyard of the old prison. The cobbled yard was dark, the low evening sun making the rooftops golden and the enclosed yard blue in the summer-evening light. Dietrich, forty-two years old, was a broad-shouldered man who'd been a manual worker for most of his life: farm laborer, petrol-pump attendant, customs officer, factory worker. Hitler had chosen him as a personal bodyguard back in the days when he needed physical protection at his meetings. Now Dietrich was an SS general, but he'd not lost the common touch. When Pauli found him, he was smoking a cigarette and chatting in Bavarian dialect with six of his black-uniformed soldiers and a tall young subaltern with shiny new officer's badges.

"Hello, Pauli," said Dietrich, still speaking in his strong Bavarian accent. He prided himself on his informality. "It looks like we're ready to go." He threw down his cigarette and ground it under the heel of his polished boot. The firing squad picked up their rifles. "I want it all neat and tidy," said Dietrich. He put an arm round Pauli's shoulder and walked him away from the soldiers and the young officer.

"Yes, Gruppenführer," said Pauli.

"You're the legal expert. I want it all neat and tidy." He looked into Pauli's watery eyes and, to be sure that it was clear, said, "We're executing these SA people. Not Röhm: he stays in custody while the Führer thinks it over. What's the normal procedure?"

"A trial and a verdict," said Pauli.

Dietrich was a simple man, and now he smiled as if Pauli had made a subtle joke. "The Führer has tried them and found them guilty," he said.

Pauli wiped his nose and his eyes. Dietrich was staring at him as if he might be crying. He felt a fool. "Do you have orders?"

"I don't want the Public Prosecutor chasing me," said Dietrich, turning his back and lowering his voice. With remarkable bravery, the Munich Public Prosecutor had persuaded the Ministry of Justice to file cases for "incitement to murder" against the Dachau camp commandant and two of his officials.

"Don't worry," said Pauli. "The Minister of the Interior told the Cabinet that any investigation of Dachau must be refused for reasons of state policy. This will come under the same heading."

"But the camp commandant was sacked," said Dietrich, scowling. He didn't want to risk the same fate.

"It will be all right," said Pauli, who wanted only to go home and go to bed. "But, for legal reasons, your officer had better read the sentence to each man before the execution takes place." Pauli felt a sneeze building up and had his handkerchief ready for it. He sneezed.

"Gesundheit!" said Dietrich politely, and beckoned the young officer over to them. "Tell him what to say," he instructed Pauli.

Thinking quickly, Pauli said, "Something like 'You have been condemned to death by the Führer.' " He blew his nose.

"Is that enough?" said Dietrich doubtfully.

"They only have to be told the sentence," said Pauli. "That's the law."

" 'Heil Hitler' at the end," said Dietrich. " 'You have been condemned to death by the Führer. Sentence to be carried out herewith. Heil Hitler.' Got it?"

"Yes, Gruppenführer," said the subaltern.

Crack! The sound of the rifles echoed round and round the narrow prison courtyard. The small barred windows were silent and dark, with bright-orange rust marks disfiguring the gray bricks. Yet Pauli could not get over the feeling that he was being watched by many eyes.

Next! Next! Next! Hurry! Hurry! Hurry! Cold and wet from a quick drenching under a cold shower, the SA leaders arrived one by one in the yard doorway, frightened and bewildered. The young SS officer's face was impassive, but he gabbled too quickly through the sentences and sometimes stumbled over the words.

More than one of the prisoners stood erect and met the bullets with a Nazi salute and a shouted "Heil Hitler!"—believing that they—and their Führer, too—were the victims of an SS coup.

Pauli had qualms when Edmund Heines crumpled under the bullets. As well as being SA-Obergruppenführer, Heines was the Police President of Breslau. And even Dietrich's iron nerve seemed to go as SA-Obergruppenführer Schneidhuber faced the firing squad. Schneidhuber was Police President of Munich.

But the shooting went on. Pauli watched it dispassionately. Better men than this had died alongside him in the war, he reminded himself. If the truth was known, some of the British and Frenchmen he'd killed were more to be pitied. Only when Captain Graf came into the courtyard did Pauli feel like turning his eyes away. But he didn't. He watched Graf standing erect in front of the wall that was now chipped and broken with rifle fire. The dust of the broken brickwork hung in the air like smoke, and mingled with the cordite to make a unique stink that he never forgot.

Graf refused a blindfold. He looked at Pauli right to the end. And Pauli stared back at him. Graf didn't shout "Heil Hitler!" or give the Nazi salute. He had never been a great admirer of Hitler, or of the men around him. Graf was one hundred percent soldier; the Freikorps and the SA were just ways of holding on to a soldier's mode of life. When the volley came, Graf was torn in two and the blood spurted like a fountain. His death seemed bloodier than the others. Perhaps because a chance bullet clipped an artery—or perhaps because Pauli felt it more. Graf had been a comrade, a good comrade, and a man does not lightly lose a friend. But Graf was a soldier; it was a good enough way for a soldier to go.

"Leave the presidency vacant—what a great idea."

It wasn't turning out to be the successful dinner party that Inge had planned, and she was unhappy. It was the first time that they had had guests in this new Berlin apartment that had been redecorated to her own wishes, and she'd had her dress made specially for the occasion. It was a long slinky bias-cut gold satin gown that hugged her figure. Sleeveless, with a plunging neckline, it revealed her wonderful skin. Inge had invited her sister Lisl with her husband, Erich Hennig. The guest of honor was to be Reichsminister Fritz Esser, now one of the party luminaries, a member of the cabinet, and a close associate of the Führer. But Fritz Esser had sent a huge bunch of flowers and a note that said he was delayed in meetings at the Reichskanzlei and wouldn't arrive until after dinner.

"It's because the President is so sick," Inge explained to Erich, her brother-in-law, as if she was well informed about the state of President Hindenburg's health. "I feel so concerned about the Führer. He looks tired." The two sisters always spoke of Hitler as a couple of starry-eyed schoolgirls might speak of an adorable hockey coach. It was a competition between them, a contest in which a curiously large proportion of Germany's female population also participated.

"I know," said Lisl Hennig. "We're hoping Erich will play before the Führer next year at the Bach Festival in Leipzig."

Lisl was always saying that her husband would be playing at one of the concerts Hitler attended. It would be impetus enough to put Erich Hennig far ahead of his rivals. But Adolf Hitler did not attend many such musical events, and Erich's career was at present in the doldrums. Hennig's piano recitals, and his occasional performances with large orchestras, were to be heard in far-off German provinces, while Berlin's concert halls were monopolized by more famous performers of a previous generation.

In the hope of pleasing his musical guest, Pauli said, "Fritz Esser was with the Führer at Bayreuth last week. They saw *Das Rheingold.* Fritz said it was the best ever."

It proved not so pleasing. "Fritz Esser!" said Hennig contemptuously. "And how many other productions of *Das Rheingold* has he seen?"

335

Pauli smiled and poured more wine. Inge had always said the Hennigs were jealous of Pauli's longterm friendship with the very influential Fritz Esser. To say nothing of Pauli's regular meetings with Heydrich, Himmler, and Josef Goebbels. Perhaps it was true.

It was a warm summer evening, uncomfortably warm, and the Winters' apartment had the windows open to catch the breeze. Their new cook was determined to show her skills for such a celebrated guest and had produced an exquisite meal of fresh tomato soup, trout, and then roast beef, with Pauli's favorite chocolate cake to follow.

The absence of Fritz was a disappointment to all, but it gave the two sisters a chance to talk about family matters. The Hennigs now had a four-year-old son, and their present apartment was not big enough. Also, Frau Wisliceny had died the previous month, and now that the initial shock was over, they were able to discuss more practical problems.

"Papa has enough money," said Lisl Hennig. "He has the pension and his investments."

"But not enough to keep that big house going," added Erich Hennig quickly. Lisl and Erich had discussed it before coming tonight, thought Pauli. Erich was shrewd. Peter had always hated him, of course, and sometimes Pauli could see what his brother disliked. Politics, business, or the custody of his father-in-law's house, Erich Hennig would always manage it to his own advantage.

"He told me he wanted to go in one of those new service apartments round the corner, on Prenzlauer Promenade," said Pauli in an innocent voice.

It amused him to see that this had exactly the effect he expected. "One bedroom, one bathroom, one drawing room, and a tiny little kitchen!" said Erich excitedly. "He'd go crazy in a tiny place like that."

Just to keep Erich agitated, Pauli said, "He said he'd eat most of his meals downstairs in the restaurant."

"Ridiculous!" said Erich Hennig. "He says that now, but wait until he's tried it for a few months."

It was quite amusing to bait Erich, thought Pauli. He decided to memorize every word: it would amuse Peter no end. "But he eats in restaurants now," said Pauli. "He likes restaurants. Even before your poor mama died, they went to restaurants a lot."

"Leave the presidency vacant—what a great idea."

Inge knew what Pauli was doing, of course, and now she indicated that it had gone far enough. "Let's hear what Lisl thinks," said Inge.

"We were thinking of moving in with Papa," said Lisl. "He needs someone to look after him. He could eat with us, and we could see to his laundry and so on. The maid we have is a wonderful laundress. She even does Erich's dress shirts for his concert performances."

"That would mean a lot of extra work for you," said Inge. "It's such a big house."

Lisl said, "It wouldn't mean any extra work. We'd keep Papa's two girls, so we'd have three staff."

"Couldn't Papa move to your apartment?" said Pauli.

"We're too cramped already," said Erich.

"I know what you're thinking," said Lisl. "Papa's house is partly Inge's; of course it is."

"Professor Wisliceny is getting old," said Erich. "He can't last that much longer."

Lisl said, "When Papa dies, Inge, then we wouldn't expect to keep the house."

Erich was not prepared to be a party to such rash and selfless promises. He said, "On the other hand, looking after your father will be a lot of extra work for Lisl."

"She just said it wouldn't be any extra work," said Pauli.

"Be quiet, Pauli," said Inge. She'd already been considering how much to spend, and where to invest the remainder of the proceeds of her share of the big Wisliceny house. Similar houses round the corner from Papa, in Kant Strasse, were fetching high prices nowadays. The Ku-damm area had gone up and up. Some speculator would buy it to convert to apartments, or even into a hotel.

"We need a room for our little one and two rooms for the nanny," said Lisl. "And it would help Erich to prepare for his concert."

"What concert?" asked Inge.

"Erich has this wonderful chance to play the Mozart wind quintet in Breslau," said Lisl. "But the new tenants downstairs have been complaining about the piano."

"If you are thinking of having wind quintets playing there, you'll have Professor Wisliceny's neighbors complaining, too," said Pauli.

"It's the Köchel 452," said Erich Hennig slowly and patiently. "Piano with wind instruments. I would only be practicing the piano part. We have rehearsal rooms for the ensemble." He smiled as a children's photographer smiles at a particularly difficult sitter.

"In Papa's house the walls are so much thicker," said Lisl resolutely. "Think of the times Mama had musical events there."

"If Papa agrees, then of course you must," said Inge suddenly. "You need the extra rooms."

Pauli looked at her with some surprise, but Inge always gave in to her younger sister, or so it seemed to him. He wondered if that was the way other people saw the relationship between him and Peter.

"Thank you, Inge," said Lisl.

"We'll drink to it," said Inge, reaching for the wine. In some ways the decision was a relief to her. It would mean that Papa would be properly looked after. She would have been worried to have her father living alone. "When you move out, we'll sell and share the money." The Hennigs drank the wine, but Pauli noticed that they didn't confirm the idea of eventually sharing the money.

After the Hennigs had gone, Inge seemed to regret her impulsive generosity. She was often like that: she gave away things she treasured and then regretted it, venting her consequent anger not upon herself but upon the person to whom she'd been so generous. Pauli poured a nightcap for her, and they sat together in the study while he glanced through some papers from his office.

"They'll never move out," said Inge sadly. "We'll never see a pfennig from Papa's lovely house." She was also thinking about the extra space they'd need when she had babies, but she didn't say that.

"I doubt if they'll be able to afford it after your father goes, darling. It must cost a lot of money to keep up. I remember your father complaining about the enormous bill for that new roof a couple of years ago."

"Well, at least they won't have the roof to worry about," said Inge.

Pauli laughed. His wife was determined to be downhearted.

"I'm going to bed, darling," she said. "Don't be long." She smiled and kissed him. Some husbands might have scolded a wife who'd so foolishly abandoned a large part of her inheritance, but Pauli would never look at it like that. Pauli didn't care much about possessions, beyond his basic comfort. Sometimes she felt he wouldn't even care if he lost her.

It was half past midnight when Fritz Esser rang the bell. Inge was in bed and asleep. Pauli was sitting in his tiny study, reading through a sheaf of regulations and amendments; these now appeared on his desk in ever-increasing amounts.

Fritz Esser stood in the hallway with a stupid grin on his face. At first Pauli thought he was drunk, but no one ever came drunk from a meeting with the Führer, except drunk with happiness.

"I pissed myself laughing," shouted Esser as Pauli showed him into the little study and brought out a bottle of fine old French brandy. Fritz was forty last birthday. He laughed. Except for his dark eyes and his amazing collection of crowded, broken, and irregular teeth, this man was scarcely recognizable as the lean youth who'd pulled the Winter boys out of the Baltic so long ago. Esser had put on weight to a point where his suits had to be tailored for him. They were all made by one of Berlin's best tailors. When Pauli's weight went up, Inge nagged him to diet, but Esser was unmarried and had no such restrictions. Still, Esser was tall and big-boned: he could put on this much weight without appearing ridiculous.

"What happened?" said Pauli.

"It's not what's happened," said Esser, "it's what's going to happen tomorrow. The Chancellery is a madhouse: generals, admirals, Gauleiters, and all the press and propaganda bigwigs."

"Hindenburg? Has he gone?" Hindenburg was dying; everyone knew that it was just a matter of time.

"Those army bastards," said Esser. He drank some brandy and laughed again. It was Fritz Esser's naughty-boy laugh, with something of a snigger in it. "Those generals are too stupid to know when it's raining. Which of those idiots chose tomorrow as the day for their big military celebration? They haven't won a war for over half a century. They certainly can't celebrate victory day for the last show—which they lost—so they decide to celebrate the twentieth anniversary of the day the Kaiser ordered mobilization." He laughed again, a loud, hearty laugh that suited his big frame. He picked up the brandy bottle—Fritz had developed a taste for brandy—and poured more for himself. They knew each other well.

In Pauli Winter's house he didn't have to ask for what he wanted: he helped himself. "Remember mobilization day, 1914?"

"I remember," said Pauli. That fateful day in 1914 was etched deeply into his memory. At the Lichterfelde cadet school there had been a special parade. His parents had attended; Mama had cried.

"So now all the toy generals are taken out of their boxes and wound up, ready to march backwards and forwards to the music of their tin-soldier bands. The generals have put on their nicest uniforms and groomed their pet donkeys. . . . And what's going to happen? That inconsiderate old bastard Paul Ludwig Hans von Beneckendorff und von Hindenburg is going to snuff it . . . and screw up the whole bloody show. Ha, ha, ha! It's the best laugh I've had since they shot that bastard Röhm last month."

"Are you sure about Hindenburg?"

"I was with the Führer when the latest doctor's bulletin was delivered. The army will look such fools. Blomberg, that wonderful War Minister of ours, is in the Bendlerblock sending teleprinter messages to every army unit in Germany canceling the celebration and ordering them to prepare funeral ceremonies instead."

"What did the Führer say?"

"Oh, naturally, the Führer was very upset," said Esser, in a voice that indicated that the Führer wasn't upset at all. "The Führer will become president now and probably combine the rank of chancellor with it."

"That would be illegal," said Pauli.

"Are you sure?" He stopped drinking, put the glass down, and wiped his mouth.

"You should know that, Fritz. You were a deputy in 1932, when the Reichstag passed the amendment. It said that in the event of the President's death, the duties of president will be performed by the president of the High Court of Justice until a new election is held."

"Authority doesn't automatically pass to the Chancellor?"

"No, it doesn't."

"President of the High Court of Justice? You can't be serious."

"I'm perfectly serious," said Pauli.

"You're forgetting the 'Enabling Act,' " said Fritz Esser. "That gives him power to do anything he wants."

"Except interfere with the authority of the presidency. That was specifically excluded."

"Jesus Christ! An election? That could ruin everything. I'd better go back and make sure the Führer knows."

"Sit down and relax a moment, Fritz." Fritz Esser cautiously sipped at his brandy and sat down to think it over.

"Better not to become president," said Pauli, to make conversation. "If Adolf Hitler becomes president, he'll have to take an oath to uphold the constitution. That will limit his powers."

"How could he avoid it?"

"He could leave the presidency vacant and create a new office."

"For instance?"

"Just call himself Führer, for instance."

"Führer. Yes, excellent. Chancellor and Führer—he could combine those roles. He's sending for the service chiefs. He's going to make them swear an oath of allegiance."

"That would be a way round it," said Pauli.

"A way round what?" said Esser.

"Normally the army swears an oath of allegiance to the presidency and, as a safeguard, the President takes an oath to uphold the constitution. That's how the system works."

"You mean, get the army to swear an oath to the Führer, then leave the presidency vacant, so that he doesn't have to promise to uphold the constitution. That's damned clever, Pauli. The Führer will like that."

He picked up his glass, then, remembering his Führer's abstinence, put it down again. "I'd better get going. There's going to be the devil of a lot to do. It's a good thing I didn't let my driver off for an hour; I usually do when I come to see you."

"If you must go, Fritz."

"You're too bright for that job you're doing with the Gestapo, Pauli. I'll have to find you something better than that."

"I'm okay, Fritz. It's interesting and I'm good at it."

"Leave the presidency vacant—what a great idea."

1936

"Rinse and spit out."

"Rinse and spit out," said Dr. Volkmann. "Don't eat on that side for an hour or two. I'll need to see you one more time." He pressed the foot pedal, and the dentist's chair slowly resumed the upright position.

"Thank you," said Peter Winter. He washed out his mouth and wiped his lips.

"You can go, Ursula," Volkmann told his nurse.

"Thank you, Herr Doktor."

When they heard the outer door close after her, Isaac Volkmann said, "Her mother's sick, and I have no more patients this afternoon."

Peter looked at the clock. It was only three-fifteen.

Volkmann said, "I've lost a lot of patients over the last six months. I'm seriously considering whether I should move out of the Ku-damm area."

"But your sort of patients expect to come here, to a smart address."

"The radio, film, and theatre crowd, you mean? I'm afraid I've already lost a lot of those."

"I'm sorry," said Peter.

"I don't exactly blame them," said Volkmann. "They depend on the Nazis for their living, and Goebbels is one of the worst anti-Semites of the lot. And now young Ursula has given notice. She's been with me for over three years, but her father says he doesn't want her working for a Jew."

"She's lucky to have a job at all," said Peter.

"She'll get another job all right. The Nazis have reduced unemployment, Peter—we have to be fair about that."

"And how have they done it?" said Peter. "By drafting men to work on the land or to build the *Autobahnen.* Or by giving them jobs working at the local Nazi Party office for little or no wages."

"I have to be thankful I'm not in the army or the civil service," said Volkmann, "or I'd be unemployed, too. At least they are allowing me to work."

"These people are mad," said Peter.

Volkmann smiled ruefully. "The funny thing is that in many ways I agree with this Hitler fellow. I am proud to be a German nationalist. I resent every last clause of that damned Versailles Treaty. I, too, hate the communists, and despise the pseudo-intellectuals and their café-society Marxism. There are many ways in which I support Hitler; why must he pursue this insane vendetta against us?"

"I don't know," said Peter.

"And shall I tell you something, Peter, old friend. When I switched on the radio last Saturday and heard that our soldiers had marched into the Rhineland, I exulted. He was right to take our sacred German soil back from the French."

"I suppose so," said Peter. He was always embarrassed when Isaac became emotional, as he so often did on the subject of his homeland.

"And you are busy?"

Peter nodded. "We are hoping to get some contracts for coal by-products. It would make a great difference to next year's shareholders' report."

"What sort of by-products: oil?"

"Yes, and now I. G. Farben have discovered how to make very good synthetic rubber, too."

"Is it cheap?"

"No, thank goodness," said Peter, and laughed. "It's damned expensive."

"So why don't we buy rubber and oil on the world market?"

"Germany has a lot of coal, Isaac. It will keep our miners employed."

"That's not the reason, my friend, and you know it. This fellow is determined to fight a war."

"We must be ready to defend ourselves, Isaac. The Russians and Poles are not to be trusted."

"I hope to God I'm wrong," said Volkmann. "Oh, I almost forgot. I must return Lottie's passport."

"Lottie's passport?"

Volkmann had already reached it from where it was hidden in his locked drugs cabinet before he looked up and registered Peter's surprise. "Oh dear! Didn't you know?"

"What? What's it all about, Isaac?"

Volkmann stood uncertain whether to hand him the package. "I would hate to be the cause of a disagreement between you, Peter. You are our best and most loyal friends."

"What are you doing with Lottie's U.S. passport, Isaac?"

Again the dentist hesitated, but decided that he had no choice but to tell everything. "Your wife loaned her passport to a friend of mine. We have been looking at the visas in it."

"Don't talk in riddles, Isaac. You mean you've been copying the visas to make forgeries?"

"Yes, that is what I mean, Peter. I thought you knew about it. I suppose it must come as a shock to you."

"And forging U.S. passports, too?"

"Some of my people are desperate, Peter. Terrible things are happening in this country of ours."

"You've no right to put my wife in danger."

"I didn't put her in danger. Lottie insisted that her passport be used, and as a Jew she has the right to decide such things."

"She is my wife, and we have a young child. What would happen if . . ."

"I know, I know. . . ."

"You should not have encouraged her."

"I did everything I could to dissuade her, Peter. Everything! I swear I did. I thought she must have discussed it with you."

"And you should not be mixed up in such activity, Isaac. These people are criminals and you are an accessory."

"Do not quote the letter of the law, my friend, when justice lies bleeding at my feet."

"For such things people go to prison for life, Isaac."

"For the sin of being born a Jew, people are being done to death.

Should I shun my duty as a Jew, to serve a regime that is murdering my people?"

Peter took the passport and put it into his pocket. "Please, Isaac. No more. She is a Jew, but she is also my wife."

Isaac Volkmann did not give Peter Winter the assurance he sought. "Shall we say next Tuesday at 2:30 p.m.? It gives you a chance to lunch. There is very little to do except scaling, but I'd like to look again."

"That will be very convenient," said Peter. He took his hat and gloves from the stand in the hall. Volkmann followed him to see him out.

"Your wife is a very determined woman, Peter," he said.

"Next week, then," said Peter. He nodded to Volkmann and departed. Usually he shook hands when he said goodbye, but today he didn't; and he didn't say goodbye, either.

1937

"You know what these old cops are like."

The Geheimes Staatspolizeiamt—the Gestapa, or what people called the Gestapo—had taken over the huge art school in Prinz-Albrecht-Strasse, and Pauli Winter had been assigned an office on the third floor, overlooking the magnificent gardens they shared with the adjoining little palace Heydrich had taken over for his SD.

Now that the Nazis had consolidated their political control of the nation, fundamental changes were made to police forces, too. Pauli Winter—aided by six clerks and the two young lawyers who worked under him—had spent long working weeks, over many months, tackling the organization plan for the Security Police (Sipo). At one time this authority had included the whole police organization, from traffic police to *Gendarmerie.* But now that all the German police forces had come under the command of SS-Reichsführer Himmler, a new sort of Sipo was being formed from just the most powerful units—the Criminal Police (Kripo) and the Political Police.

This newly created Sipo, under the direction of Heydrich's Hauptamt Sicherheitspolizei, ranked as a ministerial authority and came directly under the Reich's Ministry of the Interior.

It made the Sipo potentially one of the most powerful instruments of repression ever seen in modern society. But it was Pauli Winter's report, based upon the legal restrictions of Paragraph 42 of the Reich Criminal Code, that enabled Himmler's policemen to be their own judge and jury.

Paragraph 42 authorized law courts throughout Germany to

order the "preventive arrest" of habitual criminals and other potential troublemakers. But it was the legal work of Dr. Pauli Winter that provided the notion that, under the *völkisch* concept of German law, people and police must work together to maintain law and order. So, argued Winter's long and carefully worded report, in the case of a preventive arrest, the Sipo represented the police and the arrested person the "people." Thus it was lawful for the Hauptamt Sicherheitspolizei to order preventive arrest without going to the law courts. This was a triumph for Himmler, the SS-Reichsführer—a triumph of bureaucracy.

To avoid too much discussion about guilt or innocence, the arrested persons were usually categorized as *Volksschädling* (antisocial malefactors), a description that included prostitutes, beggars, homosexuals, traffic offenders, psychopaths, grumblers, the tellers of anti-Nazi jokes, and anyone who'd "refused without adequate reason employment offered to them on two occasions."

The difficulties that would have come from delivering prisoners to prisons without the necessary court documents were avoided by delivering the arrested people to concentration camps, which also came under the SS-Reichsführer's command. The Ministry of Justice objected to this, but their objections were ignored.

So, by 1937 in Nazi Germany, or what the Goebbels propaganda machine preferred to call the Third Reich, the courts and the whole legal system had been short-circuited. The powers of arrest, judgment, and punishment—terrible punishment, torture, and death—could be instantly used against anyone the Nazis didn't like.

It was March 9, 1937, when the new powers were first put into effect. From the Berlin Police Headquarters in Alexanderplatz, Kripo offices throughout Germany were instructed to take into preventive arrest two thousand people who might commit a crime, might offend against morality, or might otherwise act against the Nazi regime. They were delivered by the police to the nearest concentration camp. It was only the beginning.

For Pauli Winter, March 1937 marked the end of a lot of thankless and tedious administrative work. Up on the third floor he missed the excitement of real police work, and it was years since he'd pitted his wits against some lawyer in the rough and tumble of the local courts.

347

He missed Lothar Koch, too. Lothar could have come up here to where the decisions were made, and there would have been more pay, too. But Lothar was smart: he chose to remain downstairs and deal with people every day. Up here was just a corridor of cramped offices where self-important bureaucrats dictated long documents that were sent to policemen who would manage better without them.

"Pauli?" It was the end of a long day, and Pauli was putting a few things into a briefcase before going home to dinner. The offices, hastily converted to provide extra accommodation, were small and ill-lit, and his visitor was in the shadow, out of range of his desktop light.

"Lothar. What are you doing up here? Want some coffee?" He was always pleased to see Lothar, and the more downcast he looked, with his big mournful eyes and shaggy eyebrows, the more Pauli wanted to laugh at him. "Come in, come in."

"I had to see you. It's urgent."

"What is it? Who have you got out there?" Pauli peered. The offices all had glass panels through which people could be seen walking down the corridor.

"Can I bring him in? It's one of my detectives."

"If you wish," said Pauli, disappointed that he was not going to have the pleasure of a chat.

The detective came in. He was deferential. Everyone knew Pauli Winter by reputation. Pauli was a minor celebrity: Pauli was the man who knew Fritz Esser, Pauli had cracked Para 42, Pauli was the man who lunched with Heydrich, Pauli had a house on the Obersalzberg.

The detective was named Theodor Steiner, a beer-bellied old-timer who'd got into the plainclothes force after many years on the street. A red-faced man with a big rosy nose and circular-shaped horn-rimmed glasses that he had to wear when reading from his notebook.

"Steiner is going to pull in that forgery ring who've been doing the travel documents. Do you know about that?"

"No," said Pauli. "Should I know about it?" He indicated two little caneback chairs, but his visitors remained standing.

"It's been on the sheets for months. They've been leading us a merry dance."

"Travel documents?" said Pauli. He was puzzled.

"Even American passports. One of our undercover agents at the

Hamburg-Amerika Line offices picked up the first one. He wasn't suspicious: he just started talking to this 'American' and found he couldn't speak a word of English."

"He was an illegal?"

"You bet he was. It's neat, isn't it? With a U.S. passport he doesn't need a U.S. visa or a letter of invitation or any of the papers to authorize the export of jewelry, currency, or other valuables. He's an American tourist, going home. You can see the beauty of it, can't you?"

"Yes, I can," said Pauli.

"Well, Steiner here has busted them. He's found the printshop. A printer named Geschke—not even a Jew—in Dietrich-Eckart-Strasse, near the Wittenau station. They're there now, working away: we've got men outside. This will be a big bust, Pauli. Steiner here might get a promotion."

"Congratulations, Steiner. How did you do it?"

"I have an inside man: a Jew, of course."

"That's probably the only way," said Pauli.

"It is with this crowd," said Steiner. Steiner had a thin, chirruping voice that was unexpected from such a big-framed fellow. "They're very cautious, and very skilled." He offered Pauli a passport and other papers.

"This is one of their forgeries?"

"It is."

"Take a look," Koch told him, and Pauli moved his briefcase in order to spread the papers across his desk, under the light of the green-shaded lamp. There was the forged blank U.S. passport, a sheet of clear rubber-stamp marks photographed on line film, and photos of a genuine passport, page by page.

"What do you think?" Koch asked.

Pauli glanced up at him. Koch's face was set in an inscrutable grimace: the sort of face he always pulled when telling one of his jokes. Now that Koch was nearer to the desk light, his face could be seen more clearly. How strange that, while his hair was growing grayer and grayer, his big eyebrows remained coal-black.

Pauli looked down again. It was Lottie Winter staring at him from the photograph in the genuine passport. And there was her name: Charlotte Sarah Winter. Born 1902, Los Angeles, California. Pauli looked up. "They are there now? At the printing shop in Tegel?"

"Yes," said Koch. "The owner, Geschke, and his son, four other men, and this woman." He indicated the photo of Lottie.

"What has the woman to do with it?" Pauli asked Steiner.

"She's one of them. Also, she tells the people who use the passports how to pretend they are American."

"How do you know that?" asked Pauli sharply.

"My inside man," said Steiner.

"Your inside man, yes, of course."

"Steiner has a preventive-arrest order. He was on his way over there when I met him. I said you might want to talk to him."

"I don't want this done by preventive-arrest order," said Pauli. "This is too important for that. These people are enemies of the state. They must be arrested by the police. I'll talk to the Kripo desk right away."

"I don't think that's the way to do it," said Steiner. His rank was nothing, but he spoke with the assurance of a lifetime of police work. "If the Kripo handle it, they'll take the credit. And it will have to go through the courts."

"What's wrong with that?" said Pauli.

The merest trace of a smile passed over Steiner's big, round, inscrutable face. "Nothing, except that my boys will have to type out all the reports and spend a lot of time in the courtroom giving evidence."

"This is an American citizen," said Pauli. He tapped the forged passport with his fingertips.

"German resident," said Steiner doggedly. "She's not a tourist, she's a German resident. When a resident commits a crime, it doesn't matter what color her passport is."

"Technically," interjected Koch, "technically, Detective Constable Steiner has the right to decide."

"And on February 26 this year," said the stolid Steiner, "SS-Gruppenführer Heydrich issued an order that said that no future use was to be made of police arrest, 'so as to avoid the necessity for subsequent examination by the courts of measures taken by the police.' "

"Yes, I know," said Pauli, who'd had too long with his law books to be outwitted by a mere detective. "But the Interior Minister's decree of April 12, 1934, said that 'preventive arrest shall not be used as a punishment for criminal offenses.' This is a serious criminal offense with a foreign national involved. You must use a proper warrant."

There was a long silence. They all knew that, although Pauli was theoretically correct, and although the Sipo came under the direct orders of Interior Minister Dr. Wilhelm Frick, Frick's authority was flouted, his 1934 decree ignored.

Pauli stared at Steiner, and Steiner, like many before him, was alarmed to recognize in Pauli a man who was entirely devoid of the restrictions that fear usually imposes upon even the bravest of men. Steiner looked into Pauli's cold, colorless eyes and felt uneasy. Eventually Steiner said, "Very well. I'll go down to the Kripo desk. Will they give me the warrant there, or do I have to go through all the business of getting an authorized signature?"

"It's urgent," said Pauli. "I'll phone and arrange everything."

Steiner sighed, picked up the photos, and went out.

"Will he do it my way?" Pauli asked Koch after the surly detective had departed.

"He knew she was your sister-in-law. You realize that, don't you?"

"Did he? Winter—it's a common enough name."

"Steiner's no fool. He's been on the Berlin force for over thirty years. He knows everything that happens round here."

"But he'll do it?"

"Oh, he'll do it your way. I know Steiner well enough to be sure of that. He's not going to make an enemy up here on the executive level. But he'll mark it up as something you owe him. In due time he'll come to collect a favor or two. You know what these old cops are like."

"No," said Pauli. "What are they like?"

"They are like you," said Koch, and he laughed.

Pauli Winter phoned Inge to say he was delayed and then went to see his brother. Breaking the news of Lottie's arrest was one of the most painful moments of his life. Peter seemed to think that Pauli could have done more. It was impossible to make Peter see that no one could have done more.

When Peter opened the door to his brother, he was dressed in a blue silk dressing gown with a red scarf tied at his throat. He

looked like a prosperous actor. Pauli found it surprising that someone could take so much trouble with his appearance when he was
alone in the house, but Peter had always been like that.

"Peter. I've got something to tell you."

Peter let him in, saying, "I've been looking for the coffee. I can't
find it anywhere, and Lottie is with Mama."

"She's not with Mama. It's Lottie I want to talk about."

"Then goodness knows where she's got to. I do wish she'd tell
me what she's doing. The girl is not here, and the omelet I made
turned out a terrible mess." The radio was playing "The Way You
Look Tonight."

"Lottie has been arrested, Peter."

"Oh my God! Are you sure?" Peter turned away to compose
himself. His hands were trembling as he switched off the music.

"You aren't mixed up with it, are you?" asked Pauli.

"What is she charged with?" Peter replied. He pushed his hands
into the pockets of his dressing gown.

"The charges are not drawn up yet."

"Is it something to do with passports?" said Peter.

"You'd better sit down, Peter." Peter had gone very pale.

"I think I will." He sat down and took a cigarette from a box on
the table.

"Yes, forging passports." Pauli lit his brother's cigarette for him.

"I must go to her."

"They won't let you see her tonight. She's being questioned."

"I thought she was with Mama."

Pauli said nothing. He'd never seen his brother so upset, and it
caused him pain.

"Are you sure they won't let me see her tonight? Poor, darling
Lottie."

"At the remand prison? You know what they're like. Of course
they won't."

"Not even if I am her defense lawyer?"

"Peter, be sensible."

"I can't think straight."

"Did you know she was doing this kind of thing?" But before
Peter could answer, he held up a hand to silence him and added,
"No, I don't want to know the answer to that. Forget I asked."

"She'll think I've deserted her. Only last night I scolded her about the housekeeping accounts. If only I'd known what was going to happen."

"Pull yourself together, Peter, for God's sake!" said Pauli sharply.

"You're right: I must. For Lottie's sake I must."

"I insisted that the Criminal Police arrest her, using a warrant from a law court. That means she'll get a fair trial, Peter. And she's being held in the remand prison. If they'd used a protective-custody order and taken her to a concentration camp, you'd probably never see her again."

"They'll give her life imprisonment," said Peter.

"We don't know what sentence she'll get; we both know how unpredictable the courts are. But we do know she'll serve her time in a proper, civilized prison," said Pauli. He couldn't seem to make his brother understand how lucky she was.

"Who shall I get to handle her defense?"

"She's guilty, Peter. You do realize that, don't you?"

Peter nodded.

"There's no lawyer in the world who is going to get her released."

"She must have the best."

"I'll find someone. But not many lawyers want to defend 'enemies of the state.' It might be difficult."

"You mustn't get involved, Pauli. I realize your job makes it difficult for you."

"I like Lottie: I've always liked her."

Peter looked round at him. "But you think that as a foreigner, and a Jew, she should have kept out of German politics?"

"I didn't say that, Peter: you said it."

"But that's what you think, isn't it?"

"I don't know what I think."

"How can you work for those Nazis?" said Peter and then regretted it. He was just taking out his frustrated rage and misery on his younger brother. It was stupid and unfair.

Pauli blinked but didn't respond to his brother's flash of anger. He said calmly, "You must realize, Peter, that we are not restricting the emigration of Jews. The SD has an office that does everything it can to encourage emigration. The problem is that no country wants them. The real reason these people were forging American passports was because they can't get entry permits on a German one."

"Does Inge know what's happened?"

"No. I must be getting along."

"Thanks, Pauli."

"Did you ever think about living abroad?"

"Is that your advice, Pauli?"

"I'm thinking of Helena . . . schools and so on."

"I will have to see what happens to Lottie."

"If you went now it would probably be easy. But if and when Lottie is convicted, you might find it impossible to get permission to leave, even as a tourist."

"I can't think about such things at this time."

"This will make a difference in other ways, too, Peter. Be prepared for that."

"What exactly do you mean?"

"There will be publicity, and it won't be helpful. The company might have complaints from shareholders. I've seen it all happen before. A thing like this makes a lot of ripples in the pool."

"I'll be ready."

"If I can help . . ."

"Thanks, Pauli. You already have."

"And, Peter, you see Isaac Volkmann now and again, don't you?"

"I'm one of his patients," said Peter defensively.

"I hear that he's looking for somewhere to live."

"Yes, poor Isaac. Their landlord has thrown them out with only a month's notice."

"I wonder if he's ever thought of living in a lock-up shop?"

"Why?"

"Shopowners don't have to register tenants with the police the way people have to with apartments and houses."

"Live in a shop? Like a fugitive? Is that really necessary?"

"No, it's precautionary. There will be more and more pressure brought on Jews. Life might become intolerable for them."

"Is this an instruction," said Peter, carefully choosing his words, "or just information?"

"It's advice," said Pauli unhesitatingly.

"I'll pass your message on."

"Better not say it's from me, Peter."

"I can't believe the Volkmanns will go to live in a shop."

"You never know," said Pauli.

"Lottie is so headstrong," said Peter. "She wouldn't listen to me."

When Pauli finally got home he was exhausted. He let himself into the apartment and entered the drawing room. The room was dark except for a pool of light on the sofa, where Inge was lounging. Next to her sat Fritz Esser, his jacket off and necktie loosened. They were laughing: laughing in a way he'd never heard either of them laugh before. When they looked up to see him the laughter stopped, and their faces were frozen in a circle of yellow light from the parchment-shaded table lamps. He felt like a stranger, an intruder almost.

"Pauli darling." said Inge. She got up hurriedly and smoothed her skirt. "We heard about Lottie."

"I've been with Peter," explained Pauli.

"Have you eaten?"

"I don't want anything." All he needed was a stiff drink. There was an assortment of drinks on a side table, but Pauli hesitated. He'd been drinking far too much lately. It would be better to have coffee.

"How is Peter taking it?" Inge asked.

"It's a shock for him."

"It's a shock for all of us," said Fritz Esser. He got up unsteadily. He'd been drinking.

"Did you want me, Fritz?" Pauli asked.

"Fritz came to ask if he could help in any way," said Inge.

"That was very kind of you, Fritz," said Pauli. He looked at the brandy decanter and decided to have a proper drink. After a day like this one, a man was entitled to get a little drunk.

1938

"Being innocent is no defense."

Riding across the snow-covered German countryside on a good horse was one of life's finest pleasures. It was white everywhere, with not a human habitation in sight. Sometimes it was hard to believe such open country existed so near to the heart of Berlin.

Despite the loose zipper jacket he wore and his red silk scarf, a careful observer would have recognized the horseman's riding breeches and high boots as belonging to an officer's uniform. He always came here in uniform straight from church. It was a part of his long-established routine.

Colonel Alex Horner had spent too long in the War Office. The introduction of compulsory military service had expanded the German army to almost unmanageable size, and the paperwork was overwhelming. The Bendlerblock had become a madhouse. Some of his fellow desk-bound officers—especially the older ones—liked being at the center of things, delighted in the petty departmental squabbling, and enjoyed the sophisticated pleasures of life in the capital. But such desk work was too tiresome for any fit young officer, and too constricting for the energetic and ambitious Horner.

To make it worse, the civil war in Spain had been going on for over a year, and the German army had been using this foreign battlefield to test its men, its commanders, its tactics, and its equipment. Now, when he seemed to have arranged a posting there, Horner's wife, Chrisi, had announced that she was pregnant. It would make no difference to his determination to go—that his career came first had been agreed at the time of their marriage—but she had no relatives in Berlin, and it seemed unkind to leave her.

He was thinking of these things while riding Pola, a wonderful chestnut roan, back to the Bernau stables near Berlin. He relished these Sunday-morning outings. He loved his wife, but he also cherished the opportunity to be alone now and again. And these Sunday-morning rides were the only chance he got to withdraw from his demanding daily life.

The stables were run by ex–Sergeant Major Winkel, a comrade from the war. It was funny to think that Winkel had come back to Berlin suffering so badly from British chlorine gas that the doctors had almost given him up for dead. Six months, they'd said, or maybe a year, providing he got out of the filthy *Braunkohle* fumes that Berlin's factories and power stations spread over the city like a brown blanket.

So Winkel took his hundred-percent-disability pension, such as it was, and a pretty young farmer's daughter, and the two good-tempered horses that came as her dowry, and set up his riding stables out here in what had then been open countryside. And now, twenty years after the war ended, Winkel was looking as well as ever he looked, and raking in the cash from officers like Horner who wanted a decent horse, rather than the mounts the army provided for such exercise.

It was January and the air was cold. He'd given the horse a good chase, and now, for the final kilometer, he let her walk to cool off. She knew the way home even better than he did. It was a chance for Alex to think his own thoughts about Spain, changing tactics, Germany's Condor Legion, and his contemporaries who were building reputations there. Soon—too soon—the white-painted gates of the stables came into sight, and another Sunday-morning excursion was ended.

He let the horse find her own pace as her feet encountered the uncertain surface of the cobbles. The experts said horses liked cobbles, but Pola seemed to be an exception. As he rode into the yard, he saw Winkel and his teen-age son trying to find the leak in a bicycle tire by holding it in a tin bath of water.

"Leave her to me, Winkel," said Horner, waving away assistance. Winkel always made sure that Horner had his favorite, Pola, and Horner liked to look after her. He liked the stables, the smells of sweat and dung and old harness. He liked to see ex–Sergeant Major Winkel, too. Winkel's comfortable existence confirmed for Alex Horner that the army looked after its own. Bernau was outside the city limits of Gross-Berlin, half an hour on the train from the Stettiner station, and yet enough officers came here to make sure that Winkel flourished. It was just one more tiny example of the way the army looked after its own.

Now that his father was dead, and his elder brother—who'd inherited the estate in East Prussia—wrote to him only once a year, it was this feeling about the close comradeship of the army that made life worth living for Alex Horner. Once, many years ago, during the terrible time when the army was being torn apart by Bolsheviks and revolutionaries, a fierce artillery colonel had asked him whether he would be prepared to die for his country. It was the sort of question only an old man who'd spent the war years at a divisional HQ twenty miles behind the fighting would put to a very young infantry subaltern who'd seen as much front-line service as Horner. Horner—a mere Leutnant at the time—had immediately given an answer in the affirmative, but a more truthful answer might have expressed his willingness to die for the army. He loved the army, and perhaps it was a significant reflection upon his relationship with his father that his proudest memory was of his father's words of praise after Alex graduated from Lichterfelde and went home wearing his regimental uniform.

As he rode Pola into the dark stables, his eyes adjusting to the gloom, he didn't for a moment see the figure standing near the ladder that led up to the hayloft.

"Hello, Alex."

It was a man of about his own age. A man wearing a gray felt hat and black leather overcoat with a gray knitted scarf wrapped around his neck in that careless style sometimes affected by students.

"Pauli?"

Pauli took the horse without answering, but now Alex Horner recognized his old friend.

"How did you find me here, Pauli?" He swung down off the horse and they shook hands and exchanged greetings. Then Alex Horner turned back to his horse again. He released the girth and hauled the saddle off.

Pauli took the saddle from him and hung it on the half-door. "So Winkel's still got this place," said Pauli. They'd both known Sergeant Major Winkel in the war. Long ago Pauli had ridden with Alex for a few Sunday-morning rides. But Inge felt neglected, so he stopped.

Pauli took off his overcoat and hat, and started to help. He grabbed some straw and began rubbing the horse down. On the other side of the horse, Alex did the same. For a few minutes the men worked on in silence; then Alex, finding the silence discomforting, said, "Let me guess what you've come to tell me. Have you come to give me the inside story on the downfall of our beloved War Minister?"

"That's another matter," said Pauli. "Field Marshal von Blomberg is finished; no one can do anything to help him. He'll have to resign."

"Blomberg must have guessed she was a whore before marrying her, don't you think?"

"I'm not an expert on women, or on the working of army officers' minds," said Pauli.

Alex gave a brief smile. "But still . . . he surely must have . . ." He waited.

"Men don't usually check with the Identification Office of the Kripo before proposing marriage," said Pauli.

"Was it just bad luck that someone saw her antics on old porno photos and then recognized her in the wedding-group photo?"

"There was no marriage photo, as far as I know. It was a very private ceremony."

"Very private," said Alex sarcastically, "with the Führer and General Göring as witnesses." He paused and waited until Pauli smiled at the notion of Göring as a general. "So how did the police find out?"

"The change-of-address card," said Pauli.

"Well, Blomberg is big enough and old enough to look after himself," said Alex. "Let him resign. There are plenty of other men to fill his job. I don't want people pointing a finger at the War Minister and saying, There's Generalfeldmarschall Werner von Blomberg, the old fool who married the whore. It makes the army look ridiculous."

"The Frau Generalfeldmarschall was never a whore, as far as police records go," said Pauli patiently. "She posed for pornographic photos."

"Then she must be a damned odd one," said Alex.

"After working for the Gestapo, you start realizing how many odd people there are about," said Pauli.

"I don't approve of this so-called tolerant society. I never did." Alex threw down his handful of straw and moved away.

"You're a stuffed shirt, Alex; you always were," said Pauli.

"You say that about everyone. You used to say that about your brother." His voice was raised as he went out through the door and into the locker room beyond.

"I still do," called Pauli.

"Have a drink." Alex Horner came back with his army tunic over his arm and a hip flask in his hand.

"I've stopped drinking; I really have."

"One schnapps won't hurt you. It would be better than all those cigarettes you smoke." Alex carefully removed the silver cup from the flask and poured a measure into it. After offering it again to Pauli, he downed it in one gulp. This also was a part of Alex Horner's Sunday-morning routine.

"Cigarettes don't spoil my judgment, Alex."

"Would the occasional spoiled judgment be so bad? You're not on the battlefield."

"Oh, but I am, Alex." Pauli watched Colonel Alex Horner put on his beautifully tailored tunic. Pauli felt a twinge of envy. But for one isolated piece of bad judgment, plus the spiteful officiousness of that swine Brand, Pauli might have been wearing that same colonel's uniform and been working alongside his friend. But Pauli didn't dwell upon it: he'd never wasted much time feeling sorry for himself. He'd grown up under the shadow of his academically brilliant brother. Considering his meager assets, Pauli was satisfied with his good fortune. Still, Colonel Horner looked damned good, even if he did have to wear those ridiculous little swastika badges. Despite his own party affiliation, Pauli felt that von Blomberg should never have agreed to making the German army wear political-party insignia: it was undignified.

"Won't you come back and have lunch with us? Chrisi is only cooking home-made soup and some bratwurst. There will be plenty."

"I have to get back to the office, Alex. Thank you."

"Chrisi is keen that you and Inge come to dinner."

"Next month things will be easier."

"It's Sunday! My goodness, you people work hard. The Gestapo now, is it?"

"I'm trying to keep my SD desk running, too. It's the devil of a lot of work."

"Then you'd better tell me your news."

"How close are you to von Fritsch?"

"No one is close to von Fritsch," said Alex without hesitation. Colonel General Werner Freiherr von Fritsch, the Commander in Chief of the German army, was a forbidding figure.

"Is he a homosexual?"

"No. Fritsch, a homosexual? It's out of the question."

"He's not married," said Pauli.

"Is this official?"

"I'm trying to help."

"Well, Fritsch is not a homosexual; I'd bet anything on that. Now, what else can I tell you?" It was one of those rare moments when Alex Horner revealed a hint of displeasure.

"It's not official, Alex. We're old friends. I wanted to talk with you."

"About the C in C?"

"The railway police at Wannsee picked up some little piece of rubbish named Otto Schmidt. He was hanging around the station there. He makes a living by blackmailing homosexuals. In the course of his interrogation he started name-dropping. One of the names was Fritsch."

Alex Horner showed both relief and exasperation. "Good God, Pauli, you're surely not going to take that seriously. He just wanted them to think he had influence. What other names did he drop?"

"Lots of other names: the Potsdam Police President and the Minister of Economics."

"There you are." Alex poured some more schnapps from the flask, then held it up, but Pauli shook his head to decline again. Alex drank. Usually on Sunday he limited himself to only one drink, but today was different.

"Not quite," said Pauli. "The police pushed him along to the Gestapo desk that deals with the suppression of homosexuality. . . ."

"Is there such a department?" He wiped his lips on the back of his hand.

"We think of everything," said Pauli sardonically. He watched Alex carefully; Pauli had become an expert observer. In the next stall a restless horse put its weight against the wooden partition so that it creaked. "And they showed him photos. He picked out the photo of the C in C."

"Hardly reliable evidence."

Still studying his friend's face, Pauli said, "He is prepared to say he saw Fritsch committing a homosexual act with a youth he picked up at the Wannsee station."

"Oh," said Alex, keeping his emotions under control. "What will happen now?"

"Quite a lot has happened already. A file on the case went to the Führer. Reichsführer Himmler took it to him personally, so we kept the tightest security."

"And?"

"The Führer said, 'Burn this muck.' "

"Good for the Führer. Was it burned?"

"We don't burn anything."

Alex sighed. "Oh, come along, Pauli, old friend. Some things get burned in the Third Reich. Didn't I see big piles of books by Jewish authors being burned in Unter den Linden not so long ago? At Opernplatz; I stopped to watch. A big bonfire. I noticed quite a few books there I rather fancied. Freud, Gide, Proust, Zola, Wells, Zweig, Mann . . ."

"I wish you'd trust me, Alex."

"What do you want me to do?"

It was not easy to help people; Pauli had found that again and again. They all acted as though Pauli were talking to them in some incomprehensible foreign tongue. "Warn Colonel General Fritsch."

"You expect me to walk into his office and tell him that Hitler suspects him of committing homosexual acts at the Wannsee station?"

Alex still couldn't get it into his head. All these years in the army seemed to have made him incapable of understanding the simple facts of German political life. Pauli explained it as simply as he could. "Now that it seems as if von Blomberg must go, Göring will persuade Himmler to bring up the Fritsch business again."

"But why?"

"Don't be naïve, Alex. Göring wants Blomberg's ministry, and Fritsch is next in line right now. 'War Minister Göring': he'd love that."

"And how would Himmler benefit?"

"If Fritsch went, the Reichsführer-SS would also take the opportunity to extend his powers."

"Himmler, extend his powers? My God, the fellow has taken over all the police forces in Germany. And now he's expanded this SS army of his to three regiments, plus a combat-engineer company and a communications unit."

"Top marks to the Abwehr, Alex. They keep you well informed." He took out a cigarette, lit it, and blew smoke. "And the concentration camps, too. The Totenkopfverbände who guard the camps are also part of his command."

"And you, too?"

"Yes, me, too."

"Then why are you here?"

"Don't you know that, Alex?"

Alex paused. "The army? Does it mean so much to you still?"

"I don't know, Alex. Perhaps I simply want to prove I can be my own master sometimes. Inge keeps telling me I should be my own master." He got up, took his overcoat off the hook.

Alex watched his friend putting the heavy leather overcoat on. Pauli moved like an infirm old man. Goodness knows what he was doing these days, but he looked as if he was working too damned hard. Even the Bendlerblock let its inmates spend Sunday at home. "You don't believe it, either, do you?"

"About Fritsch? No, it's all nonsense. The man who paid blackmail money to this Schmidt filth is someone quite different; a retired Captain von Frisch."

"How did you find out?"

"His address was in Schmidt's original statement. I went along to the address and spoke with him. After a little questioning he admitted it, and we got his bank statements to prove the payments."

"Then it will be all right," said Alex. Pauli patted the horse and it nuzzled him affectionately. He loved horses; he always had.

"No, it will not be all right. Someone had better tell Fritsch."

"Tell him what? He's innocent. You've just said so."

"Tell him that being innocent is no defense." Pauli smiled, buttoned his coat, and decided to say no more about it. Already he'd said too much.

Alex nodded and took another drink. The world had gone mad.

Case Otto.

On the evening of Friday, March 11, 1938, the most splendid social event in Berlin was undoubtedly the lavish party given at the newly named and redecorated Haus der Flieger—the old Prussian Diet building on Prinz-Albrecht-Strasse—by Hermann Göring.

Göring himself, forty-five years old, Commander in Chief of the newly created Luftwaffe and in charge of all civil aviation, too, had recently been made a field marshal. The promotion was to compensate him for his disappointment at not taking over von Blomberg's job as War Minister (Hitler had taken that authority for himself). This night he arrived at his gala pink-faced and excited. He was wearing his new field-marshal uniform, complete with an array of medals. At his neck there was the Orden Pour le Mérite, the nation's highest award for valor, which Göring had won as a fighter pilot in the war. Short in stature, as so many fighters pilots are, and very overweight, Göring this night was the essence of charm.

It was a sumptuous affair: more than a thousand guests, including diplomats and high-ranking officials, were entertained by the orchestra, singers, and ballet of the Berlin State Opera. Among the many guest performances was a Beethoven piano sonata played by Erich Hennig.

Ever since playing before the Führer at the Bach Festival in Leipzig in June 1935, Erich Hennig had been a celebrity of the Third Reich. Once Hitler had admired him, he'd become noted as an interpreter of Bach as well as of Beethoven and Mozart, and Hennig was regularly to be heard on the radio. A handsome man, thin and rather drawn, with a carefully trimmed mustache and intense black eyes, Hennig had cultivated the appearance that audiences expected of a concert pianist. It was his appearance—and such mannerisms as flicking his coat tails and "washing" his hands quickly before the piano's first entry—as much as his talent, that had earned him a regular place on the new entertainment medium, television. On March 22, 1935, Germany had started the first regular public TV broadcasting system in the world. Despite the small number of TV receivers in use, performers such as Erich Hennig were becoming famous "personalities."

And so, when Hennig took the stage that evening, this familiar figure was given a welcoming applause that outmatched that given to any other performer.

"Erich would have got tickets for you," Lisl Hennig told her sister Inge after showing her some snapshots of the Hennigs' eight-year-old son.

"We were invited anyway," said Inge haughtily. "Pauli gets tickets for all the big events."

"How wonderful," said Lisl as she put the photos back in her handbag. Inge sometimes liked to pretend she preferred the freedom of being childless, but her face, as she looked at Lisl's snapshots, made it obvious how much she wanted a baby. And Pauli—unlike Erich—was wonderful with children. "Forgive me for the way I keep watching the stage, but Erich will probably be presented to Field Marshal Göring, and he'll want me to be with him."

"How is Papa?" asked Inge to change the subject.

"He misses Mama terribly. Though he hardly ever mentions her, he just isn't the same without her. It's easy to forget how old he is, but his memory is going. He has no sense of time. Last week I mentioned that I'd seen you buying fish in Ka-De-We and he said, 'Is Inge going to marry that young Peter Winter? He's a polite young fellow.' I replied, 'She's married his brother.' Papa said, 'Oh, is that legal?' We laughed. We were eating dinner at the time. Erich laughed so much I thought he would choke. Yes, Papa says odd things at times." Lisl chuckled.

Inge didn't laugh. She said, "Pauli couldn't come. Pauli's packing to go to Vienna." She shouldn't have said it, really—Pauli had sworn her to secrecy—but she'd suffered enough of her sister's tormenting.

"Vienna? So the *Anschluss* is happening?"

"At dawn tomorrow, our troops cross the border. Please God the Austrians won't start shooting."

"Start shooting? You can't be serious, Inge. The Austrians will love to become a part of the Reich." She looked at Inge. "Why is Pauli going there?"

"He's taking into custody the dissidents, the Marxists, and troublemakers. A lot of German criminals have gone there to hide."

"And Jews," said Lisl.

"Yes. The Gestapo have nearly a hundred thousand names with Vienna addresses," said Inge.

"So Pauli will be there for a long time."

"No, thank goodness. The SS-Reichsführer has promised that Vienna will be safe for the Führer to visit by Tuesday. I couldn't bear to have Pauli away for a week. I miss him dreadfully, and he needs me, Lisl. Without me the poor darling doesn't even remember to change his linen, and he never eats properly when he's away from home."

At ten-thirty that evening, those favored musicians and members of the *corps de ballet* and *corps diplomatique* who'd been alerted to the prospect of shaking hands with Field Marshal Göring were told that plans for these formal presentations had been canceled.

Although no reason was given, it was because Göring—who'd taken a major role in the planning for the annexation of Austria—was closeted with one of his guests. Göring was determined to persuade Dr. Mastny, the Czechoslovak ambassador, that Germany's aggression boded no such similar fate for his country. This was just a "family matter," said Göring—the Austrians were in fact Germans—and Germany was determined to have excellent relations with Czechoslovakia. He hoped that there would be no question of Czechoslovakia's mobilizing against this entirely German affair.

Dr. Mastny was not entirely convinced.

"It's a lovely dress, Inge," Lisl told her, and there was no doubt of her sincerity. It was a floor-length dress of gray shot-silk that shimmered in the light of the chandeliers. The bodice front was buttoned high to the neck in a style based deliberately upon some of the old German country costumes. It was a "model dress" exclusive to her. Inge had chosen it from one of the expensive couturiers in Ku-damm. She had in mind taking it with her when they next went to the Obersalzberg. She knew it was the sort of dress the Führer would approve of. "It must have cost a fortune."

"Well, I told Pauli that now he's an important man in the administration, I have to dress accordingly."

"You're lucky," said Lisl. "Erich is awfully mean about my clothes."

"You must speak with him," said Inge. "You entertain all sorts of interesting artists. And if you are going to come to events like this, where there are lots of foreigners, it's important that you look your best. Germans must show them that we have a new place in the world."

"That's all right for Pauli," said Lisl, "but you'd never get away with that with Erich. If I said I had nothing suitable to wear, Erich would just leave me behind."

Colonel Alex Horner first heard officially on Thursday, March 10. It all started just before 9:00 a.m., when General Wilhelm Keitel arrived. Although Keitel was officially styled the chief of the Armed Forces Command (the OKW, an office that Hitler created to replace von Blomberg's War Ministry), everyone knew that Keitel was no more than Hitler's office boy.

But, as Alex Horner noted, "Hitler's office boy" could certainly make the Bendlerblock come alive. When Hitler had got rid of Fritsch and Blomberg, he'd ruthlessly purged the generals: there had been fifty transfers and forced retirements. Now, when Keitel came through the door unexpected, the anxiety could be smelled in every corridor.

The Austrians were planning a plebiscite on Sunday as a way to appeal to world opinion and so counter the German ultimatum. The Führer had decided that, to prevent it, the army must occupy Austria by Saturday. It was already mid-morning Thursday. Colonel Horner's immediate superior—an elegant and cultured old general whom Horner had come to distrust if not despise—sent for him urgently.

"Anything on Austria, Colonel Horner?"

"Nothing in the way of military plans, Herr General."

"No contingency plans against the Austrians? Nothing at all?" He was trying to maintain his usual supercilious, patronizing manner, but to Horner he sounded desperate.

"Nothing, Herr General."

"Come along, Horner. General Jodl says there is something."

"Did he say what it was, Herr General?"

"I gather it is a rather impractical scheme that was prepared when there were rumors that the Austrians were planning to restore Otto of Habsburg to the throne."

"I don't remember it, Herr General," said Horner.

"He thinks it's called Case Otto. Perhaps it's filed downstairs in one of the storerooms. Get some reliable officers to go through the filing cabinets downstairs."

"Immediately, Herr General."

"And Colonel Horner. I've decided to deny that application for you to go to Spain."

"As the general wishes."

"Oh, I know you must be disappointed, but with your wife pregnant with a first child, and the High Command's decision to cut back on the forces in Spain . . ."

"I understand, Herr General." His general was not the sort of man who considered the feelings of pregnant wives; he simply had another protégé lined up for the Spanish posting.

"What would you say to a weekend in Vienna instead? It looks as if the army is heading that way."

"Vienna, Herr General?"

"Type yourself some orders for attachment to one of the units in the order of battle. I'd choose one of these panzer outfits, unless you relish some hard marching."

"The Herr General is very kind."

"Lots of time for Spain, Horner. That young General Franco is not going to beat the Reds for a long time yet, judging by the way the Russians are putting material into the fighting."

"Yes, Herr General."

"You don't want to go to Spain, Colonel Horner. It's full of flies and beggars. The food's terrible, too: olive oil and rice with odds and ends in it. Go to Vienna: better food, decent music, and far more beautiful women."

"I'll get started on the search for the plans for Case Otto, Herr General."

"Don't break your heart on it, Colonel. If those plans were here, I would have seen them; and I don't remember them."

"I thought General Jodl . . ."

"General Jodl is getting old, Colonel. You go and dust off your dancing pumps. Send a couple of officers downstairs, then go and prepare your orders, and get me to sign them while I'm still in a good mood."

"Yes, Herr General. Thank you."

Meanwhile, Keitel had left the building to hurry across to the Reichskanzlei for his ten o'clock meeting with the Führer and was relieved to hear that Hitler would be satisfied with Case Otto. But when he returned to Bendlerstrasse, no one had found it, and despite more searching the plans were never located.

"It's a typical Bendlerstrasse balls-up," Alex Horner told the two young officers who'd emerged from the storerooms with hands and faces blackened by the dirt and dust of filth-encrusted bundles of old documents.

Keitel went into immediate conference with General Beck, chief of the General Staff. When Beck was summoned to see the Führer, he had the luck to grab General Erich von Manstein—the army's most capable general—to go with him.

Manstein was supposed to be on his way out of Bendlerstrasse, where, until Hitler's purge, he'd been deputy chief of the General Staff. By now he should have been on the train to Liegnitz, to the humiliatingly low job of commanding the 18th Infantry Division.

It took Manstein five hours to draft the plans, which, to conceal the fact that the original was lost, were called Case Otto. By 6:30 p.m. orders were on the teleprinters to mobilize three army corps and the necessary air-force units.

Alex Horner found an excuse to go into the room where the fabled General Manstein was at work. He was a ferocious-looking man with gray hair, bushy eyebrows, and a big beak of a nose. But Manstein's ferocity was not selectively targeted. Everyone remembered that it was the lonely voice of Manstein who'd objected to the order that in 1934 had dismissed Jews from the army. And Manstein was not afraid to put his objection in writing and send it to the High Command. He protested the meting out of such treatment to men who'd proved, by voluntary enlistment, that they were ready to give their lives for Germany—and added that the army had shown cowardice in surrendering to the Nazi Party on such an issue. Manstein's courageous protest had alarmed those generals who were frightened to rock the boat. War Minister Blomberg was furious and ordered General Werner von Fritsch (the army C in C) to take disciplinary action against Manstein, but the stalwart Fritsch said it was none of the War Minister's business.

Now Blomberg had gone, and Fritsch had gone, too, and Manstein was perfecting Hitler's plans for the invasion of Austria.

TOP SECRET

§ If other measures prove unsuccessful I intend to invade Austria with armed forces to establish constitutional conditions and to prevent further outrages against the pro-German population.

§ The forces of the army and air force detailed for this operation must be ready for invasion on March 12, 1938, at the latest by 1200 hours.

It all seemed a long time ago, thought Colonel Alex Horner as he sat by the roadside perched upon the hull of a broken-down tank.

Alongside him sat his old friend Captain von Kleindorf, wearing the black uniform of the tank men. "They're not tanks at all," complained von Kleindorf, thumping the thin steel of the PzKw IA with his fist. "Five meters long, and armed with nothing better than a couple of machine guns. The damned thing only weighs six tons! Look at it."

Alex didn't want to look at it: he hated it and all the other miserable little steel boxes like it. "So why have we got them?"

"Ask your friends in the Bendlerblock," said von Kleindorf. "For parades past the newsreel cameras, I suppose. We've got fifteen hundred of these useless little two-man machines, and hundreds of them still have the rotten little four-cylinder Krupp engine, like this one."

"I know," said Alex. He didn't exactly know, but he'd seen so many of them broken down on the roadsides of South Germany that the figure didn't surprise him.

A company of infantry marched past. They'd been getting ready to jeer and catcall the men on the broken tank but, recognizing the uniforms of the two officers, the sergeant called the marching men to attention.

"And the damned SS soldiers are all in trucks," said von Kleindorf bitterly. "And they're wearing proper field-gray army uniforms!"

"Guderian shouldn't have agreed to have SS units with us in the corps," said Alex.

"What option did he have?" said von Kleindorf. "The tanks need motorized infantry in support, and Himmler seems to know where to get his hands on trucks. Our poor devils have to march." It wasn't exactly true—most of the infantry units passing them were using horse-drawn vehicles—but Alex had been up all night, he was tired, and he was not in the mood for arguing.

"You two officers! Quickly!" Two large open-top staff cars had stopped. The second one had hit a mud patch and almost skidded into the other. Staff officers leapt out in the way that staff officers do when they want to impress their commander.

"He wants us," said von Kleindorf.

"*Ja!*" shouted Alex Horner, and jumped to the ground.

"Come here!"

They ran to him. He was a Generalleutnant, his overcoat collar open to reveal the huge crimson lapels that are the insignia of the rank of general. He stood up in the open Mercedes with one arm resting along the top of the windscreen and the other hand impatiently shaking a pair of expensive kid gloves. His face, like his uniform, bore splashes of mud.

Magisterially the general said, "A colonel authorized tank commanders to break the locks on civilian gas pumps and steal petrol from service stations. A colonel with a helmet painted dark green, I was told. Was it one of you two officers?"

Alex Horner's helmet was painted dark green, as it had been for autumn maneuvers last year. All around him the soldiers of the corps had their helmets the same shade of brownish gray. "Yes, Herr General," said Alex. "I authorized it."

"From civilian gas pumps?"

"There is no fuel convoy, Herr General."

"That's theft!"

"Yes, Herr General."

"Your name?"

"Colonel Horner, Herr General."

"Who is your commander?"

"I am attached from Berlin, Herr General, OKW Operations Office."

"Oh, you're a tourist, Colonel? Just here to try the schnitzels, I suppose. Well, you confine your damned criminal activities to the Bendlerblock. Perhaps that's the way they do things there. But meanwhile, when a court of inquiry starts asking for compensation for those civilians, I'll make sure it's your head that's on the block. Is that clear, Colonel Horner?"

"Yes, Herr General." Behind this truculent general, one of his aides stood smirking at Alex's discomfort.

"What are you waiting here for?"

"The maintenance section. A track has broken and we've no spare links, Herr General."

"They won't need you to help them fix it. Get into my car; I'll take you up to Divisional HQ if we can find them. Have you got any kit?"

"No, Herr General."

"Go, driver!" Even before the doors slammed, the general's driver had let in the clutch and the car roared away. In the mirror Alex glimpsed the second car chasing after them.

"And your name, Captain?" shouted the general as the car bumped and skidded along the narrow road.

"Captain von Kleindorf, Herr General."

"Kleindorf? Is General von Kleindorf your father? We were together in 1918. Is he well?"

"Yes, Herr General."

"You give him my respects next time you write."

"Yes, Herr General."

"Look at these damned fools. Stop, driver!" The car skidded to a halt, and again the one behind narrowly avoided a collision. "Where's your commander, Sergeant? Get him immediately. Why are you stopped? Out of fuel? Good God, man, why don't you get fuel as you go? Get motor spirit from one of these civilian service stations. If they won't let you have it on signature, take it at gunpoint. Do you understand? Good. Go, driver!" And the car leapt forward again.

"Stop, driver! Come here, Sergeant. Don't you know that all vehicles must be garlanded with flowers or flags or, failing that, leaves? Haven't you been told that all units are to have a joyful appearance? Get greenery and have it done right away. Smile, Sergeant. You heard me, smile! That's right. Now, you keep that smile on your face until you're in Vienna. We want those damned dumpling-eaters to celebrate our arrival. It's better than fighting them. Carry on, Sergeant. Go, driver!"

It was the same all along the road, with the general chivvying his columns into action. But many of the breakdowns had mechanical causes too grave to be got moving by the general's sharp tongue. This day Alex Horner saw broken tanks and trucks all along the road to Vienna.

"And who is that civilian, Captain? An Austrian mechanic fixing your truck? Why can't you fix it yourself? You're a damned disgrace to your uniform, Captain. No, don't stop him. If your fool of a driver can't mend it, then let the Austrian do it. But don't count on that kind of help from the Polacks when we invade Poland, Captain."

"Poland, General?"

"Don't look so worried, Captain. It's just a joke. At least, it's just a joke until the Führer decides it isn't a joke. Go, driver!"

With his head lolling back against the leather seat, the general put a question to his passenger. "So what do you think of our big new army of conscripts, now that you've seen them in action, Colonel Horner?"

"There are problems, Herr General."

"So! Even a man from the Bendlerblock can see it! That's reassuring anyway. Yes, there are problems, Colonel. From what I can see, about fifty percent of our motorized and armored force has suffered breakdowns. The machinery is second-rate, the maintenance is poor, and the army have had to promote competent private soldiers to be incompetent NCOs, and competent young subalterns to be incompetent captains. That's what conscription has done to the army. The average young officer hasn't got enough initiative to blow his own nose."

"The general is perhaps too critical," ventured Alex bravely.

"Rubbish! Look for yourself. Did you see that sergeant back there? He couldn't have been much more than nineteen years old, and he's in charge of thirty men. What can a boy like that know about commanding soldiers?"

"He might have served in Hitler Youth, Herr General," said Alex.

"Don't talk to me about Hitler Youth," said the general. "I'm always getting complaints about the way the little swines report chance remarks by their NCOs, and their officers, too. I stamp on that! I'll tell you—and I don't care if you're a Nazi or not—I stamp on it. I won't have these little freshly recruited bastards snooping on my trained men."

"Of course not, Herr General."

"Nor will I give the conceited little Nazi tykes quick promotions."

"No, Herr General."

"Ah! You agree, Horner. So! Is that the official attitude of the

Bendlerblock? Can I take that as being the official reaction of the OKW?"

"No, Herr General. I have no idea what is the official attitude to such matters."

"Neither do I, Horner. That's my dilemma, you see. You might say that's the army's dilemma. We wear these pretty little silver Nazi eagles and swastikas on our chests, and we are not our own men anymore. Follow me, Horner?"

"Yes, Herr General. I follow you."

"Don't work too hard, Pauli Winter."

Damned German tourists: they were everywhere. They must have followed within hours of the soldiers crossing the border. Or perhaps the shrewder ones had contrived to be in Vienna already. Here they were: eating, eating, eating, as if they were starved. It's true, the food was better than in the Reich, but only marginally so. Of course, the rate of exchange was good, so the Reichsmark bought more. Even so, Pauli Winter disapproved of the way that the restaurants and shops were crowded with Germans. It was undignified and uncomfortably like the profiteers in Berlin in those awful days of 1919.

Nor did he like the way that so many of the German businessmen he knew wanted him to help them buy out Jewish businesses at knockdown prices. He'd upset some of them with his unequivocal refusals. He'd sent them packing with a few home truths ringing in their ears. He smiled to himself as he thought about it. No doubt those outbursts had made for him a few bitter enemies, but he was confident that they'd do nothing about it. That was one consolation about this rather dull job of his: no sane man wanted to get on the wrong side of a senior executive of the Gestapo.

Pauli Winter was enjoying this visit to the city of his birth. He remembered it well enough, even though he'd not been here for nearly five years. Past the Opera to the Ringstrasse. A bearded gypsy violinist was standing on the corner playing a sad melody. He should have been arrested as a vagrant, but Pauli put some coins into the tin. Though it was a chilly day, the sun was bright and there was a feeling of excitement in the air. Pauli's enjoyment was somewhat marred by the sight of elderly Jews on their knees scrubbing the pavement, supervised by uniformed Austrian Nazis, while passers-by stopped to look and sometimes jeer.

The Jews were mostly harmless. They chose university professors and professional men to set to scrubbing the streets and cleaning out public toilets, because their respectable appearance made them look more ridiculous. Pauli knew they were harmless: anyone with a record of even the mildest anti-Nazi word or action had been rounded up and put under lock and key within hours of Pauli's arrival.

Soon, when the new concentration camp at Mauthausen—on the Danube, near Enns—was ready, it would all be much easier. There would not be the long train journeys to take prisoners to camps in Germany. Furthermore, the prisoners would be able to work in the Mauthausen stone quarry. That could be said to be Pauli Winter's idea. It was Pauli's long analysis of the concentration-camp accounts that had ended with a suggestion that all the camps eventually become self-financing. In an appendix at the end he'd listed the sort of labor-intensive enterprises that the SS should obtain—perhaps by confiscation from Jewish owners—with a view to using free concentration-camp labor for increased profit. Quarries, any sort of quarries, and such firms as the Meissen porcelain works were especially desirable. The SS-Reichsführer had sent a letter of interest and appreciation, and Heydrich had suggested that Pauli resign his job with the Gestapo post and work only for his Sicherheitsdienst. It was a great compliment, but Pauli politely declined, pointing out that the Gestapo (a state organization) carried the full state pension rights that were granted to such public employees, whereas the SD (a Nazi Party organization) had no such guaranteed long-term benefits. This was particularly unfair now that the concentration-camp guards—unemployable riffraff for the most part—were officially recognized as civil servants, with all the rights and privileges of that elite fraternity.

For Pauli the operation in Vienna had all gone smoothly. By this afternoon the men would have finished moving all the confiscated silver, paintings, furniture, and carpets from the Rothschilds' palace in Prinz-Eugen-Strasse so that the building could be used as offices for the Sipo and SD. Pauli wondered what would happen to all those priceless things he'd watched the SS men loading onto trucks. Judging by the care they'd taken, the antiques were already earmarked for some Nazi Party leader. Even more valuable plunder was going to Germans who knew the right people. The German company I. G. Farben was to be given Skodawerke Wetzler AG chemical works in exchange for a promise to replace all Jews in the management and bring this huge gunpowder works into the Nazi four-year plan. Rothschild's steel rolling mills in Czechoslovakia had been promised to Field Marshal Göring. That would be the price for Baron de Rothschild's freedom.

Now he had to stop and ask the way. Kärtnerstrasse. He knew it was near the boulevard, but it was long time since he'd been in this part of the city. The woman who directed him there had a strong Viennese accent. She asked him if he was a German. "We are all Germans now," Pauli replied.

"On the left," said the woman, "just fifty meters along the street."

He went up to the fourth floor. The name tab on the bell had been peeled away. From the apartment upstairs he could hear American dance music—"Thanks for the Memory." He pressed the bell, and after a long delay the door was opened by a youngish man in plain tie, white shirt, and the sort of hard-wearing dark serge suit that employers furnish to domestic servants.

"Yes?"

"My name is Winter," said Pauli with careful politeness. He gave the man his visiting card. It bore only his name—Dr. iur. Paul Winter—and his private Berlin address and phone number. His employer—the Gestapo—and office address were discreetly omitted.

"Please wait," said the man.

"Forgive me," said the woman who eventually emerged from behind the bead curtain at the end of the hall. In her mid-fifties, she was very small, slim, and still beautiful, even if she wore a little too much rouge and lipstick. Her hair was lustrous but it was too dark and too wavy and too tight against her head. She wore a wonderful old silk negligee patterned with fierce Chinese tigers. "I tell Boris he must always look through the peephole before answering the door." She'd never shed the Hungarian accent; for some it is difficult.

"That's sensible," said Pauli.

"Come into the drawing room," she said. She looked down at

"Don't work too hard, Pauli Winter."

Pauli's card and fingered the name on it as if it were Braille. "We will have tea and we will talk." Then she looked at Pauli, trying to see his father in him.

Pauli was half prepared for the room. Once his father, in some uncharacteristic moment of revelation, had confided something of the wonderful things he'd bought when young. But he did not think it would be like this. "It's magnificent!"

It was a museum, but far better than any museum could ever be: this perfect example of Viennese Art Nouveau, complete with two small Klimt murals, some exquisite Schiele drawings, and Josef Hoffmann furniture, had never had to endure the ceaseless burden of uninvited visitors.

Soon Boris appeared with a silver tray and tea things. Pauli got a better look at him this time. Thirty-five, maybe younger. Dark hair. Not particularly handsome or attractive in any way. A boring sort of fellow. If he was her lover there was no sign of it. And yet there was no sign of anything. She hardly looked at the man. Was that because she was frightened of revealing their true relationship? Or had he worked for her so long that she no longer noticed his existence?

"With lemon?" Martha Somló fitted into the scheme perfectly. She sat in her favorite chair and poured tea, impaled slices of lemon on a silver fork, and carefully positioned perfectly shaped pieces of cake upon the Art Nouveau plates.

"Yes, lemon."

"Harry—your father—loved it, of course. Back in the old days we had dinner parties. Artists came. I met them all. The dining room is the finest example anywhere, Harry says. Mind you, people said he was crazy when he bought all this stuff. Me, too. I didn't tell him, but I hated it at first. But after nearly forty years . . . Did he send you? Did Harry send you?"

"He was worried."

"About me? That's a surprise." She said it without rancor. "Does he still come?"

"To see me? Sure. But not often. I love him, you see. Sometimes I even think that he loves me."

Pauli picked up his tea and took his time squeezing lemon into it to avoid having to reply.

"Does that offend you, Herr Pauli Winter?"

So she knew he was called Pauli. He wondered how much his

father had told her about him. A lot, perhaps. He wondered if his father knew about the presence of the manservant. "No, it doesn't. Of course not. Not at all."

"Did you ever see me before?"

"No, I don't think so."

"I just wondered. You see, long ago, the year before you were born, your mother used to come and stand out there on the boulevard, looking up at the window. She was pregnant, I suppose. I felt sorry for her. I think she wanted to see what I looked like. One day I went down and crossed the road and passed near her. I looked at her and she looked at me. I didn't see any hatred there. I suppose we both pitied each other, in that insane way in which women are able to convince themselves that they have the best part of any deal. She never came again after that." She picked up her tea and stirred it and then let the tea leaves settle in the bottom of the cup. She looked down into the tea before drinking it. Pauli wondered if she was trying to read her fortune there.

"I work for the German police," said Pauli tentatively.

"Well, you'll be kept busy," said Martha. She looked up at him evenly. There was no fear in her face, although Pauli knew somehow that she was frightened. He'd seen too many frightened people not to be able to recognize fear in all its guises.

"My father asked me to give you my protection. I promised him that I would."

"What do you do for the German police, that you can protect me?"

"I am a Regierungsdirektor working in the Gestapo. I also hold SS-Standartenführer rank for my work with the SD."

"What a mouthful. It sounds very important."

He was being mocked, but he didn't mind that. He found her attractive, this little woman with her large eyes that challenged him and tried to see inside him. Until now he'd not realized that his father needed a woman like this, a strong, challenging personality who let you know she would fight back. And yet her assumed fearlessness was curiously disconcerting. "I might be useful, Frau Somló."

"I call myself Frau Winter."

"Frau Winter. Good. Yes, that is clear. It might be possible to find completely new papers for you."

"You are going to convert me from being a Jew?"

"I will try. Do you see any difficulty?"

"Difficulty?"

"Yes," said Pauli. My God, but people could be stupid when it came to the important things in life. "Are you registered or listed anywhere as a Jew? Do you go to the synagogue? Jewish societies? Do your neighbors know you as a Jew?"

"Synagogue: no. Societies: never. Neighbors . . . The Bergers upstairs know. We talked about it one evening. Years ago."

Pauli brought out his notebook and crossed his legs to balance it on his knee. "Bergers? One floor up? Number eight? What is the first name of the father?"

For a moment Martha Somló stared at him with her big eyes. Calmly and softly she said, "No, no, no, Herr Regierungsdirektor-working-in-the-Gestapo Pauli Winter. I don't want anything unpleasant to happen to my friends upstairs."

"They will simply be moved," said Pauli. "No one will be harmed."

She was fishing the lemon from her empty teacup, apparently giving it all her attention. "I said no."

He laid his thin gold pencil upon the open notebook. "Frau Somló—Frau Winter, that is—I came here to help."

She looked up at him again, and, in a small theatrical gesture, she touched the wedge of lemon to her mouth to taste its sourness. She smiled and said, "You came here because your father asked you to come."

"That is correct."

"So don't make yourself into an altruistic benefactor."

Pedantically he said, "I came here to help because my father asked me."

"Not at the price of my neighbors, Pauli Winter. Do you think I could sit here waiting for footsteps on the stairs? Knowing I sent them?"

"Not to hurt them."

"No, I said no. You just get out of here and leave me alone."

Pauli felt humiliated. His face went pale and he stood up to take his leave. "You misunderstand me," he said.

"Perhaps I do." She looked at him. So this was the one who had come back so changed by the war. From where in the family did he

379

get that wonderful blond hair? It made him look perpetually young. Still, he was Harry's boy. She could see Harry Winter in him—in the way he moved, the way he spoke, and he had Harry's touchiness—but it was a Harry Winter without that ruthless determination.

"I'll give you my office card. . . ." He got one from his waistcoat pocket. It had his rank and his Gestapo office on it. On the back of it, in his minute handwriting, he put "Frau Winter/Somló is under my protection. Contact with this office mandatory before action." Then he signed it and passed it to her.

She took the card without thanking him and put it into her handbag. "Is your mother well?" She didn't ring for the man: she went and got his hat and overcoat from the hall.

He took the coat and put it on. All the time he was waiting for her to change her mind. People often did.

"She is. Thank you." He took the dark roll-brim hat that Inge had bought for him because it made him "look important." When she'd opened the door he took Martha Somló's hand gently. "Goodbye, Frau Winter." From upstairs came the same vocalist singing "Thanks for the Memory." It was a gramophone record.

"Goodbye, young Pauli. Don't work too hard," she said.

It was another of her jokes, of course. She knew what he'd been sent to Vienna to do.

Once he'd gone, her face fell. She went back into the drawing room and poured herself another cup of tea. Boris came from the kitchen and held up his cup. She poured tea for him, too. "It's cold. I'll boil up more water," he offered.

"This will do," she said.

"So he came?"

"Yes, he came." She sighed and sank down on the chair. She wrapped the silk dressing gown across her knees; the tigers smiled contemptuously.

"You shouldn't have got angry, Mother. It never does any good."

"I know."

"He wanted to help."

"How can I be sure?"

"Father asked him to come." He sat down beside her, wanting to comfort her but not being sure how to go about it.

"Don't work too hard, Pauli Winter."

"I should have told him who you were," she said.

"Perhaps it's better he doesn't know."

She put an arm around him and kissed him on the ear. "Wonderful Boris. You never complain about your stupid old mother."

He smiled and drank his tea.

"Harry should have told him, and told Peter, too. Sometimes I wonder how Harry has kept you a secret for so long."

1939

"Moscow?" said Pauli.

"Well, I said we'd do it and we have," said Fritz Esser rubbing his big hands together in glee. Today he was wearing another of his seemingly endless supply of new, beautifully tailored suits, but his hair was thinning so that he was almost bald at the front.

Pauli Winter faced him across the huge desk in the Ministry of the Interior and poured out two glasses of schnapps. He seldom drank nowadays, but this was a celebration. "To the next Minister of the Interior," toasted Pauli.

Fritz Esser held his drink high. The August sunshine caught the cut glass and made it sparkle. "To the next Minister of the Interior," he said, "as long as it's me."

Both men laughed and drank. It was a good big room in the Interior Ministry, a corner room in one of the best positions in the city. From one of these two big windows there was a view of the traffic along Unter den Linden, and through the other they could see Pariser Platz and the Brandenburg Gate. Since Hitler's fiftieth birthday in April, when the remarkable "East-West Boulevard" had been opened by a military parade that took four hours to pass through that gate, this had been the center of a new, vigorous Imperial Germany. But inside the Ministry it all looked as it must have looked for many generations, with paneled walls, rich carpets, and comfortable chairs. Only the formal sepia photograph of Adolf Hitler on the wall looked new.

"Moscow?" said Pauli.

"The minister won't last long," said Pauli, "and the Führer wants you in the job."

"That's what he said."

"Then the job is yours," said Pauli.

Esser looked round the room. "The Führer can't always be relied on to say exactly what he means," said Esser cautiously. "He likes to play off one against the other. I can't be sure he hasn't promised the job to someone else . . . to Heini or Reini, for instance."

"They have enough on their plates," said Pauli. He'd got used to Fritz Esser's calling people by their first names and knew that he meant SS-Reichsführer Heinrich Himmler and SS-Gruppenführer Reinhard Heydrich respectively. Sometimes Fritz Esser wanted everything formal: everyone addressed by rank and title. Some days, when visitors were present, Pauli was addressed as Dr. Winter or just as Winter. On other days it was exactly the reverse, and Fritz would even refer to the Führer as Dolfo. "And now that we're working together at last, we'll show what we can do around here," said Pauli.

"You'll be back and forth to Prinz-Albrecht-Strasse, I'm afraid," said Esser. "They wanted you officially reassigned to Heydrich's SD and given an office there in Wilhelmstrasse, but I said you'd prefer to remain as you were."

"I've been through all that with them," said Pauli. "The SD is still a party organization. Heydrich still depends on party funds. I wouldn't like to have my future so unsure. I'll stay with the Gestapo and get my state pension and medical insurance."

"Yes," said Esser.

"I'm nearly forty, I have to be practical," said Pauli. And then, to change the subject, he said, "How did the meeting go?"

"Shall I tell you something that always amazes me?" said Esser, pouring another drink, and continued without waiting for a reaction. "It's the way everyone I meet has some secret desire to be a member of the army's General Staff."

"Do they?" said Pauli. Who, in his secret dreams, had that very notion.

"Everyone bows and scrapes to the generals: it makes me sick."

"Not the SS-Reichsführer?" said Pauli. Esser had just come from a meeting with Himmler.

"He's just as bad. They all treat the soldiers like little tin gods. And Heini's latest obsession is to have his own soldier boys."

"He's got them already."

"He wants a whole bloody army corps of his own. Then he says they'll have to make him a member of the General Staff. Why the hell do you want to be a member of the bloody General Staff, I asked him." Esser pulled a mournful face and imitated Himmler's high voice: "You wouldn't understand, Esser: you're not an army man." Esser laughed. "Silly old goat! I felt like saying he'd never been an army man, either, except for a few weeks of cadet school at the end of the war."

"He's given them field-gray uniforms; the army is furious," said Pauli.

" 'Waffen SS,' he says he'll call them. But that's as far as it will get: a name. The army have already made sure that that stupid idea will come to nothing."

"Have they?"

"Well, Heini can't draft men, can he? Conscription has completely stifled any idea of an SS army. As Heini himself says, just as he gets his kids indoctrinated and trained, the army grabs them, and they're lost to him."

"They can join the SS when they come out of the army," said Pauli.

Fritz Esser pulled a face at him. "*When* they get out of the army? *If* they get out of the army. Heini doesn't want the army's leftovers; he wants a proper army of his own. He's quite crazy. You know how he gets these crackpot ideas, and then he can't think of anything else."

"It shouldn't be difficult to get round the problem," said Pauli.

"How?" Fritz Esser sniffed. "The army's legal department keep screaming that they have the sole right to conscript men. And Heini's been all through it with his best lawyers looking for loopholes."

"Best lawyers?" said Pauli. "Those shysters in the SS legal department?"

"But the army have the sole right to draft men," said Esser in that dogged way in which people say things they desperately hope will be contradicted.

"Yes," said Pauli. "The army have the right to call fit men of military age into the army, but some men are exempt."

"Moscow?" said Pauli.

"Only the unfit," said Esser. "He's been all through that."

"No, not only the unfit," insisted Pauli. "Policemen are exempt."

"You can't run a country without a police force," said Esser.

Pauli smiled. "You're right, but Himmler is the head of all German police forces. He could draft his policemen into this army he wants to set up, and then recruit more policemen to replace them."

Fritz looked at him with a set expression on his face. "Would that be legal?"

"More or less," said Pauli, his mind working on the possibilities. "And he could do the same thing with his concentration-camp guards. They sign up for twelve years, don't they? He could make his five SS-Totenkopf regiments into the cadre, and form a division round that. Then he could recruit more guards for the camps."

"That would give him a large Totenkopf battalion plus a Polizeidivision?" said Esser. "He'd almost have the SS corps he's talking about." He was still doubtful. "You say it's legal to do that?"

"Yes," said Pauli.

"Heini will kiss you if you're right," said Esser.

"Then tell him it's your idea," said Pauli.

"It would give him almost two divisions."

"Now that Czechoslovakia is no more, he could recruit in the new Reichsprotektorat and perhaps in the Slovak Republic, too. With the *Volksdeutsche* living there as well, he'd certainly get enough for two divisions."

"*Volksdeutsche.* That would be legal, wouldn't it?" Esser touched the top of his head, where his few remaining strands of hair were carefully arranged.

"Yes, the army could hardly complain about that. The army is only permitted to recruit within the borders of Germany—they have no right to draft Germans who live in other countries."

A sly smile had come over Fritz's large moonlike face as he envisaged telling all this to the ambitious Himmler. "That's wonderful, Pauli."

"Is it? I'm not sure we should be encouraging the SS-Reichs-führer to encroach upon the army's preserves."

"Nonsense!" said Esser happily. "Let's give him an army to organize; he needs something to do. Could you get these ideas of yours typed out into a short report, and have an appendix giving the necessary legal references? And seal it up and put it into my private safe—I don't want some snooper reading it."

"If that's what you want, Fritz, I'll dictate it this afternoon."

"The end of the week will do. I'm going to the Obersalzberg for a meeting with the Führer and then, as soon as I return, I'm flying to Moscow with Ribbentrop and his gang."

"Moscow?" said Pauli.

Fritz Esser winked.

Pauli smiled and decided that it was one of Fritz's jokes, the sort of thing he said when he was going to disappear for a few days with a new girlfriend.

"If I'm not back for Inge's birthday, give her a big kiss and tell her that I won't forget." It had always been something of a mystery to Pauli that Inge and Fritz always got along well together. She really seemed to like him, despite his rough accent, coarse manners, and ribald jokes. I wish I'd seen you before Pauli here, he'd often say with a saucy wink, and give her a slap on the behind. "Tell her happy birthday."

Pauli sometimes forgot the date of his wife's birthday, so nowadays he arranged that the florist sent lots of flowers and a card every year on that date. Sometimes it proved inappropriate—for instance, the time when they went away to Italy and came back to a house filled with dead blooms, and another time when the flowers arrived while they were having a row.

But usually it worked well. This time he had arrived home to find carefully arranged flowers around the house and Inge in a particularly happy mood. They went to change to go out to dinner. Inge was sitting in front of the mirror in her petticoat, applying makeup. She'd let her hair grow out so it was loosely curled over her ears and the nape of her neck, a more feminine style. It did need more visits to the hairdresser, but they could afford such little luxuries.

Around the dressing-table mirror, birthday cards were arranged—birthday greetings from both sides of the family. The Winters always sent jewelry: this year a watch. Professor Wisliceny had sent a valuable antique vase filled with flowers. Pauli had paid the bill for her new dress, and Fritz had sent a kilo tin of Russian caviar. There were cards from everyone: even the Horners had remembered, and Peter and Lisl and Erich, too.

"Moscow?" said Pauli.

On the bed Inge had laid out her husband's formal evening dress, complete with starched dress shirt and black silk socks. Pauli was searching through the chest of drawers to find all the necessary accessories: tie, pearl shirt-studs, gold cuff links, and the pocket watch that he'd bought after Inge told him that only waiters wore wristwatches with their evening clothes.

Inge was in her underwear—silk, black, lacy, and expensive— sitting at her dressing table penciling her eyebrows. She moved like a cat; sometimes Pauli wondered if she contrived these feline manners. On a hanger by the door was Inge's new dress. Instead of the clinging bias-cut dresses she usually wore, she had this latest fashion: double-tier full skirt with ruched bodice, low straight neckline, and halter strap. Inge had spent two hours this afternoon trying on various jackets with it to see which she preferred. She was very happy. Pauli took advantage of her good will to ask a favor: "I'd like to invite my brother to dinner at the weekend, darling."

"Of course, Pauli, if that's what you want."

"It might be the last time we'll get the opportunity for some while. He's got his cabin booked: he's going to America."

"When?"

"Next week. Grandfather sent the tickets. First class: promenade deck. The *Bremen,* I think it is."

"Is it something about Lottie?" said Inge. It would have to be about Lottie. Peter had never adjusted to Lottie's going to prison. Inge stood up and smoothed the petticoat over her hips while looking at her reflection. She was forty-two and regretted that her prayers about having a baby had not been answered, but at least she had a good figure, better than her younger sister Lisl, who was getting plump. "America. Yes, well, he's pestered everyone in Germany about her." It was a cruel little jest, and she felt self-conscious as soon as she'd said it. But Inge had never really forgiven Peter for choosing Lottie in preference to her. Even though she'd got over her love for him, that feeling of injured pride and resentment remained.

Pauli said, "I talked with him about it last week. Grandfather will be eighty-nine this year. He still has all his faculties. He was a personal friend of Herbert Hoover. Peter is hoping that he can get the State Department to petition for Lottie's release, on condition that she returns to live in America." He struggled into his stiffly starched dress shirt and started pushing the buttons through the buttonholes. It wasn't easy.

"Would Peter live there?" Inge had never been able to cope with foreign languages, and the idea of living anywhere other than Germany was appalling to her.

"If Lottie was there, yes. I encouraged him. He stands a better chance of doing things at diplomatic-corps level. Getting someone out of prison through regular channels is impossible. The Ministry of Justice will never cooperate with us. I told Peter even the SS-Reichsführer can't get prisoners out of prison. I know—I've seen him try."

"Who did the Reichsführer want to release?" said Inge, always keen for the latest gossip.

Pauli had the shirt on and the cuff links done up. He began trying to get the stiff collar onto the back stud. The effort, with his arms twisted round his head, made him puff. He was terribly out of condition. He decided to take more exercise, starting next Monday. "Release? No one. I'm talking about when we've tried to get people out of prisons to send them to concentration camps. People the SS particularly dislike."

Inge nodded gravely before lifting the dress above her head and letting it slide down over her, careful not to disarrange hair or makeup. "Is he taking Helena?"

"Yes, I arranged the travel documents."

Inge's head emerged from the dress and she said, "She's only twelve: thirteen in September."

"Lottie's mother and everyone will want to see her. And the sea voyage will do her good. She's not been too well, lately. She's never really got over having her mother taken away."

"Poor child," said Inge. "How could Lottie have been so irresponsible? And the way Peter sits around moping all the time doesn't help anyone."

"Peter works hard," said Pauli.

"He's in that apartment playing the piano half the night. He doesn't eat properly, and his work is neglected. The other directors only keep him on the board because your papa founded the company."

Pauli corrected her. "They keep him on the board because Peter knows more about running those companies than all the others put together."

"He's lucky they didn't force him to resign when he married Lottie."

Pauli laughed; sometimes his wife got carried away. "They'd hardly do that, darling. That's years before Hitler came to power."

"Isn't he frightened there might be a war?" said Inge. "He'd be trapped in America."

"There'll be no war," said Pauli. "Peter knows that: everyone knows that."

"The Poles will never give in about the corridor," said Inge. "I know what the Poles are like."

"Leave it to the Führer," said Pauli. "The Austrians gave way, the Czechs gave way. We occupied Memel. Who will help the Poles if they fight us?"

"The British."

For the fourth time he tried to do up the bow tie, and again it was uneven. He tugged it undone again. "Don't be silly, Inge. How can the British do anything? Look at the map and see for yourself."

"And France. France could attack the Western Front, as they did last time. Look at the map for yourself," she replied rudely. She hated to be treated as if a woman's opinion was of no account.

"Come here, Inge, and I'll tell you a secret. A real secret this time." He went to the door and looked to make sure that the maid's room was unoccupied. It was her evening off, but you couldn't be too careful. "Fritz just flew back from Moscow. He was a special plenipotentiary from the Führer, sent to keep an eye on that fool Ribbentrop. A pact will be signed: Stalin has agreed to everything. Poland will be split down the middle, one-half for Russia and one-half for us."

"A pact with Stalin?" Inge almost dropped the earrings she was holding.

"You're surprised, aren't you? And think how surprised the French and the British will be. The Führer will announce it just before our troops move across the frontier. The Western powers will all be too terrified to do anything. They are worms! The Führer said that himself. 'Our opponents are little worms,' he told the generals. 'Close your hearts to pity. Proceed brutally.'"

"What did he mean?" said Inge.

"I don't know," said Pauli, "but he knows how to talk to the generals. Someone has to put some guts into them." He abandoned the bow tie and took the shoe horn to put his patent-leather shoes on. It was such a business dressing up, but Inge liked it.

"With Stalin? A pact?" said Inge. She simply couldn't come to terms with the idea. Everyone knew that the Russians were bestial subhumans and that Stalin was the devil incarnate.

"Fritz said they were received in Moscow with open arms. Not just the usual diplomatic exchanges—such celebrations that he could hardly believe it. Drink, caviar, wonderful food. Parties going on until the morning, and the Russians embracing our people like long-lost brothers. Stalin toasted the Führer's health. Fritz said the Russians were wonderful: it was just like being with old Nazi Party comrades."

"You didn't tell Peter all this?"

"Fritz only got back last night." He loosened the laces fully and slipped the shoes on.

"Did you ask Fritz about time off in September?"

"Our vacation on the Obersalzberg?" He stood up and stamped, first one foot, then the other.

"If we leave it too late, the Führer won't be there. It's so much more exciting when he's there."

She meant, of course, that she wanted another of those invitations to tea. Usually Bormann would arrange for the Winters to be included, but last year Bormann had taken Pauli aside and asked him about buying his house. He said the Führer wanted to acquire the whole hillside, which was now being referred to as the Führergebiet. The process had been going on since 1933. Bormann was ruthless: some of the houses had been obtained by threats, and others had been seized. Inge was appalled at the idea of losing their holiday home. She had decided to take the Führer aside and talk to him about it, and Pauli dreaded the thought of such a conversation. Inge sometimes went too far. And on the subject of their country house—and its proximity to the Führer's Berghof—Inge felt passionate. How would she ever be able to tell Lisl that they no longer had that wonderful status symbol?

"I can't see how I'll get my desk cleared, darling. The Führer has sent this damned note about euthanasia to Philip Bouhler—head of Chancellery—and it's landed on my desk."

"Why your desk, darling?" She lifted her skirt very high to adjust her garter belt. Pauli watched her. She saw him looking at her and smiled.

"Moscow?" said Pauli.

"Fritz was with Reichsführer Himmler. He offered to take it over. And when Fritz takes on some task, I do it."

"How tiresome." She stroked her silk stockings and straightened the seams.

"There's no one to help."

"It can't take the whole month, Pauli. If we could get away by Saturday, September 9 . . ." She let the new dress fall properly, and it looked fine. She twisted her head to see the back in the mirror.

Speaking to Inge's reflection, Pauli said, "Darling, be reasonable. The Führer's ordered that all the chronically insane and incurables in Germany must be put to death. And it's to be done by SS doctors. Can you imagine how much work that's going to make for me?"

"Not a whole month." She went to him and kissed him on the tip of his nose—or, rather, almost kissed him, so she didn't leave her lipstick mark. Then she effortlessly did up his bow tie.

Pauli was indignant. His wife didn't seem to understand how hard he worked. He reached for his jacket. "Just for a start: I'm going to have to draw up some sort of legal definition of what is incurable, and what is insane."

"Surely it should be obvious," said Inge petulantly.

"It's no good my telling the doctors that it should be obvious," said Pauli. He shook his cuffs out of his jacket and then straightened up to look at himself in the mirror. He could do with a new dinner suit: a bigger one. "They'll want me to put a definition in writing. How do I do that? I've had no medical training."

"I didn't think of that," said Inge.

"No, exactly," said Pauli, somewhat mollified. "People say these things without realizing what's involved at the administration end. Incurable—what's that mean? Someone might have a pain in the ass that's incurable: does that mean I get Fritz to sign an order for the man to die, just because some doctor says he can't cure it? And there is the task of setting up euthanasia centers. The first one will be at Schloss Hartheim, near Linz, but one won't be enough. It will be a lot of work finding suitable buildings and equipping them. Someone will have to do a lot of traveling. I just hope it won't be me. Then we'll have to explain it carefully to the SS doctors, so they don't start complaining. These damned doctors stick together. Suppose they all said they didn't want to do it?"

"Poor darling," said Inge, going to him to put an arm around his waist and hug him. "The doctors won't mind doing it if it's what the Führer wants." She could see he'd become agitated and decided to return to the subject of his annual leave after dinner. He would be in a better mood after dinner. Perhaps she'd wait till they were in bed.

Pauli grunted and studied himself in the mirror.

"So how long will Peter be gone?" she said, to change the subject.

"He'll have to go to California and see Lottie's mother. And Mama has made him promise to make the rounds of all the Rensselaer family. She feels guilty about not going back herself, I suppose. Papa insists that Peter take a good long rest, because he hasn't had a break for so long. I doubt if he'll be back much before Christmas."

"Do you think he'll really get her out of prison?"

"I didn't think so at first. But you know what Peter is like; he's been writing to Granddad and Uncle Glenn. Uncle Glenn has good contacts in the State Department. They both seemed quite hopeful, but they say they can't do anything without more details. They insist he go in person. They say that a personal approach to the right people in Washington would make a lot of difference."

"And Peter speaks good English."

"Oh, yes, no problem there, completely fluent. Much better than mine." He smiled as he remembered something. "Granddad used to dislike Peter. I remember Peter kicking him when we were tiny. But now the old man has decided that Peter is the one he likes. I'm the bad Nazi." He chuckled at the thought of it. "Bad Nazi. He actually said 'bad Nazi.'"

"Peter told you that?"

"Peter's mail is intercepted, Inge darling. All of it is opened. Anyone with a wife in prison for crimes against the state can't write letters to overseas addresses without our seeing what it's about."

"Did you arrange that?" She held up to herself first the earrings and then the gold necklace. One or the other, she decided, not both.

"No, a wretch named Steiner, an old cop, arranged that I saw the interceptions. He's the one who arrested Lottie. He does me a favor every now and again, but he makes sure that for every favor he does for me, I do two or three for him. I thought I'd got rid of him when I went into Fritz's new department, but he still comes and finds me."

She decided on the necklace. Gold always looked good: it was rich but discreetly so. "What sort of favors?" She looked at Pauli. He seemed to be ready, too. For once they'd arrive at the restaurant on time. They were going to Medvedj, her favorite Russian restaurant; it seemed an appropriate choice after hearing Pauli's amazing news.

"Nothing that takes me more than a moment. I shouldn't complain, I suppose. Signatures on protective-custody orders and that sort of thing. Usually things he couldn't get past his own superior. He waits an opportunity and then brings them up to me." He shrugged. "They settle old scores that way. People they don't like disappear."

"You should send him after Brand," said Inge flippantly. She twirled to let Pauli admire the lovely new dress he'd bought her.

"Yes," said Pauli. "I should send him after Brand."

1940

The sound stage.

"Folks around these parts said I was nuts . . ." said Mrs. Nita Danziger. She let the sentence tail away. She obviously wasn't nuts; there was no need to say so. She'd been relating the story of returning alone to California from Berlin after the Wall Street crash had impoverished her. "Simon's stockbroker advised me to do exactly the opposite. He said to sell my shares in the movie company and hold on to the house. My lawyers said the same thing. But I'd had enough of their advice by that time. From here on I play things my way, I told them, and . . ."

"And you did," said Glenn Rensselaer. Like so many people talking to Nita Danziger, he felt the need to finish her sentences for her. "But you're still living here," he said. He moved his shoulders to get some air on his body: his lightweight clothes were sticking to him. He'd never get used to this sort of weather. Her "ranch house" was on a hill but on windless days like this the thermometer soared.

She smiled and got up to close the flyscreen and wedge open the door so that there would be a movement of air. There were two large electric fans going, but her visitor was obviously uncomfortable. It was September, the first heavy rainstorms had come out of the Pacific Ocean and passed, leaving clear skies and hot sunshine. Nita Danziger seemed unaffected by the heat. She was dressed in a brown skirt and an English wool sweater with pearls. Her hair was perfectly arranged, as if she'd just come from the hairdresser. "Sure. I bought the old place back again. I paid nearly double for it, but it was worth it. This house holds a million memories for me. Memories like that . . ."

For a few minutes they didn't speak. They'd known each other a long time. Her late husband—Simon Danziger—had known Glenn's father for ages, but for a very long time there had been an insurmountable barrier between them. The Danzigers had set their minds on Lottie's marrying a Jewish boy. They blamed Glenn for encouraging the marriage with Peter Winter. Now Nita, although only a stepmother, and despite her affection for Peter, still felt bitter about the tragedy that had come of that marriage. Perhaps that's why she persisted in calling him "Mr."

"Your hunch was right," said Glenn.

"I've always been crazy about movies, Mr. Rensselaer. And those young fellows at the studio were making the kind of movies I like. My lawyer called them 'trashy' and maybe he was right, but folks have a right to see trashy movies if they like them. And I like them."

"So you sold the house and bought more movie shares."

"They were so cheap. One of the partners took a beating in the crash, the way so many of us did. He preferred to sell his holding to me. . . ."

"You did everything right, Mrs. Danziger."

"There were some tough decisions. Remember that trip on the *Graf Zeppelin*? That day we sat talking? I'm glad I didn't know what I was about to go through." She tried to pour coffee for him, but the pot was empty. "More coffee?"

"No thanks, Mrs. Danziger."

"I guess you didn't visit with me to hear all this old family history. You came to see Peter."

"It's good to see you again," said Glenn. He'd called on Mrs. Danziger before going to see Peter. There was something he wanted to find out.

"Like I told you on the phone, he's settled down real well now; but it hasn't been easy for him."

"It's a year since he left Berlin."

"No one could have figured on little Helena's being sick."

"Has the war made a difference to him?" asked Glenn.

"The war with England? Sure. It shook us all, didn't it? But now that France has surrendered they say it will soon be possible to get to Germany via Portugal."

"The British navy have a blockade," said Glenn.

"Peter went through all that with the German consul. He said it wasn't something Peter should try along with a sick little girl."

"I'd say that's good advice," said Glenn.

"The German consul said he should wait until the British surrender, too."

Glenn would not be drawn into that kind of speculation. He said, "I'm hoping that Peter will stay on here. Do you know his plans?"

"He's reconciled to staying here through Christmas. The doctor said Helena wouldn't be fit to travel before then."

"You see," said Glenn, having decided to enlist Mrs. Danziger's aid, "I'm hoping he'll stay longer than that. Lottie will be released from prison in 1942, and the American ambassador in Berlin has been told—unofficially—that she'll certainly be deported. Where will that leave Peter? He's a German citizen: I can't imagine the Nazis will let him go with her. They might even draft him into the navy; he still has a reserve commission, I guess."

"He worries about Lottie. He worries about her all the time."

"He must stay here in America," said Glenn. "Even if Peter goes back to Berlin, he won't be with Lottie."

"That's easy to say, Mr. Rensselaer. But it's only natural that Peter should want to be near her. He loves her to distraction. It's pitiful to see him sometimes. It's only work that's helped him through the last few months."

"I need to know if he expresses any opinion about the Nazis. Don't think I'm snooping on him. But if I'm to help him I need to know his state of mind. Does he feel he should be back in Germany fighting the British? That's what I need to know."

"He doesn't like Hitler and the Nazis. That's something I am sure about."

"Are you, Mrs. Danziger?"

"Yes, I am sure." He'd never heard her so resolute. She stood up to adjust the fan. "I'm a Jew, Mr. Rensselaer. I'll do anything you suggest that might prevent my little Helena from going back to Nazi Germany."

Glenn Rensselaer looked at his watch. "Peter is giving me a tour of the studio, so I mustn't be late."

"Peter Winter is a fine man, Mr. Rensselaer."

The sound stage.

"I know." He indicated the parcel he'd been carrying. "I brought a little gift for Helena. She probably has enough dolls already, but . . ."

"No little girls have enough dolls," said Nita Danziger. "I'll get her."

While Mrs. Danziger went to get Peter's daughter, Glenn looked around the room. It never changed. After buying the house for a second time, she'd restored it to exactly what it had been like before. There was a certain absurdity in such dedication, for the house had never been tastefully arranged or even very comfortable. It was a gloomy place, built for a silent-movie star back in the days when any Hollywood star living out here in Ventura County was considered an eccentric recluse. The house had a Western motif: leather bar-stools, like saddles, arranged down a long counter that was said to have come from an authentic cowboy bar in Deadwood City, or some such remote place that the movies had invested with a mytho-logical significance. On the walls were paintings depicting scenes from the Old West and half a dozen dusty mounted heads of long-horn steers. They glowered myopically across the room, as if resent-ing the prospect of being castrated and cut into steaks.

"You remember your uncle Glenn," Mrs. Danziger prompted.

Helena was almost fourteen years old, a shy little girl with Peter's pale-blue Rensselaer eyes and her mother's wavy jet-black hair. "Of course I do," said Helena confidently. She came to him and kissed him sedately.

"I brought you a doll. Do you still play with dolls?"

"Sometimes."

"I hear you've been sick."

"I'm going to school again now," she said. She had the careful, almost accentless voice of the language student, and her phrases seemed to have been adopted whole from the speech of the grown-ups around her.

"Well, that's great," said Glenn.

"Just three mornings a week," said Nita Danziger. "Next month maybe she'll start dancing class."

"Do you like dancing?" said Glenn.

"I want to be a dancer," said Helena.

Glenn smiled. Nita Danziger had been a dancer in her younger days. He suspected that the motivation came from her. He gave Helena the doll. It wasn't much of a present: a blank-faced ballerina

397

he'd bought hurriedly in a downtown department store. And it was obvious that she considered herself too old for such things.

"It's perfectly lovely," she said politely and cuddled the doll.

"Your English is wonderful," said Glenn.

"My accent is swell, but my grammar needs working on."

"She studies very hard at it," said Mrs. Danziger approvingly.

"Have you been to Europe lately?" Helena asked.

"Yup!"

"Did you see my mommy?"

"Maybe next time," said Glenn awkwardly.

"She's serving a sentence in prison," said Helena.

"That's a kind of misunderstanding," said Glenn.

"She's a victim of the Nazis," said Helena. "That's what I told the girls at school."

"What did they say?" said Glenn.

"They said she was a spy."

"What did you tell them?"

"I said yes, she was," said Helena, and in a sophisticated aside added, "It was better to say that. The girls at school thought that was exciting."

"Well, keep working on the English," said Glenn, looking at his watch again. "I have to go and see your father now."

"Thank you for the doll, Uncle Glenn. It was very thoughtful of you." She gave a stately bow.

"Sure," said Glenn.

To anyone who'd not seen a movie studio before it was all quite staggering. Right in the center of the San Fernando Valley, amid orange groves that seemed to reach as far as the San Gabriel Mountains, there were these three great buildings, each as high as a city block and almost as extensive. These were the sound stages, and each had cost half a million dollars. Behind them were almost a hundred acres of land: ponds, hills, a Western street, and the derelict rear half of a gigantic Spanish galleon complete with sails that were now shredded and stained. On the back lot, the filming that had been abandoned because of the rain was now resumed, and a posse of bandits galloped through the street there for the mute camera.

The big red lights on the wall went out, and two men emerged from the building upon which the words "Stage Two" had been painted in huge letters. Despite the arc-lit stage from which they'd come, the two men were blinking in the even brighter sunlight. Glenn Rensselaer had not changed much over the years, but a year in the United States had completely transformed his nephew Peter. He'd spent a couple of weeks with Cy Rensselaer and Dot, but it was when he got to California that he felt reborn. Forty-four years old, he looked at least ten years younger. His hair was short, trimmed close to the skull the way the local college boys liked it these days, with a short-sleeved, open-neck white shirt and bright-blue-and-white-striped trousers with white canvas shoes. Peter's face and arms were tanned, and he no longer seemed so self-conscious about his crippled hand.

"I certainly am glad you showed me around, Peter. I've never seen a movie being shot before."

"This will be the studio's first large-scale Technicolor musical," said Peter. "It's a big investment and we don't want too many people in the industry knowing exactly what we're doing." He looked at his uncle. He'd guessed that Glenn was bringing news about Lottie, but he didn't press him. Glenn had this strange need to get himself prepared for important conversations, and Peter knew that.

"You already talk like a movie executive," said Glenn.

"That's what I am," said Peter. "Thanks to my father-in-law. I wish I'd known poor Simon Danziger better. He must have had an amazing business brain."

"Really?" said Glenn.

"He sold these orange groves to the movie company, and kept a large piece of the equity. How many people saw what profits were going to come from movie-making? And that was back in the days of silent films. What foresight! Mrs. Danziger is a very rich woman now."

Glenn looked at his nephew and decided that there was nothing to be gained from telling him how his father-in-law's fiscal recklessness had led to despair and suicide, that his ownership of the stock in the movie company was due only to the buyer's lack of liquidity. "Yeah," said Glenn. "It worked out real well for her."

A small electric tractor went buzzing past them, towing a train containing racks filled with eighteenth-century costumes: crinolines, naval uniforms, and other gorgeous garments of doubtful historical accuracy. "Some of the studios are switching to war movies," said Peter, "but we're sticking to what they call 'escapism' here." He laughed at the strange word.

"So I see."

"When they asked me to become a vice-president, I knew it was only because of Mrs. Danziger's holdings," said Peter. "But since then I've saved them from some bad mistakes. They were going to sell the old studio in Culver City, but I persuaded them to lease it to a company that will build offices there. We did very well on the lease. I believe that real-estate values in the Los Angeles region will soar in value one day. And I went into the contract department and found that no one working there speaks any foreign language. No one! So I sorted out their European distribution contracts. Can you believe that when the war began they were talking about cutting their losses and withdrawing from the European market? In fact, of course, the war has meant more and more people going to the movies. Soldiers, factory workers, refugees, and evacuated people— the movies are their only entertainment. And the Rensselaer brothers have been wonderful. Having the support of the bank made me indispensable." Peter smiled.

"And now you're writing tunes."

"Who told you that?"

"Nita Danziger. She showed me the publicity with your name on it."

Peter smiled modestly. "They let me try my hand when they needed music urgently. One or two numbers have been popular."

They looked up at the sound of aircraft engines. Overhead, four brightly painted naval biplanes flew in a wobbly formation. "Trainers," said Glenn.

"That's why the sound stages were built," said Peter. "Planes didn't matter in the old days of silent movies."

"I'd say you've become an American," said Glenn.

Peter answered literally, as he always did. "I am going to take out papers. Helena is at school. She has private English lessons and she manages the language very well. It has taken her a long time to learn that English has so few rules. One of the Rensselaers has a son born the same year as Helena, and they seem to like each other. When Lottie comes out of Germany we'll live here. I haven't said that to anyone but you, Glenn. But I have made up my mind." It was fitting that he should confide his secret first to Glenn Rensselaer. During the time they'd spent in Washington they'd become very close. Peter had been touched to discover how hard and how long his uncle had worked trying to get Lottie released.

"But you're happy?"

"If Lottie was with me I'd be in paradise." He looked at Glenn. Now surely he would tell him what was happening about getting Lottie released.

"The reason I'm asking you, Peter, is because I'd like you to come to Washington."

"What is the latest news about Lottie?"

"This isn't about Lottie exactly. Except that it's about thousands of Lotties, I suppose."

"What do you mean?"

"You saw the newsreels of the German army's victory march through Paris. The news agencies say a German invasion fleet is massing along the Channel coast. There are people in Washington, plenty of people, who are convinced that the British are not going to be able to last much longer."

"I know."

"How do you feel about that, Peter?"

"Hitler will have to be stopped. He's a madman."

"Stopped or defeated?"

"What do you mean, Glenn?"

"We all want to see Hitler stopped, but now it looks like the only way to stop him is to defeat him. That means defeating Germany: shooting bullets, dropping bombs, sinking ships, and killing Germans. What I mean is, how far will you go in stopping him?"

"I have already given your question a great deal of thought. I want Hitler stopped. You tell me that the only way to stop him is to defeat Germany. I think you are right. My poor Fatherland will have to suffer defeat all over again. I cry for them."

"There are people in Washington who think that the U.S. will have to fight, too. Soon, perhaps." They moved well aside for a truck delivering fully grown trees for the next sequences of the Western being shot on the back lot.

"Against Germany?"

"Yes, against Germany. Our intelligence-collecting organization is more or less useless. We know nothing about Germany except what the embassy sends us, and that's not much. The President has now authorized the formation of a secret intelligence outfit. Even

Congress doesn't know about us. Our state of ignorance is such that only by employing people like yourself, who've recently come from Germany, can we be ready to train our youngsters."

"And you want me to join?" They'd arrived at Glenn's car, a big V-8 Cadillac with air conditioning and all the extras that only Cadillacs have.

"There's not much money in it. No uniforms, badges, or medals. We'd probably be able to get your citizenship through more quickly—although even that I can't promise—and I can offer you only the salary of a U.S. Army major. But we are a rather informal group of warriors. If you wanted to take the American bar exams, I could get you tuition and time off. I might be able to arrange for you to come back here and dabble in your movie-making every few months. And we'd give you travel expenses: airplane, not that damned train."

"You Americans are a strange people, Glenn."

"Yeah, so I've heard." He got in the car and brought down the electric window so they could talk. Now he would tell him about Lottie. This was the way Uncle Glenn always did things.

Peter leaned down to him. "And I am very German. The idea of being an officer in an army run in such a fashion that its officers are civilians when they prefer it, is more than I can comprehend."

"So what do you say?"

"I'll try," said Peter.

Glenn let in the clutch so that the car started to move. It was only then that Peter finally realized there was as yet no news of her. He felt physically sick with disappointment.

1941

"It was on the radio."

Lottie had fought the system. She'd not been insolent or disobedient: she'd fought the prison routine by not submitting to it. She went out of her way to be friendly and helpful to the other prisoners. She laughed and joked and kept smiling, the way her father had said you keep smiling in the face of rudeness or hostility. But she'd been in prison a long time now and she was getting tired. And today it was hot; damned hot. The sort of day to go sailing, swimming, or sunbathing on Berlin's wonderful lakes.

"You get used to it. That's the trouble," said the plump woman.

"No talking!" The loud voice of the prison guard echoed across the cobbled yard as the four prisoners walked smartly and quickly, as regulations prescribed, towards the kitchen. It was hot and humid; the women felt sticky in their clothes. Everything was tiring.

Once they were delivered to the warder in the kitchen and the door was locked behind them, discipline relaxed. The big kitchen was like nowhere else in the whole prison. Only here was there daylight in abundance; sunlight streamed down through the skylight and made all the spotlessly clean wooden tables and the steaming pots gleam and shine. But even with the skylights wide open, the air was hotter and wetter here than anywhere else in the whole prison.

"What do you mean?" said Lottie to the buxom woman who'd been reprimanded in the yard.

"Prison. You get to depend on it. You never have to think for yourself: just obey orders."

"But that's just what it's like outside," said Lottie.

The woman did not smile. She was an enthusiastic Nazi and did not hold against them her imprisonment for being an abortionist. The fact that her last patient had died from infection was bad luck. It was something to be blamed on fate or God or the careless young soldier—nothing to do with the police, the court, or the Nazis.

"Which of you two made the goulash yesterday?" This woman was a Female Police Auxiliary, a neurotic, fidgety individual who took great pride in her smart police-green uniform with the small side cap that she wore perched on her forehead.

"I did," said Lottie.

"Come with me." She was a stern-faced woman of about forty, but she was not unfriendly. She'd told Lottie the previous day that her husband was a tank gunner with a division stationed in occupied Poland, far away from the war against England, and she thanked God for that.

She took off her uniform jacket and arranged it on a hanger before putting on her white apron. Then she led Lottie into the bread store and started her weighing up the ingredients for 1,220 *Leberknödel.* "Half these girls in here can't read or write," she complained.

Lottie smiled and said nothing. The woman's eyes were reddened, as if she'd been crying.

"I can't trust them to weigh ingredients." She watched Lottie putting breadcrumbs into a box to weigh them on the scales. There would not be much liver in the "Bavarian liver dumplings"; they'd be bread and garlic with some chopped fat, the way they'd been since the war began in 1939.

"Is everything all right for you at home?" said Lottie in her fluent but imperfect German.

The woman corrected Lottie's grammar, in a flat, fast, automatic way, without seeming to notice she was doing so. "Yes, everything is in order," she added.

Lottie continued the weighing in silence. Then the woman looked round the storeroom furtively and said, "We've invaded Russia!"

"What?" said Lottie.

"They told us not to tell the prisoners." The woman picked up a measure and started shoveling the crumbs.

"Are you sure?" Lottie wondered if she'd misunderstood the German. She did sometimes.

"It was on the radio. Fanfares every few minutes. Dr. Goebbels read the Führer's proclamation over all stations this morning. It's the biggest offensive in the history of the world." The woman had been dying to tell someone; you could tell that by the way she said it.

"Russia!" said Lottie, trying to understand what it meant.

"At dawn this morning. My Karl will be in the thick of it. The tanks always are." Her fears were tinged with pride. The propaganda service had singled out the panzer divisions for special praise since the victories in France the previous year.

"I'm sure he'll be safe," said Lottie.

"We have four children," said the woman. There was sweat on her brow. "Four, seven, ten, and thirteen. I couldn't manage without Karl." She kept on shoveling the crumbs, working fast, as if trying to set Lottie a good example.

"You mustn't worry," said Lottie.

"Army Group Center," said the woman mechanically, "Second Armored Group. By Christmas they say they'll be in Moscow."

Lottie looked down and saw that the distraught woman had been tipping the breadcrumbs onto the floor.

"Yes, Heil Hitler, Colonel Weizsäcker."

It was December. The isolated little farm was half buried under deep drifts of snow, and yet still more snow came. Inside the dark farmhouse a small group of staff officers stood round a kitchen table, stamping their feet and slapping themselves to keep warm while they awaited the arrival of their divisional commander. It was daylight outside, but the windows had been boarded up in an attempt to keep out the cruel Russian winds. The talk was about the 258th Infantry Division, which had got a reconnaissance battalion as far as the Moscow suburb of Khimki.

"One of the soldiers went to the streetcar stop and picked up a ticket. He's been showing it to everyone." The signals captain spoke loudly because of the noise of the wind.

"There'll be plenty of streetcar tickets for everyone when we get there," growled Colonel Weizsäcker, who after the recent casualties had become the senior officer of this detached "battle group."

"They weren't there long," said a captain from the panzer regiment, showing a perverse pride in his weaponry. "The Russki tanks pushed them out right away." He touched his nose. It was frostbitten. He must find the doctor immediately the conference ended. He hoped he wouldn't lose it, the way some of the frostbitten soldiers had lost toes, fingers, and noses. There was something not suitably heroic about going home with a nose missing due to frostbite.

"This is Moscow," said Weizsäcker. "They'll fight harder for Moscow. We all know that."

They heard the sentry shuffle to attention in the snow outside, and then there was a flash of light as the door opened and the general appeared, like a demon king in a children's pantomime.

The officers came to attention and saluted. They were all a little afraid of General Alexander Horner. He was tall and slim, an intimidating figure with a tight-skinned, skull-like face, and a saber-scarred cheek. The sort of Prussian officer they used to see depicted in political cartoons back in the time when such cartoons were permitted.

The general had been off somewhere in his half-track vehicle. God knows where he went on these jaunts; he took no one with him, and asking his driver was useless. Young Winkel was the son of one of the general's first war comrades, and treated everything the general did as a military secret.

"Good morning, gentlemen. Have we received the situation reports yet?" He took off his helmet and fastidiously knocked snow from the shoulders of his greatcoat.

"The radio is kaputt, Herr General!" The frightened young boy who was crouched in the far corner looked up at him as if terrified of being blamed.

"Have you tried other crystals?" Horner had to shout: the wind was louder now, screaming like a thousand banshees, and there was the steady thump of the generator, too. The light was inadequate but there was enough to see the maps, the throbbing generator, and the cables linking it to the lights and radio. And enough light to see the splashes and stains along the wall where animals had been tethered, and the dirt floor that probably stank when it wasn't so cold. It was hard to believe that humans lived in such squalor, alongside their animals, but there was a rough wooden rack on the wall, bunks in which six Russian peasants had slept.

"I've tried most of them, Herr General."

Horner glanced down at the blank message pad. Only the date had been filled in there. December 6, 1941. Not much chance now of fulfilling that toast—Christmas Day in Moscow—that that fool Weizsäcker had proposed back in June, when the German armies moved forward. "Keep trying."

"Yes, Herr General."

General Alex Horner turned back to the other officers, who were standing round the table. They were all bundled up into every stitch of clothing they possessed. Some of them had also found, bought, or stolen civilian clothes—scarves, knitted gloves, and sweaters. What a sight they were, more like a rabble of refugees than German officers. Horner looked at the map and continued to stare at it for a long, long time. He closed his eyes. He was becoming hypnotized by the map, obsessed with it. He'd seen the same thing happen in the first war, commanders just staring at maps, frozen as a driver or pilot freezes at the controls, incapable of thinking a rational thought or giving a sensible command. He pushed the map aside angrily. Without proper reports from his headquarters, and contact with the front-line positions, the map was useless.

"Do you have dispatch riders who know the HQs, Colonel?"

"Yes, Herr General." Of course he did—he wasn't a complete blockhead.

"We'll pull back as far as the river."

"Everyone, Herr General?"

"No, not everyone. A rearguard will remain. One of your rifle regiments should be enough."

"Yes, Herr General." Colonel Weizsäcker was too inexperienced. He'd thought that they'd be marching into the Kremlin by now, the way—as a captain—Weizsäcker had led his company into Paris, smiling at the pretty girls and keeping an eye open for a suitable restaurant to eat in that evening. Well, this one wasn't like that.

Horner went to the window and found a narrow gap in the boards through which to squint. The artillery fire continued all the time, and the flickering light of it made the dark-gray sky lighten along the horizon. Yesterday the thermometer had gone down to thirty-two degrees below zero, but today was even colder. It was damned dark; he looked at his watch hardly able to believe that it was eleven o'clock in the morning. The whole landscape was gray with snow. It wasn't like the snow he'd known as a child in East Prussia, or like the snow he'd pushed down Pauli Winter's neck at Lichterfelde on the day when they went up a class and received their bayonets. This wasn't the sort of snow he'd galloped Pola through at Bernau near Berlin. This snow was gray: ask any of the thousands of German soldiers who were out there frozen to death under that stuff. Ask the pinched, blue-faced sentry standing here at the farm-house door with his feet wrapped up in huge bundles of straw in the hope that his toes wouldn't come off with his boots. Ask any of the shivering men who were still in their summer uniforms because winter uniforms were in short supply, or the luckier ones, nearer the supply depots, who were now discovering that the German-issue winter clothing was never intended for these arctic temperatures.

He came back to the table and tried to see the map with a fresh eye. Field Marshal Walther von Brauchitsch had suffered a heart attack and had requested that he be relieved. Well, it wasn't difficult to see why. The armies round Moscow were in a damned perilous position, and German soldiers were simply not trained or equipped for fighting, or even existing, in these conditions.

"Supply troops first, Herr General?"

"No," said Horner. He paused as the reciprocating engine of the generator missed a beat or two and the bulb went dull yellow and then orange and red before going out completely. For a moment it was dark, the interior lit only by slatted beams of light that came through the boarded window. Then the engine picked up and the light brightened. Horner said, "We must assume we'll have to fight our way through."

"Fight to our rear, Herr General?"

"Look for yourself," he said tonelessly. "No radio messages from the second panzer regiment or from the engineers. Then the rifle-regiment headquarters also goes silent. What do you make of it? Look for yourself, Colonel." It all made sense. He'd felt the front tightening over the last few days. All patrols and reconaissance units had been repulsed with unusual promptness: he should have guessed what was coming, and might have done so, except that 4th Army intelligence kept insisting that the Red Army had nothing left to fight with. Nothing!

"Damn these radios," said Colonel Weizsäcker. He was puzzled. Had the Russians used some secret weapon to render the radios useless, or was it this terrible weather?

"Don't you understand?" said Horner. "Look, man. Look!" He lifted his arm and slowly brought it down upon the map so that all the silent positions were covered. They were silent because all the units, including the headquarters troops, were on the move. The alternative explanation for their silence was too terrible to contemplate.

"My God!" said the colonel. The other officers said nothing. They were youngsters, except for a couple of old men from the Reserve. Perhaps they didn't fully understand what it meant. But Weizsäcker understood: he'd been in France in 1940. That's what Guderian had done to the French.

To eliminate any possibility of a misunderstanding, Horner said, "The Russians have launched an attack and sliced right through our front."

"In this weather? It's not possible."

"They're probably using sledges: sledge-borne infantry, sledge-mounted artillery, and ski troops reinforcing Cossack divisions." Weizsäcker made no response. "Making for the river," said Horner. He had no evidence to support this assertion, but he knew it was right.

"Jesus Christ! Begging the general's pardon."

"The Almighty is fully occupied right now," said Horner grimly. "We must save what we can, and try and re-form along the riverbank here." He shouldn't have used the word "try." He must be positive, assertive, and confident. "Re-form along here, fight and die holding the line."

Colonel Weizsäcker glanced at his general, surprised by this dramatic prose style. "The bridges are here . . . and here," said the colonel, pointing to another section of the river.

Horner nodded. "Yes, we'll send the Feldgendarmerie to the bridges." He paused. He had no military police. He was exhausted. He'd forgotten for a moment that he wasn't with von Kleindorf at Divisional Headquarters, he was with these idiots at the headquarters of his "battle group." On paper it comprised a rifle regiment, a panzer regiment plus engineers, some signals troops, and an artillery battalion. In fact it was a collection of military oddments suffering fatigue, shock, frostbite, frozen diesel oil, and cracked engines, and it was scattered over too large a front, with its radios giving frequent trouble. "Organize a company of infantry to block the bridges. No one will cross either bridge. No one, whatever his rank, his injuries, or his written or oral authority. No one. They will shoot anyone who comes within one hundred meters of the ridge this side of the riverbank. Get on to that immediately. Send someone reliable." He paused. "Make it two companies. Some bloody fools might be desperate enough to try the ice floes."

"I have just the right man, Herr General."

Horner turned back to the staff. "Infantry first, of course. If there are not enough half-track vehicles serviceable, the rest must go on foot. The tanks will keep to the roads, such as they are. Keep visual contact. Von Kleindorf will probably start pulling back, too, as soon as they realize what is happening. Tell the commanders that movement on the northeast might be our own people. Although in this damned weather God knows how close you have to get to see anything properly." He looked at his watch. "The infantry must start at 1300 hours." He looked at the colonel. "You're in command, Weizsäcker."

"And the general?" Colonel Weizsäcker wet his lips.

"I'll take my chance to the north," said Horner.

"As the general chooses," said Weizsäcker, "but surely that will lead you straight into the center of the Red advance." He was nervous, thought Horner. He didn't want to take the battle group back to the river line. He didn't want to take anyone anywhere. Was that because he had no confidence in Horner's plan, because he didn't believe Horner's diagnosis, or because he was shit-scared?

Horner looked at the battle-group commander trying to decide. Should he relieve him? It was a terrible thing to do to an officer. Weizsäcker's military career would end there and then. And which of the others would do better? He looked at the faces: eager young men with amazing reserves of energy and enthusiasm. But now they were bewildered. Not demoralized yet, but bewildered. None of them had ever faced this sort of war, or even dreamed what it might be like. Neither had Horner. No one had, except the Russians. "I don't think so, Colonel. If I was the Red commander I'd leave my center weak and put everything on the flank, to break right through to the river. He doesn't want to push our center back or try to capture Divisional HQ. By now von Kleindorf should have begun to pull back. And that means he'll bring Divisional HQ through the crossroads where we lost all those tank destroyers that would be so useful now. There is no other way for him to go."

"Except cross-country," said the colonel.

"I hope to God he doesn't try that with HQ transport," said Horner. "You'll hold to this side of the river, Colonel Weizsäcker. When I find Divisional HQ, their communications will enable me to re-form and reinforce you. Whether I succeed or not makes no difference to your task. Is that clear?" He looked at the colonel and then at the rest of them. "No man of this division will retire across that river, under the penalty of death."

"Heil Hitler!" said Weizsäcker nervously. He raised his arm in the Nazi-style salute, but no one responded.

Was the man mad? Horner gave one of his rare smiles. "Yes, Heil Hitler, Colonel Weizsäcker. And may God be with you."

"Just discussing strategy."

It was the enterprising Obergefreiter Winkel who found the place for General Horner's next Divisional Headquarters. Winkel had joined the army expecting to be able to use the expertise with horses that he'd learned in his father's riding stables. But, typically, the army had sent him to a panzer division, and he spent all his time driving General Horner's half-track command car.

The place he found was a very large country house. It was easy to visualize how magnificent it must have been in tsarist times, but it had been abandoned by the owners during the revolution, and since then had become progressively more derelict. Recently artillery fire had razed most of the main buildings. But Winkel had discovered the cellars: huge, rambling, and relatively dry, they provided somewhere for the whole staff to disappear. The only problem was disguising the telltale footmarks from the Red Army's reconnaissance aircraft that buzzed over whenever there was a break in the weather.

Miracle upon miracle, the engineers had demolished an underground wall and discovered a wine cellar. The false wall must have been erected at the rear end of the wine cellar back in 1917, to hide the finest vintages from the advancing Reds.

It was Christmas, and the abstemious General Horner had given orders that the wine be distributed to all units for consumption in small amounts. Not that large amounts made much difference in this sort of weather. A drunk had only to raise his head above ground level, and be exposed to the subarctic winds, to become stone sober.

"Happy Christmas, von Kleindorf."

"A Happy Christmas, Herr General." The two men were sitting in a long, narrow, cobwebbed cellar on two delicate little chairs that someone had found in the barn. Between them was a table upon which von Kleindorf had arranged a dozen of the most amazing vintage wines. Some of them had spoiled, but the sound ones were magnificent.

"I'm giving you the division: it is a good present." It was an odd way to transfer command, sitting in a cellar drinking wine. But von Kleindorf was the only one he revealed himself to, and, beyond sometimes using first names, he didn't unbend very much with von Kleindorf. This was one of the penalties of command.

"Indeed it is, Herr General." Although he looked much older, General Horner was only forty-two years old. If eventually he got a promotion to go with his corps command, he'd be one of the army's success stories.

"And Colonel Weizsäcker comes with it," Horner told von Kleindorf. "All in all, he did reasonably well when the attack started. But I'm glad we didn't have to leave him too long holding the river line. If men had started crossing the river, the whole division would have disintegrated. You realize that, von Kleindorf?"

"Yes, Herr General."

"And in any case, in our present state, you can ill afford a detached battle group."

"No, Herr General."

"First rifle regiment is overworked," said Horner. He rummaged through the array of bottles, studying the wonderful labels and the venerable vintages. Choosing one, he drew the cork and sampled it.

"Because they are fully motorized," said von Kleindorf. "It's inevitable."

"Don't wear them right down," said Horner. "You'll need them, and the combat engineers, more than ever now." He tasted the wine and looked at his second in command. He would, of course, prefer to take him to Corps HQ, but he must be given a chance at his first general command. Getting a division was the most coveted step in an officer's career.

"There is all the paper," von Kleindorf reminded him dutifully. "Some of it you perhaps would like to look at before you go." He'd brought it back from his visit to Army HQ. It was stacked in the gray-painted steel boxes to which the German army consigned its treasured paperwork. Special orders, supplementary orders, revisions to standing orders, intelligence summaries—all the wastepaper with which the rear echelons fought their war. Almost all of it had been written before the Red Army launched its momentous counterattack on December 6 and had become irrelevant except to the men who lived on paperwork.

"I will of course recommend that you continue to command the division, but it will not be in my gift." Horner put his booted feet up on the table. He did this with some difficulty, getting first one foot there, and then—with agonizing slowness, and awkwardness—the second.

"I will be content to work with whoever the army sends."

"I know that, von Kleindorf, and I appreciate your loyalty to me and to the division. What else did you hear at Corps HQ?" Horner asked. "Apart from von Bock's taking over the Fourth Army?"

"General Hoepner has been dismissed, stripped of his rank, and forbidden to wear an army uniform again."

"Hoepner got closer to Moscow than anyone did," said Horner. He tipped back on the little chair. Von Kleindorf thought he was going to overbalance, but he recovered.

"And Guderian has been cashiered."

"I can't believe it," said Horner. "This is the end of the army as we knew it, von Kleindorf. Eventually, we'll fight our way into Moscow and beat the Russians, because our soldiers never let us down. But the army will never be the same again—we have lost too much. And the Russians have got our measure. They know the terrain and they are prepared for the weather. We might sit here for weeks, even months, before we break into the city." He wiped his nose. He had a cold; he was surrounded by a desolation of snow and ice. His wife, Chrisi, kept writing to ask if he was safe. There was a patent medicine that he would dearly love to have right now—in Berlin he'd found it unfailingly effective against these runny noses—but could he seriously write and tell her he had a headcold?

"I have never congratulated you on getting the corps, Herr General."

"Save your congratulations until we see how long I last," said
Horner. He drew the cork from a famous Burgundy and tasted it.
It had gone sour or corked or something. He spat it on the floor and
selected another.

"You saved the division, Herr General."

Ah, this was better. He ran it round his mouth before swallowing
it. "We serve in an army that does not usually reward commanders
who withdraw from captured territory, no matter what is otherwise
gained."

"Intelligence have now revised their enemy-battle-order assess-
ment. They say that they are not sure how many Red Army divisions
were employed in the offensive of December 6. They have identified
eighteen divisions the Red Army used. I have the latest bulletins."

Horner smiled. "I saw them at close quarters back in the 1920s,
when we were teaching them how to drive tanks. They proved apt
pupils, eh, Kleindorf?"

"What were they like, Herr General?"

Horner swirled the Burgundy in his glass, just for the pleasure
of looking at it. "Moody," he said at last. "Either they are desolate
and melancholy and incapable of doing even the simplest thing
right, or they are jubilant and indomitable." Horner reached for
another bottle of wine. "So far we've only encountered a sad and
shocked Ivan, but a successful battle in front of Moscow could
transform the whole nation into a far more formidable enemy."
Horner sniffed at the wine. What was this fine old medley of half-
forgotten smells? A Médoc. His father used to let him open the
wines when he was small. Once he'd got up out of bed in the middle
of the night and went round the vacated dining room trying the
unfinished drinks. They found him in the morning, drunk and snoring. His father had been furious. Why did he care so much what his
father thought? He'd always known that the estate would go to his
elder brother. And yet . . . Did second children always spend their
lives looking for reassurance and approval? Was that why he'd
joined the army, and why Pauli Winter was working for those dreadful people in the Ministry of the Interior? "You weren't at Lichterfelde, von Kleindorf?"

"Alas, no, Herr General."

"It made me into a man."

"Indeed, Herr General."

"I went past the old barracks a couple of years ago. There are fellows in black uniforms using the place nowadays: 'Leibstandarte Adolf Hitler,' they call themselves."

"I heard the LAH were there," said von Kleindorf.

"Scoundrels," said Alex Horner.

Von Kleindorf noticed that his commander was getting progressively drunk. He'd never seen Horner drunk and was undecided what he should do about it. His general had to be on his way before dawn, to take up his new command back at Corps Headquarters. He wouldn't want to do that journey with a hangover. And yet von Kleindorf didn't feel that he could mention his concerns. "Yes, Herr General."

Horner went quiet and drank some more of the wine. "We're facing a new Russki commander; I feel it in my guts."

"The monitoring service heard Radio Moscow announce that Marshal Timoshenko has been replaced. A general named Zhukov has been named commander of their Central Front."

"Aha! So heads roll on both sides of the line, von Kleindorf. Mark that, my lad!"

"Yes, Herr General, I shall."

Horner belched but seemed unaware that his second in command might have noticed it. "The bridges, for instance. It's interesting, isn't it?" General Horner had been attacking the next bottle of wine with the corkscrew, but finally he gave up and passed bottle and corkscrew to von Kleindorf.

"In what way, Herr General?"

"They've not bombed those damned bridges, von Kleindorf."

"Some strafing attacks," said von Kleindorf, who'd narrowly missed being killed in one such attack.

"I mean serious attacks—bombing raids to destroy them."

"No, sir, that's true." He passed the open bottle back to his commander.

Horner poured the wine carefully. "Why? Tell me why?"

"I hadn't thought about it, General."

"Think about everything, old lad. Everything. Why haven't they tried to destroy those bridges? Because they want us to run away over them when they attack? No, they've enough strength to fight us, they don't have to chase us away. Because they hope to come through so fast that they will capture the bridges and not have to build their own? I don't think so. The Ivans are not opportunists: they work to plan. Why, then?"

"Do you have a theory, Herr General?"

"Suppose they attacked in a pincer movement: both pincers coming down the other side of the river?"

"That would be a very big pincer movement, General."

"I estimate the December 6 offensive must have used about one hundred divisions."

"One hundred divisions?" Von Kleindorf shifted in his seat. The general was not a man who made reckless estimations. But one hundred divisions was a gigantic force for the Russians suddenly to produce out of nowhere. Germany's momentous assault on Russia—"Barbarossa"—had used only 153 divisions.

"On a two-hundred-mile front. With air forces and artillery and everything Comrade Zhukov asked for. We do not, unfortunately, have a monopoly on encirclement tactics."

"Where would they get them?"

"From their eastern provinces. Divisions manning the frontiers with the Chinese and Japanese."

"That's quite a thought, Herr General."

"Enough for a big pincer movement, eh?"

"Indeed, General." Von Kleindorf looked at his chief. He didn't look drunk. If it wasn't for those occasional slurred words, he wouldn't have even guessed the general had been drinking.

"We are to blame. The army is at fault. General Marcks, our chief of planning, said we could conquer Russia in nine weeks . . . seventeen weeks at the most. I saw the report. The Soviets, it said, would not have time to deploy their reserves. The Führer believes us when we tell him such things." Horner belched.

"Indeed he does, Herr General."

Horner drank more wine, an old Burgundy this time, and handed the bottle to von Kleindorf. "Is there any news about who will become C in C when Brauchitsch goes?"

"Yes, the Führer," said von Kleindorf. He pretended to drink but only let the wine touch his lips. He'd decided that one of them must stay sober.

"C in C of the army, I mean."

"Yes, the Führer has assumed that command, too."

Horner could hardly believe it. "He's Head of State, Minister of War, and Supreme Commander of the Armed Forces. And now you say the man has made himself commander in chief of the army too?"

"Oh, and there was something else, General. The Americans

and the Japanese are fighting each other. On Sunday morning, Japanese naval aircraft flying off carriers attacked American naval bases in the Pacific. I haven't got any better details, but the reports sound accurate. All the news services have been carrying them."

"So the whole world is at war," said Horner gloomily.

"That's right. And on Thursday the Führer declared war on America, too."

"What?" said General Horner, spilling his drink down the bright-red lapels of his greatcoat.

"In a speech to the Reichstag."

"Declared war on the U.S.A.?"

"Yes, it's official."

"Ha, ha, ha!" said General Horner. He laughed so much that he spilled his drink again and very nearly fell off his chair. "Ha, ha, ha!" The tears came to his eyes as he laughed. "The British are bombing our cities, and our armies are stretched from Africa to Norway's North Cape, and we are stuck in the Russian snow facing a hundred fresh divisions on this front alone. And the little Austrian corporal has chosen this moment to declare war upon the greatest industrial power in the world. Ha, ha, ha! Ha, ha, ha!" He clutched his stomach and laughed until von Kleindorf joined in, too.

They made so much noise that Obergefreiter Winkel, Horner's driver, came down to see if there was something wrong.

"No, it's all right, Winkel," said General Horner. "The chief of staff and I were just discussing strategy."

417

1942

"I knew you'd wait."

The night was dark. It was February, and East Prussia was covered with its regular blanket of snow and ice. The German railway system, burdened by the ever-growing needs of the war against Russia, was showing signs of strain. Trains were crowded, dirty, and late.

The railway-station platform at Königshof was illuminated only by gas lamps and some of these were not working. Inge Winter rubbed condensation from the window, and cupped her face with her hands, to see into the darkness.

"Is this Königshof?" she asked the young Stuka pilot dozing in the seat opposite her. He jumped to his feet and opened the window to lean out. Cold air, smelly with soot from the locomotive, came into the compartment.

"Hey you!" shouted the officer. "Is this Königshof?"

"Königshof," called a woman railway official obligingly. And then, just in case any passengers from the Berlin train wished to alight at this rural town, she called more loudly: "Königshof! Königshof!"

Inge stood up and put on her fur coat while the young flier got her leather bag down from the rack and opened the door for her. He smiled and said goodbye reluctantly, for Inge in her mid-forties was a very attractive woman. She was slim, with a pale face and naturally wavy hair. But most of all he'd remember her for those deep, luminous gray eyes that seemed to be for him alone.

Inge was cheerful and self-sufficient, almost defiant of the world about her. It was this wonderful confidence that so many people, such as Pauli, saw and admired. That was what had made Pauli want to marry her, and that was what made casual acquaintances, such as the Stuka pilot, her willing slave.

By the time Inge had stepped down from the train, the handsome young pilot was forgotten. Her mind was on other things, not the least of which was the speech she'd be making to the local RADwJ—young women enlisted as an agricultural labor force and factory workers. This would be the biggest audience she'd ever addressed.

She began to pick her way between the heaps of snow. It was dark; a thick layer of cloud obscured moon and stars. Whistles were blowing to announce the train's departure, and the signals were green. There were no porters, so she carried her own bag: she was used to it by now, it was the war.

"All blackout blinds down!"

Steam enveloped her, and the train jolted forward, its wheels screaming and groaning upon the icy metals.

She seemed to be the only passenger getting off at this remote place. The passengers were all soldiers, or civilians on official business like her. There were no spare seats nowadays on the express trains. People stared out the windows as the train clanked past, reluctant to close the blackout blinds. In another hour or so these men would be in Königsberg, East Prussia, and transferred to trains that would take them to the fighting front.

She pushed her way through the heavy sprung doors and then put her bag down for a moment. It was warmer inside the station building, and the air smelled of wartime cigarettes and unwashed human bodies. The concourse was crowded with people waiting for the local trains. Civilians of one sort or another, going back to their little towns and villages after a day's shopping. Farmers and agricultural workers from the huge estates that made up this part of Prussia. All of them were prosperous nowadays, benefiting from the boom that had come with Germany's assault upon the U.S.S.R. The German army needed food, fodder, and all kinds of horses, in ever-increasing amounts. Whenever possible they favored German suppliers. So here, in that part of North Germany closest to the fighting, the hotels and restaurants were kept full by army procurement officials being feted by those with something to sell.

Yet it was amazing how many of these civilians had contrived to wear a uniform: forestry and falconry officials, brownshirts, women auxiliaries, Hitler Youth, and part-time SS men in their forbidding black uniforms.

Inge looked around expectantly. "Under the clock," the message said, but there was no one there except two steely-eyed Feldgendarmerie sergeants, with their metal gorgets, and two men of the railway police, who were questioning two flashy young girls.

She looked at her watch. The train was late. She hated to be kept waiting, especially in public places like this. Already some of the soldiers sitting on a mountain of kit were appraising her and smiling invitingly. Any moment now those policemen would turn their attentions to her. Not because she might be a whore, a spy, or a fugitive, but just to pry and be officious. Military policemen were all bastards; Pauli had told her that and he knew.

It was five minutes before a pot-bellied brownshirt came huffing and puffing and apologizing abjectly.

"Frau Winter?"

She stared at him and said nothing. The man, a red-faced fellow too old for the army, picked up her case and, using his free arm, pushed a way through the crowd. She followed him.

In the station forecourt was a superb old Mercedes: shiny black paintwork, with an official pennant affixed to the front. The brownshirt opened the luggage compartment and put her case inside. Then he opened the door for her to get in.

"Did you have a good journey?" said the man sitting in the back seat.

"No. I bloody well did not," said Inge. "And you're late."

"I knew you'd wait," said the man. He grinned. He liked to annoy her.

"Go to hell," she said. No one who knew her as the self-confident girl who needed nothing and no one would have recognized her now.

The man laughed.

"You'll regret it, mark my words."

Lothar Koch knew that there was always an array of drinks in Fritz Esser's corner cupboard and that Pauli had a key to it. Lothar would never have dared to drop in and ask the deputy minister for a drink, but recently, on his regular visits from Gestapo Headquarters, three blocks away, he'd call on Pauli to see if Esser was out and suggest that they have a schnapps. Pauli found it irritating sometimes, but he never said so. He wished Lothar would go. He looked out the window. In the street below, the linden trees were in full leaf, and the windows were open to let in the warm, sweet-smelling air.

Today the usually melancholy Lothar was excited and outgoing, wearing a new suit. He stood in the middle of Fritz Esser's large office, gesticulating and pulling appropriate faces. Lothar liked to go into Esser's office when it was unoccupied. He pretended to himself that he was the deputy minister. Lothar was like that. "So the Führer went out in the street to ask passers-by what they think of Hitler. He is disguised with a false beard and so on."

"Lothar, you are quite hopeless at telling jokes," said Pauli, whose mind was on the work that he should be catching up with.

It was no use: Lothar thought he was rather good at telling stories. "Listen," said Lothar. "The Führer goes up to the first fellow he sees, and says, 'What do you think of this chap Hitler?' The man grabs the Führer by the arm and takes him to the Tiergarten. He goes across the grass until they can be quite sure that there's no one in earshot. Then the fellow leans close to the Führer and whispers, 'For myself, I don't too much mind him!' " Lothar cackled loudly and slapped his thigh.

"I heard it before," said Pauli.

" 'I don't too much mind him!' " said Lothar, repeating the punch line and smiling enough to show his gold teeth.

"They arrested the comic at the Admiralspalast last week," said Pauli, who was drinking Apollinaris water.

"So I heard. What was he saying? Was it funny?" Lothar asked.

"He came on the stage and looked at the audience in silence for several minutes; then, when everyone was getting nervous, he'd say, 'Well, that's enough of the political discussions; now we'll tell the jokes.' "

"And for that they arrested him?" said Lothar. "That's rough."

"There was a group of party leaders there with their wives after dinner. There were complaints. Fritz thought we ought to do something."

"Did he go to a camp?"

"It would never have stood up in court," said Pauli.

"I suppose not. It's rough, though. And he wasn't even Jewish."
Lothar took his glass over to the cupboard, where there was a sink
and a glass rack. He rinsed it off and put it in the rack. He never had
a second drink. That was part of his training as a cop: one free drink
was a perquisite; two was corruption.

Suddenly, while Koch's back was turned, Pauli said, "By the way,
Lothar, is it true that Jews are being systematically killed in the
camps?" Lothar always seemed to know what was going on.

Lothar Koch looked at him for a long time before answering.
"Yes, it's true. At certain camps."

"Systematic killing?"

Again Lothar Koch paused. "It was a top-level decision. Heydrich chaired meetings at Wannsee in January. *Endlösung*—a final
solution to the Jewish problem—it's being kept very secret. How did
you hear?" Koch had become more sober now. He was back to
being his old mournful, wary self.

"I didn't. But I've had the lawyers from I. G. Farben up here.
They've been supplying one of their patent chemicals to the camps.
Now there's an argument about it."

"Lawyers?"

"Fritz had been handling it, but once Farben brought their lawyers into it he dumped it on me. You know what he's like."

"A legal opinion about chemicals?"

"It's a poison gas: a vermin exterminator called Zyklon-B. Now,
there is a very big order for it, but the camps want it supplied
without its 'indicator'—that's some kind of noxious smell that warns
humans of its presence in the air. Farben won't supply it until
they're sure that omitting the indicator won't endanger the company's rights to the patent. I've been in and out of the Patents Office
on Gitschiner Strasse so many times, and read so many specifica-
tions, that I found myself wondering what the hell it's all about. I
started wondering what the camps are doing with all that odorless
poison gas."

"Why not ask Fritz Esser?"

"I did. He laughed and told me to buy some shares in Degesch."

"Degesch?"

"That's the Farben subsidiary that manufactures the stuff."

Lothar Koch turned away and said, "Esser knows all about it."

"You'll regret it, mark my words."

"What do you know about it? Look at me, Lothar. What do you know about it?"

"Not much. Except that I heard that the wife of a German officer was pushed into one of the death-camp trains by mistake. When she got to the other end, the senior officer said she must go with the others. That's how secret it is."

"Could it be true? Good God, what would she have witnessed? Is there killing on such a scale?"

Lothar shrugged. "I hear stories like that, and I know what I'm told by my men who take prisoners to the camps. But it's better not to know too much, and my people don't see the extermination camps. They're too far away."

"Where?"

"Always outside the borders of the Reich," said Lothar. "Fritz Esser settled all that—you must have been in on the meetings. There was a man handling it for the insurance companies. I saw him in your office."

"The insurance companies were complaining about how many life-insurance policies they were paying out because of deaths in the camps."

"Exactly. And you told Fritz Esser that under the present law people emigrating from Germany lost all their civil rights. Fritz Esser told everyone how clever you were."

"I didn't know that had anything to do with killing prisoners. Fritz said that there were a lot of old, sick people in the camps. I thought he was talking about natural deaths."

"Well, now they make sure all these special extermination camps are outside the Reich. They transport them to Poland mostly. Then they die across the border and the insurance companies don't have to pay anyone anything."

"What bastards they are."

"The insurance companies?"

Pauli didn't answer the question. "Lothar, my sister-in-law is being released next month. What do you think will happen to her?"

"Next month? Let's see, she's serving her sentence here in Berlin, so that means the women's prison in Barnimstrasse. Probably she'll be picked up at the prison gates by one of our people with a protective-custody order. That's the usual procedure nowadays."

"And taken to a camp?"

"Where else?"

"Could you find out the day and time of release, and get the number of the protective-custody order from Registry in Prinz-Albrecht-Strasse?"

He offered Pauli one of his stinking little cheroots. Pauli took one. "Forget it, Pauli. It's too dangerous."

"It's very conspicuous for me to make inquiries over there, because she's a Winter, too. People notice I have the same name. And I'm not over there as much as I used to be. For you it's easy."

"She's an enemy alien, Pauli. Convicted of a crime against the state."

"She's Peter's wife."

"Forget it, Pauli. Listen to the advice of a friend. This is not like the old days, when we forged signatures and got extra overtime or shuffled paperwork to suit ourselves. It's different now, and it's all done on orders from the top, Pauli. The very top. If you get yourself into this and upset someone, you won't get out alive." He paused while the truth of that got into Pauli's head. "You haven't seen what happens at the other end of all this paperwork. It gets very rough. I'm serious."

Pauli seemed not to have heard his urgent warning. "Just type it on one of my daily sheets: prison, date, and time. Then delete the custody order on the register. If I go in there they'll wonder why, but you're in and out of Registry every day. Okay?"

"No, it's not okay."

"Please, Lothar."

Lothar Koch lit his cheroot and blew some smoke before responding to Pauli's plea. "You've got this nice office on Unter den Linden. You don't come over to Prinz-Albrecht-Strasse so much these days, Pauli. And when you do come, you go up to the third floor and smoke a nice cigar with one of the top brass and look out at the gardens and talk about the finer points of the law. Let me take you down to the basement sometime."

"What's in the basement?" said Pauli. He sank down into the soft leather chair that Fritz kept for visitors.

"You know what's in the basement as well as I do."

"I've never been in the basement."

"No, you make sure you keep your hands clean. You stay over here in the Interior Ministry, where the basement is full of archives and the only thing that happens to people in the basement is that they get their hands dusty. In Prinz-Albrecht-Strasse they have rooms in that basement where they torture prisoners when you, or people like you, are in a hurry for a statement. It's not pretty down there, Pauli. A lot of prisoners don't survive that sort of interrogation. I stay clear as much as I can, so I don't blame you for doing the same, but don't look me in the eye and say you don't know what goes on. And I'm not going to get a protective-custody order so that you can tear it into shreds and hope it all goes unnoticed when your sister-in-law Frau Winter isn't delivered to Oranienburg at the stated date."

"I'm sorry, Lothar. I shouldn't have asked."

Pauli's soft apology made Lothar Koch feel ashamed at letting his friend down. "I might be able to get the order and the delivery sheet, but I can't delete anything in Registry. Falsifying such a document in wartime is probably treason. People are being executed for that kind of thing, Pauli. Plenty of them." He smiled nervously. "Better that she gets into trouble in prison and gets her sentence extended. Tell her to hit a prison guard; it's common enough nowadays, when people guess that they'll be picked up at the gates and taken to a concentration camp. Hit a prison guard, that's the best thing for her to do."

"Get the order and the delivery sheet. What will it say—Frau Winter, Jew, non-German by race and nationality?"

"I don't know what the hell you're up to Pauli, and I don't want to know anything about it. When your Frau Winter doesn't arrive at the Oranienburg camp on time they will raise hell. Believe me, I know what they're like. You can't get away with releasing a prisoner."

"Thanks, Lothar."

"You'll regret it, mark my words."

"Couldn't Inge work in Berlin?"

Pauli loved his father and his mother, he loved them with all his heart, and yet he had never been able to convey this to them. Now that his father was not well, he visited them almost every day, but still he wasn't able to voice his innermost thought.

This Sunday afternoon in early June he'd taken his oldest friend, Alex Horner, there to tea. Horner was in the magnificent uniform that the German army has traditionally provided to its generals. His collar had the patches that only generals wear, and his trousers bore the coveted wide red stripe. But General Horner had paid a grim price for his rank, his authority, and his medals. Alex Horner's service on the Russian Front had aged him beyond his years.

Pauli sat beside his friend, and opposite them sat Harald Winter. Pauli's father had had his favorite armchair brought into the drawing room and, despite the bright sunshine that fell across the carpet on this wonderful June afternoon, he sat there swaddled in blankets. The chintz-covered wing armchair looked incongruous amid the jazzy chrome Bauhaus furniture, mirrors with shiny black-lacquered frames, and on the wall not paintings but old advertisement posters, one of them for the *Graf Zeppelin*'s service to South America.

Harald Winter was too stubborn to obey his doctor's orders and remain in bed. He was only seventy-two, he kept reminding the doctors, not an extreme old age. In these days of modern medicine, seventy-two was no more than advanced middle age.

"Your Field Marshal Göring made the greatest mistake of his life when he destroyed the airships in 1940," said Harald Winter, noticing his younger son looking at the zeppelin poster on the wall.

Pauli noted that Göring was his field marshal, a sure sign that the old man was feeling argumentative. Perhaps that was a good sign. Perhaps he was on the mend. "The Luftwaffe needed the aluminum alloy," said Pauli.

"Ha!" said his father. "My factories were supplying the aircraft manufacturers with more than they could use until the Air Ministry appointed all those tame Nazis to the boards."

"That was the reason given," said Pauli, who didn't care either way.

"Göring couldn't make the Zeppelin companies dance to his tune; that's the truth of it, and good for them! Göring's the worst possible man for that job. That fat clown is still living up in the clouds, flying his Fokker Triplane in 1918."

"You're right," said Pauli. His father hated Göring. This aversion had come from dealing with the incompetent bureaucrats in Göring's vast Air Ministry, which now filled a whole city block in Wilhelmstrasse—ten times the size of the other ministry buildings.

"Rouge and powder on his face, and painted fingernails."

"I know," said Pauli. He glanced at his friend Alex but didn't smile in case his father saw it.

"Disgusting!" said his father.

"It's better not to talk about it," said Pauli, who knew that people were in prison for saying less than that.

"Better for whom?"

"Better for you," said Pauli. "We're at war, Papa. Such talk can be misconstrued as treason."

His father said, "And a thousand RAF bombers attacked Cologne last Sunday. It's terrible, they say. Ask Göring about that!"

"Thirty-seven British planes were shot down," said Pauli, who'd had an internal SD memo saying the raid had caused "serious fear" among German civilians.

"Rouge and powder. It's disgusting, disgusting!" said his father again, like a petulant child who'd been told not to swear. "And this fat fool likes to be called the Iron Man." He gave another little laugh and repeated it: "Der Eiserne!"

Veronica Winter returned from the kitchen carrying a large silver tray upon which were cups and saucers, cakes and tea. "Let me take that, Mama," said Pauli, jumping to his feet. He was shocked to see his mother engaged in such domestic chores. "Where are the servants?"

Veronica didn't give Pauli the tray. No matter that he was now a middle-aged man—Veronica still thought of him as the awkward, clumsy child who had dropped and broken her precious china. She said, "The parlormaid's fiancé is home on leave from the Eastern Front. I had to give her the time off. And the young one is sick, and Cook is at the market lining up for things off-ration. I can't ask Hauser to work in the kitchen—it would be like telling him to take orders from Cook. Servants are so touchy. And it's not easy to get staff nowadays. Girls prefer to go into factories; I don't understand why. Thank you, Pauli dear. Put the flowers on the side table—it will make more room. That's better. Give Alex a cup and I'll pour."

"But, Mama, you mustn't do housework. I never let Inge fetch and carry."

"Lucky Inge," said Veronica, pouring tea. "It's very weak, I'm afraid. Do you know, I was having tea with Baronin Munte last week, and she had lemons. A relative had brought them from Greece or somewhere. I'd almost forgotten what a lemon tasted like. Do you get lemons in Russia, Alex?"

"No, Frau Winter, we don't."

"The tea we get on the ration is not real tea, it's herbal-leaf tea, and it doesn't taste of anything much without lemon. I've started putting milk in again, the way they do in England."

"You could have *Ostarbeiter* working in the house. There are lots of them now," said Pauli.

Veronica said, "Your father won't have Polish people in the house; he says they smell."

"It's nonsense," said Pauli. He looked at his father and said it again. "Nonsense!"

"I know it is, dear," said his mother, "but I can't go against your father's wishes." In fact, Veronica Winter had decided that she couldn't have a Polish girl in the house because it would make her uneasy. Now that the United States was fighting against Germany, the Poles were *de facto* allies. It wouldn't be right to have a Polish girl assigned there, working for little or no pay like a slave. Technically Veronica was German now, but she remained American enough to believe that labor must be hired for a negotiated wage. She changed the subject: "Is Inge back yet?"

"She'll be back on Sunday night," said Pauli.

"She's away a lot lately."

"She hates the traveling, but she insisted upon doing something to help with the war effort."

"I don't know exactly what she does," said Veronica. She went to the window and closed it, despite the heat. There was so much noise from the street nowadays: cars, trucks, horses, marching men. It was a pandemonium.

"It's a party job. She works for the central office of the League of German Girls and coordinates their work with other women's organizations."

"Wouldn't it be better if she stayed at home and looked after you, Pauli?" his mother asked.

"We all have to do something for the war, Mama, and we have no children. Inge wanted to do it."

"But the traveling . . . Silesia, the Rhineland . . . Couldn't Inge work in Berlin?"

It was impossible to explain such things to his parents. They remained relatively unaffected by the war, except for the hardships of rationing and a bomb now and again. And his mother was always delighted by a chance to criticize poor Inge. "Fritz explained all that, Mama. Though there was a job in Berlin available, it wouldn't have been suited to someone with an education like Inge's. I miss her when she's away, but it won't be forever."

Veronica turned to their visitor and said, "What about your little son, Alex? How old is he now?"

"Our Christian will be four years old on Saturday."

"Is it four years?" said Pauli. He knew that Alex was remembering the day he'd waited for him in the stables at Bernau. How could he ever have expected Alex to warn Fritsch? What a stupid idea it had been to try to do anything to stop it all from happening. Now he knew better. Now he kept out of trouble . . . or at least he tried to.

"How wonderful that you are on leave. Your wife is surely delighted. You must bring her along to see us before your leave is up. Did you specially arrange to come home for the little one's birthday, General Horner?" said Veronica rather archly.

"Don't be silly, Mama. I told you, Alex is here for the state funeral on Tuesday."

"The funeral of Heydrich, the SS leader. Of course."

"Alex is an official representative of the Wehrmacht," said Pauli proudly.

If Alex Horner imagined that the eccentricities of Harald Winter were those of a senile man, he was now to think differently. Winter leaned forward and said, "What happened to Heydrich, then?"

"He was shot, Herr Winter," said Alex, who felt no sense of loss at the death of the SS leader.

"I know that, Alex, I'm not in my dotage. Who shot him and why?"

"It's a bit early to be sure, Herr Winter, but the Abwehr say the assassins were Czechs, dropped by parachute."

"So the newspapers have got it right. From Russia?"

"No. Not from Russia. The Soviets do not have the right men or the right aircraft for such an operation."

"From England, then?"

"Yes, London. They think the Czechoslovak government in exile under Eduard Beneš was getting worried about Heydrich's popularity."

"I thought he went there to crush all resistance," said Harald Winter.

"At first he took the stick to them," said Pauli. "But after he'd rooted out the troublemakers, he reorganized the social-security system for Czech workers and peasants. Heydrich became remarkably popular. There is no terrorism against us in Bohemia and Moravia."

"There will be now," said Alex Horner dolefully. "There's bound to be a crackdown, and that's just what the British want."

"It's started already," said Pauli. "They've rounded up thousands of Czechs, and hundreds have been shot."

"How dreadful," said Veronica.

"It's the way war is," said Harald Winter. "Am I right, General Horner?"

"I'm afraid so, Herr Winter. We lose a lot of soldiers killed by the Russian partisans. In the rear areas there are special SS units that do nothing but fight the guerrillas. It's a messy, bloody, repugnant business, and not the sort of war the army wants, I assure you."

"When do you return to the Eastern Front, General Horner?" said Harald Winter.

"I am to be reassigned," he said.

"I do hope you stay in Berlin," said Veronica. "Children grow up so quickly."

"Mama had a letter from Peter," Pauli told his friend. "Did I tell you?"

"Yes, but is it possible?" said Alex. "He's in the U.S.A., isn't he?"

"There is a mail service to enemy countries through a mailbox in Lisbon," said Veronica. She put her teacup on the glass-topped table and produced the letter from her handbag, took it from the envelope, and unfolded it carefully. It was fragile now, for she'd read it over and over again, and kept it like a lucky piece. "It takes ages. I suppose everything has to be checked for invisible inks and codes and so on. But it was wonderful to hear from him. Can you read English, Alex?"

"I'm afraid not, Frau Winter."

"Then there is no point in showing you." She was grateful for an excuse to read the letter yet again. She spread it on her knees and bent over it. Peter's small, neat writing was unmistakable; across the page there was a yellow diagonal stripe of some chemical that would detect secret inks. "He says only that he is well and that little Helena is at school in California. He saw his grandfather, who is ninety-one years old; isn't that remarkable?"

"There you are," said Harald Winter. "People live longer nowadays. We eat better food and take care of ourselves."

Veronica paused long enough to be sure that her husband had finished and then went on about Peter. "He says he plays the piano a lot and has a job with a film company. It's all very general, of course. I suppose he was afraid the censor's office would intercept it and stop it from getting through if he said anything specific. He asks us to look after his wife, Lottie. She's in prison, you know." Veronica looked up.

"Yes, I know," said Alex Horner. She looked at him; he looked so much older than Pauli, his contemporary. From what she'd heard about Russia, nothing could be worse than fighting there, except perhaps sending other young fellows off to do so. What terrible stroke of fate had sent this poor man—and the rest of his generation—twice into the slaughteryards of world war?

"But the prison authorities haven't answered my letters, so I can't find out when she's to be released."

"Leave it with me, Mama," Pauli told her. "I told you to leave it with me."

"But if we don't know . . ."

"I'll see to it."

"Now, don't get yourself into trouble, Pauli," said Veronica.

"Don't fuss, Mama."

"Pauli is such a darling," Veronica told General Alex Horner.

"People need cheering up these days."

The big house off Kant Strasse was not the glittering showplace it had been when Frau Wisliceny's "salons" attracted the greatest artists, musicians, writers, and intellectuals of the city. With America's entry into the war, and the departure of the Latin American diplomats, too, Berlin's sparkling social life guttered and died. Even here in the heart of the capital the war had brought drab austerity.

Professor Wisliceny had died, but the Hennigs remained in the house. Inge had not pressed them to sell it, for such Berlin properties were fetching very poor prices nowadays. Berliners were dispersed across the world battlefronts. Some people were moving out of the city to avoid the air raids that they said would inevitably come to Berlin next winter, and those who nowadays crowded Berlin's streets didn't buy houses.

Even if Erich Hennig had still been earning his fat performance fees, it would have been difficult to keep up the interior. Ordinary items, such as paint, were in short supply, and the craftsmen who might have redone the beautiful ceilings, cleaned the carpets, or repaired the valuable chandeliers were all in the army or in the war factories.

Besides, Erich Hennig was not earning any performance fees at present. He had trouble with his arm. He couldn't lift it above his head, and the wrist sometimes pained him. The doctor was optimistic, advising rest, a set of exercises that took two hours, hot baths containing some foul-smelling crystals, and a noxious ointment that had to be rubbed into his arm muscles every night before bed.

"In six months—perhaps less—Erich will be fit and well again," said Lisl. "It's good for him to have a rest. It was going round the war factories that started his trouble. Sleeping in damp sheets— that's what I think it was."

"Do you still practice, Erich?" Pauli asked him. They were sitting round the scrubbed kitchen table after one of Lisl's *Eintopf* dinners. The big dining room next door was dark. Pauli wondered if he'd ever again see it the way it had been for Frau Wisliceny's formal dinner parties.

"Every day without fail," said Erich Hennig.

"And he's teaching our little Theo to play," said Lisl proudly. "Erich says he has real talent."

"That's wonderful," said Pauli. He liked the Hennigs' twelve-year-old son and had become a beloved uncle.

"Erich could give a recital, but the doctor says it would be bad for the arm."

"I'm not sure I could," said Erich, "unless it was of short pieces. I couldn't manage a long work."

"Erich was in Warsaw," said Lisl proudly. "Six concerts for the soldiers. He met General Steflea, the Rumanian chief of staff."

"How wonderful," said Pauli, who had never heard of the fellow.

"And all the top field marshals and generals," added Lisl when she saw that her brother-in-law wasn't very impressed.

Pauli pushed his plate away. Clearing a space on the table before saying something important was a mannerism he'd had since childhood. "I hear you've converted the top floor into an apartment," he said.

"Now, wait a moment, Pauli," said Erich defensively. "It's just until I'm back at work again."

"It's not for the rent," said Lisl. "I needed someone living in, now that Erich has to have someone to look after him."

"I haven't come to ask you for a share of the rent money," said Pauli. "I want you to find a bed for someone. I'll pay you if you wish."

"It wouldn't be possible," said Erich hastily.

"Of course it would," said Pauli. He drank the water in his glass and reached for the jug to pour more.

"Won't you have a glass of wine?" said Erich. As he was pouring some for himself, his hand shook.

"I don't drink," said Pauli.

"I wish Erich wouldn't drink," said Lisl. "The doctor said it's not good for him."

"The doctor knows nothing," said Erich bitterly. "He doesn't even know what's wrong with me."

"The apartment is occupied," said Lisl. She looked at Erich, and then Erich looked away and drank his wine.

"They'll have to move out," said Pauli. He was determined to have the matter settled the way he wanted it, and his tone of voice revealed that determination.

"They can't move out," said Lisl. "They are refugees—they have no proper papers and nowhere to go."

"*Ostarbeiter?*" said Pauli.

"Dr. Volkmann and the Frau Doktor are living up there," said Lisl, blurting it out defiantly. And yet Pauli didn't miss the fear in her voice. He was the Gestapo man to them, and to many other people, too. People were frightened of him. No matter how he tried to reassure them, it was no good.

"Volkmann? The dentist?"

It was Lisl who spoke. Her husband kept a discreet silence. Erich had never been noted for his heroism. After the zeppelin crash, Erich Hennig had run for his life. He'd run nearly two kilometers before falling into a ditch and breaking his ankle. But Lisl had mettle enough for both of them. Defiantly she said, "They had nowhere to go. Men went to arrest them, but they weren't at home. The girl who worked for them ran to his surgery to warn him and they never went home again."

"I didn't know about that," said Pauli. "I started going to another dentist a long time ago. I lost touch."

"If we put them out on the street they'll be picked up. Is that what you want?" Lisl asked.

"Whatever made you take the Volkmanns in?" Pauli asked, still trying to get used to the idea.

"He was always so kind and patient with Papa," said Lisl. "I couldn't say no to them."

What an amazing reason for putting yourself in jeopardy, thought Pauli, but he wasn't surprised. Most such reckless courses were started upon for small personal reasons rather than for moral or political ones. His time with the Gestapo had demonstrated that over and over again. "Do they never go out?" said Pauli.

"Dr. Volkmann goes to work at the Jewish cemetery at Weissensee," said Erich. "He says he's safe there. Is that true, Pauli?"

"Yes, he's safe. They certainly won't allow Aryans to dig graves for Jews, so as long as there are Jews to be buried they'll let the Jewish cemetery-workers and undertakers continue in safety."

"Frau Volkmann helps me in the house," said Lisl.

"Working in the house? Cooking and washing, Frau Volkmann?" said Pauli. She'd been so delicate and ladylike.

"Things change," said Erich, having decided that Pauli was not going to report them for harboring the Volkmanns. He didn't look at them. He was getting very drunk.

"They'll have to make room for another person," said Pauli. "Lottie is coming out of prison. She'll have to be hidden."

"Lottie is coming out?" It was Lisl's turn to be surprised.

Pauli nodded. "I have to find somewhere she can hide. I didn't know about the Volkmanns, but perhaps that makes it easier for everyone."

Erich was still staring at nothing in particular and sipping his wine. Eventually Lisl said, "And Peter is still in America?"

"Yes, Mama had a letter. It was posted months ago, but it got through. She was very excited."

"Poor Peter," said Lisl. "I suppose he worries about Lottie."

"She'll be all right if you let her stay with the Volkmanns."

"They haven't got much room up there, Pauli."

"People need cheering up these days."

"They'll have to manage," said Pauli. "It's better than being in a camp, isn't it?"

"What about rations?" said Lisl. "It's difficult enough with the Volkmanns."

"I'll see what I can do about that. I know someone who works in the department that deals with rationing. We might get some emergency cards, like they give to air-raid evacuees. It would help out."

"And I'll need some extra blankets," said Lisl. "It's all right for the time being, while the weather is warm, but it gets cold at the top of the house in winter, and we can't keep the heating on all the time."

"We have lots of blankets," said Pauli. "And sheets and things, too. I'll talk to Inge when she gets back."

"You're going to tell Inge, then?" said Lisl.

"Of course I am. Why not?"

"We never told her about the Volkmanns," said Lisl. "She's my own sister, but she can be unpredictable about this sort of thing."

"What sort of thing?" said Pauli.

"The regime," answered Lisl without hesitation. "Inge won't hear a word said against the regime; you must know that, Pauli. I told her a joke once, a silly joke about the Führer. . . . She flared up and gave me a lecture about the war effort. For a moment I thought she was going down to the People's Court to report me!" Lisl laughed. It was a joke, of course: she didn't really think her sister would report her to the notorious Volksgericht.

"I'll talk to Inge when she gets back," said Pauli, although in the back of his mind was the notion that it might be better not to talk to her.

"What I'd really like to do," said Lisl, leaning forward as if to demonstrate her earnestness, "is to start a tea room."

"Not again," said Erich, without turning to look at them.

"Tea room?" said Pauli.

"It would be perfect. We're only a step away from Kant Strasse and not far from Ku-damm. It wouldn't cost much to make it look really grand."

"A tea room?" said Pauli again. "Here?"

"Downstairs."

His back still turned to them, Erich said, "Not being far from

435

Ku-damm won't help. People don't stroll past here the way they stroll on Ku-damm."

Pauli realized that his presence was providing them with an excuse to argue through him. It was a device that married couples sometimes resorted to; he remembered doing the same sort of thing himself at times.

"They would come if it was a nice place. There are so many people walking about aimlessly—soldiers and their girls, war workers on vacation, and foreigners. A tea room wouldn't be much work: afternoons and early evenings. And I'd use the two downstairs rooms that we never go into now. I'd enjoy doing it, Pauli, and it might bring in some money."

Erich turned round to face them again. He'd finished the wine in his glass and now he poured himself more. It was French wine, Pauli noticed. The Hennigs might have been short of money, but they lived well nevertheless. "What will people say when it gets round that Erich Hennig the concert pianist is running a tea room?" he said.

"Be reasonable, Erich darling," Lisl said. "You won't let me take a job, and a little extra money would solve all our problems."

"You'd need a license," said Erich. He was bent very low over the table, so that he only had to lift the glass a tiny way to his lips.

"Leave all that to me," she said. "Will you let me try, Erich?"

He pulled a face. "The rooms downstairs are in a terrible mess."

"The Volkmanns would help me. Dr. Volkmann is good at decorating, and Lily will help me clear it all up."

Erich Hennig was softening. "You mustn't put the best furniture in there. Certainly not those valuable dining-room chairs."

"Do you think I'm stupid, Erich darling? Of course I won't put the dining-room chairs in there—they were Mother's dearest possession. I can rent or borrow what I need. Or there are places where they sell furniture from places damaged in the air raids. Some of it is very good."

"Where will you put that old upright piano?"

"I thought of leaving it there, Erich. If things went well, I might get a pianist, or even a trio, to play. People need cheering up these days."

"What do you think, Pauli?" Erich asked.

"It's worth a try," said Pauli. "I'll bring Fritz Esser along. If he started bringing his girlfriends here, you'd become famous."

"I don't want Fritz Esser and his girlfriends," said Lisl. "It's not going to be that sort of place." Though she smiled enough to make it a joke, there was an underlying sincerity in her voice. Pauli wondered what she meant, but he didn't ask.

"You're an old man now, Peter."

"You look the part, Peter," Glenn Rensselaer told him as they walked along Baker Street, London. Rensselaer, sixty-two years old, wore a well-cut English herringbone-weave three-piece suit, a brown felt hat, and brogues. There were crowds on the street, mostly in uniform of some kind or other: Women's Royal Naval Service officers with their schoolgirl-style brimmed hats, bearded Norwegians, Australian airmen in their special dark blue, Canadians with their green-tinted khaki, Polish officers in their spiky caps, and, looking in the shopwindows, pretty girls in fur coats, who always lingered where the soldiers passed.

"I feel like a fraud," said Peter Winter, who was dressed as a colonel of the U.S. Army. "And everyone treats me like a fraud. Or at least the Americans do." They stopped, waiting for a break in the traffic before they crossed the road.

"It's your accent," said Glenn. "If you spoke stumbling English with a heavy German accent you'd be immediately accepted. Army intelligence, as you well know, is filled with German emigrants. But you speak excellent English with a very British accent. That's darned difficult for a GI to reconcile with an American colonel's uniform."

"I'll have to take elocution lessons," said Peter. "And why don't you wear a uniform? Tell me that, Uncle Glenn." There was a break between a red double-decker bus and a transporter lumbering under the weight of a Matilda tank, and the two men dashed across the road, narrowly avoiding a woman dispatch rider on a powerful motorcycle.

"Cut out the 'Uncle,' will you, Peter. Uniform? Well, I learned my lesson about uniforms back in the old days. If we sent a lieutenant to a meeting, the British sent a captain, and so on and so on. Finally I decided to drop my honorary rank and revert to civilian. That way the British don't know how much authority I have, and I don't get brass hats breathing down my neck."

"I wish you'd told me," said Peter.

"You'll be all right, Colonel. You've got me to back you up: I've got no one to back me up."

"I thought you were the big boss."

"Yes, but I'm the boss of nothing. For the time being we are the poor relations here. We have to use RAF planes to drop our agents, and that means we have to line up, cap in hand, along with the Free French, the Poles, the Czechs, the Dutch, and all the governments in exile."

"Why don't we use American planes?" Peter asked.

"Hallelujah! Walking into that RAF group captain's office and telling that toffee-nosed SOB what he can do with his airplanes is a pleasure I'm much looking forward to. But the RAF are flying over Germany every night. They have all kinds of magic boxes, so they can find a map reference and put an agent down right where he must be. Our flyboys are trained to fly in daylight. And they fly in formation, which means only the formation leader has to know where he is—and even then he can use the maps to help him find his way. No, Peter, agents have to be dropped in the dark, and for the time being that puts us into the hands of the British, including that pretentious goldbrick we just talked with."

They came to a small, rather smart block of flats, its windows covered with the sticky net cloth that was supposed to prevent glass from flying when bombs exploded. They went up the short flight of steps—each bearing a strip of new white paint to help in the blacked-out streets—and pushed open the doors. From outside, the building looked like many of the other small blocks of expensive apartments in Saint Marylebone, London, but like most of the others this one had been taken over for official use. Inside the door were two armed U.S. military policemen in white webbing belts and white gaiters. One of them was sitting with his feet up on a chair listening to the radio playing "I Don't Want to Set the World on Fire." He jumped to his feet and saluted, then turned the radio down, looked at their identification cards, and got them to sign the book.

"How are you doing, Sergeant?" asked Glenn amiably.

"Not bad, Mr. Rensselaer," said the cop. "Not bad at all."

"We won't wait for the elevator," said Glenn. "It's only two floors up." As they started up the stairs, "I Don't Want to Set the World on Fire" got suddenly louder.

They passed through a room where three large metal Type H containers were being packed with guns, radios, and rations before being parachuted into occupied Europe. They walked down a narrow corridor to a door marked "G. Rensselaer. Operations Staff Only." Once inside Glenn's poky little office, they sat down. Peter looked out the window onto Seymour Place.

"Want a drink? Coffee? Tea?" Glenn asked.

"No thanks. It's exciting to be in London again. And to be here! It's odd to think that we're only round the corner from Grandfather's house," said Peter. His hair was no longer cut very short, but he was still tanned from the California sun. They'd flown him over the Atlantic. That was a measure of high importance in these days of priorities.

"Yes, this section of town has been chosen by most of the exiled governments," said Glenn. "I guess they want to stick close to the British Special Operations Executive in Baker Street."

"How much do the British know?" asked Peter.

"Officially they know nothing. The deal we made with them is the same as that made by the others. The Dutch and the French don't want to reveal anything about the men they ask the RAF to drop into Europe, and we have the same arrangement. But the British are not stupid. They know that we have no underground movement over there, the way the French and the Belgians and the Dutch do. So they must guess that we are parachuting in German Americans for our own purposes. Tomorrow you'll meet a man named Piper—Sir Alan now, they gave him a knighthood last year—he's one of the top British intelligence people. You met him once. I brought him to Travemünde back when your grandmother was still alive. It was the year you had the sailing accident that made your mother go gray."

"Mama, go gray?"

"Sure, you must have noticed that."

"No, I never did. Is that the man Mama fell in love with?"

"So you knew about that?"

"Not at the time. Pauli told me many years later. I can't clearly remember him, except that he was tall and spoke German with a funny accent."

"That's the guy. He fell for your mother. I would never have taken him there if I'd guessed what was going to happen."

"Did it affect Mama so much?"

439

"I don't know. I was thinking of Piper. You know, he still has a photo of your mother in a frame."

"After all this time?"

"It's together with other pictures of friends and acquaintances, but I know him well enough to know . . ."

"And you approve?"

"Don't be such a . . ."

"A stuffed shirt?"

"Right. Don't be a stuffed shirt, Peter. Boy Piper loved Veronica, and maybe it would have been better if she'd gone off with him."

"Is that what you told her?" There was a note of displeasure in Peter's voice.

"She's your mother, but she's my sister," said Glenn doggedly. "Maybe you should remember that. And Boy never married."

"And he's a friend of yours."

"He's a good guy. You'll see that. There are plenty of wrongos in this town, but when the British get it right, they get it really right."

"I'll look forward to meeting him," said Peter.

"Well, don't upset him. Just about everything we have right now, from thumbtacks to parachute training, is because of Boy Piper's say-so."

"I won't upset him."

To change the subject Glenn said, "How are your guys coming along?"

"One of them will never be good enough, but the best three are ready. I can't teach them anything much more. What are their chances, Glenn? Of getting back, I mean."

"I wouldn't start thinking like that, Peter. You can't play God. These guys are all volunteers. They want to do something for the war, and this is the job they're best suited to do. Some of them have lost relatives—all of them have stories to tell."

"They don't talk much."

"That's good, but we're going to have to tighten it up even more. The next batch will be known only as code names, and they'll be confined to quarters from the time they arrive, in case we get another rumpus like the guy who got drunk in the pub and started telling the barmaid his life story. We can't risk that—it's too danger-ous for the others. And by the end of the month the British have promised us better quarters. I want a place out in the sticks with a lot of space around it, somewhere we can build our own training course, complete with primary parachute training—just a tower and a rail to give them the idea. That would shorten the time at Manchester. The less time our guys spend with foreigners the better."

"I suppose so."

"Last month we had a guy beaten to hamburger by a couple of Poles. They figured he was a German, and that was enough for them to start taking him apart. What could the poor kid do? We'd told all our people they were for the high jump if they told anyone who they really were."

"I didn't hear about that."

"Damn right you didn't. One rumpus like that could wreck our whole program. Suppose a newspaper man got a whiff of it. This lousy town is filled with reporters hungry for stories."

"I wish I could go," said Peter.

"Are you crazy? You're an old man now, Peter. You'd never get through the physical, let alone the training. You leave this tough-guy stuff to the youngsters."

"One of my people is forty years old."

"Müller. Sure, but he's a special case. I can't train one of these kids to be a Bavarian chemist—it takes years to learn enough chemistry. So I have to take a chemist—Müller—and use him."

"Müller's German is Berlin German, and Müller . . ."

"And Müller is Jewish and looks Jewish. Yeah, I know. I've been through this a dozen times with people from Washington. He's not exactly a perfect choice but he might make out."

"I don't think he will. He's been away too long. His German is dated and he forgets things."

"Did Müller give any sign of not wanting to go?"

"None at all, he's very keen."

"Then he'll go."

"But, Glenn . . ."

"Look, Peter. Müller saw his parents killed. I don't want to go into it, because it's Müller's personal business, and it's against standing orders to reveal an agent's background. But this is Müller's war. He knows the risks and he still wants to go. That's great with me. I need him and I'm fixing for him to go as soon as the nights get long enough."

"Müller wants to go because he's been told that the office failed to find any other person with his qualifications."

"Don't lecture me, Peter; I've got a hundred Müllers on my hands. I can't start worrying about them. And you can't either."

"I'm just saying that if Müller is suitable, I'm suitable, too."

"Jesus, Peter, you're forty-six years old and you wear eyeglasses and you're out of shape. If we get a sudden strategic need to drop an agent with a degree in corporation law and a talent for boogie-woogie piano, I'll keep you in mind. Meanwhile, Colonel Winter, just keep to your assignment."

"Yes, sir," said Peter, but he was offended. He thought that his uncle was not giving proper attention to the fact that Lottie was in Berlin somewhere and that there was no news of her. In fact, Glenn Rensselaer worried about Lottie and Veronica as much as Peter did.

1943

"A happy and victorious 1943."

January 1, 1943. It was a celebration for Pauli's forty-third birthday. His parents were there, Alex Horner was there, and so was Fritz Esser. Inge had saved up enough ration coupons to make a wonderful cake, and Harald Winter had allowed them to have a couple of bottles of French champagne from the almost empty cellar. As Pauli said in his brief welcoming speech, had Peter been there it would have been as near perfect as anyone had the right to expect in these difficult times.

They held the party in the Winters' family home. This was the only practical way to arrange things if Pauli's seventy-two-year-old father was to be present. It was difficult for him to get around nowadays, and his elaborate wooden wheelchair wouldn't fit into the elevator at Pauli's apartment building.

Peter's enforced absence in America seemed to affect Harald Winter even more than it did Veronica. Pauli had tried to fill the place in his father's life that Peter had left empty, but it was no use. He said the things that Peter used to say and tried to talk intelligently about things that Peter used to take care of. But Pauli's efforts seemed only to irritate and annoy his father, and it was as if Pauli's presence seemed only to emphasize the absence of his favored son. From time to time Pauli and his father found again the wonderful warm relationship that both strove for. But each time this gold turned back to base metal and they were as distant as ever. But tonight Pauli had new hopes that his father would love him again as he used to love him, for there was nothing Pauli wanted more than the love and respect of Harald Winter.

Dinner was served in the smaller of the two dining rooms. It was a fine room, still decorated in the old Gründerzeit style. Four columns with elaborate tops were surmounted with carved wooden angels that supported, upon their outstretched wings, each corner of the ceiling. From it an amazing glass centerpiece hung down low over the polished table and reflected in its thousand cut facets the light of the candles that made the only illumination. The Bohemian crystal glasses, Irish linen napkins, Meissen tableware, and antique silver cutlery were Mama's very finest. And she hired extra staff so that the evening would be perfect. It was a birthday to remember. Just as well perhaps, for it was to be the last such formal dinner ever served in that room.

After dinner the ladies withdrew while the men remained to smoke and talk. "You've been traveling a lot lately, Alex," Fritz Esser said to General Horner. Since Horner's assignment to the Bendlerblock in June, Fritz had cultivated a friendship with him. Esser was a power in the highest echelons of the party, a valuable contact for an army general, and Horner knew what the army was thinking. General Horner had survived the Führer's displeasure over his corps's failure to occupy impossible objectives that had been assigned to them during one of Hitler's tantrums. But Horner had almost worked the miracles demanded of him, and because the army always found ways of looking after its own, the Knight's Cross now hung from Horner's collar, and the medal of the German Cross was fastened on his pocket. Regularly they lunched together at the best Berlin restaurants and guardedly exchanged points of view. Fritz Esser, a peasant's son, got a profound sense of pleasure at calling a general by his first name, and Horner enjoyed the outrageous things that Esser said about the party and the regime.

Esser puffed smoke. Always able to provide himself with the good things of life, from powerful cars to complaisant young women, Esser had brought the cigars this evening. A friend of his in the Foreign Ministry brought them from Vichy, France, whenever he went there for meetings with the Pétain government. Now that the German army had occupied the southern part of France, the supply would probably come to an end. The soldiers would get them, the way they always did. Esser decided to speak to Horner about it: he must have contacts in the occupation army.

Horner, who'd also got his cigar going, breathed out and nodded approval. A Havana—there was no mistaking the flavor of it. "Traveling too much for my taste," said Horner.

"Chasing Der Chef," said Esser, looking round the table at Harald Winter, who sat at the end of the table in his wheelchair. Winter was not permitted to smoke, and he sniffed the air enviously.

"The Führer moved everything to the Berghof in the middle of November," said Horner. "I had to go there. I was disappointed. I was expecting to go to the HQ in East Prussia. Wolfsschanze is not so far from my family estates. I was hoping to visit my brother, and see the house again."

"The Chief moved to the mountains. I told him not to do it," said Esser, "but that damned Dr. Morell has him in the palm of his hand. From one side of Germany to the other. What a mess! What a muddle. I was there. I saw it."

"Everything?" said Harald Winter. His voice was hard and rasping.

Fritz Esser turned to him. "The whole damned Führerhauptquartier packed up and went down there."

"That was just the beginning," said Horner. "A skeleton staff from the 'small Reich chancellery.' And the special train complete with personnel from the Wehrmachtsführungstab went, too. There was no room for them, of course, not even at Berchtesgaden, so the train was parked in a siding at Salzburg. I went down there for a conference chaired by Jodl. It took hours to find the people we needed to talk to."

"Were you with Der Chef on November 22?" Esser asked.

"When the news came that the Red Army pincers had joined at Kalach? No, that's what made him take the whole headquarters back to East Prussia. That was the absurdity of it—they were only down there for a few days."

"They say he was in one of his blackest moods," said Fritz Esser.

"He was, until Göring arrived and got him in a good humor again and persuaded him that the Luftwaffe was going to supply the Stalingrad pocket by air. The Führer cheered up then, cheered up enough to reject General Paulus's request that the Sixth Army should fight westwards and break out."

"Will the Luftwaffe be able to do it?" asked Harald Winter. "What do they need, five hundred tons a day?" Pauli looked at his father respectfully. The old man's brain was still as active as ever. Pauli smiled at him and Harry nodded.

"They could probably manage on three hundred," said Horner. "I saw the Operations Staff estimates. But the Luftwaffe won't be able to do that, even if the Sixth Army keep the airfields going. We're only flying at night, or with heavy cloud cover. As soon as the Russians see what we're trying to do, they'll bring in fighter planes from other fronts. I dread to think what might happen."

"But they won't be besieged for long, now that von Manstein has been given Army Group Don," said the always optimistic Pauli. He knew that Alex Horner adored the old general. "He'll fight his way through and lift the siege."

"And all living Germans have him in their hearts," said Horner. "But he can't work miracles. The Russians have encircled an army of two hundred and fifty thousand men, and they'll hold on tenaciously. I know these people. Forget what Dr. Goebbels's propaganda machine says about the Russian *Untermensch.* The Russian soldier is a peasant, but not unintelligent. And he is hard, very hard. Manstein's soldiers are finding a wall of steel as they try to rescue their Sixth Army comrades."

"And then poor Rommel arrived at Wolfsschanze," said Pauli. He was prompting them in behalf of his father. Pauli had heard it all before.

"Not so much 'poor Rommel,' " said Fritz Esser. "The man is an intriguer. He always was. Back before the war, I remember him when he was liaison officer with Hitler Youth. He was always trying to get the Führer's attention. I never liked the fellow."

"I wasn't there," said Horner, "but it obviously was not a good time to suggest that we evacuate North Africa. And Rommel was crazy to arrive unexpectedly with such a suggestion. Whatever the military requirements, a withdrawal of the Afrika Korps now would be a terrible blow to the nation's morale."

"Will it be better to withdraw from North Africa after a debacle at Stalingrad?" asked Fritz Esser provocatively.

"Let's see what happens," said Pauli.

"Shall I tell you what will happen?" said Harald Winter. The others had moved closer together, as men do when the ladies withdraw. But Harald Winter, trapped in his wheelchair, was at the far end of the table. The candles were guttering, and Winter's blood-less face was almost lost in the gloom. "The Russians will do every-thing they can to destroy Paulus and the Sixth Army by January 30. It will be Stalin's way of celebrating the Führer's tenth anniversary."

There was a silence round the table. Erich Hennig reached for the wine bottle and poured himself a big glassful. He'd contributed nothing to the conversation. As always lately, he sat brooding and silent and got more and more drunk. Everyone had heard of this year's preparations for the tenth anniversary of the seizure of power. Each year Hitler came to Berlin and made a speech at the Sportpalast. It was the most important date in the Nazi calendar, and this year was especially important, for it would mark a decade of Nazi rule.

Finally Fritz Esser broke the strained silence: "He won't speak."

"The Führer won't speak?" said Pauli.

"He must," said Horner. "It would be terrible if he failed to come to the Sportpalast. It would be delivering a moral victory to the enemy."

"It's decided," said Esser. "He's told Göring to speak instead. Goebbels will probably read a statement from the Führer over the radio."

"Something must be done," said Horner.

"Have you suddenly become a convert to the aims and ideals of the party?" Esser asked him mockingly.

"It's not a question of politics," said Horner. He thought for a moment before continuing: even in such private company an army general had to remain circumspect. "The army did not seek this war, nor did we encourage it. But the nation required us to fight. We are fighting with all our strength, and the cost is terrible. But we live in an age when the morale of the people is a part of the weaponry of war. If the Führer fails to deliver his annual speech at the Sport-palast it will be like losing an army corps."

Fritz Esser put his cigar in his mouth in order to clap his hands. "Well said, Herr General. The Propaganda Ministry lost a star turn when your father decided to make you a soldier."

Horner smiled dutifully. He'd grown used to Esser's sarcasm but he didn't enjoy being the butt of it. The fact was that he could never reconcile himself to the idea that an uneducated *Kerl* such as Esser could be a member of the Cabinet. But most of the Nazis were such simple peasants; even Waffen-SS generals he'd worked alongside on

447

the Eastern Front often turned out to be men without any proper schooling. Some of them had difficulty reading a map.

Fritz said, "You don't know the Führer, Alex. I've known him a long time. Goebbels likes to build him up as a superman and Himmler thinks the sun shines out of his ass, but really Der Chef is a simple man with wonderful gifts of intuition. But the Führer's intuition works best when things are going well. He is not a man well equipped to sail in bad weather."

"Well, who is?" said Pauli, who hated this sort of pessimistic conversation. If the Führer hated bad weather, Pauli knew the feeling well.

"Winston Churchill," croaked Harald Winter from the other end of the table.

"Yes," said Esser somewhat doubtfully. Erich Hennig closed his eyes. He had a nasty feeling that the conversation was turning near to treason. Men had felt the weight of the executioner's ax for talk no more "defeatist" than this.

"Churchill took over when things were at their worst for England," persisted Harald Winter. It was all right for Winter to speak treason: he was so old and sick that he had nothing much to lose.

"Yes, well, let's see what he'll be like when they start winning," said Esser. There was a deathly silence. No one knew whether it was Esser's idea of a joke or a foolish *faux pas.* No one laughed.

There was a light tap at the door. Hauser, a sprightly gray-haired fellow in his mid-sixties, came in and said, "The coffee is served, Herr Winter. And Frau Winter would like the Herr Doktor to cut the cake." He looked at Pauli.

"Good!" said Pauli's father. "Let's join the ladies." Pauli jumped to his feet and grabbed the handles of his father's wheelchair. "Let Hauser do it," the old man shouted. "Push me, Hauser, and mind the carpet. It got caught in the wheel yesterday." Pauli watched Hauser push the chair out of the room. It was Pauli, of course, who yesterday got the carpet's corner jammed into the brake and the wheel.

The ladies were waiting for them in the drawing room. This was Harald's favorite room. Since being confined to his chair, he spent a lot of time here. It was a light, modern room with a newly fitted white carpet with huge zigzag patterns that crossed the room from corner to corner. There was a big chromium-and-glass construction that held some small modern sculptures—a Rodin and an Epstein—

and the walls held big abstract paintings. It was everything the Nazi regime condemned as "degenerate," and rumor said that Harald Winter had bought them at bargain prices for that very reason, but there was no mistaking how much he adored his collection.

In the corner of the room was, as always at this time of year, a Christmas tree. And, in keeping with another old tradition of the Winter family, Pauli's birthday presents were placed under it.

It made a wonderfully happy scene. The women had all made special efforts to overcome the austerity of wartime. Veronica Winter had had a lovely old pink silk dress remade. Lisl Hennig wore a gown Erich had got when he entertained German troops in Paris. Inge looked radiant. She was wearing a low-cut gold satin dress she'd had since 1934—the dinner party that Fritz Esser had missed—but it still fitted her perfectly. Chrisi Horner still showed that engaging shyness that was unexpected in a "Frau General." And when the men arrived, even the rather doleful blonde girl Fritz had brought with him cheered up.

Pauli cut the cake with great ceremony. It was as superb as cakes could be in this time of rationing, when butter was seen only in tiny cubes, and cream and chocolate seldom glimpsed. And although the coffee served from the big silver pot was ersatz—malt with some kind of fig flavoring—it tasted almost as good as the real thing.

Now came the time to serve the French champagne while Pauli opened his presents. And if these offerings were not as grand as could be remembered on other birthdays, there was no sign of it in Pauli's reaction to the gifts.

His mother and father had given him a diamond tie pin, Alex Horner gave him a leather document-case, Esser a dozen bottles of old cognac, the Hennigs some records of Erich playing Schubert piano sonatas, and Inge a gold cigarette-case engraved with his name and the date.

Even today Pauli kept to soda water, but he relished another chance to make a speech. He loved to make little speeches and tell his jokes, and he had something prepared for this occasion. They laughed and applauded the things he said, for he said nothing alarming, surprising, or revealing. This was why people all liked Pauli: he did nothing disturbing, he liked things the way they were. He kissed his mother. She was such a wonderful woman; how odd it was to think that she was a foreigner. She would be sixty-eight this coming birthday, but she was still as beautiful as anyone in the

449

room, except—he hurriedly added—perhaps for Inge. There was laughter.

And how lucky he was to have his closest friends, and dearly beloved family, around him at a time when so many people, all round the world, were separated by circumstances of the war.

They drank to Pauli's health. And he replied with this toast: "I give you a happy and victorious 1943."

They drank to that.

But the evening was marred by the tiff that Inge and Pauli had after they'd got back home. They were walking up to their apartment on the fifth floor.

Inge insisted on walking up. Lately she'd complained of claustrophobia and could no longer endure the cramped elevator car. She nagged Pauli to walk, too: it might help reduce his weight.

It was while they were walking upstairs that Pauli said, "I wish you wouldn't act the fool with Fritz."

Loudly she said, "What do you mean?" She stopped on the fourth-floor landing and looked at him.

"Those silly jokes . . . winking and patting his behind when you kiss him good night."

Inge giggled. She'd had too much to drink. "Has your mother been complaining?"

Now that he'd stopped drinking, intoxicated people seemed intolerably silly and noisy. Patiently and quietly he said, "No, but the old people don't understand those jokes you make about Fritz. Telling him to change his underwear more often. . . ."

"It's only meant in fun, Pauli. Don't be such a prude."

"Well, Fritz doesn't like it. I can tell you that." He got the keys from his pocket and went marching up the final flight of stairs to the apartment. "It makes him look a fool, and no one enjoys that."

"For resettlement in the East."

The train lurched to a stop. Colonel Rudolf Freiherr von Kleindorf, who'd been asleep while the train had roared through innumerable stations and rattled over countless crossings, now came awake in his narrow bunk. He turned over, but it was too narrow, and the sides of the bunk trapped his arms. When he put an arm out and hung it over the high wooden side of the bunk, his blood supply was constricted and his hand started to go dead, so he had to move again. He looked at his watch. There was only the very dim red bulb in the ceiling, but eventually he made out the time: two-twenty-five in the morning. Ugh!

He'd been dreaming about Moscow again, about his brief time as a division commander. Suppose he hadn't pulled back? Suppose he'd given the order to fight to the last man, the way the Führer said every unit was to do? Well, in that case he wouldn't have been disciplined and demoted to be the adjutant of a rifle regiment until getting this regimental command. No, he would be dead, together with every last man of the division. Perhaps seven months as adjutant of a rifle regiment was a cheap price to pay for the lives of so many fine young men. General Horner thought so—he'd sent von Kleindorf a letter saying exactly that—but it didn't entirely make up for commanding a division. He'd give almost anything for that pleasure and privilege.

Colonel von Kleindorf, a prematurely aged man in his late thirties, tried to get back to sleep, but he was unable to do so, and the train still didn't move: it remained where it was except to judder and shake. Every time he dozed off, there was some mechanical noise of the sort trains made: the clanking of the coupling link chains or the sudden hiss of air in the brakes. After what seemed like hours but was really a little less than thirty minutes, he swung out of his uncomfortable sleeping space and put his feet on the floor. The floor was cold. This was an army train and its furnishings didn't extend to carpeting, not even for the little sleeping cabinet provided to the officer in charge. And if the floor was cold, the air outside would be freezing. He had on underwear with long sleeves and long legs. Some of the others slept fully dressed—boots, too, in some cases—but on a journey like this Rudi von Kleindorf slept in his underwear. It was a compromise. Quite a lot of things in Rudi's life were compromises. Even going into the army had been a compromise, back in 1920.

He put the clear light bulb on. It didn't provide much more illumination: these trains were designed to go right up into the army's railheads, some of them uncomfortably close to the front line. He slipped his elastic braces over his shoulders, buttoned up his flies, and got an arm into his jacket while he was stepping into his high boots. It was all second nature to him. He could dress, and even shave, before becoming fully awake. There was a folding sink in the corner. He splashed water on his face and ran a hand back through his closely cropped hair. He rubbed his face. He needed a shave, but his hair was light and he'd probably not meet anyone who mattered. He was the regimental commander and senior officer on the train.

He was reaching for the handle on the door when a knock came. It was the duty officer: Leutnant Uhl. The young officer was surprised to find von Kleindorf fully dressed. "Herr Oberst! How did you know?"

"Commanders know everything," said von Kleindorf. It was what Horner used to say to him in the old days. He wondered how often he'd credited Horner with such prescience in similar circumstances.

Leutnant Uhl—a spindly young man with eyeglasses—said, "There's some obstruction on the line. I have put out pickets, in case it's a guerrilla ambush. The train commander has gone back to find a signal box to telephone and find out what's wrong."

"A signal box to telephone?" said von Kleindorf with a grim laugh. "Does he think he's on the S-Bahn to Wannsee?"

"He thinks he'll find one," said Uhl.

"Where are we, Uhl?"

"I don't know, Herr Oberst. Poland, I suppose, by now."

"Not many signal boxes and telephones in Poland, Uhl. You might make a note of that for future reference."

"I will, Herr Oberst." Von Kleindorf liked the kid. He was not much more than twenty years old. He'd got into medical school at some absurdly young age and then, within a year of graduating, thrown it in to join the army. What a fool.

"And no partisans this close to home. But you did the right thing, Uhl. It's good practice, and I want to keep the men alert and ready. Let the guards stay there. Men on the roof?"

"Yes, Herr Oberst. A machine-gun team, too."

"Let's go and see what the holdup is, Uhl." Von Kleindorf put on his heavy winter overcoat and turned up the fur collar.

Cautiously the two officers climbed down from the train and moved forward in the darkness. No moon tonight: such a night would be entirely suited to an ambush. But surely it couldn't happen this far in the rear areas. On the other hand, there were such curious stories. In the rear areas SS-Einsatzgruppen did nothing except summarily execute partisans and irregulars who threatened the lines of supply, and according to what he'd heard they were slaughtering people by the thousand, so it must be dangerous. Men didn't execute suspects without good reason, did they?

There was a cold wind, especially biting up here on the railway embankment. On each side of them the land was flat as far as they could see, which was not far on this dark night. As they walked past the locomotive, they felt the warmth from its boiler and looked up at the footplate, where the driver and firemen were rimmed by the orange light of the fire. Lucky devils: they'd be the only ones warm this freezing-cold night. "They've done nothing about finding out what's wrong," complained Leutnant Uhl.

"Standing orders, Uhl. Drivers and fireman have to remain on the footplate while a train is stopped. There were too many cases of loco crews being lured away and killed. Then the whole train is at the mercy of attackers."

"That's clear. Herr Oberst."

"A foul smell in the air," said von Kleindorf.

"The fields perhaps, Herr Oberst. Human fertilizer."

"At this time of year? You must be a town boy, Leutnant Uhl."

"I am, Herr Oberst."

"What a stench! It's like a battlefield."

They continued walking. The train track was roughly fashioned. By the light of his torch he could see the sleepers: rough balks of timber with patterns of holes to show that they'd been shifted and reused many times; crude wedges to hold the rails, and a total absence of the gravel fettling that ensured that wooden sleepers could be nicely adjusted for height. These were not like the railway tracks in Germany, so elaborate and well made. This was the East.

Blocking the way ahead of them was another train. A long train, perhaps a hundred freight wagons. Painted dark green and marked with the eagle insignia of the Reichsbahn.

"What's wrong?" called von Kleindorf.

"The bloody axle, that's what's wrong!" It was the voice of an ill-tempered man dragged out of bed in the middle of the cold night.

As the two officers got closer to the men, the speaker said, "Oh, I'm sorry, Herr Oberst." He was a hoarse-voiced man with a Silesian accent.

"You'll have to get it moving," said von Kleindorf. "There are other trains close behind us." The stench from the boxcar was almost overwhelming. He wondered if the whole train was like this.

A bearded man who seemed to be in charge consulted his clipboard, shining a torch upon it to see the typed sheet. "You're the HZ 1489? Advance party, Regimental HQ of the Panzer Division, Herr Oberst?" His voice was softer and authoritative.

"Yes: seventy-two trains close behind us," said von Kleindorf, although he had no doubt that the railway workers knew how many trains it needed to move an armored division.

"Can you tell me where the armor is loaded, Herr Oberst?" said the man, who then cupped his hands together and blew into them to warm them.

Von Kleindorf hesitated. The disposition of the tanks and tracked artillery on their flatbed cars was not something to be revealed to the first person who asked. These men were undoubtedly Germans, despite their thick Silesian accents, but why would they want to know?

As if reading his mind, the man explained in more detail: "I can work ordinary freight cars, or passenger coaches, past this broken box-wagon. But your tanks will overhang their flatbeds. In the old days the smaller tanks permitted two-line working, but I can't work your large modern armor through without both up and down lines clear."

"There is armor right behind us," said von Kleindorf. There was a sound from inside the car—animals, he guessed, horses or cattle.

"And we've got more armor on the train in the siding, so I can't shunt it over there," said the bearded man, and sucked his teeth reflectively. "Then we'll have to get rid of this broken wagon," he said. He turned to his loud-voiced companion. "Any ideas, Andi?"

"The nearest crane is in the yards, but if you don't mind about salvaging it, we might bring up a winch and topple it off the track and down the slope there."

"I've got two hospital trains due," said the bearded man. He'd taken his gloves off to write. Now he put them on again. "That's the first one coming now, if I'm not mistaken. Battle casualties. That one should get priority." The sound of a train could be heard very faintly. The man's hearing was tuned to such sounds.

"We can't wait for cranes or winches," said von Kleindorf. "I'll bring up one of my combat pioneer officers and we'll put a couple of sticks of dynamite under it."

"For resettlement in the East."

"Without damaging the track, Herr Oberst?"

"My *Pioniere* can crack an egg without breaking the yolk," said von Kleindorf. "But you'll have to empty it first. Your boxcar will be no more than matchwood. What are its contents? Livestock?"

The two railway workers exchanged glances. What an odd question. Did these army officers really not know? Couldn't they smell the whole train? Didn't they know that Reichsbahn trains like this were a major part of the rail traffic eastwards nowadays, and that they returned empty? "Jews, Herr Oberst."

"Jews?"

"For resettlement in the East." He shone his torch at the Reichsbahn docket clipped to the wooden side of the boxcar. Upon it was printed "To Auschwitz-Birkenau" in large black letters.

Von Kleindorf could hear them now. What he'd thought was animals was the restless movement of people, humans who must be packed together so tight that some of them could not breathe.

"Get your saw and take the locks off," said the bearded man.

"What will we do with them?"

"Can you provide us with an armed sentry, Herr Oberst?"

"I can't leave him behind, if that's what you mean," said von Kleindorf. "Better you get a local man."

"We don't need a sentry," said the man called Andi. "They'll give us no trouble. They can go into the empty boxcar on the sidings."

It was only a two-minute job to saw through the locking bolt. But it needed the strength of both railway workers to heave the door open. And then the people spewed out, to crash onto the hard, cold ground with sickening thumps.

The sudden stench of urine, excrement, and death came like a blow. "Good God!" said Leutnant Uhl, and jumped back in alarm. Even the battle-hardened von Kleindorf gasped at the sight. Women, children, old men, young women clutching babies, all tumbled out stiff, like dressmakers' dummies, with the cold. One tall fellow in a black suit hit the ground with such force that he folded up and rolled down the embankment into the ditch.

And yet these wretched creatures nearest the door were the strongest ones. They were the men and women who'd fought and elbowed their way, or pushed their children, to where there was sometimes a crack of daylight and a thin draft of air.

"Raus! Raus!" shouted the bearded man. He shone his torch into

455

the dark confines of the boxcar, and there was the glint of frightened eyes. More people were there, dozens of them. "Out! Out! Out!" But some of them couldn't get out. Some of the old people were dead. Children, too, of course. Men and women had slipped down in the crush of bodies and suffocated there. Others had fainted and gone all the way to the floor of the car, trampled underfoot until they were unrecognizable as anything but sticky, bloody bundles of old rags.

Von Kleindorf felt physically sick. He turned on his heel and marched away. The young subaltern followed him. So that was the sort of resettlement the regime was offering the Jews. He pulled his cigarettes from his pocket. Anything to get rid of the sight and the smell. But the memory was a thing he'd never escape.

Boris Somló was just losing consciousness as they began to saw through the locking bolt from the door. He was pinned in the corner of the car. He'd always hated crowds; even when his mother had taken him to the big Vienna department stores, he'd hated being crushed close to other people. But this was hell. For a long time he'd tried to hold a small boy up, too, but that was many days ago. It was before the day they gave them water and bits of bread. That was before the first time he'd lost consciousness. Where was the child now? He could have been no more than five or six years old, a solemn little fellow who never replied to anything. Boris rubbed his face and tried to judge from his beard how many days they'd spent locked up in the cold, dark boxcar. But his beard had never been very heavy and he couldn't guess.

Boris heard the railway workers' voices, too, but he couldn't make out what they were saying, and he didn't much care. He was so weak that even his hunger had abated. Nothing mattered anymore. Nothing. So—like the rest of them—he was totally unprepared for the opening of the door.

As the door crashed open, everyone in the wagon moved, and Boris suddenly found himself swept to the doorway, watching people on each side fall into the darkness. He breathed the air, so cold it hurt his lungs, and then someone pushed from behind and he, too, was falling into the bottomless black space.

He hit the ground with a thump that took all the breath from him, but the force of landing sent him rolling down the dark embankment. At the bottom of the slope was a shallow ditch of stagnant water, its top frozen into a thin layer of ice that broke like sugar icing as he rolled over in the cold water.

Suddenly he was fully conscious, but he had very little strength left, and no determination except to scramble out of the water into the field beyond it. The warmth of the packed bodies had been keeping them all alive, and now the effect of the cold wind upon his wet clothes chilled him enough to make him gasp. He stifled a cough with his hand and crawled on.

He looked back up the railway embankment to where the men with torches were shouting into the half-empty boxcar. He got to his feet and walked very slowly away into the darkness.

Boris dragged one foot after the other until he'd walked the whole length of the "resettlement transport," his body aching with cold. Beyond it there was another train. It would be sensible to get away from the railway, and into the open country. The lines of communication were always heavily guarded—you didn't have to be a soldier to know that. But Boris could not face the open countryside in his wet clothing. He was hungry, thirsty, tired, and very weak. He knew that he couldn't survive more than another half-hour or so in this weather.

He stumbled along, without thinking of what he was doing or where he was going. He got to the second train without knowing why he was heading towards it, except that he could see its twinkling lights and it looked warm and inviting. It was an army train, and on the side of it there were big Red Cross signs. He approached it carefully. He'd learned now the danger that sentries represented, but there were no sentries except for two armed men on the roofs of the carriages. He supposed that hospital trains did not have manpower enough to supply sentries every time the train came to a stop.

Some of the windows had open blinds and he could see soldiers inside. The train was jammed full of men; gray-clad men were strewn everywhere, like broken soldiers thrown into a toybox.

Many of them were bandaged; most of them were sleeping. There was no movement anywhere. He walked along, staying away from the locomotive. The locomotive would have men who were on duty and awake. The next carriage was fitted with bunk beds for casualties who couldn't walk. This was as crowded as the previous one, with soldiers packed together as close as possible. All the men

457

were wrapped in gray blankets and crammed into the bunks together, looking curiously like tinned sardines.

The door of the third carriage was open, and the light spilled out. Two medical orderlies were seated on the steps, both smoking with the dedication that comes after lengthy denial. In the doorway behind the orderlies, Boris could see an open cupboard, its shelves filled with army blankets. He coveted one of those thick, warm blankets more than anything he could think of in the world.

He waited for a long time, the icy wind cutting through him like a thousand knives. Eventually the orderlies finished their cigarettes and went back into the train. He could see them through the windows, moving along the train. This was his chance, and he got up on the steps and tried the door. It was unlocked. He opened it carefully and stepped inside and up the steps. To his right was a toilet, and behind him the communicating doors to the next carriage. From here he could see right down into the train. He felt the warmth of the heating and heard the snoring, soft moans and restless movements of the injured men. No one was looking this way. He stepped into the soft yellow light and opened the cupboard. He pulled a blanket out slowly, holding the others back with his free hand. It fell out and opened. He dragged it back into the space provided by the doorway. But as he did so the train gave a jolt. From the floor nearby he heard the couplings clatter and there was a hiss of steam from the locomotive as the train jolted twice and started to move.

"Orderly! Orderly! This man needs help! He's bleeding again." It was a shrill voice, the frightened voice of a young man.

"I'm coming, I'm coming!" An orderly had opened the communicating door from the next carriage. He stood there for a moment, and Boris could recognize him as one of the men who'd been smoking outside. The train groaned and rolled forward, clattering over the steel rails of a junction. Boris stepped back into the shadow and pulled the blanket round him to completely cover his black suit, stinking now and soiled with vomit and excrement, his and other people's. The orderly passed Boris with scarcely a glance at him. Even his disgusting smell attracted no attention here, amongst the sick and injured.

"Bleeding?" said the orderly when he got to the frightened young man. "Where is he bleeding?" The train was picking up speed now. It would soon be going too fast for him to jump without the probability of a damaged leg or foot. He looked out the window. They were passing another train: a troop train filled with soldiers. They stared at him, as they stared at all the wounded, wondering if this was the way they would come back.

Blood had come from the bunk above and made a spotty pattern on the young soldier's face and the blanket. "That's nothing," the medical orderly said. "I'll change his dressing in the morning."

"I want to move," said the frightened boy.

"If you can find a place, move," said the orderly. He smoothed the blankets in the fussy little movements that come automatically to trained nurses.

"You've shit yourself again, haven't you?" said the orderly.

"I couldn't help it," said the frightened boy.

"You'd better get yourself fresh pajamas. But this is the last change you get, understand?"

"Yes," said the boy.

The orderly came back past Boris, but before he opened the communicating door he paused to look at him. Boris met the orderly's eyes and his stomach churned in fear. "I know your damned tricks," the orderly said angrily. "You're not allowed to smoke in there. Get back to your bed or your compartment or wherever you're from. You know the regulations."

Boris nodded.

The orderly slammed the heavy connecting door and disappeared into the next carriage.

Boris watched the boy getting out of the bunk to get fresh pajamas. If Boris could get army pajamas, and hide this black suit, perhaps they'd feed him along with the rest of them. If he could get something to eat, he'd be able to think more clearly.

He looked out the window. There was another army train waiting on a siding. This one consisted of tanks chained down upon flatbed wagons. His train rumbled past them slowly, hundreds of them. It was as if the whole world were nothing but tanks.

"You're the only real friend I've got, Lottie."

Pauli Winter could cheer people up. It was a magical gift. Now that he came to the Hennigs' house two or three times a week to visit Lottie, she found life much more endurable. Pauli told her jokes,

Pauli provided her with stories and gossip and scandal, and Pauli showed her silly magic tricks that made a coin disappear and then come out of his ear . . . or her ear! And it was Pauli who'd sent most of the books, especially the ones in English, which (unknown to Lottie) had been confiscated from their previous owners in police raids. And Pauli had sent the cushions and a red velvet armchair with a built-in footrest, two framed van Gogh prints, and some dance-music records and an old wind-up gramophone. These things had helped to transform Lottie's two cramped garret rooms at the top of the Hennigs' house into a reasonably comfortable little apartment.

When Pauli came, he liked to sit in the red armchair and put his feet up. The gramophone was playing "Jeepers Creepers." Lottie was at the little electric ring making eggless pancakes to go with their ersatz coffee. She had become rather good at cooking in prison, where they had, for a spell, allowed her to work, and even to do some cooking, in the kitchens. Sometimes she had a meal with the Volkmanns, who occupied the adjoining rooms and shared her bathroom. And sometimes she was invited downstairs to eat with the Hennigs, but most of the time Lottie was alone. She liked to sit near the dormer window and stare across the crooked roofs and identify the spires and the shapes of the taller buildings on Ku-damm. It gave her a lot of time to think. "I sometimes wonder if there are any other Americans here in the city," she said as she tipped the pancake onto a plate. The music stopped and she turned the record over, but she didn't start it going again.

"I shouldn't think so," said Pauli, although he knew from the ministry records that there were some. The chances were that they were foreign nationals classified as friendly by the Gestapo, or they were German emigrants who'd returned to Germany because of Hitler's New Order, and they were not the sort of friends he wanted Lottie to make. He didn't want her to start thinking about contacting any other people in the town. The Hennigs were sworn to secrecy, and the Volkmanns knew how to behave like fugitives. Even Mama saw Lottie only twice a month. It was better that way. No alert, much less a custody order, had been issued for her—there was that to be thankful for. But the identity card that Pauli had given her bore a big "J" mark across the front and certainly wouldn't bear up under the sort of close scrutiny that German policemen gave to cards with

"J" on them. Perhaps it didn't matter that her first name was given as Martha instead of Charlotte Sarah, but her age was given as sixty instead of forty, and the photo was of a much older women who bore no resemblance to her.

If she stayed inside she'd probably be safe, but if she went out walking there was always the danger of her being rounded up in the street and bundled off to a camp. The fate of the Jews had become a subject of argument and rivalry amongst the various SS factions, but the dispute was only over whether they should be done to death immediately in an extermination camp or worked to death in a labor camp.

By now Pauli's ideas about the camps' becoming self-financing had been extended so that the SS had become the owner of a great industrial empire that, in its concentration camps, used slave labor to manufacture everything from cheap furniture to forged foreign paper money. Prisoners quarried stone, made synthetic rubber, and sewed army uniforms. The SS owned the Meissen porcelain company, and was on the way to monopolizing the manufacture of soda water, starting with the Apollinaris concern.

"That's what I thought," said Lottie. "Imagine if I was the only one here. Why, I could write a book, *The Only American in Wartime Berlin*—can you imagine that? I'd be famous."

Pauli knew she was only joking, so he laughed. But he added, "I wouldn't write anything down, Lottie. Not for the time being."

From downstairs came the sound of the Hennigs' child practicing the piano. Erich said the boy was musically talented, but it was not easy to believe it when listening to this performance of "Für Elise."

"There hasn't been another letter, I suppose?"

"From Peter? No, nothing. But he's safe in the U.S.A. The Americans won't make him go into the army. He's probably sitting in California with your mother, wondering what we're doing."

"I suppose so. It seems so long since I saw him. And Helena will be seventeen in September. I can hardly believe it. She was only ten when I went to prison. I have missed all those years of watching her grow up. I wish I had a more recent photo of them both." She put the pancake and coffee at Pauli's side and he thanked her warmly. "Seventeen. She was a beautiful little child."

"And now she's a beautiful young woman," said Pauli.

"Yes, I'm sure she must be, Pauli. She was always so perfect. She never cried the way some babies do. She was so . . . I don't know . . . so adult, so mature."

"Yes," said Pauli. Lottie liked to talk, so he drank his coffee and let her talk. It must have been very boring for her, sitting here alone for so much of the time. And it amused him to hear her speak in fluent German that came complete with all the Berlin slang and underworld argot.

"If I hadn't got pregnant we would have gone to America," said Lottie. "Uncle Glenn advised against it, but Peter would have taken that job. Think of that—another year and Helena would have been born an American. I wish Dad could have seen her."

"Yes," said Pauli. He watched Lottie with some apprehension. On his last visit she'd asked Pauli to put some flowers on her father's grave. She'd asked about the other Jewish cemeteries and he'd had to tell her that the old Jewish cemetery in Grosse-Hamburger-Strasse, which had been there since the seventeenth century, was now no more. The bodies had been dug up and disposed of, and the cemetery was declared *judenrein,* cleared of Jews. Lottie had been terribly distressed. Perhaps he shouldn't have told her, but he'd been frightened that she might make an expedition there and be questioned. "It was lucky that Peter took her with him," said Pauli.

"I think about that a lot. Could Peter have guessed?"

"Guessed that the Japanese would attack Pearl Harbor and that the Führer would follow up by declaring war on the Americans? I don't think anyone could have guessed that, Lottie."

"No, I suppose he couldn't have."

"He took Helena with him so that Granddad, and your mother, could see her."

"And now she'll be an American. I can just imagine her at her high-school dances. But what about Peter? What must it be like for him?"

Pauli drank some coffee. "Peter will be all right. I suppose people will treat him badly because he's a German, but from what I read in the Foreign Ministry intelligence bulletins, there's been no large-scale internment of Germans there."

Lottie was scornful. "People won't treat him badly simply because he's a German. It's only you Germans who have that deep-down fear and mistrust of foreigners that makes you treat strangers so badly. That's how this whole Hitler business got started. It's people like Hitler who hate foreigners, and too many Germans supported his hate program. Americans like Europeans. The U.S. is a place where Europeans went to get away from pogroms and prejudice. My dad was never treated badly in the first war. I was a teen-ager then; I remember it well. We never had any problems." She stopped. How could she make dear Pauli the butt of her anger? Pauli had risked everything for her.

"We had a Scottish nanny," said Pauli. He smiled. He took no offense at her scolding; he supposed it was justified. Most of the scolding he'd suffered throughout his life had been justified. "You remind me of her sometimes. 'You Germans,' she used to say, 'you think only of making wars.' She was a wonderful woman. She packed up and went home when the first war began. I never even said goodbye to her properly, but when I looked back afterwards I saw how much of her life she'd given up for us. I wonder what makes a woman sacrifice so much to look after other people's children."

"Perhaps she couldn't have children of her own," said Lottie, and then regretted saying it as she remembered how much Pauli and Inge had wanted children.

"Perhaps," said Pauli. "Lisl told me that Mrs. Volkmann is having a baby."

"Yes, the Volkmanns are very excited. It will give them something to live for again."

"So miracles happen," said Pauli. "How old is Dr. Volkmann? He must be nearly fifty."

"Yes, I suppose so. But Lily is much younger than him. I do hope it all goes well for her."

"How will the Hennigs manage without her?"

"The tea room, you mean? Yes, she makes most of the cakes and breads for the tea room. I will help out as best I can—I told Lisl that. It's been a tremendous success. Lisl is so pleased that Erich plays the piano there now."

"Erich Hennig plays in the tea room?" Pauli was surprised. Erich had been so scornful about Lisl's new enterprise.

"As of last month. Didn't you know? They were paying the other pianist much too much money, and he wasn't even reliable. Then Lisl fired him for arriving late, and they had no one for three weeks. But business fell off so much that Erich finally consented to play for the time being."

"I must drop in and have tea one afternoon."

"Erich says it's just for the time being, but his arm has got worse. I don't think he'll ever give a recital again."

"He didn't mention it to me," said Pauli.

"He still doesn't like the idea," said Lottie. "But they need the money, and Lisl loves running the place. She doesn't open until noon and closes at six-thirty, so it doesn't take up too much of her time. Anyway, she doesn't have to go out and visit people: all her old friends come here. And she goes table-hopping and exchanging all the latest gossip. Dr. Volkmann says it's one of the most fashionable places in Berlin."

"Here? The most fashionable place in Berlin?" said Pauli. "Is that what he hears from the people he works with in the Weissensee cemetery?"

"Don't be awful, Pauli," said Lottie, laughing. "He's exaggerating, of course. It's not like the Kaiserhof or the Kempi, but Lisl has worked wonders. Oh, I just remembered, your mother sent some brownies for me. Would you like one?"

"No thanks. I'm getting too fat."

"Even when I was in prison she sent them. Not real chocolate, of course, but it's wonderful of her. A taste of the U.S.A., she calls them. I love your mother."

"She wanted to come and see you more often," said Pauli, "but I told her to make it no more than twice a month. For the time being I want you to be extra cautious."

"Whatever you say, Pauli." In prison she'd heard what happened to certain categories of prisoners when they'd finished serving their sentences. But instead of an SS man with a custody order, it was Pauli whom she found waiting in a car outside the prison in Barnimstrasse. He'd brought her straight here to the Hennigs' house. She'd never asked him how he'd arranged things so that she wasn't taken to a camp. She just did as he suggested and thanked God for the miracle.

"Things are tightening up. The war is not going as well as was expected. The whole of the Sixth Army perished at Stalingrad: twenty-four German generals surrendered to the Reds. Some of the boys I knew at Lichterfelde were there. It must be the worst disaster in German history. Fritz Esser says that in the final days Hitler got the message that his nephew, Leo Raubal, was amongst the injured, but he refused to evacuate him by air. God knows what will happen to the man if the Russians discover who he is. Then, in May, a quarter of a million more German soldiers surrendered to the British and Americans in Tunisia. More friends gone, Lottie. Will I ever see them again, I wonder?"

"But no invasion?" said Lottie.

"Of France? I don't think that will ever happen. Think how many ships they'd need, and the whole coastline is heavily fortified. I saw the defenses on the newsreel last week. But Dr. Goebbels has decreed 'Total War,' whatever that means, and everyone from sixteen to sixty-five has to register for service. Even poor old Hauser has to register. More registrations means more spot checks." Pauli finished his ersatz coffee and got up. He hoped the mention of the spot checks would be enough to keep Lottie inside. He knew from Lisl that she'd taken little Theo out shopping, and for walks in the Tiergarten. This reckless behavior appalled Pauli, but he didn't know how to persuade Lottie to stay indoors.

"You're not going already, Pauli?"

"I'd better. I walk to work nowadays. I'm trying to cut my weight down, but it means I have to leave home earlier."

"Poor Inge. So she has to get up earlier, too."

"I'm on my own at present."

"Inge works too hard, Pauli."

He looked at her for a moment. "Inge spends most of her free time with Fritz these days."

"What do you mean, Pauli?"

"She sleeps at Fritz Esser's apartment."

She looked at him. Did he really mean what she thought he meant? "Pauli! You can't be serious."

"Yes, I'm serious. I suppose I should have guessed what was going on when she was out of town so much. But it never occurred to me that she was always away at the same time that Fritz was on a trip. Why should it?"

"Oh, Pauli!"

"I accused her, and she laughed and said that they'd both wondered how much longer it would be before I guessed."

"Oh, Pauli," she said again. She couldn't think of what else to say. He looked so pathetic. How could anyone do that to Pauli? His face was tight—the face of a little boy whose world has come to an end. She put her arms round him, and he embraced her tightly.

"She laughed," said Pauli, still holding her tightly. "I asked how long had it been going on, and she said for years. She laughed. I told her that I'd never been unfaithful to her, and she just said, Then you must be a fool."

"But Inge . . ." Lottie's mind went spinning. She'd not seen Inge for many years. "I thought she adored you. I'm sure she did."

"Perhaps if we'd had a child . . ."

"How could she be so cruel?" said Lottie, still holding him. She could feel his heart beating.

"She loved me once, she said, but Fritz Esser is more of a real man. I don't know what she's talking about, Lottie."

"Sit down again, Pauli. You can't leave like this. You look awful. There's some schnapps. . . ."

"I never drink alcohol."

"You need a drink, Pauli."

"Perhaps just one small measure." He sat down.

"Does Lisl know?"

"Good God, no. She'd tell absolutely everyone."

"Who else knows?"

"No one," said Pauli. "Alex is not in Berlin, and apart from him you're the only real friend I've got, Lottie. I mean, you're family, aren't you?"

"Yes, Pauli, I am."

He smiled. "I feel better, now I've told someone. I was bottling it up . . ."

"Come and see me more often, Pauli. I love to talk with you."

"Yes, I will, Lottie."

"I've never been able to please you, have I?"

Pauli Winter's deep and solemn love for his father had always been tinged with a trace of fear. If he ever had children he would do everything possible to liberate them from this feeling of anxiety that he always had when face to face with his father. Even now, with Harald Winter an invalid in a wheelchair, and Pauli, forty-three years old, a senior officer in the Interior Ministry of which the universally feared Heinrich Himmler had recently become head, he still found himself nervous in his father's presence. It was ridiculous.

His father had said very little during this Sunday outing in the

Tiergarten. He sat, a wizened figure hunched inside a large blanket, his hat slightly askew, as hats are when put on by a wife. He stared at the world disapprovingly. Pauli was pushing him; his heavy wooden wheelchair was too heavy for Veronica, who walked alongside Pauli, enjoying the sunshine and the greenery. The Tiergarten was at its best. The trees were intensely lit with sun that came under the clouds and made each leaf and blade of grass unnaturally sharp, like a world underwater. Whatever else had changed, this wonderful green park, in the very heart of the city, remained as glorious as ever. Pauli had been brought here in the pram by Nanny, even before he'd learned to walk. He knew each tree and bush, and the water that looped in its surprising shapes, and the ducks and birds that lingered there waiting to be fed on bits of bread hoarded from nursery teas. Sometimes, on the way home, they'd heard the lions growling in the zoo.

That summer of 1943 was perfect. This day had been wonderful, with warm sun and blue skies. But now the spell of perfect weather was coming to an end. Today the air was turbulent with the gusty breeze that comes before a storm. There was thunder in the air and the sky was darkening. For this reason Pauli had suggested they shorten their excursion. They could turn at the Siegessäule and head straight towards Budapester Strasse. But his parents dismissed the threat of rain: his mother because she knew how much Harald liked these outings, and Harald because he readily accepted such concessions from her. He always had. He was selfish. Sometimes Pauli wondered why his mother didn't rebel against his father's self-centeredness.

"I wish we'd spoken English more often at home," Veronica was saying. "It would have been good for you, Pauli, and good for your father, too. And I confess my English is getting rusty these days. It's a sin."

His mother was wearing a smart new coat and a brown felt hat with the wide brim that was fashionable these days. When the wind gusted, she had to hold the brim or it would have been whisked off her head. She was sixty-eight years old, but she'd kept the same slim, upright figure that she'd had as a young girl. Pauli was proud of her. "There is a joke going the rounds," Pauli offered, "that the optimists are learning English and the pessimists learning Russian."

"That's a perfectly awful thing to say, Pauli. And I'm sure it's not true."

"I'm sorry, Mama. I said it was a joke. I'm sure we'll soon be pushing the Russians back again." The sky was getting blacker every moment, and the thunder came again; this time a flash of lightning preceded it. They would get wet if it rained: there was nowhere nearby to shelter.

"I don't even look at the newspapers anymore," she said. "All those maps . . . Did I tell you that Hugo—the young footman who worked so hard to convert the wine cellar into an air-raid shelter for us—was killed? He went into the navy and was killed in that terrible air raid on Hamburg. He must have put us down as his next of kin. Poor little Hugo—I didn't know he had no family. That's why he wrote to us so often, I suppose."

At the mention of the series of air raids that had devastated Hamburg—and caused widespread alarm throughout the German population—Harald Winter showed interest in the conversation. "What do you know about Hamburg, Pauli? What's the truth of it? Eh? Eh?"

Pauli didn't soften the hard truth. "Kauffmann, the Hamburg Gauleiter, reported having eight hundred thousand homeless wandering around the streets and needing food, clothes, and shelter. What could we tell him? We sent blankets and medical supplies and so on. But our people in the ministry don't know how to cope with that sort of catastrophe. The fellow we sent didn't help them much, I'm afraid: he came back quite shaken and said the damage was unimaginable. He brought photos. The whole city has been razed. But they're gradually getting it back to work. No one will ever know how many died. People leapt into the canals to escape from the flames, but they didn't escape, and the canals were filled with corpses next morning."

His father growled. Every such disaster was to be blamed on that "fat fool" Göring, Commander in Chief of the sorely pressed German air force. His mother didn't respond. Perhaps he shouldn't have told either of them. Some people preferred to be ignorant of the facts about everything. A plane flew over. He looked up. It was a Junkers transport. He'd seen hundreds of them, but each time he saw one his mind went back to that dreadful morning in 1934 when the Führer had flown into Munich to wreak a terrible vengeance upon his brownshirts. Again he saw poor old Graf fold up and spurt blood. And the others . . . "Heil Hitler!" they'd screamed as the firing squad squeezed the triggers. Poor deluded devils. And what for? Had Röhm's cronies really been planning a coup, or was it just another example of the Führer's notorious paranoia?

"Will the Führer ask for terms?" his mother asked.

"Peace terms?" Pauli was surprised at such a question. The possibility had never seriously entered his mind. "No, I don't think so. He's always said he'll fight to the last drop of blood, and he'll demand the same from us."

"But they will keep on bombing, won't they? Suppose all our cities are attacked by thousands of bombers, the way that Hamburg was attacked?"

"We're safe in Berlin, Mama."

"But the Luftwaffe started bombing London years ago. I can't think that the English will want to spare us."

"Hamburg is on the sea, Mama. It's easier for them to attack Hamburg—they don't have to penetrate our main air-defense zones."

"You're always so confident, Pauli, but I fear the worst."

"What is the worst, Mama?"

"That the Russians will get here," said Veronica without hesitation.

Pauli laughed. "Come along, Mama. You can't really believe that the Russians could get all the way to Berlin. The Cossacks are coming: that's the sort of story Berlin mothers used to frighten their naughty children with." There was another flash of lightning, and this time the soft drumroll of thunder went on for a long time.

Another plane came over. Veronica said, "Perhaps they are hurrying to land before the rain starts."

He didn't laugh at her. "Perhaps they are, Mama," he said. The plane was very low; it was a huge four-engined Focke-Wulf transport coming in to land at Tempelhof. Its camouflage painting was streaked with dirt and oil, and it bore the marks of recent damage. These long-range aircraft that carried senior officers and urgent supplies between Berlin's *Zentral-Flughafen* and the battlefront reminded every Berliner who cared to look up how near the fighting was.

469

His mother said, "Germany is fighting a two-front war, Pauli. I can remember when everyone said that a two-front war is always fatal for Germany."

"We haven't got a two-front war, Mama. The British and the American armies are still in England."

"They are not there on vacation, Pauli," said his mother sharply.

"You're not secretly hoping that the Amis will win, are you, Mama?"

"No, of course not, Pauli, but I wish the Führer would start thinking about peace."

"I wouldn't say anything like that in public, Mama."

She looked at him. It was terrible when a mother couldn't reveal her true thoughts to her own son, but she could see that, on this subject, Pauli's mind was closed. "No, I won't, Pauli," she promised.

He looked at her and touched her arm. He loved his mother. But, like too many other people he knew, she simply didn't know the difference between what was expedient and what was downright foolish. Suppose everyone in Germany went round saying exactly what he or she thought? The cellars of the Prinz-Albrecht-Strasse wouldn't have room enough to lock them up.

"It's going to rain hard," said Pauli. "Did you bring the umbrella?"

"No, but it doesn't matter."

"We'll get wet," said Pauli.

Four young soldiers and their girls, anxious to avoid the rainstorm, came hurrying past them as they crossed the little bridge. They were noisy and excited as only young couples can be. Pauli turned his head to watch them as they pushed one another and chased along the path. Pauli had never known that sort of carefree, youthful exuberance. His whole life had been spent in thrall to authority.

When they reached the rose gardens everyone had gone, the seats were all empty. Pauli sat down alongside his father's wheelchair while his mother strolled around the flower beds. Harald's outing to the Tiergarten had become a set routine. Mama liked to examine the flowers: she remembered all the bushes like children, and remarked upon their progress. While Pauli talked to his father, they watched his mother on her tour of inspection. She showed no sign of hurry, despite the black sky and the thunder that was getting nearer all the time. It was characteristic of her: she was a very determined woman. One day Pauli would confide in her about Inge's infidelity, and she would provide renewed strength for him— but not yet.

"Have you visited Lottie recently?" his father asked him. It was a surprising question. Although Harald Winter had been informed that his daughter-in-law was living in Berlin, he'd shown no interest in seeing her, and her name was seldom mentioned in his presence. When Veronica went to visit Lottie, she went alone.

"I take food for her," said Pauli nervously.

His father's eyes shone with an intensity that did nothing to allay Pauli's fears of him. Other old men had vague, watery old eyes, but Harald Winter had the same piercing gaze that had sent Pauli running to Nanny. "You got her out of prison, didn't you?" Harald Winter said, showing no sign of pleasure.

"She was released. Her sentence was fully commuted for good behavior." Pauli's speech was hasty and nervous. He knew his father had an ear tuned to nervousness in anyone, and that made Pauli more diffident.

Harald Winter looked round to see where his wife was. She was well out of earshot, but even so he whispered. "What happened to Martha?"

"Martha?"

"Don't pretend to me, you swine!"

"Oh, Martha. Your Martha."

"What happened to her?"

"I don't know. Why?"

"You went there, you went to Vienna. I heard all about it."

"That was years ago. . . . That was the *Anschluss.*"

"You gave her a card and offered her protection."

"Yes." Pauli smiled nervously. Surely now he would be praised.

"She was arrested. She phoned you in Berlin."

"No!"

"Don't deny it: I have a witness," said his father.

"I wasn't there."

"I know you weren't there. I say she phoned you."

"I wasn't in the office, I mean."

"Don't tell me lies. She spoke with you. The man who arrested her let her use the phone to call you in Berlin. You told her that nothing could be done."

Why was his father blaming him for everything? Pauli corrected him. "I told her that I would try to help her."

"You did nothing."

"I did what I could."

"You did nothing."

Now it was Pauli's turn to become resentful. "You think it's so easy, don't you? Why didn't you do something to help her? She's your mistress." Harald Winter reeled back as if struck in the face. Pauli had never spoken to him like this, at least not since that terrible night when Hauser was stabbed by one of Pauli's Nazi comrades.

"Don't talk to me like that," said Harald Winter.

So great was Pauli's sense of injustice that the sort of hurt and anger that he'd harbored so long came pouring out. "I'll talk to you any way I like. I'm not a child any longer. She was taken into custody because she was a foreign national of Jewish race. If you'd married her she would have had a German passport and the protection of a mixed marriage."

"Are you trying to blame me for what happened to her?"

"I don't know what happened to her," insisted Pauli.

Harald Winter stiffened; his hands clenched tight and his voice went quiet. "You never could face the truth, Pauli."

"I tell you I don't know."

"She was taken to a camp and sent east for resettlement."

"There was nothing I could do."

Softly Harald Winter said, "Your signature was on the protective-custody order. Can you explain that?"

"It's not true."

"There was a witness to the arrest. You didn't calculate on that when you sent one of your tame gangsters to Vienna to arrest her. You didn't think of that, did you?" He gave a grim, mirthless smile, a bleak smile of triumph.

"It's not true."

"You think I don't know what happened? You think I don't know how your warped mind works?"

"What?" Pauli's world was falling to pieces.

"You disgusting little swine. You've the moral code of a snake."

"What?"

"Mrs. Winter: foreign national, female, Jew. Do you think I'm stupid? Do you think I can't add it up? You had Martha arrested and sent her to the camp where Lottie was expected."

Pauli wet his lips. "What if I did? I saved Lottie, Peter's wife, didn't I?" He heard his own voice: high and shrill, betraying everything he wanted to hide most, the fact that he was still the scared schoolboy he'd always been, and had always hated.

He looked at his father, even at this point hoping for a reprieve. His father's lips twisted with scorn. "You swine!"

"Peter's wife." He waited for his father to understand, but Harald Winter's fury and contempt were unabated. Pauli said, "Your mistress—and she wasn't the only one you had—for Peter's wife. Your Martha was old . . . sixty years old."

"I never want to see you again," said his father quietly.

"Who was this witness? Can I be told that?" said Pauli sarcastically.

"No."

"Boris, I suppose."

"Yes, Boris."

"Her fancy man."

Harald Winter looked hard at his son before deciding how to reply. "So that's what you thought." He wiped his mouth as if trying to keep words from escaping. "Boris is my son: her son."

"Boris is your son?" said Pauli hoarsely.

"Your half-brother," said his father, twisting the knife.

"He was probably only taken because he couldn't prove he was half Aryan. It's your fault if he was taken: if you'd acknowledged him as your son, he'd have been registered as a *Mischling* and got identity papers. *Mischlinge* aren't usually taken to the camps."

"He was taken."

"Then how do you know about all this?"

"He escaped."

"They never escape."

"Some do. Tell your masters that. Some will be there to watch you hanged."

Pauli took a handkerchief from his pocket and wiped his nose. "I've never been able to please you, have I? No matter what I do, it's wrong. I pass out of Lichterfelde and you tell me I got low marks; I fight in the war and you wonder why I don't get a medal; I pass my law exams and you say that criminal law is easy; I become a civil

servant and you call me a bureaucrat; I work hard and get promoted
and you say I'm a Nazi swine! I never got a word of praise from you,
and I suppose I'll never hear one."

"Get away from me." The first drops of rain started. Huge spots
like shiny coins were scattered on the dusty path.

"I saved Lottie, your daughter-in-law." His father's face showed
no change. He stared at his son with a curious blankness. There was
no hatred there, just indifference. Pauli said, "And what's more, I
destroyed the file on you."

"The file on me?" Harald Winter said contemptuously. All Pauli
wanted was a word of praise, or some small gesture of appreciation.
The risk he'd taken in removing the file—like the risks he'd taken
in a whole lot of things, from warning Alex Horner about the frame-
up of General von Fritsch to saving poor Lottie—was considerable,
but his father was unyielding.

"In Vienna. The Emperor's secret police had a thick file on you,
right from the time you joined the Silver Eagle Society as a student."

"Ha!" Harald Winter looked at his son and remembered the
conversation with Count Kupka in the club. That was on New Year's
Eve, just before Pauli was born. He could remember the clangor of
all those damned church bells. And he could remember that fool of
a gynecologist who said, Your baby will be born in 1900: a child of
the new century. Well, perhaps he was right, and what a damnable
century it had been.

He wished his son had never been born. "Get away, I say!"

"Mama can't manage the wheelchair."

"She'll manage. Get out of my sight! And stay away from my
house until I'm dead." The rain started in earnest. "That's not
much to ask, is it?"

"Where's Fritz?"

That Sunday evening marked the end of the wonderful summer
weather. By the time Pauli returned to his apartment, near Bismarckplatz, the rain was heavy and unrelenting. He went up in the
lift and let himself in. He was surprised to find all the lights burning
and a smell of coffee lingering in the air. In the kitchen was an
opened cake-box on the table; its wrappings were in the bin.

"Pauli?" He went into the drawing room. Inge was sitting on the sofa, dressed in a sober brown-striped, button-through dress that suited the hot weather, but her hair was bedraggled. "Did you get wet? I got absolutely soaked."

"Inge! What are you doing here?"

"It's my home," she said defiantly.

"Where's Fritz?"

"He's in Hamburg."

"Doing what?"

"Doing something very predictable with a willing blonde nineteen-year-old who works in the typing pool at the Blohm and Voss aircraft factory."

"I see." He looked at her; this crestfallen Inge was someone he'd never seen before.

"That's what he's doing." She laughed. She must have got used to Fritz's endless affairs, for there was not much bitterness in the laugh. "We went together. He made a speech to war workers and then took one of his audience off to bed." She was still lovely. How could that stupid Fritz prefer anyone else to this wonderful creature? On the low table was a *Gugelhupf* with a slice or two missing. There was a pot of coffee and two cups with saucers. How could she have guessed when he'd arrive? She couldn't possibly have known; but Inge had always been lucky in small things. It was the important things that went wrong for her: Peter, Pauli, and now Fritz and the baby that she wanted so much.

"Beneath the ashes fires still rage," said Pauli.

Inge smiled. It was a quote from Fritz Esser's speech, a speech he repeated when he couldn't think of anything new to say.

"Is it over?" Pauli asked.

"I don't know." She touched her hair, conscious of what a sight it must look.

"I don't think I could . . ."

"I need somewhere to stay."

"Fritz won't marry you, if that's what you are still hoping for."

"He won't even come looking for me," she said sadly. "I know that."

"The Führer said he doesn't want any more messy divorces."

"He's a puritan. Yes, I know. Fritz won't even take me to see him in case he gets asked awkward questions."

"I thought Fritz was 'a real man.' Is he so intimidated by the Führer?"

"I'm sorry if I hurt you, Pauli. I didn't want to."

"Didn't you?" He remembered the way she'd humiliated him. He remembered her taunting him about his "manhood."

"You've lost weight," she said and poured coffee for him. It wasn't real coffee, but it was very good.

"Worry and hard work." He sipped the coffee and eyed the cake without taking a piece.

"Worry?"

"I've just had an awful row with Papa. He says he never wants to see me again."

"Poor Pauli."

"He means it."

She laughed, trying to make light of his misery. "We're both feeling rejected, aren't we? Let's go to bed and forget it all. It's another day tomorrow."

It was typical of her that she bestowed her favors on him with such condescension. He loved and wanted her, but it would all be different from now on. He would never adore her as once he'd done, because he didn't want to be hurt again. "I've a lot of paperwork to do," he said. "I'll sleep on the folding bed."

She smiled. She didn't mind too much: Inge had learned to take things as they came. Today all she needed was a place to sleep.

1944

"We're all serious."

"Berlin again tonight," said the RAF flight lieutenant. An elderly man, he wore the Observer air-crew badge of the first war and the sort of medals that go with it. Now he worked in the Operations Block as an intelligence officer but, apart from briefing crews when his colleague was away, his duties were not much more than those of a high-ranking clerk. He was wearing a battle-dress blouse of the sort that the air crews wore, instead of the more usual officer's tunic. It was an affectation, like the "handlebar" mustache he'd cultivated.

"So I heard," said Colonel Peter Winter. There was no need to ask him what he meant. Ever since November 1943, Berlin had been the focus of the Allied air bombardment. Enough heavy bombers had found their way to the German capital—despite the cloud that is a regular feature of Berlin winters, and the extensive built-up areas that made the city difficult to discern on the H2S radar screens—to devastate whole areas of the city. Most of the ministries were, at least temporarily, rendered uninhabitable, and so was one-fifth of Berlin's living accommodation. The British information services were calling this series of air attacks "the Battle of Berlin."

"The long winter nights, you see," said the man. "It gives them a chance to hit the distant targets and get home in the dark."

"I suppose so," said Peter.

"You're waiting for General Rensselaer, aren't you?"

"Yes," said Peter. He leaned closer to his copy of *Picture Post* magazine in the hope that the man would stop talking. The airfield

477

was quiet now and the Operations Block silent. The bombers were all in the air, and there was no work to do until they returned.

"But you're not a Yank?" It was an odd thing to say to a man dressed in the uniform, patches, and badges of the U.S. Army Signal Corps, but all sorts of strange fellows, in unlikely costumes, had passed through this RAF Bomber Command airfield.

"Yes, I am," said Peter.

"You don't talk like a Yank."

"I went to school in Europe," said Peter.

"Ah, that's it," said the man. "Where, may I ask?"

"Where?"

"Did you go to school. It's a personal question, I know, but I'm just curious about where you learned to speak such good English."

"My mother is American," said Peter. Although tempted to say that he'd learned his good English from a Scots nanny in Berlin, he'd discovered from previous encounters that this only led to endless well-meaning questions that he didn't want to answer. And he'd been warned a thousand times that his job was top-secret, and that meant his background and country of birth were top-secret, too.

"Yes, Berlin is getting it again tonight. Serves the bastards right, I say."

"Yes," said Peter. "It serves the bastards right."

"It's my boy I worry about."

"Your boy?"

"My son. He flies Lancasters. He's done fourteen ops. I worry about him. The Jerries call them 'terror fliers,' you know. We've heard of cases where our boys have been killed out of hand after parachuting. It's against the rules of war, but your Hun is like that."

"It's hot in here," said Peter. He put down his magazine. The man was determined to chatter. "It's stuffy, there's no ventilation."

"Can't take the blackout boards down."

"Couldn't you black out the windows with curtains and let air in?"

"We tried that, but there were always chinks."

"Chinks?" said Peter. That was the difficulty about English: they were always inventing new words.

"Chinks that let the light through."

"Oh, I see."

"Not Chinese chinks," said the man. "You've not been in England long, I can see."

"It seems long," said Peter.

"That's the war," said the man. "Sometimes I think it will still be going on after I'm dead. I'm getting on for sixty."

"Really? You look younger."

"Yes, a lot of people tell me that. It's my hair, I think." He looked at Peter's empty teacup. Peter had been given a saucer, too; he'd learned that this was something that was accorded to him because of his rank. The British did not give every visitor a saucer. "More tea, Colonel?"

"No, thank you."

"You drink it without milk, I notice."

"I don't like the powdered milk."

"The Germans drink it like that. Were you by any chance born in Germany?"

"Encino, California." He always gave Encino as his place of birth. It was a place he could describe, and it was about as far away from Europe as one could get.

"I just remember the Germans always drinking their tea black." He got to his feet. "Are you sure you won't have one? I'm going to get my girl to brew more. I'm a teapot."

"No thanks."

"Would you prefer coffee?"

"I don't like coffee."

"The Germans love coffee. I hear the German prisoners of war just can't believe that we've gone right through all these years of war and never rationed coffee."

"They'd believe it if they tasted it," said Peter with feeling.

"Ah!" He looked puzzled for a moment, then laughed briefly. "I see what you mean. Yes."

The British didn't like jokes about their coffee. Peter had noticed that before. You could make jokes about their uncomfortably cold houses, about the miserably inefficient telephones and postal service, about the government and even about the King; but jokes about the British cooking or their inability to make coffee were not considered polite. "I never drink coffee," said Peter.

It was at this moment that the door opened and Glenn Rensselaer came in. His opposition to wearing a uniform had waned since he was made a brigadier general. He looked strong, smart, and solidly. His graying hair made him distinguished, rather than old, and he still had the easy smile.

479

"I'm just brewing up, General Rensselaer," offered the man.

"No thanks, Mr. Parker. We must hurry. Come along, Colonel. Have you got your overnight things?"

"Your driver put them in the car," replied Peter.

"Let's go, I'm driving. Wrap up. We're in a jeep, and that's as cold as an English bedroom."

The night was dark. Glenn Rensselaer dismissed his driver and got behind the wheel himself. It was a long drive to London, but Glenn Rensselaer didn't mind driving, even on the narrow, twisting, blacked-out roads of England. His "jeep" turned out to be the slightly more roomy, and very slightly more comfortable, Dodge three-quarter-ton weapons carrier, but it still had canvas top and sides against which the cold night air drummed a tattoo before striking the occupants like a stream of ice-cold water. It was warmer in the front, Glenn told his nephew. Peter nodded and buttoned up his collar.

They drove in silence for a while. Peter was thinking about Lottie. By deducting the maximum reduction of sentence for good behavior, she'd be out of prison by now. He'd written to his mother asking for news, but he couldn't be sure the letters got there. He wondered what the RAF flight lieutenant would have said had he been able to see into his thoughts.

"He guessed I was German," said Peter suddenly.

"Who? Nosy? He likes to see what he can find out. Next time he sees me he'll take me aside and tell me that he knows all about you. He used to be an interrogator in a POW camp. When he was there he wanted to be here; now he's here he wishes he'd stayed there. You know the type."

"You called him 'Mr.' "

"That's the British style for officers below field rank."

"He speaks German?"

"Fluently. He was a flier, shot down in 1916. Spent the rest of the war behind barbed wire. He thinks he's an expert on 'the German mind.' "

"He's very persistent."

"An RAF flight lieutenant is no more than a captain. You're a colonel. Just tell him to shut up."

"I don't feel like a colonel."

"By now you should feel like one."

"I see him sitting there with a chestful of ribbons and his wing."

"Do you want to wear your ribbons and your Zeppelin Division insignia?"

"That's different."

"It's not different. You don't have to take any backchat from Nosy, or anyone like him."

"Did SIXPACK get away okay?"

"Yup! We got the radio signal from the plane to say he dropped on time. Now we wait and see."

"He'll be all right," said Peter.

"Oh! That's unusual coming from you. Why are you so confident about SIXPACK?"

"He's a crook," said Peter. "He has no intention of following his orders. He's on the make."

"How exactly?"

"I don't know how. But some of them are like that, Glenn. They are opportunists. They'll hang on to the money and lie low."

"Have you told anyone else what you think about these agents of ours?"

"They're not all like that. But I don't think we should put any follow-up into SIXPACK unless we're sure of what we're getting."

"Money, you mean?"

"Sure. He'll ask for money, and more money. You'll see."

"I hope you're wrong."

"It doesn't matter too much, does it?"

"SIXPACK knows a few faces, doesn't he?" said Glenn Rensselaer.

"He won't turn himself in. He'll go to ground."

"You've got a good instinct for these guys, Peter." Peter's previous predictions had so far proved right.

"It's not instinct, Glenn, it's judgment. I've lived among Germans all my life. I can recognize one from another, just as you can with Americans."

"I guess so." Glenn slowed up as they came to the circular junction that the British called "roundabouts." A lot of Americans, encountering such unexpected obstructions for the first time, continued straight on, and ended up as a traffic casualty on the central reservation. "I would appreciate a little of that 'judgment' on the can of worms facing me tomorrow. Something real big has come up." Glenn slowed the car and cruised along slowly until he found a place where he could pull off the road.

"I didn't want my driver with us," said Glenn, "because this is really hot." He switched off the engine. The countryside was black and the night was silent, except for a nearby owl and the distant sound of trains shunting.

"Whatever is it?"

"For over a year now the British have been getting feelers about some kind of peace deal."

"From Hitler?"

"No, not from Hitler. These are people who plan to overthrow Adolf and then come to terms."

"Who are they?"

"Right. Who are they? There are different groups. One is called the Kreisau Circle, pacifists and intellectuals with a lot of 'vons' and 'counts' and stuff. Big names they tell me. Okay."

"Von Moltke," said Peter.

"Maybe."

"The Moltke estate is at Kreisau, in Silesia," said Peter.

"Is that right?" said Glenn. "Sounds like they need a little tighter security, if you can guess it in one go."

"Am I right?"

General Rensselaer didn't answer the question. "These Kreisau guys got a couple of high-up church leaders to go to Stockholm, Sweden. They talked to some British bishop who was on a trip there. He brought their message back to London."

"How did they get permission to leave Germany?"

"It's a question that kind of troubles me, too. Anyway, there are other contacts. Have you heard of a guy named Goerdeler?"

"Carl Goerdeler, yes. Onetime mayor of Leipzig. Protestant, monarchist, and anti-Hitler."

"What's he like?"

"Tough, brave, active, intelligent."

"Sounds good."

"But noisy and impulsive. Too conspicuous, as an anti-Hitler man, to be a suitable rallying point for a secret coup."

"Okay, but what if Goerdeler got together with the army?"

"The army?"

"Goerdeler has been trying to sell his revolution to the generals. He even went to Smolensk to recruit Field Marshal Kluge, commander of Army Group Center on the Eastern Front."

"With what success?" asked Peter.

"We don't know. We know, or we think, that Ludwig Beck, who used to be chief of staff, is a convert."

"What power does he have nowadays?"

"Influence, they say. The idea is that they knock Hitler off, use General Fromm's Replacement Army to take over in Berlin, then ask for terms. We say yes immediately and they consolidate power."

"The Replacement Army is just recruits and transfers."

"But it's got guns, and it's right there in Berlin, and other big cities."

"And is all this going on without the Nazis knowing?"

"The experts say Himmler won't wield the dagger that cuts Hitler down but he'll willingly take over the government when, and if, someone does the job for him."

Peter said, "This is the man they call Loyal Heinrich."

"Well, maybe Himmler is a question mark, but Admiral Canaris is with the plotters."

"Canaris? Who's he?"

"Chief of the Abwehr. That's why the generals feel so confident. The chief of army intelligence is one of the plotters."

"What's all this got to do with us?"

"It didn't have anything to do with us—it was strictly a British headache—until these guys found our OSS office in Berne, Switzerland, and tried to hurry things along. Our man in Berne told Washington, and now Washington is asking us if it's kosher."

"Washington is prepared to do a deal?"

"Washington is an eagle with many heads. My guess is that they want to keep the conspirators simmering on the back burner."

"To see if they can take over?"

"An unequivocal no might send them marching off to talk to Uncle Joe in Moscow."

"Is Washington that cynical?"

"Yes."

"So what are we supposed to do?"

"The conspirators are going to bump off Adolf very soon, March, maybe: exact date and method yet to be fixed. They want us to supply an agent and a radio link. They'll want to have a communiqué about a cease-fire issued pronto. Then, if the SS remain loyal to the Hitler regime and fight back, these boys expect quick military help. What do you say?"

"I knew it would happen." Peter managed to conceal his happiness. He'd always hoped that the Germans would come to their senses and get rid of the Nazi gangsters. Now the old Germany—the Imperial Germany he'd grown up to love and honor—would be restored to its rightful place in the world.

"Well, it hasn't happened yet. But let's keep our fingers crossed. A political solution like this could save us from invading the Continent. Maybe it would save a million lives."

"What about the Russians?"

"I was hoping you wouldn't ask that, Peter."

"I'm serious."

"Sure you are; so am I. We're all serious—the Limeys, the Russkis, and maybe even Washington. But are these sons of bitches in Berlin serious? That's what we need to know, Peter."

"March—that doesn't leave much time."

General Glenn Rensselaer didn't answer. He turned the key in the ignition and resumed the journey, leaving Peter Winter to stare into the dark night and think about it.

They reached London in the early hours of the morning. The sky was streaked with pink and there was the noise of pigeons, starlings, and sparrows from the trees in the square. Cyrus Rensselaer's London house had been turned over to the American Red Cross as an Officers' Club. But Glenn had kept possession of the mews house in the narrow cobbled street at the back of it. He opened the doors of what had once been stables and drove the Dodge inside.

"If I leave it on the street, regulations say I have to remove the rotor arm," he told Peter, "and, to tell you the truth, I don't have the faintest idea what a rotor arm is."

Peter smiled and helped close the doors. He wasn't always sure whether to believe his uncle's self-deprecatory remarks. Self-conscious about his age—sixty-four next birthday—Glenn had lately begun to refer to himself as if he were a blundering old idiot. Perhaps it was because the war was being taken over by youngsters. They flew the planes and commanded the ships and won the medals. Now even some of the generals were little more than kids.

"Rotor arms!" Glenn Rensselaer continued. "Why, some crook with a pocketful of rotor arms could go around the streets helping himself to any vehicle he fancied."

He led the way up the creaky wooden staircase. The place had hardly been changed from the time when it was coach house and stables: the stalls, feed troughs, and drains all remained in place.

"Ah, good! Sally has been here," he said.

"Sally? Who is Sally?"

"Not my fancy woman," said Glenn, and laughed. "What the British call a charlady—the old woman who cleans up for me." He went over to the sink and nodded approvingly at how clean and tidy everything was, then switched on the lights. "These mews flats are always dark. It's the worst fault with them."

"It's very pleasant," said Peter. He looked around doubtfully. It was not only dark but also incredibly cramped: the "kitchen" was just a stove on the landing, the bathroom no more than a small closet. The ever-adaptable Glenn—who'd spent his life in improvised lodgings—didn't seem to notice these disadvantages. "Who lived here?"

"Dad's chauffeur and his wife and kids!" Glenn took a bottle of Scotch from his overcoat and put it on the table. "When gas rationing started, he got another job and moved." Standing precariously on a chair, Glenn reached a cupboard and opened it to reveal electric meters and a tangle of ancient wiring. He switched on a box crudely labeled "hot water." Then he stepped down, red-faced with the effort, and looked through the mail that his char had put on the little writing desk he'd rescued from his father's house. He shuffled quickly through the letters and put a copy of the *Saturday Evening Post* on a pile of magazines that remained unopened. "Dad sends magazines," Glenn explained. "He says it's to help me remember where my roots are." Glenn laughed and switched on an electric fire. "It will soon warm up." Then, in anticipation of its warming up, he took off his short overcoat, and tunic, and threw them over a chair. Then he looked in the tiny refrigerator to confirm that she'd bought him milk. Americans were addicted to dairy foods, Peter noticed. Even the men ordered glasses of milk in restaurants or went into drugstores just to have an ice-cream sundae. After some thumping with a dinner knife, Glenn loosened a tiny ice tray and slid it out. "Charlady," he said reflectively, putting the accent on "lady." "Don't these British kill you? Even the men's urinals here are marked 'Gentlemen.'" He held the ice under the water tap. "Take off your coat, make yourself comfortable. Whisky?"

"No thanks."

Glenn put some ice cubes in a tall glass. "Maybe you want to hit the hay?"

"No," said Peter.

"If you're hungry, there are some real eggs here. Sally gets them on the black market."

"I'm fine, thank you."

Outside, in the cobbled street, were the sounds of taxicabs arriving, and the loud voices of people saying goodbye after a party that had lasted all night. Peter pushed aside the net curtain to see through the window. Outside the house opposite, a chauffeur was hosing down a Daimler while two children raced matchsticks in the fast-running water of the gutter. Getting into the taxis were women in fur coats, a couple of scruffy-looking British army officers, a Polish sailor, and a man in evening clothes, tails and white tie. London was like that nowadays—a curious mélange of incompatible elements—and these converted mews houses were often rented for short periods to such transient people.

"I'm talking to Boy Piper at noon. I must have a tub and get cleaned up." Glenn opened his bottle of PX Scotch, poured some on the ice, loosened his tie, and sat down on an armchair. He put his feet on a low table and sipped his drink.

"About the anti-Hitler putsch?" said Peter.

"Yes. The arrangement is that I have to keep him informed."

"Is Sir Alan still running things for the British?"

"Not officially, but his successor has assigned areas of responsibility to him. The British are good at dividing command without quarreling about it. It's something we could learn from them. On their tank-carrying ships the senior army and navy officers have equal say. Try that on a U.S. boat and you'd have a knock-down, drag-out fistfight."

"But the final word is yours?"

"I know what's in your mind, Peter, but forget it."

"The final word is yours?"

"When we have a plan worked out, I will put it to Boy and he'll okay it."

"And if he doesn't okay it?"

"It will be because he has good reason, so I'll look at it again."

"You trust him, don't you?"

"Sure. He's an old buddy. Any reason I shouldn't trust him?"

Peter didn't reply. He still felt bitter about Boy and his brief affair with Veronica. "What kind of man will you drop to make contact with these people?"

"No one big. Washington sent strict instructions about what we mustn't do. It mustn't be a politician or even a political adviser. It mustn't be an officer of high rank. Just a radio operator; someone expendable, I guess."

Peter was appalled. "Those people won't negotiate with some tech. sergeant from the Signals Corps," he said.

"For God's sake, take off your coat and sit down and relax. You make me nervous standing there like you're on guard duty." As if to emphasize this, Glenn pulled off his own shoes and tossed them into a corner of the room, near the chair where he'd put his overcoat and tunic. "Negotiate? Who's talking about negotiations?"

"In effect, whoever you send will be a representative of the Allied governments."

"No, they won't!"

"You're avoiding the truth, because you want to avoid the truth. These generals and field marshals are not even going to say good day to the sort of man you're talking about."

"Then let them go to hell!"

"Is that official policy? Would you really prefer that this had never happened? Do you want to ensure that it all collapses? Is this your way of showing them that the Allies want no part of their conspiracy to get rid of Hitler? You send them an uneducated, time-serving, noncommissioned radio operator?"

"Peter, you're a goddamned snob."

"You told me last night that this could save a million lives." Peter took off his jacket. American informality went much too far; what made them relaxed made him uncomfortable.

"I don't know what to think, Peter, and that's the truth."

"You must treat it seriously, Glenn. It would be terrible to leave these people unsupported. They're risking their lives, and the lives of their families, too. We know the way the Gestapo work."

"So you'd send a U.S. general?"

"You must have a general who speaks German."

"And what a propaganda coup capturing him would make for Goebbels."

"Not such a coup as having Deputy Führer Hess fly to Scotland. The Nazi regime survived that."

"A general."

"Or someone they'd consider a social equal," persisted Peter. "Germany is the most class-conscious nation in the world—no matter what they may say about the British class system—and the German officer corps is the most sensitive element of it."

"I guess you know about these things better than I do."

"Yes, Glenn. I know about them."

"But to you this is a chance for Germans to show the world that they are not behind Hitler?"

"Yes, good Germans."

"You mean upper-class Germans: the Prussian Officer Corps, intellectuals, academics, and men with the right backgrounds."

"What if I do? What's wrong with that?"

"Nothing. I just want to get the terminology right."

"There have been plenty of chances for the workers to overthrow Hitler, and nothing has come of them, because Hitler is popular with the working class. Hitler has eliminated unemployment and he's given the workers the best living standards in Europe—far higher than England's—and workers with high living standards don't urgently want freedom of speech and a choice of literature."

"That sounds kind of sad."

"Well, it's true," said Peter.

"And so the counterrevolution depends upon the generals?" Glenn said with just a hint of mockery.

"You find it amusing," said Peter. "Perhaps you don't realize what dangers the conspirators face."

"Okay, Peter. You're right, I guess. But I have a hunch that if I told you we were parachuting the Kaiser back into Berlin to lead a revolution against Hitler, you'd be even more enthusiastic."

"The Kaiser died in Holland in 1941," Peter corrected him soberly, half hoping that his uncle would tell him he was wrong.

"And people say you Germans have no sense of humor," said Glenn.

"You must let me go," said Peter, ignoring the gibe.

"Well, we've both known what was in your mind since I first mentioned it last night, but I don't think that would be a good idea."

"The people you're talking about are likely to be of my age and from my class. I'm a German, I can speak to them."

"You're a defector."

"No, I'm not," said Peter in what was almost a cry of pain.

"In their eyes you are," persisted his uncle.

"I was trapped in the U.S.A. by the outbreak of war."

"Peter! You're wearing the uniform of a colonel of the U.S. Army. We're at war with Germany. Can you really expect your people to see that as a trick of fate?"

Peter said, "I will have a drink, if you will permit."

"All the rest of the booze is in the writing desk. I have to lock it away, or Sally takes it home for her husband's flu. He suffers a lot with flu. The glasses are in the cupboard, over the sink. Hit me with another Scotch, too, please."

"I can parachute," said Peter when he came back with the Scotch.

"I know. I watched you. You scared the shit out of me."

"I did?" He poured more whisky for his uncle and a small measure for himself.

"You were scheduled to take that group to Wales the following week. If you'd broken your neck, there was no one else but me to go. And I hate those trips to Wales."

"I could do it, Uncle Glenn."

"So it's 'Uncle Glenn' now?"

"Seriously."

"Peter. I wasn't kidding when I said that this was a job for someone expendable. You're not expendable."

"It's worth the risk."

"You think it's worth the risk, but you're not running the department. I'm running the department, and I say it's not worth the risk. Dropping someone in there is easy enough, but if this military uprising fails, the Nazis will clamp down real tight. And then there will be no way of getting our guy out."

"In such a case no one would have such a good chance of survival as me. I know Berlin, I've lived there, I have family there who would shelter me."

"And your mother is my sister."

"Yes," said Peter, and knew that any chance of endangering Veronica would count very much against his going. He picked up his Scotch, but the moment he caught the heavy, sweet smell of it his stomach revolted. He put the glass down again.

His uncle was watching him very carefully. "Oh, sure, there are reasons why you would be a good choice, but the reasons against are even more persuasive."

"Tell me the reasons."

"That you should go?" Glenn Rensselaer had walked right into that one, but there was no getting out of it now. Peter expected to be treated like an equal, and that's the way he'd be treated. "General Fromm is heavily committed to the conspiracy. On his staff he has a general named Horner who was at cadet school with your brother."

"Horner? Alex Horner? Yes, I know him. He's one of the very best types of Prussian: honorable, clever, restrained. He would never be a party to something that might easily fail."

"Take it easy. We don't know that Horner is one of them. We only know that Fromm is, and Horner's on his staff."

"And my brother?"

"Pauli? No, no indication that Pauli is involved."

"Horner is just about his closest friend. I thought . . ."

"Politics divides friends and families," said Rensselaer. "I guess you've discovered that already."

"Yes, a long time ago."

"Pauli is not the revolutionary type, Peter. You know that. Pauli swims with the tide."

"He pulled me out of the sea."

"Okay, that wasn't the right analogy, but Pauli is not the type who joins a coup. Pauli is the bloodhound type, who smells out what's going on and dutifully reports to his superiors."

"That's not fair, Uncle Glenn. Pauli is the kindest and most liberal of men."

"I confess I'd worry if I heard that Pauli was involved in this business. I like him, Peter, I really like him. But Pauli has his own ways of doing things. They can be great, but guys who have their own way of doing things can't be relied upon."

"I want to go. Officially. I'm asking to go."

"Take it easy, Peter. We'll talk again tomorrow."

Peter was persistent. "Tell Boy Piper that I want to go. See what he says."

"I know what he says," said Glenn.

"What?"

"He chose you right from the word go."

"Well, then."

"One other thing," said Glenn Rensselaer, who now felt bound to put all the cards on the table. "We have no one to receive an agent in the Berlin region. The British would have to organize the reception at Bernau, which they like because it's on the main line into Berlin. I'm reliably informed that their man there is that fellow Samson."

"Brian Samson? The man I employed at the Bremen factory?"

"That's the one. He was sent back in, about six months ago."

"Why can't Samson do it?"

Glenn finished his drink and pulled a face. "Samson knows nothing of this business, and anyway he has his own work to do. He can't be compromised by revealing his true identity to these conspirators. Whoever goes in will need a lengthy briefing. Samson may not even have a radio. He probably hasn't been trained to operate a radio. There's no way to tell him the wavelengths. There are a million reasons . . . but even if they were all overcome, the British wouldn't let one of their SIS people do anything like this. The British keep their operations entirely separate from the collection of intelligence. All 'Operations' are done by SOE, out of that office on Baker Street, and they concentrate on the occupied countries. They don't operate anywhere near Berlin at present."

"Samson," said Peter. "I would trust Samson."

"But would he trust you?" said Rensselaer. "Up till now, the British SIS have refused to work with our guys, because they say we are amateurs and the agents we use are renegades." He looked at his watch. "I wonder if that water is warm by now. I've got to get my act together if I'm to keep all my appointments today."

"You'll talk to Boy Piper," insisted Peter.

Glenn Rensselaer looked at him. Lottie's name had not been mentioned. It was better that it not be. "I'll talk to him," Rensselaer promised. He switched on the radio to get the news. It was tuned to the American Forces Network, a big band playing "Do Nothing Till You Hear from Me."

General Glenn Rensselaer was late arriving at his meeting with Sir Alan Piper, or "Sir Boy," as some of the wags called him. Glenn hated to be late, but he told himself his conversation with Peter made the delay worthwhile. He was shown into his friend's new office, a room facing a weed-filled bombed site at the back, now that Piper was no longer running the show.

Though this room was smaller than his previous one, it shared a landing with the kitchen and the ladies who supplied tea. On the whole, Piper, a dedicated tea drinker, had decided it was a change for the better. There were other changes, too, notably a wide-eyed young man with a thin nose and lank hair who had been appointed as Piper's special assistant. Glenn Rensselaer shook hands gravely with the nervous youth, who had come down from university with unprecedented high marks in Greek. To Glenn it seemed a weird recommendation for an important job in the Secret Intelligence Service, but the British seemed to prefer men who had spent their college days doing something conspicuously impractical. "This is Mr. Frank Harrington," said Piper. "He'll sit in and take notes, if that's all right with you."

"Sure thing," said Glenn, and the young man took his coat and went to get them the inevitable cups of tea.

"He's a clever young man," said Piper defensively after Harrington went out. "He's one of the youngsters selected for security work in Germany after the war is won. We plan to have an office in Berlin with Gaunt, whom you know, in charge. Young Harrington and a few other selected people will work there."

"Has it got as far as that?" said Rensselaer in surprise. "Jesus. We haven't even invaded the Continent yet."

"I know," said Piper. "These preparations for the future make me feel old sometimes."

Glenn Rensselaer looked at his friend and smiled. Piper was seventy. Goodness knows how he'd fixed permission to go on working all this time. It was the war, he supposed, the same war that had given him new work to do when he was past retirement age. Harrington came in, balancing two cups of tea. Respectfully he put them on the desk and went to get a tin of homemade biscuits that was kept for special guests.

"Well, what did he say?" Piper asked.

"Young Winter? He said yes, just as we both knew he would. I practically had to tie him down to prevent him from coming along here and giving you his lecture."

"What kind of lecture?"

"The same one you gave me, with a few modifications."

"Yes, there would be a few modifications. I can't imagine any German seeing it my way exactly."

"I've never been able to hate the Germans the way you hate them, Boy," Rensselaer told his friend.

"I don't hate the Germans, but I hate their attitude to the rest of the world. I hate the crocodile tears they shed for their own victims. Everywhere I went in Germany before the war, I saw big signs that said, 'The Jews are our misfortune.' They victimize the Jews, steal from them, lock them up, and kill them. But the Jews are *their* misfortune: that's what I hate about the Germans." He found a box of cigars in the drawer of his desk and offered them to Rensselaer. It was a gesture of concern. He knew Glenn was worried. "And God only knows what we're going to find in these concentration camps when we get there. The reports we're getting are too horrible to contemplate, but every day we hear more of the same sort of thing. It's almost as if the Germans are trying to exterminate the whole Jewish population—all of them, from the whole of Europe!"

Rensselaer took a cigar and toyed with it but did not light it. Lighted cigars were for reflection, contemplation, or satisfaction, not for times of anxiety like this. Piper waited for him, giving him time to think. For a moment Rensselaer stared in silence. Damn! Why had he been faced with such a conundrum? Peter was part of his own family. "I'd like to have a couple of days looking for an alternative," he said.

Piper nodded and poured tea. "Oh, of course. It's hard for you, old chap, I know it is. But your nephew seems to be an ideal choice."

"We have to put him in by air, don't we?" said Glenn. Politely he took the proffered tea and put it on the table. He could not face a cup of strong English tea.

"I'm afraid we do, Glenn. Whoever goes will have to parachute. There again your nephew fits the bill."

"Have you ever dropped people untrained?"

"Yes. They always get hurt. Sometimes only a sprained ankle, but that's enough to write a man's death warrant when he's lying crippled in the dropping zone. The radio side is much easier. Nowadays we have sets that even a child can operate." Piper smiled and drank tea. Piper—like so many of his countrymen—seemed to flourish on this stuff.

"And back through Switzerland?"

"If possible, but I think I should be quite frank with you, Glenn. The chances of getting him back safely are not one hundred percent."

"I thought Samson was coming back. You said Samson's wife was having a baby. You said you'd promised to bring him back."

"Samson is a special case. He's proved to be one of our very best

493

people. We flew him to Stockholm in a Mosquito, and he went straight to Germany on a Swedish steamship. He has first-rate identity papers and he will come out very soon. Silas Gaunt wants Samson as his number one, and these Military Government security teams must be ready by the time we invade the Continent, and they have a lot of preparatory work to do. I couldn't endanger him to help the fellow you send. . . . Your chap's identity papers will be produced in a hurry. I couldn't risk it, Glenn, I really couldn't."

Glenn's stomach turned over. He'd always taken great pride in having an impassive professional attitude towards everything he did. But Peter was his own family, and over the past year Glenn had become more and more attached to him. "He's expendable, you mean?" He kept his voice flat and unemotional.

"You know I don't mean that. We'll do everything we can to get your fellow out, but the chances are not good."

Glenn tapped the unlit cigar upon the back of his hand and gave it all his attention. He said, "Shall I take it, from everything you've just said, that you don't rate the chances of this assassination of Hitler very high?"

Piper got up from his desk, walked to the window, and looked down at the empty place where not so long ago a fine Queen Anne house had stood. Now it was flattened and the rubble removed; it had become a thick tangle of nettles and willow herb. "Not very high. It's a long shot. Hope for the best; plan for the worst. That's all we can do, isn't it?"

He turned and noticed that his friend's fingers had started to unravel the cigar. It was unsmokable now.

"Until the Führer is dead."

From a distance the two horsemen looked like bugs on a bedcover, a rumpled green blanket dotted with bare trees and small farms. They were Germans and, characteristically, the two men rode with that desperate competition that not even the Latin races aspire to. They chased across the fields and jumped hedges and gates with a calculated skill and a daring that bordered upon the foolish.

A third man watched them through field glasses. He was in his mid-sixties, a soldierly sort of figure, but not in uniform. Though he was wearing rough country clothes and rubber boots, he was certainly not a peasant. He was standing on a hillock at the end of the churchyard that marks the very edge of the village of Hohendorf, on the road from Bernau to Biesenthal. When the horsemen went out of sight over the hill, he put his field glasses back into their case and strapped the case closed. Then he turned and walked back slowly through the churchyard, stopping now and again to look at the headstones. A sudden shower of rain began to fall, but he still didn't hurry. When he got to the little village church, he peered inside.

The church was quiet and unlit. The last morning service had ended and the lights were out. The man went into the church. Though it was empty, he could smell smoke from the recently extinguished candles. Candle wax was in short supply—no one wasted it. He found a place at the very back where he could see everything. Then he kneeled down to say a long prayer. That finished, he sat back on the hard wooden seat and started thinking. He had a lot to think about.

The man was Baron Wilhelm von Munte; his son was a senior official in the Reichsbank. The von Muntes were wealthy. They'd owned a big house here for many years, and their estate in Pomerania went back many generations. Von Munte had a lot to lose if his plans went wrong.

Outside, where the brief shower had passed and the sun was brightening the dull colors of the wintry landscape, the two horsemen had stopped and were talking.

"I would never have done this if you hadn't suggested it," said Pauli.

"And suggested it and suggested it and suggested . . ." said General Alex Horner. He got down from his saddle and stood, enjoying the air. There was only a small patch of blue sky. The sun would vanish, and there was much more rain to come, but it didn't matter.

"Yes, I know. I'm sorry. But when the Reichsführer became Minister of the Interior last year, it created a lot of work, and we are still not clear." He got down, too. Pauli was puffed. That chase had taken it out of him, though he would never admit it.

"But you're all right?" Alex asked.

"Oh, you heard about the scourging of the lawyers. Yes, he got

495

rid of all those lawyers in the Administration and Legal Section of Hauptamt Orpo, but that was long overdue."

"Fritz was disappointed," said Horner. "He wanted to be minister."

"Once he saw that the Reichsführer was determined to take over, Fritz was sensible enough to stay clear of the struggle. But Fritz has done well enough. He's still deputy, and so much extra power has been given to the RSHA that Fritz Esser has become more powerful than before."

"That's not evident."

"I don't think Fritz minds that."

"I don't think Fritz minds anything as long as he can live in high style," said Horner. "I went to a party there last month; I've seldom seen such food and wine. You'd never know there was a war on."

"Fritz takes what he can get," said Pauli feelingly. "My God, but it's wonderful to be out here in the open country again. I feared I might have forgotten how to ride."

"It's not something you forget, Pauli. We were lucky to have learned so young. And the cadet school taught everything properly. I wonder what the old riding stables are used for, now that the SS soldiers are there." When Pauli didn't respond he said, "My little Christian will be six in June. I've promised him his first riding lesson then. Chrisi is making him a riding outfit for his birthday."

Pauli still did not respond. They got back on the horses and rode slowly to let them cool a little after their furious ride. At the brim of the next rise Horner dismounted again and stood looking over the landscape before them. He looked with a soldier's eye. The only way he could interpret landscape nowadays was in terms of covered ground, observation points, artillery positioning, and antitank defenses. But this wasn't a battlefield, this was the homeland, and he tried to see it in other terms. He relished it as one of the things he was fighting for.

"It's over between me and Inge," said Pauli. There, he'd said it at last.

"I didn't mean . . ."

"It's all right, Alex. I don't mind talking about it."

"But I thought she'd . . ."

"Come back to live with me? Yes, she has. It's convenient for both of us now that she's not living with Fritz."

"It's tragic, Pauli. I'm so sorry."

"Until the Führer is dead."

"The marriage will never be anything but a sham. I don't blame Fritz," said Pauli. "Inge threw herself at him. She told me so. But Fritz became tired of her. I knew he would. Fritz has hundreds of women: it's the way he is. You know him."

"Yes, I know him," said Horner. "We had lunch the other day. He said that Germany now had no chance of winning the war."

"I wouldn't take that too seriously," Pauli warned him. "Fritz says all sorts of things he doesn't mean."

"I think he meant it this time," said Horner.

There was a pause as Horner waited for Pauli to respond. "Things are not too good at present," said Pauli. "But there are so many things in our favor."

"For instance?"

"If the Americans try an invasion, we'll thrash them as they come ashore. I'm convinced it will be the greatest tragedy they've ever suffered."

"I wish I felt as confident," said Horner. "I was in France looking at the defenses last month."

"I saw the newsreel," said Pauli. "It's magnificent."

"The piece they film for the newsreels is," said Horner, "but we don't know where the Allies will strike. It's possible that they'll land an airborne army in our rear. And much of the coast is manned by Russian volunteers. We can't expect them to fight to the last drop of blood to defend occupied France for us."

"You think the landing will succeed?"

"I think it has far better than a fifty-percent chance. And if they get a beach head they will land such an amount of men and material that our forces in the West could be overwhelmed."

"Are their armies to compare to the Russian armies?" said Pauli scornfully, hoping to end his friend's pessimistic arguments. "Are you saying that these Americans, and the Tommies that we chased out of France in 1940, can compare to the German soldier?"

"Not man for man. But the Amis fight with machines. Our army is still mostly horse-drawn. The Anglo-American armies have got rid of their horses. Everyone is moved by road; sometimes whole divisions of infantry advance in armored carriers. Their artillery has an abundance of shells, there will be endless supplies of bullets, and their supply forces will use planes and trucks to keep the pressure up. In the West, where the roads are good, we'll find it difficult to withstand them."

497

"We also have planes to attack them. The beaches will make a juicy target for our bombers. And we have the miracle weapons."

"That the Führer has promised. Yes, the miracle weapons. I wonder what kind of miracles they will perform, and how long we will have to wait for them."

"Are you really so despondent, Alex?"

"Fritz is right, Pauli. Perhaps the war is not yet lost; but the war cannot be won. If only the people at the top would make the Führer see it."

"The Führer is determined," said Pauli.

"Then perhaps someone must make the Führer step aside, and do it in his behalf," said Alex Horner.

"What do you mean, Alex?"

"I see divisions mangled every day. The German army is being destroyed. Our losses are gigantic, Pauli. Germany is losing its soldiers: and with such wholesale conscription, its soldiers are its entire male population. We can't go on like this. Germany is dying. Dying, Pauli!"

"But what can we do?"

"Have you ever heard of the opposition groups?"

"The Kreisau Circle?" said Pauli.

"Yes," said Horner guardedly.

"Or do you mean what Goerdeler and Beck are doing?"

Horner was silent, and like the skillful interrogator he'd become, Pauli gave his friend a few moments to reflect. But then he continued the pressure. "Are you one of them, Alex?"

"I've been approached, Pauli," said Alex Horner.

"Oh my God, Alex. How can you be such a fool?"

"Turn me over to your Gestapo if you like, but you'll get nothing out of me."

"I'm not going to turn you over to anyone, you fool. But how can you get mixed up with treason? You didn't tell Fritz any of this?"

"No, of course not."

"Cut your connections with these people, Alex. We've had the Beck-Goerdeler group and the Kreisau Circle under observation for months. Just go sick or think of some other way to do it."

"Is that your best advice?"

"Beck is too old and Goerdeler too indiscreet. They'll talk and talk until their activities can't be ignored any longer, and then they'll be thrown into a camp. They won't do anything. It's all for nothing, Alex."

"I'm glad I talked to you, Pauli. You didn't mind, did you?"

"Those people have been under observation for over a year. 'Gestapo' Müller was bragging about it only last week, when I was over there. He was showing us his dossiers and playing the wiretaps. He knows all about those people."

"I feel better now, Pauli."

"Depend on the Führer," said Pauli. "Some people are too ready to discount him, but he's never been wrong yet."

"Race you to that clump of trees?"

"Let's go."

Both men swung up into the saddle with such energy that the horses reared. Then they pounded across the fields, their horses neck and neck.

Pauli felt good, really good; this time he'd done something useful to help his friend.

"And?" said the old man who sat waiting for General Horner in the back pew of the empty church.

"He's a careful one," said Horner.

"He won't join us?" said von Munte. He fiddled with the strap of the field glasses.

"No, but he'll keep it to himself. I would trust him with my life."

"You have," said the old man dryly.

"He knows about the Kreisau Circle and the Beck-Goerdeler group. The Gestapo know, too. He says they have recordings of phone calls and everything."

"Poor devils. But nothing about us?"

"I'm sure he would have mentioned it."

"It's been worth all the trouble to maintain security."

"But now I am compromised," said General Horner.

"Yes, we should assume that your friend will betray you. It's safer that way. But it doesn't matter, General. You will be in Berlin. There will be no need for you to do anything until the Führer is dead."

"Wipe out these vermin."

"You've been working hard, Koch."

"Yes, Herr Deputy Minister," said Koch, his doleful expression unchanging. He was becoming more canine everyday, thought Fritz Esser as he looked at the little man hunched in the center of the sofa. Koch's dark-ringed eyes and bushy eyebrows made him look like a dutiful wolfhound waiting for the command to bite.

Fritz Esser picked up the papers that Koch had spread over his antique desk and piled them together. "I'll think about it." Esser picked up the phone that connected him to his secretary in the outer office and said, "Send Herr Doktor Winter in." He looked up at Koch. "Leave now, Koch." He nodded to the other door, which led to the corridor. "I want your part in this kept secret."

Koch had to move fast to pick up his Tirolean hat and leather coat and get out through the door before Pauli arrived. Koch was not surprised at this instruction. Fritz Esser's obsession with secrecy was well known. His assistants made jokes about it when he was not around.

It was the first time that Pauli Winter had seen Fritz Esser's new accommodation. Far more comfortable than any previous office, it had room for a leather sofa in addition to matching black leather armchairs. And there was a low table so that Esser could sit with his visitors and drink coffee when he wanted an atmosphere of informality that could not be achieved from behind his magnificent desk. On his desk now, alongside the dossier that Lothar Koch had brought, was a loosely wrapped brown paper parcel.

They shook hands and exchanged greetings. Pauli had promised himself that Inge's infidelity would make no difference to his friendship with Fritz. Fritz had said the same thing a million times. But it did make a difference. Pauli saw Fritz in a new light these days. He was aware of the deviousness and cunning that were hidden under Fritz's noisy, outspoken friendliness. Hunched over his desk, this man whom Pauli had always likened to a moth-eaten bear looked like a toad. "It's wonderful, Fritz," Pauli said, looking round at the modern lithographs on the wall—a series of National Socialist heroes, from a tank commander to a shapely swimming champion—

and the silver-framed photo, signed with fraternal greetings from the Führer, that had a place of honor on the side table.

"Yes," said Fritz Esser awkwardly, "you haven't seen it before, have you?" Pauli realized that the decoration must have been arranged by Inge. The carpets, the tapestry that hung behind his desk, and the lithographs: it was all very much Inge's style. Some of these items were things she'd always wanted Pauli to have in his office.

The windows were big and the view of Unter den Linden high enough to see over the famous lime trees. Across the road, men were repairing the two badly burned upper stories of a building that had been hit by a cluster of incendiary bombs. Nowhere was it safe from the Allied bombers now. "I came as soon as I could," said Pauli.

"Yes, good," said Fritz. "Drink?"

"No thanks." It was the usual routine, but Fritz always offered. He reached for the bottle and topped his own drink up. "I have some new reports on the conspiracy."

"Better than the last lot?" said Pauli, referring to some hysterical rumors that informers had brought here in January, and which had provoked first alarm and then anger from SS-Reichsführer Himmler.

Fritz ignored this remark. He said, "Would you believe that the army—Army Group Center, those rattlesnakes around Kluge—are preparing a coup?" He said it without much anger in his voice and looked up to see how Pauli reacted.

"Any evidence?" said Pauli. He'd heard such stories before. Berlin was full of rumors these days, and Pauli encountered most of them in his rounds of the Gestapo building and the ministry.

Fritz sighed at this "lawyer's reaction." "They have a bomb: two bombs, in fact."

"They have?" said Pauli.

"British bombs."

"Is the army so short of bombs?" said Pauli.

"It is no laughing matter," said Fritz Esser sternly and then, having said it so sternly, found he couldn't keep a straight face. Collecting himself, he said, "These British devices are dropped for the terrorists. I have a sample one here." He unwrapped the parcel that was on his desk. There were two metal cylinders inside, and Esser grabbed one to show him. When Pauli showed some alarm

Fritz reassured him: "These have been emptied. But let me show you how they work."

"Very well," said Pauli. Fritz Esser did not have the sort of brain that could cope with the intricacies of mechanical engineering, but these bombs were simple enough for him to understand the way they functioned, and he proudly explained the workings to Pauli. "You press here and the little bottle breaks. Then acid eats into the restraining wire until the wire . . . There, that's it—see? Lets the spring bring the . . . Wait a moment. Yes, that's it. The striker there hits the detonator. Detonator explodes and up goes the bomb. What do you think?"

"Very crude. It looks as if a schoolboy made it. Is this the best the British can do?"

"Crude, yes. They make them by the thousands, and it costs them almost nothing. They drop them into France, Belgium, Holland, Norway, and so on. These hoodlums use them against us while the British rub their hands and laugh."

"Are you saying there's to be an attempt to kill the Führer?"

"It's silent. That's what you've missed, Pauli. No ticking or whirring of clockwork. Absolutely silent. And this wire can be changed so that the timing can be anything you want, from ten minutes to an hour or two."

"Can I ask how you came by this infernal machine?"

"The Abwehr have intercepted thousands of them."

"The Abwehr." Since February 18, the army's intelligence service had been amalgamated with the SD, the SS intelligence service, and now came into Himmler's ever-growing empire.

"The Abwehr are a part of the conspiracy against the Führer. Sometime last year there was a conference of intelligence officers at Smolensk—Army Group Center—and two of these bombs were taken there. That's where the army swines did their plotting. They might have already tried and failed. We have trouble infiltrating these army circles, of course. They close ranks against us."

"What do they plan?" asked Pauli.

"I don't know, but there has already been some contact between certain of these traitors and the Western governments."

"How do you know?"

"The Ausland-SD and the Gestapo both agree on that."

"Will there be arrests?"

"Not yet," said Esser. "The SS-Reichsführer says that nothing is to be done until we are quite ready."

"The Führer's life is in danger," said Pauli, appalled at the risk.

Fritz drank some of his drink. It was brandy; Pauli could smell it. Then Fritz leaned forward and in a low voice said, "Suppose I told you that the SS-Reichsführer himself has been in contact with the Americans?" Pauli was not shocked; he didn't believe it. It was one of Fritz Esser's stories.

"To discuss making peace with them?"

"He sent Dr. Carl Langbehn—a Berlin lawyer—to Switzerland to talk to an American named Dulles who claims to speak on behalf of President Roosevelt."

Was it true? Could it be? "I can't believe it. But Langbehn was arrested. . . ."

"Listen, Pauli, listen. Langbehn went to Switzerland with the SS-Reichsführer's blessing. But the Gestapo monitoring service picked up a radio broadcast. No one knows how, why, or what the source was, but the British have always opposed any dealings with the SS-Reichsführer, so it looks like the British wanted to sabotage the Langbehn talks and sent the message so it could be monitored by our listening service. . . . The Gestapo sent the intercepted message to Führer HQ, and we had no alternative but to arrest Langbehn and send him to a camp." Fritz grinned to reveal his bent teeth. "The SS-Reichsführer was very worried. Yes, I've never seen Heini so scared. Since then he's had no contact at all with any other of the groups."

Pauli was overwhelmed. His world was falling to pieces. "This is all true? I can hardly believe it."

"Well, believe it: it's true, every word. But Heini's problem has always been his oath to the Führer. He wouldn't listen to any plans that included doing harm to the Führer."

"I should think not," said Pauli.

"And yet, while the Führer is there, no one will be allowed to do what has to be done." Fritz Esser leaned forward across his desk and touched his fingertips together while he smiled. "But suppose something like this . . ." He touched the bomb delicately, as if it might explode. "Suppose the person we're talking about was no more." Even Fritz couldn't bring himself to say it in plainer words.

"Then we could arrest the culprits and provide the SS-Reichsführer with the mission that I believe is his."

Pauli looked at Fritz Esser as he realized what Fritz meant. He wanted the Führer to be assassinated, to make way for Himmler. What a hypocrite he was, and what a cynic. How much of this had come from the SS-Reichsführer, and how much of it had been planted in Heini's mind by the cunning Fritz? But it made sense—it was crude and cunning but it made sense—and what Fritz had told him fitted together with other things he'd come across in his official duties.

"Why are you telling me this, Fritz?"

"I want you to take over the investigation of these treacherous opposition groups."

"Me?"

"You'll have all the authority and all the staff you need."

"No, Fritz, no. Please."

"Pauli, it's got to be someone I can trust."

"What do you want me to do?"

"Isn't it obvious?"

"No."

"I want you to wipe out these vermin, whether they are in the army, the Abwehr, the church, the universities, or anywhere else. Even if they are in the SD or the Gestapo, you will have authority to question who you like. No one will be empowered to challenge your authority. I want the Führer to know that the party's police apparatus is in control of the state."

"You want me to smash these organizations?"

"Investigate them," Fritz corrected him gently. "There are influential people involved: high churchmen, field marshals, and aristocrats. Don't underestimate their power. There will have to be a proper trial. The party can't afford to look foolish in court."

"So I shall bring them to trial?"

"Yes, but not too quickly." He smiled that inimitable cunning smile. "Give them time to do something we can charge them with."

Across the road the workmen were boarding up the top stories of the ministry; the upper part of the building was being closed and abandoned. It was eyeless, its boarded-up windows here in the Government Quarter a reminder to every passer-by that the Allied bombers could bring the war to the heart of the Reich.

"We don't need any help in killing Hitler."

"Do you understand?" asked Fritz.

"I understand," said Pauli.

"We don't need any help in killing Hitler."

Before the coming of the Nazi regime, the inhabitants of Berlin's Wedding were reliably communist in sympathy. It was a district of huge old apartment blocks, barracklike buildings that had been hurriedly built in the previous century to house the seemingly endless waves of peasants who swarmed into Berlin looking for jobs in the new factories. Since they were designed in a honeycomb style, shafts of daylight could sometimes reach into their courtyards and scatter light into their tiny, squalid rooms, where men crowded together in dozens. Now these apartment houses were not so crowded or so squalid as they once had been, but there was no comfort here in the grim stone monoliths, and the inhabitants were thankful that summer was coming, bringing with it more light and warmth.

A room at the very top of one such building was, on this chilly spring evening, occupied by two men. One was some sort of foreign seaman, a tall, cheerful man, about thirty-five years old, with a large mustache and steel-rimmed circular glasses, excellent German—usually an impossible language for foreigners to master—and a clever way of making rude jokes that were particularly *berlinerisch*. With him there was a German fellow, getting on for fifty, with wavy gray hair and the sort of Berlin accent that you'd expect to hear in Grunewald, rather than in a grimy place like this.

Living together in the same room for nearly two weeks had not made the men friends. The stress did not help, nor did the smell from the toilet on the landing, the dirty sheets on the bed, and the stuffy atmosphere of this room in which they slept, ate, played cards, and tried not to argue.

"What's the time?" said Peter Winter, the elder of the men. He was wearing a dark-gray suit. It was baggy and in places threadbare, but it was one of the few suits that had fitted him when the Special Operations Executive in London offered him their selection of German-made clothes with German labels. It might help him sustain the fiction that he was the senior costing clerk that his forged identity papers described. But respectable-looking clerks were not easily

505

provided for. Most of the clothes available came from refugees, and refugees are not noted for their sartorial elegance.

"Twenty-five minutes past," replied Brian Samson testily. It was the third time Winter had asked him that question in the previous quarter of an hour. Samson had a white roll-neck seaman's sweater and brown corduroy trousers and heavy boots with studs that in the last resort he could use as a weapon. He was sitting immediately under the light, darning a sock while holding it stretched over an empty tumbler.

"They should have sent someone by now." Winter looked at the radio transmitter in the corner. If they were caught with that, and the antenna that was fixed to the guttering outside the window, they'd be executed without trial. He looked at Samson. There was no anxiety to be seen; it wasn't nerves that made him so bad-tempered. If the door crashed down now, Brian Samson would smile and do his Swedish seaman act and get away with it, with laughs and salutes all round. Samson had the "common touch," and Peter Winter envied him that gift. In the dangerous game of espionage, the "common touch" could be a trump card.

"Perhaps Hitler canceled the meeting and went back to Wolfs-schanze," said Samson. He said the name of the Führer's headquarters with unconcealed contempt. "Wolf's Lair"—the name that Hitler had given to his headquarters—was a measure of the fantasy world in which these madmen lived.

"To Rastenburg in East Prussia? No, that's out of the question. Everything is done from the Berghof at this time of year. The Führer is spending more and more time there these days. The generals say the Führer won't go back east until the summer offensive begins."

"I wish you wouldn't keep calling that bastard the Führer. He's not my Führer."

Peter Winter didn't argue, but it was difficult to get out of such ingrained habits. "That's why this is such a good time for the army to do it. He'll be at the Berghof until about July, and the security there is not so rigorous."

"I see," said Samson sardonically, without looking up from his darning.

Winter looked down at the crippled fingers of his left hand. Handling the harness and shroud lines for his parachute drop had proved difficult, and this maimed hand was red and sore with the exertion of it. For years he'd been able to forget about the deformity, but now—under the critical gaze of Samson—he was self-conscious again. "It's a young captain. . . . He's demonstrating a new antitank weapon to Hitler. . . ." He got it right this time, "Hitler," not "Führer." "The bomb is concealed in one of the ammunition boxes that are part of the demonstration."

"Sounds good," said Samson in an offhand way.

"The officer will lose his own life," persisted Peter. He looked at his companion in the hope that he'd show more interest and compassion.

Samson looked up from his darning, stared at Peter, and said, "You really believe all this shit, don't you?"

"What do you mean?"

"Do our people in London believe all this rubbish you keep telling me?" And then, in answer to his own question, "I suppose they must do, or they wouldn't have given me all the extra work of looking after you."

Peter resented that. It was typical of Samson that everything was measured by his work and his inconvenience. "Why wouldn't they believe it?"

"The Yanks sent you, didn't they? They'll believe anything. If someone told those Yanks in London that Hitler was really a tame gorilla, they'd send a zoologist over here."

"The army are determined . . ."

"The army! Don't tell me about the bloody army. Those spine-less bastards didn't discover that there was anything wrong with Hitler until the Red Army started showing them how to fight battles, and the RAF started bombing their precious German towns. Now they've decided that they want to get rid of him. Typically German, that: fair-weather friends, the Germans."

"They've tried before," said Peter. He knew that a lot of it was just Samson letting off steam, but it hurt just the same.

"And how they've tried before! I've heard so many stories about the army's attempts to assassinate Hitler that I can't keep account of them."

"His security is so tight nowadays."

"So why weren't they trying to kill the bastard back in 1940, when security wasn't so tight? Too busy marching into Poland, Norway, France, Belgium, and Holland, that's why."

"Perhaps."

"No 'perhaps' about it. These bloody aristocratic army officers are not going to kill Hitler. They haven't got the guts. If the generals were going to kill Hitler, they would have done it by now. My God, they've been discussing it long enough. Would you like to know when I first heard those stories?"

Peter, who didn't want to hear how long ago that was, said, "It's not only the army. A lot of Germans are making efforts to get an armistice."

"An 'armistice' is the right word," said Samson. "A suspension of hostilities. That's what they want—a breathing space before going back to war again. I've got no time for any of them: generals, landed gentry, churchmen, intellectuals, liberals, and all that crowd. I wouldn't listen to any of them. A kick up the arse is what they need."

"Don't you want the war to end?"

"Yes, I want the war to end. But I want it to end at the right time, at the right place, and with the right people ending it. We've stated our war policy—unconditional surrender. We don't want any of this damned armistice nonsense. We had an armistice in 1918, and look what happened. It only needed a few years of reorganization and rearmament and you bloody Germans were on the march again. No, no, no. Let's not make the same mistake again. The hell with this clique of well-born officers, and the rest of them. Sod them! We don't need any help in killing Hitler. We'll do it in our own way and in our own good time."

"Is that what most of your countrymen feel?"

"My countrymen? Yes, it is. And if you think we're a bit lacking of the Old World courtesies, you should talk to the Poles and the Czechs and the rest of the poor devils you've walked over."

"I didn't realize how strongly you feel. Under the circumstances I must thank you again for everything you've done for me."

"I did what I had to do." He looked at his watch. "They're not going to kill Hitler. They'll have some wonderful excuses, of course—they always do. If they spent as much time on their assassination plots as they do on their excuses, Hitler would have been eaten by the maggots long ago."

"We'll see."

Seeing that his outburst had failed to anger Winter, Samson was a fraction more conciliatory. "You see, these staff officers you think so much of—they don't want to make Germany into any sort of democracy. I don't have to tell you that; you remember what most army officers thought about the Weimar government."

"They don't like Hitler," said Winter.

"No, he's the wrong rank for them. They don't hate Hitler because he invaded neutral countries or because of what he's doing to the Jews. They hate him because he's a rough-spoken Austrian country yokel who doesn't respect their noble ancestry and admire their mastery of the art of war."

"That's silly talk."

"The German generals don't want to end the war: they want help to fight it. You told me yourself that they propose to go on fighting the Russians as a 'bulwark to communism' while making peace with the Western powers."

"Yes."

"Well, what does that mean, except us helping them fight the Reds?"

"I suppose you're right, but we can't let the Russians keep coming. They will have to be held back. A lot of people in America agree."

"Forget it. The British public wouldn't stand for it; they think Joe Stalin is their savior. And the government would never try it on. No matter what sort of havoc the Red Army are creating for you, there's not a chance in hell of a separate peace without the Russians. Churchill, Roosevelt, and Stalin spelled out their unconditional-surrender message long ago. If they didn't modify that when they were losing, why the hell would they do so now, when they're winning?"

It was not encouraging to listen to this man, thought Winter. If there were many others like him, Winter's mission was doomed to failure right from the start. And he had the feeling that there were a lot of others like him.

"Love him? I detest him!"

In another part of the city a Mercedes 320 convertible, one of the smarter types of staff car used by the army, went slowly along Unter den Linden. The lime-tree blooms smelled strong at this time of evening. There was a lot of traffic tonight. People were coming out of the Opera and flooding across Unter den Linden, oblivious of the traffic, their heads full of music. It was Mozart tonight. Not *The Magic Flute,* of course—that was banned because of the Masonic references—and not *The Marriage of Figaro* or *Così fan tutti,* because the libretto had been written by da Ponte, a baptized Jew. Tonight it was *Die Entführung.* Berlin audiences had always liked that, and it was sung in a language they could understand.

General Horner, seated in the back of the slowly moving car, looked at the buildings as the car went along. He could never get used to the terrible damage that the winter of air attacks had wrought. So much of the city had been destroyed, whole districts had gone, so many killed and injured, but even worse was the loss of confidence that these sustained air attacks had inflicted. Berliners being Berliners, they had met their hardships with smiles and jokes. But the jokes were different from the old jokes. Scratch a smiling Berliner and you'll find a cynic underneath, and Berlin jokes were becoming bitter. And the jokes were not just jokes about Hermann Göring and the Luftwaffe's defense system; they were farther-ranging than that, and they were about defeat. "Jewish jokes," some people called them, and perhaps they were right.

There were more people on the street in the evenings now that winter had passed. Night bombing was done by the British, and Berliners realized that the RAF's heavy bombers could get as far as this only under cover of the long winter nights. Now it was possible to get a proper night's sleep, except when sometimes light aircraft were sent over to drop a few bombs and sound the alarms just for the nuisance of it. Well, it was good tactics, he supposed. It was worth losing a small aircraft in exchange for having the whole city's workforce bleary-eyed next morning. And, as everyone knew, the British didn't lose even their light aircraft. These damned RAF Mosquitoes flew too high for the Luftwaffe's night fighters to reach them.

As for the Americans, they were crossing the Reich to bomb Poland in broad daylight! The implication was frightening: the Allies were getting virtual control of the air.

Even Unter den Linden had not escaped the bombs. Kranzler Corner had been demolished, he noticed. He'd not sit there again, eating cream cakes and watching the girls strolling past, as he'd so often done with Pauli Winter when they were young cadets. In those days wars were fought on battlefronts: the enemy didn't come and destroy a man's home while he was hundreds of miles away fighting for his country. The effect of the bombing upon soldiers serving on the Russian Front was only too evident from the extracts and samples that the field post-office censors sent back for analysis. Every way he looked, reason said the war must end. And if there was only one way to end it, then so be it, oath to the Führer or no oath.

"Hurry, driver! I told you it was urgent."

"*Ja,* Herr General."

After they were past Pariser Platz the traffic thinned a bit, and they roared through the dark Tiergarten, where the shielded headlights picked out a few couples strolling arm in arm, round past the Eden Hotel and the scaffolding where they were repairing the bomb damage to the zoo. The Zoo Palast cinema was emptying, and the Ku-damm was filled with traffic; the streetcars slowed everything even more. But the evening was not yet over, and more people were arriving here in the entertainment district. The dark-green Mercedes halted behind a streetcar and waited while the alighting passengers walked to the curb before resuming the journey. Some of the streetcar passengers were dressed up: it had become difficult to get motor fuel for anything but important official journeys nowadays.

His driver knew the way. He turned off at Hubertus Allee and went around the circle at Bismarckplatz and to the expensive little apartment block where Pauli Winter lived. The driver jumped out and ran round to hold the door open. Damn, it was cold, thought Alex Horner as he got out of the car. He should have worn his overcoat.

General Horner went and rang the bell. The janitor let him in, bowing in deference to the general in his uniform with the breeches and polished high boots, and the Knight's Cross dangling from his collar. The janitor opened the grille of the lift. "Good evening, Herr General." Alex nodded and pressed the button; there was a grinding noise and a lurch before the tiny lift went up to Pauli's apartment on the fifth floor.

Pauli opened the door. "Alex! Hello!"

"Are you alone?" he asked.

"Yes," said Pauli. "Come in. Inge's gone to the cinema."

"I can't stay, but I couldn't tell you on the phone." Horner put his peaked cap on the hall stand before going into the drawing room.

"A drink?"

"No. Pauli—there has been another attempt on the Führer's life. This afternoon at four o'clock. At the Berghof."

"It failed?"

"Yes, it failed."

"I've heard nothing so far," said Pauli. He looked at his friend quizzically. Was that all? Had he dashed across Berlin to tell him that another of the army's attempts on the Führer's life had ended in failure?

"I will have that drink," said Alex. "Brandy, if you have it."

"Sit down, Alex." Pauli poured a glass and opened an Apollinaris water for himself. Ever since the SS had acquired the mineral-water company, Fritz Esser had arranged that everyone on his staff got crates and crates of the stuff.

"It's rather complicated, Pauli. It was a demonstration for the Führer—an antitank rocket weapon, an elaborate version of the Panzerfaust. . . . You know how he likes to be shown these things so that he can lecture all present and display his knowledge."

"Yes, I know," said Pauli. He watched Horner drink his brandy-and-soda in two or three gulps and put the empty glass down. Pauli lit a cigarette. For a moment the two men stood facing each other and not speaking. It had become a strange relationship. Although the deep and long-lasting friendship provided a fundamentally sound basis of trust, there was an element of bluff and double bluff, too. General Alex Horner was single-minded and at ease. He was loyally serving the army, and more specially the group of plotters to which he reported. If Himmler wanted to monitor the plot through Pauli Winter, that was all right, for Alex was kept at arm's length from the plotters, just in case his old friendship proved not enough protection. And if Himmler felt he was going to step in and eliminate the army's men after the deed was done, then he might find himself outmaneuvered.

Pauli Winter's loyalties were less easily defined. He also revered the army, and his training at Lichterfelde bound him to the Prussian Officer Corps in the same way that it bound Horner. But Pauli Winter had other allegiances, too: in the postwar years the Nazi regime had provided him with renewed self-respect, at a time when he needed help most. He'd become one of the party's elite, part of the state within a state. The apparatus that the SS-Reichsführer had brought under his direct control now included the black-uniformed

Allgemeine SS, the field-gray-uniformed Waffen-SS, the concentration and extermination camps, the SD intelligence organization, the Ministry of the Interior, the Gestapo, and various police organizations that came under Himmler in his role of minister. Added to this were commercial companies that made everything from cheap furniture to uniforms and firearms.

Himmler was now more powerful than any army general could ever have hoped to become, and Pauli admired the quiet, modest little Heini in his pince-nez and the uniform that he so liked to wear. If Himmler wanted his men to do nothing while the army tried to assassinate the Führer, then Pauli would do exactly that. He had come to see the logic of it. Himmler had already taken over *de facto* control of the Third Reich; it was just a matter of time before he took over entirely. And if the SS-Reichsführer then negotiated peace with the Western powers, doubtless he would do it with the same skill he'd shown in climbing to his present position.

So Pauli Winter was able to treat Alex Horner's determination to kill the head of state with equanimity. And yet he would not rejoice at Hitler's death. He'd be saddened, as he'd been saddened at the necessary death of old Graf before a firing squad in the prison in Munich.

General Horner had declined the invitation to sit down. He moved about the room, looking at pictures and books without actually seeing them, and moving his lips without speaking. Now he turned, fists pushed into the front pockets of his breeches, and said, "The weapons were displayed—no firing, of course, just a display of prototypes—and the bomb's time fuse was set. The demonstration was in the SS barracks yard behind the Platterhof. Then, just as the demonstration was about to begin, the Führer was called back inside the barracks building to take an important phone call from the Chancellery. You can't change the fuse once it's started."

"It went off?"

"Just half a kilo or so of explosive, but the officer was badly hurt."

"He's not dead?"

"No, he's 'being questioned,' Pauli."

"I can do nothing for him, Alex. I really can't. I have authority to investigate plans for attempts against the Führer's life, but this is something quite different. Questioning your man will be done under the orders of the SS officer in charge of security there. Even the Gestapo couldn't get access to such a prisoner until the officer there is satisfied that the immediate danger is past and no other bombs are planted in the vicinity."

"I didn't come to ask you to interfere at the Berghof, Pauli. But the trouble is that this officer has had contact with other people here in Berlin."

"You'd better get them to some area where the army have complete control: France might be best."

"One of the people was your brother."

"My brother? Peter? How?"

"Peter is in Berlin. He was sent to make contact on behalf of the Western powers."

"Peter?" It was bewildering.

"And Peter met the officer concerned. If they make him talk he will describe Peter. It's for you to decide, Pauli. You might want to get your brother out of danger."

"What is he doing here?"

"He has a radio. He was to radio to London the news of the assassination and then remain as the liaison with the army here in Berlin. He would stay until the army radio established a direct link with London."

"Do you know where he is?"

"In Wedding. There's no phone."

"No phone—how absurd."

"It was more secure," explained Alex Horner.

"And damned inconvenient. Didn't they take into account that something like this would happen?"

"No, they didn't. They thought it would be successful."

Pauli looked at him. "Yes, they always think it will be successful." He was tempted to add some sarcastic remark about the army's similar optimism, and lack of success, against the Russians, but he knew that Alex Horner would not welcome it, and he was too fond of Alex to erode their precious friendship.

In the moments of silence that followed there was the sound of the lift motor. Outside on the landing the metal grille slammed, and then the voices got louder until Inge came into the room, and Fritz Esser followed her. He made some sort of joke and they both laughed.

"General Horner?" said Inge in the stagy voice that she often adopted after a few drinks. "What are you doing here?" She was dressed up: they both were.

"Alex called in for a drink, darling," said Pauli. "But I thought you were going to have a late dinner and go dancing."

"We were," said Inge, "but some tiresome man brought Fritz a message." She looked in the mirror and touched her hair. She was forty-seven and had begun to tint the graying places. They'd been to see *Romanze in Moll.* Inge loved it and identified with the doomed heroine, the unfaithful wife of a civil servant. But her lover—a musical genius writing a "romance"—could hardly be compared to Fritz Esser. Inge was annoyed at missing the rejected wife's suicide, even if she had already seen the film three times. She smiled wanly at her reflection.

"To the cinema," said Fritz after he'd greeted Horner. "They stopped the film and put a slide on the screen asking me to contact the manager."

"What is it?" said Pauli.

Fritz Esser looked from General Horner to Pauli and back to Horner. He guessed what had brought Horner here, but he went through the motions, since that was the way they wanted it. "An attempt on the Führer's life. It's not being announced officially. An army captain with a bomb. A staff officer, but an ex–front-line soldier: the usual Knight's Cross and all that ironware. The poor little swine got his arm blown off. The Führer was inside taking a shit at the time. He must have wondered what he'd eaten when he heard that one go off, eh?" The Führer's diet of salads, and the chronic flatulence that resulted, was well known to those in his immediate circle, and Fritz laughed loudly, exposing his teeth. He'd had a great deal of expensive dental work done lately. At Inge's urging, his old bad, crooked, broken tombstones were now being systematically replaced with even, regular ones. Many of them were gold.

"How do you know all the details?" Pauli asked.

"I phoned Bormann. Bormann's the only one who knows what he's doing down there in the Berghof. It's a circus! Those Bavarians couldn't run a candy store, but the Führer doesn't seem to mind the way they screw everything up. And they're the only ones who can understand the Führer's accent," said Fritz, and laughed again. "Give me a drink, Pauli, will you? I'll be up half the night. They have the poor bastard in custody, but we'll have to send someone down there to investigate, just for the look of the thing. Do you think our pal Koch could handle it?" He looked at his watch and then poured the drink himself. He knew where everything was kept. "I must go."

"Koch's not a very good investigator," said Pauli. "And he sometimes upsets people. Don't send him to the Berghof. I've put him behind a desk and let him shuffle paper. Leave him there."

"I'll find someone," said Fritz, drinking his large measure of schnapps.

"I've got to go out with Alex," Pauli announced.

"Where to?" asked Inge petulantly. She would be left alone, and she hated to be alone. That was why she stayed with Pauli and put up with this absurd pretense of marriage.

"Out," said Pauli.

"You don't have to be so damned rude," said Inge shrilly. Any sort of rejection hurt her deeply.

"Now, now, now," said Fritz Esser, who often found himself keeping the peace between them. "Pauli never asks us where we're going, Inge, my love. You must let him live his own life."

"We should have been divorced ages ago," she said.

Alex Horner had picked up his cap. He stood in the hall, staring at an engraving of Vienna—a present from Inge for Pauli's birthday long ago—his face blank, as if he were not hearing the conversation.

"Forget about divorces," Fritz Esser told her. "The Führer doesn't approve of divorces: it would affect your husband's career, and maybe mine, too." He grinned. This might have been a joke—it was not always possible to know with Fritz—but at least she could be sure that his injunction was sincere, and she didn't pursue the topic.

Inge looked at Pauli with a smile that was too sweet. "So Peter is here in Berlin?" she said suddenly.

"What's that?" bellowed Fritz Esser.

Alex Horner continued to study the engraving and Pauli said, "Peter? In Berlin? No." But Pauli had never been a very good liar, and Fritz's genuine surprise showed Pauli's denials for what they were.

"I heard you talking," said Inge. "I came up the stairs—I can't go into that lift anymore—and let myself in while Fritz was parking the car. I heard you."

"Yes, he's here." Pauli's voice was devoid of emotion. It was the voice he'd used so often during the rows they'd had.

"Is that where you're going?" she asked.

"Yes," said Pauli. "I'm going to see my brother."

"Are you going to tell him that Lottie is dead?"

"I don't know."

"Murdered by American bombs: make sure he understands that," she said cruelly.

Pauli looked at her. Poor Inge. "Do you still love him?" he asked.

"Love him? I detest him!"

"Like you detest me?" Pauli asked her.

"Yes, like I detest you."

Fritz Esser gulped his schnapps, put the glass on the table, grabbed Inge by the arm, and shook her so hard that her teeth snapped together. "Now, you listen to me, you silly girl," he said. "This is state business, not romantic stories from the ladies' magazines. You keep your mouth shut." He shook her roughly. "Tight shut! You mention the name of Peter Winter and I'll beat the daylights out of you. Understand, you little bitch?"

Fritz released his grip on her arm and she backed away from him fearfully, rubbing the arm where he'd hurt her. To Pauli's surprise, Inge smiled—a bitter smile, but a smile nevertheless. "You make everything so clear, Fritz darling," she said.

"She'll be all right, Pauli," Fritz assured him without even looking at her. "You get going and do what you have to do. Where is he?"

"Where is he?" Pauli in turn asked Alex Horner.

Horner hesitated and then said, "Wedding: an apartment block, between Saint Josef's Church and the subway station."

"I need to know, if I'm to keep the bloodhounds away from you," explained Fritz Esser without saying how he intended to do it.

"The officer held in custody—the injured one at the Berghof—has met Peter," said Pauli.

"Don't worry about him," said Fritz. "He's already taken care of." He glanced at General Horner, but Horner remained as stiff as a rod, in that tense and formal military attitude that the Germans call *zackig.*

Pauli looked at Horner, too, and felt embarrassed. There was no doubt what Fritz meant: plans had been put under way to ensure that the officer died as quickly as possible and so obviate any chance of further complications. General Horner understood, of course—he was not a fool—but he gave no sign of emotion.

"Go to bed, Inge," Fritz Esser said; when she remained in the room fidgeting with the empty glasses, as if trying to decide whether to clear them away, he said, "Did you hear me? I said go to bed."

"Yes, Fritz. Good night, General Horner." Horner bowed without a word. "Good night, Pauli."

"Good night, Inge."

"And keep that big mouth of yours shut," said Fritz before she could say good night to him. To the others he said, "Come along. I take it you've got a car, Alex?"

"Yes, I have."

"Good luck to you both," said Fritz. "It's going to be a damned long night."

"Who was the Swedish fellow?"

The Bodensee is a large gloomy-looking lake that forms the boundary between southwestern Germany and the German-speaking cantons of Switzerland. Its waters are frequently made dangerous by storms that spring up quickly from the snow-tipped Alps that serrate the southern horizon. From Friedrichshafen—a small town on the German side—a ferryboat goes regularly to the Swiss town of Romanshorn. This June evening the air had turned suddenly cooler, and the water had the curious milky look that local people say is the presage of a storm. The air was full of tiny flying insects, and there were birds swooping low over the smooth lake water preying upon them. The threat of rain had kept everyone indoors except two men. The waterfront was theirs alone.

The men were strolling along under the trees. One was shortish, plump, and in his mid-forties. An untidy-looking fellow, he wore a good suit of the same black worsted as lawyers favor throughout the world. His blond hair was going white, and he moved his hands a lot as he spoke. The other man was slightly older, a thin-faced man with eyeglasses; he was shabbily dressed but tall and slim, and he carried himself more gracefully, the way an actor or a dancer might walk. When they got to the wall, they turned and started coming back towards the big black BMW with the Berlin registration plates that was parked near the church.

"The immigration officer on this side is named Schanz," Pauli told his brother. "A tall fellow with a mustache . . . about sixty years old. He used to work for Papa at the factory here in town. He's friendly. Tell him you are going to Switzerland for the company. If there's any trouble I will intercede, but let's hope it will be all right without me."

"I don't want to get you into trouble," Peter said.

"I can look after myself," said Pauli.

"I wouldn't have got out of Berlin without you."

"Who was the Swedish fellow?"

"A seaman. He was trying to sell me tins of butter and bacon."

"He slipped away very quietly," said Pauli.

"Black market. He was afraid of getting picked up, I suppose."

"I thought I knew his face," said Pauli.

"Perhaps he's sold you butter and bacon."

Pauli smiled. "That must be it." He looked across the water again. They were on the strand near the Schlosskirche, at the very spot where Mama had sat in Papa's wonderful Italian motorcar watching the zeppelin so many years ago. Where was the old car now? Pauli wondered. In a museum, perhaps. Once, during the Berlin fighting in 1919, he'd glimpsed it driving through the Tiergarten with half a dozen soldiers piled in it. "You say you'll be all right on the other side. . . . If you have any trouble there, ask for a man named Becheler. He's a police inspector who is always somewhere near the customs office. Tell him you know me. He's a sullen young bastard, but we pay him."

"The Gestapo?"

"Yes. He helps us from time to time. His parents live in Innsbruck: he won't do anything that might upset us," said Pauli ominously.

Peter looked at his pocket watch—a cheap steel one, but it worked all right, just as London said it would. "The boat will be leaving soon. I wish you'd come, too, Pauli."

"We've been through all that, Peter."

"I wish you'd come. I could make it all right for you, whatever you've done."

Good grief! How could Peter be urging his younger brother to flee from his native land and join his country's enemies? Surely it would make more sense for Peter to stay here and let Pauli protect him. The world was turning upside down. "I've done nothing I'm ashamed of," said Pauli.

Peter looked at his brother. He wished he could make Pauli understand what was waiting for the SS and the Gestapo and all Himmler's minions. "They hate us, Pauli."

"Who? The Americans?"

"Everyone hates us. No one respects the Germans any longer. They call us names—Krauts, Huns, Boches, Jerries—and they despise us."

"We'll see about that when we've won the war," said Pauli defiantly.

Pauli's childish optimism irritated Peter. He wanted to shake some sense into him. "The war is lost, Pauli. Surely you must see that by now."

"Is it, Peter?"

Poor Pauli. He looked lost. Peter had always taken his brother's respect, love, and loyalty for granted; perhaps he'd not given enough in return. Perhaps none of the family had. Suddenly he felt protective of his younger brother in a way he'd never felt before. He put an arm round Pauli's shoulder and said gently, "God knows what is going to happen to Germany. Come with me! What have you got to stay here for?"

"Nothing. I've lost Inge; I have no children; Father won't permit me in his house. But I can't go with you. I'm too old to adapt to another country and another language. Too old and too stupid. I'll stay with Mama. She'll need comforting when Father dies. He won't last another winter; the doctor told Mama that."

"The boat is coming now. I wish I could have seen him . . . and Mama. Perhaps you could find some way of telling her."

"The fewer people who know, the better, Peter."

"I suppose you're right. But it's terrible to think I may never see him again."

"I didn't want to argue with Father, but he blamed me for things that were not my fault. It wasn't fair."

"He's old, Pauli. And old people become crotchety."

"I did what I could."

"I'm sure you did, Pauli. We'd better go along to the pier."

Pauli stopped strolling. He turned to his brother and said, "I loved Lottie. I really loved her."

"I'm sure you did, Pauli. No one blames you for anything."

"You don't understand: I loved her!"

"We must go, Pauli. The ferryboat is almost here."

"If she'd stayed at Lisl Hennig's she would have been all right, but she was feeling low, and Lisl's little boy said he'd take her to the cinema. She never went out, but it was a color film, a musical. Little Theo said it would cheer her up."

Peter closed his eyes and tried not to hear Pauli's words. It was too painful. "You told me."

"And then the Americans came over. It was a bad raid. They both must have died instantly: the whole cinema got it—a direct hit."

Peter opened his eyes to look at his brother. "No one blames you, Pauli. It's the war. I understand." Peter had forced the news of Lottie's death into some dark recess of his mind. He'd grieve for her at another time and in another place.

"I would have done anything, Peter. You know that."

"I know, Pauli."

"There is a visitor."

The big house in downtown New York City had become something of a curiosity, for all around it were tall apartment blocks and office buildings. In a bedroom on the second floor of the old house, Cyrus Rensselaer was in bed. He was ninety-three years old and in amazing physical shape for a man of his years. Almost every day he got up and, with a little help from a servant, got dressed and came downstairs in the newly installed elevator to have luncheon. But for the last two weeks he'd not managed that feat. He'd remained in bed and had *The New York Times* and *The Wall Street Journal* read to him. He'd eaten only soft-boiled eggs and a little chicken soup with dry toast. The doctor visited him every day. At first he'd said that his patient was in fine shape, but on Tuesday Cyrus Rensselaer grew weaker.

He liked to have the mail brought up to him. Sometimes there was a letter from Glenn. It didn't say very much, of course—Glenn had never been very good about writing letters, and now that he was engaged in secret work in England, his letters were both short and uninformative. A couple of times he'd said that all the family could be proud of Peter Winter, and once, very recently, he'd written to say that Peter was in England, safe and sound. But since they'd never heard that Peter was out of England, or in danger, this letter of reassurance meant little to anyone.

On Friday morning Cyrus Rensselaer received the sort of letter he liked: a big fat letter from an old friend who'd been on a business trip to Portugal. This long letter, written in a bold, flowing hand on a dozen sheets of bright-blue airmail paper, contained all sorts of information about European people, places, and corporations known to Cyrus. The latest doings of his business rivals were catalogued there, and near the end his friend had written: ". . . no one gets to Berlin these days, but I met a fellow who told me that Harald Winter's funeral was something of an event in that miserable town. Your daughter, Veronica, was there and looking well, I'm delighted to tell you, but you probably know all this already."

Cyrus put the letter down. So Harald had died. Soon the war would be over and Veronica would come home. Life would be better then. He'd be back on his feet once Veronica was in the house again. He could clearly remember the sounds of her voice from the days when she was a child. Singing and chattering—such a noisy little girl. He smiled at the memory. The house had never been the same since she'd gone off to college. There was so much to talk to her about.

They found Cyrus Rensselaer dead when they took his light lunch to the bedroom. His eyeglasses were still on his nose; he'd died peacefully. The blue sheets of writing paper had fallen to the floor. Some people who read the letter thought that perhaps the news of his son-in-law's funeral had killed him, but more perceptive people said that he'd died happy knowing that his old enemy Harald had gone before him.

The news of Cyrus Rensselaer's death reached London more quickly than the news of Harald Winter's death had crossed the Atlantic Ocean. For Cyrus Rensselaer was a name known to the world of business and beyond. In London an obituary appeared in *The Times* and in *The Financial Times,* too. *The Economist* ran a short article about "A Wizard of Wall Street." But it took much longer for Glenn to find out that the old man's fortune had been made over to his wife, Dot. For Glenn there was no more than a small annuity, and for Veronica, who, as his will said, had never returned to her homeland, there was nothing at all.

In London that long and anxious summer of 1944, Glenn Rensselaer and Peter Winter were too occupied to spend much time with condolences, mourning, or celebration. June 6 was D-Day, when the Anglo-American armies invaded France, and Germany had the two-front war that most strategists thought must prove fatal.

Colonel Rudolf von Kleindorf had been amongst the first to encounter the newly arrived foe. He was the commander of a battalion that was engaged close to the beach in the early hours of the battle. On the day following D-Day, he made a personal reconnaissance of the ground to the south of Omaha Beach, where the American assault had gone very wrong. It was easy to get lost in the leafy, hedge-lined lanes, and the German defenders were under constant attack by Allied fighter planes, which ground-strafed anything that moved. In one such low-level attack, von Kleindorf's armored car was hit by machine-gun bullets and went off the road and overturned. He and his driver spent four hours hiding in a shell crater, hoping to get back to their own lines under cover of darkness.

But darkness comes very late in a June evening in Normandy. Advancing American infantry captured the two men, and a corporal took from Kleindorf his medals, his gold signet ring with the Kleindorf family crest, and his wristwatch and stuffed them in the pocket of his jacket. When von Kleindorf objected vociferously to this theft of his personal possessions, an infantry soldier named Weinberger from Chicago swore at him in fluent, colloquial Berlin German before hitting him in the face with a rifle butt, causing Kleindorf to suffer a broken jaw, broken nose, broken cheekbones, some lost teeth, and multiple cuts and bruises. He was left unconscious at the roadside, and the infantry platoon moved forward again.

The armies of the Western powers had broken through the "Atlantic Wall" without pausing. The Anglo-American navies permitted no German ship within striking distance of the vast invasion fleet that filled the Channel, and the sky belonged to their air forces. Two weeks later, on June 20, the Red Army's summer offensive began on the Eastern Front. The Red Army smashed into Army Group Center, where the German army's power was concentrated. The German front gave way, and Poland and the German Reich were laid open to the Russian advance.

On July 20 the army conspirators tried again to kill Adolf Hitler. Another of the English-made bombs obtained from Abwehr sources was exploded by time fuse during a conference at the "Wolf's Lair" at Rastenburg in East Prussia. This attempt was only marginally more successful than all the previous ones. Hitler was injured, but survived and maintained control of his regime.

This time, however, the conspirators bungled not only the assassination but the seizure of power, too. The messages, proclamations, and orders that had been so carefully prepared by the plotters were not issued. It was a hot, humid day in Berlin, and in the offices and corridors of the Replacement Army in the Bendlerblock, officers stood around discussing what to do and waiting for orders that did not come. No attempt was made to seize the radio-broadcasting offices or the post, telephone, and telegram service. No one arrested Nazi ministers, and Berlin's chief of police, who was a party to the conspiracy, waited in vain for orders to act.

Only after Count von Stauffenberg—who had put the bomb alongside Hitler—returned to Berlin did the coup attempt start. By that time it was too late. News had reached Berlin that Hitler was alive and kicking. Now the conspiracy fell to pieces, and soon the notorious basement of the Gestapo building in Prinz-Albrecht-Strasse was filled with high-ranking army officers. The questioning to which they were subjected was hurried and ruthless. Shorthand clerks wrote rapidly while the professional torturers performed their tasks.

None of the men involved got anything resembling a fair trial: it was feared that the opportunities for public speaking might incite others to resist the regime. At the Volksgerichtshof—the People's Court—the accused were not tried; they were simply abused and reviled, a process in which the so-called defense lawyers joined. Conspirators were tortured, sentenced, and executed by such barbarous methods as slow strangulation. Generals and field marshals were hung from meathooks by piano wire and filmed in their death agonies so that Adolf Hitler could have the satisfaction of seeing them die many times over. Not only the guilty were made to suffer. Relatives and friends in the thousands were executed or sent to concentration camps. Many died simply because they had the same name as one of the accused.

General Alex Horner's assignment to command an army corps in France took him away from Berlin and the attempted putsch. When news of it came, Horner—a corps commander—was desperately trying to counter General Bradley's breakthrough of the front at Saint-Lô and stem General Patton's Third Army, which came charging through the gap. Constantly aware of the risk that his name might be revealed by the continuing interrogations of his fellow officers in Berlin, and knowing that his superior, Field Marshal Kluge, was a suspect, Alex Horner nevertheless gave all his attention to the battlefield. But every night he found a few minutes to write a letter to his wife, Chrisi, and always he drew at the bottom of the page some silly picture for his six-year-old son, Christian.

It was warm this evening, so warm that he could smell the ripe cherries on the trees of the orchard in which he was bivouacked. Even through the green canvas, the flashes of a new American artillery bombardment lit his tent. And the noise of the gunfire came like thunder; sometimes the explosions were so close together that it was impossible to distinguish one from another.

He'd finished writing his letter when young Winkel came into the tent. "Herr General?"

"Yes, Winkel. What is it?" The boy was getting to look exactly like his father. Too much beer, that was the trouble. No matter: the days of beer and roses had gone, never to return.

"There is a visitor."

"Who?"

"A general, an SS-Gruppenführer."

The SS officer pushed past Winkel. "General Horner?" he said brusquely. His face registered surprise, but Alex Horner was used to that. Forty-five-year-old generals were not yet a common sight, even in this new age of National Socialism.

"Yes?"

"Heil Hitler," said the officer, extending his arm in the salute that, since the bomb attempt on Hitler's life, had become mandatory for the army as well as the SS.

"Good evening," said Horner, remaining seated. He licked the flap of the envelope. "What is it?"

"I'm bringing my division up on your left tomorrow, General." Horner was senior to him in rank and was his corps commander, but the newcomer called him "General," not "Herr General." That was the SS style: they did it amongst themselves and to the army, too. He was about sixty years old, clean-shaven, with a bony nose in a long leathery face that had rounded and wrinkled with time. He spoke in the thick, inarticulate mumble of Bavaria. On his head he had a well-worn "Afrika Korps"–style cap at a jaunty angle; he wore the mottled camouflage smock that was issued only to the Waffen-SS, and the SS insignia and his rank badge were crudely stenciled on its collar. He had a pistol on his hip and laced high boots that were nonregulation. Despite his age, he looked like a fighting soldier or a brigand. Horner looked at him but was not impressed. Some of them chose to look like infantry veterans, but it meant nothing: generals won battles by using their brains, and a pistol on the hip got in the way when you were leaning over a map table.

"Yes, I was expecting you two days ago," said Horner.

"There were unforeseen transportation problems."

"Have a drink," said Horner.

"Is that real French brandy?"

"Bring two glasses, Winkel," Horner called. He knew that his driver would be picking cherries as an excuse to eavesdrop, but Winkel knew how to hold his tongue, so Horner tolerated his nosiness. To the newcomer Horner said, "Where have you come from?"

"Northern Italy: near Milan. We were in reserve, trying to get ourselves sorted out. We took a pounding on the Eastern Front. We're nowhere near full strength."

"Panzer grenadiers?"

"On paper." Winkel brought the glasses and the two men looked at each other as they drank. The new man had small, active eyes: cunning? piglike? Or was Horner too prejudiced against these political soldiers? He didn't relish the prospect of having a Waffen-SS division in his corps, despite their undoubted capacity for battle. Waffen-SS units had a tiresome habit of ignoring orders when it didn't suit them: of occupying towns they were ordered not to enter, and failing to enter ones they were told to attack. The SS-Gruppenführer drank some cognac and wiped his mouth on the back of his hand. "That's good stuff." And then, "But we'll manage, General; my boys know how to fight."

"As long as you don't think it's easy here," said Horner. "The Americans are young and inexperienced. Sometimes they are stupid, and they continue to make a lot of mistakes, but they have youthful energy and boldness, too, and they learn fast. More important, they seem to have an endless supply of everything. It's different from the Eastern Front, but don't think it's easier."

"My men will hold your line for you." Horner noted the way that these SS soldiers would be holding "his" line "for him." He watched as the man helped himself to another brandy without asking for it. It was often said that Prussians were too cold and aloof but, faced with a fellow like this, it was difficult for Horner to resist his father's theory that all Bavarians were stupid, hostile, sour-faced pigs.

"I'm sure they will," said Horner.

"The 'fire brigade,' they call us. We rush from front to front, wherever the army need help. And we fight to the last bullet."

"One thing must be understood, Herr Gruppenführer," Horner said coldly. "I don't want any shooting of prisoners. There'll be no atrocities on my sector of front."

"These things happen," said the SS-Gruppenführer. "My men fight to win."

"If they happen on my front there will be a field court-martial."

"Right. No shooting of prisoners."

"I hope you understand, Herr Gruppenführer. I will court-martial any officer who disobeys my orders. Whatever his rank."

"You don't recognize me, do you, General Horner?"

Horner's life had been crowded with faces, fleeting glimpses of men of all ranks, shapes, and sizes, but he'd never had command of an SS division before. He stared at the man. "No, I don't, Herr Gruppenführer."

"Brand is the name; General Heinrich Brand, Crazy Heini! I was teaching you about trench warfare when you were scarcely out of your nappies and bibs."

Yes, it was Brand. He'd changed a lot, but Horner should have recognized those mad, constantly moving eyes. What bad luck to meet up with that insolent swine again after all these years. "You'd better start moving up into position right away," said Horner.

"My men are still arriving."

"You'll need the cover of darkness. In this sector, enemy air activity is fierce as soon as there's light enough for them to see. They come in relays, squadron after squadron . . . rocket-firing planes, sometimes. Anything that's moving will be attacked. And it's like that all day."

"Where's the damned Luftwaffe?"

"They have unforeseen transportation problems, too," said Horner. "They get shot down every time they come near."

"My flak . . ."

"Never mind trying to stem the air attacks—leave that for the day following," said Horner sarcastically. "Just get your forward positions in place before daylight. We're all ready for you; we're considerably overextended. I have an officer fully briefed; I'll send him with you. Do as he says. You'll have to keep them all moving."

"I don't need any help," said Brand.

"I didn't ask if you needed help," said Horner. "I said I'll send one of my staff officers with you. I'll expect you to be holding the front-line positions by dawn."

"That's not much time," said Brand.

"It's the regular army procedure," said Horner, to goad him more.

"Where's the officer?"

"Winkel!" called Horner. "I want you to take the Herr General to the command post." To Brand he said, "Send a runner when you are in position. Then come to the staff conference at 0730 hours."

"Yes, Herr General," said Brand. He bared his teeth in a fierce smile.

A very proud parent.

Veronica Winter peeped into the room that Harald Winter had used as a study ever since they'd moved in. The room was little changed from the way it had been just after they married. Everything was in place: Harry's library; the valuable carpets, now a little worn; and the wonderful inlaid desk where Pauli was sitting. He'd been sitting there for nearly half an hour, trying to summon up the courage or the will, or whatever it was he needed, to unlock his father's desk and sort out his private papers.

Pauli would have given almost anything to have someone else do this sad task. His mother refused to go through Harald's desk. He supposed she dreaded finding love letters, or other compromising material, from Harald's notorious love affairs. Veronica had taken her husband's death stoically. She'd loved him with that tenderness and loyalty that her generation were taught a provider deserved. Though she wept for him, Harry's death marked the end of her bondage.

Pauli noticed the new strength of his mother, but he could not account for it. He took it for granted that Veronica would be as devastated by Harald Winter's death as he was. Often, ever since he was a small child, he'd wondered how he would cope with his father's death. At one time it had been the ultimate nightmare. But always he'd comforted himself with the thought that, when the time came, it would be Peter's duty.

He took his father's keys and put the tiny one into the lock. How familiar those keys were to him. Ever since Pauli could remember, Papa had worn them on the gold chain that stretched across his waistcoat. Now the keys and the chain were his, but Pauli didn't enjoy handling them.

Methodically he started going through the desk: onyx cuff links in a tiny box bearing the name of a Paris jeweler; a horn-handled letter opener; a Zeiss magnifying glass held alongside a spare pair of eyeglasses by a thick rubber band; an ivory slide rule worn and discolored from constant use; a small calfskin address book that fitted Papa's waistcoat pockets, filled with Papa's tiny writing; letters put back into their envelopes with penciled notes on the outside; deeds of the house, a carbon copy of a letter about Harry's shares in the Winter companies, and a long agreement about the partnership signed by all the directors and affixed with a red wax seal; photo postcards of all the old zeppelins, one of them bearing a note and the complex signature of the old Count; a sepia studio photo of Veronica before they were married.

Pauli went through everything piece by piece, trying not to think about the father he would never see again, trying not to wonder where the relationship had started to go wrong. What did Harald expect of him? What does any father expect of his son? Far, far too much. If Harald had just taken Pauli's love and respect for what they were worth, and thanked God for a loyal and trusting son, it would have all been wonderful. But for Pauli life with Harald Winter had been one long, unrelenting examination. Their relationship had always been a series of tests, invented, conducted, and judged with Godlike impartiality by Harald Winter in person.

At the back of the desk were four large plainly bound books, their leather covers showing varying degrees of wear. At first glance they might have been ledgers, which is why Pauli, who was not very skilled at reading accounts, left them to last. But when he opened the heavy pages he was in for the biggest surprise of his life. They were scrapbooks. Neatly pasted onto each page were newspaper and magazine cuttings. There were photos, too, and even a couple of signed menus and a home-made birthday card that nine-year-old Pauli had sent to his father so many years ago.

The four books contained what was virtually a history of Pauli's life. School reports from Lichterfelde, letters he'd written from the trenches, newspaper cuttings reporting his graduation from law school. Newspaper photos of Pauli's magnificent wedding. There were even tiny cuttings from the SS newspaper that announced each of Pauli's promotions and his honorary appointment to SS rank. He didn't know that his father had even seen a copy of *Das Schwarze Korps*, let alone got a copy and cut it up. Pauli was astounded. He read the four books all the way through. There were some cuttings and mementos concerning Peter, but it was mostly about Pauli. And there was nothing to cast a shadow upon Pauli's career. It was the sort of thing that only a very proud parent would compile.

1945

"It's a labor of love."

In the middle of January 1945, the Red Army launched the greatest Russian offensive of the war. One hundred eighty divisions were used in an attack that within two weeks cut East Prussia away from the Reich and gave the Russians the Silesian industrial region, which supplied most of the coal and steel for Germany's war effort.

Adolf Hitler's command post had been moved back to the Reichs-kanzlei and the bunker under it. On January 19, Eva Braun, Hitler's mistress, and Martin Bormann arrived from the Obersalzberg to be with him. On the afternoon of January 27, maps on the wall of the newly equipped Berlin operations room were revised to show that reconnaissance units of Zhukov's Red Army's spearheads had crossed the river Oder and were now only a hundred miles from the city. As the month ended, Hitler made one of his rare excursions: he went to tea with Dr. Josef Goebbels at the Goebbels home at Schwanenwerder, an island in the Havel. Distrustful of poisoners, Hitler took with him a vacuum flask of tea and a bag of biscuits.

On that same day, in Weissensee, on the other side of Berlin, another doctor was entertaining colleagues to tea. There was no funeral that day in Berlin's big Jewish cemetery. Dr. Isaac Volk-mann, who'd once been a highly regarded dentist in the town, was celebrating his birthday. For some years Volkmann had worked as a gravedigger here, and he was grateful to God for this opportunity to survive. He'd brought a handful of tea with him today. Not real

531

tea, of course—a mixture of mint leaf and other herbs that Germans had learned to drink without complaint.

Volkmann had a lot to be grateful for. He went home each night to his wife and his baby son, and the hard work of digging and working as a general laborer came more easily to him than it did to some of the others. Volkmann had always been stocky and muscular. At college he'd excelled at games: hockey, rowing, and athletics. For some of the others it was more difficult. There was Benjamin the rabbi, with his arthritic shoulder; old Simon "the professor," who'd had a chair in physics at Frankfurt an der Oder, with his bronchial cough that left him gasping for breath; and Dr. Sigmund Weiss, who was frightened to go to hospital with his chest pains in case he was taken straight off to a camp.

It was three other men who did most of the digging. They were younger, working-class lads who'd grown up to the prospect of such hard work. The only misfit was the seventh man, the strange Boris Somló, who was the most awkward fellow here. Dr. Volkmann wondered about Somló. He was officially known as "Fromm," but Volkmann had seen his real name on an old Austrian driving license that had fallen from his pocket one day. It dated from before the *Anschluss* and was no longer valid. The man was a fool to keep it. There had been photos, too, all of them of a woman who looked very like him. It must have been his mother.

The mystery about the furtive Boris Somló was that he once said his father wasn't a Jew. As a *Mischling* he could probably have lived and worked a more normal life, without persecution. It wasn't absolutely necessary for him to work here in the cemetery. It wasn't the difference between life and death, as it was for the rest of them. Dr. Weiss said it was a disgrace. Weiss said that Boris should get out, and so provide a safe place for some real Jew who was in danger, but Boris said that he'd been on a transportation train and he didn't want to risk it again. No one believed him, but that was his story. Transportation train: no one got off transportation trains and came back to tell the tale. It had taken a long time to comprehend fully what was happening to the Jewish families who went off to be "resettled in the East," but who never wrote letters or postcards to say they'd arrived. Now they knew, however, and they knew that no one ever came back. That's why they didn't believe Boris.

Isaac Volkmann was the only one who befriended Boris at the cemetery. He felt sorry for him. Although over forty years old, Boris was an unlucky bungler who seemed unable to organize for himself such things as clean linen or even regular shaves. He was—said the others, when Boris was out of earshot—a shlemiel.

Boris's helpless demeanor might not have made him such a figure of fun had it not been for that dreadful Viennese accent, a nasal whine that made even Isaac Volkmann grin sometimes, despite his determination not to make the poor chap's life more difficult.

But today, with mugs of hot tea in their hands and the door closed against the awful Berlin cold, they were all in a good mood. Volkmann looked round at them. They were good men, although none of them had had what he would regard as proper dental care. They stood in the shed behind the mortuary that afternoon talking about the Russian advance—or, rather, about the rumors of it, for none of them had heard anything about the Red Army's crossing of the Oder on the German radio at first hand. Perhaps some had heard the BBC, but none would admit to it, even to these close friends and fellow sufferers.

What would they do if the Russians got here, to Berlin? It was still "if," despite the closeness of the enemy. "The Russians are barbarians," said Dr. Weiss, who had a cousin in the army. "They will kill everyone if they get here."

"Not us," said the professor, "not Jews." The revolution in Russia had been founded upon the intellect and dynamism of the Jews. "The Red Army will not harm Jews."

"How will they know who are Jews?" asked Dr. Weiss.

"We must not be afraid," said Benjamin the rabbi. Benjamin was the last rabbi alive and free in the whole of Berlin. For all he knew, he was the last surviving rabbi in the whole of Germany. He was always cheerful.

It was while they were talking that Boris went to the metal lockers in the side room where the men kept their street clothes. He unlocked the door of his locker and reached inside for a brown paper parcel. They watched him in silence as he laboriously untied the string around the parcel. Inside it was what appeared to be a bundle of bright-red cloth. He took it by one edge and, holding it high, let the other end fall to the floor.

There was a gasp of surprise, and of fear, too, when they saw what he displayed. It was a full-size red flag, complete with hammer and sickle.

"Where did you get this?" asked Dr. Weiss.

"I made it," said Boris.

There was no laughing at his accent now. Weiss leaned over and touched the hem of the flag as if it might explode. "You made it?"

They could all see now that it had been assembled from small pieces of cloth sewn together with remarkable skill. The hammer-and-sickle insignia was put together from bright-yellow cloth that shone like gold. Thousands of tiny stitches had gone into the effort. It was a labor of love, and the professor respectfully said so.

"When they come, we will fly it from the flagpole," said Boris.

"It's a labor of love," repeated the professor.

"They'll know then," said Boris.

"Put it away quickly," said Benjamin the rabbi, who was by common consent the voice of authority and wisdom. "Good work, Boris. Now put it away until we need it."

"Good work, Boris," said the others. There was a new respect in their voices. Who would have guessed that such a slow and lugubrious fellow could have fashioned that magnificent flag in secret, and brought it here without their knowing?

But Isaac Volkmann now thought he saw a reason for the *Mischling*'s exaggerated fears, and his change of name. He guessed that Boris Somló had been an active member of the Communist Party in Austria before the *Anschluss.* If that was the case, his fears made sense.

"It doesn't look like gold."

For any superstitious Nazi like Fritz Esser, Friday, April 13, 1945, fulfilled its awful promise. The U.S. Army was across the Berlin Dessau autobahn, and from Bendlerstrasse there came the order to destroy the army's two explosives factories, which were imminently threatened by the American advance. These were the army's last two powder factories; there would be no more ammunition for the German guns.

Berlin was a maze of fires and bombed buildings. The Chancellery was badly damaged—Hitler was in the bunker—and in the nearby Adlon Hotel, Louis Adlon walked through scorched carpeting, shattered mirror, and broken brickwork to see what might be salvaged of what had once been the most magnificent hotel in

Europe. Potsdamer Platz was unrecognizable, its trees gone and surrounding hotels and offices gutted. The famous Messel façade of Wertheims department store was no more. Most of the ministries had already begun to move their documents and personnel out of Berlin. Hitler's personal staff had gone to the Obersalzberg to prepare for his arrival there on April 20, his fifty-sixth birthday. A cake was made ready: Adolf Hitler loved cakes.

The morning of Friday, April 13, dawned blood-red. The RAF squadrons that had lit up the skies with marker flares, and the ground with their phosphorus bombs and high explosive, had gone. In the street Fritz Esser, in his big six-wheel Mercedes, steered carefully around the huge mountains of old rubble and fresh wreckage. He was on his way to pick up Pauli Winter. Public transport could no longer be relied upon, although the efforts of the transport workers were almost superhuman. Esser's car passed a large group of children—fourteen-, fifteen-, and sixteen-year-olds—straggling along Keith Strasse towards their homes in badly damaged Schöneberg. It had been a bad night: some were to find their homes had disappeared. They were dressed in absurdly ill-fitting uniforms and carried helmets too heavy for them to wear comfortably on their heads. They were the schoolchildren lately assigned to crew the heavy anti-aircraft guns in the Tiergarten. The last of the children were crossing Cornelius Bridge. Under it the Landwehr Canal was dry, the machinery that controlled its flow bombed and useless.

Fritz Esser stopped his car and backed up. He felt a sudden impulse to give the children something: they looked so pathetic. They stared at the car—it was the same model that the Führer had used in the days when he could be seen riding through the city. They realized that Esser must be a high-ranking official. They grouped around him respectfully. In the boot of the car was a large box of chocolates that he'd obtained for Inge. He gave them to the children and they ate them ravenously. Some of them had never seen chocolate before. One pale-faced fifteen-year-old, discovering the taste for the first time, laughed as if someone had played a joke upon him, as, in a way, the little Austrian corporal had played a joke upon all of them. Fritz laughed, too. What else was there to do except cry?

"Goebbels is still sitting in his office in Wilhelmplatz, drinking champagne," said Fritz. He was in the car with Pauli, outside the Interior Ministry building. They were waiting for the offices to open and the staff to arrive. "He phoned the Führer and told him that it was written in the stars that mid-April would see a change in our fortunes. He says the death of Roosevelt corresponds to the death of the Tsaritsa during the Seven Years' War, and it will bring victory to the Führer as it did to Frederick the Great."

"I'm sure that went down well," said Pauli. The doorman came out and opened up the ministry at exactly 8:30 a.m. and an organ grinder began playing in the hope of getting a few coins from the office workers.

"He's had someone dig out the Führer's horoscope for January 30, 1933. It says the same thing."

"Does Goebbels believe in all that horoscope stuff?" said Pauli.

"Goebbels is shit-scared of the Russkis," said Fritz. "He's doing everything he can to convince himself that they'll never get here."

"But Goebbels is an educated man."

"Goebbels believes his own propaganda," said Fritz. It cast a new light on the Reichsminister for Public Enlightenment and Propaganda. Pauli had always thought Goebbels, with his virulent anti-Semitism, was a cynic like Fritz.

"I never realized that." Pauli coughed. They were both smoking, and the interior of the car was blue with tobacco smoke.

"They are all mad," said Fritz. "That's why I'm clearing out."

"I thought you were going to the Obersalzberg with the Führer."

"He'll never go. I should have seen that before. He'll stay down inside that damned bunker until the Russian tanks roll over us."

"I thought he'd arranged to be there for his fifty-sixth birthday."

"That's what he said, but he'll not go now. I should have realized what he really intended when Eva Braun arrived here back in January. He usually keeps her locked up in the Berghof."

"Who's Eva Braun?" said Pauli.

"The Führer's mistress: his fancy woman."

"Mistress? The Führer? Are you sure?"

"It's been a well-kept secret, hasn't it? He's had that lovely little piece tucked away in the Berghof for twelve years or so, yet very few people know."

"Where will you go?"

"South. Once the American spearheads join the Russians, we'll never get through."

"Through to where?"

"I don't know . . . Switzerland, or Italy. I want false papers. Do you think Lothar Koch could fix something for me?"

"I should think so; he's done it for others, and for himself. He has papers to show he's been a clerk for the last twelve years, and a hotel reception clerk before that. Who knows, someone might believe him. Go up and see him now. He's been sleeping in his office since the the S-Bahn stopped."

"I want you to come, too, Pauli."

"I can't, Fritz."

"Wait until you see what I've got." Fritz grinned. "Look in the sacks." The whole rear seat was taken up by small sacks tied loosely with rope. Pauli grabbed one and looked inside. At first he couldn't distinguish what was there. It was damned heavy but it looked like scrambled egg—dirty scrambled egg.

"What is it?"

"Gold."

"Gold? It doesn't look like gold," said Pauli.

"Teeth and stuff, gold spectacle frames, a lot of junk the SD had stored in the Reichsbank."

"How did you get it?"

"Reichsminister Funk has ordered that all gold, silver, foreign paper money, and valuables stored in their vaults be moved south."

"Where to?"

"It's all being put in salt mines and caves. Hidden away."

"And this?"

"It doesn't belong to the Reichsbank: it belongs to us. I gave them a receipt on Sicherheitsdienst notepaper. No one cared as long as they had a receipt."

"The SD? There will be terrible trouble when they find out, Fritz."

"Don't be so stupid, Pauli." He lit a new cigarette from the butt before stubbing it into the ashtray with exaggerated force. "It's all over. And this is what we need to finance us. Reichsmarks are not going to be worth a thing once we stop fighting."

"But you've stolen it."

"Who else needs it? Come along, we'll share. Feel the weight of it."

"Teeth? Gold teeth?"

"From prisoners who died in the camps."

"Ugh!"

"Don't go squeamish. You fought in the war, didn't you?"

"Prisoners? People who died in the camps? It's horrible. They stored it in the Reichsbank?"

"There's tons of it there. This is all I could manage. Come with me, Pauli. I have plenty of gas for the car."

"I have to stay here, Fritz. I have to look after my mama." Pauli wound the window down to let some of the smoke out. The sound of the little barrel organ sounded louder.

"You'll never have a chance like this again, Pauli. The Russians will kill everyone in the city."

"My mother's too old to go anywhere."

Fritz didn't argue that point. He had no intention of taking Pauli's mother anywhere. Hell, she must weigh at least fifty kilos, and think what that would be worth in gold.

Pauli closed the neck of the sack. He found it disturbing to look at these pathetic and grotesque bits and pieces now that he knew what they were. He tied the sack carefully and pushed it aside. "Thanks again, Fritz, but I have to stay here with her. There's no one to look after her now that Papa is dead."

"I'll need a gun, Pauli."

"I thought you had one."

"Something more effective—a machine gun." They looked at each other and Fritz said, "People will kill for this much gold."

"Will they, Fritz?"

"Not here in the city . . . not yet. But I'm going south, where the fighting is." People were arriving for work. A bus stopped and a dozen or more clerks got off it. It was amazing how people just carried on, despite the imminent collapse of the nation.

"See Koch. Tell him to phone the armory at Prinz-Albrecht-Strasse—he knows who to speak with—and say I said it was all right for you to have whatever you want."

"I knew you'd be able to fix it, Pauli." He tugged at the steering wheel, as if impatient to start.

"Then it's goodbye?"

"Yes. I'm off as soon as I get documents and a gun." Fritz tapped ash from the end of his cigarette in the little ashtray. It was an unusual gesture for Fritz, who usually let ash fly where it might.

"We had some good times, Fritz."

"And we'll have lots more, Pauli. It will work out, you'll see. I'll write to you at your mother's house. Okay?"

"Is Inge going with you?"

"She left yesterday. By train. I managed to get her a seat and papers. I'll meet her in Mittenwald on the weekend."

"Tell her good luck, too." Pauli opened the car door and got out. "Goodbye, Fritz." The organ was playing "Lilli Marlene." Pauli had lots of work to do. Perhaps it would be more sensible to get false papers and flee, the way Fritz was doing, but for Pauli work came first. It always had.

"A time to be brave."

On April 20, Adolf Hitler's birthday was celebrated in Berlin, and all the top Nazi leaders were with him in the bunker: Göring, Himmler, Ribbentrop, Bormann, and Goebbels, as well as the senior military commanders. But that night many of them left the city. Göring, in a long caravan of motor vehicles, was taking some choice pieces of plundered art to the Obersalzberg, while Himmler headed north to Lübeck, where he was to discuss peace terms in the Swedish consulate.

Such extra space made available in the Führerbunker meant that the entire Goebbels family was invited to move in from their damaged house in the Wilhelmstrasse garden. Two days later, Russian tanks broke through the outer defenses and got inside the city limits. By this time artillery shells were falling in the center of Berlin.

The men who worked at the Weissensee cemetery continued to go to work even when there was German field artillery in nearby Berliner Allee firing at targets in the open ground at Wartenberg, to the north of the freight railway lines. The shots were falling in the vegetable patches, and the loose earth made great black clouds as each one exploded in the dry dirt.

"Infantry," said Dr. Volkmann. The others listened respectfully. In the first war he'd won the Iron Cross first class while serving on the Western Front. "High-explosive shells; and that sort is used against soft targets. Russian infantry."

"Poor devils," said Benjamin the rabbi.

The poor devils must have been radioing for help, for hardly

were the words out of his mouth when great fireballs began arcing
across the dark sky, their trajectories ending in the approximate
position of the German guns. The mysterious fiery missiles made
loud screaming sounds as they came racing through the air.

"Counterbattery fire," said Dr. Volkmann. "Rockets. They call
them 'Stalin Organs.' I think we'd better get back to the mortuary.
There must be tanks behind the infantry. Can you hear it? One of
the guns has started to fire armor-piercing rounds."

"The infantry will be behind the tanks, surely," said the professor, who never liked to be left out of a conversation too long.

"No, no, no," said Volkmann. "Infantry first, then tanks." He
didn't intend to turn it into the sort of academic discussion that the
professor enjoyed. "I'm getting back."

Boris Somló had been carrying his big red flag wrapped in brown
paper. Now he untied the string and was ready to unfold it. The
others stayed close to him.

Dr. Volkmann asked if anyone was coming with him.

"We have to face them sometime, Dr. Volkmann," said Benjamin the rabbi.

"Better here in the open," said Dr. Weiss. "Perhaps they'll give
us some form of *laissez-passer* that will keep us safe. By tomorrow
everyone will be clamoring for special treatment." He looked at
Boris. There was a hard, determined expression on his face, a look
the others had never seen before.

"I'm going back," said Volkmann. "Who's coming with me?" No
one answered.

"This is a time to be brave," said Benjamin the rabbi.

As Benjamin said it, Boris moved forward, with the flag thrown
back over his shoulder like a blanket roll. The others followed him,
heading for the railway lines. Boris had decided that the embankment would be a good place to confront the oncoming Soviet soldiers. They would have enough time to see the flag if it was draped
across the embankment. By tacit consent Boris had become the
leader of the group.

Dr. Volkmann went back. He didn't want to confront the Red
Army soldiers. He wanted to get back to his wife and baby son.

Volkmann hurried along Berliner Allee, hoping for a lift into the
center of town, but the only traffic on the street was the army: trucks
filled with infantry, some ten-centimeter guns being towed behind
big half-tracks, and five tanks coming down Virchow Strasse from

the Friedrichs Hain, which had been made into a vehicle park for the army. The tracks were damaging the road surface, but it didn't matter now, he supposed. Nothing mattered. When he got to the Horst Wessel Hospital on Landsberger Allee he saw men strung up on the lampposts. The bodies were swaying in the breeze and on each one a hastily scrawled white card was tied. It said, "I deserted my post and paid the price." He'd heard that there were "flying tribunals" serving out summary death sentences in the streets, but this was the first evidence he'd seen of their work. He shuddered and hurried on, skirting round a place near the Alexanderplatz where a bus had fallen into an exposed section of the underground railway. Teno crews—specially trained and equipped engineers— had erected lifting tackle and were working to release people trapped in the twisted wreckage.

On the west side of the wide intersection, two streetcars had been shifted off their tracks to improvise a barrier. Hitler Youth and elderly men wearing old Imperial Army greatcoats, "Afrika Korps" caps, and Volkssturm armbands were filling the streetcars with rubble and bits of broken paving. In the middle of the road were three dead horses and the pieces of an army wagon. A shallow crater marked the place where the stray round from some Red Army gun had found them.

As Dr. Volkmann reached the next corner, there was the sudden sound of rifle fire. Just a ragged volley of about half a dozen gunshots, but it was so near at hand that Volkmann stopped in his tracks, frightened that he was coming into a line of fire. Surely the Russians hadn't got this far so suddenly, though there had been wild rumors about parachute troops dropping into the city at night.

He looked around in time to see six soldiers scrambling over a pile of rubble to get back to the street from some wrecked houses. They were tough-looking fellows, their uniforms stained and dusty, their boots dirty and scuffed.

"Hey, you!" one of them shouted.

Volkmann turned.

"Don't move!" Two of them had their rifles raised and pointed at him in a businesslike way. They'd been through this routine before.

Volkmann raised his hands well above his head and waited. As they got closer he could see that their uniforms were green and they wore police badges on their sleeves, but they weren't ordinary policemen: they were members of one of the special "police regiments" formed for service in the occupied Eastern territories. They were fierce-looking men who well knew the terrible reputation they'd earned in the regions where they were employed to protect the army's lines of communication.

One of them—a tall NCO with the rank badges of a Wachtmeister—prodded Volkmann with the muzzle of his rifle, and in doing so deliberately pushed back his coat lapel to expose fully the large yellow cloth star of David that all Jews were compelled by law to wear outdoors.

"Where are you going, Jew?" he demanded roughly in the singsong accent of the Rhineland.

"Home, Herr Major."

The other men gave grim, mirthless chuckles. Volkmann knew the man wasn't a major—he wasn't even an officer—but it seemed expedient to flatter him. Jews, those who'd survived, had learned to flatter every official they encountered, so now their fellow Germans expected such subservience.

"All the way to Palestine?" said the Wachtmeister, and the other men laughed dutifully.

Volkmann smiled to show what a good joke it was, and said, "To Neuer Westen, Herr Major."

"New West End!" said the Wachtmeister, and sucked his teeth in mock respect at the mention of such a grand district. "The Jews are back in New West End already. They must think the war is lost." To Volkmann he said, "Jews aren't allowed on the street." As the soldiers crowded closer round him, Volkmann grew aware of how tall they were. He became frightened, as they intended he should be.

"I work at the Weissensee cemetery," said Volkmann. "I have my papers."

"Shoot the little bastard," said one of them, "and tomorrow he'll ride to work in a hearse." He laughed at his own joke.

Volkmann looked round at the men. He knew now beyond doubt what the volley of rifle shots were: this was a "flying tribunal" executing stragglers, deserters, or any unfortunate who could not satisfy them with his credentials.

The constant drumbeat of distant bombardments was suddenly obliterated by the closer, sharper bangs of field artillery. The soldiers looked back across the Alexanderplatz. The Volkssturm men working on the barricade had crouched down at the sudden sound. The Wachtmeister laughed at such nervousness. He spat on the ground, and as he wiped his mouth Volkmann saw a tattoo on the back of his hand: "Mother." The Wachtmeister took out his notebook. He opened it at a dog-eared page and began a litany: "In the name of the Führer and the Reich . . ."

"Oh my God!" said Volkmann.

"Better wait for the officer," one of the men warned the Wachtmeister. The officer emerged from a piece of wall behind which, with an exaggerated modesty considering the circumstances, he'd retired to urinate. His pistol belt was thrown over his shoulder and his overcoat was flapping open as he fastened his flies. He was a big fellow with a round face, narrow eyes, and a thin pointed nose. His uniform was not like the others': it was the ordinary German-army field gray, and his badges and piping were those of an artillery captain. When he'd fastened his overcoat, he left the top three buttons undone and the lapels fully open. It was a privilege extended only to generals and field marshals and to heroes who had Germany's most coveted medal for valor hanging at their collar.

"A Jew," the Wachtmeister reported. "No proper papers: shoot him?" His voice betrayed the very limited respect these men of the police regiment had for the regular army. The Wachtmeister would have very much resented being sent out on patrol under the orders of a mere gunnery officer had it not been for the "tin necktie"—the Knight's Cross with oak leaves—and all the other paraphernalia that he was wearing.

"I have papers," said Volkmann shrilly, although he knew the officer was more likely to believe his NCO.

Heavy trucks lumbered past, towing guns. Inside the trucks the crews looked tired, pale, and apprehensive. "What's your name?" said the officer. Volkmann was slightly reassured to hear the accent of Berlin in his voice. Berlin—a cosmopolitan city—had never been as hostile to the Jews as some other regions.

"Volkmann. Isaac Volkmann. I work at the cemetery. My papers are in order, Herr Hauptmann." He almost added that he was an ex-officer and a holder of the Iron Cross, but even now, with death so close, Isaac Volkmann's pride prevented him from saying it. Besides, such claims were unlikely to impress this fellow. Better, perhaps, simply to show these riffraff that a Jewish officer could die with his dignity and self-assurance intact.

The artillery captain stared at him disdainfully. "You work at the cemetery?" he asked as though he didn't believe it. "The cemetery?"

"Yes, Herr Hauptmann."

"You're Dr. Volkmann the dentist," he said accusingly.

"Yes, I was."

"You did my teeth. When I was tiny. My father took me to your surgery in Ku-damm. Mauser; Rolf Mauser. Remember me?"

"Perhaps," said Volkmann.

"Rolf Mauser. You photographed my teeth. You said you were going to use the photo slide in a lecture."

"I lectured a lot at one time," said Volkmann.

"Some special sort of root treatment. You never sent a bill," said the officer.

"Perhaps the school sent you," said Volkmann. The field artillery fired again. It was closer this time. It must be on tracks: only self-propelled guns could change position and fire so quickly afterwards.

"Lichtenberg," said one of the soldiers to the unasked question. "Over open sights . . . and that means Russki tanks . . . at close range."

"Get along home," said the officer. "Now the bill is paid. Right?"

"Thank you, Herr Hauptmann."

"Go home and stay home. Protect your wife and your family. When the Ivans arrive, God help all of us."

By the time Volkmann got back to the Hennigs', the first platoon of Red Army infantry had reached the railway embankment at Weissensee. They were veterans. Some of them had fought all the way from Moscow. They had dreamed of this day. They thought only of the women and the drink that were awaiting them just along the road in the center of this great metropolis. They had been promised full liberty to take anything they wanted from the "German criminals." There would be no restrictions. It was to be three days of raping, killing, looting, and drinking; three days that would make up for the misery they'd suffered, the years without leave, the comrades lost.

But the Germans were still fighting hard. It would be tragic to die on this day, so near the end. That was why the Red infantry took no chances. That was why it was better to shoot at anything that moved. That was why they didn't hesitate to kill the small bunch of old men in civilian clothes who were crouched behind the railway embankment. One long burst of fire was all that was needed, but a couple of hand grenades made sure of them. After that the whole platoon came across the railway in one wild dash. An embankment like that can be dangerous. There is a moment when each infantry man becomes silhouetted against the southern sky. German snipers, and an MG 42, were firing from the roofs of houses in Franz Josef Strasse. But of the first Russian infantry platoon across the railway embankment only one man was killed. The fatality was a fifty-year-old senior NCO from Odessa. It was his bad luck to get his feet entangled in a big red cloth.

When the burial party picked up his body nearly three weeks later—when fears of typhoid and typhus forced the Soviet authorities to hurry up the burying of the dead—they found his feet tangled in a flag, a crude home-made red flag. The burial party didn't waste any time wondering what it was. The Red Army didn't encourage men to wonder about such things.

She was not young or even middle-aged.

When the fighting, and its horrendous aftermath, ended, Berlin was like a Hollywood film set. To the casual observer appeared streets and houses. But a closer inspection revealed that most of the houses were no more than hollow shells open to the sky: a honeycomb of enclosed empty spaces. Sometimes the whole sides of big blocks had slid away to reveal sinks and baths hanging from their plumbing lines. Paintings, and even mirrors, had survived on walls unaffected by the blast, and upper floors hung out over the street like tongues extended in a last rude, defiant grimace at the city's tormentors.

It was spring. For many of the inhabitants, the coming of summer would provide a chance to survive and prepare for the sort of raw temperatures that Berlin suffers in winter, but the summer would bring the sun and the flies, and it would make the stench of the city something that Berliners there at that time would never forget.

Already it smelled bad. It smelled of the unburied dead, the dust of ancient brickwork and burned timbers, and of the stink from broken, overflowing sewers. But the conquering armies had become used to that. The sour smell of feces, wreckage, and putrefying flesh was a smell all soldiers knew: it was the smell of war.

For most of the American, Russian, and British soldiers, Berlin was just another German town. It was smelly and very badly damaged by bombing and shelling, but so were many of the other towns through which they'd fought. The only changes were the ones that occupying armies brought to all conquered towns: whores, beggars, and black-marketeers.

But not all the soldiers who walked between the huge mountains of rubble were indifferent to the city's plight. Sir Alan "Boy" Piper felt the city's agonies as a chronic stab of pain. It was like seeing some beautiful friend who'd narrowly survived a disfiguring accident. One recognized every feature, but where did one look? What did one say?

Piper was dressed as an Intelligence Corps major. His actual equivalent rank was brigadier general, but he felt far too conspicuous in such a uniform. For the time being at least, the military command was insisting that everyone wear a uniform of some sort, so Piper, as an important figure in the military government, felt unable to flout the regulations. He'd chosen to be a major. Colonels attracted far too much attention, but this field rank gave him admittance to clubs and offices where a captain would find it difficult to get in.

But if Piper thought this device would render him inconspicuous, he was mistaken. Piper was upright and healthy—they'd made him take a physical before allowing him to come overseas—and he managed a soldier's stride and had abundant white hair and bright-blue eyes that seemed to glitter when he smiled, but Piper was as old as Methuselah. Though soldiers were used to seeing very elderly brigadiers, such a very elderly major made heads turn. By now he'd realized this—and he was frequently stopped by military police and asked to show his papers—but he didn't care. He preferred being a major. People talked to majors in a way they didn't talk to generals; Piper liked talking to people, and his German was excellent.

At the Kempinski Hotel he turned off Ku-damm and went up the side street until he came to the tea room. It was in a dilapidated condition, but someone had been trying to repair the ceiling and get it back into shape. What's more, the tea room was functioning: a handwritten sign said it opened at noon. There were chairs and tables with newly washed cloths and some primroses in tumblers on each one. In the corner was a big cracked Chinese pot containing an aspidistra plant. There was even a fellow tuning the piano. Piper watched him for a moment as he took a moment off from his work and played a few bars of Beethoven—"Für Elise."

"That's damned good!" said Piper when the piano tuner ended his little recital.

"Thank you, Herr Major," said Erich Hennig.

"I'm looking for Frau Winter. Frau Veronica Winter. She isn't in her own home. I understand she's staying here."

"The second floor. Are you a relative?"

"Alas, no," said Piper, "an old friend."

"At the back, on the second floor. Mind the loose stair carpet, Herr Major: it's dangerous."

"Thank you," said Piper. "I shall."

As he went up the stairs, he was humming to himself. You old fool, he thought, you are like some wretched eighteen-year-old on his first date. But he couldn't help feeling excited. He'd spent his life thinking about Veronica, one way or another. He'd even contrived to see her brother as often as possible because he was so like her in looks and in manner. Now the moment had finally come and he was preparing himself for a rude shock. Preparing himself for a rude shock, and yet not actually expecting it. "Hope for the best and prepare for the worst"—his niece had embroidered that at school on a small sampler that she later gave him. He'd had it hanging on the wall of his London office ever since.

He reached the dark landing, knocked, and after a moment or so called: "Frau Winter?"

She was a long time coming to the door. What had he expected: that beautiful, animated creature who'd turned his head in 1910 and occupied his mind ever since?

She was not young or even middle-aged, that woman who answered the door to him: she was white-haired.

"Yes?" Old and frail but unmistakably her. She held the door open. She was not as tall as the woman he remembered, but she had the same wide, bony face and the same Rensselaer jaw and mouth. She was still beautiful.

"Veronica. Do you remember me?"

547

It took her a moment to adjust herself to speaking in English. "Are you a friend of my brother's? . . . I am sorry I am in such muddle. I have just moved here. . . . Everything is . . ."

"Veronica. It's Alan Piper—'Boy.' You remember . . . ?"

"Yes, Boy." She frowned. She recalled the voice so clearly. It was a wonderful voice, low and clear and mellow. Without her glasses she couldn't see him distinctly in the darkness of the landing. But when she leaned closer her face lit up and she smiled the sort of sad, reflective smile that he remembered so well. "Do come in. . . . You're in the army. Come in. . . . It's all such a muddle, I have just moved in."

"Thank you, but I mustn't stay. I came to see that you were all right. I promised your brother."

"How did you find me? This house belongs to the Hennig family."

"The ration cards."

"Oh, of course." She took his peaked cap from him and indicated that he should sit down on the battered sofa. The room *was* in a terrible muddle. There were two trunks open on one side of the room. From them she'd been taking linen and some oddments of personal possessions. Otherwise the room was relatively bare. Apart from the sofa, there were three hard wooden chairs and a table propped up under a broken leg. A picture of a rather grand wedding group was occupying pride of place on a small inlaid side table. There was no frame for the photo: she'd sold the silver frame to give the Hennigs something to help, and show her appreciation. Close inspection revealed that the groom was Paul, in his army uniform. The bride looked radiant, and there was a big crowd of smiling faces and an escort of army officers with drawn swords.

"And I wanted to tell you that your sons are safe and well," he said.

"Safe and well," she repeated, and sat down as if dazed. "Safe and well. Both of them?"

"Peter is in the American army. He's with your brother in the American Zone—Munich or somewhere near there. I'm sure they'll both visit you as soon as they get a chance."

"Peter, yes, I'd heard he was with the army."

"A full colonel. He's been assigned to the International Military Tribunal."

"That sounds very grand."

She was not young or even middle-aged.

"The war crimes trials at Nuremberg. It won't start for a long time yet, and it will go on for ages. You'll see a lot of him, I should think, unless you've decided to be repatriated."

"To the U.S.?"

"It wouldn't be difficult to arrange, Veronica. If that's what you want."

"You said both boys were safe."

"Paul is in a prison camp near Cologne. He'll probably be taken to England eventually."

"To England?" The poor woman was confused. It was all too much for her.

"Shall I put the stove on and boil some water?" he offered. "I brought some coffee with me."

"Real coffee?"

"Yes indeed."

"It's a pressure stove. You won't be able to work it."

"Stay where you are, Veronica. I was working these stoves when I was at Boy Scout camp, and that was a long time ago."

She laughed. It was a sweet, girlish laugh. "Yes, it must have been a long time ago."

She watched him as he made the coffee. It gave her a moment to compose herself. It was all so unexpected. Why hadn't he written? She would have worn something better, and asked Lisl to do her hair for her. There was a sudden loud hissing as he got the pressure stove started. He tried the tap, but there was no water.

"In the jug on the drain board," she called. As well as a two-pound package of coffee, he'd brought a can of evaporated milk and a bag of sugar. He was so precise and methodical. "The can opener is in the drawer."

"Stay where you are, Veronica. I can manage."

"And you are in the army?" she said.

"Don't I look like a soldier?"

"Of course you do," she said, although in fact he didn't. He looked like an elderly matinee idol playing the role of one.

He brought the pot of coffee, and the milk in a jug. She said, "Tell me about Pauli."

He looked at her. It was better to tell her the whole truth; she wasn't the sort of woman who refused to face reality. "He's being interrogated. . . . Oh, don't be frightened, Veronica. That doesn't mean ill-treated. He's being questioned."

"About what?"

"Paul was a high official of the Gestapo. He was at a decision-making level in the Ministry of the Interior."

"He's not a criminal," she said softly. "He was just a civil servant: a bureaucrat."

"There are Nazi Party organizations, Veronica. It's routine, but he'll have to be questioned."

"You know a lot about him."

"I poked my nose into it. They let me look at the files. One of my young men, a fellow named Brian Samson, is what, in this hateful modern jargon, they are calling 'a de-Nazification expert.' "

"Samson. The name is familiar. Do I know him?"

"Possibly. He used to work in one of Harald's factories."

She looked at him in mild surprise; she could believe anything by now. "An Englishman. Yes, I met him once or twice. So he was one of your people?"

"Yes," said Piper.

"Harald always said you were a spy. I laughed at him. We quarreled about it."

"I'm sorry."

"For being a spy?"

"That you quarreled."

"It doesn't matter." She picked up the coffee, smelled it for a moment, and then drank some greedily. It was the first taste of real fresh coffee she'd had in a long, long time. "Do you have a family?" she asked.

"No, I never married. There was always so much work. Girlfriends wouldn't put up with me."

"I'm sure that's not true."

He tried to think of something to say. Something that would smoothly lead to his being able to tell her that no one he'd ever met could measure up to her. But he couldn't bring himself to say it. He only had two days here in Berlin, and he'd vowed to tell her that there had been no one else in his life. He watched her, savoring the sight of her. She had drunk all her coffee already and he'd not even tasted his own. He smiled and poured more for her.

"That coffee tastes so good," she said.

"And you never married again?" he asked.

"Me? No." She decided that her second cup would have evaporated milk in it. "Do you take cream?"

She was not young or even middle-aged.

"Thank you, yes."

She poured some for him. "Enough?"

"Yes."

"It's so good to speak English again." She poured some of the tinned milk for herself, then touched her hair. "I must look terrible. It's so dusty, and everything is such a mess."

"You look wonderful, Veronica."

"I wish I could offer you something."

"I'll send you some food. I have such a lot. Do you smoke?"

"No," she said.

"I'll let you have some cigarettes anyway. They say you can get anything done for cigarettes."

"Yes, there's no doubt about that." She sighed. "There is no self-discipline, no faith, no dignity, no self-respect anymore. The Germany that I once knew is gone."

"Was it anything but our self-deception, Veronica? I loved Germany, too, but now I ask myself if that Germany I loved so much ever existed."

"What will happen to him?"

"To Paul? It's difficult to guess. There is talk of declaring the SS an illegal organization, but I don't see how they could punish every member of the SS, could they?"

"Harald said that once about the Jews. He said that Hitler and his Nazis could hardly punish every one of them, but he did, didn't he?"

"Nearly every one, yes, but we're not Hitler."

"Pauli's wife left him. She went off with a man he worked for, Fritz Esser, the deputy minister. Now I see that Fritz Esser is going to be charged with crimes against humanity." She picked up her coffee and sipped some. "I worry about Pauli. He's a wonderful boy; there is no wickedness in him."

"And I'm sure he'll come to no harm."

"When the Russian soldiers came to the old house, he stayed with me, locked up in the attic. He had a gun. Eventually they went away."

"It must have been terrible."

"People were being raped and murdered. We could hear them screaming and shouting. It was a nightmare, and it went on for days and nights, but Pauli stayed with me. Then, when the British soldiers arrived, an English officer and police came. They searched the house and took Pauli away." She was distressed at the memory.

He said, "Better us than the Russians."

"Pauli said that, too. Then the English came back and commandeered the whole house. They'd noticed that I was there alone and that it wasn't too badly damaged. They gave me forty-eight hours to get out. I had to come over here to live with the Hennigs."

"Berlin will not be a good place to live, Veronica. Accommodation will become more and more difficult, and when winter comes life will be hard."

"I'm sure you're right," she said. She looked at him and smiled.

He wondered if this was the right time for him to say that he loved her, that he adored her, that he wanted to marry her, that she was the only woman he'd ever wanted. But he wasn't sure it was the right time. He was English: an elderly Englishman who was frightened of making a fool of himself. He decided to leave it for another time. The thought of her laughing at him was unendurable. Better, perhaps, to live without her than to risk the destruction of his dream.

"I'm going to Cologne tomorrow for a conference," he said. He mustn't outstay his welcome. Perhaps it was a mistake to come without warning. He got to his feet. "If I can get any news of your son, I will let you know."

"Thank you. You're forgetting your package of coffee."

"Please, keep it if you'd like it."

"It was wonderful to see you again, Boy." She couldn't offer him a meal; she had no food and no money to buy any. She wondered where would be the best place to sell the coffee. With that money she'd have enough to give him a snack of some kind next time he came.

"I'll keep in touch," he promised. She was close to him, and he wondered whether he should kiss her, but it might offend her. He decided to shake hands instead.

"Everyone is being damned vindictive."

Colonel Peter Winter could never get over the Americans, their profligate use of money and the hardware, and convenience, that money could buy. When he went to collect his brother, the U.S. Army provided him with the exclusive use of a plane to Nuremberg.

It was not a small communications plane, either, but a large Douglas DC3 transport.

Pauli Winter's months in custody had made him thin, wiry, and fit—he looked like the young soldier who'd marched off to fight in World War I—but he was no longer the careless, cheerful man he'd once been. Confinement did not suit Pauli's restless, undisciplined spirit, and now he'd become moody and subdued; even the presence of Peter hadn't restored his confident good humor. He'd chosen a seat by the window, and now he watched the land pass beneath in breathless horror. Nothing he'd read or heard had prepared him for the reality of this war-ravaged, pockmarked land that once had been Germany. The light dusting of snow revealed every crater and roofless farm building, every broken spire and lifeless village. To Pauli it was as if someone had taken a pot of white paint to mark each wound and say to him, "German, this is your punishment—repent!"

Peter Winter and his brother, Pauli, sat side by side. Behind them sat Brian Samson, who wore the uniform of a British army captain. The people in London had been reluctant to let Paul Winter go, and eventually Peter had eased the situation by suggesting that Brian Samson come, too. Samson didn't want to go to Nuremberg, but he'd been ordered to do so. It was, someone had said, important not to create a precedent. Senior staff from the Ministry of the Interior were important catches. Such categorized German prisoners would not be released to the Americans on receipt of a request. Paul Winter was not released to the Americans: he was still in the direct custody of Captain Brian Samson and would remain so until further notice.

Suddenly Pauli dragged his eyes away from the ground below and asked, "Wouldn't it have been better if I'd stayed in London and faced this de-Nazification inquiry?"

Peter was tired. There were rings under his eyes, and his face was wrinkled, as was his uniform. Worry about Pauli and grief for Lottie, concern for his daughter and his mother, had put such a multitude of burdens upon him that he sometimes felt he could no longer cope. For the last week or so he'd been subjected to Glenn Rensselaer's long and bitter tirades about Dot and the way she'd managed to become the sole beneficiary of Cy Rensselaer's fortune. She'd already made it clear that she'd do nothing to rectify the old man's harsh decision to omit Glenn and Veronica from the will. The money was destined for her three sons. Glenn, who'd never concerned himself with money, was furious. He wanted to contest the will and urged Peter to join him in the action. Peter was too tired even to argue about it. But collecting Pauli had concentrated his mind. For the time being Pauli was the focus of his anxieties. He loved Pauli and had missed him very much.

"No, it wouldn't," said Peter. "Everyone is being damned vindictive at the moment. Let a few months go by and they will simmer down a little. Instead of hanging people they'll be giving out shorter and shorter prison sentences. If I can keep you in Nuremberg until the IMT is finished, everyone will be getting bored with de-Nazification. I know the Americans. Do as I say."

"Did you tell Fritz Esser to ask for me?"

"I had someone remind him that it was his right to have any defense lawyer who would agree to serve. He didn't have to be told that you would be a good choice."

"He could have had anyone?"

"Even a German serving a sentence would be temporarily released."

"So it will be a fair trial?"

"A fair trial? In Nuremberg?" Peter looked at his younger brother and gave him a weary smile. "Yes, they'll get a fair trial, and then they'll be hanged."

"Do you mean that?"

"It will be a fiasco," said Peter. "The Russians are sitting in judgment. The Russians! They were Hitler's allies. Stalin sent Hitler a message of congratulation when France surrendered to the panzers. Stalin's concentration camps have slaughtered more victims than Himmler's have. They will be the judges."

"But still . . ."

"Wait till you get there; you'll see. Each of the accused has one lawyer. You won't even be able to talk to Fritz Esser in private: you'll be in a noisy room, crowded together with other accused men trying to talk to their lawyers. There will be a guard sitting alongside you to make sure that he hears everything you say. And, to make sure you don't get close enough to whisper, they'll put a sheet of armored glass in front of your face."

"That won't help them. . . ."

"And you'll see what the prosecution team is like. There are hundreds of lawyers, and hundreds of researchers, translators, and secretarial staff. Money is being spent without restriction; this is the trial that justifies the war, you see. So the prosecution staff are living in the fancy hotels and throwing wild parties every night. French champagne and American rations. Cigarettes by the carton. Oh, yes, the lawyers will have a fair trial; it will be something to talk about when they're back home in America. But for the accused it will be a travesty of justice."

"It can't be true," said Pauli.

"It's true. I'm on the prosecution staff, so I know," said Peter.

"Are you trying to depress me?"

"I just don't want you to imagine that you are going to go to Nuremberg and do some kind of wonderful legal work and bring Esser out of court a free man. You're not. Esser will go to the gallows. The International Military Tribunal at Nuremberg is just a fancy way of sending him there."

There was a new voice, soft but angry. "Is that what you think, Colonel Winter?" said Brian Samson from the seat behind them.

"Yes, it is," said Peter Winter. He'd known that Samson was listening to him. In fact, his tirade wasn't entirely designed to disillusion Pauli, but partly to provoke and irritate Brian Samson. And he'd succeeded. The two men knew exactly how to annoy each other. They'd had a lot of practice.

"Spring will be a little late this year."

The jail was five spokes radiating from a central rotunda, each with three levels of cells. There was heavy-duty wire mesh overhead to frustrate suicide jumps. The guards were uniformed American soldiers, and from the office at the end came the resonant sound of music: "Spring Will Be a Little Late This Year." It was one of the hit tunes. Fritz Esser was on the bottom level, near the end. The cell floor was uneven flagstones, and the walls rough plaster with damp patches under the tiny window set high in the wall. In the corner was a toilet that smelled of a powerful disinfectant.

Pauli entered the prison cell unprepared for the change that the short period of imprisonment had wrought. Fritz Esser was only fifty-two years old and looked at least sixty. He was an old man. He was sitting on the iron frame bed, sallow and shrunken. His elbows were resting on his knees and one hand was propped under his unshaven chin. The prison authorities had taken from him his belt, his braces, and his necktie, and the expensive custom-made suit from Berlin's most famous tailor was now stained and baggy. And yet the dark-underlined eyes were the same, and the pointed cleft chin made him immediately recognizable as a celebrity of the Third Reich, one of Hitler's most reliable associates.

He waited for Fritz Esser to speak but he said nothing. Finally Pauli said, "You sent for me, Herr Reichsminister?"

The prisoner looked up. "The Reich is kaputt, Germany is kaputt, and I'm not a minister: I'm just a number." Pauli Winter could think of no way to respond to this bitterness. He'd become used to seeing him sitting behind the magnificent hand-carved desk in the tapestry-hung room in the ministry, surrounded by aides, secretaries, and assistants. "Yes, I sent for you, Herr Doktor Winter. Sit down."

He sat down. So he'd guessed right. Fritz Esser wanted to keep it all formal: Herr Doktor Winter, not Pauli. Well, that was just as well. It was better kept formal if you were talking to your former boss in prison.

"I sent for you, Winter, and I'll tell you why. They told me you were in prison in London awaiting interrogation. They said that any of us on trial here could choose any German national we wanted for our defense counsel, and that if the one we chose was being held in prison they'd release him to do it. It seemed to me that a man in prison might know what it's like for me in here."

Pauli looked at him. Fritz reminded Pauli of someone he'd known a long time ago, and as Fritz looked up he realized who: he had become the very image of his father, the pig man. Pauli wondered if he should offer the ex-Reichminister a cigarette, but when—still undecided—he produced his precious cigarettes, the military policeman in the corridor shouted through the open door, "No smoking, buddy!"

The ex-Reichsminister gave no sign of having heard the prison guard's voice. He carried on with his explanation. "Two, you speak American . . . speak it fluently. Three, you're a damned good lawyer, as I know from working with you for many years. Four, and this is the most important, you are an Obersturmbannführer in the SS. . . ." He saw Winter's face change and said, "Is there something wrong, Winter?"

Pauli leaned forward; it was a gesture of confidentiality and commitment. "At this very moment, just a few hundred yards from here, there are a hundred or more American lawyers drafting the prosecution's case for declaring the SS an illegal organization. Such a verdict would mean prison, and perhaps death sentences, for everyone who was ever a member."

"Very well," said the prisoner testily. He'd always hated what he called "unimportant pettifogging details." "But you're not going to suddenly claim you weren't a member of the SS, are you?"

For the first time since the message had come that Fritz Esser wanted him as defense counsel, Winter felt alarmed. He looked round the cell to see if there were microphones. There were bound to be. He remembered this building from the time when he'd been working with the Nuremberg Gestapo. That was the summer when old Graf and the rest of them were executed. Half the material used in the trial of the other disgruntled brownshirts had come from shorthand clerks who had listened to the prisoners over hidden microphones. "I can't answer that," said Winter softly.

"Don't give me that yes-sir, no-sir, I-don't-know-sir. I don't want some woolly-minded, fainthearted, Jew-loving liberal trying to get my case thrown out of court on some obscure technicality. I sent for you because you got me into all this. I remembered your hard work for the party. I remembered the good times we had long before we dreamed of coming to power. I remembered the way your father lent me money back when no one else would even let me into their office. Pull yourself together, Winter. Either put your guts into the effort for my defense or get out of here!"

So his father had given money to the party, despite everything that Pauli had done and advised. And Fritz had been the one who handled it: how typical of his father, and typical of Fritz. And typical of the party, too! God, how devious everyone was.

"Did you hear me?" he said.

"Yes." Pauli smiled encouragement. He admired his old friend's spirit. Appearances could be deceptive: he wasn't the broken-spirited shell that Winter had thought; he was still the same ruthless old bastard that he had worked for. He remembered that first political meeting in the Potsdamer Platz in the 1920s and the speech he'd given: "Beneath the ashes fires still rage." It had been a recurring theme in his speeches right up until 1945.

"We'll fight them," said Pauli. "We'll grab those judges by the ankles and shake them until their loose change falls to the floor."

"That's right," said Esser. It was another one of his pet expres-

557

sions. Is that what he'd done to Papa: shaken him until the loose change fell to the floor? "That's right," repeated Esser and almost smiled. How like a bear he was. Not now the elegant bruin who pawed live fish from fast streams; more like the moth-eaten old specimens behind bars in the zoo. But the claws and teeth were still sharp, and so was the mind.

"Time's up, buddy!"

Pauli looked at his watch. There was another two minutes to go. The Americans were like that. Peter's little outburst on the plane—never since repeated—had been one hundred percent correct. They talked about justice and freedom, democracy and liberty, but they never gave an inch. There was no point in arguing: they were the victors. The whole damned Nuremberg trial was just a fiasco, just an opportunity for the Americans and the British and the French and the Russians to make an elaborate pretense of legal rectitude before executing the vanquished. But it was better that the ex-Reichsminister didn't fully realize the inevitable verdict and sentence. Better to fight them all the way and go down fighting. At least that would keep his spirits alive. With this resolved, Pauli felt better, too. It would be a chance to relive the old days, if only in memories.

When Pauli got to the cell door, Esser called out to him, "One last thing, Winter." Pauli turned to face him. "I hear stories about some aggressive American colonel on the prosecution staff, a tall, thin one with a beautifully tailored uniform and manicured fingernails . . . a man who speaks perfect German with a Berlin accent. They say he hates all Germans and makes no allowances for anything; he treats everyone to a tongue-lashing every time he sends for them. Now they tell me he's been sent from Washington just to frame the prosecution's case against me. . . ." He paused and stared. He was working himself up into the sort of rage that had sent fear into every corner of his ministry and far beyond. "Not for Göring, Speer, Hess, or any of the others, just for me. What do you know about that shit-face *Schweinehund?*"

"Yes, I know him. It's my brother."

He almost enjoyed the consternation on Fritz Esser's face. "Your brother? Peter?"

"That's him." A prison guard strolled past, whistling tunelessly.

"The Americans made him a colonel in their army? He's a German."

"The Americans do things differently, Fritz. It takes a bit of getting used to."

"Jesus Christ, it does! He was some kind of spy! I saved the bastard's life. Last year: that night in Berlin. I saved his life. You got him away."

"He knows that."

"I wonder if he does," said Esser.

"You didn't do it for *him,* did you?" It was a question: not rhetoric. "It was for the SS-Reichsführer."

Esser pointed a stubby finger. "You saved his life."

"Never mind the pettifogging details," said Pauli.

Fritz Esser managed a brief grin. My God! How like the pig man he looked. Pauli wondered if he was now beginning to resemble Harald Winter to the same extent.

"A good German, a man of honor."

Considering that he'd been left unconscious on the battlefield, suffered shell-splinter wounds, and been identified as a live enemy casualty by an American burial party, Rudolf Freiherr von Kleindorf had made an amazing recovery. But he'd spent five months in hospital, and even now he was subject to giddiness and fainting. That's why he'd been repatriated and officially made into a civilian at a time when most of the German army were still in Allied prison camps.

Armed with an official pass issued by the Allied Military Command in Berlin, he had come into the Russian Zone of Germany to find a man he'd never met: Baron Wilhelm von Munte, a landed aristocrat who'd lived here, near Bernau, for many generations.

What in former times was a commuter ride from central Berlin had taken von Kleindorf four hours. It was a miserable gray day with low cloud and the easterly wind that always brings low temperatures in that region. The only train that Germans were permitted to use was over an hour late, and he'd had to walk all the way from the station, much of the way in thick mud. Four times he'd been stopped by Russian military policemen, and they not only wanted to see his papers but phoned to their headquarters before allowing him to continue his journey.

Even when he reached the address he'd been given he was held

559

up and questioned by the Russian soldiers, for the Munte family home had been taken over by the Red Army. They were front-line soldiers, curious-looking fellows who toyed with their guns, smoked cheroots, and, unlike the men Kleindorf had commanded, were unshaven and smelled of drink.

Old von Munte was in bed in a room in the tiny gate-lodge. Although his grand mansion had been taken over by the Red Army, they'd not objected to the Muntes' living nearby. They'd even allowed him to bring a few armfuls of books from his library. The books were stacked on the floor along one wall of this cramped, dark bedroom. But it was too dark to read. There was no electricity anywhere in this part of the country, and none was promised for the immediate future. The Russians were not trying to get the electricity stations going: they were dismantling them and shipping them back to Russia. Heat was sometimes provided by a tiny woodstove that today—despite the bitter cold—was unlit, and light by a big brass oil lamp that was in pieces on top of the side table, waiting to be cleaned.

The old man was recovering slowly from some unidentified virus, but he was lucky enough to have a competent local physician to attend him, and even luckier to have his son Walter von Munte looking after him so attentively. It was Walter who answered the door and who warned von Kleindorf that his father was not fit to talk for more than a few minutes.

Walter had been a brilliant student who'd got high marks in his final exams and, by war's end, a senior position in the Reichsbank. Married very young—because his girlfriend, Ida, became pregnant—he'd lost her when she was killed in Berlin in one of the first of the really bad air raids. She'd been a dancer, and had gone back to work after the baby was born. There had been fierce family rows—the old man had always hated his new daughter-in-law—but Walter worshipped her and now worshipped her memory and the son she'd given him. Then, at the very end of the fighting, came another terrible tragedy. Walter's young brother had been killed in the fighting. The fifteen-year-old child had been the very essence of the old man's life. The loss had deprived him of the will to go on. Since then Walter had lived with his father and looked after him— and his own motherless baby son—with great devotion. But it was agony that bound the two men, agony that bordered on the edge of despair.

And so von Kleindorf faced the obstructions of the son, as well as the gloom of the father, in his request that old Wilhelm von Munte come to Hamburg to give evidence at the war-crimes trial of General Alex Horner.

Von Kleindorf was standing, head bent, cautiously avoiding the place where the wooden ceiling beam had already caused him to strike his head. No one had invited him to sit down so he stood, arms at his side in a formal pose that befitted one Prussian aristocrat paying a call upon another.

"What makes you think it's not true?" asked the younger man. Walter was sitting in the corner, a heavily built man balanced on a little wooden kitchen chair. The hard light that comes before a storm lit one side of his face and reflected from the bare floorboards to make golden patterns on the ceiling. For a few moments the room was suffused with a curious shadowless light. It made the old man, propped on the lace-trimmed pillow in the brass bed, look like a long-dead saint, desiccated and displayed for some holy celebration.

Von Kleindorf had been speaking to the old man in the bed, but the old man said nothing. It was always his son who replied. Though the son must be young, he didn't look young. He was a heavy, saturnine figure, the sort of man who never looked young.

Kleindorf looked at him. What was the fellow up to: was he testing him? "I didn't say it wasn't true," said Kleindorf patiently. "I said he wasn't guilty."

"Of shooting the British prisoners?"

"There was an SS division in Horner's corps. They shot the prisoners: Australian prisoners."

"What does the SS commander say?"

"The SS commander is dead. The Divisional Headquarters staff fought to the last man. When the Corps Headquarters was overrun, General Horner was using a rifle. It's an amazing story. They fought to the very end."

"The commander gets the blame for any atrocities in his sector," said Walter.

"It's not right," said von Kleindorf. "It's not fair."

Walter von Munte didn't bother to respond. Of course it wasn't right or fair; almost nothing was right or fair. "When is this trial?"

"In about two months' time. The date's not fixed yet."

"In Hamburg?"

"Yes, in Hamburg." Would the fact that the trial would provide a visit to the British Zone make the old man more interested? he wondered.

"I fail to see what my father can actually do there."

Von Kleindorf was tired of having his questions answered by the younger man. He looked directly at Wilhelm, propped up in the bed. "Baron Munte," he said. "You know General Horner. He was in the anti-Hitler conspiracy with you. I simply want you to tell the court that."

The old man cleared his throat and said, "Will the British believe that no anti-Nazi conspirator could shoot prisoners?" It was a croaky voice and his tone was mocking.

"I don't know, Baron Munte. I'm just trying to help a good man, a good German, a man of honor."

"All the good Germans are dead," said the Baron. It was an old man's response, a provocative, mischievous dismissal.

Von Kleindorf said nothing.

"Why did Horner send you?" asked the old man querulously, as if slighted that the imprisoned general had not come in person.

"He didn't send me: I came."

"Why you?"

"It was my duty."

"Do you have any cigarettes?" croaked the old man.

"No, I can't afford them," said von Kleindorf.

Walter said, "The Russians will not allow my father to go." Behind him, rain pattered on the window and then developed into a tattoo.

"The British will request it."

"They still won't allow him to go. When they hear he's a defense witness for a German, they will obstruct things, the way they always do."

"Always do?" said von Kleindorf. The room had grown much darker, now that the rain was heavy. The figures of the two men were almost lost in the gloom. Only the rails of the brass bedstead shone in the light.

"You don't live here in the Russian Zone," said the son, "or you'd know that already."

"Will you agree to come?" von Kleindorf asked the old man.

Old Wilhelm leaned back and closed his eyes as he thought about it. He was a calculating old devil, wondering to what extent such evidence would be of benefit to his reputation and to that of his family. "I will let you know," he said.

Kleindorf clicked his heels and bowed. "Thank you, Baron Munte."

"Perhaps a written deposition," offered the son as von Kleindorf turned to go.

"And no one knows who those three are."

It was one of the American lawyers, Colonel Bill Callaghan, who had made the fuss about Pauli Winter. It was he who suggested that Pauli Winter should be ordered to sign in and out of the accommodation he'd been given, and sign in and out at the Palace of Justice. But for that, no one would have reported him gone before the trial resumed the next morning.

But Pauli Winter didn't go back to his billet that evening, and Colonel Peter Winter, U.S. Army, disappeared, too. Brian Samson cursed. On paper, Samson was the one responsible for Paul Winter, and here in Nuremberg paper was the only thing that mattered.

It was bright moonlight. Three big trucks, despite their all-weather tires and four-wheel drives, found the narrow Bavarian country road difficult going in the deep snow. Samson had picked up this hastily assigned detail, and the trucks, from the barracks in Bad Reichenhall. The drivers were not used to the sort of weather to be faced here in the Bavarian Alps at this time of year, and the soldiers were an assorted collection of men from outfits far and wide with nothing in common but a ticket to go home. They were jumpy and ill-tempered at being pulled out of their warm barracks on such a night.

Leading the trucks was a jeep—General Glenn Rensselaer's Buick staff car would never have made it through this sort of terrain—with Captain Brian Samson and General Rensselaer riding in the back of it. In front, beside the driver, a map and a flashlight on his knee, was a young pink-faced New Yorker: a first lieutenant of the C.I.C. named Busby. He was twenty-eight years old, an ex-cop, pushy the way cops so often become in big cities, but, on the basis of a few hours in his company, Brian Samson had decided that Busby was good at catching fugitives, and that was the task they'd been set.

"How did you trace them?" General Rensselaer asked Busby.

"There's an engineering battalion repairing that section of the highway near the Chiemsee. Everyone that goes along it has to wait until they give the okay."

"And these engineers identified them?"

"Military Police control the traffic."

"Yes, of course."

"A colonel and a middle-aged German civilian: short and blond. Oh, they're your guys, all right. Don't worry."

Brian Samson stole a glance at General Rensselaer. Rensselaer would probably have preferred a less convincing description. He was still trying to believe that it was all a mistake.

"It's happened before," said Busby. "These sons of bitches head for the Austrian border, hoping eventually to turn west for good old Switzerland, or south into Italy. We usually get them at one of the passes. There are not so many ways through the mountains still open at this time of year. But why the U.S. colonel? Is he a hostage or something?"

"We don't know," said General Rensselaer hurriedly.

"That would be a new twist," said Busby. "Or are they in some kind of racket together? Jesus! I had to arrest a colonel last week: he had a truckload of narcotics, and he tried to bawl me out—can you believe it?"

Rensselaer didn't respond. Busby used the flashlight for a quick look at the map, then carefully extinguished it again, as regulations dictated. The official instructions were that all transport moving after dark should be on the lookout for units of the werewolf. These werewolf units, the intelligence bulletins said, were highly organized, well-equipped groups of dedicated and specially chosen German soldiers and SS men who'd gone to ground at the end of the war in order to stage a massive uprising against the occupation forces when the time was ripe. The fact that the werewolf existed only in the minds of Allied intelligence officers had not prevented many soldiers from reporting its activity whenever the night was dark enough and the drink strong.

"The cops at the Chiemsee roadworks noticed that they had a spade and tools on the jeep," added Busby.

"Don't all jeeps have a spade?" Rensselaer asked. "This one does."

"Yeah, maybe they do. But if they are digging up some of those

Reichsbank gold bars we keep hearing about, I'll call in for metal detectors. The other jeep has a radio."

"We won't need metal detectors," said Rensselaer. He turned to Samson and quietly said, "What do you make of it, Brian?"

"Paul Winter was facing serious charges in London. It would be tempting for him to try to escape."

"You don't believe that, Brian?" It was a plea. "And why Peter, too?"

"I don't know, General. But Pauli saved his brother's life, not once but several times. Peter knows that. He carries that obligation like a burden round his neck."

"So he'd help, you mean?"

"Yes, he'd help, General."

"I guess you know Peter as well as I do—better, maybe."

"You get to know someone when you are shut up in a room together."

"And you don't like him."

"I've had Germans up to here, General Rensselaer." He held a hand up to the level of his nose. "When my contract ends I'm going to ask to go somewhere a long way away. Or I'll go into some other business."

Rensselaer said, "You say that now, but I'll bet you'll end your days as a German specialist. Maybe living here in Germany."

"God forbid," said Samson.

Rensselaer leaned forward to speak to the lieutenant. "When we get there, you spread your men out the way I showed you on the map. I'll go up to the house with Captain Samson. We know these two men. We'll talk to them."

"Whatever way you want it, General," said Busby. "But you'd better be armed."

"Captain Samson has his revolver. That will be enough."

"If you say so, General, but I'll have an awful lot of questions to answer if these sons of bitches nail you."

"Just make sure no one gets past."

"Sure thing, General. My men won't let a gopher past. My boys have done all this before. There's no way your guys can get over to Austria except through Kniepass way to the west, or through Hallein. Even in high summer I doubt if anyone can hike over those mountains. Your Nazis will either have to come back this way or stay where they are until their butts freeze."

"They're not exactly Nazis," said Rensselaer gently.

"No! Sure!" said Lieutenant Busby. "Speaking with these Krauts has convinced me that there were only three Nazis in the whole of Germany, and no one knows who those three are."

Rensselaer was angry, but he bit his lip and kept his anger under control. It wasn't appropriate for a general to bawl out a junior officer in such circumstances. And Samson couldn't be expected to reprimand the lieutenant: Samson wasn't even in the same army. In any case, it was a touchy subject.

They reached Berchtesgaden. The lights were on, but the curfew had cleared the streets of Germans, and Americans, too, except for a sergeant in a jeep waiting outside the Berchtesgaden Hof, now a rest center for 101st Airborne Division officers.

"Hello, Siggi!" the lieutenant called when they reached the sergeant. There was a brief exchange. Siggi, a master sergeant, was a tiny man: he stood on the running board to talk to Busby. Then he got in his jeep and led the procession.

It was still a distance to go to the Obersalzberg. They were climbing now. The road was steep and twisting, with hairpins. The trucks needed low gear and growled at the dark hillsides, and the snowclad trees growled back.

They passed the roofed gate and sentry box that had once barred the way to the "Führer District"; now it was damaged and empty. When they reached some old farm buildings, they slowed down. Then the jeep ahead went bouncing through an open gate and across the cobbled yard. Siggi, arm outstretched from the moving jeep, pointed to show them the trail. It was a long time since the two fugitives had gone across the farm, but their footprints were still visible in the snow.

When the jeep got to the second yard, on the far side of the deserted farm, the convoy halted. There was no road beyond this that the trucks could possibly follow. From here the ground rose sharply, first to thickly forested slopes, and beyond that to where the snowy Hohe Göll and Hohe Brett looked gigantic and threatening in the bright moonlight.

The lieutenant jumped out, slung his carbine over his shoulder, and, with the help of his top sergeant, positioned his platoon along the cart track that marked the edge of the high summer pasture. When they were in a long line at the bottom of the slope, he advanced them uphill slowly until they were out of sight. The men had parkas, and the bitter cold made them pull the hoods over their heads and tie the laces tight. They stood under the trees, stamping and thumping their arms against their bodies in an effort to stay warm. More than one of them took a swig from a flask.

Captain Samson took off his overcoat and put it on the back seat of the jeep. Then he strapped his webbing belt, shoulder strap, and pistol back on over his battle dress.

"Good luck, sir," said Busby as Rensselaer and Samson started trudging up the steep path.

Over his shoulder Rensselaer said, "Just make sure you don't shoot my ass off, lieutenant."

"Yes, sir," said Busby, and saluted. His breath came as white smoke on the cold night air.

The path was slippery and the ice cracked underfoot, and lots of snow fell from the trees, so that it seemed as if it had begun to snow again. After about fifteen minutes they were into the dark, thickly forested mountainside. It was not snowy underfoot here; the trees closed overhead.

When they reached a firebreak, Rensselaer stopped to admire the view. Looking back, with the mountainside bathed in moonlight, they could see the whole "Führergebiet": the Hitler Berghof, Bormann's house (characteristically close to his master), Göring's flamboyant hunting lodge, the austere Party Guest House, and the huge SS barracks blocks surrounding the parade ground. All roofless ruins now, in a cratered landscape. The snowfall emphasized the destruction.

To the northwest the lights of Berchtesgaden were as clear as the clustered stars. Behind the little town rose the mighty Lattengebirge. There were mountains on every side. It was the view Hitler had had from the terrace of his Berghof. Why did Germans love to hide themselves in such mountain scenery? thought Samson. Was it something to do with their fundamental paranoia?

"What a view, Brian," said Rensselaer, although they both knew that in reality the elder man needed a break to catch his breath. "You were smart to leave your overcoat behind."

Samson nodded.

When they started again, the path was even steeper. Without the snow it was no longer possible to see the footprints of the two brothers, but even in the depths of winter the underbrush was thick enough to see that no one had recently ventured far off the narrow track.

They stopped again, and this time Rensselaer made no attempt to hide his breathlessness. He unbuttoned his short overcoat and leaned against a tree. "If you know what this is all about, Brian, this might be the time to tell me."

Brian Samson looked at him as if trying to decide what to say. Then he said, "I don't know Paul Winter personally—I only met him briefly a long time ago—but from what I hear he's never been able to face the real world. Now he's facing punishment, so he's running."

"You make him sound like a small child," said Rensselaer.

"That's what everyone tells me he is," said Samson.

"You're a hard man, Captain Samson," said Rensselaer. "I wouldn't like to have you sit in judgment on me."

"I'm not sitting in judgment on anyone," said Samson. "But Winter is in my custody and I'm determined to bring him in."

"Everything by the book, eh?" It wasn't sarcastic: Rensselaer was trying to understand him.

"You're not suggesting that we turn him loose, General?"

"No. But did you have to sound reveille for this three-ring circus?"

"Nuremberg C-in-C office is my official contact number. Lieutenant Busby is the duty-operations officer today."

"You could have phoned me, Samson. At my apartment. You have the number."

"I have your phone number, General Rensselaer, and I phoned you immediately after talking to the C in C."

"A pity it wasn't *before* you phoned the C in C."

"That's not reasonable, General. You know as well as I do that Paul Winter was under surveillance. And that surveillance was ordered by an American officer: Colonel Bill Callaghan. It wasn't anything that was requested by my superiors, or by me."

"How did you come to know that, Captain?"

"I made it my business to find out, General Rensselaer. When someone interferes with the processing of a prisoner in my custody, I like to know what it's all about."

Glenn Rensselaer nodded. This Englishman was an abrasive guy. No wonder Peter had never been able to hit it off with him. But he was right, of course. He knew his facts; that was why it was so miserable to argue with him. It was like trying to talk back to a speak-your-weight machine. "I guess you're right, Captain. I shouldn't have brought it up." He looked up the path and said, "Okay. Let's go, then. The sooner we find out the answers to this mystery, the better."

The first thing they came to was a little log cabin, primitive accommodation used by the cow herds in the summer months, when the cattle go to graze on the higher slopes. It stood in the middle of a small clearing. At the side of the cabin, cut wood had been stacked in the astonishingly careful way it is always arranged in this part of Europe. The cut ends of the logs made a pattern of golden crescents.

There were a few stone steps and wrought-iron gates on a decorative brickwork porch. Over the porch was a beautifully carved log incised with the words "Haus Pauli," and carved edelweiss flowers each side. Then, beyond the porch, higher up still, was the house that Harald Winter had given to his son. The windows were dark, but the shutters on one window had been opened, as if to let the moonlight in.

Samson drew his Webley service revolver and called, "Winter! Come out with your hands up."

Nothing happened.

Then Rensselaer tried: "Pauli, it's Glenn! Come on out. It's going to be okay."

Still nothing.

"Maybe they can't hear. The windows are closed." Rensselaer walked to the door of the house. It was unlocked. He opened it, but Samson pushed past him and went in, gun ready. It was dark inside. He went through the lobby to the big sitting room. The light through the window showed that the place was empty. Curtains, carpets, books, pictures, and furniture had all been stolen by the sort of thieves who call themselves souvenir hunters. Even a gilded lamp bracket had been torn out of the plaster, broken, and left dangling.

They went upstairs. It was the same throughout the house. Only one bedroom had been recently occupied. In it was an iron bed, some used bedding, two wooden chairs, and a dented metal steamer trunk in the corner. The trunk was dirty and looked as if it had been dug out of the hard, frozen ground. They went across to it, and

Rensselaer shone his flashlight inside. It was empty except for an old brass padlock with a key still in it.

"They collected something," said Samson.

"It looks that way." Glenn Rensselaer opened the closet door. There were clothes hanging there: a gray suit and some working trousers. There were women's clothes, too, black dresses and a petticoat that would fit someone of Inge's shape and size.

"They must be Reichsminister Esser's clothes," said Captain Samson. "He was arrested in this house."

"It's Pauli Winter's house," said Glenn Rensselaer.

"Yes, I know," said Captain Samson.

"You know everything, don't you?" said Glenn Rensselaer.

"About Paul Winter? Yes, I do."

"Then maybe you could tell me where his wife, Inge, is."

"Garmisch: the White Horse Inn."

"The what?"

"It's an expensive nightclub for black-marketeers and other lowlife. They feature a dance band. She sings there."

"Sings! Inge Winter? Jesus, she's a middle-aged woman."

"There's no law against old ladies' singing," said Samson.

Rensselaer said nothing for fear of showing his anger. He resented Captain Samson's manner, just as he resented Lieutenant Busby's impertinence. It had become a young man's world: courtesy had gone.

After another quick look round the house, the two men came outside, looking for footprints. They found them too late.

The sound of the shooting was loud in the bright, still night. Samson recognized it: a Browning automatic rifle; they made a distinctive noise.

"Oh my God!" said Rensselaer. He was a tired old man, but his anxiety made him go hurrying back down the treacherous path, sliding sometimes as he missed his footing.

Captain Samson didn't hurry. Whatever had happened would be waiting for him when he got there. Right from the start he'd had the feeling that Lieutenant Busby's men were too damned jumpy.

The two bodies were close together, sprawled in the snow at that place on the mountainside where the trees opened up and gave way to the snow-covered open grass of the upper pastures. One of the men—the blond one—had bled to form a large patch of colored snow that had melted and quickly refrozen, so that it shone with a smooth, glossy surface. Neither man was armed. Peter was wearing a pale khaki trenchcoat; it wasn't easy to distinguish him as an officer in uniform. The coat was unbuttoned and had opened to its full shape, like wings.

Pauli was wearing an old blue overcoat, the same one he'd been wearing for years. It was an expensive loden that Inge had chosen at a time when she chose just about everything.

Pauli was huddled on his side; his arms had twisted under him as he fell. His knees were drawn up in the fetal position, the muscles constricted in the way that so often comes with the final moments of such deaths. Peter, immediately behind him, was spread-eagled, face down. To General Glenn Rensselaer it seemed as if Peter's arm was reaching out towards his younger brother's shoulder.

A NOTE ON THE TYPE

This book was set in a digitized version of a type face
called Baskerville. The face itself is a facsimile
reproduction of types cast from molds made for John
Baskerville (1706–1775) from his designs. Baskerville's
original face was one of the forerunners of the type style
known to printers as "modern face"—a "modern" of the
period A.D. 1800.

Composed, printed, and bound by
The Haddon Craftsmen, Inc.,
Scranton, Pennsylvania

Designed by Marysarah Quinn